PENGUIN 🐧

A MODEST PROPOSAL AND OTHER WRITINGS

JONATHAN SWIFT was born in Dublin on 30 November 1667, some months after his father's death. He was sent to Kilkenny Grammar School when he was six and later attended Trinity College, Dublin, where he received his BA degree in 1686. When civil war broke out between the forces of William III and the Catholic James II in 1688, Swift fled to England, where he took up employment in the household of Sir William Temple and first met Esther Johnson, later to be immortalized as 'Stella' in the birthday poems and London journal he addressed to her. Ordained in Ireland in 1694, he spent an unhappy year as an Anglican churchman in largely Presbyterian Kilroot, near Belfast, before returning to Temple's service, where he became involved in the Ancients–Moderns controversy, for which he wrote *A Tale of a Tub* and *The Battel of the Books*. Having obtained his Doctor of Divinity degree from Trinity College in 1702, he was sent to England as an emissary of the Church of Ireland in order to win remission of the First Fruits (a tax paid by the Irish clergy to Queen Anne): an aim he achieved during his extended stay in London (1710–14) while supporting the Tory ministry through his periodical *The Examiner*. During his stay he was actively involved in London's literary scene, becoming a member of the Scriblerus Club and forming close ties with writers such as Alexander Pope, John Gay and Joseph Addison. Following the ministry's fall in the summer of 1714, Swift returned to Ireland to take up his post as Dean of St Patrick's cathedral in Dublin, where (except for two extended visits to England in 1726 and 1727) he remained for the rest of his life. It was during this final period that Swift achieved his greatest successes: first as the Drapier, whose galvanizing *Letters* helped prevent the circulation of potentially worthless half-pence made in England for Irish consumption (1724); later, as the author of *Gulliver's Travels* (1726), an enormously popular work in its day that has resonated with both young and old for centuries thereafter. His widespread reputation as 'Hibernian Patriot' grew out of the numerous tracts and satires he wrote against British oppressive and venal policies in Ireland, and which *osal*

(1729). Swift died on 19 October 1745 and was buried in St Patrick's cathedral under an epitaph he himself composed, which acknowledged a life of 'savage indignation' and exalted his role as a strenuous champion of liberty.

CAROLE FABRICANT is Professor of English at the University of California, Riverside. She is the author of *Swift's Landscape* (originally published by the Johns Hopkins University Press in 1982; reissued in paperback with a new introduction by the University of Notre Dame Press in 1995) and has published widely on a number of eighteenth-century writers, including Alexander Pope, Edmund Burke and Bishop Berkeley, as well as on topics such as landscape gardening, travel, tourism and questions of colonialism and race in the eighteenth century, especially as they relate to British–Irish relations during the period.

JONATHAN SWIFT

A Modest Proposal and Other Writings

Edited with an Introduction by
CAROLE FABRICANT

PENGUIN BOOKS

PENGUIN CLASSICS

Published by the Penguin Group
Penguin Books Ltd, 80 Strand, London WC2R ORL, England
Penguin Group (USA) Inc., 375 Hudson Street, New York, New York 10014, USA
Penguin Group (Canada), 90 Eglinton Avenue East, Suite 700, Toronto, Ontario, Canada M4P 2Y3
(a division of Pearson Penguin Canada Inc.)
Penguin Ireland, 25 St Stephen's Green, Dublin 2, Ireland
(a division of Penguin Books Ltd)
Penguin Group (Australia), 250 Camberwell Road, Camberwell, Victoria 3124, Australia
(a division of Pearson Australia Group Pty Ltd)
Penguin Books India Pvt Ltd, 11 Community Centre, Panchsheel Park, New Delhi – 110 017, India
Penguin Group (NZ), 67 Apollo Drive, Rosedale, North Shore 0632, New Zealand
(a division of Pearson New Zealand Ltd)
Penguin Books (South Africa) (Pty) Ltd, 24 Sturdee Avenue, Rosebank, Johannesburg 2196, South Africa

Penguin Books Ltd, Registered Offices: 80 Strand, London WC2R ORL, England

www.penguin.com

This edition first published in Penguin Classics 2009
1

Selection and editorial material copyright © Carole Fabricant, 2009
All rights reserved

The moral right of the editor has been asserted

Set in 10.25/12.25 pt PostScript Adobe Sabon
Typeset by Rowland Phototypesetting Ltd, Bury St Edmunds, Suffolk
Printed in England by Clays Ltd, St Ives plc

ISBN: 978-0-140-43642-6

www.greenpenguin.co.uk

Penguin Books is committed to a sustainable future
for our business, our readers and our planet.
The book in your hands is made from paper
certified by the Forest Stewardship Council.

Contents

A MODEST PROPOSAL
AND OTHER WRITINGS

Acknowledgements

Over the long and sometimes frustrating course of preparing this edition, many friends and colleagues have provided assistance and support of various kinds. For bibliographic assistance and help with manuscript preparation I wish to thank Kristin Brunnemer, Jay Conway, Tracy Curtis, Lora Geriguis, Corrinne Harol, Marilyn Kim, Mark Quigley and Jackie Stallcup. For advice about translations I am indebted to John Ganim and (especially) Harold Donoghue. For responding to my queries of a factual or textual nature I want to thank Andrew Carpenter, Ralph Hanna, Robert Mahony and James Woolley. Many offered moral support and a sympathetic ear, chief among them Lois Chaber, Maryann Griffo, Stephanie Kay, Felicity Nussbaum, Paul and Ruth Von Blum and Alice Wexler. I owe a special debt of gratitude to Sean Shesgreen for his heroic efforts in helping me cut this edition down to length specifications. For first encouraging me to take on this project, I am deeply grateful to Aaron Walden; my only regret is that he did not live to see the project to its end. And for first introducing me to the brilliance of Swift's satire and inspiring me to devote the past four decades to writing about it, I owe a continuing debt of gratitude to Ronald Paulson.

I would also like to thank the helpful staff at a number of research institutions, including the William Andrews Clark Memorial Library; the Huntington Library; the Charles E. Young Research Library at the University of California, Los Angeles; the Pierpont Morgan Library; the National Library of Ireland; Trinity College Library, Dublin; Marsh's Library; the British Library; the National Art Library at the Victoria and

Albert Museum; the Royal College of Surgeons of England; and the Wren Library of Trinity College, Cambridge. Plates 1 and 3 are reproduced here by permission of the Department of Special Collections, Charles E. Young Research Library, University of California, Los Angeles; Plate 2 is reproduced by permission of The Huntington Library, San Marino, California; Plate 4 is reproduced by permission of the Pierpont Morgan Library, New York. Finally, I would like to thank the Academic Senate Research Committee at the University of California, Riverside for grants that have helped defray travel and other expenses incurred in the course of putting together this edition.

Chronology

1667 Born in Hoey's Court, Dublin, on 30 November to Abigail Swift (*née* Erich), seven months after the death of his father, Jonathan Swift.

1673 Sent to Kilkenny Grammar School (remains there until 1682).

1682 Enters Trinity College, Dublin.

1685 Death of Charles II (6 Feb.); accession of his Roman Catholic brother, James II.

1686 Swift obtains BA degree, *speciali gratia* ('by special grace'); continues at Trinity College.

1688 The 'Glorious Revolution': accession to the throne of William of Orange (as William III) and his wife (as Mary II); James II flees to France.

1688–9 Swift leaves for England to escape the civil strife following James II's arrival in Ireland.

1689 Enters household of Sir William Temple at Moor Park in Surrey, where he first meets Esther Johnson ('Stella'), then eight years old.

1690 Returns to Ireland; William III defeats James II at the Battle of the Boyne (1 July).

1691 Swift returns to Moor Park to work as Temple's secretary; the Treaty of Limerick (3 Oct.) ends the civil strife in Ireland after the defeat of the Jacobite army.

1692 Swift receives MA degree from Hart Hall, Oxford University; publishes 'Ode to the Athenian Society', his first work to appear in print.

1694 Returns to Ireland and is ordained deacon (28 Oct.); death of Queen Mary (28 Dec.)

1695 Swift is ordained priest (13 Jan.) and appointed to the prebend of Kilroot, near Belfast; enactment of first of the Penal Laws in Ireland.

1696 Swift returns to Moor Park (June), where over the next three years he contributes to the Ancients–Moderns controversy by writing *The Battel of the Books* and (most of) *A Tale of a Tub*.

1699 Death of Temple (27 Jan.); Swift returns to Ireland as chaplain to the Earl of Berkeley, Lord Justice of Ireland; passage of Woollen Act restricting Irish trade.

1700 Swift is presented to the church livings of Laracor, Rathbeggan and Agher (Feb.); installed as prebendary of St Patrick's cathedral, Dublin (22 Oct.); death of John Dryden (1 May).

1701 Swift returns to England; publishes *A Discourse of the Contests and Dissensions in Athens and Rome*, defending several impeached Whig statesmen; Esther Johnson moves to Dublin, accompanied by Rebecca Dingley; death of James II (16 Sept.).

1702 Swift receives Doctor of Divinity degree at Trinity College (16 Feb.); English Parliament declares war on France; death of William III (8 Mar.) and accession of Queen Anne.

1704 Publication of the volume containing *A Tale of a Tub*, *The Battel of the Books* and *The Mechanical Operation of the Spirit*; the Test Act is passed in Ireland.

1707 Swift arrives in London in November with commission from the Church of Ireland to solicit remission of the 'First Fruits' from Queen Anne, remaining for a year and a half; the Union of England and Scotland prompts *The Story of the Injured Lady* (published posthumously).

1708–9 Swift develops close ties with Addison, Steele and other prominent writers and wits; publishes *The Bickerstaff Papers* and several tracts related to the Church; writes *An Argument against Abolishing Christianity* (published in 1711); contributes to Steele's *Tatler* with 'A Description of the Morning'; returns to Ireland (June 1709).

1710 Returns to London (Sept.) and joins forces with the new Tory ministry (led by Robert Harley and Henry St John), on whose behalf he writes partisan essays for *The Examiner* (from 2 Nov. until 14 June 1711); starts the *Journal to Stella* on 2 September (runs to 6 June 1713); writes 'A Description of a City Shower' for *The Tatler*; publication of the fifth edition of *A Tale of a Tub*, with the 'Apology' added.

1711 Swift publishes his *Miscellanies in Prose and Verse*; begins his involvement with Esther Vanhomrigh ('Vanessa'); circulates his highly effective pro-peace polemic, *The Conduct of the Allies* (Nov.); Duke of Marlborough dismissed (Dec.); Addison's and Steele's *The Spectator* appears on 1 March (runs to 6 Dec. 1712; briefly revived in 1714); Harley made Earl of Oxford.

1713 Swift's membership (with Pope, Gay, Arbuthnot and Parnell) in the Scriblerus Club; his attacks on Steele's Whig journalism; Treaty of Peace with France, ending the War of the Spanish Succession, signed at Utrecht (11 Apr.), celebrated by Pope in *Windsor-Forest*; Swift installed as Dean of St Patrick's cathedral, Dublin (13 June); returns to London (9 Sept.).

1714 Collapse of Tory ministry (July); death of Queen Anne (1 Aug.) and accession of the Hanoverian George I; Swift has price placed on his head for writing *The Public Spirit of the Whigs*; leaves for Dublin (16 Aug.) to assume his new post; personal and political tensions between Swift and his 'boss' William King, Archbishop of Dublin (later eased through their mutual exertions on behalf of the 'Irish interest').

1715 Former Tory ministers impeached; Bolingbroke flees to France to join the Pretender and Oxford is imprisoned in the Tower (released in 1717); Jacobite Rebellion in Scotland; death of Louis XIV of France (1 Sept.).

1720 Publication of Swift's *A Proposal for the Universal Use of Irish Manufacture* (May), shortly after passage of the Declaratory Act, strengthening Britain's legislative power over Ireland; prosecution of the printer; South Sea Bubble (Sept.).

1721 Robert Walpole appointed First Lord of the Treasury and begins his de-facto tenure as Prime Minister of Britain (until 1742); he will become a target of Swift's satire and wrath throughout the 1720s.

1722 William Wood receives royal patent to coin copper half-pence for Ireland (July); opposition to the patent begins to emerge among all segments of the Irish population.

1723 Swift embarks on a four-month tour of southern Ireland following the death of Esther Vanhomrigh at her Celbridge home near Dublin (2 June).

1724 Writes *The Drapier's Letters* attacking Wood's patent; Carteret arrives in Dublin as Lord-Lieutenant of Ireland (Oct.); reward of £300 (unclaimed) offered for discovery of the Drapier; Harding jailed and prosecuted for printing *Drapier's Letter IV* (Nov.); Swift attains hero status as the 'Hibernian Patriot'; death of Earl of Oxford (21 May).

1725 Wood's patent surrendered (Aug.); Swift works on manuscript of *Gulliver's Travels* during a five-month visit to Sheridan in Co. Cavan (late Apr. to early Oct.).

1726 Visits England (Mar.–Aug.); stays with Pope at Twicken-ham; has disastrous meeting with Walpole to discuss the Irish situation; *Gulliver's Travels* published in London (28 Oct.) and becomes an instant sensation, with two Dublin editions following shortly thereafter.

1727 Swift's final visit to England (Apr.–Sept.); returns to Dublin to a seriously ailing Esther Johnson via a trip recorded in the *Holyhead Journal*; death of George I (11 June) and accession of George II; onset of a severe famine in Ireland.

1728 Death of Esther Johnson (28 Jan.); Swift publishes *A Short View of the State of Ireland* (Mar.) and writes other Irish tracts on the worsening conditions in the country; collaborates with Sheridan on the periodical, *The Intelligencer* (lasts for one year, beginning 11 May); opening of Gay's *The Beggar's Opera* in London; publication of Pope's *The Dunciad* (3-canto version).

1729 Publication of *A Modest Proposal* (Oct.); death of Archbishop King (8 May).

1731 Swift writes *Verses on the Death of Dr Swift* (published in 1739).

1732 Publication of *The Lady's Dressing Room*, one of his most popular poems during his lifetime and a prime example of his so-called 'excremental' poems; death of Gay (4 Dec.).

1735 Publication of George Faulkner's 4-volume Dublin edition of Swift's *Works*.

1736 Publication of the poem *A Character . . . of the Legion Club*, Swift's scathing satire on the Irish House of Commons.

1738 Publication of Swift's *Polite Conversation*; death of Sheridan (10 Oct.).

1740 Swift makes his last will (3 May), directing that the bulk of his estate be used for the construction of St Patrick's Hospital; severe weather results in widespread disease and famine throughout Ireland.

1742 Swift declared 'of unsound mind and memory' (17 Aug.) and delivered to the care of guardians; Walpole forced to resign (1 Feb.); Handel in Dublin oversees the first performance of his *Messiah* (13 Apr.); publication of Pope's *New Dunciad* (Book IV).

1744 Death of Pope (30 May).

1745 Death of Swift (19 Oct.); burial in St Patrick's cathedral, beneath the famous epitaph he himself composed; publication of his unfinished *Directions to Servants*; death of Walpole (18 Mar.); the final, abortive Jacobite uprising in Britain, led by the 'Young Pretender'.

Abbreviations

Apperson	G. L. Apperson, *The Wordsworth Dictionary of Proverbs* (Ware, Hertfordshire: Wordsworth, 1993)
Ball	F. Elrington Ball (ed.), *The Correspondence of Jonathan Swift*, 6 vols. (London: Bell, 1910–14)
BL	British Library
Brewer/Evans	*The Wordsworth Dictionary of Phrase & Fable, Based on the original book by Ebenezer Cobham Brewer*, rev. Ivor H. Evans (Ware, Hertfordshire: Wordsworth, 1993)
C	*The Correspondence of Jonathan Swift* (see Williams, below)
CD	*A New Canting Dictionary* (London, 1725)
Davis	Herbert Davis (ed.), *The Prose Works of Jonathan Swift*, 14 vols. (Oxford: Blackwell, 1939–74)
DS [date]	Volumes in Hawkesworth's *The Works of Jonathan Swift* (see below), edited by Deane Swift
Ehrenpreis	Irvin Ehrenpreis, *Swift: The Man, his Work, and the Age*, 3 vols. (Cambridge, Mass.: Harvard University Press, 1962–83)
F '35	*The Works of Jonathan Swift*, 4 vols., ed. George Faulkner (Dublin, 1735);

	subsequent editions by Faulkner are indicated by *F* followed by the relevant year
Ferguson	Oliver W. Ferguson, *Jonathan Swift and Ireland* (Urbana: University of Illinois Press, 1962)
Forster	Manuscript collection housed in the Victoria and Albert Museum, London
GT	*Gulliver's Travels*; in *Prose Works*, ed. Davis (see above)
H [date]	*The Works of Jonathan Swift*, ed. John Hawkesworth, 6 vols. (London, 1755); 12 vols. (London, 1765–75)
Hob-Job	Henry Yule and A. C. Burnett, *Hobson-Jobson: The Anglo-Indian Dictionary* (1903; Ware, Hertfordshire: Wordsworth, 1996)
Hunter-Baillie	Manuscript collection housed in the Royal College of Surgeons of England, London
JN [date]	*A Supplement to Dr. Swift's Works*, ed. John Nichols, 2 vols. (London, 1776–9)
Johnson	*Samuel Johnson's Dictionary of the English Language*, ed. Alexander Chalmers (London: Studio Editions, 1994)
JS	Jonathan Swift, *The Journal to Stella* (see Williams, below)
Kelly	James Kelly, *A Complete Collection of Scottish Proverbs* (London, 1721)
Landa	Louis A. Landa, *Swift and the Church of Ireland* (Oxford: Oxford University Press, 1954)
M'11	Swift, *Miscellanies in Prose and Verse* (London, 1711)
M.: *Burnet*	Swift's 'Marginalia' to Gilbert Burnet, *History of His Own Times* (London, 1724–34)

M.: *Clarendon*	Swift's 'Marginalia' to Edward Hyde, Earl of Clarendon, *History of the Rebellion* (London, 1707)
M.: *Macky*	Swift's 'Marginalia' to John Macky, *Characters of the Court of Britain, &c.* (London, 1733)
Molyneux	William Molyneux, *The Case of Ireland's Being Bound by Acts of Parliament in England, Stated* (Dublin, 1698)
ODEP	*The Oxford Dictionary of English Proverbs*, compiled William George Smith; intro. Janet E. Heseltine; second edition revised Sir Paul Harvey (Oxford: Clarendon Press, 1952)
OED	*The Oxford English Dictionary*
Partridge	Eric Partridge (ed.), *Swift's Polite Conversation* (London: André Deutsch, 1963)
Pierpont Morgan	The Pierpont Morgan Library, New York City
PW	*The Prose Works of Jonathan Swift* (see Davis, above)
Ray	John Ray, *A Collection of English Proverbs* (London, 1670); reissued as *A Hand-Book of Proverbs*, ed. Henry G. Bohn (London: H. G. Bohn, 1855; New York: AMS Press, 1968); second edition of Ray's collection published in 1678
Rothschild	Manuscript collection housed in Trinity College Library, Cambridge
Tilley	Morris Palmer Tilley, *A Dictionary of the Proverbs in England in the Sixteenth and Seventeenth Centuries: A Collection of the Proverbs Found in English Literature and the Dictionaries of the Period* (Ann Arbor: University of Michigan Press, 1950)
Williams	Harold Williams, ed., *The Correspondence of Jonathan Swift*, 5 vols. (Oxford:

Clarendon Press, 1963–5); *Journal to Stella*, 2 vols. (Oxford: Clarendon Press, 1948); repr. as vols. 15–16 of *Prose Works of Jonathan Swift*.

Woolley   James Woolley (ed.), Swift and Thomas Sheridan, *The Intelligencer* (Oxford: Clarendon Press, 1992)

NB Swift's poetry is quoted from *The Poems of Jonathan Swift*, ed. Harold Williams, 2nd edn. (Oxford: Clarendon Press, 1958).

Introduction

Any mention of Swift as prose writer is likely to call to mind a small handful of canonical works that confirm his status as one of the greatest satirists in the English language. But these texts constitute only a tiny portion of Swift's total prose output, which was voluminous, generically and thematically varied and reflective of both learned and popular traditions. This edition is designed to display the full range of these writings. The deliberate omission of *Gulliver's Travels* and *A Tale of a Tub*—two pieces readily available elsewhere—has allowed for the inclusion of many of Swift's less familiar works, along with several texts that have not appeared before in popular editions. The selections in this edition are intended to reveal both the towering figure who lent his name to an age, becoming one of the most eminent authors in the Great Literary Tradition, and the gadfly who flitted along the margins of respectable literary (and political) society, engaged in activities that alternated between falling under the radar screen and falling foul of established canonical institutions. Swift may be numbered among a group of great thinkers and writers—Edmund Burke, Karl Marx, Mark Twain, George Orwell—who, while quite capable of producing lengthy, even magisterial works that have become anointed as 'classics', spent much of their careers in the trenches (as it were), writing political pamphlets and journalistic essays in crisis situations that demanded quick-witted responses (often laced with satire) rather than lengthy artistic contemplation. It is therefore not coincidental that Swift was as much associated with printers of cheap ephemera (John Waters, Sarah Harding) as with publishers of artful editions designed for posterity (George Faulkner).

For Swift, prose writing was not simply an exercise in creative expression, nor was it only an activity periodically indulged in for purposes of instruction, amusement or profit. It was one of his most important ways of being and acting in the world, of positioning himself in relation to the people, events and material conditions of his life. This intimate bond between author and work was tacitly acknowledged by Swift himself in his statement in *A Letter to a Young Gentleman, Lately entered into Holy Orders* that reading a book is largely meaningless 'without entering into the Genius and Spirit of the Author' (p. 122) and in his promise made in the *Journal to Stella*, 'I'll come again to-night in a fine clean sheet of paper' (*JS* 1: 154). At the same time, one should avoid a simplistic equation of the author and his work that ignores the mediating effects of language and the ways in which even explicitly autobiographical pieces rely on rhetorical and fictional techniques to convey their picture of 'truth'. Swift's regular use of complex irony, intricate wordplay and fictive speakers undermines any simple, clear-cut interpretation of his writings and helps explain the often widely divergent meanings that readers have derived from them.

Swift's prose works exemplify all the different ways in which written texts can intersect with the world. History functions in these works, not as an inert background or external set of references, but as an integral part of both their form and content. With few exceptions, Swift's texts dramatize the social and public function of writing. Even an ostensibly private work such as the *Journal to Stella*, filled with verbal intimacies meant to be unintelligible to an outside reader, insists upon its status as an important chronicle of events. Thus Swift assures his correspondent, Esther Johnson, that a particular letter of his will be 'a good history' to show her the significant political changes occurring in England at the time (*JS* 2: 436). Swift's often-cited advocacy of 'Proper Words in proper Places' in *Letter to a Young Gentleman* has less to do with a narrowly defined stylistic or generic decorum than with his acute sense of language's social context, and of the need to use words in a manner appropriate to the specific setting and occasion at hand. The 'Places' he refers to include all those social spaces—the marketplace, the coffee house, the church, for example—where words are publicly exchanged and communal meanings are produced. In writing separate letters to distinct groups in Irish society as the Drapier, Swift conveyed his awareness that the propriety of his own words was to be measured, not against some abstract norm of stylistic or rhetorical correctness, but according to their effectiveness in reaching real-life audiences made up of particular classes and economic interests.

As writings that tend to call attention to their status as occasional works tied to specific contemporary events, Swift's prose pieces encourage us to rethink the nature and meaning of a 'literary classic', which has traditionally been associated with ideas of aesthetic transcendence and universality. The reason his works have endured for almost three centuries and remain relevant to us today is not because they make sweepingly general statements about 'the nature of man' but because, in their very concern for showing individual men (and women) acting within concretely defined sets of circumstances, they are able to present situations that everyone living in a world of power and privation must in some way contend with. The society of Swift's day was, after all, hardly the last or the only one to be faced with the recalcitrant fact that, in Gulliver's words, '*Poor* Nations are *Hungry*, and *rich* Nations are *proud*; and Pride and Hunger will ever be at Variance' (*PW* 11: 246). It is stark realities such as these that inhabit much of Swift's (especially later) prose, presented not as eternal truths but in all the blood and guts of their particularity. Edward Said has commented that 'too many claims are made for Swift as a moralist and thinker who peddled one or another final view of human nature' and suggests instead the idea of Swift as 'a kind of local activist, a columnist, a pamphleteer, a caricaturist'.[1] Though wrong to deny the clear evidence of larger ideological commitments and coherencies in Swift, Said offers a useful corrective to conventional views of Swift as a producer of thoughts and writings that lend themselves to general labels ('Christian humanist', 'Augustan', etc.). His view allows us to understand Swift as an

organic as well as a traditional intellectual—as someone who
helped formulate the new ideas of an emerging class as well as
someone who defended the status quo—and to appreciate his
role as a fighter against what Jean-Paul Sartre called 'the terror-
ist practice' of 'liquidating the particularity'.[2] Sartre's comment
that 'At one time this intellectual terror corresponded to "the
physical liquidation" of particular people' brings to mind
Swift's graphic examples of such 'liquidation': the Modest Pro-
poser in his scheme to cannibalize Irish Catholic infants, the
Houyhnhnms debating 'Whether the *Yahoos* should be exter-
minated from the Face of the Earth', and the colonialist-
butchers depicted at the end of *Gulliver's Travels*, who give
'free Licence . . . to all Acts of Inhumanity and Lust', leaving
'the Earth reeking with the Blood of its Inhabitants' (*PW* 11:
271; 294).

Swift's resistance to the 'terrorism' of abstraction resulted in
writings distinctive for their concreteness and immediacy. Their
contributions to Irish nationalist, anti-colonialist and anti-war
ideologies are universal in scope while at all times remaining
firmly tied to the specific conditions in which Swift lived and
worked. In contrast to Pope, who regularly wrote, revised and
published his works governed by the idea that 'We who are
Writers ought to love Posterity, that Posterity may love us',
Swift produced the majority of his prose works for immediate
impact rather than for artistic immortality.[3] He was generally
more concerned about their influence on the thoughts and
actions of his present readers than about their place in some
future pantheon of Great Literature. As he remarked in
Thoughts on Various Subjects: 'It is pleasant to observe, how
free the present Age is in laying Taxes on the next. *Future Ages
shall talk of this: This shall be famous to all Posterity*. Whereas,
their Time and Thoughts will be taken up about present Things,
as ours are now' (*PW* 1: 243). Not that Swift was indifferent
to fame, or content to let his works pass out of existence along
with the occasions that produced them. The persona of *A Tale
of a Tub* dramatizes the plight not only of the Grub Street
Hack but of all occasional writers when he complains to Prince
Posterity of the disappearance of the Moderns' productions

without a trace after being mercilessly devoured by Father Time. Along with its obvious function as a satire on ephemeral scribblers, this lament surely reflects something of Swift's own anxiety and dread when faced with the threat of historical extinction. In the Drapier's wish that readers of his *First Letter* keep it 'carefully by them to refresh their Memories' in times to come (p. 164), we can see evidence of the occasional writer's paradoxical desire to preserve the ephemeral; to speak to the immediate moment while creating a more lasting memorial for future ages. Swift's reluctance to let the Drapier 'die' even after his political *raison d'être* had ceased to exist (he continued invoking the latter's presence and authority long after *The Drapier's Letters* had accomplished their goal), and his concern with creating an enduring image of himself as an Irish Patriot in works such as the *Verses on the Death of Dr Swift*, point to an interest in the perpetuation of his memory which invites comparison with Pope's desire for immortality. Where they differ is in Swift's insistence upon situating his fame in the very heart of the mundane, transient circumstances of his life rather than in an aesthetic transformation of them. Swift entertained little notion of the transcendence of his work to some other-worldly status, in the way (for example) that the apotheosis of Belinda's lock into the heavens, at the end of *The Rape of the Lock*, suggests the elevation of Pope's poetry itself to a kind of divine status—or at least to the airy realms of high culture. Swift's version of this apotheosis—his poetic depiction of the astrologer Partridge's ascent into the spheres, where he appears as a '*Triumphant* Star' ('An Elegy on Mr Partrige')—functions as pure mockery, ridiculing all claims to supposedly prophetic vision and underscoring the absurdity of attempts to soar beyond earthly bounds.

Swift's particular understanding of worldly realities, especially those growing out of the inequalities of power and wealth, was derived from his concrete situation in the world as an Anglo-Irishman whose life and career, shaped (and fissured) by the political and ethnic conflicts between England and Ireland, as well as those within Ireland itself, serve to magnify the problematic nature of colonial identity in eighteenth-century

Ireland. Swift was born on 30 November 1667 in Hoey's Court
in Dublin, to a father who had emigrated from England to
Ireland some half-dozen years earlier and to an Irish-born
mother from an old English family from Leicestershire. He was
in many ways fated by historical circumstances to a life of social
dislocations and uncertainties. The Dublin in which Swift grew
up was an expanding colonial city, the fortified centre of the
English settlement in Ireland known as 'the Pale' and the site
of the main institutions of Anglican power. At the same time
the city functioned as a bilingual community of English- and
Gaelic-speaking inhabitants which included a growing number
of Catholic merchants, artisans and servants as well as a significant Dissenting element, such as the Huguenot weavers whose
dire plight was later to have a galvanizing effect on Swift's
exertions on behalf of Ireland's economic independence. Since
his father died before he was born and his mother was left with
few resources, Swift was exposed from an early age to the
ignominies of financial dependency—an experience whose
indelible mark could later be discerned in his often scathing
view of the patronage system, his resentment towards those in
whose service he toiled and his passionate rejection of the idea
of Ireland as a *depending Kingdom* in the *Fourth Drapier's
Letter* (p. 174). With the help of his well-to-do uncle, Godwin,
Swift was able to attend Kilkenny School and Trinity College,
Dublin, elite institutions committed to inculcating the religious
and cultural values of Ireland's governing class. At the same
time his tenure at Trinity College exposed him to modes of
parody, wit and wordplay that were uniquely Irish in form and
cadence.

An indifferent student, Swift scraped by in his studies to
obtain his Bachelor of Arts degree at Trinity, but his academic
career was dramatically interrupted by the upheavals following
upon the 'Glorious Revolution' of 1688, when the Catholic
monarch James II was forced to flee England, making way for
the joint rule of his Protestant daughter Mary and her husband
William of Orange (William III). This event had a profound
effect on the course of English history, but its most immediate
and destructive consequences were felt in Ireland, which served

as the battleground for the forces of James and William. Forty years later, Swift would say that this contention was decided 'with such ravages and ruin executed on both sides, as to leave the kingdom a desert' (*PW* 12: 132). Along with many others of his class Swift fled to England, where he began his lengthy tenure working for the son of a family friend, the noted Whig diplomat and man of letters Sir William Temple, at his country seat, Moor Park, in Surrey. It was here that Swift first met the then eight-year-old Esther Johnson, who was to play so significant a role in his life and become immortalized in his writings as 'Stella'. Through his contact with Temple (and with Temple's essays on history and literature, which he had frequent occasion to read, transcribe and later edit), Swift was ushered into the world of the scholar-dilettante, at once connected with and detached from affairs of state. Moreover, Temple's involvement in what came to be known as the Ancients–Moderns controversy through his essays championing the superiority of Ancient learning fuelled Swift's great satires on the Moderns, *A Tale of a Tub* and *The Battel of the Books*.

Temple, despite (or perhaps because of) his own Anglo-Irish lineage, projected the very model of an English country gentleman, Whig in outlook, epicurean in mode of living, expressing a casual contempt for the Irish that was endemic to his class. It was a model that must have held no small appeal for Swift, then eager for entrée into English society, but it proved to be as ill-fitting for him as the 'embroidered coat' worn by the man 'begging out of Newgate [Prison] in an old shoe' described in *A Proposal to the Ladies of Ireland* (*PW* 12: 127), and in later years he would construct a life—as a Dubliner, a fierce critic of English policies in Ireland, a Tory and an Anglican churchman—which rejected most aspects of the Temple model of existence. Moreover, Temple tended to be haughty and patronizing in his behaviour towards Swift, who a dozen years later warned that he 'would not be treated like a school-boy' by Lord Bolingbroke since he had 'felt too much of that in [his] life already (meaning from sir William Temple)' (*JS* 1: 230). This treatment, combined with Temple's failure to help him obtain suitable preferment, resulted in Swift's departure from Moor

Park and return to Ireland after taking holy orders in 1693. Swift's first church living was in remote Kilroot near Belfast, an inhospitable area dominated by the Presbyterian kirk. This experience proved bitterly disappointing to Swift, reinforcing his aversion to religious Dissent and prompting his return to Moor Park, where he resumed his former duties until Temple's death in 1699. Immediately thereafter he accompanied the Earl of Berkeley to Ireland as his chaplain, and in the following year he was named vicar of Laracor, a village in County Meath near Dublin.

The ensuing decade was crucial to Swift's development as a churchman, a political activist and a writer. As the chosen representative of the Church of Ireland in its solicitation for remission of certain taxes (known as the 'First Fruits and Twentieth Parts') then being paid to the Crown, he was given the opportunity to live for lengthy periods of time in London. His indefatigable efforts on behalf of the Church were ultimately successful, but not before his disillusionment with those he initially viewed as allies—the Whig politicians who were willing to aid his cause only if he agreed to support a repeal of the Test Act, which made the taking of the sacrament according to Anglican ritual a prerequisite for holding public office— prompted his switch in allegiance to the Tory Party.

Swift's embrace of the Tory ministry at the moment of its ascendancy was no doubt motivated at least in part by political self-interest, as well as by personal factors such as vanity and resentment. Robert Harley, Lord Treasurer of the Tory ministry, showered him with attention and treated him as an important personage, while the leader of the Whig Junto, Sidney Godolphin, was barely civil to him in their one meeting about the 'First Fruits' matter. But mixed together with these personal and narrowly political motives were more general beliefs— about the necessary role of an Established Church, the destructiveness of a new economic system based on speculation and credit, and the need to subordinate the military to civilian authority and severely curtail the power of a standing army— which made Swift's embrace of the Tory position at this moment in history consistent with larger and long-standing ideological allegiances. Indeed, it is as well to keep in mind that Swift in later life did not explicitly identify himself as a Tory, despite the fact that he was regularly branded and ostracized as one. Instead he insisted, not without justification, that it was the Whig Party, not his own political beliefs, that had changed. As late as 1733 he could write to a friend, 'I am of the old Whig principles, without the modern articles and refinements' (C 4: 100).

The years 1710–14 were among the most active and productive in Swift's life, marking his highly visible emergence into public life and into the vibrant literary world centred in London. Swift pursued a busy schedule as chief political writer for the Tory ministry, which included penning essays for the government periodical he edited, *The Examiner*, and weighing in on the side of a peace treaty with France to end the War of the Spanish Succession—most notably through his highly influential tract, *The Conduct of the Allies* (1711). He simultaneously enjoyed the life of a London wit, developing friendships with noted writers of all political persuasions, including Alexander Pope, John Gay, Richard Steele, Joseph Addison, Nicholas Rowe and Matthew Prior. During this period, his authorship of *The Bickerstaff Papers*, a brilliantly effective parody of astrological almanacs, along with poems such as 'A Description of the Morning', 'A Description of a City Shower' and 'The Virtues of Sid Hamet the Magician's Rod' (a political lampoon on Sidney Godolphin) readily demonstrated Swift's unique imaginative powers and his particular genius for satire—one already amply displayed in his earlier, anonymously published *A Tale of a Tub*. It was also during this period that Swift, through his participation in the Scriblerus Club, a literary group whose members included Pope, Gay, John Arbuthnot and Thomas Parnell, collaborated on pieces satirizing perceived abuses in modern learning.

Yet for all the heady excitement and rich promise of these years in London, the period was marked by often profound frustrations for Swift, some of which were bitterly reminiscent of earlier disappointments with patrons and modes of employment. Growing conflicts between the two leaders of the Tory ministry, Henry St John (by this time Viscount Bolingbroke) and Harley (now Earl of Oxford), and their continual delays in finding suitable preferment for him, made Swift increasingly cynical about both political and personal prospects. As he wryly observed to Esther Johnson, 'They call me nothing but Jonathan; and I said, I believed they would leave me Jonathan as they found me' (*JS* 1: 193–4). Moreover, even as he expressed a fondness for many aspects of London life and fantasized about obtaining a church living somewhere nearby, his *Journal to Stella* is filled with recurring nostalgic recollections of his gardens at Laracor and with eager anticipations of his return to Ireland: 'Oh, that we were at Laracor this fine day! the willows begin to peep, and the quicks to bud' (*JS* 1: 220). When the Tory government began disintegrating as a result of warring factions within it, Swift realized the futility of his continued stay in England and, shortly after Queen Anne's death in the summer of 1714, sailed for Ireland to take up the post of Dean of St Patrick's cathedral, Dublin, which he had earlier obtained, not through his employers' English connections, but through the Irish-born Duke of Ormonde, in whose gift the Deanship resided.

The first years of Swift's return to Ireland were difficult ones for him, marked by jurisdictional struggles within the cathedral hierarchy (highlighted by tensions with his 'boss', William King, Archbishop of Dublin) and by various forms of harassment and persecution, including interception of his mail, because of his Tory associations in London and the consequent unfounded suspicions that he was a Jacobite sympathizer (that is, a supporter of the exiled Stuarts). Forced to keep a low profile, he professed indifference to all public affairs, assuring one correspondent (albeit somewhat disingenuously), 'I am the only man in this kingdom who is not a politician, and therefore I only keep such company as will suffer me to suspend their politics' (*C* 2: 294). By late 1719, however, there was the more candid admission to his friend Charles Ford, 'But as the World is now turned, no Cloyster is retired enough to keep Politicks out, and I will own they raise my Passions whenever they come in my way' (*C* 2: 330). And indeed, it was only a matter of months after this observation that Swift acted on his political 'passions' by publishing the first of his Irish political tracts, *A Proposal for the Universal Use of Irish Manufacture*, which attacked England's legislative restrictions on Ireland's trade and urged a national boycott of English clothing goods. Almost immediately the target of a high-profile government prosecution that landed its printer in jail, the *Proposal* was deemed by the English authorities and the so-called 'English interest' in Ireland as an incendiary call to arms—literally as well as figuratively, since it cited the 'pleasant Observation of some Body's; *that* Ireland *wou'd never be happy 'till a Law were made for* burning *every Thing that came from* England, *except their* People *and their* Coals', adding the wryly ominous comment (omitted in later printings), 'Nor am I *even yet* for lessening the Number of those Exceptions' (p. 132). Although published anonymously, the *Proposal* marked Swift's dramatic entrance onto the Irish political stage, initiating a decade of polemical and creative outpourings far more prolific even than his years in London.

During the next ten years Swift wrote over sixty tracts dealing with Irish affairs, including his mercilessly demystifying account, *A Short View of the State of Ireland* (1728), and his most brilliant short satire, *A Modest Proposal* (1729). This was also the period in which he achieved his two greatest successes. The first of these took place on the political level, with the appearance of *The Drapier's Letters* (1724), which helped defeat an English-sponsored coinage scheme that was threatening to flood Ireland with worthless half-pence and which transformed Swift into the 'Hibernian Patriot', a kind of folk hero widely celebrated in print and song for his defiance of the highest authorities in the land and their futile offer of a large (but unclaimed) reward for his discovery. On the literary level, his success came with the publication in 1726 of *Travels into Several Remote Nations of the World*, better known as *Gulliver's Travels*, an instant best-seller appealing to all segments of the reading public and reflecting the influence of both Swift's earlier satiric experiments as a member of the Scriblerus Club and his subsequent role as wry observer of the Irish as well as the English political scene. (A passage in Part III, depicting the victory over England in the Drapier's affair through the figure of the Lindalinians' revolt, was suppressed for fear of government reprisals and did not appear in print until a century and a half later.) Swift's literary fame, already widespread, was secured in 1735 with the appearance of a four-volume edition of his *Works* published by George Faulkner—the 'Prince of Dublin printers', as Swift characterized him (C 4: 222).

Throughout this period Swift, writing to friends in England, periodically bemoaned his situation as 'a stranger in a strange land' or used black humour to portray himself as 'a poisoned rat in a hole' (C 3: 341; 383). More often, however, he referred affectionately to the Irish under-class as 'my old friends the rabble' and assured Ford that, though he lacked sufficient funds to travel abroad, 'there is one comfort here [in Dublin], that I am at home' (C 4: 537; 212). It is only fitting, then, that he chose as his final resting place St Patrick's cathedral, where (as he self-mockingly put it) he had reigned as 'absolute Lord' for over thirty years (C 4: 171). In the will drawn up in 1740, five years prior to his death, he not only specified the exact spot in the cathedral where he wished his body placed but also provided the epitaph to be inscribed on a tablet above his remains—one subsequently made famous in W. B. Yeats' poetic rendering: 'Swift has sailed into his rest;/Savage indignation there/Cannot lacerate his breast./Imitate him if you dare,/World-besotted traveller; he/Served human liberty.'[4] On the one hand, the 'savage indignation' referred to here suggests a Juvenalian satirist who, in the face of intolerable provocation, cannot refrain from venting his outrage at what he sees around him, and thereby links him to an important classical satiric tradition. On the other hand, it evokes no less pronounced associations with the old Irish poet, or *fili*, whose purported ability to rhyme enemies to death points to the power and the deadly precision of Swift's satiric weaponry.

This brief sketch of Swift's life underscores the importance of certain watershed dates in it—perhaps none more so than 1714, when he departed England for permanent resettlement in Ireland. (Except for two lengthy visits to London in 1726 and 1727, he remained in his native land for the rest of his long life.) It is tempting to draw a clear-cut distinction between the pre- and post-1714 Swift, separating his life into an 'English' and an 'Irish', a conservative and a progressive period; and no doubt this division has some validity, as well as a certain usefulness in interpreting his works. The strong defence of the British Crown and its policies which runs throughout the essays in *The Examiner* could only have appeared in Swift's pre-1714 writings, just as the proto-nationalist and anti-colonialist sentiments we find in his Irish tracts were most overtly and consistently expressed in works written after Swift had left England behind and came to realize that his future lay in Ireland. Nevertheless, one must keep in mind that there was also considerable overlap between the two periods. Thus a work such as *The Story of the Injured Lady* (1707) reflects Swift's fairly early preoccupation with the question of what it meant to be an Irishman trapped in an abusive relationship with England, while his renewed involvement in revising *The Four Last Years of the Queen* in the 1730s—many years after his emergence as the Hibernian Patriot—reveals his ongoing interest in commemorating the period when he came closest to being accepted as a member of English society. And although Swift's agitational style and his pronouncements against established authority are most obvious in his Irish tracts of the 1720s, it is *A Tale of a Tub*, published in 1704 but written much earlier, that best embodies his anarchic energies and his refusal to be contained within conventional structures. (It is hardly coincidental that many of England's highest authorities, including Queen Anne, viewed this work as blasphemous and subversive despite its ostensibly conservative norms.)

The same holds true for Swift's attitude towards and use of language. While his most conservative pronouncements were written during his London period whereas his most explicit deviations from standard linguistic norms appear in his later works (compare *A Proposal for Correcting . . . the English Tongue* (1712), which urges the establishment of a committee 'for *Ascertaining* and *Fixing* our Language for ever' (*P W* 4: 14), with poems and prose pieces from the 1720s that incorporate

Gaelic words, Irish rhymes and dialectal expressions, and use forms of Hiberno-English speech), his writings in fact reveal more of an alternation between these different linguistic practices than a linear development from one to the other. Swift's belief in the need to stabilize and standardize language (mainly to ensure understandable communication between different social groups and generations) was sincere, but it coexisted with a delight in exploiting the vagaries and eccentricities of language, and it never prevented him from bending language to his own idiosyncratic ends, as we can see from his creation of a private language of seeming nonsense words in the *Journal to Stella*, his invention of several different 'foreign' languages in *Gulliver's Travels* and his gleeful indulgence in word games—in playful deformations of language—with the London wits and the circle of punsters he befriended in Ireland. In all phases of his life, Swift demonstrated an unmistakable pleasure in exploring the very non-standardized forms of English he attacked in pieces like *The Tatler, No. CCXXX*. No doubt Swift's linguistic attitudes and practices were shaped to a significant degree by his years at Trinity College, Dublin, which introduced him to the multi-lingual wit play of the university scholars and the dexterous verbal exercises that were a required part of the curriculum.[5]

The seemingly contradictory mix of public and private languages in Swift's writings points to a broader (apparent) conflict informing his works, between the public and private spheres more generally. Although we tend to associate these writings with strikingly individualistic forms of thought and expression, they most consistently emphasize the importance of the public sphere by arguing for the need to subordinate the self to a wider network of communal relationships. That Swift's rebellious and highly idiosyncratic personality was ill-suited for quiet subordination to any larger social entity in no way undermined his communitarian vision; it merely rooted it in paradox. Over the course of his career the nature of this perceived community underwent significant changes, but what did not alter was his portrayal of it as an embodiment of positive values: as a symbol of the public good, perennially threatened by the forces of political faction, individual greed and private self-interest. As Swift remarked in *Thoughts on Various Subjects*, 'In all well-instituted Commonwealths, Care hath been taken to limit Mens Possessions . . . Because when Bounds are set to Mens desires, after they have acquired as much as the Laws will permit them, their private Interest is at an End; and they have nothing to do, but to take care of the Publick' (*PW*, 1: 243). In 1701, in *A Discourse of the Contests and Dissensions . . . in Athens and Rome*, the community was represented by a group of Whig statesmen whose wrongful impeachment threatened to upset the political balance that ensured the harmonious coexistence of all segments of society. In the period from 1710 to 1714, as portrayed in *The Examiner*, the community was the Tory establishment supported by the full symbolism of the British monarchy, exposed to the snarling resentments of a disgruntled faction. A decade later, in 1724, the community was re-envisioned in *Drapier's Letter IV* as 'the whole People of Ireland', threatened with ruin by the corrupt schemes of an insignificant but malevolent individual (William Wood) and his powerful backers in England. The community being defended was now Irish rather than English and had metamorphosed from being a cohesive social group originating from above to one developing from below, as a grass-roots movement that included all parts of Irish society, but the ideal of a public good opposed to the disintegrating forces of a private interest persisted. Moreover, similar images appear in the writings of both periods to dramatize this opposition. In *Contests and Dissensions*, for example, Swift urged the importance of 'a Ballance of Power' within the state, warning that 'When the Ballance is broke, whether by the Negligence, Folly, or Weakness of the Hand that held it, or by mighty Weights fallen into either Scale', the result will be tyranny (*PW* 1: 197). A decade later, in 1711, while arguing for peace in *The Conduct of the Allies*, he was once again holding up the scales of power to scrutiny in castigating the advocates of war: 'And this is what we charge them with as answerable to God, their Country, and Posterity, that the bleeding Condition of their Fellow-Subjects, was a Feather in the Balance with their private Ends' (*PW* 6:

59). And another dozen years later, the Drapier likewise weighed the public against the private interest, finding a similarly scandalous imbalance crying out for redress: 'It would be very hard, if all *Ireland* should be put into *One Scale*, and *this sorry Fellow* WOOD *into the other*: That Mr. WOOD should weigh down *this whole Kingdom*, by which *England* gets above a Million of good Money every Year clear into their *Pockets*' (p. 160).

To be sure, in the 1710–14 period, the collective body being put forward as a bulwark against the private machinations was a partisan group (the Tory Party) with a limited membership, which was soon to be defeated and marginalized. In the example cited from *The Drapier's Letters*, the community Swift so passionately defended was a society governed by a small Anglican minority in a country predominantly Roman Catholic. How are we to reconcile Swift's claim to be speaking for the collective interest or the 'whole people' with his complicity with groups that historically represented a relatively small and privileged segment of the society in which he lived? One way is to view this claim in purely polemical and rhetorical terms, as a particularly effective means of legitimizing a minority position by presenting it as congruent with the interests of the nation as a whole. Swift was, after all, a consummate political animal, and certainly knew how to advance his views in the most forceful and persuasive way possible. Nevertheless, it would be wrong to dismiss his notion of community as simply a polemical ploy. Its varied and recurring representations throughout the Swift canon point to the central role it played in his ideological imagination and underscore the importance he placed on its capacity to strike a sympathetic chord in his readers, whom he envisioned as a diverse body extending well beyond the privileged circle to which he belonged. Thus his espousal of a Tory ideology in works from the 1710–14 period not only expressed the views of an elite but also struck a populist chord with all those groups who felt exploited or disadvantaged by the new capitalist and professional military classes. In Swift's later tracts, the protest against England's subordination of Ireland to the status of a 'depending Kingdom' expressed not only the resentment of the country's Protestant elite, who chafed at being treated as inferior to their English counterparts, but also the interests of other segments of Irish society which (as the persona of *Intelligencer, No. 19* pointedly observes) were suffering in a far more immediate way from the ill effects of England's colonialist policies, including 'the *Buyers* and *Sellers*, at *Fairs* and *Markets*; the *Shopkeepers* in every *Town*; the *Farmers* in general', as well as 'common Labourers' (*PW* 12: 54–5). This shared body of concerns allowed Swift to characterize Ireland in *Drapier's Letter IV*—in terms calculated for rhetorical effect but going beyond mere rhetoric—as 'a Country, where the People of all Ranks, Parties, and Denominations' (p. 172) have come together to defeat a common enemy.

Swift's active participation in multiple (political, social, cultural and linguistic) communities throughout his lifetime gives the lie to the monolithic and static labels regularly imposed on him. Even the portrayal of him as 'Anglo-Irish', while essential to understanding his identity and writings, suggests a binary character that unduly limits the range of his perspectives and allegiances. Like his many different satiric personae, Swift was able to penetrate and exist in varied worlds, moving in and out of the realms of classical and popular culture, of socially dominant and downtrodden classes, of the metropolis and the periphery. The writings he produced as a result point to ways of bridging the gap between these worlds but without erasing their distinctiveness and without imposing false notions of unity rooted in vapid generalizations. These writings suggest that our commonality as human beings resides, not in an abstractly conceived set of characteristics, but in the very features that differentiate us as individuals confined within a particular body and occupying a particular time and place in history. Swift's oft-cited comment, 'I hate and detest that animal called Man, although I heartily love John, Peter, Thomas, and so forth' (pp. 189–90) should be understood not as an embrace of the individual to the exclusion of society or the human family, but as a recognition that such an embrace is the necessary first step towards affirming larger allegiances. As his compatriot Edmund

Burke put it, 'To be attached to the subdivision, to love the little platoon we belong to in society, is . . . the first link in the series by which we proceed towards a love to our country and to mankind.'[6] For all his notoriously misanthropic tendencies, Swift's prose writings show us that love of country and mankind can exist shorn of the usual cant and sentimentality, able to survive even the boiling cauldron of his corrosive satire.

NOTES

1. Edward W. Said, 'Swift as Intellectual', in *The World, the Text, and the Critic* (Cambridge, Mass.: Harvard University Press, 1983), 77.

2. Jean-Paul Sartre, *Search for a Method*, trans. Hazel E. Barnes (New York: Random House (Vintage Books), 1968), 28. For the distinction between organic and traditional intellectuals, see Antonio Gramsci, *Selections from the 'Prison Notebooks'*, ed. Quintin Hoare and Geoffrey Nowell Smith (New York: International Publishers, 1971; 1976), 5–14.

3. *The Correspondence of Alexander Pope*, ed. George Sherburn, 5 vols. (Oxford: Clarendon Press, 1956), 3: 135.

4. 'Swift's Epitaph', in *The Collected Poems of W. B. Yeats*, ed. Richard J. Finneran, revised 2nd edn. (New York: Scribner, 1996), 245–6.

5. See Andrew Carpenter, '*A Tale of a Tub* as an Irish Text', in *Swift Studies* (2005), 30–40.

6. Edmund Burke, *Reflections on the Revolution in France*, ed. Conor Cruise O'Brien (London: Penguin Classics, 1986), 135.

Further Reading

BIBLIOGRAPHIES AND
REFERENCE MATERIALS

Berwick, Donald M., *The Reputation of Jonathan Swift, 1781–1882* (Philadelphia: University of Pennsylvania Press, 1941; repr. New York: Haskell House, 1965).

Landa, Louis A., and Tobin, James Edward, *Jonathan Swift: A List of Critical Studies Published from 1895 to 1945* (repr. New York: Octagon Books, 1975 [1945]).

LeFanu, William R., *A Catalogue of Books Belonging to Dr Jonathan Swift: Dean of St Patrick's* (Cambridge: Cambridge Bibliographic Society, 1988).

Rodino, Richard H., *Swift Studies 1965–1980: An Annotated Bibliography* (New York: Garland, 1984).

Stathis, James J., *A Bibliography of Swift Studies 1945–1965* (Nashville: Vanderbilt University Press, 1967).

Teerink, H., and Scouten, Arthur H., *A Bibliography of the Writings of Jonathan Swift* (2nd edn, Philadelphia: University of Pennsylvania Press, 1963).

Voigt, Milton, *Swift and the Twentieth Century* (Detroit: Wayne State University Press, 1964).

Williams, Harold, *Dean Swift's Library* (Cambridge: Cambridge University Press, 1932).

Williams, Kathleen (ed.), *Swift: The Critical Heritage* (London: Routledge, 1970).

MODERN EDITIONS OF SWIFT

Collected Works

The Prose Works of Jonathan Swift, ed. Herbert Davis, 14 vols. (Oxford: Blackwell's, 1939–74).

The Correspondence of Jonathan Swift, ed. Harold Williams, 5 vols. (Oxford: Clarendon Press, 1963–5).

The Correspondence of Jonathan Swift, ed. David Woolley, 4 vols. (Frankfurt am Main and New York: Peter Lang, 1999–2007).

The Poems of Jonathan Swift, ed. Harold Williams, 3 vols. (Oxford: Clarendon Press, 1937; rev. edn. 1958).

Jonathan Swift: The Complete Poems, ed. Pat Rogers (London and New York: Penguin, 1983).

Individual Works

The Account Books of Jonathan Swift, ed. Dorothy Thompson and Paul Thompson (Newark: University of Delaware Press, 1984).

A Discourse of the Contests and Dissensions Between the Nobles and the Commons in Athens and Rome, ed. Frank H. Ellis (Oxford: Clarendon Press, 1967).

The Drapier's Letters, ed. Herbert Davis (Oxford: Clarendon Press, 1935).

Gulliver's Travels, ed. Robert A. Greenberg (New York: Norton Critical Edition, 1961; 1970); ed. Albert J. Rivero (2001).

Gulliver's Travels, ed. Paul Turner (Oxford and New York: Oxford University Press, 1971; Oxford's World's Classics, 1994).

The Intelligencer (with Thomas Sheridan), ed. James Woolley (Oxford: Clarendon Press, 1992).

Journal to Stella, ed. Harold Williams, 2 vols. (Oxford: Clarendon Press, 1948; repr. as vols. 15–16 of *Prose Works of Jonathan Swift*).

The Letters of Jonathan Swift to Charles Ford, ed. David Nichol Smith (Oxford: Clarendon Press, 1935; repr. Folcroft Press, 1969).

Swift's Polite Conversation, ed. Eric Partridge (London: André Deutsch, 1963).

A Tale of a Tub (et al.), ed. A. C. Guthkelch and D. Nichol Smith (Oxford: Clarendon Press, 1920; rev. edn. 1958).

MODERN BIOGRAPHIES

Downie, J. A., *Jonathan Swift: Political Writer* (London: Routledge & Kegan Paul, 1984).

Ehrenpreis, Irvin, *Swift: The Man, His Works, and the Age*, 3 vols. (Cambridge, Mass.: Harvard University Press, 1962–83).

Elias, A. C., Jr., *Swift at Moor Park: Problems in Biography and Criticism* (Philadelphia: University of Pennsylvania Press, 1982).

Glendinning, Victoria, *Jonathan Swift* (London: Hutchinson, 1998).

McMinn, Joseph, *Jonathan Swift: A Literary Life* (Basingstoke: Macmillan; New York: St Martin's Press, 1991).

Nokes, David, *Jonathan Swift, A Hypocrite Reversed: A Critical Biography* (Oxford: Oxford University Press, 1985).

CRITICISM AND COMMENTARY

NB This list does not contain studies focused on *A Tale of a Tub*, *Gulliver's Travels* or Swift's poetry.

Collections of Essays

Connery, Brian A. (ed.), *Representations of Swift* (Newark: University of Delaware Press, 2002).

Douglas, Aileen, Kelly, Patrick, and Ross, Ian Campbell (eds.), *Locating Swift: Essays from Dublin on the 250th Anniversary*

of the Death of Jonathan Swift, 1667–1745 (Dublin: Four
Courts Press, 1998).

Fox, Christopher, and Tooley, Brenda (eds.), *Walking Naboth's Vineyard: New Studies of Swift* (Notre Dame, Ind.: University of Notre Dame Press, 1995).

Jeffares, A. Norman (ed.), *Fair Liberty Was All His Cry: A Tercentenary Tribute to Jonathan Swift, 1667–1745* (London: Macmillan; New York: St Martin's Press, 1967).

McHugh, Roger, and Edwards, Philip (eds.), *Jonathan Swift, 1667–1745: A Dublin Tercentenary Tribute* (Dublin: Dolmen Press; Oxford: Oxford University Press, 1967).

Palmieri, Frank (ed.), *Critical Essays on Jonathan Swift* (New York: G. K. Hall, 1993).

Probyn, Clive T. (ed.), *The Art of Jonathan Swift* (London: Vision Press, 1978).

Rawson, Claude J. (ed.), *The Character of Swift's Satire: A Revised Focus* (Newark: University of Delaware Press, 1983).

Tuveson, Ernest (ed.), *Swift: A Collection of Critical Essays* (Englewood Cliffs, NJ: Prentice Hall, 1964).

Vickers, Brian (ed.), *The World of Jonathan Swift: Essays for the Tercentenary* (Oxford: Blackwell, 1968).

General Studies of Swift's Satire and Prose Writings

Bullitt, John M., *Jonathan Swift and the Anatomy of Satire: A Study of Satiric Technique* (Cambridge, Mass.: Harvard University Press, 1953).

Davis, Herbert, *Jonathan Swift: Essays on His Satire and Other Studies* (Oxford: Oxford University Press, 1964).

Donoghue, Denis, *Jonathan Swift: A Critical Introduction* (Cambridge: Cambridge University Press, 1969).

Fabricant, Carole, *Swift's Landscape* (Baltimore and London: Johns Hopkins University Press, 1982; repr. with new introduction, Notre Dame, Ind.: University of Notre Dame Press, 1995).

Kelly, Ann Cline, *Swift and the English Language* (Philadelphia: University of Pennsylvania Press, 1988).

Price, Martin, *Swift's Rhetorical Art: A Study in Structure and Meaning* (New Haven: Yale University Press, 1953).

Quintana, Ricardo, *Swift: An Introduction* (London: Oxford University Press, 1955).

Rawson, C. J., *Gulliver and the Gentle Reader: Studies in Swift and Our Time* (London and Boston: Routledge & Kegan Paul, 1973).

Reilly, Patrick, *Jonathan Swift: The Brave Desponder* (Manchester: Manchester University Press, 1982).

Rosenheim, Edward W., *Swift and the Satirist's Art* (Chicago: University of Chicago Press, 1963).

Steele, Peter, *Jonathan Swift: Preacher and Jester* (Oxford: Clarendon Press, 1978).

Williams, Kathleen, *Jonathan Swift and the Age of Compromise* (London: Constable, 1959).

Wyrick, Deborah Baker, *Jonathan Swift and the Vested Word* (Chapel Hill and London: University of North Carolina Press, 1988).

Historical, Political and Literary Backgrounds

Armitage, David, *The Ideological Origins of the British Empire* (New York and Cambridge: Cambridge University Press, 2000).

Beckett, J. C., *The Anglo-Irish Tradition* (London: Faber, 1976).

Brewer, John, *The Sinews of Power: War, Money and the English State, 1688–1783* (Cambridge, Mass.: Harvard University Press, 1988 [1990]).

Connolly, S. J., *Religion, Law, and Power: The Making of Protestant Ireland 1660–1760* (Oxford: Oxford University Press, 1992; Clarendon Press, 1995).

Craig, Maurice, *Dublin 1660–1860: A Social and Architectural History* (Dublin: Allen Figgis, 1969).

Elliot, Robert C., *The Power of Satire: Magic, Literature, Art* (Princeton: Princeton University Press, 1960).

Fauske, Christopher J., *Jonathan Swift and the Church of*

Ireland, 1710–1724 (Dublin and Portland, Ore.: Irish Academic Press, 2002).

Ferguson, Oliver W., *Jonathan Swift and Ireland* (Urbana: University of Illinois Press, 1962).

Fox, Christopher (ed.), *The Cambridge Companion to Jonathan Swift* (Cambridge: Cambridge University Press, 2003).

Goldgar, Bertrand A., *Walpole and the Wits: The Relation of Politics to Literature, 1722–1742* (Lincoln: University of Nebraska Press, 1976).

Higgins, Ian, *Swift's Politics: A Study in Disaffection* (Cambridge: Cambridge University Press, 1994).

Hill, Christopher, *The Century of Revolution 1603–1714*, Norton Library History of England (New York: Norton, 1961).

James, Francis Godwin, *Ireland in the Empire, 1688–1770: A History of Ireland from the Williamite Wars to the Eve of the American Revolution* (Cambridge, Mass.: Harvard University Press, 1973).

Johnston, Edith Mary, *Ireland in the Eighteenth Century* (Dublin: Gill and Macmillan, 1974).

Landa, Louis A., *Swift and the Church of Ireland* (Oxford: Oxford University Press, 1954).

Leerssen, Joep, *Mere Irish and Fior-Ghael: Studies in the Idea of Irish Nationality, its Development and Literary Expression prior to the Nineteenth Century* (Cork: Cork University Press, Notre Dame: University of Notre Dame Press [Field Day Monographs], 1997 [1984]).

McLoughlin, Thomas, *Contesting Ireland: Irish Voices against England in the Eighteenth Century* (Dublin: Four Courts Press, 1999).

Mahony, Robert, *Jonathan Swift: The Irish Identity* (New Haven and London: Yale University Press, 1995).

Mercier, Vivian, *The Irish Comic Tradition* (Oxford: Clarendon Press, 1962; repr. 1992).

Nokes, David, *Raillery and Rage: A Study of Eighteenth-Century Satire* (New York: St Martin's Press, 1987).

Paulson, Ronald, *The Fictions of Satire* (Baltimore: Johns Hopkins University Press, 1967).

Rogers, Pat, *Grub Street: Studies in a Subculture* (London: Methuen, 1972); abridged as *Hacks and Dunces: Pope, Swift and Grub Street* (London: Methuen, 1980).

Speck, W. A., *Stability and Strife: England 1714–1760* (London: Edward Arnold, 1977; rev. edn. 1984).

Note on the Text

Most of the texts in this volume are based on the George Faulkner edition of 1735, whose publication Swift assisted with in a variety of ways; unless otherwise noted, the copy-text for a given work is this edition. For pieces not appearing in this edition I have used other eighteenth-century editions or autograph copies, which are identified in the headnotes to the works.

I have generally avoided normalizing such features of the copy-text as spelling, capitalization, punctuation and use of italics in order to retain important aspects of Swift's personal, at times idiosyncratic style as well as to demonstrate certain common writing and printing practices in Swift's time. In extreme cases, such normalization can destroy the meaning as well as the form of the text, as in *A Famous Prediction of Merlin*, where archaic words and spellings, not to mention the 'black-letter' typography evident in Plate 2, are essential to Swift's satiric point. So too is Swift's use of word forms that evoke colloquial or dialectal speech, spellings that underscore puns integral to a work's multiple levels of meaning and the deliberate use of certain written and print forms for purposes of emphasis. At the same time, there is no reason to treat as sacrosanct every aspect of a printed text—things like punctuation practices and capitalizations could vary greatly among eighteenth-century printers, and even change from one edition to another by the same printer. I have therefore not hesitated on occasion to make very minor alterations in these areas in order to ensure a readable and understandable text. With regard to punctuation, the very heavy use of semicolons as substitutes for both commas and (especially) periods, as well as the gratuitous use of commas in the body of a sentence ('Not that I am, in the least of Opinion with those . . .'), can create needless obstacles to comprehension for the modern reader, and this has on occasion resulted in slight editorial changes. In the case of inordinately long sentences that in some instances continue for several pages, I have, when deemed appropriate, replaced semicolons with commas or periods to clarify the relationship among the sentence's numerous clauses and to preclude unnecessary confusion for the reader. Obvious printer errors have been silently corrected.

Needless abridgements of Swift's works have been avoided. Lengthy works such as the *Journal to Stella* and *Polite Conversation* which could not here be reproduced whole are represented by complete segments; in the former case, by complete 'Letters', in the latter, by the 'Second Conversation' in its entirety. The same principle applies to Swift's contributions to various periodicals, represented here by complete essays. In the case of *Directions to Servants*, which contains some rather fragmentary material, two of the work's most complete sections ('Rules that Concern All Servants in General' and 'Directions to the Footman') are included.

Since any attempt to group Swift's writings according to theme or genre is largely futile given their tendency to traverse formal boundaries and deal with a number of interrelated themes within a single text, the works are arranged chronologically, according to their date of composition as far as it is ascertainable. This arrangement helps to underscore these works' inextricable ties to a particular moment and set of circumstances in history. I have not, however, applied this organizing principle so rigidly that the relative integrity of works consisting of multiple parts is interrupted. Thus, for example, all selections from the *Journal to Stella*, *The Examiner* and *The Intelligencer* have been placed together in sequence. Nor is a strict adherence to chronology possible in all instances, given that we can only conjecture about the composition date of certain pieces, while others were written and revised over a lengthy period of time.

Along with notes contextualizing Swift's works and identifying references in them, a 'Glossary' and a 'Biographical Dictionary' appear at the end of the volume. Included in the former are not only words requiring definition but also some important historical terms, places and events crucial to Swift's writings. Unfamiliar phrases, as well as certain words having a special meaning within their immediate context, are glossed in the Notes. The 'Biographical Dictionary' is limited to figures cited by and roughly contemporary with Swift who played a significant role in his life or writings, or who have a particular historic or literary importance; others are briefly identified in the Notes.

In Swift's time the beginning of the year was computed from 25 March rather than 1 January. In recording dates that fall within this nearly three-month period, I have adhered to current practice.

List of Illustrations

A MODEST PROPOSAL
AND OTHER WRITINGS

NOT to marry a young Woman.

Not to keep young Company unless they really desire it.

Not to be peevish, or morose, or suspicious.

Not to scorn present Ways, or Wits, or Fashions, or Men or War, &c.

Not to be fond of Children, or let them come near me hardly.[1]

Not to tell the same Story over & over to the same People.

Not to be covetous.

Not to neglect decency, or cleanlyness, for fear of falling into Nastyness.

Not to be over severe with young People, but give Allowances for their youthfull follyes, and Weaknesses.

Not to be influenced by, or give ear to knavish tatling Servants, or others.

Not to be too free of advise nor trouble any but those that desire it.

To desire some good Friends to inform me wch of these Resolutions I break, or neglect, & wherein; and reform accordingly.

Not to talk much, nor of my self.

Not to boast of my former beauty, or strength, or favor with Ladyes, &c.

Not to hearken to Flatteryes, nor conceive I can be beloved by a young woman. et eos qui hereditatem captant odisse ac vitare.[2]

Not to be positive or opiniatre.[3]

Not to set up for observing all these Rules; for fear I should observe none.

THE
WORKS

OF

J.S, D.D, D.S.P.D.

IN

FOUR VOLUMES.

CONTAINING,

I. The Author's MISCELLANIES in PROSE.

II. His POETICAL WRITINGS.

III. The TRAVELS of Captain *Lemuel Gulliver.*

IV. His Papers relating to *Ireland*, confifting of
feveral Treatifes; among which are, The
DRAPIER's LETTERS to the People of *Ireland*
againft receiving *Wood*'s Half-pence: Alfo,
two Original DRAPIER's LETTERS, never before publifhed.

In this Edition are great Alterations and Additions; and likewife many Pieces in each Volume, never before publifhed

---

DUBLIN:

Printed by and for GEORGE FAULKNER, Printer
and Bookfeller, in ESSEX-STREET, oppofite to
the Bridge, M DCC XXXV.

Plate 1. Title page of the Faulkner edition of
The Works of Jonathan Swift (1735)

A MEDITATION UPON
A BROOM-STICK

ACCORDING TO

The Style and Manner of the Honourable
Robert Boyle's *Meditations*

THIS single Stick, which you now behold ingloriously lying in
that neglected Corner, I once knew in a flourishing State in a
Forest: It was full of Sap, full of Leaves, and full of Boughs: But
now, in vain does the busy Art of Man pretend to vye with
Nature, by tying that withered Bundle of Twigs to its sapless
Trunk: It is now at best but the Reverse of what it was; a Tree
turned upside down, the Branches on the Earth, and the Root
in the Air: It is now handled by every dirty Wench, condemned
to do her Drudgery; and by a capricious Kind of Fate, destined
to make other Things clean, and be nasty it self. At length,
worn to the Stumps in the Service of the Maids, it is either
thrown out of Doors, or condemned to the last Use of kindling
a Fire. When I beheld this, I sighed, and said within my self,
SURELY MORTAL MAN IS A BROOMSTICK! Nature sent him
into the World strong and lusty, in a thriving Condition, wearing his own Hair on his Head, the proper Branches of this
reasoning Vegetable; till the Axe of Intemperance has lopped
off his Green Boughs, and left him a withered Trunk: He then
flies to Art, and puts on a *Perriwig*; valuing himself upon an
unnatural Bundle of Hairs, all covered with Powder, that never
grew on his Head. But now, should this our *Broom-stick* pretend to enter the Scene, proud of those *Birchen* Spoils it never
bore, and all covered with Dust, though the Sweepings of the
finest Lady's Chamber, we should be apt to ridicule and despise
its Vanity: Partial Judges that we are of our own Excellencies,
and other Mens Defaults!

BUT a *Broom-stick*, perhaps you will say, is an Emblem
of a Tree standing on its Head; and pray what is Man but

a topsy-turvy Creature? His Animal Faculties perpetually
mounted on his Rational; his Head where his Heels should be,
groveling on the Earth. And yet, with all his Faults, he sets up
to be a universal Reformer and Correcter of Abuses; a Remover
of Grievances; rakes into every Slut's Corner of Nature, bringing hidden Corruptions to the Light, and raiseth a mighty Dust
where there was none before; sharing deeply all the while in the
very same Pollutions he pretends to sweep away.[1] His last
Days are spent in Slavery to Women, and generally the least
deserving; till worn to the Stumps, like his Brother *Bezom*, he
is either kicked out of Doors, or made use of to kindle Flames
for others to warm themselves by.[2]

THE STORY OF THE INJURED LADY

Written by HERSELF

In a LETTER to her *Friend*, with his ANSWER

SIR,

BEING ruined by the Inconstancy and Unkindness of a Lover, I hope a true and plain Relation of my Misfortunes may be of Use and Warning to credulous Maids, never to put too much Trust in deceitful Men.

A Gentleman in the Neighbourhood had two Mistresses, another and myself; and he pretended honourable Love to us both. Our three Houses stood pretty near one another; his was parted from mine by a River, and from my Rival's by an old broken Wall. But before I enter into the Particulars of this Gentleman's hard Usage of me, I will give a very just impartial Character of my Rival and Myself.

As to her Person she is tall and lean, and very ill shaped; she hath bad Features, and a worse Complexion; she hath a stinking Breath, and twenty ill Smells about her besides, which are yet more unsufferable by her natural Sluttishness; for she is always Lousy, and never without the Itch. As to her other Qualities, she hath no Reputation either for Virtue, Honesty, Truth, or Manners; and it is no Wonder, considering what her Education hath been. Scolding and Cursing are her common Conversation. To sum up all, she is poor and beggarly, and gets a sorry Maintenance by pilfering wherever she comes. As for this Gentleman who is now so fond of her, she still beareth him an invincible Hatred, revileth him to his Face, and raileth at him in all Companies. Her House is frequented by a Company of Rogues and Thieves, and Pickpockets, whom she encourageth to rob his Hen-roosts, steal his Corn and Cattle, and do him all manner of Mischief.[1] She hath been known to come at the Head of these Rascals, and beat her Lover until he was sore from Head to Foot, and then force him to pay for the Trouble she was at. Once, attended with a Crew of Raggamuffins, she broke into his House, turned all Things topsy-turvy, and then set it

on Fire.[2] At the same Time she told so many Lies among his
Servants, that it set them all by the Ears, and his poor Steward
was knocked on the Head,[3] for which I think, and so doth all
the Country, that she ought to be answerable. To conclude her
Character, she is of a different Religion, being a Presbyterian
of the most rank and virulent Kind, and consequently having
an inveterate Hatred to the Church; yet, I am sure, I have been
always told, that in Marriage there ought to be an Union of
Minds as well as of Persons.

I will now give my own Character, and shall do it in few
Words, and with Modesty and Truth.

I was reckoned to be as handsome as any in our Neighbourhood, until I became pale and thin with Grief and ill Usage. I
am still fair enough, and have, I think, no very ill Feature about
me. They that see me now will hardly allow me ever to have
had any great Share of Beauty; for besides being so much
altered, I go always mobbed and in an Undress, as well out of
Neglect, as indeed for want of Cloaths to appear in. I might
add to all this, that I was born to a good Estate, although it
now turneth to little Account under the Oppressions I endure,
and hath been the true Cause of all my Misfortunes.

Some Years ago, this Gentleman taking a Fancy either to my
Person or Fortune, made his Addresses to me, which, being
then young and foolish, I too readily admitted; he seemed to
use me with so much Tenderness, and his Conversation was so
very engaging, that all my Constancy and Virtue were too soon
overcome; and, to dwell no longer upon a Theme that causeth
such bitter Reflections, I must confess with Shame, that I was
undone by the common Arts practised upon all easy credulous
Virgins, half by Force, and half by Consent, after solemn Vows
and Protestations of Marriage. When he had once got Possession, he soon began to play the usual Part of a too fortunate
Lover, affecting on all Occasions to shew his Authority, and to
act like a Conqueror.[4] First, he found Fault with the Government of my Family, which to grant, was none of the best,
consisting of ignorant illiterate Creatures; for at that Time, I
knew but little of the World. In compliance to him, therefore,
I agreed to fall into his Ways and Methods of Living; I consented

that his Steward should govern my House, and have Liberty to employ an Under-Steward, who should receive his Directions.[5] My Lover proceeded further, turning away several old Servants and Tenants, and supplying me with others from his own House. These grew so domineering and unreasonable, that there was no Quiet, and I heard of nothing but perpetual Quarrels, which although I could not possibly help, yet my Lover laid all the Blame and Punishment upon me; and upon every Falling out, still turned away more of my People, and supplied me in their Stead with a Number of Fellows and Dependents of his own, whom he had no other Way to provide for. Overcome by Love, and to avoid Noise and Contention, I yielded to all his Usurpations, and finding it in vain to resist, I thought it my best Policy to make my Court to my new Servants, and draw them to my Interests; I fed them from my own Table with the best I had, put my new Tenants on the choice Parts of my Land, and treated them all so kindly, that they began to love me as well as their Master. In process of Time, all my old Servants were gone, and I had not a Creature about me, nor above one or two Tenants but what were of his chusing; yet I had the good Luck by gentle Usage to bring over the greatest Part of them to my Side. When my Lover observed this, he began to alter his Language; and, to those who enquired about me, he would answer, that I was an old Dependent upon his Family, whom he had placed on some Concerns of his own; and he began to use me accordingly, neglecting by Degrees all common Civility in his Behaviour. I shall never forget the Speech he made me one Morning, which he delivered with all the Gravity in the World. He put me in Mind of the vast Obligations I lay under to him, in sending me so many of his People for my own Good, and to teach me Manners: That it had cost him ten Times more than I was worth to maintain me: That it had been much better for him if I had been damned, or burnt, or sunk to the Bottom of the Sea: That it was but reasonable I should strain myself as far as I was able, to reimburse him some of his Charges: That from henceforward he expected his Word should be a Law to me in all Things: That I must maintain a Parish-watch against Thieves and Robbers, and give Salaries to an Overseer, a Constable, and Others, all of his own chusing, whom he would send from Time to Time to be Spies upon me: That to enable me the better in supporting these Expences, my Tenants shall be obliged to carry all their Goods cross the River to his Town-market, and pay Toll on both Sides, and then sell them at half Value. But because we were a nasty Sort of People, and that he could not endure to touch any Thing we had a Hand in, and likewise, because he wanted Work to employ his own Folks, therefore we must send all our Goods to his Market just in their Naturals; the Milk immediately from the Cow without making it into Cheese or Butter; the Corn in the Ear; the Grass as it is mowed; the Wool as it cometh from the Sheeps Back, and bring the Fruit upon the Branch, that he might not be obliged to eat it after our filthy Hands:[6] That, if a Tenant carried but a Piece of Bread and Cheese to eat by the Way, or an Inch of Worsted to mend his Stockings, he should forfeit his whole Parcel: And because a Company of Rogues usually plyed on the River between us, who often robbed my Tenants of their Goods and Boats, he ordered a Waterman of his to guard them, whose Manner was to be out of the Way until the poor Wretches were plundered; then to overtake the Thieves, and seize all as lawful Prize to his Master and himself. It would be endless to repeat a hundred other Hardships he hath put upon me; but it is a general Rule, that whenever he imagines the smallest Advantage will redound to one of his Foot-boys by any new Oppression of me and my whole Family and Estate, he never disputeth it a Moment. All this hath rendered me so very insignificant and contemptible at Home, that some Servants to whom I pay the greatest Wages, and many Tenants who have the most beneficial Leases, are gone over to live with him; yet I am bound to continue their Wages, and pay their Rents; by which Means one third Part of my whole Income is spent on his Estate;[7] and above another Third by his Tolls and Markets; and my poor Tenants are so sunk and impoverished, that, instead of maintaining me suitable to my Quality, they can hardly find me Cloaths to keep me warm, or provide the common Necessaries of Life for themselves.

Matters being in this Posture between me and my Lover,

I received Intelligence that he had been for some Time making very pressing Overtures of Marriage to my Rival, until there happened some Misunderstandings between them; she gave him ill Words, and threatened to break off all Commerce with him. He, on the other Side, having either acquired Courage by his Triumphs over me, or supposing her as tame a Fool as I, thought at first to carry it with a high Hand;[8] but hearing at the same Time, that she had Thoughts of making some private Proposals to join with me against him, and doubting with very good Reason that I would readily accept them, he seemed very much disconcerted. This I thought was a proper Occasion to shew some great Example of Generosity and Love; and so, without further Consideration, I sent him Word, that hearing there was like to be a Quarrel between him and my Rival, notwithstanding all that had passed, and without binding him to any Conditions in my own Favour, I would stand by him against her and all the World, while I had a Penny in my Purse, or a Petticoat to pawn. This Message was subscribed by all my chief Tenants, and proved so powerful, that my Rival immediately grew more tractable upon it.[9] The Result of which was, that there is now a Treaty of Marriage concluded between them, the Wedding Cloaths are bought, and nothing remaineth but to perform the Ceremony, which is put off for some Days, because they design it to be a publick Wedding. And to reward my Love, Constancy, and Generosity, he hath bestowed on me the Office of being Sempstress to his Grooms and Footmen, which I am forced to accept or starve. Yet, in the Midst of this my Situation, I cannot but have some Pity for this deluded Man, to cast himself away on an infamous Creature, who, whatever she pretendeth, I can prove, would at this very Minute rather be a Whore to a certain Great Man, that shall be nameless, if she might have her Will.[10] For my Part, I think, and so doth all the Country too, that the Man is possessed; at least none of us are able to imagine what he can possibly see in her, unless she hath bewitched him, or given him some Powder.

I am sure, I never sought his Alliance, and you can bear me Witness, that I might have had other Matches; nay, if I were lightly disposed, I could still perhaps have Offers that some, who hold their Heads higher, would be glad to accept. But alas, I never had any such wicked Thought; all I now desire is only to enjoy a little Quiet, to be free from the Persecutions of this unreasonable Man, and that he will let me manage my own little Fortune to the best Advantage; for which I will undertake to pay him a considerable Pension every Year, much more considerable than what he now gets by his Oppressions; for he must needs find himself a Loser at last, when he hath drained me and my Tenants so dry, that we shall not have a Penny for him or ourselves. There is one Imposition of his, I had almost forgot, which I think unsufferable, and will appeal to you or any reasonable Person, whether it be so or not. I told you before, that by an old Compact we agreed to have the same Steward, at which Time I consented likewise to regulate my Family and Estate by the same Method with him, which he then shewed me writ down in Form, and I approved of.[11] Now, the Turn he thinks fit to give this Compact of ours is very extraordinary; for he pretends that whatever Orders he shall think fit to prescribe for the future in his Family, he may, if he will, compel mine to observe them, without asking my Advice or hearing my Reasons. So that, I must not make a Lease without his Consent, or give any Directions for the well-governing of my Family, but what he countermands whenever he pleaseth. This leaveth me at such Confusion and Uncertainty, that my Servants know not when to obey me, and my Tenants, although many of them be very well inclined, seem quite at a Loss.

But, I am too tedious upon this melancholy Subject, which however, I hope you will forgive, since the Happiness of my whole Life dependeth upon it. I desire you will think a while, and give your best Advice what Measures I shall take with Prudence, Justice, Courage, and Honour, to protect my Liberty and Fortune against the Hardships and Severities I lie under from that unkind, inconstant Man.

THE ANSWER
TO THE *Injured Lady*

MADAM,

I HAVE received your Ladyship's Letter, and carefully considered every Part of it, and shall give you my Opinion how you ought to proceed for your own Security. But first, I must beg leave to tell your Ladyship, that you were guilty of an unpardonable Weakness t'other Day in making that Offer to your Lover, of standing by him in any Quarrel he might have with your Rival. You know very well, that she began to apprehend he had Designs of using her as he had done you; and common Prudence might have directed you rather to have entered into some Measures with her for joining against him, until he might at least be brought to some reasonable Terms: But your invincible Hatred to that Lady hath carried your Resentments so high, as to be the Cause of your Ruin; yet, if you please to consider, this Aversion of yours began a good while before she became your Rival, and was taken up by you and your Family in a sort of Compliment to your Lover, who formerly had a great Abhorrence for her. It is true, since that Time you have suffered very much by her Encroachments upon your Estate, but she never pretended to govern or direct you:[12] And now you have drawn a new Enemy upon yourself; for I think you may count upon all the ill Offices she can possibly do you by her Credit with her Husband; whereas, if, instead of openly declaring against her without any Provocation, you had but sat still a while, and said nothing, that Gentleman would have lessened his Severity to you out of perfect Fear. This Weakness of yours, you call Generosity; but I doubt there was more in the Matter. In short, Madam, I have good Reasons to think you were betrayed to it by the pernicious Counsels of some about you: For to my certain Knowledge, several of your Tenants and Servants, to whom you have been very kind, are as arrant Rascals as any in the Country. I cannot but observe what a mighty Difference there is in one Particular between your Ladyship and your Rival. Having yielded up your Person, you thought nothing else worth defending, and therefore you will not now insist upon those very Conditions for which you yielded at first. But your Ladyship cannot be ignorant, that some Years since your Rival did the same Thing, and upon no Conditions at all; nay, this Gentleman kept her as a Miss, and yet made her pay for her very Diet and Lodging.[13] But, it being at a Time when he had no Steward, and his Family out of Order, she stole away, and hath now got the Trick very well known among Women of the Town, to grant a Man the Favour over Night and the next Day have the Impudence to deny it to his Face. But, it is too late to reproach you with any former Oversights, which cannot now be rectified. I know the Matters of Fact as you relate them are true and fairly represented. My Advice therefore is this. Get your Tenants together as soon as you conveniently can, and make them agree to the following Resolutions.

First, That your Family and Tenants have no Dependence upon the said Gentleman, further than by the old Agreement, which obligeth you to have the same Steward, and to regulate your Houshold by such Methods as you shall both agree to.

Secondly, That you will not carry your Goods to the Market of his Town, unless you please, nor be hindered from carrying them any where else.

Thirdly, That the Servants you pay Wages to shall live at Home, or forfeit their Places.

Fourthly, That whatever Lease you make to a Tenant, it shall not be in his Power to break it.

If he will agree to these Articles, I advise you to contribute as largely as you can to all Charges of Parish and County.

I can assure you, several of that Gentleman's ablest Tenants and Servants are against his severe Usage of you, and would be glad of an Occasion to convince the rest of their Error, if you will not be wanting to yourself.

If the Gentleman refuses these just and reasonable Offers, pray let me know it, and perhaps I may think of something else that will be more effectual.

> I am,
> MADAM,
> *Your Ladyship's*, &c.

THE BICKERSTAFF PAPERS

PREDICTIONS FOR THE YEAR 1708

Wherein the Month, and Day of the Month, are set
down, the Persons named, and the great Actions
and Events of next Year particularly related as they
will come to pass

Written to prevent the People of England *from being
farther imposed on by vulgar Almanack-Makers*

By ISAAC BICKERSTAFF, Esq.[1]

HAVING long considered the gross Abuse of Astrology in this
Kingdom; upon debating the Matter with my self, I could not
possibly lay the Fault upon the Art, but upon those gross Impostors, who set up to be the Artists. I know several learned Men
have contended that the whole is a Cheat; that it is absurd and
ridiculous to imagine, the Stars can have any Influence at all
upon human Actions, Thoughts, or Inclinations: And whoever
hath not bent his Studies that Way, may be excused for thinking
so, when he sees in how wretched a Manner this noble Art is
treated, by a few mean illiterate Traders between us and the
Stars; who import a yearly Stock of Nonsense, Lies, Folly, and
Impertinence, which they offer to the World as genuine from
the Planets; although they descend from no greater a Height
than their own Brains.

I INTEND, in a short Time, to publish a large and rational
Defence of this Art; and therefore, shall say no more in its
Justification at present, than that it hath been in all Ages
defended by many learned Men; and among the rest, by *Socrates*
himself; whom I look upon as undoubtedly the wisest of unin-
spired Mortals: To which if we add, that those who have condemned this Art, although otherwise learned, having been such
as either did not apply their Studies this Way; or at least did
not succeed in their Applications; their Testimony will not

be of much Weight to its Disadvantage, since they are liable to the common Objection of condemning what they did not understand.

NOR am I at all offended, or think it an Injury to the Art, when I see the common Dealers in it, the *Students in Astrology*, the *Philomaths*, and the rest of that Tribe, treated by wise Men with the utmost Scorn and Contempt: But I rather wonder, when I observe Gentlemen in the Country, rich enough to serve the Nation in Parliament, poring in *Partrige*'s Almanack, to find out the Events of the Year at Home and Abroad; not daring to propose a Hunting-Match, until *Gadbury*, or he, hath fixed the Weather.[2]

I WILL allow either of the Two I have mentioned, or any other of the Fraternity, to be not only Astrologers, but Conjurers too, if I do not produce an Hundred Instances in all their Almanacks, to convince any reasonable Man, that they do not so much as understand Grammar and Syntax; that they are not able to spell any Word out of the usual Road; nor even in their Prefaces to write common Sense, or intelligible *English*. Then, for their Observations and Predictions, they are such as will equally suit any Age, or Country in the World. *This Month a certain great Person will be threatned with Death, or Sickness*. This the News-Paper will tell them; for there we find at the End of the Year, that no Month passes without the Death of some Person of Note; and it would be hard if it should be otherwise, when there are at least two Thousand Persons of Note in this Kingdom, many of them old; and the Almanack-maker has the Liberty of chusing the sickliest Season of the Year where he may fix his Prediction. Again, *This Month an eminent Clergyman will be preferred*; of which there may be some Hundreds, Half of them with one Foot in the Grave. Then, *Such a Planet in such a House shews great Machinations, Plots and Conspiracies, that may in Time be brought to Light*: After which, if we hear of any Discovery, the Astrologer gets the Honour; if not, his Prediction still stands good. And at last, *God preserve King* William *from all his open and Secret Enemies, Amen*. When if the King should happen to have died, the Astrologer plainly foretold it; otherwise, it passeth but for the pious Ejaculation of a loyal Subject: Although it unluckily happened in some of their Almanacks, that poor King *William* was prayed for many Months after he was dead; because it fell out that he died about the Beginning of the Year.

To mention no more of their impertinent Predictions: What have we to do with their Advertisements about *Pills, and Drink for the Venereal Disease*, or their mutual Quarrels in Verse and Prose of *Whig* and *Tory*? wherewith the Stars have little to do.[3]

HAVING long observed and lamented these, and a hundred other Abuses of this Art, too tedious to repeat, I resolved to proceed in a new Way; which I doubt not will be to the general Satisfaction of the Kingdom. I can this Year produce but a Specimen of what I design for the future, having employed most Part of my Time in adjusting and correcting the Calculations I made for some Years past; because I would offer nothing to the World of which I am not as fully satisfied as that I am now alive. For these two last Years I have not failed in above one or two Particulars, and those of no very great Moment. I exactly foretold the Miscarriage at *Toulon*, with all its Particulars; and the Loss of Admiral *Shovel*;[4] although I was mistaken as to the Day, placing that Accident about thirty six Hours sooner than it happened; but upon reviewing my Schemes, I quickly found the Cause of that Error. I likewise foretold the Battle at *Almanza* to the very Day and Hour, with the Loss on both Sides, and the Consequences thereof.[5] All which I shewed to some Friends many Months before they happened; that is, I gave them Papers sealed up, to open at such a Time, after which they were at liberty to read them; and there they found my Predictions true in every Article, except one or two, very minute.

As for the few following Predictions I now offer the World, I forbore to publish them, till I had perused the several Almanacks for the Year we are now entered upon: I found them all in the usual Strain, and I beg the Reader will compare their Manner with mine. And here I make bold to tell the World, that I lay the whole Credit of my Art upon the Truth of these Predictions; and I will be content that *Partrige*, and the rest of his Clan, may hoot me for a Cheat and Impostor, if I fail in any single Particular of Moment. I believe any Man who reads this

Paper, will look upon me to be at least a Person of as much Honesty and Understanding, as a common Maker of Almanacks. I do not lurk in the Dark; I am not wholly unknown in the World; I have set my Name at length, to be a Mark of Infamy to Mankind, if they shall find I deceive them.

IN one point I must desire to be forgiven, that I talk more sparingly of Home Affairs. As it would be Imprudence to discover Secrets of State, so it might be dangerous to my Person: But in smaller Matters, and such as are not of publick Consequence, I shall be very free: And the Truth of my Conjectures will as much appear from these as the other. As for the most signal Events abroad in *France*, *Flanders*, *Italy* and *Spain*, I shall make no Scruple to predict them in plain Terms: Some of them are of Importance, and I hope I shall seldom mistake the Day they will happen: Therefore, I think good to inform the Reader, that I all along make use of the *Old Stile* observed in *England*, which I desire he will compare with that of the News-Papers, at the Time they relate the Actions I mention.[6]

I MUST add one Word more: I know it hath been the Opinion of several learned Persons, who think well enough of the true Art of Astrology, That the Stars do only *incline*, and not *force*, the Actions or Wills of Men: And therefore, however I may proceed by right Rules, yet I cannot in Prudence so confidently assure that the Events will follow exactly as I predict them.

I HOPE I have maturely considered this Objection, which in some Cases is of no little Weight. For Example: A Man may, by the Influence of an over-ruling Planet, be disposed or inclined to Lust, Rage, or Avarice; and yet by the Force of Reason overcome that evil Influence: And this was the Case of *Socrates*. But the great Events of the World usually depending upon Numbers of Men, it cannot be expected they should all unite to cross their Inclinations, from pursuing a general Design, wherein they unanimously agree. Besides, the Influence of the Stars reacheth to many Actions and Events, which are not any way in the Power of Reason; as Sickness, Death, and what we commonly call Accidents; with many more needless to repeat.

BUT now it is Time to proceed to my Predictions, which I have begun to calculate from the Time that the *Sun* enters into

Aries. And this I take to be properly the Beginning of the natural Year.[7] I pursue them to the Time that he enters *Libra*, or somewhat more, which is the busy Period of the Year. The Remainder I have not yet adjusted upon Account of several Impediments needless here to mention. Besides, I must remind the Reader again, that this is but a Specimen of what I design in succeeding Years to treat more at large, if I may have Liberty and Encouragement.

MY first Prediction is but a Trifle; yet I will mention it, to shew how ignorant those sottish Pretenders to Astrology are in their own Concerns: It relates to *Partrige* the Almanack-Maker. I have consulted the Star of his Nativity by my own Rules, and find he will infallibly die upon the 29th of *March* next, about eleven at Night, of a raging Fever: Therefore I advise him to consider of it, and settle his Affairs in Time.

THE Month of *APRIL* will be observable for the Death of many great Persons. On the 4th will die the Cardinal *de Noailles*, Archbishop of *Paris:* On the 11th the young Prince of *Asturias*, Son to the Duke of *Anjou:*[8] On the 14th a great Peer of this Realm will die at his Country-House: On the 19th an old *Layman* of great Fame for Learning: And on the 23d an eminent Goldsmith in *Lombard Street*. I could mention others, both at home and abroad, if I did not consider such Events of very little Use or Instruction to the Reader, or to the World.

As to publick Affairs: On the 7th of this Month, there will be an Insurrection in *Dauphine*, occasioned by the Oppressions of the People; which will not be quieted some Months.[9]

ON the 15th will be a violent Storm on the South-East Coast of *France*; which will destroy many of their Ships, and some in the very Harbour.

THE 19th will be famous for the Revolt of a whole Province or Kingdom, excepting one City; by which the Affairs of a certain Prince in the Alliance will take a better Face.

MAY, against common Conjectures, will be no very busy Month in *Europe*, but very signal for the Death of the *Dauphin*, which will happen on the 7th, after a short Fit of Sickness, and grievous Torments with the Strangury. He dies less lamented by the Court than the Kingdom.[10]

ON the 9th a *Mareschal* of *France* will break his Leg by a Fall from his Horse. I have not been able to discover whether he will then die or not.

ON the 11th will begin a most important Siege, which the Eyes of all *Europe* will be upon: I cannot be more particular; for in relating Affairs that so nearly concern the *Confederates*, and consequently this Kingdom, I am forced to confine my self, for several Reasons very obvious to the Reader.

ON the 15th News will arrive of a very *surprizing Event*, than which nothing could be more unexpected.

ON the 19th, three Noble Ladies of this Kingdom, will, against all Expectation, prove with Child, to the great Joy of their Husbands.

ON the 23d, a famous Buffoon of the Play-House will die a ridiculous Death, suitable to his Vocation.

JUNE. This Month will be distinguished at home, by the utter dispersing of those ridiculous deluded Enthusiasts, commonly called the *Prophets*; occasioned chiefly by seeing the Time come, when many of their Prophecies were to be fulfilled; and then finding themselves deceived by contrary Events.[11] It is indeed to be admired how any Deceiver can be so weak to foretel Things near at hand, when a very few Months must of Necessity discover the Imposture to all the World: In this Point less prudent than common Almanack-Makers, who are so wise to wander in Generals, talk dubiously, and leave to the Reader the Business of interpreting.

ON the 1st of this Month a *French* General will be killed by a random Shot of a Cannon-Ball.

ON the 6th a Fire will break out in the Suburbs of *Paris*, which will destroy above a thousand Houses; and seems to be the Foreboding of what will happen, to the Surprize of all *Europe*, about the End of the following Month.

ON the 10th a great Battle will be fought, which will begin at four of the Clock in the Afternoon, and last till nine at Night with great Obstinacy, but no very decisive Event. I shall not name the Place, for the Reasons aforesaid; but the Commanders on each left Wing will be killed. —— I see Bonfires and hear the Noise of Guns for a Victory.

ON the 14th there will be a false Report of the *French* King's Death.

ON the 20th Cardinal *Portocarero* will die of a Dissentery, with great Suspicion of Poison; but the Report of his Intention to revolt to King *Charles* will prove false.[12]

JULY. The 6th of this Month a *certain General* will, by a glorious Action, recover the Reputation he lost by former Misfortunes.

ON the 12th a *great Commander* will die a Prisoner in the Hands of his Enemies.

ON the 14th a shameful Discovery will be made of a *French* Jesuit giving Poison to a great Foreign General; and when he is put to the Torture, will make wonderful Discoveries.

IN short, this will prove a Month of great Action, if I might have Liberty to relate the Particulars.

AT home, the Death of an old famous Senator will happen on the 15th at his Country-House, worn with Age and Diseases.

BUT that which will make this Month memorable to all Posterity, is the Death of the *French* King *Lewis* the Fourteenth, after a Week's Sickness at *Marli*; which will happen on the 29th, about six a-Clock in the Evening. It seems to be an Effect of the Gout in his Stomach, followed by a Flux. And in three Days after, Monsieur *Chamillard* will follow his Master, dying suddenly of an Apoplexy.

IN this Month likewise an *Ambassador* will die in *London*; but I cannot assign the Day.

AUGUST. The Affairs of *France* will seem to suffer no Change for a while under the Duke of *Burgundy*'s Administration.[13] But the Genius that animated the whole Machine being gone, will be the Cause of mighty Turns and Revolutions in the following Year. The new King makes yet little Change either in the Army or the Ministry; but the Libels against his Grandfather, that fly about his very Court, give him Uneasiness.

I SEE an Express in mighty Haste, with Joy and Wonder in his Looks, arriving by the Break of Day, on the 26th of this Month, having travelled in three Days a prodigious Journey by Land and Sea. In the Evening I hear Bells and Guns, and see the Blazing of a Thousand Bonfires.

A YOUNG Admiral, of noble Birth, does likewise this Month gain immortal Honour, by a great Atchievement.

THE Affairs of *Poland* are this Month entirely settled: *Augustus* resigns his Pretensions, which he had again taken up for some Time; *Stanislaus* is peaceably possessed of the Throne; and the King of *Sweden* declares for the Emperor.[14]

I CANNOT omit one particular Accident here at home; that near the End of this Month much Mischief will be done at *Bartholomew* Fair, by the Fall of a Booth.

SEPTEMBER. This Month begins with a very surprizing Fit of frosty Weather, which will last near twelve Days.

THE Pope having long languished last Month, the Swellings in his Legs breaking, and the Flesh mortifying, will die on the 11th Instant: And in three Weeks Time, after a mighty Contest, be succeeded by a Cardinal of the *Imperial* Faction, but Native of *Tuscany*, who is now about Sixty-One Years old.[15]

THE *French* Army acts now wholly on the Defensive, strongly fortified in their Trenches; and the young *French* King sends Overtures for a Treaty of Peace, by the Duke of *Mantua*; which because it is a Matter of State that concerns us here at home, I shall speak no farther of it.

I SHALL add but one Prediction more, and that in mystical Terms, which shall be included in a Verse out of *Virgil*.

> *Alter erit jam Tethys, & altera quæ vehat Argo,*
> *Delectos Heroas.*[16]

UPON the 25th Day of this Month, the fulfilling of this Prediction will be manifest to every Body.

THIS is the farthest I have proceeded in my Calculations for the present Year. I do not pretend that these are all the great Events which will happen in this Period, but that those I have set down will infallibly come to pass. It may, perhaps, still be objected, why I have not spoke more particularly of Affairs at home, or of the Success of our Armies abroad; which I might, and could very largely have done. But those in Power have wisely discouraged Men from meddling in publick Concerns; and I was resolved, by no Means, to give the least Offence. This

I will venture to say; that it will be a glorious Campaign for the Allies; wherein the *English* Forces, both by Sea and Land, will have their full Share of Honour: That Her Majesty Queen ANNE will continue in Health and Prosperity: And that no ill Accident will arrive to any in the chief Ministry.

As to the particular Events I have mentioned, the Readers may judge by the fulfilling of them, whether I am of the Level with common Astrologers; who, with an old paultry Cant, and a few Pot-hooks for Planets to amuse the Vulgar, have, in my Opinion, too long been suffered to abuse the World. But an honest Physician ought not to be despised, because there are such Things as Mountebanks. I hope I have some Share of Reputation, which I would not willingly forfeit for a Frolick or Humour: And I believe no Gentleman, who reads this Paper, will look upon it to be of the same Cast or Mold with the common Scribbles that are every Day hawked about. My Fortune hath placed me above the little Regard of writing for a few Pence, which I neither value nor want: Therefore, let not wise Men too hastily condemn this Essay, intended for a good Design, to cultivate and improve an antient Art, long in Disgrace by having fallen into mean unskilful Hands. A little Time will determine whether I have deceived others, or my self; and I think it is no very unreasonable Request, that Men would please to suspend their Judgments till then. I was once of the Opinion with those who despise all Predictions from the Stars, till in the Year 1686, a Man of Quality shewed me, written in his *Album*, that the most learned Astronomer, Captain *Hally*, assured him, He would never believe any thing of the Stars Influence, if there were not a great Revolution in *England* in the Year 1688.[17] Since that Time I began to have other Thoughts; and after Eighteen Years diligent Study and Application, I think I have no Reason to repent of my Pains. I shall detain the Reader no longer than to let him know, that the Account I design to give of next Year's Events, shall take in the principal Affairs that happen in *Europe*: And if I be denied the Liberty of offering it to my own Country, I shall appeal to the learned World by publishing it in *Latin*, and giving Order to have it printed in *Holland*.[18]

THE ACCOMPLISHMENT OF
THE FIRST OF MR. BICKERSTAFF'S
PREDICTIONS

BEING AN ACCOUNT OF THE Death of Mr. *Partrige*,
the Almanack-maker, upon the 29th Inst.

In a Letter to a Person of Honour

Written in the Year 1708

My LORD,

IN Obedience to your Lordship's Commands, as well as to
satisfy my own Curiosity, I have for some Days past enquired
constantly after *Partrige* the Almanack-maker; of whom it was
foretold in Mr. *Bickerstaff*'s Predictions, published about a
Month ago, that he should die the 29th Instant, about Eleven
at Night, of a raging Fever. I had some Sort of Knowledge of
him when I was employed in the Revenue; because he used
every Year to present me with his Almanack, as he did other
Gentlemen upon the score of some little Gratuity we gave him.
I saw him accidentally once or twice about ten Days before he
died; and observed he began very much to droop and languish,
although I hear his Friends did not seem to apprehend him in
any Danger. About two or three Days ago he grew ill; was
confined first to his Chamber, and in a few Hours after to his
Bed; where Dr. *Case* and Mrs. *Kirleus* were sent for to visit,
and to prescribe to him.[1] Upon this Intelligence I sent thrice
every Day one Servant or other to enquire after his Health; and
Yesterday about four in the Afternoon, Word was brought me
that he was past Hopes: Upon which I prevailed with my self
to go and see him; partly out of Commiseration, and, I confess,
partly out of Curiosity. He knew me very well, seemed surprized
at my Condescension, and made me Compliments upon it as
well as he could in the Condition he was. The People about him
said, he had been for some Time delirious; but when I saw him,

he had his Understanding as well as ever I knew, and spoke strong and hearty, without any seeming Uneasiness or Constraint. After I had told him I was sorry to see him in those melancholy Circumstances, and said some other Civilities, suitable to the Occasion; I desired him to tell me freely and ingenuously whether the Predictions Mr. *Bickerstaff* had published relating to his Death, had not too much affected and worked on his Imagination. He confessed he often had it in his Head, but never with much Apprehension till about a Fortnight before; since which Time it had the perpetual Possession of his Mind and Thoughts, and he did verily believe was the true natural Cause of his present Distemper: For, said he, I am thoroughly persuaded, and I think I have very good Reasons, that Mr. *Bickerstaff* spoke altogether by guess, and knew no more what will happen this Year than I did my self. I told him his Discourse surprized me; and I would be glad he were in a State of Health to be able to tell me what Reason he had to be convinced of Mr. *Bickerstaff*'s Ignorance. He replied, I am a poor ignorant Fellow, bred to a mean Trade;[2] yet I have Sense enough to know, that all Pretences of foretelling by Astrology are Deceits, for this manifest Reason, because the Wise and Learned, who can only judge whether there be any Truth in this Science, do all unanimously agree to laugh at and despise it; and none but the poor ignorant Vulgar give it any Credit, and that only upon the Word of such silly Wretches as I and my Fellows, who can hardly write or read. I then asked him, why he had not calculated his own Nativity, to see whether it agreed with *Bickerstaff*'s Predictions? At which he shook his Head, and said, O! Sir, this is no Time for jesting, but for repenting those Fooleries, as I do now from the very Bottom of my Heart. By what I can gather from you, said I, the Observations and Predictions you printed with your Almanacks were meer Impositions upon the People. He replied, if it were otherwise, I should have the less to answer for. We have a common Form for all those Things: As to foretelling the Weather, we never meddle with that, but leave it to the Printer, who takes it out of any old Almanack as he thinks fit: The rest was my own Invention to make my Almanack sell, having a Wife to

maintain, and no other Way to get my Bread; for mending old
Shoes is a poor Livelihood: And (added he, sighing) I wish I
may not have done more Mischief by my Physick than my
Astrology; although I had some good Receipts from my Grandmother, and my own Compositions were such, as I thought
could at least do no Hurt.

I HAD some other Discourse with him, which now I cannot
call to Mind; and I fear I have already tired your Lordship. I
shall only add one Circumstance, That on his Death-Bed he
declared himself a Nonconformist, and had a fanatick Preacher
to be his spiritual Guide. After half an Hour's Conversation, I
took my Leave, being almost stifled by the Closeness of the
Room. I imagined he could not hold out long; and therefore
withdrew to a little Coffee-House hard by, leaving a Servant at
the House with Orders to come immediately, and tell me, as
near as he could, the Minute when *Partrige* should expire,
which was not above two Hours after; when looking upon my
Watch, I found it to be above five Minutes after Seven: By
which it is clear, that Mr. *Bickerstaff* was mistaken almost four
Hours in his Calculation. In the other Circumstances he was
exact enough. But whether he hath not been the Cause of
this poor Man's Death, as well as the Predictor, may be very
reasonably disputed. However, it must be confessed, the Matter
is odd enough, whether we should endeavour to account for it
by Chance or the Effect of Imagination: For my own Part,
although I believe no Man hath less Faith in these Matters; yet
I shall wait with some Impatience, and not without Expectation,
the fulfilling of Mr. *Bickerstaff*'s second Prediction, that the
Cardinal *de Noailles* is to die upon the 4th of *April*; and if that
should be verified as exactly as this of poor *Partrige*, I must
own, I should be wholly surprized, and at a Loss, and infallibly
expect the Accomplishment of all the rest.

A VINDICATION OF ISAAC
BICKERSTAFF, ESQ.

AGAINST What is objected to him by Mr. *Partrige*, in his
Almanack for the present Year 1709

By the said ISAAC BICKERSTAFF, *Esq.*

Written in the Year 1709

MR. *Partrige* hath been lately pleased to treat me after a very
rough Manner, in *that which is called* His Almanack for the
present Year: Such Usage is very undecent from *one Gentleman
to another*, and doth not at all contribute to the Discovery of
Truth, which ought to be the great End in all Disputes of the
Learned.[1] To call a Man *Fool* and *Villain*, and *impudent Fellow*,
only for differing from him in a Point meerly speculative, is, in
my humble Opinion, a very improper Stile for a Person of *his
Education*. I appeal to the *learned* World, whether in my last
Year's Predictions, I gave him the least Provocation for such
unworthy Treatment. Philosophers have differed in all Ages,
but the discreetest among them have always differed as became
Philosophers. Scurrility and Passion, in a Controversy among
Scholars, is just so much of nothing to the Purpose; and, at
best, a tacit Confession of a weak Cause. My Concern is not
so much for my own Reputation, as that of the *Republick
of Letters*, which Mr. *Partrige* hath endeavoured to wound
through my Sides. If Men of publick Spirit must be supercili-
ously treated for their ingenious Attempts, how will true useful
Knowledge be ever advanced? I wish Mr. *Partrige* knew the
Thoughts which *foreign Universities* have conceived of his
ungenerous Proceedings with me; but I am too tender of his
Reputation to publish them to the World. That Spirit of Envy
and Pride, which blasts so many rising Genius's in our Nation,
is yet unknown among *Professors* abroad: The Necessity of
justifying my self, will excuse my Vanity, when I tell the Reader,
that I have near an Hundred *honorary* Letters from several
Parts of *Europe* (some as far as *Muscovy*) in Praise of my

Performance. Besides several others, which, as I have been credibly informed, were opened in the Post-Office and never sent me. It is true, the *Inquisition* in *Portugal* was pleased to burn my Predictions, and condemn the Author and Readers of them;[2] but, I hope, at the same Time, it will be considered in how deplorable a State *Learning* lies at present in that Kingdom: And with the profoundest Veneration for *crowned Heads*, I will presume to add, that it a little concerned *his Majesty of Portugal*, to interpose his Authority in Behalf of a *Scholar* and a *Gentleman*, the Subject of a Nation with which he is now in so strict an Alliance.[3] But the other Kingdoms and States of *Europe* have treated me with more Candour and Generosity. If I had leave to print the *Latin* Letters transmitted to me from foreign Parts, they would fill a Volume, and be a full Defence against all that Mr. *Partrige*, or his Accomplices of the *Portugal Inquisition*, will be ever able to object; who, by the way, are the only Enemies my Predictions have ever met with at home or abroad. But, I hope, I know better what is due to the Honour of a *learned Correspondence*, in so tender a Point. Yet, some of those illustrious Persons will, perhaps, excuse me for transcribing a Passage or two in my own Vindication.[4] The most learned Monsieur *Leibnitz*[5] thus addresseth to me his third Letter: *Illustrissimo Bickerstaffio Astrologiæ Instauratori*, &c.[6] Monsieur *le Clerc*, quoting my Predictions in a Treatise he published last Year, is pleased to say, *Ità nuperimè Bickerstaffius, magnum illud Angliæ sidus*.[7] Another great Professor writing of me, has these Words: *Bickerstaffius, nobilis Anglus, Astrologorum hujusce Seculi facilè Princeps*.[8] Signior *Magliabecchi*, the *Great Duke*'s famous Library-keeper, spends almost his whole Letter in Compliments and Praises.[9] It is true, the renowned *Professor* of Astronomy at *Utrecht* seems to differ from me in one Article; but it is after the modest Manner that becomes a Philosopher; as, *Pace tanti viri dixerim*:[10] And, *Page* 55, he seems to lay the Error upon the Printer, (as indeed it ought) and says, *Vel forsan error Typographi, cum alioquin Bickerstaffius vir doctissimus*, &c.[11]

IF Mr. *Partrige* had followed these Examples in the Controversy between us, he might have spared me the Trouble of

justifying my self in so publick a Manner. I believe few Men
are readier to own their Error than I, or more thankful to
those who will please to inform him of them. But it seems this
Gentleman, instead of encouraging the Progress of his own Art,
is pleased to look upon all Attempts of that Kind, as an Invasion
of his Province. He hath been indeed so wise, to make no
Objection against the Truth of my Predictions, except in one
single Point, relating to himself: And to demonstrate how much
Men are blinded by their own Partiality, I do solemnly assure
the Reader, that he is the *only* Person from whom I ever heard
that Objection offered; which Consideration alone, I think, will
take off all its Weight.

WITH my utmost Endeavours, I have not been able to trace
above two Objections ever made against the Truth of my last
Year's Prophecies: The first is of a *French* Man, who was
pleased to publish to the World, That *the Cardinal* de Noailles
*was still alive, notwithstanding the pretended Prophecy of
Monsieur* Biquerstaffe: But how far a *French* Man, a *Papist*,
and an *Enemy*, is to be believed in his own Cause, against an
English Protestant, who is *true to the Government*, I shall leave
to the candid and impartial Reader.

THE other Objection, is the unhappy Occasion of this Discourse; and relates to an Article in my Predictions, which foretold the Death of Mr. *Partrige* to happen on *March* 29, 1708.
This he is pleased to contradict absolutely in the Almanack he
hath published for the present Year; and in that ungentlemanly
Manner, (pardon the Expression) as I have above related. In
that Work, he very roundly asserts, That he *is not only now
alive, but was likewise alive upon that very 29th of* March,
when I had foretold he should die. This is the Subject of the
present Controversy between us; which I design to handle with
all Brevity, Perspicuity, and Calmness: In this Dispute, I am
sensible, the Eyes not only of *England*, but of all *Europe*, will
be upon us: And the *Learned* in every Country will, I doubt
not, take Part on that Side where they find most Appearance of
Reason and Truth.

WITHOUT entering into Criticisms of *Chronology* about the
Hour of his Death, I shall only prove that Mr. *Partrige* is

not alive. And my first Argument is thus: Above a Thousand
Gentlemen having bought his Almanacks for this Year, meerly
to find what he said against me; at every Line they read, they
would lift up their Eyes, and cry out, betwixt Rage and Laughter, *They were sure no Man* alive *ever writ such damned Stuff
as this*. Neither did I ever hear that Opinion disputed: So that
Mr. *Partrige* lies under a *Dilemma*, either of disowning his
Almanack, or allowing himself to be *no Man alive*. But now, if
an *uninformed* Carcass walks still about, and is pleased to call
it self *Partrige*, Mr. *Bickerstaff* does not think himself any way
answerable for that. Neither had the said Carcass any Right to
beat the poor Boy, who happened to pass by it in the Street,
crying, *A full and true Account of Dr.* Partrige's *Death*, &c.

SECONDLY, Mr. *Partrige* pretends to tell Fortunes, and
recover stolen Goods; which all the Parish says he must do by
conversing with the Devil, and other evil Spirits: And no wise
Man will ever allow he could converse personally with either,
till after he was dead.

THIRDLY, I will plainly prove him to be dead, out of his own
Almanack for this Year, and from the very Passage which he
produceth to make us think him alive. He there says, *He is not
only* now *alive, but was also alive upon that very 29th of*
March, *which I foretold* he *should die on*: By this, he declares
his Opinion, that a Man may be alive *now*, who was not alive
a Twelve-month ago. And, indeed, there lies the Sophistry of
his Argument. He dares not assert, he was alive ever since the
29th of *March*, but that he *is now alive, and was so on that
Day*: I grant the latter, for he did not die till Night, as appears
by the printed Account of his Death, in a *Letter to a Lord*; and
whether he be since revived, I leave the World to judge. This
indeed, is perfect cavilling, and I am ashamed to dwell any
longer upon it.

FOURTHLY, I will appeal to Mr. *Partrige* himself, whether it
be probable I could have been so indiscreet, to begin my Predictions with the *only* Falshood that ever was pretended to be in
them; and this in an Affair at Home, where I had so many
Opportunities to be exact; and must have given such Advantages against me to a Person of Mr. *Partrige*'s Wit and Learning,

who, if he could possibly have raised one single Objection more against the Truth of my Prophecies, would hardly have spared me.

AND here I must take Occasion to reprove the abovementioned Writer of the Relation of Mr. *Partrige*'s Death, in a *Letter to a Lord*, who was pleased to tax me with a Mistake of *four whole Hours* in my Calculation of that Event. I must confess, this Censure, pronounced with an Air of Certainty, in a Matter that so nearly concerned me, and by a *grave judicious Author*, moved me not a little. But although I was at that Time out of Town, yet several of my Friends, whose Curiosity had led them to be exactly informed, (for as to my own Part, having no doubt at all in the Matter, I never once thought of it,) assured me I computed to something under half an Hour; which (I speak my private Opinion) is an Error of no very great Magnitude, that Men should raise Clamour about it. I shall only say, it would not be amiss, if that Author would henceforth be more tender of other Mens Reputation as well as his own. It is well there were no more Mistakes of that Kind; if there had, I presume he would have told me of them with as little Ceremony.

THERE is one Objection against Mr. *Partrige*'s Death, which I have sometimes met with, although indeed very slightly offered; That he still continues to write Almanacks. But this is no more than what is common to all of that Profession; *Gadbury, Poor Robin, Dove, Wing*, and several others, do yearly publish their Almanacks, although several of them have been dead since before the *Revolution*.[12] Now the natural Reason of this I take to be, that whereas it is the Privilege of other Authors, *to live after their Deaths*, Almanack-makers are alone excluded; because their Dissertations, treating only upon the Minutes as they pass, become useless as those go off. In consideration of which, *Time*, whose *Registers* they are, gives them a Lease in Reversion, to continue their Works after their Death.

I SHOULD not have given the Publick or my self the Trouble of this Vindication, if my Name had not been made use of by several Persons, to whom I never lent it; one of which, a few Days ago, was pleased to father on me a new Set of Predictions.[13] But I think these are Things too serious to be trifled with. It grieved me to the Heart, when I saw my Labours, which had cost me so much Thought and Watching, bawled about by common Hawkers, which I only intended for the weighty Consideration of the gravest Persons. This prejudiced the World so much at first, that several of my Friends had the Assurance to ask me, Whether I were in jest? To which I only answered coldly, *That the Event will shew*. But it is the Talent of our Age and Nation, to turn Things of the greatest Importance into Ridicule. When the End of the Year had *verified all my Predictions*, out comes Mr. *Partrige*'s Almanack, disputing the Point of his Death; so that I am employed, like the General who was forced to kill his Enemies twice over, whom a *Necromancer* had raised to Life. If Mr. *Partrige* hath practised the same Experiment upon himself, and be again alive, long may he continue so; but that doth not in the least contradict my Veracity: For I think I have clearly proved, by *invincible Demonstration*, that he died at farthest within half an Hour of the Time I foretold; and not four Hours sooner, as the above-mentioned Author, in his Letter to a Lord, hath maliciously suggested, with Design to blast my Credit, by charging me with so gross a Mistake.

A FAMOUS PREDICTION OF MERLIN, THE BRITISH WIZARD

Written above a thousand Years ago, and relating to the Year 1709

With Explanatory Notes. By T. N. *Philomath*

Written in the Year 1709

LAST Year was published a Paper of Predictions, pretended to be written by one *Isaac Bickerstaff*, Esq.; but the true Design of it was to ridicule the Art of Astrology, and expose its Professors as ignorant, or Impostors. Against this Imputation, Dr. *Partrige* hath learnedly vindicated himself in his Almanack for that Year.

FOR a farther Defence of this famous Art, I have thought fit
to present the World with the following Prophecy. The Original
is said to be of the famous *Merlin*, who lived about a thousand
Years ago: And the following Translation is two hundred Years
old; for it seems to be written near the End of *Henry* the Seventh's
Reign. I found it in an old Edition of *Merlin*'s Prophecies;
imprinted at *London* by *Johan Haukyns*, in the Year 1530.[1] *Page*
39. I set it down Word for Word in the old Orthography, and
shall take leave to subjoin a few explanatory Notes.

SEVEN and TEN addyd to NINE,
Of Fraunce hir Woe thys is the Sygne,
Tamys Rivere twys y-frozen,
Walke sans wetyng Shoes ne Hosen,
Then cometh foorthe, Ich understonde,
From Toune of Stoffe to fattyn Londe,
An herdie Chiftan, woe the Morne
To Fraunce, that evere he was borne.
Then shall the Fyshe beweyle his Bosse;
Nor shal grin Berrys make up the Losse.
Yonge Symnele shall again miscarrye:
And Norways Pryd again shall marrey.
And from the Tree where Blosums fele,
Ripe Fruit shall come, and all is wele.
Reaums shall daunce honde in honde,
And it shall be merye in old Inglonde.
Then old Inglonde shall be no more,
And no Man shall be sorie therefore.
Geryon shall have three Hedes agayne,
Till Hapsburge makyth them but twayne.

[SEVEN and TEN addyd to NINE,
Of Fraunce hir Woe thys is the Sygne,
Tamys Rivere twys y-frozen,
Walke sans wetyng Shoes ne Hosen,
Then cometh foorthe, Ich understonde,
From Toune of Stoffe to fattyn Londe,
An herdie Chiftan, woe the Morne

To Fraunce, that evere he was borne.
Then shall the Fyshe beweyle his Bosse;
Nor shal grin Berrys make up the Losse.
Yonge Symnele shall again miscarrye:
And Norways Pryd again shall marrey.
And from the Tree where Blosums fele,
Ripe Fruit shall come, and all is wele.
Reaums shall daunce honde in honde,
And it shall be merye in old Inglonde.
Then old Inglonde shall be no more,
And no Man shall be sorie therefore.
Geryon shall have three Hedes agayne,
Till Hapsburge makyth them but twayne.]

Explanatory NOTES

Seven and Ten. This Line describes the Year when these Events shall happen. Seven and Ten make Seventeen, which I explain seventeen Hundred, and this Number added to Nine makes the Year we are now in; for it must be understood of the Natural Year, which begins the First of *January*.

Tamys Ryvere twys, &c. The River *Thames* frozen twice in one Year, so as Men to walk on it, is a very signal Accident; which perhaps hath not fallen out for several Hundred Years before; and is the Reason why some Astrologers have thought that this Prophecy could never be fulfilled, because they imagined such a Thing could never happen in our Climate.

From Toune of Stoffe, &c. This is a plain Designation of the Duke of *Marlborough.* One Kind of Stuff used to fatten Land is called *Marle,* and every Body knows that *Borough* is a Name for a Town; and this Way of Expression is after the usual dark Manner of old Astrological Predictions.

Then shall the Fyshe, &c. By the *Fish* is understood the *Dauphin* of *France,* as the Kings eldest Sons are called: It is here said, he shall lament the Loss of the Duke of *Burgundy,* called the *Bosse,* which is an old *English* Word for *Hump shoulder,* or *Crook-back,* as that Duke is known to be: And the Prophecy seems to mean, that he should be overcome, or slain.

By the *Grin Berrys*, in the next Line, is meant the young Duke of *Berry*, the *Dauphin*'s third Son, who shall not have Valour or Fortune enough to supply the Loss of his eldest Brother.

Yonge Symnele, &c. By *Symnele* is meant the pretended Prince of *Wales*; who, if he offers to attempt any Thing against *England*, shall miscarry as he did before. *Lambert Symnel* is the Name of a young Man noted in our Histories for personating the Son (as I remember) of *Edward* the Fourth.[2]

And Norways Pryd, &c.[3] I cannot guess who is meant by *Norways Pride*; perhaps the Reader may, as well as the Sense of the two following Lines.

Reaums shall, &c. *Reaums*, or as the Word is now, *Realms*, is the old Name for *Kingdoms:* And this is a very plain Prediction of our happy *Union*, with the Felicities that shall attend it. It is added, that *Old England* shall be no more, and yet no Man shall be sorry for it. And, indeed, properly speaking, *England* is now no more; for the whole Island is one Kingdom, under the Name of *Britain*.[4]

Geryon shall, &c. This Prediction, though somewhat obscure, is wonderfully adapt. *Geryon* is said to have been a King of *Spain*, whom *Hercules* slew. It was a Fiction of the Poets, that he had three Heads, which the Author says he shall have again.[5] That is, *Spain* shall have three Kings; which is now wonderfully verified: For, besides the King of *Portugal*, which properly is Part of *Spain*, there are now two Rivals for *Spain*; *Charles* and *Philip*. But *Charles*, being descended from the Count of *Hapsburgh*, Founder of the *Austrian* Family, shall soon make those Heads but two; by overturning *Philip*, and driving him out of *Spain*.[6]

SOME of these Predictions are already fulfilled, and it is highly probable the rest may be in due Time: And, I think, I have not forced the Words, by my Explication, into any other Sense than what they will naturally bear. If this be granted, I am sure it must be also allowed, that the Author (whoever he were) was a Person of extraordinary Sagacity; and that Astrology brought to such Perfection as this, is, by no Means, an Art to be despised; whatever Mr. *Bickerstaff*, or other merry Gentlemen, are pleased to think. As to the Tradition of these

Lines having been writ in the Original by *Merlin*; I confess I lay not much Weight upon it: But it is enough to justify their Authority, that the Book from whence I have transcribed them, was printed 170 Years ago, as appears by the Title-Page. For the Satisfaction of any Gentleman, who may be either doubtful of the Truth, or curious to be informed, I shall give Order to have the very Book sent to the Printer of this Paper, with Directions to let any Body see it that pleases; because I believe it is pretty scarce.

A Famous Prediction of *MERLIN*, the *British* Wizard,
written above a Thoufand Years ago, and relating to this
prefent Year.

With Explanatory Notes. By *T. N.* Philomath.

LAST Year was publifh'd a Paper of Predictions pretended to be written by
one *Ifaac Bickerftaff*, Efq; but the true Defign of it was to Ridicule the Art
of Aftrology, and Expofe its Profeffors as Ignorant, or Impoftors. Againft
this Imputation, Dr. *Partridge* hath vindicated himfelf in his Almanack
for the prefent Year.

For a further Vindication of this famous Art, I have thought fit to prefent the
World with the following Prophecy. The Original is faid to be of the famous *Mer-
lin*, who lived about a Thoufand Years ago : And the following Tranflation is Two
Hundred Years old ; for it feems to be written near the End of *Henry* the Seventh's
Reign. I found it in an Old Edition of *Merlin*'s Prophecies; imprinted at *London* by
Johan Haukyns, in the Year 1530. *Page* 39. I fet it down Word for Word in the
Old Orthography, and fhall take Leave to fubjoin a few Explanatory Notes.

> Seben and Ten addyd to nyne,
> Of fraunce hir woe thys is the fygne,
> Tamys ribere twys y-frozen,
> Walke fans wetynge Shoes ne hozen.
> Then compth foorthe, Ich underftonde,
> From Toune of Stoffe to fattyn Londe
> An herdie Chiftan, woe the mozne
> To fraunce, that evere he was bozne.
> Than fhall the fyfhe bewayle hys Boffe;
> Nor fhall grin Berris make up the Loffe.
> Yonge Symnele fhall agayne mifcarrye :
> And Norways pryd agayne fhall marreye.
> And from the Tree where Bloffums feie,
> Ripe fruit fhall come, and all is wele.
> Reaums fhall daunce honde in honde,
> And it fhall be merye in olde Inglonde.
> Then olde Inglonde fhall be noe moze,
> And no Man fhall be fozie therefoze.
> Geryon fhall habe thzee Hedes agayne
> Till Hapsburge makyth them but twayne.

Expla-

AN ARGUMENT TO PROVE, THAT THE ABOLISHING OF CHRISTIANITY IN ENGLAND

May, as Things now stand, be attended with some
Inconveniencies, and perhaps, not produce those many
good Effects proposed thereby

Written in the YEAR 1708

I AM very sensible what a Weakness and Presumption it is, to
reason against the general Humour and Disposition of the
World. I remember it was with great Justice, and a due Regard
to the Freedom both of the Publick and the Press, forbidden
upon severe Penalties to write or discourse, or lay Wagers
against the *Union*, even before it was confirmed by Parliament:
Because that was looked upon as a Design to oppose the Current
of the People; which besides the Folly of it, is a manifest Breach
of the Fundamental Law, that makes this Majority of Opinion
the Voice of God.[1] In like Manner, and for the very same
Reasons, it may perhaps be neither safe nor prudent to argue
against the Abolishing of Christianity, at a Juncture when all
Parties appear so unanimously determined upon the Point; as
we cannot but allow from their Actions, their Discourses, and
their Writings. However, I know not how, whether from the
Affectation of Singularity, or the Perverseness of human
Nature; but so it unhappily falls out, that I cannot be entirely
of this Opinion. Nay, although I were sure an Order were issued
out for my immediate Prosecution by the Attorney-General, I
should still confess that in the present Posture of our Affairs at
home or abroad, I do not yet see the absolute Necessity of
extirpating the Christian Religion from among us.

THIS perhaps may appear too great a Paradox even for our
wise and paradoxical Age to endure: Therefore I shall handle
it with all Tenderness, and with the utmost Deference to that
great and profound Majority, which is of another Sentiment.

AND yet the Curious may please to observe, how much the

Genius of a Nation is liable to alter in half an Age: I have heard it affirmed for certain by some very old People, that the contrary Opinion was even in their Memories as much in Vogue as the other is now; and that a Project for the Abolishing of Christianity would then have appeared as singular, and been thought as absurd, as it would be at this Time to write or discourse in its Defence.

THEREFORE I freely own, that all Appearances are against me. The System of the Gospel, after the Fate of other Systems, is generally antiquated and exploded; and the Mass or Body of the common People, among whom it seems to have had its latest Credit, are now grown as much ashamed of it as their Betters: Opinions, like Fashions, always descending from those of Quality to the middle Sort, and thence to the Vulgar, where at length they are dropt and vanish.

BUT here I would not be mistaken; and must therefore be so bold as to borrow a Distinction from the Writers on the other Side, when they make a Difference between nominal and real *Trinitarians*.[2] I hope, no Reader imagines me so weak to stand up in the Defence of *real* Christianity; such as used in primitive Times (if we may believe the Authors of those Ages) to have an Influence upon Mens Belief and Actions: To offer at the restoring of That, would indeed be a wild Project; it would be to dig up Foundations; to destroy at one Blow *all* the Wit, and *half* the Learning of the Kingdom; to break the entire Frame and Constitution of Things; to ruin Trade; extinguish Arts and Sciences with the Professors of them; in short, to turn our Courts, Exchanges and Shops into Desarts: And would be full as absurd as the Proposal of *Horace*, where he advises the *Romans*, all in a Body, to leave their City, and seek a new Seat in some remote Part of the World, by Way of a Cure for the Corruption of their Manners.[3]

THEREFORE, I think this Caution was in it self altogether unnecessary, (which I have inserted only to prevent all Possibility of cavilling) since every candid Reader will easily understand my Discourse to be intended only in Defence of *nominal* Christianity; the other having been for some Time wholly laid aside by general Consent, as utterly inconsistent with our present Schemes of Wealth and Power.[4]

But why we should therefore cast off the Name and Title of Christians, although the general Opinion and Resolution be so violent for it, I confess I cannot (with Submission) apprehend the Consequence necessary. However, since the Undertakers propose such wonderful Advantages to the Nation by this Project; and advance many plausible Objections against the System of Christianity; I shall briefly consider the Strength of both, fairly allow them their greatest Weight, and offer such Answers as I think most reasonable. After which I will beg leave to shew what Inconveniencies may possibly happen by such an Innovation, in the present Posture of our Affairs.

First, One great Advantage proposed by the Abolishing of Christianity is, That it would very much enlarge and establish Liberty of Conscience, that great Bulwark of our Nation, and of the *Protestant* Religion, which is still too much limited by *Priest-Craft*, notwithstanding all the good Intentions of the Legislature; as we have lately found by a severe Instance.[5] For it is confidently reported, that two young Gentlemen of great Hopes, bright Wit, and profound Judgment, who upon a thorough Examination of Causes and Effects, and by the meer Force of natural Abilities, without the least Tincture of Learning; having made a Discovery, that there was no God, and generously communicating their Thoughts for the Good of the Publick; were some Time ago, by an unparalleled Severity, and upon I know not what *obsolete* Law, broke *only* for *Blasphemy*.[6] And as it hath been wisely observed, if Persecution once begins, no Man alive knows how far it may reach, or where it will end.

In Answer to all which, with Deference to wiser Judgments; I think this rather shews the Necessity of a *nominal* Religion among us. Great Wits love to be free with the highest Objects; and if they cannot be allowed a *God* to revile or renounce, they will *speak Evil of Dignities*, abuse the Government, and reflect upon the Ministry; which, I am sure, few will deny to be of much more pernicious Consequence; according to the Saying of *Tiberius*, *Deorum offensa Diis curæ*.[7] As to the particular Fact related; I think it is not fair to argue from one Instance; perhaps another cannot be produced; yet (to the Comfort of all those, who may be apprehensive of Persecution) Blasphemy we know is freely spoke a Million of Times in every Coffee-House and Tavern, or where-ever else *good Company* meet. It must be allowed indeed, that to break an *English Free-born* Officer only for Blasphemy, was, to speak the gentlest of such an Action, a very high Strain of absolute Power. Little can be said in Excuse for the General; perhaps he was afraid it might give Offence to the Allies, among whom, for ought I know, it may be the Custom of the Country to believe a God. But if he argued, as some have done, upon a mistaken Principle, that an Officer who is guilty of speaking Blasphemy, may, some Time or other, proceed so far as to raise a Mutiny; the Consequence is, by no Means, to be admitted: For surely, the Commander of an *English* Army is like to be but ill obeyed, whose Soldiers fear and reverence him as little as they do a Deity.

IT is further objected against the Gospel System, that it obliges Men to the Belief of Things too difficult for Free-Thinkers, and such who have shaken off the Prejudices that usually cling to a confined Education. To which I answer, that Men should be cautious how they raise Objections, which reflect upon the Wisdom of the Nation. Is not every Body freely allowed to believe whatever he pleaseth; and to publish his Belief to the World whenever he thinks fit; especially if it serve to strengthen the Party which is in the Right? Would any indifferent Foreigner, who should read the Trumpery lately written by *Asgill, Tindall, Toland, Coward,*[8] and Forty more, imagine the Gospel to be our Rule of Faith, and confirmed by Parliaments? Does any Man either believe, or say he believes, or desire to have it thought that he says he believes one Syllable of the Matter? And is any Man worse received upon that Score; or does he find his Want of *Nominal* Faith a Disadvantage to him, in the Pursuit of any Civil, or Military Employment? What if there be an old dormant Statute or two against him? Are they not now obsolete, to a Degree that *Empson* and *Dudley* themselves, if they were now alive, would find it impossible to put them in Execution?[9]

IT is likewise urged, that there are, by Computation, in this Kingdom, above ten Thousand Parsons; whose Revenues added to those of my Lords the Bishops, would suffice to maintain, at least, two Hundred young Gentlemen of Wit and Pleasure, and Free-thinking; Enemies to Priest-craft, narrow Principles, Pedantry, and Prejudices; who might be an Ornament to the Court and Town: And then again, so great a Number of able (bodied) Divines might be a Recruit to our Fleet and Armies. This, indeed, appears to be a Consideration of some Weight: But then, on the other Side, several Things deserve to be considered likewise: As, First, Whether it may not be thought necessary, that in certain Tracts of Country, like what we call Parishes, there should be *one* Man at least of Abilities to read and write. Then, it seems a wrong Computation, that the Revenues of the Church throughout this Island would be large enough to maintain two Hundred young Gentlemen, or even Half that Number, after the present refined Way of Living; that is, to allow each of them such a Rent, as, in the modern Form of Speech, would make them *easy*. But still, there is in this Project a greater Mischief behind; and we ought to beware of the Woman's Folly, who killed the Hen, that every Morning laid her a Golden Egg. For, pray, what would become of the Race of Men in the next Age, if we had nothing to trust to, besides the scrophulous consumptive Productions furnished by our Men of Wit and Pleasure; when having squandered away their Vigour, Health, and Estates; they are forced, by some disagreeable Marriage, to piece up their broken Fortunes, and entail Rottenness and Politeness on their Posterity? Now, here are ten Thousand Persons reduced by the wise Regulations of *Henry* the Eighth to the Necessity of a low Diet and moderate Exercise, who are the only great Restorers of our Breed; without which, the Nation would, in an Age or two, become but one great Hospital.[10]

ANOTHER Advantage proposed by the abolishing of Christianity, is the clear Gain of one Day in Seven, which is now entirely lost, and consequently the Kingdom one Seventh less considerable in Trade, Business, and Pleasure; beside the Loss to the Publick of so many stately Structures now in the Hands of the Clergy; which might be converted into Theatres, Exchanges, Market-houses, common Dormitories, and other publick Edifices.

I HOPE I shall be forgiven a hard Word, if I call this a perfect Cavil. I readily own there hath been an old Custom, Time out of Mind, for People to assemble in the Churches every *Sunday*, and that Shops are still frequently shut; in order, as it is conceived, to preserve the Memory of that antient Practice; but how this can prove a Hindrance to Business, or Pleasure, is hard to imagine. What if the Men of Pleasure are forced, one Day in the Week, to game at home instead of the *Chocolate-House*? Are not the *Taverns* and *Coffee-Houses* open? Can there be a more convenient Season for taking a Dose of Physick? Are fewer Claps got upon *Sundays* than other Days? Is not that the chief Day for Traders to sum up the Accounts of the Week; and for Lawyers to prepare their Briefs? But I would fain know how it can be pretended that the Churches are misapplied. Where are more Appointments and Rendezvouzes of Gallantry? Where more Care to appear in the foremost Box with greater Advantage of Dress? Where more Meetings for Business? Where more Bargains driven of all Sorts? And where so many Conveniences, or Incitements to sleep?

THERE is one Advantage, greater than any of the foregoing, proposed by the abolishing of Christianity; that it will utterly extinguish Parties among us, by removing those factious Distinctions of High and Low Church, of *Whig* and *Tory*, *Presbyterian* and *Church-of-England*, which are now so many grievous Clogs upon publick Proceedings, and dispose Men to prefer the gratifying themselves, or depressing their Adversaries, before the most important Interest of the State.

I CONFESS, if it were certain that so great an Advantage would redound to the Nation by this Expedient, I would submit and be silent: But, will any Man say, that if the Words *Whoring*, *Drinking*, *Cheating*, *Lying*, *Stealing*, were, by Act of Parliament, ejected out of the *English* Tongue and Dictionaries, we should all awake next Morning chaste and temperate, honest and just, and Lovers of Truth? Is this a fair Consequence? Or if the Physicians would forbid us to pronounce the Words *Pox*, *Gout*, *Rheumatism*, and *Stone*; would that Expedient serve like so many *Talismans* to destroy the Diseases themselves? Are Party and Faction rooted in Mens Hearts no deeper than

Phrases borrowed from Religion, or founded upon no firmer Principles? And is our Language so poor, that we cannot find other Terms to express them? Are Envy, Pride, Avarice and Ambition, such ill Nomenclators, that they cannot furnish Appellations for their Owners? Will not *Heydukes* and *Mamalukes*, *Mandarins* and *Potshaws*, or any other Words formed at Pleasure, serve to distinguish those who are in the *Ministry* from others who *would be in* it *if they could?* What, for Instance, is easier than to vary the Form of Speech, and instead of the Word *Church*, make it a Question in Politicks, Whether the *Monument* be in Danger?[11] Because Religion was nearest at Hand to furnish a few convenient Phrases, is our Invention so barren, we can find no other? Suppose, for Argument Sake, that the *Tories* favoured *Margarita*, the *Whigs* Mrs. *Tofts*, and the *Trimmers Valentini*;[12] would not *Margaritians*, *Toftians*, and *Valentinians*, be very tolerable Marks of Distinction? The *Prasini* and *Veneti*, two most virulent Factions in *Italy*, began (if I remember right) by a Distinction of Colours in Ribbonds; which we might do, with as good a Grace, about the Dignity of the *Blue* and the *Green*;[13] and would serve as properly to divide the Court, the Parliament, and the Kingdom between them, as any Terms of Art whatsoever, borrowed from Religion. Therefore, I think there is little Force in this Objection against *Christianity*; or Prospect of so great an Advantage as is proposed in the Abolishing of it.

IT is again objected, as a very absurd, ridiculous Custom, that a Set of Men should be suffered, much less employed, and hired to bawl one Day in Seven against the Lawfulness of those Methods most in Use towards the Pursuit of Greatness, Riches, and Pleasure; which are the constant Practice of all Men alive on the other Six. But this Objection is, I think, a little unworthy so refined an Age as ours. Let us argue this Matter calmly. I appeal to the Breast of any polite Free-Thinker, whether in the Pursuit of gratifying a predominant Passion, he hath not always felt a wonderful Incitement, by reflecting it was a Thing forbidden: And therefore we see, in order to cultivate this Taste, the Wisdom of the Nation hath taken special Care, that the Ladies should be furnished with prohibited Silks, and the Men with prohibited Wine:[14] And, indeed, it were to be wished, that some other Prohibitions were promoted in order to improve the Pleasures of the Town; which, for want of such Expedients, begin already, as I am told, to flag and grow languid; giving way daily to cruel Inroads from the Spleen.

IT is likewise proposed, as a great Advantage to the Publick, that if we once discard the System of the Gospel, all Religion will, of Course, be banished for ever; and consequently along with it, those grievous Prejudices of Education, which, under the Names of Virtue, Conscience, Honour, Justice, and the like, are so apt to disturb the Peace of human Minds; and the Notions whereof are so hard to be eradicated by right Reason, or Freethinking, sometimes during the whole Course of our Lives.

HERE, first, I observe how difficult it is to get rid of a Phrase, which the World is once grown fond of, although the Occasion that first produced it be entirely taken away. For several Years past, if a Man had but an ill-favoured Nose, the deep Thinkers of the Age would, some way or other, contrive to impute the Cause to the Prejudice of his Education. From this Fountain are said to be derived all our foolish Notions of Justice, Piety, Love of our Country; all our Opinions of God, or a future State, Heaven, Hell, and the like: And there might formerly, perhaps, have been some Pretence for this Charge. But so effectual Care hath been since taken, to remove those Prejudices by an entire Change in the Methods of Education, that (with Honour I mention it to our polite Innovators) the young Gentlemen, who are now on the Scene, seem to have not the least Tincture left of those Infusions, or String of those Weeds; and, by Consequence, the Reason for abolishing *Nominal* Christianity upon that Pretext, is wholly ceased.

FOR the rest, it may perhaps admit a Controversy, whether the Banishing all Notions of Religion whatsoever, would be convenient for the Vulgar. Not that I am in the least of Opinion with those, who hold Religion to have been the Invention of Politicians, to keep the lower Part of the World in Awe, by the Fear of invisible Powers; unless Mankind were then very different from what it is now: For I look upon the Mass, or Body of our People here in *England*, to be as Free-Thinkers, that is to say, as staunch Unbelievers, as any of the highest Rank. But I conceive some scattered Notions about a superior Power to be of singular Use for the common People, as furnishing excellent Materials to keep Children quiet, when they grow peevish, and providing Topicks of Amusement in a tedious Winter Night.

LASTLY, It is proposed as a singular Advantage, that the Abolishing of Christianity, will very much contribute to the uniting of *Protestants*, by enlarging the Terms of Communion, so as to take in all Sorts of *Dissenters*; who are now shut out of the Pale upon Account of a few Ceremonies, which all Sides confess to be Things indifferent: That this alone will effectually answer the great Ends of a Scheme for Comprehension, by opening a large noble Gate, at which all Bodies may enter;[15] whereas the chaffering with *Dissenters*, and dodging about this or the other Ceremony, is but like opening a few Wickets, and leaving them at jar, by which no more than one can get in at a Time, and that not without stooping, and sideling, and squeezing his Body.

To all this I answer, That there is one darling Inclination of Mankind, which usually affects to be a Retainer to Religion, although she be neither its Parent, its Godmother, or its Friend; I mean the Spirit of Opposition, that lived long before Christianity, and can easily subsist without it. Let us, for Instance, examine wherein the Opposition of Sectaries among us consists; we shall find Christianity to have no Share in it at all. Does the Gospel any where prescribe a starched squeezed Countenance, a stiff formal Gait, a Singularity of Manners and Habit, or any affected Modes of Speech, different from the reasonable Part of Mankind?[16] Yet, if Christianity did not lend its Name to stand in the Gap, and to employ or divert these Humours, they must of Necessity be spent in Contraventions to the Laws of the Land, and Disturbance of the publick Peace. There is a Portion of Enthusiasm assigned to every Nation, which if it hath not proper Objects to work on, will burst out, and set all in a Flame. If the Quiet of a State can be bought by only flinging Men a few Ceremonies to devour, it is a Purchase no wise Man would refuse. Let the Mastiffs amuse themselves about a

Sheep-skin stuffed with Hay, provided it will keep them from worrying the Flock.[17] The Institution of Convents abroad, seems in one Point a Strain of great Wisdom; there being few Irregularities in human Passions, that may not have recourse to vent themselves in some of those Orders; which are so many Retreats for the Speculative, the Melancholy, the Proud, the Silent, the Politick and the Morose, to spend themselves, and evaporate the noxious Particles; for each of whom, we in this Island are forced to provide a several Sect of Religion, to keep them quiet. And whenever Christianity shall be abolished, the Legislature must find some other Expedient to employ and entertain them. For what imports it how large a Gate you open, if there will be always left a Number, who place a Pride and a Merit in refusing to enter?

HAVING thus considered the most important Objections against Christianity, and the chief Advantages proposed by the Abolishing thereof; I shall now with equal Deference and Submission to wiser Judgments as before, proceed to mention a few Inconveniences that may happen, if the Gospel should be repealed; which perhaps the Projectors may not have sufficiently considered.

AND first, I am very sensible how much the Gentlemen of Wit and Pleasure are apt to murmur, and be choqued at the Sight of so many daggled-tail Parsons, who happen to fall in their Way, and offend their Eyes: But at the same Time these wise Reformers do not consider what an Advantage and Felicity it is, for great Wits to be always provided with Objects of Scorn and Contempt, in order to exercise and improve their Talents, and divert their Spleen from falling on each other, or on themselves; especially when all this may be done without the least imaginable *Danger to their Persons*.

AND to urge another Argument of a parallel Nature: If Christianity were once abolished, how could the Free-Thinkers, the strong Reasoners, and the Men of profound Learning be able to find another Subject so calculated in all Points whereon to display their Abilities? What wonderful Productions of Wit should we be deprived of, from those whose Genius, by continual Practice hath been wholly turned upon Raillery and

Invectives against Religion; and would therefore never be able to shine or distinguish themselves upon any other Subject? We are daily complaining of the great Decline of Wit among us; and would we take away the greatest, perhaps the only Topick we have left? Who would ever have suspected *Asgill* for a Wit, or *Toland* for a Philosopher, if the inexhaustible Stock of Christianity had not been at hand to provide them with Materials? What other Subject through all Art or Nature could have produced *Tindal* for a profound Author, or furnished him with Readers? It is the wise Choice of the Subject that alone adorns and distinguishes the Writer. For had an hundred such Pens as these been employed on the Side of Religion, they would have immediately sunk into Silence and Oblivion.

NOR do I think it wholly groundless, or my Fears altogether imaginary, that the Abolishing of Christianity may perhaps bring the Church in Danger; or at least put the Senate to the Trouble of another Securing Vote.[18] I desire, I may not be mistaken; I am far from presuming to affirm or think, that the Church is in Danger at present, or as Things now stand; but we know not how soon it may be so, when the Christian Religion is repealed. As plausible as this Project seems, there may a dangerous Design lurk under it. Nothing can be more notorious, than that the *Atheists*, *Deists*, *Socinians*, *Anti-Trinitarians*, and other Subdivisions of Free-Thinkers, are Persons of little Zeal for the present Ecclesiastical Establishment: Their declared Opinion is for repealing the Sacramental Test; they are very indifferent with regard to Ceremonies; nor do they hold the *Jus Divinum* of Episcopacy.[19] Therefore this may be intended as one politick Step towards altering the Constitution of the Church Established, and setting up *Presbytery* in the stead; which I leave to be further considered by those at the Helm.

IN the last Place, I think nothing can be more plain, than that by this Expedient, we shall run into the Evil we chiefly pretend to avoid; and that the Abolishment of the Christian Religion, will be the readiest Course we can take to introduce Popery. And I am the more inclined to this Opinion, because we know it hath been the constant Practice of the *Jesuits* to send over Emissaries, with Instructions to personate themselves Members of the several prevailing Sects amongst us.[20] So it is recorded, that they have at sundry Times appeared in the Guise of *Presbyterians*, *Anabaptists*, *Independents*, and *Quakers*, according as any of these were most in Credit: So, since the Fashion hath been taken up of exploding Religion, the *Popish* Missionaries have not been wanting to mix with the Free-Thinkers; among whom *Toland*, the great Oracle of the *Anti-Christians*, is an *Irish* Priest, the Son of an *Irish* Priest; and the most learned and ingenious Author of a Book, called the *Rights of the Christian Church*, was, in a proper Juncture, reconciled to the *Romish* Faith; whose true Son, as appears by an Hundred Passages in his Treatise, he still continues.[21] Perhaps I could add some others to the Number; but the Fact is beyond Dispute; and the Reasoning they proceed by, is right: For, supposing Christianity to be extinguished, the People will never be at Ease, till they find out some other Method of Worship; which will as infallibly produce Superstition, as this will end in *Popery*.

AND therefore, if notwithstanding all I have said, it shall still be thought necessary to have a Bill brought in for repealing Christianity; I would humbly offer an Amendment, that instead of the Word *Christianity*, may be put *Religion* in general; which I conceive, will much better answer all the good Ends proposed by the Projectors of it. For, as long as we leave in being a God and his Providence, with all the necessary Consequences, which curious and inquisitive Men will be apt to draw from such Premises; we do not strike at the Root of the Evil, although we should ever so effectually annihilate the present Scheme of the Gospel. For, of what Use is Freedom of Thought, if it will not produce Freedom of Action; which is the sole End, how remote soever in Appearance, of all Objections against Christianity? And therefore, the Free-Thinkers consider it as a Sort of Edifice, wherein all the Parts have such a mutual Dependance on each other, that if you happen to pull out one single Nail, the whole Fabrick must fall to the Ground. This was happily expressed by him, who had heard of a Text brought for Proof of the Trinity, which in an antient Manuscript was differently read; he thereupon immediately took the Hint, and by a sudden Deduction of a long *Sorites*, most logically concluded: Why, if it be as you say, I may safely whore and drink on, and defy the Parson. From which, and many the like Instances easy to be produced, I think nothing can be more manifest, than that the Quarrel is not against any particular Points of hard Digestion in the Christian System, but against Religion in general; which, by laying Restraints on human Nature, is supposed the great Enemy to the Freedom of Thought and Action.

UPON the whole; if it shall still be thought for the Benefit of Church and State, that Christianity be abolished; I conceive, however, it may be more convenient to defer the Execution to a Time of Peace; and not venture in this Conjuncture to dis-oblige our Allies; who, as it falls out, are all Christians; and many of them, by the Prejudices of their Education, so bigotted, as to place a Sort of Pride in the Appellation. If, upon being rejected by them, we are to trust to an Alliance with the *Turk*, we shall find our selves much deceived: For, as he is too remote, and generally engaged in War with the *Persian* Emperor; so his People would be more scandalized at our Infidelity, than our Christian Neighbours. Because, the *Turks* are not only strict Observers of religious Worship; but, what is worse, believe a God; which is more than is required of us, even while we preserve the Name of Christians.

To conclude: Whatever some may think of the great Advan-tages to Trade, by this favourite Scheme, I do very much appre-hend, that in six Months Time, after the Act is past for the Extirpation of the Gospel, the Bank and *East-India* Stock may fall at least One *per Cent*.[22] And since that is Fifty Times more than ever the Wisdom of our Age thought fit to venture for the *Preservation* of Christianity, there is no Reason we should be at so great a Loss, meerly for the Sake of *destroying* it.

THE TATLER, NUMBER CCXXX

Thursday, September 28, 1710

From my own Apartment, Sept. 27

THE following Letter hath laid before me many great and manifest Evils, in the World of Letters which I had overlooked; but they open to me a very busy Scene, and it will require no small Care and Application to amend Errors which are become so universal. The Affectation of Politeness, is exposed in this Epistle with a great deal of Wit and Discernment; so that, whatever Discourses I may fall into hereafter upon the Subjects the Writer treats of, I shall at present lay the Matter before the World, without the least Alteration from the Words of my Correspondent.

To ISAAC BICKERSTAFF, *Esq;*

SIR,

THERE are some Abuses among us of great Consequence, the Reformation of which is properly your Province; although, as far as I have been conversant in your Papers, you have not yet considered them. These are the deplorable Ignorance that for some Years hath reigned among our English *Writers; the great Depravity of our Taste; and the continual Corruption of our Style. I say nothing here of those who handle particular Sciences, Divinity, Law, Physick, and the like; I mean the Traders in History and Politics, and the* Belles Lettres; *together with those by whom Books are not translated, but (as the common Expressions are)* Done out of French, Latin, *or other Language, and* made English. *I cannot but observe to you, that until of late Years, a* Grub-street *Book was always bound in Sheep-skin, with suitable Print and Paper; the Price never above a Shilling; and taken off wholly by common Tradesmen, or Country Pedlars. But now they appear in all Sizes and Shapes, and in all Places: They are handed about from Lapfulls in every Coffee house to Persons of Quality; are shewn in* Westminster-Hall, *and the Court of Requests. You may see them gilt, and in Royal*

Paper of five or six Hundred Pages, and rated accordingly. I would engage to furnish you with a Catalogue of English *Books published within the Compass of seven Years past, which at the first Hand would cost you an Hundred Pounds; wherein you shall not be able to find ten Lines together of common Grammar, or common Sense.*

THESE two Evils, Ignorance and want of Taste, have produced a Third; I mean the continual Corruption of our English *Tongue; which, without some timely Remedy, will suffer more by the false Refinements of Twenty Years past, than it hath been improved in the foregoing Hundred. And this is what I design chiefly to enlarge upon, leaving the former Evils to your Animadversion.*

BUT, instead of giving you a List of the late Refinements crept into our Language, I here send you the Copy of a Letter I received some Time ago from a most accomplished Person in this Way of Writing; upon which I shall make some Remarks. It is in these Terms: ˙

SIR,
I *Cou'dn't* get the Things you sent for all *about Town.*—I *thot* to *ha'* come down my self, and then *I'd ha' bro't 'um;* but I *ha'n't don't,* and I believe I *can't do't,* that's *pozz* —— *Tom* begins to *gi'mself* Airs, because *he's* going with the *Plenipo's.*[1] —— 'Tis said the *French* King[2] will *bamboozel us agen,* which *causes many Speculations.* The *Jacks,* and others of that *Kidney,* are very *uppish,* and *alert upon't,* as you may see by their *Phizz's.*[3] —— *Will Hazard* has got the *Hipps,*[4] having lost *to the Tune of* five Hundr'd Pound, *tho'* he understands Play very well, *no Body better.* He has promis't me upon *Rep,*[5] to leave off Play; but you know 'tis a Weakness *he's* too apt to *give into, tho'* he has as much Wit as any Man, *no body more.* He has lain *incog*[6] ever since.—The *Mob's* very quiet with us now. —— I believe you *tho't* I *banter'd* you in my last like a *Country Put.* —— I *shan't* leave Town this Month, &c.

THIS Letter is in every Point an admirable Pattern of the present polite Way of Writing; nor is it of less Authority for

being an Epistle: You may gather every Flower of it, with a
Thousand more of equal Sweetness, from the Books, Pamphlets,
and single Papers offered us every Day in the Coffee-houses:
And these are the Beauties introduced to supply the Want of
Wit, Sense, Humour and Learning; which formerly were looked
upon as Qualifications for a Writer. If a Man of Wit, who died
Forty Years ago, were to rise from the Grave on Purpose, how
would he be able to read this Letter? And after he had got
through that Difficulty, how would he be able to understand
it? The first Thing that strikes your Eye, is the *Breaks* at the
End of almost every Sentence; of which I know not the Use,
only that it is a Refinement, and very frequently practised.
Then you will observe the Abbreviations and Elisions, by which
Consonants of most obdurate Sound are joined together, without one softening Vowel to intervene: And all this only to make
one Syllable of two, directly contrary to the Example of the
Greeks and *Romans*; altogether of the *Gothick* Strain, and
a natural Tendency towards relapsing into Barbarity, which
delights in Monosyllables, and uniting of mute Consonants; as
it is observable in all the *Northern* Languages.[7] And this is
still more visible in the next Refinement, which consisteth in
pronouncing the first Syllable in a Word that hath many, and
dismissing the rest; such as *Phizz, Hipps, Mobb, Pozz, Rep*,
and many more; when we are already over-loaded with Monosyllables, which are the Disgrace of our Language. Thus we
cram one Syllable, and cut off the rest, as the Owl fattened her
Mice after she had bit off their Legs, to prevent them from
running away; and if ours be the same Reason for maiming of
Words, it will certainly answer the End, for I am sure no other
Nation will desire to borrow them. Some Words are hitherto
but fairly split; and therefore only in their Way to Perfection;
as *Incog.* and *Plenipo's*: But in a short Time, it is to be hoped,
they will be further docked to *Inc* and *Plen*. This Reflection has
made me, of late Years, very impatient for a Peace; which I
believe would save the Lives of many brave Words, as well as
Men. The War hath introduced abundance of Polysyllables,
which will never be able to live many more Campaigns. *Speculations, Operations, Preliminaries, Ambassadors, Pallisadoes,*

Communication, Circumvallation, Battallions, as numerous as they are, if they attack us too frequently in our Coffee-houses, we shall certainly put them to Flight, and cut off the Rear.

THE third Refinement observeable in the Letter I send you, consisteth in the Choice of certain Words invented by some *pretty Fellows*, such as *Banter, Bamboozle, Country Put*, and *Kidney*, as it is there applied; some of which are now struggling for the Vogue, and others are in Possession of it. I have done my utmost for some Years past, to stop the Progress of *Mob* and *Banter*;[8] but have been plainly born down by Numbers, and betrayed by those who promised to assist me.

IN the last Place, you are to take Notice of certain choice Phrases scattered through the Letter; some of them tolerable enough, till they were worn to Rags by servile Imitators. You might easily find them, although they were not in a different Print; and therefore I need not disturb them.

THESE are the false Refinements in our Style which you ought to correct: First, by Arguments and fair Means; but if those fail, I think you are to make Use of your Authority as Censor, and by an annual *Index Expurgatorius*, expunge all Words and Phrases that are offensive to good Sense, and condemn those barbarous Mutilations of Vowels and Syllables.[9] In this last Point, the usual Pretence is, that they spell as they speak: A noble Standard for Language! To depend upon the Caprice of every Coxcomb; who, because Words are the Cloathing of our Thoughts, cuts them out, and shapes them as he pleases, and changes them oftner than his Dress. I believe, all reasonable People would be content, that such Refiners were more sparing of their Words, and liberal in their Syllables. On this Head, I should be glad you would bestow some Advice upon several young Readers in our Churches; who coming up from the University, full fraught with Admiration of our Town Politeness, will needs correct the Style of their Prayer-Books. In reading the Absolution, they are very careful to say *Pardons* and *Absolves*; and in the Prayer for the Royal Family, it must be *endue'm, enrich'um, prosper'um*, and *bring'um*. Then, in their Sermons, they use all the modern Terms of Art; *Sham, Banter, Mob, Bubble, Bully, Cutting, Shuffling*, and *Palming*:

All which, and many more of the like Stamp, as I have heard them often in the Pulpit from some young Sophisters; so I have read them in some of *those Sermons that have made a great Noise of late*. The Design, it seems, is to avoid the dreadful Imputation of Pedantry; to shew us, that they *know the Town, understand Men and Manners*, and have not been poring upon old unfashionable Books in the University.[10]

I SHOULD be glad to see you the Instrument of introducing into our Style, that Simplicity which is the best and truest Ornament of most Things in human Life, which the politer Ages always aimed at in their Building and Dress, (*Simplex munditiis*[11]) as well as their Productions of Wit. It is manifest, that all new affected Modes of Speech, whether borrowed from the Court, the Town, or the Theatre, are the first perishing Parts in any Language; and, as I could prove by many Hundred Instances, have been so in ours. The Writings of *Hooker*, who was a Country Clergyman, and of *Parsons* the Jesuit,[12] both in the Reign of Queen *Elizabeth*, are in a Style that, with very few Allowances, would not offend any present Reader; much more clear and intelligible than those of Sir *H. Wooton*, Sir *Robert Naunton, Osborn, Daniel* the Historian,[13] and several others who writ later; but being Men of the Court, and affecting the Phrases then in Fashion, they are often either not to be understood, or appear perfectly ridiculous.

WHAT Remedies are to be applied to these Evils, I have not Room to consider; having, I fear, already taken up most of your Paper. Besides, I think it is our Office only to represent Abuses, and yours to redress them. I am, with great Respect,

SIR,

Yours, &c.

THE EXAMINER

NUMBER 13

Thursday, November 2, 1710

—— *Longa est Injuria, longæ*
Ambages, sed summa sequar fastigia rerum.[1]

It is a Practice I have generally followed, to converse in equal
Freedom with the deserving Men of both Parties; and it was
never without some Contempt, that I have observed Persons
wholly out of Employment, affect to do otherwise: I doubted
whether any Man could owe so much to the Side he was of,
altho' he were retained by it; but without some great Point of
Interest, either in Possession or Prospect, I thought it was the
Mark of a low and narrow Spirit.

It is hard, that for some Weeks past, I have been forced, in
my own Defence, to follow a Proceeding that I have so much
condemned in others. But several of my Acquaintance, among
the declining Party,[2] are grown so insufferably Peevish and
Splenetick, profess such violent Apprehensions for the Publick,
and represent the State of Things in such formidable Ideas, that
I find myself disposed to Share in their Afflictions, although I
know them to be groundless and imaginary; or, which is
worse, purely affected. To offer them Comfort one by one,
would be not only an endless, but a disobliging Task. Some
of them, I am convinced, would be less melancholy, if there
were more Occasion. I shall therefore, instead of hearkning to
further Complaints, employ some Part of this Paper for the
Future, in letting such Men see, that their natural or acquired
Fears are ill-grounded, and their artificial Ones as ill-intended.
That all our present Inconveniencies are the Consequence of
the very Counsels they so much admire, which would still
have encreased, if those had continued: And that neither our
Constitution in Church or State, could probably have been

long preserved, without such Methods as have been already taken.

THE late Revolutions at Court, have given Room to some specious Objections, which I have heard repeated by well-meaning Men, just as they had taken them up on the Credit of others, who have worse Designs. They wonder the Queen would chuse to change her Ministry at this Juncture, and thereby give Uneasiness to a General who hath been so long successful Abroad; and might think himself injured, if the entire Ministry were not of his own Nomination.[3] That there were few Complaints of any Consequence against the late Men in Power, and none at all in Parliament; which on the Contrary, passed Votes in favour of the Chief Minister. That if her Majesty had a Mind to introduce the other Party, it would have been more seasonable after a Peace, which now we have made desperate, by spiriting the *French*, who rejoice at these Changes, and by the Fall of our Credit, which unqualifies us for continuing the War. That the Parliament, so untimely dissolved, had been diligent in their Supplies, and dutiful in their Behaviour. That, one Consequence of these Changes appears already in the Fall of the Stocks. That, we may soon expect more and worse: And lastly, That, all this naturally tends to break the Settlement of the Crown, and call over the *Pretender*.[4]

THESE and the like Notions are plentifully scattered abroad by the Malice of a ruined Party, to render the QUEEN and her Administration odious, and to inflame the Nation. And these are what, upon Occasion, I shall endeavour to overthrow, by discovering the Falshood and Absurdity of them.

IT is a great Unhappiness, when in a Government constituted like ours, it should be so brought about, that the Continuance of a War must be for the Interest of vast Numbers (Civil as well as Military) who otherwise would have been as unknown as their Original.[5] I think our present Condition of Affairs, is admirably described by two Verses in *Lucan*.[6]

> *Hinc usura Vorax, avidumque in tempore fœnus,*
> *Hinc concussa fides, & multis utile bellum.*

Which, without any great Force upon the Words, may be thus translated.

Hence are derived those exorbitant Interests and Annuities; hence those large Discounts for Advances and prompt Payment; hence publick Credit is shaken; and hence great Numbers find their Profit in prolonging the War.

IT is odd, that among a free Trading People, as we call ourselves, there should so many be found to close in with those Counsels, who have been ever averse from all Overtures towards a Peace. But yet there is no great Mystery in the Matter. Let any Man observe the Equipages in this Town; he shall find the greater Number of those who make a Figure, to be a Species of Men quite different from any that were ever known before the Revolution; consisting either of Generals and Colonels, or of such whose whole Fortunes lie in Funds and Stocks: So that *Power*, which, according to the old Maxim, was used to follow *Land*, is now gone over to *Money*; and the Country Gentleman is in the Condition of a young Heir, out of whose Estate a Scrivener receives half the Rents for Interest, and hath a Mortgage on the Whole; and is therefore always ready to feed his Vices and Extravagancies while there is any Thing left. So that if the War continue some Years longer, a landed Man will be little better than a Farmer at a rack Rent, to the Army, and to the publick Funds.

IT may perhaps be worth inquiring from what Beginnings, and by what Steps we have been brought into this desperate Condition: And in search of this we must run up as high as the Revolution.[7]

MOST of the Nobility and Gentry who invited over the Prince of *Orange*, or attended him in his Expedition, were true Lovers of their Country and its Constitution, in Church and State; and were brought to yield to those Breaches in the Succession of the Crown, out of a Regard to the Necessity of the Kingdom, and the Safety of the People, which did, and could only, make them lawful; but without Intention of drawing such a Practice into Precedent, or making it a standing Measure by which to proceed

in all Times to come; and therefore we find their Counsels ever
tended to keep Things as much as possible in the old Course.
But soon after, an under Sett of Men, who had nothing to lose,
and had neither born the Burthen nor Heat of the Day, found
means to whisper in the King's Ear, that the Principles of
Loyalty in the Church of *England*, were wholly inconsistent
with the *Revolution*. Hence began the early Practice of caress-
ing the Dissenters, reviling the Universities as Maintainers of
Arbitrary Power, and reproaching the Clergy with the Doctrines
of Divine-Right, Passive-Obedience, and Non-Resistance.[8] At
the same Time, in order to fasten wealthy People to the New
Government, they proposed those pernicious Expedients of
borrowing Money by vast *Premiums*, and at exorbitant Interest:
A Practice as old as *Eumenes*, one of *Alexander*'s Captains,
who setting up for himself after the Death of his Master, persuaded his principal Officers to lend him great Sums, after
which they were forced to follow him for their own Security.[9]

   THIS introduced a Number of new dextrous Men into
Business and Credit: It was argued, that the War could not last
above two or three Campaigns; and that it was easier for the
Subject to raise a Fund for paying Interest, than to tax them
annually to the full Expence of the War. Several Persons who
had small or encumbred Estates, sold them, and turned their
Money into those Funds to great Advantage: Merchants, as
well as other monied Men, finding Trade was dangerous, pursued the same Method: But the War continuing, and growing
more expensive, Taxes were encreased, and Funds multiplied
every Year, 'till they have arrived at the monstrous Height we
now behold them. And that which was at first a Corruption, is
at last grown necessary, and what every good Subject must now
fall in with, although he may be allowed to wish it might soon
have an End; because it is with a Kingdom, as with a private
Fortune, where every new Incumbrance adds a double Weight.
By this Means the Wealth of a Nation, that used to be reckoned
by the Value of Land, is now computed by the Rise and Fall
of Stocks: And although the Foundation of Credit be still the
same, and upon a Bottom that can never be shaken; and
although all Interest be duly paid by the Publick, yet through

the Contrivance and Cunning of *Stock-Jobbers*, there hath been brought in such a Complication of Knavery and Couzenage, such a Mystery of Iniquity, and such an unintelligible *Jargon* of Terms to involve it in, as were never known in any other Age or Country of the World. I have heard it affirmed by Persons skilled in these Calculations, that if the Funds appropriated to the Payment of Interest and Annuities, were added to the yearly Taxes, and the Four-Shilling Aid strictly exacted in all Counties of the Kingdom,[10] it would very near, if not fully, supply the Occasions of the War, at least such a Part, as in the Opinion of very able Persons, had been at that Time prudent not to exceed. For I make it a Question, whether any wise Prince or State, in the Continuance of a War, which was not purely defensive, or immediately at his own Door, did ever propose that his Expence should perpetually exceed what he was able to impose annually upon his Subjects? Neither if the War last many Years longer, do I see how the next Generation will be able to begin another; which in the Course of human Affairs, and according to the various Interests and Ambition of Princes, may be as necessary for them as it hath been for us. And if our Fathers had left us as deeply involved as we are like to leave our Children, I appeal to any Man what sort of Figure we should have been able to make these twenty Years past.[11] Besides, neither our Enemies, nor Allies, are upon the same Foot with us in this Particular. *France* and *Holland*, our nearest Neighbours, and the farthest engaged, will much sooner recover themselves after a War. The first, by the absolute Power of the Prince, who being Master of the Lives and Fortunes of his Subjects, will quickly find Expedients to pay his Debts: And so will the other, by their prudent Administration, the Greatness of their Trade, their wonderful Parsimony, the Willingness of their People to undergo all kind of Taxes, and their Justice in applotting as well as collecting them. But above all, we are to consider, that *France* and *Holland* fight in the Continent, either upon, or near their own Territories; and the greatest Part of the Money circulates among themselves; whereas ours crosses the Sea, either to *Flanders, Spain*, or *Portugal*; and every Penny of it, whether in Specie or Returns, is so much lost to the Nation for ever.

UPON these Considerations alone, it was the most prudent Course imaginable in the QUEEN, to lay hold of the Disposition of the People for changing the Parliament and Ministry at this Juncture; and extricating her self as soon as possible out of the Pupilage of those who found their Accounts only in perpetuating the War. Neither have we the least Reason to doubt, but the ensuing Parliament will assist her MAJESTY with the utmost Vigour, until her Enemies *again* be brought to sue for Peace, and *again* offer such Terms as will make it both honourable and lasting; only with this Difference, that the Ministry perhaps will not *again* refuse them.[12]

Audiet pugnas vitio parentum
Rara Juventus.[13]

NUMBER 14
Thursday, November 9, 1710

E quibus hi vacuas implent Sermonibus aures,
Hi narrata ferunt alio: mensuraque ficti
Crescit, & auditis aliquid novus adjicit autor,
Illic Credulitas, illic temerarius Error,
Vanaque Lætitia est, consternatique Timores,
Seditioque recens, dubioque autore susurri.[1]

I AM prevailed on, through the Importunity of Friends, to interrupt the Scheme I had begun in my last Paper, by an Essay upon the Art of *Political Lying*. We are told, *The Devil is the Father of Lyes*, and *was a Lyar from the Beginning*; so that, beyond Contradiction, the Invention is old: And, which is more, his first Essay of it was purely *Political*, employed in undermining the Authority of his Prince, and seducing a third Part of the Subjects from their Obedience. For which he was driven down from Heaven, where (as *Milton* expresseth it) he had been VICEROY of a great *Western Province*; and forced to exercise his Talent in inferior Regions among *other fallen Spirits*, or *poor deluded Men*, whom he still daily tempts to *his own Sin*, and will ever do so till he be *chained in the bottomless Pit*.[2]

BUT although the Devil be the Father of *Lyes*, he seems, like other great Inventors, to have lost much of his Reputation, by the continual Improvements that have been made upon him.

WHO first reduced *Lying* into an Art, and adapted it to *Politicks*, is not so clear from History; although I have made some diligent Enquiries: I shall therefore consider it only according to the modern System, as it hath been cultivated these twenty Years past in the Southern Part of our own Island.

THE Poets tell us, That after the Giants were overthrown by the Gods, the *Earth* in revenge produced her last Offspring, which was *Fame*.[3] And the Fable is thus interpreted; That when Tumults and Seditions are quieted, Rumours and false Reports are plentifully spread through a Nation. So that by this Account, *Lying* is the last Relief of a *routed*, *earth-born*, *rebellious Party* in a State. But here, the Moderns have made great Additions, applying this Art to the gaining of Power, and preserving it, as well as revenging themselves after they have lost it: As the same Instruments are made use of by Animals to feed themselves when they are hungry, and bite those that tread upon them.

BUT the same Genealogy cannot always be admitted for *Political Lying*; I shall therefore desire to refine upon it, by adding some Circumstances of its Birth and Parents. A *Political Lye* is sometimes born out of a discarded Statesman's Head, and thence delivered to be nursed and dandled by the *Rabble*. Sometimes it is produced a Monster, and *licked* into Shape; at other Times it comes into the World compleatly formed, and is spoiled in the *licking*. It is often born an Infant in the regular Way, and requires Time to mature it: And often it sees the Light in its full Growth, but dwindles away by Degrees. Sometimes it is of noble Birth; and sometimes the Spawn of a *Stock-jobber*. *Here*, it screams aloud at opening the Womb; and *there*, it is delivered with a *Whisper*. I know a *Lye* that now disturbs half the Kingdom with its Noise, which although too proud and great at present to own its Parents, I can remember in its *Whisperhood*. To conclude the Nativity of this Monster; when it comes into the World without a *Sting*, it is still-born; and whenever it loses its *Sting*, it dies.

No Wonder, if an Infant so miraculous in its Birth, should be destined for great Adventures: And accordingly we see it hath been the *Guardian Spirit* of a *prevailing Party* for almost twenty Years.[4] It can conquer Kingdoms without Fighting, and sometimes with the Loss of a Battle: It gives and resumes Employments; can sink a Mountain to a Mole-hill, and raise a Mole-hill to a Mountain; hath presided for many Years at Committees of Elections; can wash a *Black-a-moor* white; make a Saint of an Atheist, and a Patriot of a Profligate; can furnish *Foreign Ministers* with Intelligence; and raise or let fall the Credit of the Nation. This Goddess flies with a huge *Looking-glass* in her Hands to dazzle the Crowd, and make them see, according as she turns it, their Ruin in their Interest, and their Interest in their Ruin. In this Glass you will behold your best Friends clad in Coats powdered with *Flower-de-Luce*'s and *Triple Crowns*; their Girdles hung round with *Chains*, and *Beads*, and *wooden Shoes:* And your worst Enemies adorned with the Ensigns of *Liberty, Property, Indulgence, Moderation*, and a *Cornucopia* in their Hands.[5] Her large Wings, like those of a flying Fish, are of no Use but while they are moist; she therefore dips them in *Mud*, and soaring aloft scatters it in the Eyes of the Multitude, flying with great Swiftness; but at every Turn is forced to stoop in *dirty Ways* for new Supplies.

I HAVE been sometimes thinking, if a Man had the Art of the *Second Sight* for seeing *Lyes*, as they have in *Scotland* for seeing Spirits;[6] how admirably he might entertain himself in this Town; to observe the different Shapes, Sizes, and Colours, of those Swarms of *Lyes* which buz about the Heads of *some People*, like Flies about a Horse's Ears in Summer: Or those Legions hovering every Afternoon in *Exchange-Alley*, enough to darken the Air; or over a Club of discontented Grandees, and thence sent down in Cargoes to be scattered at Elections.[7]

THERE is one essential Point wherein a *Political Lyar* differs from others of the Faculty; That he ought to have but a short Memory, which is necessary according to the various Occasions he meets with every Hour, of differing from himself, and swearing to both Sides of a Contradiction, as he finds the Persons disposed, with whom he hath to deal. In describing the Virtues and Vices of Mankind, it is convenient, upon every Article, to have some eminent Person in our Eye, from whence we copy our Description. I have strictly observed this Rule; and my Imagination this Minute represents before me a certain *Great Man* famous for this Talent, to the constant Practice of which he owes his twenty Years Reputation of the most skilful Head in *England* for the Management of nice Affairs.[8] The Superiority of his Genius consists in nothing else but an inexhaustible Fund of *Political Lyes*, which he plentifully distributes every Minute he speaks, and by an unparallelled Generosity forgets, and consequently contradicts the next half Hour. He never yet considered whether any Proposition were True or False, but whether it were convenient for the present Minute or Company to affirm or deny it; so that if you think to refine upon him, by interpreting every Thing he says, as we do Dreams, by the Contrary, you are still to seek, and will find your self equally deceived, whether you believe or no: The only Remedy is to suppose that you have heard some inarticulate Sounds, without any Meaning at all. And besides, that will take off the Horror you might be apt to conceive at the Oaths wherewith he perpetually Tags both Ends of every *Proposition*: Although at the same Time, I think, he cannot with any Justice be taxed for Perjury, when he invokes *God* and *Christ*; because he hath often fairly given publick Notice to the World, that he believes in neither.[9]

SOME People may think that such an Accomplishment as this, can be of no great Use to the Owner or his Party, after it hath been often practised and is become notorious; but they are widely mistaken: Few *Lyes* carry the Inventor's Mark; and the most prostitute Enemy to Truth may spread a Thousand without being known for the Author. Besides, as the vilest Writer hath his Readers, so the greatest *Lyar* hath his Believers; and it often happens, that if a *Lye* be believed only for an Hour, it hath done its Work, and there is no farther Occasion for it. *Falshood flies*, and *Truth* comes *limping* after it; so that when Men come to be undeceived, it is too late, the Jest is over, and the Tale has had its Effect: Like a Man who has thought of a good Repartee, when the Discourse is changed, or the Company parted: Or, like a physician who hath found out an infallible Medicine after the Patient is dead.

CONSIDERING that natural Disposition in many Men to *Lye*, and in Multitudes to *Believe*; I have been perplexed what to do with that Maxim, so frequent in every Bodies Mouth, That *Truth will at last prevail*. Here, has this Island of ours, for the greatest Part of twenty Years lain under the Influence of such Counsels and Persons, whose Principle and Interest it was to corrupt our Manners, blind our Understandings, drain our Wealth, and in Time destroy our Constitution both in Church and State;[10] and we at last were brought to the very Brink of Ruin; yet by the Means of perpetual Representations, have never been able to distinguish between our Enemies and Friends. We have seen a great Part of the Nation's Money got into the Hands of those, who by their Birth, Education and Merit, could pretend no higher than to wear our Liveries. While others, who by their Credit, Quality and Fortune, were only able to give Reputation and Success to the Revolution, were not only laid aside, as dangerous and useless; but loaden with the Scandal of *Jacobites*, Men of *Arbitrary Principles*, and *Pensioners* to *France*; while Truth, who is said to *lie in a Well*, seemed now to be buried there under a heap of Stones. But I remember it was a usual Complaint among the *Whigs*, that the Bulk of Landed-men was not in their Interests, which some of the Wisest looked on as an ill Omen; and we saw it was with the utmost Difficulty that they could preserve a Majority, while the Court and Ministry were on their Side; till they had learned those admirable Expedients for deciding Elections, and influencing distant Boroughs, by *powerful Motives* from the City.[11] But all this was mere Force and Constraint, however upheld by most dextrous Artifice and Management; until the People began to apprehend their *Properties*, their *Religion*, and the *Monarchy* itself in Danger; then we saw them greedily laying hold on the first Occasion to interpose. But of this mighty Change in the Dispositions of the People, I shall discourse more at large in some following Paper; wherein I shall endeavour to undeceive or discover those deluded or deluding Persons, who hope or pretend, it is only a short Madness in the Vulgar, from which they may soon recover. Whereas, I believe, it will appear to be very different in its Causes, its Symptoms, and its Consequences; and prove a great Example to illustrate the Maxim I lately mentioned, That *Truth* (however sometimes late) *will at last prevail*.

NUMBER 20

Thursday, December 21, 1710

—— *Pugnacem scirent sapiente minorem.*[1]

I AM very much at a Loss how to proceed upon the Subject intended in this Paper, which a new Incident hath led me to engage in: The Subject I mean, is that of *Soldiers* and the *Army*; but being a Matter wholly out of my Trade, I shall handle it in as cautious a Manner as I am able.

IT is certain, that the Art of War hath suffered great Changes, almost in every Age and Country of the World; however, there are some Maxims relating to it, that will be eternal Truths, and which every reasonable Man must allow.

IN the early Times of *Greece* and *Rome*, the Armies of those States were composed of their Citizens, who took no Pay, because the Quarrel was their own; and therefore the War was usually decided in one Campaign; or, if it lasted longer, yet in Winter the Soldiers returned to their several Callings, and were not distinguished from the rest of the People. The *Gothick* Governments in *Europe*, although they were of Military Institution, yet observed almost the same Method. I shall instance only in *England*. Those who held Lands in *Capite* of the King, were obliged to attend him in his Wars with a certain Number of Men, who all held Lands from them at easy Rents on that Condition. These fought without Pay; and when the Service was over, returned again to their Farms. It is recorded of *William Rufus*, that being absent in *Normandy*, and engaged in a War with his Brother, he ordered twenty thousand Men to be raised and sent over from hence to supply his Army; but having struck up a Peace before they were embarked, he gave them leave to disband, on Condition they would pay him ten Shillings a Man; which amounted to a mighty Sum in those Days.[2]

CONSIDER a Kingdom as a great Family, whereof the Prince is the Father; and it will appear plainly, that Mercenary Troops are only *Servants armed*, either to awe the *Children* at home; or else to defend from Invaders, the Family who are otherwise employed, and chuse to contribute out of their Stock for paying their Defenders, rather than leave their Affairs to be neglected in their Absence. The Art of making Soldiery a Trade, and keeping Armies in Pay, seems in *Europe* to have had two Originals. The First was *Usurpation*, when popular Men destroyed the Liberties of their Country and seized the Power into their own Hands, which they were forced to maintain by hiring Guards to bridle the People. Such were anciently the *Tyrants* in most of the small States of *Greece*; and such were those in several Parts of *Italy*, about three or four Centuries ago, as *Machiavel* informs us.[3] The other Original of mercenary Armies, seems to have risen from larger Kingdoms or Commonwealths, which had subdued Provinces at a Distance, and were forced to maintain Troops upon them, to prevent Insurrections from the Natives: Of this Sort were *Macedon*, *Carthage* and *Rome* of old; *Venice* and *Holland* at this Day; as well as most Kingdoms of *Europe*. So that mercenary Forces in a free State, whether *Monarchy* or *Commonwealth*, seem only necessary, either for preserving their Conquests (which in such Governments it is not prudent to extend too far) or else for maintaining a War at a Distance.

IN this last, which at present is our most important Case, there are certain Maxims that all wise Governments have observed.

THE first I shall mention is, That no *private* Man should have a Commission to be *General for Life*, let his Merit and Services be ever so great.[4] Or, if a Prince be unadvisedly brought to offer such a Commission in one Hand, let him (to save Time and Blood) deliver up his *Crown* with the other. The *Romans*, in the Height and Perfection of their Government, usually sent out one of the new *Consuls* to be General against their most formidable Enemy, and recalled the old one, who often returned before the next Election; and according as he had Merit, was sent to command in some other Part; which, perhaps, was continued to him for a second, and sometimes a third Year. But if *Paulus Æmilius*, or *Scipio* himself,[5] had presumed to move the *Senate* to continue their *Commissions for Life*, they certainly would have fallen a Sacrifice to the Jealousy of the People. *Cæsar* indeed (between whom and *a certain General*, some of late with much Discretion have made a *Parallel*) had his Command in *Gaul* continued to him for five Years, and was afterwards made perpetual *Dictator*; that is to say, *General for Life*, which gave him the Power and the Will of utterly destroying the *Roman* Liberty.[6] But in his Time the *Romans* were very much degenerated; and great Corruptions had crept into their Morals and Discipline. However, we see there still were some Remains of a noble Spirit among them: For, when *Cæsar* sent to be chosen *Consul*, notwithstanding his Absence, they decreed he should come in Person, give up his Command, and *petere more majorum*.[7]

IT is not impossible but a *General* may desire such a Commission out of *Inadvertency*, at the *Instigation of his Friends*; or, perhaps of his *Enemies*; or, meerly for the *Benefit and Honour of it*, without intending any such *dreadful Consequences*; and in that Case, a wise Prince or State may barely refuse it without shewing any Marks of their Displeasure. But the Request in its own Nature is highly Criminal, and ought to be entered so upon Record, to terrify *Others* in Time to come from venturing to make it.

ANOTHER Maxim to be observed by a free State engaged in War, is to keep the Military Power in absolute Subjection to the Civil, nor ever suffer the former to influence or interfere with the latter. A General and his Army are *Servants, hired* by the Civil Power to act as they are directed from thence, and with a Commission large or limited as the Administration shall think fit; for which they are largely paid in Profit and Honour.

The whole System by which Armies are governed, is quite *alien* from the peaceful Institutions of States at home; and if the Rewards be so inviting as to tempt a *Senator* to take a Post in the Army, whilst he is there on his Duty, he ought to consider himself in no other Capacity. I know not any Sort of Men so apt as Soldiers are, to reprimand those who presume to interfere in what relates to their Trade. When they hear any of us in a Coffee House wondring that such a Victory was not pursued; complaining that such a Town cost more Men and Money than it was worth to take it; or that such an Opportunity was lost, of fighting the Enemy; they presently reprove us, and often with Justice enough, for meddling in Matters out of our Sphere; and clearly convince us in Terms of Art that none of us understand. Nor do we escape so; for they reflect with the utmost Contempt on our Ignorance, that we who sit at home in Ease and Security, never stirring from our Fire-sides, should pretend from Books, and general Reason, to argue upon Military Affairs; which after all, if we may judge from the Share of Intellectuals in some who are said to excel that Way, is not so very profound or difficult a Science. But, if there be any Weight in what they offer, as perhaps there may be a great deal; surely these Gentlemen have a much weaker Pretence to concern themselves in Matters of the Cabinet, which are always either far above, or much beside their Capacities. Soldiers may as well pretend to prescribe Rules for Trade; to determine Points in Philosophy; to be Moderators in an Assembly of Divines; or direct in a Court of Justice; as to misplace their Talent in examining Affairs of State, especially in what relates to the *Choice of Ministers*, who are never so likely to be ill chosen as when approved by them. It would be endless to shew how pernicious all Steps of this Nature have been in many Parts and Ages of the World. I shall only produce two at present, one in *Rome*, and the other in *England*. The first is of *Cæsar*, when he came to the City with his Soldiers to *settle the Ministry*, there was an End of their Liberty for ever. The second was in the great Rebellion against King *Charles* the First. The King and both Houses were agreed upon the Terms of a Peace; but the Officers of the Army, (as *Ludlow* relates it) set a Guard upon the House of Commons, took a List out of the Members, and kept all by Force out of the House, except those who were for bringing the King to a Trial.[8] Some Years after, when they erected a Military Government and ruled the Island by *Major-Generals*,[9] we received most admirable Instances of their Skill in Politicks. To say the Truth, such formidable Sticklers can have but two Reasons for desiring to interfere in the Administration; the first is that of *Cæsar* and *Cromwell*, of which, God forbid I should accuse or suspect any Body; since the second is pernicious enough, and that is, *To preserve those in Power who are for perpetuating a War, rather than see others advanced who, they are sure, will use all proper Means to promote a safe and honourable Peace.*

THIRDLY, Since it is observed of Armies, that in the present Age they are brought to some Degree of Humanity, and a more regular Demeanor to each other, and to the World, than in former Times: It is certainly a good Maxim to endeavour preserving this Temper among them; without which, they would soon degenerate into *Savages*. To this End it would be prudent, among other Things, to forbid that detestable Custom of *drinking to the Damnation or Confusion* of any Person whatsoever.

SUCH desperate Acts, and the Opinions infused along with them, into Heads already inflamed by Youth and Wine, are enough to scatter Madness and Sedition through a whole Camp. So seldom *upon their Knees to Pray*, and so often to *Curse!* This is not properly Atheism, but a Sort of *Anti-Religion* prescribed by the Devil, and which an Atheist of common Sense would scorn as an Absurdity. I have heard it mentioned as a common Practice last Autumn, *somewhere or other*, to *drink Damnation and Confusion* (and this with Circumstances very aggravating and horrid) to the *New Ministry*, and to those who *had any Hand* in turning out the *Old*; that is to say, to those Persons whom her Majesty has thought fit to employ in her greatest Affairs; with something *more than a Glance against the Queen herself*.[10] And if it be true, that these *Orgyes* were attended with certain *doubtful Words*, of *standing by their General*, who without Question abhorred them: Let any Man consider the Consequence of such Dispositions, if they should happen to spread. I could only wish, for the Honour of the

Army, as well as of the Queen and Ministry, that a Remedy had been applied to the Disease, in the *Place* and *Time* where it grew. If Men of such Principles were able to propagate them in a Camp, and were sure of a *General for Life*, who had any Tincture of Ambition, we might soon bid farewel to Ministries and Parliaments, whether new or old.

I AM only sorry such an Accident hath happened towards the Close of a War, when it is chiefly the Interest of those Gentlemen who have Posts in the Army, to behave themselves in such a Manner as might encourage the Legislature to make some Provision for them, when there will be no further need of their Service. They are to consider themselves as Persons, by their Educations, unqualified for many other Stations of Life. Their Fortunes will not suffer them to retain to a Party after its *Fall*; nor have they Weight or Abilities to help towards its *Resurrection*. Their future Dependence is wholly upon the Prince and Parliament, to which they will never make their Way by *solemn Execrations of the Ministry*; a Ministry of the Queen's own Election, and fully answering the Wishes of her People. This unhappy Step in some of *their Brethren*, may pass for an uncontroulable Argument, that Politicks are not their Business or their Element. The Fortune of War hath raised several Persons up to swelling Titles, and great Commands over Numbers of Men, which they are too apt to transfer along with them into Civil Life, and appear in all Companies as if they were at the Head of their Regiments, with a Sort of Deportment that ought to have been dropt behind, in that short Passage to *Harwich*.[11] It puts me in Mind of a Dialogue in *Lucian*,[12] where *Charon*, wafting one of their Predecessors over *Styx*, ordered him to strip off his Armour and fine Cloaths, yet still thought him too heavy; *but*, said he, *put off likewise that Pride and Presumption; those high swelling Words, and that vain Glory*; because they were of no Use on the other Side [of] the Water. Thus, if all that Array of Military Grandeur were confined to the proper Scene, it would be much more for the Interest of the Owners, and less offensive to their Fellow Subjects.

LETTER V

London, Sept. 30, 1710

HAN'T I brought myself into a fine premunire to begin writing letters in whole sheets, and now I dare not leave it off. I can't tell whether you like these journal letters: I believe they would be dull to me to read them over; but, perhaps, little *MD* is pleased to know how *Presto* passes his time in her absence.[1] I always begin my last the same day I ended my former. I told you where I dined to-day at a tavern with *Stratford: Lewis*, who is a great favourite of *Harley*'s, was to have been with us; but he was hurried to *Hampton-court*, and sent his excuse, and that next *Wednesday* he would introduce me to *Harley*. 'Tis good to see what a lamentable confession the *Whigs* all make me of my ill usage: but I mind them not. I am already represented to *Harley* as a discontented person, that was used ill for not being *Whig* enough; and I hope for good usage from him. The *Tories* dryly tell me, I may make my fortune, if I please; but I do not understand them, or rather, I do understand them.

Oct. 1. To-day I dined at *Molesworth*'s, the *Florence* envoy; and sat this evening with my friend *Darteneuf*, whom you have heard me talk of; the greatest punner of this town next myself. Have you smoakt the *Tatler* that I writ? It is much liked here, and I think it a pure one.[2] To-morrow I go with *Delaval* the *Portugal* envoy, to dine with lord *Halifax* near *Hampton-court*. Your *Manley*'s brother, a parliament-man here, has gotten an employment; and I am informed uses much interest to preserve his brother: and to-day, I spoke to the elder *Frankland* to engage his father, (post-master here) and I hope he will be safe, although he is cruelly hated by all the *Tories* of *Ireland*.[3] I have almost finished my lampoon, and will print it for revenge on a certain great person.[4] It has cost me but three shillings in meat and drink since I came here, as thin as the town is. I laugh to see myself so disengaged in these revolutions. Well, I must leave off and go write to sir *John Stanley*, to desire him to engage lady *Hyde* as my mistress to engage lord *Hyde* in favour of Mr. *Pratt*.[5]

2. Lord *Halifax* was at *Hampton-court* at his lodgings, and I dined with him there with *Methuen*, and *Delaval*, and the late attorney-general.[6] I went to the drawing-room before dinner, (for the queen was at *Hampton-court*) and expected to see *nobody*; but I met acquaintance enough. I walked in the gardens, saw the cartons of *Raphael*, and other things, and with great difficulty got from lord *Halifax*, who would have kept me to-morrow to shew me his house and park, and improvements.[7] We left *Hampton-court* at sun-set, and got here in a chariot and two horses time enough by star-light. That's something charms me mightily about *London*; that you go dine a dozen miles off in *October*, stay all day, and return so quickly: you cannot do any thing like this in *Dublin*.[8] I writ a second penny-post letter to your mother, and hear nothing of her. Did I tell you that earl *Berkeley* died last *Sunday* was se'nnight, at *Berkeley-castle*, of a dropsy? Lord *Halifax* began a health to me to-day; it was the *Resurrection of the Whigs*, which I refused unless he would add their *Reformation* too: and I told him he was the only *Whig* in *England* I loved, or had any good opinion of.

3. This morning *Stella*'s sister came to me with a letter from her mother, who is at *Sheene*; but will soon be in town, and will call to see me: she gave me a bottle of palsy water, a small one, and desired I would send it you by the first convenience, as I will; and she promises a quart bottle of the same: your sister lookt very well, and seems a good modest sort of girl.[9] I went then to Mr. *Lewis*, first secretary to lord *Dartmouth*, and favourite to Mr. *Harley*, who is to introduce me to-morrow morning. *Lewis* had with him one Mr. *Dyet*, a justice of peace worth twenty thousand pounds, a commissioner of the stamp-office, and married to a sister of sir *Philip Meadows*, envoy to the emperor. I tell you this, because it is odds but this Mr. *Dyet* will be hanged; for he is discovered to have counterfeited stampt paper, in which he was a commissioner; and, with his accom-

plices, has cheated the queen of a hundred thousand pounds. You will hear of it before this come to you, but may be not so particularly; and it is a very odd accident in such a man.[10] Smoak *Presto* writing news to *MD*. I dined to-day with lord *Mountjoy* at *Kensington*, and walked from thence this evening to town like an emperor. Remember that yesterday, *October 2*, was a cruel hard frost with ice; and six days ago I was dying with heat. As thin as the town is, I have more dinners than ever, and am asked this month by some people, without being able to come for pre-engagements. Well, but I should write plainer, when I consider *Stella* can't read,[11] and *Dingley* is not so skilful at my ugly hand. I had, to-night, a letter from Mr. *Pratt*, who tells me, *Joe* will have his money when there are trustees appointed by the lord lieutenant for receiving and disposing the linen fund; and whenever those trustees are appointed, I will solicit whoever is lord lieutenant, and am in no fear of succeeding.[12] So pray tell or write him word, and bid him not be cast down; for *Ned Southwell* and Mr. *Addison* both think *Pratt* in the right. Don't lose your money at *Manley*'s to-night, sirrahs.[13]

4. After I had put out my candle last night, my landlady came into my room with a servant of lord *Halifax*, to desire I would go dine with him at his house near *Hampton-court*; but I sent him word I had business of great importance that hindered me, &c. And, to-day, I was brought privately to Mr. *Harley*, who received me with the greatest respect and kindness imaginable: he has appointed me an hour on *Saturday* at four, afternoon, when I will open my business to him; which expression I would not use if I were a woman. I know you smoakt it, but I did not till I writ it. I dined to-day at Mr. *Delaval*'s, the envoy for *Portugal*, with *Nic. Rowe* the poet, and other friends; and I gave my lampoon to be printed. I have more mischief in my heart; and I think it shall go round with them all, as this hits, and I can find hints. I am certain I answered your 2d letter, and yet I do not find it here. I suppose it was in my 4th: and why N. 2d, 3d; is it not enough to say as I do, 1, 2, 3? &c. I am going to work at another *Tatler*:[14] I'll be far enough but I say the same thing over two or three times, just as I do when I am

talking to little *MD*; but what care I? they can read it as easily
as I can write it: I think I have brought these lines pretty straight
again. I fear it will be long before I finish two sides at this
rate. Pray, dear *MD*, when I occasionally give you any little
commission mixt with my letters, don't forget it, as that to
Morgan and *Joe*, &c. for I write just as I can remember, otherwise I would put them all together. I was to visit Mr. *Sterne*
to-day, and gave him your commission about handkerchiefs:
that of chocolate I will do myself, and send it him when he
goes, and you'll pay me when *the giver's bread*, &c.[15] To-night
I will read a pamphlet, to amuse myself. God preserve your
dear healths.

5. This morning *Delaval* came to see me, and we went together to *Kneller*'s, who was not in town. In the way we met
the electors for parliament-men: and the rabble came about our
coach, crying A *Colt*, a *Stanhope*, &c.[16] We were afraid of a
dead cat, or our glasses broken, and so were always of their
side. I dined again at *Delaval*'s; and in the evening, at the
Coffee-house, heard sir *Andrew Fountain* was come to town.
This has been but an insipid sort of day, and I have nothing to
remark upon it worth three-pence: I hope *MD* had a better,
with the dean, the bishop, or Mrs. *Walls*.[17] Why, the reason
you lost four and eight-pence last night but one at *Manley*'s,
was because you played bad games: I took notice of six that
you had ten to one against you: Would any but a mad lady go
out twice upon *Manilio*, *Basto*, and two small diamonds? Then
in that game of spades, you blundered when you had ten-ace; I
never saw the like of you: and now you are in a huff because
I tell you this. Well, here's two and eight-pence half-penny
towards your loss.[18]

6. Sir *Andrew Fountain* came this morning, and caught me
writing in bed. I went into the city with him; and we dined at
the *Chop-house* with *Will Pate*, the learned woollen-draper:
then we sauntered at *china-shops* and booksellers; went to the
tavern, drank two pints of white wine, and never parted till
ten: and now I am come home, and must copy out some papers
I intend for Mr. *Harley*, whom I am to see, as I told you,
to-morrow afternoon; so that this night I shall say little to *MD*,

but that I heartily wish myself with them, and will come as soon as I either fail or compass my business. We now hear daily of elections; and, in a list I saw yesterday of about twenty, there are seven or eight more *Tories* than in the last *Parliament*; so that I believe they need not fear a majority, with the help of those who will vote as the *Court* pleases. But I have been told that Mr. *Harley* himself would not let the *Tories* be too numerous, for fear they should be insolent, and kick against him; and for that reason they have kept several *Whigs* in employments, who expected to be turned out every day; as sir *John Holland* the comptroller, and many others. And so get you gone to your cards, and your claret and orange, at the dean's, and I'll go write.

7. I wonder when this letter will be finished: it must go by *Tuesday*, that's certain; and if I have one from *MD* before, I will not answer it, that's as certain too! 'Tis now morning, and I did not finish my papers for Mr. *Harley* last night; for you must understand *Presto* was sleepy, and made blunders and blots. Very pretty that I must be writing to young women in a morning fresh and fasting, faith. Well, good morrow to you; and so I go to business, and lay aside this paper till night, sirrahs.—At night. *Jack How* told *Harley*, that if there were a lower place in *Hell* than another, it was reserved for his porter, who tells lies so gravely, and with so civil a manner. This porter I have had to deal with, going this evening at four to visit Mr. *Harley*, by his own appointment. But the fellow told me no lie, though I suspected every word he said. He told me his master was just gone to dinner, with much company, and desired I would come an hour hence, which I did, expecting to hear Mr. *Harley* was gone out; but they had just done dinner. Mr. *Harley* came out to me, brought me in, and presented to me his son-in-law, lord *Doblane* (or some such name) and his own son, and, among others, *Will Penn* the quaker. We sat two hours drinking as good wine as you do; and two hours more he and I alone; where he heard me tell my business; entered into it with all kindness; askt for my powers, and read them; and read likewise a memorial I had drawn up, and put it in his pocket to shew the queen;[19] told me the measures he would take; and, in short,

said every thing I could wish: told me he must bring Mr. *St.
John* (secretary of state) and me acquainted; and spoke so
many things of personal kindness and esteem for me, that I am
inclined half to believe what some friends have told me, That
he would do every thing to bring me over.[20] He has desired to
dine with me (what a comical mistake was that) I mean he has
desired me to dine with him on *Tuesday*; and after four hours
being with him, set me down at *St. James's Coffee-house*, in a
hackney-coach. All this is odd and comical, if you consider him
and me. He knew my Christian name very well. I could not
forbear saying thus much upon this matter, although you will
think it tedious. But I'll tell you; you must know, 'tis fatal to
me to be a scoundrel and a prince the same day: for being to
see him at four, I could not engage myself to dine at any friend's;
so I went to *Tooke*, to give him a ballad and dine with him; but
he was not at home: so I was forced to go to a blind chophouse,
and dine for ten-pence upon gill-ale, bad broth, and three chops
of mutton; and then go reeking from thence to the first minister
of state. And now I am going in charity to send *Steele* a *Tatler*,
who is very low of late.[21] I think I am civiller than I used to be;
and have not used the expression of (*you in* Ireland) and (*we
in* England) as I did when I was here before, to your great
indignation.—They may talk of the *you know what*; but, gad,
if it had not been for that, I should never have been able to get
the access I have had; and if that helps me to succeed, then that
same thing will be serviceable to the church.[22] But how far we
must depend upon new friends, I have learnt by long practice,
though I think among great ministers, they are just as good as
old ones. And so I think this important day has made a great
hole in this side of the paper; and the fiddle faddles of to-
morrow and *Monday* will make up the rest; and, besides, I shall
see *Harley* on *Tuesday* before this letter goes.

8. I must tell you a great piece of refinement of *Harley*. He
charged me to come to him often: I told him I was loth to
trouble him in so much business as he had, and desired I might
have leave to come at his levee; which he immediately refused,
and said, That was not a place for friends to come to. 'Tis now
but morning, and I have got a foolish trick, I must say something

to *MD* when I wake, and wish them a good morrow; for this is not a shaving-day, *Sunday*, so I have time enough: but get you gone, you rogues, I must go write: yes, 'twill vex me to the blood if any of these long letters should miscarry: if they do, I will shrink to half sheets again; but then what will you do to make up the journal? there will be ten days of *Presto*'s life lost; and that will be a sad thing, faith and troth.—At night. I was at a loss to-day for a dinner, unless I would have gone a great way, so I dined with some friends that board hereabout, as a spunger; and this evening sir *Andrew Fountain* would needs have me go to the tavern, where, for two bottles of wine, *Portugal* and *Florence*, among three of us, we had sixteen shillings to pay; but if ever he catches me so again, I'll spend as many pounds; and therefore I have put it among my extraordinaries: but we had a neck of mutton drest *a la Maintenon*, that the dog could not eat: and it is now twelve o'clock, and I must go sleep. I hope this letter will go before I have *MD*'s third. Do you believe me? and yet, faith, I long for *MD*'s third too: and yet I would have it to say, that I writ five for two. I am not fond at all of *St. James*'s *Coffee-house*, as I used to be.[23] I hope it will mend in winter; but now they are all out of town at elections, or not come from their country houses. Yesterday I was going with Dr. *Garth* to dine with *Charles Main*, near the *Tower*, who has an employment there: he is of *Ireland*; the bishop of *Clogher* knows him well: an honest good-natured fellow, a thorough hearty laugher, mightily beloved by the men of wit: his mistress is never above a cook-maid. And so, good night, &c.

9. I dined to-day at sir *John Stanley*'s; my lady *Stanley* is one of my favourites: I have as many here as the bishop of *Killala* has in *Ireland*. I am thinking what scurvy company I shall be to *MD* when I come back: they know every thing of me already: I will tell you no more, or I shall have nothing to say, no story to tell, nor any kind of thing. I was very uneasy last night with ugly, nasty, filthy wine, that turned sour on my stomach. I must go to the tavern: oh, but I told you that before. To-morrow I dine at *Harley*'s, and will finish this letter at my return; but I can write no more now, because of the archbishop:[24] faith 'tis

true; for I am going now to write to him an account of what I have done in the business with *Harley:* and, faith, young women, I'll tell you what you must count upon, that I never will write one word on the third side in these long letters.

10. Poor *MD*'s letter was lying so huddled up among papers I could not find it: I mean poor *Presto*'s letter. Well, I dined with Mr. *Harley* to-day, and hope some things will be done; but I must say no more: and this letter must be sent to the post-house, and not by the bell-man. I am to dine again there on *Sunday* next; I hope to some good issue. And so now, soon as ever I can in bed, I must begin my 6th to *MD*, as gravely as if I had not written a word this month: fine doings, faith. Methinks I don't write as I should, because I am not in bed: see the ugly wide lines. God Almighty ever bless you, &c.

Faith, this is a whole treatise; I'll go reckon the lines on t'other sides. I've reckoned them.[25]

LETTER XVII

London, Feb. 24, 1710–1711

Now, young women, I gave in my sixteenth this evening. I dined with *Ford*, it was his *Opera-day* as usual; it is very convenient to me to do so, for coming home early after a walk in the *Park*,[1] which now the days will allow. I called on the secretary at his office, and he had forgot to give the memorial about *Bernage* to the duke of *Argyle*; but two days ago I met the duke, who desired I would give it him myself, which should have more power with him than all the ministry together, as he protested solemnly, repeated it two or three times, and bid me count upon it.[2] So that I verily believe *Bernage* will be in a very good way to establish himself. I think I can do no more for him at present, and there's an end of that; and so get you gone to bed, for it is late.

25. The three weeks are out yesterday since I had your last, and so now I will be expecting every day a pretty dear letter from my own *MD*, and hope to hear that *Stella* has been much better in her head and eyes; my head continues as it was, no

fits, but a little disorder every day, which I can easily bear if it will not grow worse.[3] I dined to-day with Mr. secretary *St. John*, on condition I might chuse my company, which were lord *Rivers*, lord *Carteret*, Sir *Thomas Mansel*, and Mr. *Lewis*; I invited *Masham*, *Hill*, Sir *John Stanley*, and *George Granville*, but they were engaged; and I did it in revenge of his having such bad company when I dined with him before; so we laughed, &c. And I ventured to go to church to-day, which I have not done this month before. Can you send me such a good account of *Stella*'s health, pray now? Yes, I hope, and better too. We dined (says you) at the dean's, and played at cards till twelve, and there came in Mr. *French*, and Dr. *Travors*, and Dr. *Whittingham*, and Mr. (I forget his name, that I always tell Mrs. *Walls* of) the banker's son, a pox on him. And we were so merry; I vow they are pure good company. But I lost a crown; for you must know I had always hands tempting me to go out, but never took in any thing, and often two black aces without a manilio; was not that hard, *Presto?* Hold your tongue, &c.[4]

26. I was this morning with Mr. secretary about some business, and he tells me, that colonel *Fielding* is now going to make *Bernage* his captain-lieutenant, that is, a captain by commission, and the perquisites of the company, but not captain's pay, only the first step to it.[5] I suppose he will like it, and the recommendation to the duke of *Argyle* goes on. And so trouble me no more about your *Bernage*; the jackanapes understands what fair solicitors he has got, I warrant you. Sir *Andrew Fountain* and I dined, by invitation, with Mrs. *Vanhomrigh*.[6] You say they are of no consequence: why, they keep as good female company as I do male; I see all the drabs of quality at this end of the town with them; I saw two lady *Bettys* there this afternoon; the beauty of one, the good breeding and nature of t'other, and the wit of neither, would have made a fine woman.[7] Rare walking in the *Park* now: why don't you walk in the *Green* of *St. Stephen?* The walks there are finer gravelled than the *Mall*. What beasts the *Irish* women are, never to walk!

27. *Dartineuf* and I and little *Harrison*, the new *Tatler*, and *Jervas* the painter, dined to-day with *James*, I know not his other name, but it is one of *Dartineuf*'s dining places, who is a

true epicure.[8] *James* is clerk of the kitchen to the queen, and has a little snug house at *St. James's*, and we had the queen's wine, and such very fine victuals that I could not eat it.—Three weeks and three days since my last letter from *MD*, rare doings: why truly we were so busy with poor Mrs. *Walls*, that indeed, *Presto*, we could not write, we were afraid the poor woman would have died; and it pitied us to see the archdeacon, how concerned he was. The dean never came to see her but once; but now she is up again, and we go and sit with her in the evenings. The child died the next day after it was born, and I believe, between friends, she is not very sorry for it.—Indeed, *Presto*, you are plaguy silly to-night, and han't guest one word right; for she and the child are both well, and it is a fine girl, likely to live; and the dean was godfather, and Mrs. *Catherine* and I were godmothers; I was going to say *Stoite*, but I think I have heard they don't put maids and married women together; though I know not why I think so, nor I don't care; what care I? but I must prate, &c.[9]

28. I walked to-day into the city for my health, and there dined, which I always do when the weather is fair, and business permits, that I may be under a necessity of taking a good walk, which is the best thing I can do at present for my health. Some bookseller has raked up every thing I writ and published it t'other day in one volume; but I know nothing of it, 'twas without my knowledge or consent: it makes a four shilling book, and is called *Miscellanies in Prose and Verse. Tooke* pretends he knows nothing of it, but I doubt he is at the bottom. One must have patience with these things; the best of it is, I shall be plagued no more. However, I'll bring a couple of them over with me for *MD*, perhaps you may desire to see them. I hear they sell mightily.[10]

March 1. Morning. I have been calling to *Patrick* to look in his *Almanack* for the day of the month; I did not know but it might be *Leap-year*.[11] The *Almanack* says 'tis the third after *Leap-year*, and I always thought till now, that every third year was *Leap-year*. I'm glad they come so seldom; but I'm sure 'twas otherwise when I was a young man; I see times are mightily changed since then. — Write to me, sirrahs, be sure do by the time this side is done, and I'll keep t'other side for the answer: so I'll go write to the bishop of *Clogher*; good morrow, sirrahs. —— Night. I dined to-day at Mrs. *Vanhomrigh*'s, being a rainy day, and lady *Betty Butler* knowing it, sent to let me know she expected my company in the evening, where the *Vans* (so we call them) were to be. The duchess and [she] do not go over this summer with the duke;[12] so I go to bed.

2. This rainy weather undoes me in coaches and chairs. I was traipsing to-day with your Mr. *Sterne*, to go along with them to *Moor*, and recommend his business to the treasury. *Sterne* tells me his dependence is wholly on me; but I have absolutely refused to recommend it to Mr. *Harley*, because I have troubled him lately so much with other folks affairs; and besides, to tell the truth, Mr. *Harley* told me he did not like *Sterne*'s business;[13] however, I will serve him, because I suppose *MD* would have me. But in saying his dependence lies wholly on me, he lies, and is a fool. I dined with lord *Abercorn*, whose son *Peasley* will be married at *Easter* to ten thousand pounds.

3. I forgot to tell you that yesterday morning I was at Mr. *Harley*'s levee: he swore I came in spight, to see him among a parcel of fools. My business was to desire I might let the duke of *Ormond* know how the affair stood of the *First-Fruits*. He promised to let him know it, and engaged me to dine with him to-day. Every *Saturday* lord keeper,[14] secretary *St. John*, and I dine with him, and sometimes lord *Rivers*, and they let in none else. *Patrick* brought me some letters into the *Park*, among which one was from *Walls*, and t'other, yes faith, t'other was from our little *MD*, N. 11. I read the rest in the *Park*, and *MD*'s in a chair as I went from *St. James's* to Mr. *Harley*, and glad enough I was faith to read it, and see all right: Oh, but I won't answer it these three or four days, at least, or may be sooner. An't I silly? Faith your letters would make a dog silly, if I had a dog to be silly, but it must be a little dog.—I staid with Mr. *Harley* till past nine, where we had much discourse together after the rest were gone; and I gave him very truly my opinion where he desired it. He complained he was not very well, and has engaged me to dine with him again on *Monday*. So I came home afoot, like a fine gentleman, to tell you all this.

4. I dined to-day with Mr. secretary *St. John*; and after dinner he had a note from Mr. *Harley*, that he was much out of order; pray God preserve his health, every thing depends upon it. The *Parliament* at present cannot go a step without him, nor the queen neither. I long to be in *Ireland*, but the ministry beg me to stay: however, when this parliament lurry is over, I will endeavour to steal away; by which time I hope the *First-Fruit* business will be done. This kingdom is certainly ruined as much as was ever any bankrupt merchant. We must have *Peace*, let it be a bad or a good one, though no-body dares talk of it. The nearer I look upon things, the worse I like them. I believe the confederacy will soon break to pieces, and our factions at home increase. The ministry is upon a very narrow bottom, and stand like an *Isthmus* between the *Whigs* on one side, and violent *Tories* on the other.[15] They are able seamen, but the tempest is too great, the ship too rotten, and the crew all against them. Lord *Somers* has been twice in the queen's closet, once very lately; and your duchess of *Somerset*, who now has the key, is a most insinuating woman, and I believe they will endeavour to play the same game that has been played against them.[16]—I have told them of all this, which they know already, but they cannot help it. They have cautioned the queen so much against being governed, that she observes it too much. I could talk till to-morrow upon these things, but they make me melancholy. I could not but observe that lately, after much conversation with Mr. *Harley*, though he is the most fearless man alive, and the least apt to despond, he confessed to me, that uttering his mind to me gave him ease.

5. Mr. *Harley* continues out of order, yet his affairs force him abroad: he is subject to a sore throat, and was cupped last night: I sent and called two or three times. I hear he is better this evening. I dined to-day in the city with Dr. *Freind* at a third body's house, where I was to pass for some body else, and there was a plaguy silly jest carried on that made me sick of it. Our weather grows fine, and I will walk like camomile.[17] And pray walk you to your dean's, or your *Stoyte*'s, or your *Manley*'s, or your *Walls*'. But your new lodgings make you so proud, you'll walk less than ever.[18] Come, let me go to bed, sirrahs.

6. Mr. *Harley*'s going out yesterday has put him a little backwards. I called twice, and sent, for I am in pain for him. *Ford* caught me, and made me dine with him on his *Opera-day*; so I brought Mr. *Lewis* with me, and sat with him till six. I have not seen Mr. *Addison* these three weeks; all our friendship is over.[19] I go to no *Coffee-house*. I presented a parson of the bishop of *Clogher*'s, one *Richardson*, to the duke of *Ormond* to-day: he is translating prayers and sermons into *Irish*, and has a project about instructing the *Irish* in the protestant religion.[20]

7. Morning. Faith, a little would make me, I could find in my heart, if it were not for one thing, I have a good mind, if I had not something else to do, I would answer your dear saucy letter. O Lord, I am going awry with writing in bed. O faith, but I must answer it, or I shan't have room, for it must go on *Saturday*; and don't think I'll fill the third side, I an't come to that yet, young women. Well then, as for your *Bernage*, I have said enough: I writ to him last week.—Turn over that leaf. Now, what says *MD* to the world to come? I tell you, madam *Stella*, my head is a great deal better, and I hope will keep so. How came yours to be fifteen days coming, and you had my fifteenth in seven? Answer me that, rogues. Your being with goody *Walls* is excuse enough: I find I was mistaken in the sex, 'tis a boy. Yes, I understand your cypher, and *Stella* guesses right, as she always does. He gave me al bsadnuk lboinlpl dfaonr ufainfbtoy dpion-ufnad,[21] which I sent him again by Mr. *Lewis*, to whom I writ a very complaining letter that was shewed him; and so the matter ended. He told me he had a quarrel with me; I said I had another with him, and we returned to our friendship; and I should think he loves me as well as a great minister can love a man in so short a time. Did not I do right? I am glad at heart you have got your palsey-water; pray God Almighty it may do my dearest little *Stella* good. I suppose Mrs. *Edgworth* set out last *Monday* se'nnight.[22] Yes, I do read the *Examiners*, and they are written very finely, as you judge.[23] I do not think they are too severe on the duke; they only tax him of avarice, and his avarice has ruined us.[24] You may count upon all things in them to be true. The author has said, It is not *Prior*; but perhaps it may be *Atterbury*.—Now, madam *Dingley*, says she, 'tis fine

weather, says she; yes, says she, and we have got to our new lodgings. I compute you ought to save eight pounds by being in the others five months; and you have no more done it than eight thousand. I am glad you are rid of that squinting, blinking *Frenchman*.[25] I will give you a bill on *Parvisol* for five pound for the half year. And must I go on at four shillings a week, and neither eat nor drink for it? Who the D— said *Atterbury* and your dean were alike? I never saw your chancellor, nor his chaplain.[26] The latter has a good deal of learning, and is a well-wisher to be an author: your chancellor is an excellent man. As for *Patrick*'s bird, he bought him for his tameness, and is grown the wildest I ever saw. His wings have been quilled thrice, and are now up again: he will be able to fly after us to *Ireland*, if he be willing.—Yes, Mrs. *Stella*, *Dingley* writes more like *Presto* than you; for all you superscribed the letter, as who should say, Why should not I write like our *Presto* as well as *Dingley*? You with your aukward SS⁵; can't you write them thus, SS? No, but always SSS.[27] Spiteful sluts, to affront *Presto*'s writing; as that when you shut your eyes you write most like *Presto*. I know the time when I did not write to you half so plain as I do now; but I take pity on you both. I am very much concerned for Mrs. *Walls*'s eyes. *Walls* says nothing of it to me in his letter dated after yours. You say, If she recovers she may lose her sight. I hope she is in no danger of her life. Yes, *Ford* is as sober as I please: I use him to walk with me as an easy companion, always ready for what I please, when I am weary of business and ministers. I don't go to a *Coffee-house* twice a month. I am very regular in going to sleep before eleven. —— And so you say that *Stella*'s a pretty girl; and so she be, and methinks I see her just now as handsome as the day's long. Do you know what? When I am writing in our language I make up my mouth just as if I was speaking it. I caught myself at it just now.[28] And I suppose *Dingley* is so fair and so fresh as a lass in *May*, and has her health, and no spleen.—In your account you sent do you reckon as usual from the 1st of *November* was twelvemonth?[29] Poor *Stella*, won't *Dingley* leave her a little day-light to write to *Presto*? Well, well, we'll have day-light shortly, spight of her teeth; and zoo must cly Lele, and Hele,

and Hele aden. Must loo mimitate *pdfr*, pay? Iss, and so la
shall. And so leles fol ee rettle. Dood mollow.[30]—At night. Mrs.
Barton sent this morning to invite me to dinner; and there I
dined, just in that genteel manner that *MD* used when they
would treat some better sort of body than usual.

8. O dear *MD*, my heart is almost broken. You will hear the
thing before this comes to you. I writ a full account of it this
night to the archbishop of *Dublin*; and the dean may tell you
the particulars from the archbishop. I was in a sorry way to
write, but thought it might be proper to send a true account of
the fact; for you will hear a thousand lying circumstances. 'Tis
of Mr. *Harley*'s being stabbed this afternoon at three o'clock
at a committee of the council. I was playing lady *Catherine
Morris*'s cards, where I dined, when young *Arundel* came in
with the story. I ran away immediately to the secretary, which
was in my way: no one was at home. I met Mrs. *St. John* in her
chair; she had heard it imperfectly. I took a chair to Mr. *Harley*,
who was asleep, and they hope in no danger; but he has been
out of order, and was so when he came abroad to-day, and it
may put him in a fever: I am in mortal pain for him. That
desperate *French* villain, marquis de *Guiscard*, stabbed Mr.
Harley. *Guiscard* was taken up by Mr. secretary *St. John*'s
warrant for high treason, and brought before the lords to be
examined; there he stabbed Mr. *Harley*. I have told all the
particulars already to the archbishop.[31] I have now at nine sent
again, and they tell me he is in a fair way. Pray pardon my
distraction; I now think of all his kindness to me.—The poor
creature now lies stabbed in his bed by a desperate *French*
popish villain. Good night, and God preserve you both, and
pity me; I want it.

9. Morning; seven, in bed. *Patrick* is just come from Mr.
Harley's. He slept well till four; the surgeon sat up with him:[32]
he is asleep again: he felt a pain in his wound when he waked:
they apprehend him in no danger. This account the surgeon left
with the porter, to tell people that send. Pray God preserve him.
I am rising and going to Mr. secretary *St. John*. They say
Guiscard will die with the wounds Mr. *St. John* and the rest
gave him. I shall tell you more at night.—Night. Mr. *Harley*

still continues on the mending hand; but he rested ill last night, and felt pain. I was early with the secretary this morning, and I dined with him, and he told me several particularities of this accident, too long to relate now. Mr. *Harley* is still mending this evening, but not at all out of danger; and till then I can have no peace. Good night, *&c.* and pity *Presto*.

10. Mr. *Harley* was restless last night; but he has no fever, and the hopes of his mending increase. I had a letter from Mr. *Walls*, and one from Mr. *Bernage*. I will answer them here, not having time to write. Mr. *Walls* writes about three things. First, about a hundred pounds from Dr. *Raymond*, of which I hear nothing, and 'tis now too late. Secondly, about Mr. *Clements*: I can do nothing in it, because I am not to mention Mr. *Pratt*; and I cannot recommend without knowing Mr. *Pratt*'s objections, whose relation *Clements* is, and who brought him into the place.[33] The third is about my being godfather to the child: that is in my power, and (since there is no remedy) will submit. I wish you could hinder it; but if it can't be helped, pay what you think proper, and get the provost to stand for me, and let his christian name be *Harley*, in honour to my friend, now lying stabbed and doubtful of his life. As for *Bernage*, he writes me word, that his colonel has offered to make him captain-lieutenant for a hundred pounds. He was such a fool to offer him money without writing to me till it was done, though I have had a dozen letters from him; and then he desires I would say nothing of this, for fear his colonel should be angry. People are mad. What can I do? I engaged colonel *Disney*, who was one of his solicitors to the secretary, and then told him the story. He assured me, that *Fielding* (*Bernage*'s colonel) said he might have got that sum; but on account of those great recommendations he had, would give it him for nothing: and I would have *Bernage* write him a letter of thanks, as of a thing given him for nothing, upon recommendations, *&c. Disney* tells me he will again speak to *Fielding*, and clear up this matter; and then I will write to *Bernage*. A pox on him for promising money till I had it promised to me, and then making it such a ticklish point, that one cannot expostulate with the colonel upon it: but let him do as I say, and there's an end.[34] I engaged

the secretary of state in it; and am sure it was meant a kindness to me, and that no money should be given, and a hundred pounds is too much in a *Smithfield* bargain, as a major-general told me, whose opinion I asked. I am now hurried, and can say no more. Farewel, *&c. &c.*

How shall I superscribe to your new lodgings, pray madams? Tell me but that, impudence and saucy-face.

An't you sauceboxes to write lele [i.e. *there*] like *Presto?*[35]

O poor *Presto!*

Mr. *Harley* is better to-night, that makes me so pert, you saucy *Gog* and *Magog.*[36]

A HUE AND CRY AFTER DISMAL

Being a full and true Account, how a Whig *Lord was taken at* Dunkirk, *in the Habit of a Chimney-sweeper, and carryed before General* Hill

WE have an old Saying, *That it is better to play at small Game than to stand out:*[1] And it seems, the Whigs practice accordingly, there being nothing so little or so base, that they will not attempt, to recover their Power. On Wednesday Morning the 9th Instant, we are certainly informed, that Collonell K–le–gr–w[2] (who went to France with Generall Hill) walking in Dunkirk Streets met a tall Chimney-Sweeper with his Brooms and Poles, and Bunch of Holly upon his Shoulders, who was followed by another of a shorter Size. The Tall Fellow cry'd in the French Language (which the Collonel understands) Sweep, Sweep; The Collonell thought he knew the Voice, and that the Tone of it was like one of your fine Speakers. This made him follow the Chimney-Sweeper, and examine nicely his Shape and Countenance. Besides, he conceived also that the Chimney-Sweeper's Man was not altogether unknown to him, so the Collonel went to wait on the Generall who is Governor of Dunkirk for Her Majesty, and told his Honor, that he had a strong Suspicion that he had seen 𝕯𝖎𝖘𝖒𝖆𝖑 in the Streets of Dunkirk. (Now you must know, that our Courtiers call a certain great Whig L—d by the Name of 𝕯𝖎𝖘𝖒𝖆𝖑; belike, by reason of his 𝖉𝖆𝖗𝖐 and 𝖉𝖎𝖘𝖒𝖆𝖑 Countenance). That is impossible sure, said the Governor. I am confident of it said the Collonel; nay, and what is more, the Fellow that followed him was Mr. Squash, tho' the Master was as black as his Man;[3] and if your Honor pleases, I will bring them both to you immediately, for I observed the House they went in. So, away went the Collonel with a File of Musquiteers, and found them both in an Ale-house, that was kept by a Dutch-man. He could see nothing of the Master, but a Leg upon each Stobb, the rest of the Body being out of sight;[4] the Collonel ordered him to come down, which he did, with a great heap of Soot after him. Master and

Man were immediately conducted through the Town, with a great Mob at their Heels to the Governor's Castle, where his Honor was sitting in a Chair with his English and French Nobles about him. The Governor with a stern Countenance asked the tall Man who he was! He answered he was a Savoyard, (for beyond Sea, all the Chimney-Sweepers come from Savoy, a great Town in Italy) and he spoke a sort of Gibberish like broken French. But the French Mounseers that were by, assured the Governor, he could be no French-man, no nor Savoyard neither.[5] So then the Governor spoke to him in English, said there was Witnesses ready to prove, that under pretence of sweeping Chimnyes cheaper than other People, he endeavored to persuade the Townsfolks not to let the English come into the Town, and how as that he should say, that the English would cut all the French-mens Throats, and that his Honor believed he was no Chimny-Sweeper (though that was too good a Trade for him) but some Whiggish English Traitor. The Governor then gave Command, that both of them should be washed in his Presence by two of his Guards. And first they began with the Man, and spent a whole Pail full of Water in vain: Then they used Soap and Suds, but all to no Purpose; at last they found he was a Black-a-more, and that they had been acting the Labor-in-vain. Then the Collonel whispered the Governor, your Honor may plainly see that this is Squash. (Now you must know, that Squash is the Name of a Blackamore that waits upon the L—d whom the Courtiers call 𝕯𝖎𝖘𝖒𝖆𝖑). Then with a fresh Pail they began to wash the Master; but for a while, all their Scrubbing did no good; so that they thought he was a Black-amoor too. At last they perceived some dawning of a dark sallow Brown; and the Governor immediately knew it was the L—d 𝕯𝖎𝖘𝖒𝖆𝖑, which the other, after some shuffling Excuses, confessed. The Governor then said, I am sorry to see your L—dship in such a Condition, but you are Her Majesty's Prisoner, and I will send you immediately to England, where the Queen my Liege may dispose of you according to Her Royal Pleasure. Then his Honor ordered new Cloaths to be made both for Master and Man, and sent them on Shipboard: From whence in a few Hours they landed in England.

IT is observed, that the L—d's Face, which at best is very Black and Swarthy, hath been much darker ever since, and all the Beauty-washes he uses, it is thought will never be able to restore it. Which wise Men reckon to be a just Judgment on him for his late Apostacy.

SWIFT TO THE EARL OF OXFORD

When I was with you, I have said more than once that I would never allow quality or station made any reall Difference between Men. Being now absent and forgotten, I have changed my mind; you have a thousand people who can pretend they love you, with as much appearance of sincerity as I; so that according to common justice, I can have but a thousandth part in return of what I give. And this difference is wholly owing to your station. And the misfortune is still the greater, because I always loved you just so much the worse for your station. For in your publick capacity you have often angered me to the heart, but as a private man never once.[1] So that if I only look towards myself I could wish you a private man to morrow. For I have nothing to ask, at least nothing that you will give, which is the same thing. And then you would see whether I should not with much more willingness attend you in a retirement, whenever you pleased to give me leave, than ever I did at *London* or *Windsor*. From these sentiments I will never write to you, if I can help it, otherwise than as to a private person, nor allow myself to have been obliged by you in any other capacity. The memory of one great instance of your candor and justice, I will carry to my grave; that having been in a manner domestick with you for almost four years, it was never in the power of any publick or concealed enemy to make you think ill of me, though malice and envy were often employd to that end. If I live, posterity shall know that and more; which though you and somebody that shall be nameless seem to value less than I could wish, is all the return I can make you.[2] Will you give me leave to say how I would desire to stand in your Memory? As one who was truly sensible of the honour you did him, though he was too proud to be vain upon it: As one who was neither assuming, officious, nor teazing; who never wilfully misrepresented persons or facts to you, nor consulted his passions when he gave a character: And lastly, as one whose indiscretions proceeded altogether from a weak head, and not an ill heart. I will add one thing more, which is the highest compliment I can make; that I never was afraid of offending you, nor am now in any pain for the manner I write to you in. I have said enough, and like one at your levee, having made my bow, I shrink back into the crowd.

A MODEST DEFENCE OF PUNNING

Or a compleat Answer to a scandalous and malicious
Paper called

God's Revenge against Punning

In a Letter to a Member of Parlm^t

Punica mala leges.[1] Virg.

Cambridge Nov^br 8th. 1716.

S^r

THAT Gentleman (whoever he was) who lately under the Name
of *J. Baker Knight*, thought fit to publish a Discourse entitled
God's Revenge ag^st Punning seems to have *founded* his whole
Discourse upon one grand Mistake: And therefore his whole
Discourse will be *founddead* as soon as I have removed that
Mistake; which is, that He condemns the whole Art in generall
without distinguishing Puns into Good and Bad: whereby it
appears how ignorant he is in Antiquity. The antient Romans
very well understood the Difference between the *fine* or *pretty*
Pun, and the *bad* Pun: hence we read so often of the *bellum
Punicum*, and the *malum Punicum*.[2] Of which our Author is
as ignorant as a certain Gentleman who reading of a *Roman
Scholar*, thought *Roman* was a *Waterman* and *Scholar* a *Sculler*.

The Word *Pun* appears to be of Greek Originall. Some derive
it from Πύνδαξ, which signifyes either *Fundum*, a Bottom, or
Maniebrium gladij, the handle of a Sword.[3] From the former,
because this kind of Wit is thought to lye *deeper* than any other,
I will produce an Instance in this very word, *Fundum*. When a
young Parson marryed Mrs *Sarah*— and got a Living, which is
called Smock Simony,[4] One of our Fraternity most surprisingly
sd *Sera est in Fundo Per-Simonia.* (Anglice) *Sarah* was at the
Bottom by Simony. Secondly, from the Handle of a Sword;
Because whoever *wields* it will shew something *Bright* and
sharp at the *End*: Another and more probable Opinion is that
the word *Pun* comes from Πυνθάνομαι;[5] because without

Knoledge, *hearing* and *Enquiry*, this Gift is not to be obtained. There is a more modern Etymology which I cannot altogether approve, thô it be highly ingenious: For, the Cantabrigians derive the Word from *Ponticulus* Quasi, *Pun tickle us*, which signifyes a *little Bridge*, as ours over *Cam*, where this Art is in highest Perfection. Again; others derive it from *Pungo*; because whoever lets a *Pun go* will be sure to make his Adversary *smart*. And to include this Head, I shall not conceal one Originall of this Word assigned by our Adversaryes, from the French Word *Punaise*, which signifyes a little stinking Insect that gets into the Skin, provokes continuall *Itching*, and is with great Difficulty removed. These Gentlemen affirm the same Evils to be in punning, that it is very offensive to company, that the *Itch* of it is hardly to be cured, and that the Custom of *Scratching* a man when he makes a Pun, (which is a Rudeness much practiced by Abhorrors) came from the same Originall.

To come now to our Author, *J. Baker Knight*, who usually passeth for a *Spaniard* and by the *Quarter* he meets with among certain Lords may be a *Quarter* longer, I mean a Spani - *ell*. I thought *Punnado* had been a Spanish Dish that his Stomach would *Digest*, and his *Jest dy*. I am considering what Sort of Knight he should be; when he is among his Equalls he is a Knight of *Malt*-a, when he travels, he is a Knight of *Rhodes*, Or if we allow him to be a Knight of the *Post* it must be the *Foot-post*; But being a Spaniard, perhaps he may be Knight of St *Jakes*, or if he hath been in France, they may have conferred upon him the Order of *Sans Esprit*. But for my own Part, I am apt to think that having so much in him of the Spaniard, he may be descended from the famous *Fonseca*, and that he is the Chevalier de *Fond Sec*.[6]

I shall now with as much Care and Candor as I am master of examine his Discourse. But I think I may let pass his *Petty* Accounts of the great Plague, where five Millions as he says were *Swept* away, which indeed Mr. Alexander *Broom* records, thô there *be some* who deny it, and think it a *Whisker* yet every body allows it to have been a terrible *Brush*, and that it made *clean* work, especially in *Birchin* Lane. In this Pestilence he mentions the Woman and the Jews by themselves, because indeed it was the worst of *Maladyes* for the *Mall Ladyes*, and there is no doubt but the *Jews* were put to their *Trumps*.[7]

Neither shall I *touch* the Fire he mentions, that burnt our *Metropolis* which hath already been recorded in never dying Puns by *Poor Robin* a member of our Fraternity. London was still a *Metropolis* even after it was burnt, *mais trop aux Lis* as the French express it, or rather in our Author's own Words, when the Houses were gone it was a *Few-nest* place indeed.[8]

The next Judgment our Author mentions is an *Inundation* of Obscenity, wherein I care not to *dip* my *Fingers*; and whoever cannot behold those Obscenityes upon our Walls with *chast eyes* he may justly *chastise* them. Yet Travellers inform us, the same Abominations are seen in *Italy* (though he may think *It a Ly*) and even in Rome itself, to such a degree, that many believe there is hardly a virtuous Woman in that City, according to our English Proverb, *Rome* for Cuckolds; wherein we *allude* to *a lewd* Town. However, it is plain by this wicked Practice in London that we are more addicted to *Whetstonism* than *Whistonism*.[9]

He proceeds next to the Visitation of the *nine Comets* seen *so high* as *So Ho* by Mrs *Wadlingtun* of which Appellation there may be as many women in London as there are *fat overgrown* Bawds, which Circumstance made me first suspect the Fact, and that to make it Truth we must resolve it into a *Pun*: For the Number *nine* was only the *nine* of *Diamonds*, which happens to be the best Card at *Comet*.[10] Or was this perhaps a various Reading crept from the Margin to the Text by the Ignorance of some Copyer. If I were *Bent t' lye*, what an Air of Erudition could I give my self upon such an Occasion![11] After the same Manner when this Author assures us that the Sky did *Coruscat*, it was onely a *Chorus* of *Cats* on the Tyles in *Soho* whose Eyes glistning in the Night made Mrs *Wadlington* mistake them for Stars. Had she been a Scholar she might probably have thought their Meawling to have been the Musick of the Sphears.

I have now with some difficulty traced our Author Step by Step till he is got to his Relation of severe Judgments upon Punsters. The Maxim he lyes down amounts to this: that wher-

ever a *Pun is meant*, there certainly follows a *Punishment*;
whereof he pretends to produce severall Instances. The first is
of a certain Lord, whom he onely hints at; for he leaves a blank
and does not make him *A peer*. This Noble Person our Author
is pleased to call a *Reprobat*, sed non *re probat*.[12] He Claps as
a Chastisement upon this Noble *Hero*, a *wry Nose*, as if he
would make him a *Rinoseros*; In short the Writer was determined to bring in his Lordships *wry* nose by *Hook or by Crook*,
for which he deserves to be *hisst* whether my Lord were *clapt*
or no: However I confess I should be sorry for the affirmative,
to think he had changed his *Bristow stones* for *Carbuncles*, and
his future certainty of a *Coronet* for the present possession of
a *Corona* Veneris.[13]

But pray S^r, be pleased to observe how little consistent this
Writer is with Himself. His first Instance you see is of a young
Lord who got a *Wry Nose* as a Judgment upon Punning, and
immediatly forgetting what he had said, He now produceth a
Second of another young Noble who lost his ready *Rino's* for
the same Crime, and as he expresseth it, by the Box and Dice.
So it seems what is got by the *Pox* is lost by the *Box* (according
to the Proverb). But here is another Mistake in Fact, For it is
well known how this Second young Lord came to *Cinque* his
Fortune at Dice, by some who were not his *Cater*-cousins, and
that there are sharpers allways ready to s*educe* and B*etray*
young Men of Quality and will not bate them an *Ace*; And thus
it fell out that this young *Noble* was brought to a *Ninepence*.[14]

The third Nobleman he mentions would never have fallen
into the Arms of a Dalilah, if His Lordship had not been as the
Poet says *Var vecûm in patriâ crassoq. sub aere natus*.[15] How-
ever if this Dalilah should ever have the *Barbar*ity to cutt off
His Lordships *Hair* (which our modern Dalilahs can do without
Scissors) his comfort is, that inspight of her he will be allways
Rich, and therefore he may defy the *Philistins* and *Go ly a* bed.

The grave antient Collonell[16] deserves better Treatment. He
was formerly a great *Support* to our Fraternity, two or three of
them used to *Sup Port* with him as often as He thought fit to
afford it. But since he is grown a *supporter* of Poets, I am
informed they only *Sup Porter*.

As for Thomas *Pickle*,[17] the true Reason why he went to Minorca, was because he had not a *Sowse*. To let pass his Instances of Muley Hamet and Eustace, which upon Enquiry would be found to *budge ill* as any of the rest, I dare engage that Daniel *Button* will find a *Loop-hole* to creep out of whenever this Writer is pleased to *Quote* him if I be not mistaken in his *Mold*.[18]

We are come at *Length* to a Gentleman stunted in *Stature* for attempting to Pun. But that Person cannot be called a *proper* Instance. 'Tis true, some are *longer*, and some *shorter* at Punning; And if a *Pig may* Pun, as our Detractors affirm, then certainly a *Pigmay* can.

The worst that can be said of George *Simmons* is that he *gave all the Shoes in his Shop* to be a Punster, and so would many a better Man do, and not think it *Simmony*.

As to the Reflections he is pleased to cast on our University Clergymen for being Drunkards and Toryes, I think it will be allowed that Punning is the *dryest* of all Joking, and therefore whether those Gentlemen he hints at (if there be any such) learned their *Tope*ography here we appele to the World: I know some have affirmed that we sit up at *Supper late* in the *Evening*, which is false in the *Supperlative* Degree. For his other Reflection, in calling us Toryes, thus much we declare, that His Majesty's *Liber*ality in that noble Present of *Books*, as it will make us *Lettered*, so it *Leaves* us *bound* to Him for ever, and we should be *covered* with *Gilt*, and deserve to be *bound* as Slaves in *Turkey*, if we failed in our Loyalty; and we hope the *No-Tory*-ety of our Behavior will appear by this further Declaration against all *indefesable Titles* and *Lines* except in His Majesty's *Family* and the *Books* he hath been pleased to give us.[19]

Our Author concludes with a Fact entirely false, relating to a Devonshire Man of Wit.[20] That this Gentleman fell from his Horse down a *Precipice* and broke his Neck, by which he would *press a piece* of History upon us without any *good Ground*; He likewise recites the Pun which brought on this Judgment, and had his *Horse punnd* no better, he deserved to be drownd in a *Horse-pond*. But the Story is all mistold; a Pun indeed there was, and with some Relation to a Horse; For it seems this Man of Wit happened to call the maid of the House where he lodged, a *Sow*; and then he told a Friend, that it was the *Poets Horse*, for he had called *Peg a Sus*; which was a very happy Turn of what we call the Remote or longinque kind. Neither did the Gentleman break his Neck (for the Author allows him to be a *Devonshire* man, and not from *Brecknock*) but is alive and Hearty at this present writing. So that although I cannot affirm this Writer is a Conjurer, yet I think from publishing so premeditate a falshood he may justly be called a *Neck-Romancer*.

I am with great Respect

S^r

Y^r &c.

A SERMON ON FALSE WITNESS

EXODUS xx. 16.
Thou shalt not bear false Witness against thy Neighbour.

IN those great changes that are made in a country, by the prevailing of one party over another, it is very convenient that the prince, and those who are in authority under him, should use all just and proper methods for preventing any mischief to the public from seditious men. And Governors do well, when they encourage any good subject to discover (as his duty obligeth him) whatever plots or conspiracies may be any way dangerous to the state: Neither are they to be blamed, even when they receive informations from bad men, in order to find out the truth, when it concerns the public welfare. Every one indeed is naturally inclined to have an ill opinion of an informer; although it is not impossible, but an honest man may be called by that name. For whoever knoweth any thing, the telling of which would prevent some great evil to his prince, his country, or his neighbour, is bound in conscience to reveal it. But the mischief is, that when parties are violently enflamed, which seemeth unfortunately to be our case at present, there is never wanting a sett of evil instruments, who, either out of mad zeal, private hatred, or filthy lucre, are always ready to offer their service to the prevailing side, and become accusers of their brethren without any regard to truth or charity. Holy *David* numbers this among the chief of his sufferings; *False Witnesses are risen up against me, and such as breathe out Cruelty.*[1] Our Saviour and his apostles did likewise undergo the same distress, as we read both in the Gospels and the Acts.

Now because the sin of false witnessing is so horrible and dangerous in itself, and so odious to God and man: And because the bitterness of too many among us is risen to such a height, that it is not easy to know where it will stop, or how far some weak and wicked minds may be carried by a mistaken zeal, a malicious temper, or hope of reward, to break this great commandment delivered in the text: Therefore, in order to

prevent this evil, and the consequences of it, at least among you
who are my hearers, I shall,

I. FIRST, Shew you several ways by which a man may be
called a false witness against his neighbour.

II. SECONDLY, I shall give you some rules for your conduct
and behaviour, in order to defend yourselves against the
malice and cunning of false accusers.

III. AND lastly, I shall conclude with shewing you very briefly,
how far it is your duty, as good subjects and good neighbours, to bear faithful witness, when you are lawfully
called to it by those in authority, or by the sincere advice
of your own consciences.

I. As to the first, there are several ways by which a man may
be justly called a false witness against his neighbour.

First, According to the direct meaning of the word, when a
man accuseth his neighbour without the least ground of truth.
So we read, *that* Jezabel *hired two sons of* Belial *to accuse*
Naboth *for blaspheming God and the King, for which, although
he was entirely innocent, he was stoned to death.*[2] And in our
age it is not easy to tell how many men have lost their lives, been
ruined in their fortunes, and put to ignominious punishment by
the downright perjury of false witnesses! The law itself in such
cases being not able to protect the innocent. But this is so
horrible a crime, that it doth not need to be aggravated by
words.

A second way by which a man becometh a false witness is,
when he mixeth falsehood and truth together, or concealeth
some circumstances, which, if they were told, would destroy
the falshoods he uttereth. So the two false witnesses who
accused our Saviour before the chief Priests, by a very little
perverting his words, would have made him guilty of a capital
crime; for so it was among the Jews to prophesy any evil against
the temple. *This fellow said, I am able to destroy the temple of
God, and to build it in three days*; whereas the words, as
our Saviour spoke them, were to another end, and differently
expressed: For when the Jews asked him to shew them a sign,

he said, *Destroy this temple, and in three days I will raise it up*.[3] In such cases as these, an innocent man is half confounded, and looketh as if he were guilty, since he neither can deny his words, nor perhaps readily strip them from the malicious additions of a false witness.

Thirdly, A man is a false witness, when, in accusing his neighbour, he endeavoureth to aggravate by his gestures, and tone of his voice, or when he chargeth a man with words which were only repeated or quoted from somebody else. As if any one should tell me that he heard another speak certain dangerous and seditious speeches, and I should immediately accuse him for speaking them himself; and so drop the only circumstance that made him innocent. This was the case of St. *Stephen*. The false witnesses said, *This man ceaseth not to speak blasphemous words against this holy place and the law*.[4] Whereas St. *Stephen* said no such words; but only repeated some prophesies of *Jeremiah* or *Malachi*, which threatened *Jerusalem* with destruction if it did not repent: However, by the fury of the people, this innocent holy person was stoned to death for words he never spoke.

Fourthly, The blackest kind of false witnesses are those who do the office of the Devil, by tempting their brethren in order to betray them. I cannot call to mind any instances of this kind mentioned in holy scripture. But I am afraid this vile practice hath been too much followed in the world. When a man's temper hath been so soured by misfortunes and hard usage, that perhaps he hath reason enough to complain; then one of these seducers, under the pretence of friendship, will seem to lament his case, urge the hardships he hath suffered, and endeavour to raise his passions until he hath said something that a malicious informer can pervert or aggravate against him in a court of justice.

Fifthly, Whoever beareth witness against his neighbour, out of a principle of malice and revenge, from any old grudge, or hatred to his person; such a man is a false witness in the sight of God, although what he says be true; because the motive or cause is evil, not to serve his prince or country, but to gratify his own resentments. And therefore, although a man thus

accused may be very justly punished by the law, yet this doth
by no means acquit the accuser, who, instead of regarding the
public service, intended only to glut his private rage and spight.

Sixthly, I number among false witnesses all those who make
a trade of being informers in hope of favour and reward; and
to this end employ their time, either by listening in public
places, to catch up an accidental word; or in corrupting men's
servants to discover any unwary expression of their master; or
thrusting themselves into company, and then using the most
indecent scurrilous language; fastening a thousand falshoods
and scandal upon a whole party, on purpose to provoke such
an answer as they may turn to an accusation. And truly this
ungodly race is said to be grown so numerous, that men of
different parties can hardly converse together with any security.
Even the pulpit hath not been free from the misrepresentation
of these informers; of whom the clergy have not wanted
occasions to complain with holy *David: They daily mistake my
words, all they imagine is to do me evil.*[5] Nor is it any wonder
at all, that this trade of informing should be now in a flourishing
condition, since our case is manifestly thus: We are divided into
two parties, with very little charity or temper towards each
other: The prevailing side may talk of past things as they please,
with security; and generally do it in the most provoking words
they can invent; while those who are down are sometimes
tempted to speak in favour of a lost cause, and therefore,
without great caution, must needs be often caught tripping, and
thereby furnish plenty of materials for witnesses and informers.

Lastly, Those may well be reckoned among false witnesses
against their neighbour, who bring him into trouble and punishment by such accusations as are of no consequence at all to the
public, nor can be of any other use but to create vexation.
Such witnesses are those, who cannot hear an idle intemperate
expression, but they must immediately run to the magistrate to
inform; or perhaps wrangling in their cups over night, when
they were not able to speak or apprehend three words of
common sense, will pretend to remember every thing in the
morning, and think themselves very properly qualified to be
accusers of their brethren. God be thanked, the throne of our

king is too firmly settled to be shaken by the folly and rashness of every sottish companion. And I do not in the least doubt, that when those in power begin to observe the falshood, the prevarication, the aggravating manner, the treachery and seducing, the malice and revenge, the love of lucre; and lastly, the trifling accusations in too many wicked people, they will be as ready to discourage every sort of those whom I have numbered among false witnesses, as they will be to countenance honest men, who, out of a true zeal to their prince and country, do, in the innocence of their hearts, freely discover whatever they may apprehend to be dangerous to either. A good christian will think it sufficient to reprove his brother for a rash unguarded word, where there is neither danger nor evil example to be apprehended; or, if he will not amend by reproof, avoid his conversation.

II. And thus much may serve to shew the several ways whereby a man may be said to be a false witness against his neighbour. I might have added one kind more, and it is of those who inform against their neighbour out of fear of punishment to themselves, which, although it be more excusable, and hath less of malice than any of the rest, cannot however be justified. I go on therefore upon the second head, to give you some rules for your conduct and behaviour, in order to defend yourselves against the malice and cunning of false accusers.

It is readily agreed, that innocence is the best protection in the world; yet that it is not always sufficient without some degree of prudence, our Saviour himself intimateth to us, by instructing his disciples *to be wise as serpents, as well as innocent as doves.*[6] But, if ever innocence be too weak a defence, it is chiefly so in jealous and suspicious times, when factions are arrived to an high pitch of animosity, and the minds of men, instead of being warmed by a true zeal for religion, are inflamed only by party fury. Neither is virtue itself a sufficient security in such times, because it is not allowed to be virtue, otherwise than as it hath a mixture of party.

However, although virtue and innocence are no infallible defence against perjury, malice, and subornation, yet they are great supports for enabling us to bear those evils with temper and resignation; and it is an unspeakable comfort to a good man under the malignity of evil mercenary tongues, that a few years will carry his appeal to an higher tribunal, where false witnesses, instead of daring to bring accusations before an all-seeing judge, will call for mountains to cover them. As for earthly judges, they seldom have it in their power; and, God knows, whether they have it in their will, to mingle mercy with justice; they are so far from knowing the hearts of the accuser or the accused, that they cannot know their own; and their understanding is frequently biassed, although their intentions be just. They are often prejudiced to causes, parties, and persons, through the infirmity of human nature, without being sensible themselves that they are so: And therefore, although God may pardon their errors here, he certainly will not ratify their sentences hereafter.

However, since, as we have before observed, our Saviour prescribeth to us to be not only harmless as doves, but wise as serpents, give me leave to prescribe to you some rules, which the most ignorant person may follow for the conduct of his life with safety in perilous times against false accusers.

1st, Let me advise you to have nothing at all to do with that which is commonly called politics, or the government of the world; in the nature of which it is certain you are utterly ignorant; and when your opinion is wrong, although it proceeds from ignorance, it shall be an accusation against you. Besides, opinions in government are right or wrong just according to the humour and disposition of the times; and unless you have judgment to distinguish, you may be punished at one time for what you would be rewarded in another.

2dly, Be ready at all times in your words and actions to shew your loyalty to the king that reigns over you. This is the plain manifest doctrine of holy scripture. *Submit yourselves to every ordinance of man for the Lord's sake, whether it be to the king as supreme, &c.*[7] And another apostle telleth us, *The powers that be are ordained of God.*[8] Kings are the ordinances of man by the permission of God, and they are ordained of God by his instrument man. The powers that be, the present powers, which are ordained by God, and yet in some sense are the ordinances of man, are what you must obey, without presuming to examine into rights and titles; neither can it be reasonably expected, that the powers in being, or in possession, should suffer their title to be publicly disputed by subjects without severe punishment. And to say the truth, there is no duty in religion more easy to the generality of mankind, than obedience to government: I say, to the generality of mankind; because while their law, and property, and religion are preserved, it is of no great consequence to them by whom they are governed, and therefore they are under no temptations to desire a change.

3*dly*, In order to prevent any danger from the malice of false witnesses, be sure to avoid intemperance. If it be often so hard for men to govern their tongues when they are in their right senses, how can they hope to do it when they are heated with drink? In those cases most men regard not what they say, and too many not what they swear; neither will a man's memory disordered with drunkenness serve to defend himself, or satisfy him whether he were guilty or no.

4*thly*, Avoid, as much as possible, the conversation of those people, who are given to talk of public persons and affairs, especially of those whose opinions in such matters are different from yours. I never once knew any disputes of this kind managed with tolerable temper; but on both sides they only agree as much as possible to provoke the passions of each other, indeed with this disadvantage, that he who argueth on the side of power may speak securely the utmost his malice can invent; while the other lieth every moment at the mercy of an informer; and the law in these cases will give no allowance at all for passion, inadvertency, or the highest provocation.

I come now in the last place to shew you how far it is your duty as good subjects and good neighbours to bear faithful witness, when you are lawfully called to it by those in authority, or by the sincere advice of your own consciences.

In what I have hitherto said, you easily find, that I do not talk of bearing witness in general, which is and may be lawful upon a thousand accounts in relation to property and other matters, and wherein there are many scandalous corruptions, almost peculiar to this country, which would require to be handled by themselves. But I have confined my discourse only to that branch of bearing false witness whereby the public is injured in the safety or honour of the prince, or those in authority under him.

In order therefore to be a faithful witness, it is first necessary that a man doth not undertake it from the least prospect of any private advantage to himself. The smallest mixture of that leaven will sour the whole lump. Interest will infallibly bias his judgment, although he be ever so firmly resolved to say nothing but truth. He cannot serve God and Mammon; but as interest is his chief end, he will use the most effectual means to advance it. He will aggravate circumstances to make his testimony valuable; he will be sorry if the person he accuseth should be able to clear himself; in short, he is labouring a point which he thinks necessary to his own good; and it would be a disappointment to him that his neighbour should prove innocent.

5thly, Every good subject is obliged to bear witness against his neighbour, for any action or words, the telling of which would be of advantage to the public, and the concealment dangerous, or of ill example. Of this nature are all plots and conspiracies against the peace of a nation, all disgraceful words against a prince, such as clearly discover a disloyal and rebellious heart: but where our prince and country can possibly receive no damage or disgrace; where no scandal or ill example is given; and our neighbour, it may be, provoked by us, happeneth privately to drop a rash or indiscreet word, which in strictness of law might bring him under trouble, perhaps to his utter undoing; there we are obliged, we ought, to proceed no further than warning and reproof.

In describing to you the several kinds of false witnesses, I have made it less necessary to dwell much longer upon this head; because a faithful witness, like every thing else, is known by his contrary: Therefore it would be only repetition of what I have already said to tell you, that the strictest truth is required in a witness; that he should be wholy free from the malice against the person he accuses; that he should not aggravate the smallest circumstance against the criminal, nor conceal the smallest in his favour; and, to crown all, though I have hinted it before, that the only cause or motive of his undertaking an office, so subject to censure, and so difficult to perform, should be the safety and service of his prince and country.

Under these conditions and limitations (but not otherwise) there is no manner of doubt, but a good man may lawfully and justly become a witness in behalf of the public, and may perform that office (in its own nature not very desirable) with honour and integrity. For the command in the text is positive as well as negative; that is to say, as we are directed not to bear false witness against our neighbour, so we are to bear true. Next to the word of God, and the advice of teachers, every man's conscience strictly examined will be his best director in this weighty point; and to that I shall leave him.

It might perhaps be thought proper to have added something by way of advice to those who are unhappily engaged in this abominable trade and sin of bearing false witness; but I am far from believing or supposing any of that destructive tribe are now my hearers. I look upon them as a sort of people that seldom frequent these holy places, where they can hardly pick up any materials to serve their turn, unless they think it worth their while to misrepresent or pervert the words of the preacher: And whoever is that way disposed, I doubt, cannot be in a very good condition to edify and reform himself by what he heareth. God in his mercy preserve us from all the guilt of this grievous sin forbidden in my text, and from the snares of those who are guilty of it.

I shall conclude with one or two precepts given by *Moses* from God to the children of *Israel*, in the xxiii^d of *Exodus* 1, 2.

Thou shalt not raise a false report: Put not thine hand with the wicked, to be an unrighteous witness.

Thou shalt not follow a multitude to do evil, neither shalt thou speak in a cause to decline after many, to wrest judgment.

Now to God the Father, &c.

A LETTER TO A YOUNG GENTLEMAN, LATELY ENTERED INTO HOLY ORDERS

By a Person of QUALITY

Dated *January* 9, 1719–1720

SIR,

ALTHOUGH it were against my Knowledge, or Advice, that you entered into Holy Orders, under the present Dispositions of Mankind towards the *Church*; yet, since it is now supposed too late to recede, (at least according to the general Practice and Opinion,) I cannot forbear offering my Thoughts to you upon this new Condition of Life you are engaged in.

I COULD heartily wish that the Circumstances of your Fortune had enabled you to have continued some Years longer in the University, at least until you were ten Years standing; to have laid in a competent Stock of human Learning, and some Knowledge in Divinity, before you attempted to appear in the World: For I cannot but lament the common Course, which at least Nine in Ten of those, who enter into the Ministry, are obliged to run. When they have taken a Degree, and are consequently grown a Burden to their Friends, who now think themselves fully discharged; they get into Orders as soon as they can, (upon which I shall make no Remarks,) first sollicit a Readership, and if they be very fortunate, arrive in Time to a Curacy here in Town; or else are sent to be Assistants in the Country, where they probably continue several Years (many of them their whole Lives) with thirty or forty Pounds a Year for their Support, until some Bishop, who happens to be not over-stocked with Relations, or attached to Favourites, or is content to supply his Diocese without Colonies from *England*, bestows them some inconsiderable Benefice; when it is odds they are already encumbered with a numerous Family. I would be glad to know what Intervals of Life such Persons can possibly set apart for Improvement of their Minds; or which Way they could be furnished with Books; the Library they brought with them from their College being usually not the most numerous or judiciously chosen. If such Gentlemen arrive to be great Scholars, it must, I think, be either by Means supernatural, or by a Method altogether out of any Road yet known to the Learned. But I conceive the Fact directly otherwise; and that many of them lose the greatest Part of the small Pittance they received at the University.

I TAKE it for granted, that you intend to pursue the beaten Track, and are already desirous to be seen in a Pulpit; only I hope you will think it proper to pass your Quarentine among some of the desolate Churches five Miles round this Town, where you may at least learn to *read* and to *speak*, before you venture to expose your Parts in a City-Congregation: Not that these are better Judges, but because if a Man must needs expose his Folly, it is more safe and discreet to do so before few Witnesses, and in a scattered Neighbourhood. And you will do well, if you can prevail upon some intimate and judicious Friend to be your constant Hearer, and allow him with the utmost Freedom to give you Notice of whatever he shall find amiss either in your Voice or Gesture; for want of which early Warning, many Clergymen continue defective, and sometimes ridiculous, to the End of their Lives: Neither is it rare to observe among excellent and learned Divines, a certain ungracious Manner, or an unhappy Tone of Voice, which they never have been able to shake off.

I COULD likewise have been glad, if you had applied your self a little more to the Study of the *English* Language, than I fear you have done; the Neglect whereof is one of the most general Defects among the Scholars of this Kingdom, who seem to have not the least Conception of a Stile, but run on in a flat Kind of Phraseology, often mingled with barbarous Terms and Expressions peculiar to the Nation:[1] Neither do I perceive that any Person either finds or acknowledges his Wants upon this Head, or in the least desires to have them supplyed. Proper Words in proper Places, make the true Definition of a Stile: But this would require too ample a Disquisition to be now dwelt on. However, I shall venture to name one or two Faults, which are easy to be remedied with a very small Portion of Abilities.

THE first, is the frequent Use of obscure Terms, which by the

Women are called *hard Words*, and by the better Sort of Vulgar, *fine Language*; than which I do not know a more universal, inexcusable, and unnecessary Mistake among the Clergy of all Distinctions, but especially the younger Practitioners. I have been curious enough to take a List of several hundred Words in a Sermon of a new Beginner, which not one of his Hearers among a Hundred, could possibly understand: Neither can I easily call to Mind any Clergyman of my own Acquaintance who is wholly exempt from this Error; although many of them agree with me in the Dislike of the Thing. But I am apt to put my self in the Place of the Vulgar, and think many Words difficult or obscure, which the Preacher will not allow to be so, because those Words are obvious to Schollars. I believe the Method observed by the famous Lord *Falkland*, in some of his Writings, would not be an ill one for young Divines;[2] I was assured by an old Person of Quality, who knew him well, that when he doubted whether a Word were perfectly intelligible or no, he used to consult one of his Lady's Chambermaids, (not the Waiting-woman, because it was possible she might be conversant in Romances,) and by her Judgment was guided whether to receive or reject it. And if that great Person thought such a Caution necessary in Treatises offered to the learned World; it will be sure at least as proper in Sermons, where the meanest Hearer is supposed to be concerned; and where very often a Lady's Chambermaid may be allowed to equal half the Congregation, both as to Quality and Understanding. But I know not how it comes to pass, that Professors in most Arts and Sciences are generally the worst qualified to explain their Meanings to those who are not of their Tribe: A common Farmer shall make you understand in three Words, *that his Foot is out of Joint, or his Collar-bone broken*; wherein a *Surgeon*, after a hundred Terms of Art, if you are not a Scholar, shall leave you to seek. It is frequently the same Case in Law, Physick, and even many of the meaner Arts.[3]

AND upon this Account it is, that among *hard Words*, I number likewise those which are peculiar to Divinity as it is a Science; because I have observed several Clergymen, otherwise little fond of obscure Terms, yet in their Sermons very liberal

of those which they find in Ecclesiastical Writers, as if it were
our Duty to understand them: Which I am sure it is not. And I
defy the greatest Divine, to produce any Law, either of God
or Man, which obliges me to comprehend the Meaning of
*Omniscience, Omnipresence, Ubiquity, Attribute, Beatifick
Vision*, with a Thousand others so frequent in Pulpits; any more
than that of *Excentrick, Idiosyncracy, Entity*, and the like. I
believe I may venture to insist further, that many Terms used
in Holy Writ, particularly by St. *Paul*, might with more Discretion be changed into plainer Speech, except when they are
introduced as part of a Quotation.

I AM the more earnest in this Matter, because it is a general
Complaint, and the justest in the World. For a Divine hath
nothing to say to the wisest Congregation of any Parish in
this Kingdom, which he may not express in a Manner to be
understood by the meanest among them. And this Assertion
must be true, or else God requires from us more than we are
able to perform. However, not to contend whether a Logician
might possibly put a Case that would serve for an Exception; I
will appeal to any Man of Letters, whether at least nineteen in
twenty of those perplexing Words might not be changed into
easy ones, such as naturally first occur to ordinary Men, and
probably did so at first to those very Gentlemen, who are so
fond of the former.

WE are often reproved by Divines from the Pulpits, on
Account of our Ignorance in Things sacred; and perhaps with
Justice enough: However, it is not very reasonable for them
to expect, that *common Men* should understand Expressions,
which are never made use of in *common Life*. No Gentleman
thinks it safe or prudent to send a Servant with a Message,
without repeating it more than once, and endeavouring to put
it into Terms brought down to the Capacity of the Bearer: Yet
after all this Care, it is frequent for Servants to mistake, and
sometimes occasion Misunderstandings between Friends; although the common Domesticks in some Gentlemen's Families,
may have more Opportunities of improving their Minds, than
the ordinary Sort of Tradesmen.

IT is usual for Clergymen who are taxed with this learned

Defect, to quote Dr. *Tillotson*, and other famous Divines in their Defence; without considering the Difference between elaborate Discourses upon important Occasions, delivered to Princes or Parliaments, written with a View of being made publick; and a plain Sermon intended for the Middle or lower Size of People. Neither do they seem to remember the many Alterations, Additions, and Expungings made by great Authors, in those Treatises which they prepare for the Publick. Besides, that excellent Prelate above-mentioned, was known to preach after a much more popular Manner in the City Congregations: And if in those Parts of his Works, he be any where too obscure for the Understandings of many, who may be supposed to have been his Hearers; it ought to be numbered among his Omissions.

THE Fear of being thought Pedants hath been of pernicious Consequence to young Divines. This hath wholly taken many of them off from their severer Studies in the University; which they have exchanged for Plays, Poems, and Pamphlets, in order to qualify them for Tea-Tables and Coffee-Houses. This they usually call *Polite Conversation, knowing the World*, and *reading Men instead of Books*. These Accomplishments, when applied in the Pulpit, appear by a quaint, terse, florid Style, rounded into Periods and Cadencies, commonly without either Propriety or Meaning. I have listened with my utmost Attention for half an Hour to an Orator of this Species, without being able to understand, much less to carry away one single Sentence out of a whole Sermon. Others, to shew that their Studies have not been confined to Sciences, or ancient Authors, will talk in the Style of a gaming Ordinary and *White Friars*; where I suppose the Hearers can be little edified by the Terms of *Palming, Shuffling, Biting, Bamboozling*, and the like, if they have not been sometimes conversant among Pick-pockets and Sharpers. And truly, as they say, a Man is known by his Company; so it should seem, that a Man's Company may be known by his Manner of expressing himself, either in publick Assemblies, or private Conversation.

IT would be endless to run over the several Defects of Style among us: I shall therefore say nothing of the *mean* and the *paultry*, (which are usually attended by the *fustian*,) much less of the *slovenly* or *indecent*. Two Things I will just warn you against: The first is, the Frequency of flat, unnecessary Epithets; and the other is, the Folly of using old thread-bare Phrases, which will often make you go out of your Way to find and apply them; are nauseous to rational Hearers, and will seldom express your Meaning as well as your own natural Words.

ALTHOUGH, as I have already observed, our *English* Tongue be too little cultivated in this Kingdom; yet the Faults are nine in ten owing to Affectation, and not to the want of Understanding. When a Man's Thoughts are clear, the properest Words will generally offer themselves first; and his own Judgment will direct him in what Order to place them, so as they may be best understood. Where Men err against this Method, it is usually on Purpose, and to shew their Learning, their Oratory, their Politeness, or their Knowledge of the World. In short, that Simplicity, without which no human Performance can arrive to any great Perfection, is no where more eminently useful than in this.

I HAVE been considering that Part of Oratory, which relates to the moving of the Passions: This, I observe, is in Esteem and Practice among some Church Divines, as well as among all the Preachers and Hearers of the *Fanatick* or *Enthusiastick* Strain. I will here deliver to you (perhaps with more Freedom than Prudence) my Opinion upon the Point.

THE two great Orators of *Greece* and *Rome, Demosthenes* and *Cicero*, although each of them a Leader (or, as the *Greeks* called it, a *Demagogue*) in a popular State; yet seem to differ in their Practice upon this Branch of their Art: The former, who had to deal with a People of much more Politeness, Learning, and Wit, laid the greatest Weight of his Oratory upon the Strength of his Arguments offered to their Understanding and Reason: Whereas, *Tully* considered the Dispositions of a sincere, more ignorant, and less mercurial Nation, by dwelling almost entirely on the pathetick Part.[4]

BUT the principal Thing to be remembered is, that the constant Design of both these Orators in all their Speeches, was to drive some one particular Point; either the Condemnation, or

Acquittal of an accused Person; a persuasive to War, the enforcing of a Law, and the like; which was determined upon the
Spot, according as the Orators on either Side prevailed. And
here it was often found of absolute Necessity to enflame, or
cool the Passions of the Audience; especially at *Rome*, where
Tully spoke, and with whose Writings young Divines (I mean
those among them who read old Authors) are more conversant
than with those of *Demosthenes*; who, by many Degrees,
excelled the other, at least as an Orator. But I do not see how
this Talent of moving Passions can be of any great Use towards
directing Christian Men in the Conduct of their Lives, at least
in these *Northern* Climates; where, I am confident, the strongest
Eloquence of that Kind will leave few Impressions upon any of
our Spirits, deep enough to last till the next Morning, or rather
to the next Meal.[5]

BUT what hath chiefly put me out of conceit with this moving
Manner of Preaching, is the frequent Disappointment it meets
with. I know a Gentleman, who made it a Rule in Reading, to
skip over all Sentences where he spied a Note of Admiration at
the End. I believe, those Preachers who abound in *Epiphonemas*, if they look about them, would find one Part of their
Congregation out of Countenance, and the other asleep; except,
perhaps, an old Female Beggar or two in the Isles, who (if they
be sincere) may probably groan at the Sound.

NOR is it a Wonder that this Expedient should so often
miscarry, which requires so much Art and Genius to arrive at
any Perfection in it; as every Man will find, much sooner than
learn, by consulting *Cicero* himself.

I THEREFORE entreat you to make use of this Faculty (if you
be ever so unfortunate as to think you have it) as seldom, and
with as much Caution as you can; else I may probably have
Occasion to say of you, as a great Person said of another upon
this very Subject. A Lady asked him, coming out of Church,
whether it were not a very moving Discourse? *Yes*, said he,
I was extremely sorry, for the Man is my Friend.

IF in Company you offer something for a Jest, and no body
seconds you in your own Laughter, or seems to relish what you
said; you may condemn their Taste, if you please, and appeal

to better Judgments; but, in the mean Time, it must be agreed you make a very indifferent Figure: And it is, at least, equally ridiculous to be disappointed in endeavouring to make other Folks grieve, as to make them laugh.

A PLAIN convincing Reason may possibly operate upon the Mind both of a learned and ignorant Hearer, as long as they live; and will edify a Thousand Times more than the Art of wetting the Handkerchiefs of a whole Congregation, if you were sure to attain it.

IF your Arguments be strong, in God's Name offer them in as moving a Manner as the Nature of the Subject will probably admit; wherein Reason, and good Advice will be your safest Guides: But beware of letting the pathetick Part swallow up the rational: For, I suppose, *Philosophers* have long agreed, that Passion should never prevail over Reason.

As I take it, the two principal Branches of Preaching, are first to tell the People what is their Duty; and then to convince them that it is so. The Topicks for both these, we know, are brought from *Scripture* and *Reason*. Upon the former, I wish it were often practised to instruct the Hearers in the Limits, Extent, and Compass of every Duty, which requires a good deal of Skill and Judgment: The other Branch is, I think, not so difficult. But what I would offer upon both, is this; that it seems to be in the Power of a reasonable Clergyman, if he will be at the Pains, to make the most ignorant Man comprehend what is his Duty; and to convince him by Arguments, drawn to the Level of his Understanding, that he ought to perform it.

BUT I must remember, that my Design in this *Paper* was not so much to instruct you in your Business, either as a Clergyman, or a Preacher, as to warn you against some Mistakes, which are obvious to the Generality of Mankind, as well as to me; and we, who are Hearers, may be allowed to have some Opportunities in the Quality of being Standers-by. Only, perhaps, I may now again transgress, by desiring you to express the Heads of your Divisions in as few and clear Words, as you possibly can; otherwise, I, and many Thousand others, will never be able to retain them, nor consequently to carry away a Syllable of the Sermon.

I SHALL now mention a Particular, wherein your whole Body
will be certainly against me; and the Laity, almost to a Man,
on my Side. However it came about, I cannot get over the
Prejudice of taking some little Offence at the Clergy, for perpetually reading their Sermons; perhaps, my frequent hearing
of Foreigners, who never make use of Notes, may have added
to my Disgust. And I cannot but think that whatever is read,
differs as much from what is repeated without Book, as a Copy
doth from an Original. At the same Time, I am highly sensible
what an extreme Difficulty it would be upon you to alter this
Method; and that, in such a Case, your Sermons would be
much less valuable than they are, for want of Time to improve
and correct them. I would therefore gladly come to a Compromise with you in this Matter. I knew a Clergyman of some
Distinction, who appeared to deliver his Sermon without looking into his Notes; which, when I complimented him upon, he
assured me, he could not repeat six Lines; but his Method was
to write the whole Sermon in a large plain Hand, with all the
Forms of Margin, Paragraph, marked Page, and the like; then
on *Sunday* Morning, he took care to run it over five or six
Times, which he could do in an Hour; and when he delivered
it, by pretending to turn his Face from one Side to the other, he
would (in his own Expression) pick up the Lines, and cheat his
People, by making them believe he had it all by Heart. He
farther added, that whenever he happened, by Neglect, to omit
any of these Circumstances, the Vogue of the *Parish* was, *our
Doctor gave us but an indifferent Sermon to-day*. Now among
us, many Clergymen act so directly contrary to this Method;
that from a Habit of saving *Time* and *Paper*, which they
acquired at the University, they write in so diminutive a
Manner, with such frequent Blots and Interlineations, that they
are hardly able to go on without perpetual Hesitations, or
extemporary Expletives: And I desire to know what can be
more inexcusable than to see a Divine, and a Scholar, at a Loss
in reading his own Compositions; which, it is supposed, he
hath been preparing with much *Pains* and *Thought*, for the
Instruction of his People. The Want of a little more Care in this
Article, is the Cause of much ungraceful Behaviour. You will

observe some Clergymen with their Heads held down from the Beginning to the End, within an Inch of the Cushion, to read what is hardly legible; which, besides the untoward Manner, hinders them from making the best Advantage of their Voice: Others, again, have a Trick of popping up and down every Moment, from their *Paper* to the Audience, like an idle School-Boy on a Repetition-Day.

LET me entreat you, therefore, to add one Half-Crown a Year to the Article of *Paper*; to transcribe your Sermons in as large and plain a Manner as you can, and either make no Interlineations, or change the whole Leaf: For we, your Hearers, would rather you should be less correct, than perpetually stammering; which I take to be one of the worst *Solecisms* in *Rhetorick*. And lastly, read your Sermon once or twice, for a few Days before you preach it: To which you will probably answer some Years hence, *That it was but just finished when the last Bell rang to Church*; and I shall readily believe, but not excuse you.

I CANNOT forbear warning you, in the most earnest Manner, against endeavouring at Wit in your Sermons: Because, by the strictest Computation, it is very near a Million to One, that you have none; and because too many of your Calling, have consequently made themselves everlastingly ridiculous by attempting it. I remember several young Men in this Town, who could never leave the *Pulpit* under half a Dozen *Conceits*; and this Faculty adhered to those Gentlemen a longer or shorter Time, exactly in Proportion to their several Degrees of Dulness: Accordingly, I am told that some of them retain it to this Day. I heartily wish the Brood were at an End.

BEFORE you enter into the common unsufferable Cant, of taking all Occasions to disparage the Heathen *Philosophers*, I hope you will differ from some of your Brethren, by first enquiring what those *Philosophers* can say for themselves. The System of Morality to be gathered out of the Writings, or Sayings of those antient Sages, falls undoubtedly very short of that delivered in the Gospel; and wants, besides, the Divine Sanction which our Saviour gave to his. Whatever is further related by the Evangelists, contains chiefly Matters of Fact, and conse-

quently of Faith; such as the Birth of Christ, his being the
Messiah, his Miracles, his Death, Resurrection, and Ascension:
None of which can properly come under the Appellation of
human Wisdom, being intended only to make us wise unto
Salvation. And therefore in this Point, nothing can be justly laid
to the Charge of the *Philosophers*; further, than that they were
ignorant of certain Facts which happened long after their Death.
But I am deceived, if a better Comment could be any where
collected upon the moral Part of the Gospel, than from the
Writings of those excellent Men. Even that divine Precept of
loving our Enemies, is at large insisted on by *Plato*; who puts
it, as I remember, into the Mouth of *Socrates*.[6] And as to the
Reproach of Heathenism, I doubt they had less of it than the
corrupted *Jews*, in whose Time they lived. For it is a gross Piece
of Ignorance among us, to conceive, that in those polite and
learned Ages, even Persons of any tolerable Education, much
less the wisest Philosophers, did acknowledge, or worship any
more than one Almighty Power, under several Denominations,
to whom they allowed all those Attributes we ascribe to the
Divinity: And, as I take it, human Comprehension reacheth no
further: Neither did our Saviour think it necessary to explain
to us the Nature of God; because, as I suppose, it would be
impossible, without bestowing on us other Faculties than we
possess at present. But the true Misery of the Heathen World,
appears to be what I beforementioned, the Want of a Divine
Sanction; without which, the Dictates of the Philosophers failed
in the Point of Authority; and consequently the Bulk of Mankind lay, indeed, under a great Load of Ignorance, even in the
Article of Morality; but the Philosophers themselves did not.
Take the Matter in this Light, and it will afford Field enough
for a Divine to enlarge on; by shewing the Advantages which
the Christian World hath over the Heathen; and the absolute
Necessity of Divine Revelation, to make the Knowledge of the
true God, and the Practice of Virtue more universal in the
World.[7]

I AM not ignorant how much I differ in this Opinion from
some ancient Fathers in the Church; who arguing against the
Heathens, made it a principal Topick to decry their Philosophy

as much as they could: Which, I hope, is not altogether our present Case. Besides, it is to be considered, that those Fathers lived in the Decline of *Literature*; and in my Judgment, (who should be unwilling to give the least Offence,) appear to be rather most excellent holy Persons, than of transcendent Genius and Learning.[8] Their genuine Writings (for many of them have extreamly suffered by spurious Additions) are of admirable Use for confirming the Truth of ancient Doctrines and Discipline; by shewing the State and Practice of the primitive Church. But among such of them, as have fallen in my Way, I do not remember any, whose Manner of arguing or exhorting I could heartily recommend to the Imitation of a young Divine, when he is to speak from the Pulpit. Perhaps I judge too hastily, there being several of them, in whose Writings I have made very little Progress, and in others none at all. For I perused only such as were recommended to me, at a Time when I had more Leisure, and a better Disposition to read, than have since fallen to my Share.

To return then to the Heathen Philosophers: I hope you will not only give them Quarter, but make their Works a considerable Part of your Study. To these I will venture to add the principal Orators and Historians, and perhaps a few of the Poets: By the reading of which, you will soon discover your Mind and Thoughts to be enlarged, your Imagination extended and refined, your Judgment directed, your Admiration lessened, and your Fortitude increased. All which Advantages must needs be of excellent Use to a Divine, whose Duty it is to preach and practise the Contempt of human Things.

I WOULD say something concerning Quotations; wherein I think you cannot be too sparing, except from Scripture, and the primitive Writers of the Church. As to the former, when you offer a Text as a Proof or an Illustration, we your Hearers expect to be fairly used; and sometimes think we have Reason to complain, especially of you younger Divines; which makes us fear, that some of you conceive you have no more to do than to turn over a Concordance, and there having found the principal Word, introduce as much of the Verse as will serve your Turn, although in Reality it makes nothing for you. I do not altogether disapprove the Manner of interweaving Texts of Scripture through the Style of your Sermon; wherein, however, I have sometimes observed great Instances of Indiscretion and Impropriety; against which I therefore venture to give you a Caution.

As to Quotations from antient Fathers, I think they are best brought in, to confirm some Opinion controverted by those who differ from us: In other Cases we give you full Power to adopt the Sentence for your own, rather than tell us, *as St. Austin excellently observes:*[9] But to mention modern Writers by Name, or use the Phrase of *a late excellent Prelate of our Church*, and the like, is altogether intolerable; and, for what Reason I know not, makes every rational Hearer ashamed. Of no better a Stamp is your *Heathen Philosopher*, and *famous Poet*, and *Roman Historian*; at least in common Congregations, who will rather believe you on your own Word, than on that of *Plato* or *Homer*.

I HAVE lived to see *Greek* and *Latin* almost entirely driven out of the Pulpit; for which I am heartily glad. The frequent Use of the latter was certainly a Remnant of Popery, which never admitted Scripture in the vulgar Language; and I wonder that Practice was never accordingly objected to us by the Fanaticks.

THE Mention of Quotations puts me in mind of Commonplace Books, which have been long in use by industrious young Divines, and, I hear, do still continue so; I know they are very beneficial to Lawyers and Physicians, because they are Collections of Facts or Cases, whereupon a great Part of their several Faculties depend: Of these I have seen several, but never yet any written by a Clergyman; only from what I am informed, they generally are Extracts of Theological and Moral Sentences, drawn from Ecclesiastical and other Authors reduced under proper Heads; usually begun, and perhaps, finished, while the Collectors were young in the Church; as being intended for Materials or Nurseries to stock future Sermons. You will observe the wise Editors of ancient Authors, when they meet a Sentence worthy of being distinguished, take special Care to have the first Word printed in Capital Letters, that you may not overlook it: Such, for Example, as the *Inconstancy of For-tune, the Goodness of Peace, the Excellency of Wisdom, the Certainty of Death; that Prosperity makes Men insolent, and Adversity humble*, and the like eternal Truths, which every Plowman knows well enough, although he never heard of *Aris-totle* or *Plato*. If Theological Common-Place Books be no better filled, I think they had better be laid aside: And I could wish, that Men of tolerable Intellectuals would rather trust to their own natural Reason, improved by a general Conversation with Books, to enlarge on Points which they are supposed already to understand. If a rational Man reads an excellent Author with just Application, he shall find himself extremely improved, and perhaps insensibly led to imitate that Author's Perfections; although in a little Time he should not remember one Word in the Book, nor even the Subject it handled: For, Books give the same Turn to our Thoughts and Way of Reasoning, that good and ill Company do to our Behaviour and Conversation; with-out either loading our Memories, or making us even sensible of the Change. And particularly, I have observed in Preaching, that no Men succeed better than those, who trust entirely to the Stock or Fund of their own Reason; advanced, indeed, but not overlaid by Commerce with Books. Whoever only reads, in order to transcribe wise and shining Remarks, without entering into the Genius and Spirit of the Author; as it is probable he will make no very judicious Extract, so he will be apt to trust to that Collection in all his Compositions; and be misled out of the regular Way of Thinking, in order to introduce those Materials which he hath been at the Pains to gather: And the Product of all this will be found a manifest incoherent Piece of Patchwork.

SOME Gentlemen abounding in their University Erudition, are apt to fill their Sermons with philosophical Terms, and Notions of the metaphysical or abstracted Kind; which gener-ally have one Advantage, to be equally understood by the Wise, the Vulgar, and the Preacher himself. I have been better enter-tained, and more informed by a Chapter in the *Pilgrim's Pro-gress*, than by a long Discourse upon the *Will* and the *Intellect*, and *simple* or *complex Ideas*.[10] Others again, are fond of dilating on *Matter* and *Motion*, talk of the *fortuitous Concourse of Atoms*, of *Theories*, and *Phænomena*; directly against the Advice of St. *Paul*, who yet appears to have been conversant enough in those Kinds of Studies.[11]

I DO not find that you are any where directed in the Canons, or Articles, to attempt explaining the Mysteries of the Christian Religion. And, indeed, since Providence intended there should be Mysteries; I do not see how it can be agreeable to *Piety*, *Orthodoxy*, or good *Sense*, to go about such a Work. For, to me, there seems to be a manifest Dilemma in the Case: If you explain them, they are Mysteries no longer; if you fail, you have laboured to no Purpose. What I should think most reasonable and safe for you to do, upon this Occasion, is upon solemn Days to deliver the Doctrine as the Church holds it, and confirm it by Scripture. For my Part, having considered the Matter impartially, I can see no great Reason which those Gentlemen, you call the *Free-Thinkers*, can have for their Clamour against Religious Mysteries; since it is plain they were not invented by the Clergy, to whom they bring no Profit, nor acquire any Honour. For every Clergyman is ready, either to tell us the utmost he knows, or to confess that he doth not understand them: Neither is it strange, that there should be Mysteries in Divinity, as well as in the commonest Operations of Nature.[12]

AND here I am at a Loss what to say, upon the frequent Custom of preaching against *Atheism*, *Deism*, *Free-Thinking*, and the like; as young Divines are particularly fond of doing, especially when they exercise their Talent in Churches frequented by People of Quality; which, as it is but an ill Compliment to the Audience, so I am under some doubt whether it answers the End. Because, Persons under those Imputations are generally no great Frequenters of Churches, and so the Congregation is but little edified for the Sake of three or four Fools, who are past Grace. Neither do I think it any Part of *Prudence*, to perplex the Minds of well-disposed People with Doubts, which probably would never have otherwise come into their Heads. But I am of Opinion, and dare be positive in it, that not one in a Hundred of those, who pretend to be *Free-Thinkers*, are really so in their Hearts. For there is one

Observation which I never knew to fail, and I desire you will examine it in the Course of your Life; that no Gentleman of a liberal Education, and regular in his Morals, did ever profess himself a *Free-Thinker:* Where then are these Kind of People to be found? Amongst the worst Part of the Soldiery, made up of Pages, younger Brothers of obscure Families, and others of desperate Fortunes; or else among idle Town-Fops; and now and then a drunken 'Squire of the Country. Therefore, nothing can be plainer, than that Ignorance and Vice, are two Ingredients absolutely necessary in the Composition of those you generally call *Free-Thinkers*; who, in Propriety of Speech, *are no Thinkers at all.* And, since I am in the way of it, pray consider one Thing farther: As young as you are, you cannot but have already observed, what a violent Run there is among too many weak People, against University Education: Be firmly assured, that the whole Cry is made up by those, who were either never sent to a College; or through their Irregularities and Stupidity, never made the least Improvement while they were there. I have above Forty of the latter now in my Eye; several of them in this Town, whose *Learning, Manners, Temperance, Probity, Good-nature,* and *Politicks,* are all of a-piece. Others of them in the Country, oppressing their Tenants, tyrannizing over the Neighbourhood, cheating the Vicar, talking Nonsense, and getting drunk at the Sessions. It is from such Seminaries as these, that the World is provided with the several Tribes and Denominations of *Free-Thinkers*; who, in my Judgment, are not to be reformed by Arguments offered to prove the Truth of the *Christian Religion*; because, *Reasoning* will never make a Man correct an ill Opinion, which by *Reasoning* he never acquired: For, in the Course of Things, Men always grow vicious before they become Unbelievers: But if you could once convince the Town or Country Profligate, by Topicks drawn from the View of their own *Quiet, Reputation, Health,* and *Advantage*; their *Infidelity* would soon drop off. This, I confess, is no easy Task; because it is almost in a literal Sense, to *fight with Beasts.* Now, to make it clear, that we are to look for no other Original of this *Infidelity,* whereof Divines so much complain; it is allowed on all Hands, that the People of *England* are more corrupt in their *Morals*, than any other Nation at this Day under the *Sun*: And this Corruption is manifestly owing to other Causes, both *numerous* and *obvious*, much more than to the Publication of irreligious Books; which, indeed, are but the Consequence of the former. For, all the Writers against Christianity, since the Revolution, have been of the lowest Rank among Men, in regard to *Literature*, *Wit*, and good *Sense*; and upon that Account, wholly unqualified to propagate *Heresies*, unless among People already abandoned.

IN an Age where every Thing disliked by those, who think with the Majority, is called *Disaffection*; it may perhaps be ill interpreted, when I venture to tell you, that this universal Depravation of *Manners*, is owing to the perpetual bandying of *Factions* among us for Thirty Years past; when, without weighing the *Motives of Justice*, *Law*, *Conscience*, or *Honour*, every Man adjusts his *Principles* to those of the *Party* he hath chosen, and among whom he may best find his own Account: But, by reason of our frequent Vicissitudes, Men, who were impatient to be out of Play,[13] have been forced to recant, or at least to reconcile their former Tenets with every new System of Administration. Add to this, that the old fundamental Custom of annual Parliaments being wholly laid aside, and Elections growing chargeable; since Gentlemen found that their Country *Seats* brought them in less than a *Seat* in the House; the Voters, *that is to say*, the Bulk of the common People, have been universally seduced into *Bribery*, *Perjury*, *Drunkenness*, *Malice*, and *Slander*.[14]

NOT to be further tedious, or rather invidious, these are a few, among other Causes, which have contributed to the Ruin of our *Morals*, and consequently to the Contempt of *Religion*. For, imagine to your self, if you please, a landed Youth, whom his Mother would never suffer to look into a Book, for fear of spoiling his Eyes; got into Parliament, and observing all Enemies to the Clergy heard with the utmost Applause; what Notions he must imbibe; how readily he will join in the Cry; what an Esteem he will conceive of himself; and what a Contempt he must entertain, not only for his Vicar at home, but for the whole Order.

I THEREFORE again conclude, that the Trade of *Infidelity* hath been taken up only for an Expedient to keep in Countenance that universal Corruption of *Morals*, which many other Causes first contributed to introduce, and to cultivate. And thus, Mr. *Hobbes*'s Saying upon Reason, may be much more properly applied to Religion: That, *if Religion will be against a Man, a Man will be against Religion.*[15] Although, after all, I have heard a Profligate offer much stronger Arguments against paying his Debts, than ever he was known to do against *Christianity*; indeed, the Reason was, because in that Juncture he happened to be closer pressed by the *Bailiff* than the *Parson*.

IGNORANCE may, perhaps, be the *Mother* of *Superstition*; but *Experience* hath not proved it to be so of *Devotion*: For *Christianity* always made the most easy and quickest Progress in civilized Countries. I mention this because it is affirmed, that the Clergy are in most Credit where Ignorance prevails, (and surely this Kingdom would be called the *Paradise* of Clergymen, if that Opinion were true) for which they instance *England* in the Times of *Popery*. But whoever knoweth any Thing of three or four Centuries before the Reformation, will find, the little Learning then stirring, was more equally divided between the *English* Clergy and Laity, than it is at present. There were several famous Lawyers in that *Period*, whose Writings are still in the highest Repute; and some *Historians* and *Poets*, who were not of the *Church*. Whereas, now-a-days our Education is so corrupted, that you will hardly find a young Person of Quality with the least Tincture of Knowledge; at the same Time that many of the Clergy were never more learned, or so scurvily treated. Here among Us, at least, a Man of Letters, out of the three Professions, is almost a Prodigy. And those few who have preserved any Rudiments of Learning, are (except, perhaps, one or two Smatterers) the Clergy's Friends to a Man: For, I dare appeal to any Clergyman in this Kingdom, whether the greatest Dunce in his Parish be not always the most proud, wicked, fraudulent, and intractable of his Flock.

I THINK the Clergy have almost given over perplexing themselves and their Hearers, with abstruse Points of Predestination,

Election, and the like; at least, it is time they should; and therefore, I shall not trouble you further upon this Head.

I HAVE now said all I could think convenient with relation to your Conduct in the Pulpit. Your Behaviour in the World is another Scene, upon which, I shall readily offer you my Thoughts, if you appear to desire them from me, by your Approbation of what I have here written; if not, I have already troubled you too much.

I am, SIR,

Your affectionate

Friend and Servant

SWIFT TO CHARLES FORD

Dublin Apr. 4th 1720.

I had your former Lett^r with the inclosed from our Mississipi Friend,[1] I can make no excuse for my not acknowledging it than my perpetuall ill Health. I should not scruple going abroad to mend it, if it were not for a foolish importunate Ailment that quite disspirits me; I am hardly a Month free from a Deafness which continues anoth^r month on me, and dejects me so, that I can not bear the thoughts of stirring out, or suffering any one to see me, and this is the most mortal Impediment to all Thoughts of travelling, and I should dy with Spleen to be in such a Condition in strange Places; So that I must wait till I grow better, or sink under it if I am worse. You healthy People cannot judge of the sickly. Since I had y^r last of Mar. 10th I have not been able to write; and three Days ago having invited severall Gentlemen to dinner, I was so attacked with a fitt of Giddyness for 5 Hours, that I was forced to constitute a Grattan to be my Deputy and do the Honors of the House while I lay miserable on my Bed. Your friendly Expostulations force me upon this old Woman's Talk, but I can bring all my few Friends to witness that you have heard more of it, than ever I troubled them with. I cannot understand the South-Sea Mystery, perhaps the Frolick may go round, and every Nation (except this wch is no Nation) have it's Missisippi. I believe my self not guilty of too much veneration for the Irish H— of L^{ds}, but I differ from you in Politicks; the Question is whether People ought to be Slaves or no. It is like the Quarrell against Convocations; they meet but seldom, have no Power, and for want of those Advantages, cannot make any Figure when they are suffered to assemble.[2] You fetter a Man seven years, then let him loose to shew his Skill in dancing, and because he does it awkwardly, you say he ought to be fetterd for Life. Scotland is poorer and more Northward than this Island, yet were satisfied with their own Legislature till they were united on their Conditions, wch though I think too good for them, yet they are proud enough to be ashamed of.[3] I do assure you I never saw so universall a Discontent as there is among the highest most virulent and anti-church Whigs against that Bill and every Author or Abetter of it without Exception. They say publickly that having been the most loyall submissive complying Subjects that ever Prince had, no Subjects were ever so ill treated. They tell many aggravating Circumstances relating to the manner of rejecting their Addresses &c. I who am to the last degree ignorant, was some time at a Loss how the Commons at this Juncture when the H. of L^{ds} are not very gracious with them, and at all times think not very well of their Jurisdiction, should agree to extend it. But it is easy to see why the Ministry presst it, and as easy to guess what methods a Ministry uses to succeed.[4]

I cannot help the usage which honest Mr Curl gives me. I watched for his Ears in the Queens time, and was I think once within an Inch of them.[5] There is an honest humersom Gentleman here who amuses this Town sometimes with Trifles and some Knave or Fool transmitts them to Curl with a Hint that they are mine.[6] There is one about Precedence of Doctors, we do not know who writt it; It is a very crude Piece, tho not quite so low as some others;[7] This I hear is likewise a Present of Curl to me. I would go into any Scheam you please with Mr Congreve and Mr Pope and the rest, but cannot imagine a Remedy unless he be sent to Bridewell for Life.—You will present my humble service to My Ld Arran and Ld Harley and L^{dy} Harriette, and Friend L— and the rest.[8]—I can write no more for my Head, and so much the better for you.

A PROPOSAL FOR THE UNIVERSAL USE
OF IRISH MANUFACTURE

IN Cloaths, and Furniture of Houses, &c. UTTERLY
Rejecting and *Renouncing* Every Thing wearable that
comes from
ENGLAND

Written in the Year 1720

IT is the peculiar Felicity and Prudence of the People in this
Kingdom, that whatever Commodities, or Productions, lie under
the greatest Discouragements from *England*, those are what we
are sure to be most industrious in cultivating and spreading.
Agriculture, which hath been the principal Care of all wise
Nations, and for the Encouragement whereof there are so many
Statute-Laws in *England*, we countenance so well, that the Landlords are every where, by *penal Clauses*, absolutely prohibiting
their Tenants from Plowing; not satisfied to confine them within
certain Limitations, as it is the Practice of the *English*; one
Effect of which, is already seen in the prodigious Dearness of
Corn, and the Importation of it from *London*, as the cheaper
Market: And, because People are the *Riches of a Country*, and
that our *Neighbours* have done, and are doing all that in them
lie, to make our Wool a Drug to us, and a Monopoly to them;
therefore, the politick Gentlemen of *Ireland* have depopulated
vast Tracts of the best Land, for the feeding of Sheep.[1]

I COULD fill a Volume as large as the *History of the wise
Men of Goatham*, with a Catalogue only of some *wonderful*
Laws and Customs we have observed within thirty Years past.
It is true, indeed, our beneficial Traffick of Wool with *France*,
hath been our only Support for several Years past; furnishing
us all the little Money we have to pay our Rents, and go to
Market.[2] But our Merchants assure me, *This Trade hath
received a great Damp by the present fluctuating Condition of
the Coin in* France; *and that most of their Wine is paid for in
Specie, without carrying thither any Commodity from hence.*

HOWEVER, since we are so universally bent upon enlarging our *Flocks*, it may be worth inquiring, what we shall do with our Wool, in case *Barnstable*[3] should be over-stocked, and our *French* Commerce should fail?

I SHOULD wish the Parliament had thought fit to have suspended their Regulation of *Church* Matters, and Enlargements of the *Prerogative*, until a more convenient Time, because they did not appear very pressing, (at least to the Persons *principally concerned*) and, instead of those great Refinements in *Politicks* and *Divinity*, had *amused* Themselves and their Committees a little, with the *State of the Nation*.[4] For Example: What if the House of Commons had thought fit to make a Resolution, *Nemine Contradicente*,[5] against wearing any Cloath or Stuff in their Families, which were not of the Growth and Manufacture of this Kingdom? What if they had extended it so far, as utterly to exclude all Silks, Velvets, Calicoes, and the whole *Lexicon* of Female Fopperies; and declared, that whoever acted otherwise, should be deemed and reputed *an Enemy to the Nation*?[6] What if they had sent up such a Resolution to be agreed to by the House of Lords; and by their own Practice and Encouragement, spread the Execution of it in their several Countries? What if we should agree to make *burying in Woollen* a *Fashion*, as our Neighbours have made it a *Law*?[7] What if the Ladies would be content with *Irish* Stuffs for the Furniture of their Houses, for Gowns and Petticoats to themselves and their Daughters? Upon the whole, and to crown all the rest, let a firm Resolution be taken, by *Male* and *Female*, never to appear with one single *Shred* that comes from *England; and let all the People say*, *AMEN*.

I HOPE, and believe, nothing could please his Majesty better than to hear that his loyal Subjects, of both Sexes, in this Kingdom, celebrated his *Birth-Day* (now approaching) *universally* clad in their own Manufacture. Is there Vertue enough left in this deluded People to save them from the Brink of Ruin? If the Mens Opinions may be taken, the Ladies will look as handsome in Stuffs as Brocades, and, since all will be equal, there may be room enough to employ their Wit and Fancy in chusing and matching of Patterns and Colours. I heard the late Archbishop of *Tuam* mention a pleasant Observation of some Body's; *that* Ireland *would never be happy 'till a Law were made for* burning *every Thing that came from* England, *except their* People *and their* Coals. Nor am I *even yet* for lessening the Number of those Exceptions.[8]

Non tanti mitra est, non tanti Judicis ostrum.[9]

BUT I should rejoice to see a *Stay-Lace* from *England* be thought *Scandalous*, and become a Topick for *Censure* at *Visits* and *Tea Tables*.

IF the unthinking Shopkeepers in this Town, had not been *utterly* destitute of common Sense, they would have made some *Proposal to the Parliament*, with a *Petition* to the Purpose I have mentioned; promising to improve the *Cloaths and Stuffs of the Nation, into all possible Degrees of Fineness and Colours, and engaging not to play the Knave, according to their Custom, by exacting and imposing upon the Nobility and Gentry, either as to the Prices or the Goodness.*[10] For I remember in *London*, upon a general Mourning, the *rascally Mercers* and *Woollen Drapers*, would, in Four and Twenty Hours, raise their *Cloaths* and *Silks* to above a double Price; and if the Mourning continued long, then come whingeing with *Petitions* to the *Court, that they were ready to starve, and their Fineries lay upon their Hands*.

I COULD wish our Shopkeepers would immediately think on this *Proposal*, addressing it to all Persons of Quality, and others; but first be sure to get some Body who can write Sense, to put it into Form.

I THINK it needless to exhort the *Clergy* to follow this good Example, because, *in a little Time, those among them who are so unfortunate to have had their Birth and Education in this Country, will think themselves abundantly happy when they can afford* Irish *Crape, and an* Athlone *Hat*; and as to the others, I *shall not presume* to direct them. I have, indeed, seen the present Archbishop of *Dublin* clad from Head to Foot in our own Manufacture; and yet, under the Rose be it spoken, *his Grace deserves as good a Gown, as if he had not been born among us.*[11]

I HAVE not Courage enough to offer *one Syllable* on this Subject to *their Honours* of the Army: Neither have I sufficiently considered the great Importance of *Scarlet* and *Gold Lace*.

THE Fable in *Ovid*, of *Arachne* and *Pallas*, is to this Purpose.[12] The Goddess had heard of one *Arachne*, a young Virgin, very famous for *Spinning* and *Weaving:* They both met upon a Tryal of Skill; and *Pallas* finding herself almost equalled in her own Art, stung with Rage and Envy, knockt her *Rival* down, turned her into a *Spyder*, enjoining her to *spin* and *weave* for ever, *out of her own Bowels*, and *in a very narrow Compass*. I confess, that from a Boy, I always pitied poor *Arachne*, and could never heartily love the Goddess, on Account of so *cruel and unjust a Sentence*; which, however, is *fully executed* upon *Us* by *England*, with further Additions of *Rigor* and *Severity*. For the greatest Part of *our Bowels and Vitals* is extracted, without allowing us the Liberty of *spinning* and *weaving* them.

THE Scripture tells us, that *Oppression makes a wise Man mad*;[13] therefore, consequently speaking, the Reason why some Men are not *mad*, is because they are not *wise:* However, it were to be wished that *Oppression* would, in Time, teach a little *Wisdom* to *Fools*.

I WAS much delighted with a Person, who hath a great Estate in this Kingdom, upon his Complaints to me, *how grievously POOR* England *suffers by Impositions from* Ireland.[14] *That we convey our own Wool to* France, *in Spight of all the* Harpies *at the Custom-House. That Mr.* Shutleworth, *and others on the* Cheshire *Coasts, are such Fools to sell us their* Bark *at a good Price, for tanning* our own Hydes *into Leather*; *with other Enormities of the like Weight and Kind*. To which I will venture to add more: *That the* Mayoralty *of this City is always executed by an* Inhabitant, *and often by a* Native, *which might as well be done by a* Deputy, *with a moderate Salary, whereby POOR* England *loseth, at least, one thousand Pounds a Year upon the Ballance. That the Governing of this Kingdom cost the Lord Lieutenant three Thousand six Hundred Pounds a Year, so much* net Loss *to POOR* England. *That the People of* Ireland *presume to dig for Coals in their own Grounds; and the Farmers in the County of* Wicklow *send their Turf to the very Market of* Dublin, *to the great Discouragement of the Coal Trade at* Mostyn *and* White-haven.[15] *That the Revenues of the* Post-Office *here, so righteously belonging to the* English *Treasury, as arising chiefly from our own Commerce with each other, should be remitted to* London, *clogged with that grievous Burthen of Exchange, and the Pensions paid out of the* Irish *Revenues to* English *Favourites, should lie under the same Disadvantage, to the great Loss of the Grantees. When a* Divine *is sent over to a* Bishoprick *here, with the Hopes of Five and Twenty Hundred Pounds a Year, upon his Arrival, he finds, alas! a dreadful Discount of Ten or Twelve* per Cent. *A Judge, or a* Commissioner *of the Revenue, has the same Cause of Complaint.*[16] *Lastly, The Ballad upon* Cotter *is vehemently suspected to be* Irish *Manufacture; and yet is allowed to be sung in our open Streets, under the very* Nose *of the* Government.[17]

THESE are a *few* among the many Hardships we put upon that *POOR* Kingdom of *England*; for which, I am confident, every *honest* Man wisheth a *Remedy*: And, I hear, there is a Project *on Foot* for transporting our best Wheaten *Straw*, by Sea and Land Carriage, to *Dunstable*; and *obliging us by a Law*, to take off yearly so many *Tun of Straw-Hats*, for the Use of our Women; which will be a *great Encouragement* to the Manufacture of that industrious Town.

I WOULD be glad to learn among the Divines, whether a Law *to bind Men without their own Consent*, be obligatory *in foro Conscientiæ*; because, I find *Scripture, Sanderson* and *Suarez*, are wholly silent in the Matter.[18] The Oracle of *Reason*, the great *Law of Nature*, and general Opinion of *Civilians*, wherever they treat of *limited Governments*, are, indeed, decisive enough.

IT is wonderful to observe the Biass among our People in favour of *Things, Persons*, and *Wares* of all Kinds that come from *England*. The *Printer* tells his *Hawkers*, that *he has got an excellent new Song just brought from* London. I have somewhat of a Tendency that way my self; and upon hearing a *Coxcomb* from thence displaying himself, with great Volubility, upon the *Park*, the *Play-House*, the *Opera*, the *Gaming Ordinaries*, it was apt to beget in me a Kind of Veneration for his Parts and Accomplishments. It is not many Years, since I remember a *Person* who, by his Style and Literature, seems to have been *Corrector* of a Hedge-Press, in some *Blind-Alley* about *Little-Britain*, proceed *gradually* to be an *Author*, at least a *Translator* of a lower Rate, although somewhat of a larger Bulk than any that now *flourishes* in *Grub-street*; and, upon the Strength of this Foundation, come over *here*; *erect* himself up into an *Orator* and *Politician*, and lead a *Kingdom* after him.[19] This, I am told, was the *very Motive* that prevailed on the *Author* of a Play called, *Love in a Hollow-Tree*, to do us the *Honour* of a Visit; presuming, with very good Reason, *that he was a Writer of a superior Class*.[20] I know *another*, who, for thirty Years past, hath been the *common Standard of Stupidity in England*, where he was never heard a Minute in any *Assembly*, or by any *Party*, with *common Christian Treatment*; yet, upon his Arrival hither, could put on a *Face of Importance and Authority*, talked more than Six, without either *Gracefulness, Propriety*, or *Meaning*; and, at the same Time, be admired and followed as the Pattern of *Eloquence* and *Wisdom*.

NOTHING hath humbled me so much, or shewn a greater Disposition to a *contemptuous* Treatment of *Ireland* in some chief *Governors*, than that high Style of several Speeches from the *Throne*, delivered, as usual, after the *Royal Assent*, in *some Periods* of the two last *Reigns*. Such Exaggerations of the prodigious *Condescensions* in the Prince, to pass *those good Laws*, would have but an odd Sound at *Westminster*: Neither do I apprehend, how any *good Law* can pass, wherein the *King*'s Interest is not as much concerned as that of the *People*. I remember, after a Speech on the like Occasion, delivered by my L—d W——, (I think it was his last) he desired Mr. *Addison* to *ask my Opinion of it*: My Answer was, *That his Excellency had very honestly forfeited his Head, on Account of one Paragraph; wherein he asserted, by plain Consequence, a* dispensing Power *in the Queen*.[21] His Lordship owned *it was true*, but *swore* the Words were *put into his Mouth* by direct Orders from Court. From whence it is clear, that some *Ministers* in those Times, were apt, from their *high* Elevation, to look *down* upon this Kingdom, as if it had been one of their *Colonies* of

Out-casts in *America*.[22] And I observed a little of the same Turn of Spirit in *some great Men*, from whom I expected better; although, to do them Justice, it proved no Point of Difficulty to make them *correct their Idea*, whereof the *whole Nation* quickly found the Benefit. —— But that is *forgotten*. How the Style hath since run, I am wholly a Stranger; having never seen a Speech since the last of the Queen.

I WOULD now expostulate a little with our Country Landlords; who, by unmeasurable *screwing* and *racking* their Tenants all over the Kingdom, have already reduced the miserable *People* to a *worse Condition* than the *Peasants* in *France*, or the *Vassals* in *Germany* and *Poland*;[23] so that the whole *Species* of what we call *Substantial Farmers*, will, in a very few Years, be utterly at an End. It was pleasant to observe these Gentlemen, *labouring* with all their *Might*, for preventing the *Bishops* from letting their Revenues at a moderate half Value, (whereby the whole *Order* would, in an Age, have been reduced to manifest Beggary) at the very Instant, when they were every where *canting* their own Lands upon short Leases, and sacrificing their *oldest Tenants for a Penny an Acre advance*. I know not how it comes to pass, (and yet, perhaps, I know well enough) that *Slaves* have a natural Disposition to be *Tyrants*; and that when my *Betters* give me a Kick, I am apt to revenge it with six upon my *Footman*; although, perhaps, he may be an honest and diligent Fellow. I have heard *great* Divines affirm, that *nothing is so likely to call down an universal Judgment from Heaven upon a Nation, as universal Oppression*; and whether this be not already verified in Part, *their Worships* the Landlords are *now* at full Leisure to consider. Whoever travels this Country, and observes the *Face* of Nature, or the *Faces*, and Habits, and Dwellings of the *Natives*, will hardly think himself in a Land where either *Law, Religion*, or *common Humanity* is professed.

I CANNOT forbear saying one Word upon a *Thing* they call a *Bank*, which, I hear, is projecting in this Town.[24] I never saw the *Proposals*, nor understand any one Particular of their Scheme: What I wish for, at present, is only a sufficient Provision of *Hemp*, and *Caps*, and *Bells*,[25] to distribute according to the several Degrees of *Honesty* and *Prudence* in *some Persons*. I *hear* only of a monstrous Sum already named; and, if OTHERS do not soon hear of it too, and *hear* it with a *Vengeance*, then am I a Gentleman of less Sagacity than my self, and very few besides, take me to be. And the Jest will be still the better, if it be true, as judicious Persons have assured me, that one half of this Money will be *real*, and the other half only *Gasconnade*. The Matter will be likewise much mended, if the Merchants continue to carry off our Gold, and our Goldsmiths to melt down our heavy Silver.

A LETTER FROM DR. SWIFT TO MR. POPE

Dublin, Jan. 10, 1721

A Thousand things have vexed me of late years, upon which I am determined to lay open my mind to you. I rather chuse to appeal to you than to my Lord Chief Justice Whitshed, under the situation I am in. For, I take this cause properly to lie before you: You are a much fitter Judge of what concerns the credit of a Writer, the injuries that are done him, and the reparations he ought to receive. Besides, I doubt whether the Arguments I could suggest to prove my own innocence would be of much weight from the gentlemen of the Long-robe to those in Furs,[1] upon whose decision about the difference of Style or Sentiments, I should be very unwilling to leave the merits of my Cause.

Give me leave then to put you in mind, (although you cannot easily forget it) that about ten weeks before the Queen's death, I left the town, upon occasion of that incurable breach among the great men at Court, and went down to Berkshire, where you may remember that you gave me the favour of a visit.[2] While I was in that retirement, I writ a Discourse which I thought might be useful in such a juncture of affairs, and sent it up to London; but upon some difference in opinion between me and a certain great Minister now abroad, the publishing of it was deferred so long that the Queen died, and I recalled my copy, which hath been ever since in safe hands.[3] In a few weeks after the loss of that excellent Princess, I came to my station here; where I have continued ever since in the greatest privacy, and utter ignorance of those events which are most commonly talked of in the world; I neither know the names nor number of the Family which now reigns, further than the Prayer-book informs me. I cannot tell who is Chancellor, who are Secretaries, nor with what Nations we are in peace or war. And this manner of life was not taken up out of any sort of Affectation, but meerly to avoid giving offence, and for fear of provoking Party-zeal.

I had indeed written some Memorials of the four last years

of the Queen's reign, with some other informations, which I received, as necessary materials to qualify me for doing something in an employment then designed me: But, as it was at the disposal of a person, who had not the smallest share of steddiness or sincerity, I disdained to accept it.[4]

These papers, at my few hours of health and leisure, I have been digesting into order by one sheet at a time, for I dare not venture any further, lest the humour of searching and seizing papers should revive; not that I am in pain of any danger to my self, (for they contain nothing of present times or persons, upon which I shall never lose a thought while there is a Cat or a Spaniel in the house) but to preserve them from being lost among Messengers and Clerks.

I have written in this kingdom, a discourse to persuade the wretched people to wear their own Manufactures instead of those from England:[5] This Treatise soon spread very fast, being agreeable to the sentiments of the whole nation, except of those gentlemen who had employments, or were Expectants. Upon which a person in great office here immediately took the alarm; he sent in haste for the Chief Justice, and informed him of a seditious, factious, and virulent Pamphlet, lately published with a design of setting the two kingdoms at variance, directing at the same time that the Printer should be prosecuted with the utmost rigour of law.[6] The Chief Justice had so quick an understanding, that he resolved, if possible, to out-do his orders. The Grand-Juries of the county and city were practised effectually with to represent the said Pamphlet with all aggravating Epithets, for which they had thanks sent them from England, and their Presentments published for several weeks in all the news-papers. The Printer was seized, and forced to give great bail: After his tryal the Jury brought him in Not Guilty, although they had been culled with the utmost industry; the Chief Justice sent them back nine times, and kept them eleven hours, until being perfectly tired out, they were forced to leave the matter to the mercy of the Judge, by what they call a special Verdict. During the tryal, the Chief Justice among other singularities, laid his hand on his breast, and protested solemnly that the Author's design was to bring in the Pretender; although there was not a single syllable of Party in the whole Treatise, and although it was known that the most eminent of those who professed his own principles, publickly disallowed his proceedings. But the cause being so very odious and impopular, the tryal of the Verdict was deferred from one Term to another, until upon the Duke of G—ft—n the Lord Lieutenant's arrival, his Grace after mature advice, and permission from England, was pleased to grant a *noli prosequi*.[7]

This is the more remarkable, because it is said that the man is no ill decider in common cases of property, where Party is out of the question; but when that intervenes, with ambition at heels to push it forward, it must needs confound any man of little spirit, and low birth, who hath no other endowment than that sort of Knowledge, which, however possessed in the highest degree, can possibly give no one good quality to the mind.

It is true, I have been much concerned for several years past, upon account of the publick as well as of myself, to see how ill a taste for wit and sense prevails in the world, which politicks and South-sea, and Party, and Opera's and Masquerades have introduced.[8] For, besides many insipid papers which the malice of some hath entitled me to, there are many persons appearing to wish me well, and pretending to be judges of my style and manner, who have yet ascribed some writings to me, of which any man of common sense and literature would be heartily ashamed. I cannot forbear instancing a Treatise called a Dedication upon Dedications, which many would have to be mine, although it be as empty, dry, and servile a composition, as I remember at any time to have read.[9] But above all, there is one Circumstance which maketh it impossible for me to have been Author of a Treatise, wherein there are several pages containing a Panegyrick on King George, of whose character and person I am utterly ignorant, nor ever had once the curiosity to enquire into either, living at so great a distance as I do, and having long done with whatever can relate to publick matters.

Indeed I have formerly delivered my thoughts very freely, whether I were asked or no, but never affected to be a Councellor, to which I had no manner of call. I was humbled enough to see my self so far out-done by the Earl of Oxford in my own trade as a Scholar, and too good a Courtier not to discover his contempt of those who would be men of importance out of their sphere. Besides, to say the truth, although I have known many great Ministers ready enough to hear Opinions, yet I have hardly seen one that would ever descend to take Advice; and this pedantry ariseth from a maxim themselves do not believe at the same time they practise by it, that there is something profound in politicks, which men of plain honest sense cannot arrive to.

I only wish my endeavours had succeeded better in the great point I had at heart, which was that of reconciling the Ministers to each other. This might have been done, if others who had more concern and more influence would have acted their parts; and, if this had succeeded, the publick interest both of Church and State would not have been the worse, nor the Protestant Succession endangered.

But, whatever opportunities a constant attendance of four years might have given me for endeavouring to do good offices to particular persons, I deserve at least to find tolerable quarter from those of the other Party; for many of which I was a constant advocate with the Earl of Oxford, and for this I appeal to his Lordship: He knows how often I pressed him in favour of Mr. Addison, Mr. Congreve, Mr. Row, and Mr. Steel, although I freely confess that his Lordship's kindness to them was altogether owing to his generous notions, and the esteem he had for their wit and parts, of which I could only pretend to be a remembrancer.[10] For, I can never forget the answer he gave to the late Lord Hallifax, who upon the first change of the Ministry interceded with him to spare Mr. Congreve: It was by repeating these two lines of Virgil,

> *Non obtusa adeo gestamus pectora Pæni,*
> *Nec tam aversus equos Tyria Sol jungit ab urbe.*[11]

Pursuant to which, he always treated Mr. Congreve with the greatest personal civilities, assured him of his constant favour and protection, adding that he would study to do something better for him.

I remember it was in those times a usual subject of raillery towards me among the Ministers, that I never came to them without a Whig in my sleeve; which I do not say with any view towards making my Court: For, the new Principles fixed to those of that denomination, I did then, and do now from my heart abhor, detest and abjure, as wholly degenerate from their predecessors. I have conversed in some freedom with more Ministers of State of all Parties than usually happens to men of my level, and I confess, in their capacity as Ministers, I look upon them as a race of people whose acquaintance no man would court, otherwise than upon the score of Vanity or Ambition. The first quickly wears off (and is the Vice of low minds, for a man of spirit is too proud to be vain) and the other was not my case. Besides, having never received more than one small favour, I was under no necessity of being a slave to men in power, but chose my friends by their personal merit, without examining how far their notions agreed with the politicks then in vogue. I frequently conversed with Mr. Addison, and the others I named (except Mr. Steel) during all my Lord Oxford's Ministry, and Mr. Addison's friendship to me continued inviolable, with as much kindness as when we used to meet at my Lord Sommers or Hallifax, who were leaders of the opposite Party.

I would infer from all this, that it is with great injustice I have these many years been pelted by your Pamphleteers, merely upon account of some regard which the Queen's last Ministers were pleased to have for me: and yet in my conscience I think I am a partaker in every ill design they had against the Protestant Succession, or the Liberties and Religion of their Country; and can say with Cicero, that I should be proud to be included with them in all their actions *tanquam in equo Trojano.*[12] But, if I have never discovered by my words, writings, or actions, any Party virulence, or dangerous designs against the present powers; if my friendship and conversation were equally shewn among those who liked or disapproved the proceedings then at Court, and that I was known to be a common Friend of all deserving persons of the latter sort, when they were in distress; I cannot but think it hard that I am not suffered to run quietly among the common herd of people, whose opinions unfortunately differ from those which lead to Favour and Preferment.

I ought to let you know, that the Thing we called a Whig in England is a creature altogether different from those of the same denomination here; at least it was so during the reign of Her late Majesty. Whether those on your side have changed or no, it hath not been my business to enquire. I remember my excellent friend Mr. Addison, when he first came over hither Secretary to the Earl of Wharton then Lord Lieutenant, was extremely offended at the conduct and discourse of the Chief Managers here: He told me they were a sort of people who seemed to think, that the principles of a Whig consisted in nothing else but damning the Church, reviling the Clergy, abetting the Dissenters, and speaking contemptibly of revealed Religion.

I was discoursing some years ago with a certain Minister about that whiggish or fanatical Genius so prevalent among the English of this kingdom: his Lordship accounted for it by that number of Cromwell's Soldiers, adventurers established here, who were all of the sourest Leven, and the meanest birth, and whose posterity are now in possession of their lands and their principles.[13] However, it must be confessed, that of late some people in this country are grown weary of quarrelling, because interest, the great motive of quarrelling is at an end; for, it is hardly worth contending who shall be an Excise-man, a Country-Vicar, a Cryer in the Courts, or an Under-Clerk.

You will perhaps be inclined to think, that a person so ill treated as I have been, must at some time or other have discovered very dangerous opinions in government; in answer to which, I will tell you what my Political principles were in the time of her late glorious Majesty, which I never contradicted by any action, writing or discourse.

First, I always declared my self against a Popish Successor to the Crown, whatever Title he might have by the proximity of blood: Neither did I ever regard the right line except upon two accounts; first, as it was established by law; and secondly, as it hath much weight in the opinions of the people. For necessity may abolish any Law, but cannot alter the sentiments of the vulgar; Right of inheritance being perhaps the most popular of all topicks; and therefore in great Changes when that is broke, there will remain much heart-burning and discontent among the meaner people; which (under a weak Prince and corrupt Administration) may have the worst consequences upon the peace of any state.

As to what is called a Revolution-principle, my opinion was this; That, whenever those evils which usually attend and follow a violent change of government, were not in probability so pernicious as the grievances we suffer under a present power, then the publick good will justify such a Revolution; and this I took to have been the Case in the Prince of Orange's expedition, although in the consequences it produced some very bad effects, which are likely to stick long enough by us.[14]

I had likewise in those days a mortal antipathy against Standing Armies in times of Peace. Because I always took Standing Armies to be only servants hired by the master of the family, for keeping his own children in slavery: And because, I conceived, that a Prince who could not think himself secure without Mercenary Troops, must needs have a separate interest from that of his subjects. Although I am not ignorant of those artificial Necessities which a corrupted Ministry can create, for keeping up forces to support a Faction against the publick Interest.[15]

As to Parliaments, I adored the wisdom of that Gothic Institution, which made them Annual: and I was confident our Liberty could never be placed upon a firm foundation until that ancient law were restored among us. For, who sees not, that while such assemblies are permitted to have a longer duration, there grows up a commerce of corruption between the Ministry and the Deputies, wherein they both find their accounts to the manifest danger of Liberty, which traffick would neither answer the design nor expence, if Parliaments met once a year.[16]

I ever abominated that scheme of politicks, (now about thirty years old) of setting up a monied Interest in opposition to the landed. For, I conceived, there could not be a truer maxim in our government than this, That the possessors of the soil are

the best judges of what is for the advantage of the kingdom:[17]
If others had thought the same way, Funds of Credit and
South-sea Projects would neither have been felt nor heard of.

I could never discover the necessity of suspending any Law
upon which the Liberty of the most innocent persons depended:
neither do I think this practice hath made the taste of arbitrary
power so agreeable as that we should desire to see it repeated.[18]
Every Rebellion subdued and Plot discovered, contributes to
the firmer establishment of the Prince. In the latter case, the
knot of Conspirators is entirely broke, and they are to begin
their work anew under a thousand disadvantages; so that those
diligent enquiries into remote and problematical guilt, with a
new power of enforcing them by chains and dungeons to every
person whose face a Minister thinks fit to dislike, are not only
opposite to that maxim, which declareth it better that ten guilty
men should escape, than one innocent suffer, but likewise leave
a gate wide open to the whole Tribe of Informers, the most
accursed, and prostitute, and abandoned race, that God ever
permitted to plague mankind.[19]

It is true the Romans had a custom of chusing a Dictator,
during whose administration, the Power of other Magistrates
was suspended; but this was done upon the greatest emergen-
cies; a War near their doors, or some civil Dissention: For
Armies must be governed by arbitrary power: But when the
Virtue of that Commonwealth gave place to luxury and
ambition, this very office of Dictator became perpetual in the
persons of the Cæsars and their Successors, the most infamous
tyrants that have any where appeared in story.

These are some of the sentiments I had relating to publick
affairs while I was in the world; what they are at present, is of
little importance either to that or my self; neither can I truly
say I have any at all, or if I had, I dare not venture to publish
them: For however orthodox they may be while I am now
writing, they may become criminal enough to bring me into
trouble before midsummer. And indeed I have often wished for
some time past, that a political Catechism might be published
by authority four times a year, in order to instruct us how we
are to speak and write, and act during the current quarter.

I have by experience felt the want of such an instructer: For intending to make my court to some people on the prevailing side, by advancing certain old whiggish principles, which it seems had been exploded about a month before, I have passed for a disaffected person. I am not ignorant how idle a thing it is for a man in obscurity to attempt defending his reputation as a Writer, while the spirit of Faction hath so universally possessed the minds of men, that they are not at leisure to attend to any thing else. They will just give themselves time to libel and accuse me, but cannot spare a minute to hear my defence. So in a plot-discovering age, I have often known an innocent man seized and imprisoned, and forced to lie several months in chains, while the Ministers were not at leisure to hear his petition, until they had prosecuted and hanged the number they proposed.

All I can reasonably hope for by this letter, is to convince my friends and others who are pleased to wish me well, that I have neither been so ill a Subject nor so stupid an Author, as I have been represented by the virulence of Libellers, whose malice hath taken the same train in both, by fathering dangerous principles in government upon me, which I never maintained, and insipid productions which I am not capable of writing. For, however I may have been sowered by personal ill treatment, or by melancholy prospects for the publick, I am too much a politician to expose my own safety by offensive words: and, if my genius and spirit be sunk by encreasing years, I have at least enough discretion left, not to mistake the measure of my own abilities, by attempting subjects where those talents are necessary, which perhaps I may have lost with my youth.

SWIFT TO ESTHER VANHOMRIGH

Gallstoun near Kinnegad. July. 5th. 1721

It was not convenient, hardly possible to write to you before now, though I had a more than ordinary desire to do it, considering the Disposition I found you in last, though I hope I left you in a better.[1] I must here beg you to take more Care of your Health, by Company and Exercise, or else the Spleen will get the better of you, than which there is not a more foolish or troublesome Disease; and what you have no Pretence in the World to, if all the Advantages of Life can be any Defence against it. Cad— assures me he continues to esteem and love and value you above all things, and so will do to the End of his Life; but at the same time entreats that you would not make your self or him unhappy by Imaginations.[2] The Wisest men of all Ages have thought it the best Course to Seize the Minutes as they fly, and to make every innocent action an Amusement. If you knew how I Struggle for a little Health, what uneasyness I am at in riding and walking, and refraining from every thing agreeable to my Tast, you would think it but a small thing to take a Coach now and then, and to converse with Fools or impertinents to avoid Spleen and Sickness—Without Health you will lose all desire of drinking your Coffee, and [be] *so low* as to have no Spirits—I answer all your Questions that you were used [to] ask Cad— and he protests he answers them in the Affirmative—How go your Law Affairs?[3] You were once a good Lawyer, but Cad— hath spoiled you—I had a weary Journy in an Irish Stage-Coach,[4] but am pretty well since—Pray write to me chearfully without Complaints or Expostulations or else Cad— shall know it and punish you—What is this world without being as easy in it as Prudence and Fortune can make it—I find it every day more silly and insignificant, and I conform my self to it for my own Ease; I am here as deep employd in othr Folks Plantations and Ditchings as if they were my own Concern[5] and think of my absent Friends with delight, and hopes of seeing them happy, and of being happy with them. Shall you who have so much Honor and good Sense act

otherwise to make Cad— and your self miserable?—Settle your
Affairs, and quit this scoundrel Island, and things will be as
you desire—I can say no more being called away, mais soyez
assureè que jamais personne du monde a etè aimèe honorèe
estimeè adoreè par votre amie que vous.[6] I drank no Coffee
since I left you nor intend till I see you again; there is none
worth drinking but yours, if my *self* may be the judge[7]—adieu

THE LAST SPEECH AND DYING WORDS OF
EBENEZOR ELLISTON

who was Executed the Second Day of May, 1722

Published at his Desire, for the Common Good

I AM now going to suffer the just Punishment for my Crimes prescribed by the Law of God and my Country. I know it is the constant Custom, that those who come to this Place should have Speeches made for them, and cryed about in their own Hearing, as they are carried to Execution; and truly they are such Speeches that although our Fraternity be an ignorant illiterate People, they would make a Man ashamed to have such Nonsense and false *English* charged upon him even when he is going to the Gallows: They contain a pretended Account of our Birth and Family; of the Fact for which we are to die; of our sincere Repentance; and a Declaration of our Religion. I cannot expect to avoid the same Treatment with my Predecessors. However, having had an Education one or two Degrees better than those of my Rank and Profession; I have been considering ever since my Commitment, what it might be proper for me to deliver upon this Occasion.

AND First, I cannot say from the Bottom of my Heart, that I am truly sorry for the Offence I have given to God and the World; but I am very much so, for the bad Success of my Villanies in bringing me to this untimely End. For it is plainly evident, that after having some time ago obtained a Pardon from the Crown, I again took up my old Trade; my evil Habits were so rooted in me, and I was grown so unfit for any other kind of Employment. And therefore although in Compliance with my Friends, I resolve to go to the Gallows after the usual Manner, Kneeling, with a Book in my Hand, and my Eyes lift up; yet I shall feel no more Devotion in my Heart than I have observed in some of my Comrades, who have been drunk among common Whores the very Night before their Execution. I can say further from my own Knowledge, that two of my

Fraternity after they had been hanged, and wonderfully came to Life, and made their Escapes, as it sometimes happens; proved afterwards the wickedest Rogues I ever knew, and so continued until they were hanged again for good and all; and yet they had the Impudence at both Times they went to the Gallows, to smite their Breasts, and lift up their Eyes to Heaven all the Way.[1]

SECONDLY, From the Knowledge I have of my own wicked Dispositions and that of my Comrades, I give it as my Opinion, that nothing can be more unfortunate to the Publick, than the Mercy of the Government in ever pardoning or transporting us; unless when we betray one another, as we never fail to do, if we are sure to be well paid;[2] and then a Pardon may do good; by the same Rule, *That it is better to have but one Fox in a Farm than three or four*. But we generally make a Shift to return after being transported, and are ten times greater Rogues than before, and much more cunning. Besides, I know it by Experience, that some Hopes we have of finding Mercy, when we are tryed, or after we are condemned, is always a great Encouragement to us.

THIRDLY, Nothing is more dangerous to idle young Fellows, than the Company of those odious common Whores we frequent, and of which this Town is full: These Wretches put us upon all Mischief to feed their Lusts and Extravagancies: They are ten times more bloody and cruel than Men; their Advice is always not to spare if we are pursued; they get drunk with us, and are common to us all; and yet, if they can get any Thing by it, are sure to be our Betrayers.

NOW, as I am a dying Man, something I have done which may be of good Use to the Publick. I have left with an honest Man (and indeed the only honest Man I was ever acquainted with) the Names of all my wicked Brethren, the present Places of their Abode, with a short Account of the chief Crimes they have committed; in many of which I have been their Accomplice, and heard the rest from their own Mouths: I have likewise set down the Names of those we call our Setters, of the wicked Houses we frequent, and of those who receive and buy our stolen Goods. I have solemnly charged this honest Man, and have received his Promise upon Oath, that whenever he hears of any Rogue to be tryed for robbing, or House-breaking, he will look into his List, and if he finds the Name there of the Thief concerned, to send the whole Paper to the Government. Of this I here give my Companions fair and publick Warning, and hope they will take it.

IN the Paper abovementioned, which I left with my Friend, I have also set down the Names of several Gentlemen who have been robbed in *Dublin* Streets for three Years past: I have told the Circumstances of those Robberies; and shewn plainly that nothing but the Want of common Courage was the Cause of their Misfortunes. I have therefore desired my Friend, that whenever any Gentlemen happens to be robbed in the Streets, he will get that Relation printed and published with the first Letters of those Gentlemens Names, who by their own Want of Bravery are likely to be the Cause of all the Mischief of that Kind, which may happen for the future.

I CANNOT leave the World without a short Description of that Kind of Life, which I have led for some Years past; and is exactly the same with the rest of our wicked Brethren.

ALTHOUGH we are generally so corrupted from our Childhood, as to have no Sense of Goodness; yet something heavy always hangs about us, I know not what it is, that we are never easy till we are half drunk among our Whores and Companions; nor sleep sound, unless we drink longer than we can stand. If we go abroad in the Day, a wise Man would easily find us to be Rogues by our Faces; we have such a suspicious, fearful, and constrained Countenance; often turning back, and slinking through narrow Lanes and Allies. I have never failed of knowing a Brother Thief by his Looks, though I never saw him before. Every Man among us keeps his particular Whore, who is however common to us all, when we have a mind to change. When we have got a Booty, if it be in Money, we divide it equally among our Companions, and soon squander it away on our Vices in those Houses that receive us; for the Master and Mistress, and the very Tapster, go Snacks;[3] and besides make us pay treble Reckonings. If our Plunder be Plate, Watches, Rings, Snuff-Boxes, and the like; we have Customers in all Quarters of the Town to take them off. I have seen a Tankard worth

Fifteen Pounds sold to a Fellow in —— — Street for Twenty Shillings; and a Gold Watch for Thirty. I have set down his Name, and that of several others in the Paper already mentioned. We have Setters watching in Corners, and by dead Walls, to give us Notice when a Gentleman goes by; especially if he be any thing in Drink. I believe in my Conscience, that if an Account were made of a Thousand Pounds in stolen Goods; considering the low Rates we sell them at, the Bribes we must give for Concealment, the Extortions of Ale-house Reckonings, and other necessary Charges, there would not remain Fifty Pounds clear to be divided among the Robbers. And out of this we must find Cloaths for our Whores, besides treating them from Morning to Night; who, in Requital, reward us with nothing but Treachery and the Pox. For when our Money is gone, they are every Moment threatning to inform against us, if we will not go out to look for more. If any Thing in this World be like Hell, as I have heard it described by our Clergy; the truest Picture of it must be in the Back-Room of one of our Ale-houses at Midnight; where a Crew of Robbers and their Whores are met together after a Booty, and are beginning to grow drunk; from which Time, until they are past their Senses, is such a continued horrible Noise of Cursing, Blasphemy, Lewdness, Scurrility, and brutish Behaviour; such Roaring and Confusion, such a Clatter of Mugs and Pots at each other's Heads; that *Bedlam*, in Comparison, is a sober and orderly Place: At last they all tumble from their Stools and Benches, and sleep away the rest of the Night; and generally the Landlord or his Wife, or some other Whore who has a stronger Head than the rest, picks their Pockets before they wake. The Misfortune is, that we can never be easy till we are drunk; and our Drunkenness constantly exposes us to be more easily betrayed and taken.

THIS is a short Picture of the Life I have led; which is more miserable than that of the poorest Labourer who works for four Pence a Day; and yet Custom is so strong, that I am confident, if I could make my Escape at the Foot of the Gallows, I should be following the same Course this very Evening. So that upon the whole, we ought to be looked upon as the common Enemies of Mankind; whose Interest it is to root us out like Wolves, and other mischievous Vermin, against which no fair Play is required.

IF I have done Service to Men in what I have said, I shall hope I have done Service to God; and that will be better than a silly Speech made for me full of Whining and Canting, which I utterly despise, and have never been used to; yet such a one I expect to have my Ears tormented with, as I am passing along the Streets.

GOOD People fare ye well; bad as I am, I leave many worse behind me. I hope you shall see me die like a Man, the Death of a Dog.

E.E.

Exegi Monumentum Ære perennius. Hor

Plate 3. Portrait of Swift as the Drapier from
volume 4 of the Faulkner edition (1735)

THE DRAPIER'S LETTERS

LETTER I. TO THE SHOP-KEEPERS, TRADESMEN, FARMERS, AND COMMON-PEOPLE OF IRELAND

Brethren, Friends, Countrymen, and *Fellow-Subjects*

WHAT I intend now to say to you, is, next to your Duty to God, and the Care of your Salvation, of the greatest Concern to your selves, and your Children; your *Bread* and *Cloathing*, and every common Necessary of Life entirely depend upon it. Therefore I do most earnestly exhort you as *Men*, as *Christians*, as *Parents*, and as *Lovers of your Country*, to read this Paper with the utmost Attention, or get it read to you by others; which that you may do at the less Expence, I have ordered the Printer to sell it at the lowest Rate.[1]

IT is a great Fault among you, that when a Person writes with no other Intention than *to do you Good, you will not be at the Pains to read his Advices:* One Copy of this Paper may serve a Dozen of you, which will be less than a Farthing a-piece. It is your Folly, that you have no common or general Interest in your View, not even the Wisest among you; neither do you know or enquire, or care who are your Friends, or who are your Enemies.

ABOUT four Years ago, a little Book was written to advise all People to wear the *Manufactures of this our own Dear Country:* It had no other Design, said nothing against the *King* or *Parliament*, or *any* Person whatsoever, yet the POOR PRINTER was prosecuted two Years, with the utmost Violence; and even some WEAVERS themselves, for whose Sake it was written, being upon the JURY, FOUND HIM GUILTY.[2] This would be enough to discourage any Man from endeavouring to do you Good, when you will either neglect him, or fly in his Face for his Pains; and when he must expect only *Danger to himself*, and to be fined and imprisoned, perhaps to his Ruin.

HOWEVER, I cannot but warn you once more of the manifest Destruction before your Eyes, if you do not behave yourselves as you ought.

I WILL therefore first tell you the *plain Story of the Fact*; and then I will lay before you, how you ought to act in common Prudence, and according to the *Laws of your Country*.

THE *Fact is thus*; It having been many Years since COPPER HALF-PENCE or FARTHINGS were last Coined in this *Kingdom*, they have been for some Time very scarce, and many *Counterfeits* passed about under the Name of RAPS: Several Applications were made to *England*, that we might have Liberty to *Coin New Ones*, as in former Times we did; but they did not succeed.[3] At last one Mr. WOOD, *a mean ordinary Man, a Hard-Ware Dealer*, procured a *Patent* under His MAJESTY'S BROAD SEAL, to coin 108000 *l.* in *Copper* for this *Kingdom*; which Patent however did not oblige any one here to take them, unless they pleased.[4] Now you must know, that the HALF-PENCE and FARTHINGS in *England* pass for very little more than they are worth: And if you should beat them to Pieces, and sell them to the *Brazier*, you would not lose much above a Penny in a Shilling. But Mr. WOOD made his HALF-PENCE of such *Base Metal*, and so much smaller than the *English* ones, that the *Brazier* would hardly give you above a *Penny* of good Money for a *Shilling* of his; so that this Sum of 108000 *l.* in good Gold and Silver, must be given for TRASH that will not be worth above *Eight* or *Nine Thousand Pounds* real Value.[5] But this is not the Worst; for Mr. WOOD, when he pleases, may by Stealth send over *another* 108000 *l.* and buy *all our Goods for Eleven Parts in Twelve*, under the Value. For Example, if a *Hatter* sells a Dozen of *Hats* for *Five Shillings* a-piece, which amounts to *Three Pounds*, and receives the Payment in Mr. WOOD's Coin, he really receives only the Value of *Five Shillings*.

PERHAPS you will wonder how such *an ordinary Fellow* as this Mr. WOOD could have so much Interest as to get His MAJESTY's Broad Seal for so great a Sum of bad Money, to be sent to this poor Country; and that all the *Nobility* and *Gentry* here could not obtain the same Favour, and let us make our own HALF-PENCE, as we used to do. Now I will make that Matter very plain. We are at a great Distance from the *King's Court*, and have no body there to solicit for us, although a great Number of *Lords* and *Squires*, whose Estates are here, and are our Countrymen, spend all their *Lives* and *Fortunes* there. But this same Mr. WOOD was able to attend constantly for his own Interest; he is an ENGLISHMAN and had GREAT FRIENDS, and it seems knew very well *where to give Money*, to those that would speak to OTHERS that could speak to the KING, and would tell a FAIR STORY.[6] And HIS MAJESTY, and perhaps the great Lord or Lords who advised him, might think it was for our *Country's Good*; and so, as the Lawyers express it, the KING was deceived in his Grant; which often happens in *all Reigns*.[7] And I am sure if His MAJESTY knew that such a Patent, if it should take Effect according to the Desire of Mr. WOOD, would utterly ruin this Kingdom, which hath given such great Proofs of its *Loyalty*; he would immediately recall it, and perhaps shew his Displeasure to SOME BODY OR OTHER: *But a Word to the Wise is enough*. Most of you must have heard with what Anger our *Honourable House of Commons* received an Account of this WOOD'S PATENT. There were several *Fine Speeches* made upon it, and plain Proofs, that it was all a WICKED CHEAT from the *Bottom to the Top*; and several *smart Votes* were printed, which that same WOOD had the Assurance to answer likewise in *Print*, and in so confident a Way, as if he were *a better Man than our whole Parliament* put together.[8]

THIS WOOD, as soon as his *Patent* was passed, or soon after, sends over a great many *Barrels of those* HALF-PENCE, to *Cork* and other *Sea Port Towns*, and to get them off, offered an *Hundred Pounds* in his *Coin* for *Seventy* or *Eighty* in *Silver*: But the *Collectors* of the KING'S Customs very honestly refused to take them, and so did almost every body else. And since the Parliament hath condemned them, and desired the KING that they might be stopped, all the *Kingdom* do abominate them.

BUT WOOD is still working *under hand* to force his HALF-PENCE upon us; and if he can by help of his *Friends* in *England* prevail so far as to get an Order that the *Commissioners* and *Collectors* of the *King*'s Money shall receive them, and that the

Army is to be paid with them, then he thinks *his Work shall be done*. And this is the Difficulty you will be under in such a *Case:* For the common Soldier when he goes to the *Market* or *Ale-house*, will offer this Money, and if it be refused, perhaps he will *swagger* and *hector*, and *threaten* to *beat* the *Butcher* or *Ale-wife*, or take the Goods by Force, and throw them the bad HALF-PENCE. In this and the like Cases, the *Shop-keeper*, or *Victualler*, or *any other Tradesman* has no more to do, than to demand ten times the Price of his Goods, if it is to be paid in WOOD's Money; for Example, Twenty Pence of that Money for a *Quart of Ale*, and so in all things else, and not part with his Goods till he gets the *Money*.

FOR suppose you go to an *Ale-house* with that base Money, and the *Landlord* gives you a Quart for Four of these HALF-PENCE, what must the *Victualler* do? His *Brewer* will not be paid in that Coin, or if the *Brewer* should be such a Fool, the *Farmers* will not take it from them for their *Bere*,[9] because they are bound by their Leases to pay their Rents in Good and Lawful Money of *England*, which this is not, nor of *Ireland* neither, and the *Squire their Landlord* will never be so bewitched to take such *Trash* for his Land; so that it must certainly stop somewhere or other, and wherever it stops it is the same Thing, and we are all undone.

THE common Weight of these HALF-PENCE is between four and five to an *Ounce*; suppose five, then three Shillings and four Pence will weigh a Pound, and consequently *Twenty Shillings* will weigh *Six Pounds Butter Weight*. Now there are many hundred *Farmers* who pay Two hundred Pounds a Year Rent: Therefore when one of these *Farmers* comes with his Half-Year's Rent, which is One hundred Pound, it will be at least Six hundred Pound weight, which is Three Horses Load.

IF a *Squire* has a mind to come to Town to buy Cloaths and Wine and Spices for himself and Family, or perhaps to pass the Winter here, he must bring with him five or six Horses loaden with *Sacks* as the *Farmers* bring their Corn; and when his Lady comes in her Coach to our Shops, it must be followed by a Car loaded with Mr. WOOD's Money. And I hope we shall have the Grace to take it for no more than it is worth.

THEY say SQUIRE CONOLLY has *Sixteen Thousand Pounds a Year*; now if he sends for his *Rent* to Town, *as it is likely he does*, he must have *Two Hundred and Fifty Horses* to bring up his *Half Year's Rent*, and two or three great *Cellars* in his House for Stowage.[10] But what the Bankers will do I cannot tell. For I am assured, that some great Bankers keep by them *Forty Thousand Pounds* in ready Cash to answer all Payments, which Sum in Mr. WOOD's Money, would require Twelve Hundred Horses to carry it.

FOR my own Part, I am already resolved what to do; I have a pretty good Shop of *Irish Stuffs* and *Silks*, and instead of taking Mr. WOOD's bad Copper, I intend to Truck with my Neighbours the *Butchers*, and *Bakers*, and *Brewers*, and the rest, *Goods for Goods*, and the little *Gold* and *Silver* I have, I will keep by me like my *Heart's Blood* till better Times, or until I am just ready to starve, and then I will buy Mr. WOOD's Money, as my Father did the Brass Money in King *James's* Time;[11] who could buy *Ten Pound* of it with a *Guinea*, and I hope to get as much for a *Pistole*, and so purchase *Bread* from those who will be such Fools as to sell it me.

THESE *Half-pence*, if they once pass, will soon be *Counterfeit*, because it may be cheaply done, the *Stuff* is so *Base*. The *Dutch* likewise will probably do the same thing, and send them over to us to pay for our *Goods*; and Mr. WOOD will never be at rest, but coin on: So that in some Years we shall have at least five Times 108000 *l.* of this *Lumber*. Now the current Money of this Kingdom is not reckoned to be above Four Hundred Thousand Pounds in all; and while there is a *Silver* Six-Pence left, these *Blood suckers* will never be quiet.

WHEN once the *Kingdom* is reduced to such a Condition, I will tell you what must be the End: The *Gentlemen of Estates* will all turn off their *Tenants* for want of Payment; because, as I told you before, the *Tenants* are obliged by their Leases to pay *Sterling*, which is Lawful Current Money of *England*; then they will turn their own *Farmers, as too many of them do already*, run *all* into *Sheep* where they can, keeping only such other *Cattle* as are necessary;[12] then they will be their own *Merchants*, and send their *Wool*, and *Butter*, and *Hides*, and

Linnen beyond Sea for ready *Money*, and *Wine*, and *Spices*, and *Silks*. They will keep only a few miserable *Cottagers*. The *Farmers* must *Rob* or *Beg*, or leave their *Country*. The *Shop-keepers* in this and every other Town, must *Break* and *Starve*: For it is the *Landed-man* that maintains the *Merchant*, and *Shop-keeper*, and *Handicrafts-Man*.

BUT when the *Squire* turns *Farmer* and *Merchant* himself, all the good Money he gets from abroad, he will hoard up to send for *England*, and keep some poor *Taylor* or *Weaver*, and the like, in his own House, who will be glad to get Bread at any Rate.

I SHOULD never have done, if I were to tell you all the Miseries that we shall undergo, if we be so *Foolish* and *Wicked* as to take this *Cursed Coin*. It would be very hard, if all *Ireland* should be put into *One Scale*, and *this sorry Fellow* WOOD *into the other*: That Mr. WOOD should weigh down *this whole Kingdom*, by which *England* gets above a Million of good Money every Year clear into their *Pockets*: And that is more than the *English* do by *all the World besides*.

BUT your *great Comfort is*, that, as his Majesty's *Patent* doth not oblige you to take this *Money*, so the *Laws* have not given the *Crown* a Power of forcing the *Subjects* to take what *Money* the *King* pleases: For then by the same Reason we might be bound to take *Pebble-stones*, or *Cockle-shells*, or *stamped Leather* for *Current Coin*;[13] if ever we should happen to live under an ill *Prince*; who might likewise by the same Power make a *Guinea* pass for Ten Pounds, a *Shilling* for Twenty Shillings, and so on; by which he would in a short Time get all the *Silver* and *Gold* of the *Kingdom* into his own Hands, and leave us nothing but *Brass* or *Leather*, or what he pleased. Neither is any thing reckoned more *Cruel* or *Oppressive* in the *French Government*, than their common Practice of calling in all their Money after they have sunk it very low, and then coining it a-new at a much higher Value; which however is not the Thousandth Part so wicked as this *abominable Project* of Mr. *Wood*. For the *French* give their Subjects *Silver* for *Silver*, and *Gold* for *Gold*; but this *Fellow* will not so much as give us good *Brass* or *Copper* for our *Gold* and *Silver*, nor even a Twelfth Part of their Worth.

HAVING said this much, I will now go on to tell you the Judgments of some great *Lawyers* in this Matter; whom I fee'd on purpose for your Sakes, and got their *Opinions* under their *Hands*, that I might be sure I went upon good Grounds.

A Famous Law-Book *called the* Mirrour of Justice,[14] *discoursing of the Charters (or Laws) ordained by our* Ancient Kings, *declares the* Law *to be as follows: It was ordained that no* King *of this Realm should* Change, *or* Impair *the* Money, *or make any other* Money *than of* Gold *or* Silver *without the Assent of all the Counties, that is*, as my Lord *Coke* says, *without the Assent of* Parliament.[15]

THIS Book is very Ancient, and of great Authority for the Time in which it was wrote, and with that Character is often quoted by that great Lawyer my Lord *Coke*. By the Laws of *England*, several Metals are divided into *Lawful* or *true Metal* and *unlawful* or *false Metal*; the Former comprehends *Silver* or *Gold*, the Latter all *Baser Metals:* That the Former is only to pass in Payments, appears by an Act of *Parliament* made the Twentieth Year of *Edward* the First, called the *Statute concerning the passing of Pence*; which I give you here as I got it translated into *English*; For some of our *Laws* at that time were, as I am told, writ in *Latin: Whoever in Buying or Selling presumeth to refuse an Half-penny or Farthing of Lawful Money, bearing the Stamp which it ought to have, let him be seized on as a Contemner of the King's Majesty, and cast into Prison*.

BY this *Statute*, no Person is to be reckoned a *Contemner* of the *King's Majesty*, and for that Crime to be *committed to Prison*; but he who refuseth to accept the King's Coin made of *Lawful Metal*: by which as I observed before, *Silver* and *Gold* only are intended.

THAT this is the true *Construction* of the *Act*, appears not only from the plain Meaning of the Words, but from my Lord *Coke's* Observation upon it. By this Act (says he) it appears, that no Subject can be forced to take in *Buying* or *Selling* or other *Payments*, any Money made but of lawful Metal; that is, of *Silver* or *Gold*.

THE Law of *England* gives the King all Mines of *Gold* and

Silver, but not the Mines of other *Metals*; the Reason of which *Prerogative* or *Power*, as it is given by my Lord *Coke*, is because Money can be made of *Gold* and *Silver*; but not of other Metals.[16]

PURSUANT to this Opinion, *Half-pence* and *Farthings* were anciently made of *Silver*, which is evident from the Act of *Parliament* of *Henry* the IVth. Chap. 4. whereby it is enacted as follows: *Item, for the great Scarcity that is at present within the Realm of* England *of Half-pence and Farthings of Silver; it is ordained and established, that the Third Part of all the* Money of Silver Plate *which shall be brought to the* Bullion, *Shall be made in* Half-pence *and* Farthings. This shews that by the Words *Half-penny* and *Farthing* of Lawful Money in that Statute concerning the *passing of* Pence, is meant a small Coin in *Half-pence* and *Farthings* of *Silver*.

THIS is further manifest from the Statute of the Ninth Year of *Edward* the IIId. Chap. 3. which enacts, *That no sterling* Half-penny *or* Farthing *be Molten for to make Vessels, or any other thing by the Gold-smiths, nor others, upon Forfeiture of the* Money *so molten* (*or melted.*)

By another Act in this *King's* Reign, *Black Money* was not to be current in *England*. And by an Act made in the Eleventh Year of his Reign, Chap. 5. *Galley Half-pence* were not to pass: What kind of *Coin* these were I do not know; but I presume they were made of *Base Metal*. And these Acts were no New *Laws*, but further Declarations of the old *Laws* relating to the *Coin*.

THUS the *Law* stands in Relation to *Coin*. Nor is there any Example to the contrary, except one in *Davis's Reports*; who tells us, that in the time of *Tyrone's* Rebellion,[17] *Queen Elizabeth* ordered *Money of mixt Metal* to be coined in the Tower of *London*, and sent over hither for Payment of the *Army*; obliging all People to receive it; and Commanding, that all *Silver Money* should be taken only as *Bullion*, that is, for as much as it weighed. *Davis* tells us several Particulars in this Matter too long here to trouble you with, and that the *Privy Council* of this *Kingdom* obliged a *Merchant* in *England* to receive this *mixt Money* for Goods transmitted hither.

BUT this Proceeding is rejected by all the best Lawyers, as contrary to Law, the *Privy Council* here having no such legal Power. And besides it is to be considered, that the *Queen* was then under great Difficulties by a Rebellion in this *Kingdom* assisted from *Spain*. And, whatever is done in great Exigences and dangerous Times, should never be an Example to proceed by in Seasons of *Peace* and *Quietness*.

I WILL now, my dear Friends, to save you the Trouble, set before you in short, what the *Law* obliges you to do; and what it does not oblige you to.

FIRST, you are obliged to take all Money in Payments which is coined by the *King*, and is of the *English* Standard or Weight; provided it be of *Gold* or *Silver*.

SECONDLY, you are not obliged to take any Money which is not of *Gold* or *Silver*; not only the *Half-pence* or *Farthings* of *England*, but of any other Country. And it is meerly for Convenience, or Ease, that you are content to take them; because the Custom of coining *Silver Half-pence* and *Farthings* hath long been left off; I suppose, on Account of their being subject to be lost.

THIRDLY, Much less are we obliged to take those *Vile Half-pence* of that same *Wood*, by which you must lose almost Eleven-Pence in every Shilling.

THEREFORE, my Friends, stand to it One and All: Refuse this *Filthy Trash*. It is no Treason to rebel against Mr. *Wood*. His *Majesty* in his Patent obliges no body to take these *Half-pence:* Our *Gracious Prince* hath no such ill Advisers about him; or if he had, yet you see the Laws have not left it in the *King*'s Power, to force us to take any Coin but what is Lawful, of right Standard, *Gold* and *Silver*. Therefore you have nothing to fear.

AND let me in the next Place apply my self particularly to you who are the poorer Sort of *Tradesmen:* Perhaps you may think you will not be so great Losers as the Rich, if these *Half-pence* should pass; because you seldom see any *Silver*, and your Customers come to your Shops or Stalls with nothing but *Brass*; which you likewise find hard to be got. But you may take my Word, whenever this Money gains Footing among you,

you will be utterly undone. If you carry these *Half-pence* to a Shop for *Tobacco* or *Brandy*, or any other Thing you want; the Shop-keeper will advance his Goods accordingly, or else he must break and leave the *Key under the Door*. Do you think I will sell you a Yard of Ten-penny Stuff for Twenty of Mr. *Wood*'s *Half-pence*? No, not under Two Hundred at least; neither will I be at the Trouble of counting, but weigh them in a Lump. I will tell you one Thing further; that if Mr. *Wood*'s Project should take, it will ruin even our Beggars: For when I give a Beggar a Half-penny, it will quench his Thirst, or go a good Way to fill his Belly; but the Twelfth Part of a Half-penny will do him no more Service than if I should give him three Pins out of my Sleeve.

IN short; these *Half-pence* are like the *accursed Thing*, which, as the *Scripture* tells us, the *Children of Israel* were forbidden to touch.[18] They will run about like the *Plague* and destroy every one who lays his Hands upon them. I have heard *Scholars* talk of a Man who told the King that he had invented a Way to torment People by putting them into a *Bull* of Brass with Fire under it: But the *Prince* put the *Projector* first into his own *Brazen Bull* to make the Experiment.[19] This very much resembles the Project of Mr. *Wood*; and the like of this may possibly be Mr. *Wood*'s Fate; that the *Brass* he contrived to torment this *Kingdom* with, may prove his own Torment, and his Destruction at last.

N. B. The Author of this Paper is informed by Persons who have made it their Business to be exact in their Observations on the true Value of these *Half-pence*; that any Person may expect to get a Quart of Two-penny Ale for Thirty Six of them.

I DESIRE that all Families may keep this Paper carefully by them to refresh their Memories whenever they shall have farther Notice of Mr. *Wood*'s Half-pence, or any other the like Imposture.

LETTER IV. TO THE WHOLE PEOPLE
OF IRELAND

My dear Countrymen,

HAVING already written three *Letters*, upon so disagreeable a Subject as Mr. *Wood* and his *Half-pence*; I conceived my Task was at an End:[1] But, I find that Cordials must be frequently applied to weak Constitutions *Political* as well as *Natural*. A People long used to Hardships, lose by Degrees the very Notions of *Liberty*; they look upon themselves as Creatures at Mercy; and that all Impositions laid on them by a stronger Hand, are, in the Phrase of the *Report, legal* and *obligatory*.[2] Hence proceed that *Poverty* and *Lowness of Spirit*, to which a *Kingdom* may be subject, as well as a *particular Person*. And when *Esau* came fainting from the Field, at the Point to dye, it is no Wonder that he sold his *Birth-Right for a Mess of Pottage*.[3]

I THOUGHT I had sufficiently shewn to all who could want Instruction, by what Methods they might safely proceed, whenever this *Coin* should be offered to them: And, I believe, there hath not been, for many Ages, an Example of any Kingdom so firmly united in a Point of great Importance, as this of ours is at present, against that detestable Fraud. But, however, it so happens, that some weak People begin to be alarmed a-new, by Rumours industriously spread. *Wood* prescribes to the News-Mongers in *London*, what they are to write. In one of their Papers published here by some obscure Printer, (and certainly with a bad Design) we are told, that the *Papists in* Ireland *have entered into an Association against his Coin*; although it be notoriously known, that they never once offered to stir in the Matter: So that the two Houses of Parliament, the Privy-Council, the great Numbers of Corporations, the Lord-Mayor and Aldermen of *Dublin*, the Grand-Juries, and principal Gentlemen of several Counties, are stigmatized in a Lump, under the Name of *Papists*.

THIS Impostor and his Crew, do likewise give out, that, by refusing to receive his Dross for Sterling, we *dispute the King's*

Prerogative; are grown ripe for Rebellion, and ready to shake off the Dependency of Ireland *upon the Crown of* England. To countenance which Reports, he hath published a Paragraph in another News-Paper, to let us know, that *the Lord Lieutenant is ordered to come over immediately to settle his Half-pence.*

I INTREAT you, my dear Countrymen, not to be under the least Concern upon these and the like Rumours; which are no more than the last Howls of a Dog dissected alive, as I hope he hath sufficiently been. These Calumnies are the only Reserve that is left him. For surely, our continued and (almost) unexampled Loyalty, will never be called in Question, for not suffering our selves to be robbed of all that we have, by one obscure *Ironmonger.*

As to disputing the King's *Prerogative,* give me Leave to explain to those who are ignorant, what the Meaning of that Word *Prerogative* is.[4]

THE Kings of these Realms enjoy several Powers, wherein the Laws have not interposed: So, they can make War and Peace without the Consent of Parliament; and this is a very great *Prerogative.* But if the Parliament doth not approve of the War, the King must bear the Charge of it out of his own Purse; and this is as great a Check on the Crown. So the King hath a *Prerogative* to coin Money, without Consent of Parliament: But he cannot compel the Subject to take that Money, except it be Sterling, Gold or Silver; because, herein he is limited by Law. Some Princes have, indeed, extended their *Prerogative* further than the Law allowed them: Wherein, however, the Lawyers of succeeding Ages, as fond as they are of *Precedents,* have never dared to justify them. But, to say the Truth, it is only of late Times that *Prerogative* hath been fixed and ascertained. For, whoever reads the Histories of *England,* will find that some former Kings, and those none of the worst, have, upon several Occasions, ventured to controul the Laws, with very little Ceremony or Scruple, even later than the Days of Queen *Elizabeth.* In her Reign, that pernicious Counsel of sending *base Money* hither, very narrowly failed of losing the Kingdom; being complained of by the Lord Deputy, the Council, and the whole Body of the *English* here: So that soon after her

Death, it was recalled by her Successor, and lawful Money paid in Exchange.[5]

HAVING thus given you some Notion of what is meant by the King's *Prerogative*, as far as a *Tradesman* can be thought capable of explaining it, I will only add the Opinion of the great Lord *Bacon*; that, *as God governs the World by the settled Laws of Nature, which he hath made, and never transcends those Laws, but upon high important Occasions: So, among earthly Princes, those are the Wisest and the Best, who govern by the known Laws of the Country, and seldomest make Use of their* Prerogative.[6]

Now, here you may see that the vile Accusation of *Wood* and his Accomplices, charging us with *disputing the King's Prerogative*, by refusing his Brass, can have no Place; because compelling the Subject to take any Coin, which is not Sterling, is no Part of the King's *Prerogative*; and I am very confident, if it were so, we should be the last of his People to dispute it; as well from that inviolable Loyalty we have always paid to his Majesty, as from the Treatment we might in such a Case justly expect from some, who seem to think, we have neither *common Sense*, nor *common Senses*. But, God be thanked, the best of them are only our *Fellow-Subjects*, and not our *Masters*. One great Merit I am sure we have, which those of *English* Birth can have no Pretence to; that our Ancestors reduced this Kingdom to the Obedience of ENGLAND; for which we have been rewarded with a worse Climate, the Privilege of being governed by Laws to which we do not consent; a ruined Trade, a House of *Peers* without *Jurisdiction*; almost an Incapacity for all Employments, and the Dread of *Wood*'s Half-pence.

BUT we are so far from disputing the King's *Prerogative* in coining, that we own he hath Power to give a Patent to any Man, for setting his Royal Image and Superscription upon whatever Materials he pleases; and Liberty to the Patentee to offer them in any Country from *England* to *Japan*; only attended with one small Limitation, that *no body alive is obliged to take them.*

UPON these Considerations, I was ever against all Recourse to *England* for a Remedy against the present impending Evil;

especially, when I observed, that the Addresses of both Houses, after long Expectance, produced nothing but a REPORT altogether in Favour of *Wood*; upon which, I made some Observations in a former Letter; and might at least have made as many more: For, it is a Paper of as singular a Nature as I ever beheld.

BUT I mistake; for before this *Report* was made, his Majesty's *most gracious Answer* to the House of Lords was sent over, and printed; wherein there are these Words, *granting the Patent for coining Half-pence and Farthings*, AGREEABLE TO THE PRACTICE OF HIS ROYAL PREDECESSORS, &c. That King *Charles* II, and King *James* II, (AND THEY ONLY) did grant Patents for this Purpose, is indisputable, and I have shewn it at large. Their Patents were passed under the great Seal of *Ireland*, by References to *Ireland*; the Copper to be coined in *Ireland*, the Patentee was bound, on Demand, to receive his Coin back in *Ireland*, and pay Silver and Gold in Return. *Wood*'s Patent was made under the great Seal of *England*, the Brass coined in *England*, not the least Reference made to *Ireland*; the Sum immense, and the Patentee under no Obligation to receive it again, and give good Money for it: This I only mention, because, in my private Thoughts, I have sometimes made a Query, whether the *Penner* of those Words in his Majesty's *most gracious Answer*, AGREEABLE TO THE PRACTICE OF HIS ROYAL PREDECESSORS, had maturely considered the several Circumstances; which, in my poor Opinion, seem to make a Difference.

LET me now say something concerning the other great Cause of some People's Fear; as *Wood* has taught the *London* News-Writer to express it: That *his Excellency the Lord Lieutenant is coming over to settle* Wood's *Half-pence*.

We know very well, that the Lords Lieutenants, for several Years past, have not thought this Kingdom *worthy the Honour of their Residence*, longer than was absolutely necessary for the King's Business; which consequently *wanted no Speed in the Dispatch*. And therefore, it naturally fell into most Mens Thoughts, that a new Governor coming at an *unusual* Time, must portend some *unusual* Business to be done; especially, if the common Report be true; that the Parliament prorogued to I know not when, is, by a new Summons (revoking that Prorogation) to assemble soon after his Arrival:[7] For which extraordinary Proceeding, the Lawyers on t'other Side the Water, have, by great good Fortune, found two *Precedents*.

ALL this being granted, it can never enter into my Head, that so *little a Creature as Wood* could find Credit enough with the King and his Ministers to have the Lord Lieutenant of *Ireland* sent hither in a Hurry, upon his Errand.

FOR, let us take the whole Matter nakedly, as it lies before us, without the Refinements of some People, with which we have nothing to do. Here is a Patent granted under the great Seal of *England*, upon false Suggestions, to one *William Wood*, for coining Copper Half-pence for *Ireland*: The Parliament here, upon Apprehensions of the worst Consequences from the said Patent, address the King to have it recalled: This is refused, and a Committee of the Privy-Council *report* to his Majesty, that *Wood* has performed the Conditions of his Patent. He then is left to do the best he can with his Half-pence; no Man being obliged to receive them; the People here, being likewise left to themselves, unite as one Man; resolving they will have nothing to do with his Ware. By this plain Account of the Fact, it is manifest, that the King and his Ministry are wholly out of the Case; and the Matter is left to be disputed between him and us. Will any Man therefore attempt to persuade me, that a Lord Lieutenant is to be dispatched over in great Haste, before the ordinary Time, and a Parliament summoned, by anticipating a Prorogation; merely to put an Hundred Thousand Pounds into the Pocket of a *Sharper*, by the Ruin of a most loyal Kingdom?

BUT supposing all this to be true. By what Arguments could a Lord Lieutenant prevail on the same Parliament, which addressed with so much Zeal and Earnestness against this Evil; to pass it into a Law? I am sure their Opinion of *Wood* and his Project are not mended since their last Prorogation: And supposing those *Methods* should be used, which, *Detractors* tell us, have been sometimes put in Practice for *gaining Votes*; it is well known, that in this Kingdom there are few Employments to be given; and if there were more; it is *as well known* to whose Share they must fall.[8]

BUT, because great Numbers of you are altogether ignorant in the Affairs of your Country, I will tell you some Reasons, why there are so few Employments to be disposed of in this Kingdom. All considerable Offices for Life here, are possessed by those, to whom the Reversions were granted; and these have been generally Followers of the Chief Governors, or Persons who had Interest in the Court of *England*. So the Lord *Berkely* of *Stratton*, holds that great Office of *Master of the Rolls*; the Lord *Palmerstown* is *First Remembrancer*, worth near 2000 *l. per Ann*. One *Dodington*, Secretary to the Earl of *Pembroke*, begged the Reversion of *Clerk of the Pells*, worth 2500 *l*. a Year, which he now enjoys by the Death of the Lord *Newtown*. Mr. *Southwell* is Secretary of State, and the Earl of *Burlington* Lord High Treasurer of *Ireland* by Inheritance.[9] These are only a few among many others, which I have been told of, but cannot remember. Nay the Reversion of several Employments during Pleasure are granted the same Way. This among many others, is a Circumstance whereby the Kingdom of *Ireland* is distinguished from all other Nations upon Earth; and makes it so difficult an Affair to get into a Civil Employ, that Mr. *Addison* was forced to purchase an old obscure Place, called *Keeper of the Records in* Bermingham's *Tower*, of Ten Pounds a Year, and to get a Salary of 400 *l*. annexed to it, though all the Records there are not worth Half a Crown, either for Curiosity or Use.[10] And we lately saw a *Favourite Secretary*, descend to be *Master of the Revels*,[11] which by his *Credit and Extortion* he hath made *Pretty Considerable*. I say nothing of the Under-Treasurership worth about 9000 *l*. a Year; nor the Commissioners of the Revenue, Four of whom generally live in *England:* For I think none of these are granted in Reversion. But the Jest is, that I have known upon Occasion, some of these absent Officers as *Keen* against the Interest of *Ireland*, as if they had never been indebted to Her for a *Single Groat*.

I CONFESS, I have been sometimes tempted to wish that this Project of *Wood* might succeed; because I reflected with some Pleasure, what a *Jolly Crew* it would bring over among us of *Lords* and *Squires*, and *Pensioners* of *Both Sexes*, and Officers *Civil* and *Military*; where we should live together as merry and sociable as Beggars; only with this one Abatement, that we should neither have *Meat* to feed, nor *Manufactures* to Cloath us; unless we could be content to *Prance* about in *Coats of Mail*; or eat Brass as Ostritches do Iron.

I RETURN from this Digression, to that which gave me the Occasion of making it: And I believe you are now convinced, that if the Parliament of *Ireland* were as *Temptable* as any *other* Assembly, *within a Mile of* Christendom (which God forbid) yet the *Managers* must of Necessity fail for want of *Tools* to work with. But I will yet go one Step further, by Supposing that a Hundred new Employments, were erected on Purpose to gratify *Compliers:* Yet still an insuperable Difficulty would remain. For it happens, I know not how, that *Money* is neither *Whig* nor *Tory*, neither of *Town* nor *Country Party*; and it is not improbable, that a Gentleman would rather chuse to live upon his *own Estate*, which brings him *Gold* and *Silver*, than with the Addition of an *Employment*; when his *Rents* and *Sallary* must both be paid in *Wood*'s Brass, at above Eighty *per Cent*. Discount.

FOR these, and many other Reasons, I am confident you need not be under the least Apprehensions, from the sudden Expectation of the *Lord Lieutenant*, while we continue in our present hearty Disposition; to alter which, there is no suitable Temptation can possibly be offered: And if, as I have often asserted from the best Authority, the *Law* hath not left a *Power* in the *Crown* to force any Money, except Sterling, upon the Subject; much less can the Crown *devolve* such a *Power* upon *another*.

THIS I speak with the utmost Respect to the *Person* and *Dignity* of his Excellency the Lord *Carteret*; whose Character was lately given me, by a Gentleman that hath known him from his first Appearance in the World: That Gentleman describes him as a young Man of great Accomplishments, excellent Learning, Regular in his Life, and of much Spirit and Vivacity. He hath since, as I have heard, been employed abroad; was principal Secretary of State; and is now about the 37th Year of his Age appointed Lord Lieutenant of *Ireland*. From such a Governour this Kingdom may reasonably hope for as much

Prosperity, as *under so many Discouragements* it can be capable of receiving.[12]

It is true indeed, that within the Memory of Man, there have been Governors of so much Dexterity, as to carry Points of terrible Consequence to this Kingdom, by their Power with *those who are in Office*; and by their Arts in managing or deluding others with *Oaths, Affability*, and even with *Dinners*. If *Wood*'s Brass had, in those Times, been upon the *Anvil*, it is obvious enough to conceive what Methods would have been taken. *Depending* Persons would have been told in plain Terms, *that it was a Service expected from them, under the Pain of the publick Business being put into more complying Hands*. Others would be allured by *Promises*. To the *Country Gentlemen*, besides *good Words, Burgundy* and *Closeting*; it might, perhaps, have been hinted, how *kindly it would be taken to comply with a Royal Patent, although it were not compulsory*. That if any Inconveniences ensued, it might be made up with other *Graces or Favours hereafter:* That *Gentlemen ought to consider, whether it were prudent or safe to disgust* England: They would be desired to *think of some good Bills for encouraging of Trade, and setting the Poor to work: Some further Acts against Popery, and for uniting Protestants*. There would be solemn Engagements, that we should *never be troubled with above Forty Thousand Pounds in his Coin, and all of the best and weightiest Sort; for which we should only give our Manufactures in Exchange, and keep our Gold and Silver at home.* Perhaps, *a seasonable Report of some Invasion would have been spread in the most proper Juncture*; which is a great Smoother of Rubs in publick Proceedings: And we should have been told, that *this was no Time to create Differences, when the Kingdom was in Danger*.[13]

THESE, I say, and the like Methods, would, in corrupt Times, have been taken to let in this Deluge of Brass among us: And, I am confident, would even then have not succeeded; much less under the Administration of so excellent a Person as the Lord *Carteret*; and in a Country, where the People of all Ranks, Parties, and Denominations, are convinced to a Man, that the utter undoing of themselves and their Posterity for ever, will be dated from the Admission of that execrable Coin: That if it once enters, it can be no more confined to a small or moderate Quantity, than the *Plague* can be confined to a few Families; and that no *Equivalent* can be given by any earthly Power, any more than a dead Carcass can be recovered to Life by a Cordial.

THERE is one comfortable Circumstance in this universal Opposition to Mr. *Wood*, that the People sent over hither from *England*, to *fill up our Vacancies, Ecclesiastical, Civil and Military*, are all on our Side: *Money*, the great *Divider* of the World, hath, by a strange Revolution, been the great *Uniter* of a most *divided* People. Who would leave a Hundred Pounds a Year in *England*, (*a Country of Freedom*) to be paid a Thousand in *Ireland* out of *Wood*'s Exchequer? The *Gentleman They* have lately made *Primate*,[14] would never quit his Seat in an *English* House of Lords, and his Preferments at *Oxford* and *Bristol*, worth Twelve Hundred Pounds a Year, for four Times the Denomination here, but not half the Value: Therefore, I expect to hear he will be as good an *Irishman*, at least, upon *this one Article*, as any of his Brethren; or even of *Us*, who have had the *Misfortune* to be born in this Island. For those who, in the common Phrase, do not *come hither to learn the Language*, would never change a better Country for a worse, to receive *Brass* instead of *Gold*.

ANOTHER Slander spread by *Wood* and his Emissaries is, that, by opposing him, we discover an Inclination to *shake off our Dependance upon the Crown of* England. Pray observe, how important a Person is this same *William Wood*; and how the publick Weal of two Kingdoms, is involved in his private Interest. First, all those who refuse to take his Coin *are Papists*; for he tells us, that *none but Papists are associated against him*. Secondly, they *dispute the King's Prerogative*. Thirdly, they *are ripe for Rebellion*. And Fourthly, they are going to *shake off their Dependance upon the Crown of* England; that is to say, *they are going to chuse another King*: For there can be no other Meaning in this Expression, however some may pretend to strain it.

AND this gives me an Opportunity of explaining, to those who are ignorant, another Point, which hath often *swelled in my Breast.* Those who come over hither to us from *England*, and some *weak* People among ourselves, whenever, in Discourse, we make mention of *Liberty* and *Property*, shake their Heads, and tell us, that *Ireland* is a *depending Kingdom*; as if they would seem, by this Phrase, to intend, that the People of *Ireland* is in some State of Slavery or Dependance, different from those of *England:* Whereas, a *depending Kingdom* is a *modern Term of Art*; unknown, as I have heard, to all antient *Civilians*, and *Writers upon Government*; and *Ireland* is, on the contrary, called in some Statutes an *Imperial Crown*, as held only from God; which is as high a Style, as any Kingdom is capable of receiving. Therefore by this Expression, a *depending Kingdom*, there is no more understood, than that by a Statute made here, in the 33d Year of *Henry* VIII, *The King and his Successors, are to be Kings Imperial of this Realm, as united and knit to the Imperial Crown of* England.[15] I have looked over all the *English* and *Irish* Statutes, without finding any Law that makes *Ireland depend* upon *England*; any more than *England* doth upon *Ireland*. We have, indeed, obliged ourselves to have *the same King with them*; and consequently they are obliged to have the *same King with us*. For the Law was made by *our own Parliament*; and our Ancestors then were not such Fools (*whatever they were in the preceding Reign*) to bring themselves under I know not what *Dependance*, which is now talked of, without any Ground of *Law*, *Reason*, or *common Sense.*

LET whoever think otherwise, I *M.B. Drapier*, desire to be excepted. For I declare, next under God, I *depend* only on the King my Sovereign, and on the Laws of my own Country. And I am so far from *depending* upon the People of *England*, that, if they should ever *rebel* against my Sovereign, (which GOD forbid) I would be ready at the first Command from his Majesty, to take Arms against them; as some of *my* Countrymen did against *theirs* at *Preston*.[16] And, if such a Rebellion should prove so successful as to fix the *Pretender* on the Throne of *England*; I would venture to transgress that *Statute* so far, as to lose every Drop of my Blood, to hinder him from being *King* of *Ireland*.[17]

IT is true, indeed, that within the Memory of Man, the Parliaments of *England* have *sometimes* assumed the Power of binding this Kingdom, by Laws enacted there; wherein they were, at first, openly opposed (as far as *Truth, Reason,* and *Justice* are capable of *opposing*) by the famous Mr. *Molineaux,* an *English* Gentleman born here; as well as by several of the greatest Patriots, and *best Whigs* in *England*; but the *Love and Torrent* of Power prevailed. Indeed, the Arguments on both Sides were invincible. For in *Reason,* all *Government* without the Consent of the *Governed,* is the *very Definition of Slavery:* But in *Fact, Eleven Men well armed, will certainly subdue one single Man in his Shirt.* But I have done. For those who have used *Power* to cramp *Liberty,* have gone so far as to resent even the *Liberty* of *Complaining*; although a Man upon the Rack, was never known to be refused the Liberty of *roaring* as loud as he thought fit.

AND, as we are apt to *sink* too *much* under *unreasonable* Fears, so we are too soon inclined to be *raised* by groundless Hopes, (according to the Nature of all *consumptive* Bodies like ours.) Thus, it hath been given about for several Days past, that *Somebody* in *England,* empowered a second *Somebody* to write to a third *Somebody* here, to assure us, that we *should no more be troubled with those Half-pence.* And this is reported to have been done by the *same Person,* who was said to have sworn some Months ago, that he would *ram them down our Throats,*[18] (though I doubt they would *stick in our Stomachs*). But which ever of these Reports is true or false, it is no Concern of ours. For, *in this Point,* we have nothing to do with *English Ministers:* And I should be sorry to leave it in their Power to *redress* this Grievance, or to *enforce* it: For the *Report of the Committee* hath given me a *Surfeit.* The Remedy is wholly in your own Hands; and therefore I have digressed a little, in order to refresh and continue that *Spirit* so seasonably raised amongst you; and to let you see, that by the Laws of GOD, of NATURE, of NATIONS, and of your own Country, you ARE and OUGHT to be as FREE a People as your Brethren in *England.*

IF the Pamphlets published at *London* by *Wood* and his *Journeymen,* in Defence of his Cause, were Re-printed here, and that our Countrymen could be persuaded to read them, they would convince you of his wicked Design, more than all I shall ever be able to say. In short, I make him a perfect *Saint*, in Comparison of what he appears to be, from the Writings of those whom he *Hires* to justify his *Project*. But he is so far *Master of the Field* (*let others guess the Reason*) that no *London* Printer dare publish any Paper written in Favour of *Ireland*: And here no Body hath yet been so *bold*, as to publish any Thing in *Favour* of *him*.

THERE was a few Days ago a Pamphlet sent me of near 50 Pages, written in Favour of Mr. *Wood* and his Coinage; printed in *London*:[19] It is not worth answering, because probably it will never be published here: But it gave me an Occasion, to reflect upon an Unhappiness we lie under, that the People of *England* are utterly ignorant of our Case: Which, however, is no Wonder; since it is a Point they do not in the least concern themselves about; farther than, perhaps, as a Subject of Discourse in a Coffee-House, when they have nothing else to talk of. For I have Reason to believe, that no Minister ever gave himself the Trouble of reading any Papers written in our Defence; because I suppose *their Opinions are already determined*, and are formed wholly upon the Reports of *Wood* and his Accomplices; else it would be impossible, that any Man could have the Impudence to write such a Pamphlet, as I have mentioned.

OUR *Neighbours, whose Understandings are just upon a Level with Ours* (which perhaps are none of the *Brightest*) have a strong Contempt for most Nations, but especially for *Ireland*: They look upon us as a Sort of *Savage Irish*, whom our Ancestors conquered several Hundred Years ago: And if I should describe the *Britons* to you, as they were in *Cæsar*'s Time, when they *painted their Bodies, or cloathed themselves with the Skins of Beasts*, I should act full as reasonably as they do.[20] However, they are so far to be excused, in relation to the present Subject, that, hearing only *one Side of the Cause*, and having neither Opportunity nor Curiosity to examine the *other*, they *believe a Lye*, merely for their Ease; and conclude, because Mr. *Wood* pretends to have *Power*, he hath also *Reason* on his Side.

THEREFORE, to let you see how this Case is represented in *England* by *Wood* and his Adherents, I have thought it proper to extract out of that Pamphlet, a few of those notorious Falshoods, in Point of *Fact* and *Reasoning*, contained therein; the Knowledge whereof, will confirm my Countrymen in their *Own* Right Sentiments, when they will see by comparing both, how much their *Enemies are in the Wrong*.

FIRST, The Writer positively asserts, *That* Wood's *Halfpence were current among us for several Months, with the universal Approbation of all People, without one single Gainsayer; and we all to a Man thought our selves Happy in having them.*

SECONDLY, He affirms, *That we were drawn into a Dislike of them, only by some Cunning Evil-designing Men among us, who opposed this Patent of* Wood, *to get another for themselves.*

THIRDLY, That *those who most declared at first against* WOOD's *Patent, were the very Men who intend to get another for their own Advantage.*

FOURTHLY, That *our Parliament and Privy-Council, the Lord Mayor and Aldermen of* Dublin, *the Grand-Juries and Merchants, and in short the whole Kingdom; nay, the very Dogs* (as he expresseth it) *were fond of those Half-pence, till they were inflamed by those few designing Persons aforesaid.*

FIFTHLY, He says directly, That *all those who opposed the Half-pence, were Papists, and Enemies to King* George.

THUS far I am confident, the most ignorant among you can safely swear from your own Knowledge, that the Author is a most notorious Lyar in every Article; the direct contrary being so manifest to the whole Kingdom, that if Occasion required, we might get it confirmed *under Five hundred thousand Hands*.

SIXTHLY, He would persuade us, That *if we sell Five Shillings worth of our Goods or Manufactures for Two Shillings and Four-pence worth of Copper, although the Copper were melted down, and that we could get Five Shillings in Gold and Silver for the said Goods; yet to take the said Two Shillings and Four-pence in Copper, would be greatly for our Advantage.*

AND Lastly, He makes us a very fair Offer, as empowered

by *Wood,* That *if we will take off Two hundred thousand Pounds in his Half-pence for our Goods, and likewise pay him Three* per Cent. *Interest for Thirty Years, for an hundred and Twenty thousand Pounds (at which he computes the Coinage above the intrinsick Value of the Copper) for the Loan of his Coin, he will after that Time give us good Money for what Half-pence will be then left.*

LET me place this Offer in as clear a Light as I can, to shew the unsupportable Villainy and Impudence of that incorrigible Wretch. First (says he) *I will send Two hundred thousand Pounds of my Coin into your Country: The Copper I compute to be in real Value Eighty thousand Pounds, and I charge you with an hundred and twenty thousand Pounds for the Coinage; so that you see, I lend you an hundred and twenty thousand Pounds for Thirty Years; for which you shall pay me Three* per Cent. *That is to say, Three thousand Six hundred Pounds,* per Ann. *which in Thirty Years will amount to an Hundred and eight thousand Pounds. And when these Thirty Years are expired, return me my Copper, and I will give you Good Money for it.*

THIS is the Proposal made to us by *Wood* in that Pamphlet, written by one of his *Commissioners:* And the Author is supposed to be the same Infamous *Coleby* one of his *Under-Swearers* at the *Committee of Council,* who was tryed for *Robbing the Treasury here,* where he was an Under-Clerk.[21]

BY this Proposal he will first receive Two hundred thousand Pounds, in Goods or Sterling, for as much Copper as he values at Eighty thousand Pounds; but in Reality not worth Thirty thousand Pounds. Secondly, He will receive for Interest an Hundred and Eight thousand Pounds: And when our Children come Thirty Years hence, to return his Half-pence upon his Executors (for before that Time he will be probably gone *to his own Place*) those Executors will very reasonably reject them as Raps and Counterfeits; which they will be, and Millions of them of his own Coinage.

METHINKS, I am fond of such a *Dealer* as this, who mends every Day upon our Hands, like a *Dutch* Reckoning; where, if you dispute the Unreasonableness and Exorbitance of the Bill, the Landlord shall bring it up every Time with new Additions.

ALTHOUGH these and the like Pamphlets, published by *Wood* in *London*, be altogether unknown here, where no body could read them, without as much *Indignation* as *Contempt* would allow; yet I thought it proper to give you a Specimen how the *Man* employs his Time; where he Rides alone without any Creature to contradict him; while OUR FEW FRIENDS there wonder at our Silence: And the *English* in general, if they think of this Matter at all, impute our Refusal to *Wilfulness* or *Disaffection*, just as *Wood* and his *Hirelings* are pleased to represent.

BUT although our Arguments are not suffered to be printed in *England*, yet the Consequence will be of little Moment. Let *Wood* endeavour to *persuade* the People *There*, that we ought to *Receive* his Coin; and let Me *Convince* our People *Here*, that they ought to *Reject* it under Pain of our utter Undoing. And then let him do his *Best* and his *Worst*.

BEFORE I conclude, I must beg Leave, in all Humility to tell Mr. *Wood*, that he is guilty of great *Indiscretion*, by causing so Honourable a Name as that of Mr. *Walpole* to be mentioned so often, and in such a Manner, upon his Occasion. A short Paper, printed at *Bristol*, and re-printed here, reports Mr. *Wood* to say, that he *wonders at the Impudence and Insolence of the* Irish, *in refusing his Coin*, and *what he will do when Mr.* Walpole *comes to Town*. Where, by the Way, he is mistaken; for it is the *True English People of Ireland*, who refuse it; although we take it for granted, that the *Irish* will do so too, whenever they are asked.[22] In another printed Paper of his contriving, it is roundly expressed, that Mr. *Walpole will cram his Brass down our Throats*. Sometimes it is given out, that we must *either take these Half-pence or eat our Brogues*, And, in another News-Letter but of Yesterday, we read, that the same great Man *hath sworn to make us swallow his Coin in Fire-Balls*.[23]

THIS brings to my Mind the known Story of a *Scotch* Man, who receiving Sentence of Death, with all the Circumstances of *Hanging, Beheading, Quartering, Embowelling*, and the like; cried out, *What need all this* COOKERY? And I think we have

Reason to ask the same Question: For if we believe *Wood*, here
is a *Dinner* getting ready for us, and you see the *Bill of Fare*;
and I am sorry the *Drink* was forgot, which might easily be
supplied with *Melted Lead* and *Flaming Pitch*.

WHAT vile Words are these to put into the Mouth of a great
Counsellor, in high Trust with his Majesty, and looked upon
as a prime Minister? If Mr. *Wood* hath no better a Manner of
representing his Patrons; when I come to be a *Great Man*,[24] he
shall never be suffered to attend at my *Levee*. This is not the
Style of a Great Minister; it savours too much of the *Kettle* and
the *Furnace*; and came entirely out of *Wood's Forge*.

As for the Threat of making us *eat our Brogues*, we need not
be in Pain; for if his Coin should pass, that *Unpolite Covering
for the Feet*, would no longer be a *National Reproach*; because,
then we should have neither *Shoe* nor *Brogue* left in the Kingdom. But here the Falshood of Mr. *Wood* is fairly detected; for
I am confident Mr. *Walpole* never heard of a *Brogue* in his
whole Life.

As to *Swallowing these Half-pence in Fire-balls*, it is a Story
equally improbable. For, to execute this *Operation*, the whole
Stock of Mr. *Wood*'s Coin and Metal must be melted down,
and molded into hollow *Balls* with *Wild-fire*, no bigger than a
reasonable Throat can be able to swallow. Now, the Metal he
hath prepared, and already coined, will amount to at least Fifty
Millions of Half-pence to be *Swallowed* by a Million and a
Half of People; so that allowing Two Half-pence to each *Ball*,
there will be about Seventeen *Balls* of *Wild-fire* a-piece, to be
swallowed by every Person in the Kingdom: And to administer
this Dose, there cannot be conveniently fewer than Fifty thousand *Operators*, allowing one *Operator* to every Thirty; which,
considering the *Squeamishness* of some Stomachs, and the
Peevishness of *Young Children*, is but reasonable.[25] Now, under
Correction of better Judgments, I think the Trouble and Charge
of such an Experiment, would exceed the Profit; and therefore
I take this *Report* to be *spurious*; or, at least, only a new *Scheme*
of Mr. *Wood* himself; which, to make it pass the better in
Ireland, he would Father upon a *Minister of State*.

BUT I will now demonstrate, beyond all Contradiction, that

Mr. *Walpole* is against this Project of Mr. *Wood*; and is an entire Friend to *Ireland*; only by this one invincible Argument, That he has the Universal Opinion of being a wise Man, an able Minister, and in all his Proceedings, pursuing the *True Interest* of the *King his Master*: And that, as his *Integrity* is above all *Corruption*, so is his *Fortune* above all *Temptation*. I reckon therefore, we are perfectly safe from that *Corner*; and shall never be under the Necessity of Contending with so *Formidable a Power*; but be left to possess our *Brogues* and *Potatoes* in *Peace*, as *Remote from Thunder as we are from Jupiter*.[26]

I am, My dear Countrymen, your Loving Fellow-Subject, Fellow-Sufferer, and Humble Servant,

Oct. 13, 1724.   M.B.

A FULL AND TRUE ACCOUNT OF THE SOLEMN PROCESSION TO THE GALLOWS, AT THE EXECUTION OF WILLIAM WOOD, ESQUIRE, AND HARD-WARE-MAN

Written in the Year 1724

SOME Time ago, upon a Report spread, that *William Wood*, Hard-Ware-Man, was concealed in his Brother-in-law's House here in *Dublin*;[1] a great Number of People of different Conditions, and of both Sexes, crowded about the Door, determinately bent to take Revenge upon him as a Coiner and Counterfeiter. Among the Rest, a certain curious Person, standing in a Corner, observed that they all discovered their Resentments in the proper Terms and Expressions of their several Trades and Callings; whereof he wrote down as many as he could remember; and was pleased to communicate them to me; with Leave to publish them, for the Use of those who at any Time hereafter may be at a Loss for proper Words, wherein to express their good Dispositions towards the said *William Wood*.

The People cried out to have him delivered into
their Hands.

Says the P—l—t Man,[2] *Expell* him the *House*.
2d. P—l—t Man, I second that *Motion*.
Cook. I'll *baste* him.
2d. *Cook*. I'll give him his *Belly-full*.
3d. *Cook*. I'll give him a *Lick* in the *Chops*.
4th. *Cook*. I'll *Sowce* him.
Drunken man. I'll beat him as long as I can *stand*.
Bookseller. I'll turn over a *New Leaf* with him.
Sadler. I'll *pummel* him.

Glazier. I'll make the *Light* shine through him.

Grocer. I'll *Pepper* him.

Groom. I'll *Curry* his Hide.

'Pothecary. I'll *Pound* him.

2d *'Pothecary.* I'll beat him to *Mummy.*

School-master. I'll make him an *Example.*

Rabbet-Catcher. I'll *Ferret* him.

Paver. I'll *Thump* him.

Coiner. I'll give him a *Rap.*

WHIG. Down with him.

TORY. Up with him.

Miller. I'll dash out his *Grinders.*

2d. *Miller. Dam* him.

Boat-man. Sink him.

Scavenger. Throw him in the *Kennel.*

Dyer. I'll beat him *black* and *blue.*

Bagnio-man. I'll make the *House* too *hot* for him.

Whore. Pox rot him.

2d. *Whore.* Let me *alone* with him.

3d. *Whore. Clap* him up.

Mustard-Maker. I'll have him by the *Nose.*

Curate. I'll make the *Devil come out of him.*

Popish Priest. I'll *send him* to the Devil.

Dancing-Master. I'll *teach* him *better Manners.*

2d. *Dancing-Master.* I'll make him cut a *Caper* three Story high.[3]

Farmer. I'll *thrash* him.

Taylor. I'll sit in his *Skirts.*[4]

2d. *Taylor. Hell* is too good for him.

3d. *Taylor.* I'll *pink* his *Doublet.*[5]

4th. *Taylor.* I'll make his A— make *Buttons.*[6]

Basket-Maker. I'll *hamper* him.

Fidler. I'll have him by the *Ears.*

2d. *Fidler.* I'll bang him to some *Tune.*

Barber. I'll have him by the *Beard.*

2d. *Barber.* I'll pull his *Whiskers.*

3d. *Barber.* I'll make his *Hair* stand an End.

4th. *Barber.* I'll *comb* his *Locks.*

Tinker. I'll try what *Metal* he's made of.

Cobler. I'll make an *End* of him.

Tobacconist. I'll make him *Smoak.*

2d. *Tobacconist.* I'll make him set up his *Pipes.*[7]

Gold-finder. I'll make him *Stink.*

Hackney-Coachman. I'll make him know his *Driver.*

2d. *Hackney-Coachman.* I'll *drive* him to the Devil.

Butcher. I'll have a *Limb* of him.

2d. *Butcher.* Let us *blow him up.*

3d. *Butcher.* My *Knife* in him.

Nurse. I'll *Swaddle* him.

Anabaptist. We'll *dip* the Rogue in the *Pond.*

Ostler. I'll *rub* him *down.*[8]

Shoemaker. Set him in the *Stocks.*

Banker. I'll kick him to *Half-Crowns.*[9]

2d. *Banker.* I'll *pay* him off.

Bowler. I'll have a *Rubber* with him.[10]

Gamester. I'll make his *Bones rattle.*

Bodice-maker. I'll *lace* his Sides.

Gardener. I'll make him *water his Plants.*[11]

Ale-wife. I'll *reckon* with him.

Cuckold. I'll make him pull in his *Horns.*[12]

Old-Woman. I'll *mumble* him.

Hangman. I'll *throttle* him.

BUT, at last, the People having received Assurances, that *William Wood* was neither in the House nor Kingdom, appointed certain Commissioners to hang him in Effigie; whereof the whole Ceremony and Procession, deserve to be transmitted to Posterity.

FIRST, the Way was cleared by a Detachment of the *Black-Guards*; with short Sticks in their Hands, and Cockades of Paper in their Hats.

Then appeared *William Wood*, Esq; represented to the Life by an old Piece of carved Timber, taken from the Keel of a Ship. Upon his Face, which looked very dismal, were fixed, at proper Distances, several Pieces of his own Coin, to denote who he was, and to signify his Calling, and his Crime. He wore on his Head a Peruke very artfully composed of Four old Mops; a Halter about his Neck served him for a Cravat. His Cloaths were indeed not so neat and elegant as is usual with Persons in his Condition; which some censorious People imputed to Affectation; for he was covered with a large Rugg of several Colours in Patch-Work; he was born upon the Shoulders of an able-bodied Porter. In his March by St. *Stephen's-Green*, he often bowed on both Sides, to shew his Respects to the Company; his Deportment was grave, and his Countenance though somewhat pensive, was very composed.

BEHIND him followed his Father alone, in a long mourning Cloak, with his Hat over his Nose, and a Handkerchief in his left Hand to wipe the Tears from his Face.

NEXT in Order marched the Executioner *himself in Person*; whose venerable Aspect drew the Eyes of the whole Assembly upon him; but he was further distinguished by a Halter which he bore upon his left Shoulder as the Badge of his Office.

THEN followed two Persons Hand in Hand; the one representing *William Wood*'s Brother-in-law; the other a certain Sadler, his intimate Friend, whose Name I forget. Each had a small Kettle in his Hands, wherein was a reasonable Quantity of the new Half-pence. At proper Periods they shook their Kettles, which made a melancholly Sound, like the Ringing of a Knell for their Partner and Confederate.

AFTER these followed several Officers, whose Assistance was necessary for the more decent Performance of the great Work in Hand.

THE Procession was closed with an innumerable Crowd of People, who frequently sent out loud Huzza's; which were censured by wiser Heads as a Mark of Inhumanity, and an ungenerous Triumph over the Unfortunate; without duly considering the various Vicissitudes of human Life. However, as it becomes an impartial Historian, I will not conceal one Observation, That Mr. *Wood* himself appeared wholly unmoved, without the least Alteration in his Countenance; only when he came within Sight of the fatal Tree, which happened to be of the same Species of Timber with his own Person, he seemed to be somewhat pensive.

AT the Place of Execution, he appeared undaunted, nor was seen to shed a Tear. He made no Resistance, but submitted himself, with great Resignation, to the Hangman, who was, indeed, thought to use him with too much Roughness, neither kissing him, nor asking him Pardon.[13] His dying SPEECH was printed, and deserves to be written in Letters of GOLD. Being asked whether it were his own true genuine SPEECH, he did not deny it.[14]

THOSE of the softer Sex who attended the Ceremony, lamented that so comely and well-*timbered* a Man, should come to so untimely an End. He hung but a short Time; for upon feeling his Breast, they found it cold and stiff.

IT is strange to think how this melancholly Spectacle turned the Hearts of the People to Compassion: When he was cut down, the Body was carried through the whole City to gather Contributions for his Wake; and all Sorts of People shewed their Liberality according as they were able. The Ceremony was performed in an Ale-house of Distinction, and in a Manner suitable to the Quality of the Deceased. While the Attendants were discoursing about his Funeral, a worthy Member of the Assembly stood up, and proposed, that the Body should be carried out next Day, and burned with the same Pomp and Formalities used at his Execution; which would prevent the Malice of his Enemies, and all Indignities that might be done to his Remains. This was agreed to; and about Nine a Clock on the following Morning there appeared a Second Procession. But, Burning not having been any Part of the Sentence, Authority thought fit to interpose, and the Corps was rescued by the Civil Power.

WE hear the Body is not yet interred; which occasions many Speculations. But what is more wonderful, it is positively assured by many who pretend to have been Eye-witnesses; that there does not appear the least Alteration in any one Lineament or Feature of his Countenance, nor visible Decay in his whole Frame, further than what had been made by Worms long before his Execution. The Solution of which Difficulty, I shall leave among Naturalists.

SWIFT TO THOMAS SHERIDAN

Quilca, Sept. 11, 1725.

IF you are indeed a discarded Courtier, you have reason to complain, but none at all to wonder; you are too young for many Experiences to fall in your way, yet you have read enough to make you know the Nature of Man.[1] It is safer for a Man's Interest to blaspheme God than to be of a Party out of Power, or even to be thought so. And since the last was the Case, how could you imagine that all Mouths would not be open when you were received, and in some manner preferred by the Government, altho' in a poor Way? I tell you there is hardly a Whig in *Ireland*, who would allow a Potato and Butter-milk to a reputed Tory. Neither is there any thing in your Countrymen, upon this Article, more than what is common in all other Nations, only *quoad magis & minus*.[2] Too much Advertency is not your Talent, or else you had fled from that Text as from a Rock. For, as *Don Quixote* said to *Sancho*, what Business had you to speak of a Halter, in a Family where one of it was hanged?[3] And your Innocence is a Protection that wise Men are ashamed to rely on, further than with God. It is indeed against Common Sense to think that you should chuse such a Time, when you had received a Favour from the Lord Lieutenant, and had reason to expect more, to discover your Disloyalty in the Pulpit. But what will that avail? Therefore sit down and be quiet, and mind your Business, as you [should] do, and contract your Friendships, and expect no more from Man than such an Animal is capable of, and you will every day find my Description of *Yahooes* more resembling.[4] You should think and deal with every Man as a Villain, without calling him so, or flying from him, or valuing him less. This is an old true Lesson. You believe every one will acquit you of any Regard to temporal Interest; and how came you to claim an Exception from all Mankind? I believe you value your temporal Interest as much as any body, but you have not the Arts of pursuing it. You are mistaken. Domestick Evils are no more within a Man than others; and he, who cannot bear up against the first, will sink

under the second, and in my Conscience I believe this is your
Case; for being of a weak Constitution, in an Employment
precarious and tiresome, loaden with Children, *cum uxore
neque leni neque commoda*,[5] a Man of intent and abstracted
Thinking, enslav'd by Mathematicks, and Complaint of the
World, this new Weight of Party Malice hath struck you down,
like a Feather on a Horse's Back already loaden as far as he is
able to bear. You ought to change the Apostle's Expression,
and say, *I will strive to learn in whatever State*, &c.[6]

I will bear none of your Visions; you shall live at *Quilca* but
three Fortnights and a Month in the Year; perhaps not so much.
You shall make no Entertainments but what are necessary to
your Interests; for your true Friends would rather see you over
a Piece of Mutton and a Bottle once a Quarter; you shall be
merry at the Expence of others; you shall take care of your
Health, and go early to bed, and not read late at Night; and
laugh with all Men, without trusting any, and then a Fig for
the Contrivers of your Ruin, who now have no further
Thoughts than to stop your Progress, which perhaps they may
not compass, unless I am deceiv'd more than usual. All this you
will do *si mihi credis*,[7] and not dream of printing your Sermon,
which is a Project abounding with Objections unanswerable,
and with which I could fill this Letter. You say nothing of
having preached before the Lord Lieutenant, nor whether he is
altered towards you; for you speak nothing but generals.[8] You
think all the World hath now nothing to do but to pull Mr.
Sheridan down, whereas it is nothing but a Slap in your turn,
and away. Lord *Oxford* said once to me, on an occasion: These
Fools, because they hear a Noise about their Ears of their own
making, think the whole World is full of it.—When I come to
Town we will change all this Scene, and act like Men of the
World. Grow rich, and you will have no Enemies. Go sometimes
to the Castle, keep fast Mr. *Tickel* and *Balaguer*;[9] frequent
those on the right Side, Friends to the present Powers; drop
those who are loud on the wrong Party, because they know
they can suffer nothing by it.

Sept. 29, 1725.

[Sir, I cannot guess the reason of Mr. Stopford's management, but impute it at a venture to either haste or bashfulness, in the latter of which he is excessive to a fault, although he had already gone the tour of Italy and France to harden him. Perhaps this second journey, and for a longer time, may amend him. He treated you just as he did Lord Carteret, to whom I recommended him.[1]

My letter you saw to Lord Bolingbroke has shown you the situation I am in, and the company I keep, if I do not forget some of its contents. But] I am now returning to the noble scene of Dublin, into the grand Monde, for fear of burying my parts, to signalize my self among Curates and Vicars, and correct all corruptions crept in relating to the weight of bread and butter through those dominions where I govern.[2] I have employed my time (besides ditching) in finishing, correcting, amending, and transcribing my Travels, in four parts compleat, newly augmented, and intended for the press when the world shall deserve them, or rather when a Printer shall be found brave enough to venture his ears.[3] I like your schemes of our meeting after distresses and dispersions; but the chief end I propose to my self in all my labours, is to vex the world, rather than divert it;[4] and if I could compass that design without hurting my own person or fortune, I would be the most indefatigable writer you have ever seen, without reading.[5] I am exceedingly pleased that you have done with Translations; Lord Treasurer Oxford often lamented that a rascally world should lay you under a necessity of misemploying your genius for so long a time.[6] But since you will now be so much better employed, when you think of the World, give it one lash the more at my request. I have ever hated all nations, professions and communities, and all my love is towards individuals; for instance, I hate the tribe of Lawyers, but I love Counsellor such a one, and Judge such a one; so with Physicians, (I will not speak of my own trade) Soldiers, English, Scotch, French, and the rest. But principally I hate and detest that animal called Man, although I heartily love John, Peter, Thomas, and so forth. This is the system upon which I have governed my self many years (but do not tell) and so I shall go on until I have done with them. I have got materials towards a Treatise, proving the falsity of that definition *Animale rationale*, and to shew it should be only *rationis capax*.[7] Upon this great foundation of Misanthropy (although not in Timon's manner[8]) the whole building of my Travels is erected: and I never will have peace of mind until all honest men are of my opinion. By consequence you are to embrace it immediately, and procure that all who deserve my esteem may do so too. The matter is so clear, that it will admit of little dispute; nay, I will hold a hundred pounds, that you and I agree in the point.

I did not know your Odyssey was finished, being yet in the country, which I shall leave in three days. I thank you kindly for the present, but shall like it three fourths the less, from the mixture you mention of other hands; however I am glad you saved your self so much drudgery[9]—I have been long told by Mr. Ford of your great atchievements in building and planting, and especially of your subterranean passage to your garden, whereby you turned a Blunder into a Beauty, which is a piece of *Ars Poetica*.[10]

I have almost done with Harridans, and shall soon become old enough to fall in love with girls of fourteen. The Lady whom you describe to live at court, to be deaf, and no party-woman, I take to be Mythology, but know not how to moralize it. She cannot be Mercy, for Mercy is neither deaf, nor lives at Court. Justice is blind, and perhaps deaf, but neither is she a Court lady: Fortune is both blind and deaf, and a Court lady, but then she is a most damnable Party-woman, and will never make me easy, as you promise. It must be Riches which answers all your description: I am glad she visits you, but my voice is so weak, that I doubt she will never hear me.[11]

Mr. Lewis sent me an account of Dr. Arbuthnot's illness,[12] which is a very sensible affliction to me, who by living so long out of the world, have lost that hardness of heart contracted by years, and general conversation. I am daily losing friends, and neither seeking nor getting others. Oh if the world had but a dozen Arbuthnot's in it, I would burn my Travels! But however, he is not without fault: There is a passage in Bede, highly commending the piety and learning of the Irish in that age, where after abundance of praises he overthrows them all by lamenting that, alas, they kept Easter at a wrong time of the year.[13] So our Doctor hath every quality and virtue that can make a man amiable or useful, but alas, he hath a sort of slouch in his walk. I pray God protect him, for he is an excellent Christian, although not a Catholick, and as fit a man either to dy or live as ever I knew.[14]

I hear nothing of our friend Gay, but I find the Court keeps him at hard meat. I advised him to come over here with a Lord Lieutenant.[15] [Mr. Tickell is in a very good office. I have not seen Philips, tho' formerly we were so intimate. He has got nothing, and by what I find will get nothing though] he writes little Flams (as Lord Leicester called those sort of verses) on Miss Carteret and others.[16] It is remarkable and deserves recording that a Dublin Blacksmith, a great Poet, hath imitated his manner in a poem to the same Miss. Philips is a complainer, and on this occasion I told Lord Carteret that complainers never succeeded at court, although railers do.

Are you altogether a country gentleman that I must address to you out of London, to the hazard of your losing this precious letter, which I will now conclude although so much paper is left. I have an ill name, and therefore shall not subscribe it,[17] but you will guess it comes from one who esteems and loves you about half as much as you deserve, I mean as much as he can.

I am in great concern at what I am just told is in some of the news-papers, that Lord Bolingbroke is much hurt by a fall in hunting. I am glad he hath so much youth and vigour left, (of which he hath not been thrifty) but I wonder he hath no more Discretion.

HOLYHEAD JOURNAL, 1727

I DO here give notice to posterity, that having been the author of severall writings, both in prose and verse, which have passed with good Success, it hath drawn upon me the censure of innumerable attempters and imitatorers and censurers, many of whose names I know, but shall in this be wiser than Virgil and Horace, by not delivering their names down to future ages, and at the same time disappoint that tribe of writers whose chief end next to that of getting bread, was an ambition of having their names upon record by answering or retorting their Scurrilityes; and would slily have made use of my resentment to let the future world know that there were such Persons now in being.[1] I do therefore charge my Successors in fame, by virtue of being an antient 200 years hence, to follow the same method. Dennis, Blackmore, Bentley, and severall others, will reap great advantage by those who have not observed my rule: And heaven forgive Mr. Pope, who hath so grievously transgressed it, by transmitting so many names of forgotten memory, full at length, to be known by Readers in succeeding times, who perhaps may be seduced to Ducklane and Grubstreet, and there find some of the very Treatises he mentions in his Satyrs.[2] I heartily applaud my own innocency and prudence upon this occasion, who never named above 6 authors of remarkable worthlessness; let the Fame of the rest be upon Mr. Pope and his Children. Mr. Gay, although more sparingly, hath gone upon the same mistake.

THE JOURNAL

Friday, at 11 in the morning I left Chester. It was Sept. 22^d 1727.

I bated at a blind ale-house 7 miles from Chester. I thence rode to Ridland; in all 22 miles. I lay there, had bad meat, and tolerable wine. I left Ridland a quarter after 4 morn. on Saturday; stopt on Penmenmawr, examined about my sign verses; the Inn is to be on t' other side therefore the verses to

be changed. I baited at Conway. The Guide going to anoth^r
Inn, the Maid of the old Inn saw me in the Street, and said that
was my Horse she knew me; there I dined, and send for Ned
Holland, a Squire famous for being mentioned in Mr Lyndsay's
verses to Davy Morice. I there again saw Hook's Tomb, who
was the 41st Child of his Mother, and had himself 27 Children;
he dyed about 1638. There is a nota bene that one of his
posterity new furbishd up the Inscription.^{3} I had read in A.Bp
Williams Life that he was buried in an obscure Church in
North Wales. I enquired, and heard it was at —— Church
within a mile of Bangor, whither I was going; I went to the
Church, the Guide grumbling; I saw the Tomb with his Statue
kneeling (in marble). It began thus: [Hospes lege et relege quod
in hoc obscuro sacello non expectares. Hic jacet omnium Præsu-
lum celeberrimus].^{4} I came to Bangor, and crossed the Ferry a
mile from it, where there is an Inn, which if it be well kept will
break Bangor. There I lay,—it was 22 miles from Holyhead. I
was on horseback at 4 in the morning, resolving to be at Church
at Holyhead, but to shew Wat Owen Tudor's Tomb at Penmany.^{5} We passt the place (being a little out of the way) by the
Guides knavery, who had no mind to stay. I was now so weary
with riding, that I was forced to stop at Langueveny, 7 miles
from the Ferry, and rest 2 hours. Then I went on very weary,
but in a few miles more, Watt's Horse lost his two foreshoes,
so the Horse was forced to limp after us.^{6} The Guide was less
concerned than I. In a few miles more, my Horse lost a fore-
shoe; and could not go on the rocky ways. I walked above 2
miles to spare him. It was Sunday, and no Smith to be got. At
last there was a Smith in the way; we left the Guide to shoe the
horses, and walked to a hedge Inn 3 miles from Holyhead;
There I stayd an hour, with no ale to be drunk. a Boat offered,
and I went by Sea and Sayl in it to Holyhead. The guide came
about the same time. I dined with an old Inkeeper, Mrs. Welch,
about 3, on a Loyn of mutton, very good, but the worst ale in
the world, and no wine, for the day before I came here, a vast
number went to Ireld after having drank out all the wine. There
was Stale beer, and I tryed a receit of Oyster shells which I got
powderd on purpose; but it was good for nothing. I walked on

the rocks in the evening, and then went to bed, and dreamt (he) I had got 20 falls from my Horse.

Monday, Septr 25. The Captain talks of sailing at 12. The talk goes off, the Wind is fair, but he says it is too fierce; I believe he wants more company. I had a raw chicken for dinner, and Brandy with water for my drink. I walkt morning and afternoon among the rocks. This evening Watt tells me that my Landlady whispered him that the Grafton packet boat, just come in, had brought her 18 bottles of Irish Claret. I secured one, and supped on part of a neat's tongue, which a friend at London had given Watt to put up for me, and drank a pint of the wine, which was bad enough. Not a soul is yet come to Holyhead, except a young fellow who smiles when he meets me, and would fain be my companion; but it is not come to that yet. I writ abundance of verses this day; and severall usefull hints (thô I say it). I went to bed at 10, and dreamt abundance of nonsense.

Tuesd. 26th. I am forced to wear a shirt 3 days; for fear of being lowsy. I was sparing of them all the way. It was a mercy there were 6 clean when I left London; otherwise Watt (whose blunders would bear an history) would have put them all in the great Box of goods which goes by the Carrier to Chester. He brought but one cravat, and the reason he gave was because the rest were foul, and he thought he should not put foul linnen into the Portmanteau. For, he never dreamt it might be washed on the way. My shirts are all foul now, and by his reasoning, I fear he will leave them at Holyhead when we go. I got anoth^r Loyn of mutton, but so tough I could not chew it, and drank my 2^d pint of wine. I walked this morning a great way among the rocks, and to a hole in one of them from whence at certain periods the water spurted up severall foot high. It raind all night, and hath rained since dinner. But now the sun shines, and I will take my afternoons walk. It was fairer and milder weather than yesterday yet the Captain never dreams of Sailing. To say the truth Michaelmas is the worst season in the year. Is this strange stuff? Why, what would you have me do. I have writt verses, and put down hints till I am weary. I see no creature, I cannot read by candle-light. Sleeping will make me sick. I reckon my self fixed here: and have a mind like Marechall Tallard to take a house and garden.[7] I wish you a merry Christmas, and expect to see you by Candlemas. I have walked this evening again about 3 miles on the rocks, my giddyness God be thanked is almost gone, & my hearing continues;[8] I am now retired to my Chamber to scribble or sit hum-drum. The night is fair, and they pretend to have some hopes of going to-morrow.

Sept[r]. 26th. Thoughts upon being confind at Holyhead. If this were to be my settlement during life, I could amuse my self a while by forming some conveniencyes to be easy; and should not be frighted either by the solitude, or the meaness of lodging, eating or drinking. I shall say nothing upon the suspense I am in about my dearest friend; because that is a case extraordinary, and therefore by way of amusem[t], I will speak as if it were not in my thoughts, and only as a passenger who is in a scurvy unprovided comfortless place without one companion, and who therefore wants to be at home, where he hath all conveniences there proper for a Gentleman of quality. I cannot read at night, and I have no books to read in the day. I have no subject in my head at present to write on. I dare not send my Linnen to be washed for fear of being called away at half an hours warning, and then I must leave them behind me, which is a serious point; in the mean time I am in danger of being lowsy, which is a ticklish Point. I live at great expense without one comfortable bit or sup. I am afraid of joyning with passengers for fear of getting acquaintance with Irish. The Days are short, and I have five hours at night to spend by my self before I go to bed. I should be glad to converse with Farmers or shopkeepers, but none of them speak English. A Dog is better company than the Vicar, for I remembr him of old. What can I do but write every thing that comes into my head. Watt is a Booby of that Species which I dare not suffer to be familiar with me, for he would ramp on my shoulders[9] in half an hour. But the worst part is my half hourly longing, and hopes and vain expectations of a wind; so that I live in suspense which is the worst circumstance of human nature. I am a little vicious [?] from two scurvy disorders, and if I should relapse, there is no[t] a welch house curr that would not have more care taken of him than I, and whose loss would not be more lamented. I confine my self to my narrow chambr in all unwalkable hours. The Master of the pacquet boat, one Jones, hath not treated me with the least civility, altho Watt gave him my name. In short: I come from being used like an Emperor to be used worse than a Dog at Holyhead. Yet my hat is worn to pieces by answering the civilityes of the poor inhabitants as they pass by. The Women might be safe enough, who all wear hats yet never pull them off, if the dirty streets did not foul their petticoats by courtisying so low. Look you; be not impatient, for I onely wait till my watch marks 10, and then I will give you ease, and my self sleep, if I can. On my conscience you may know a Welch dog as well as a Welch man or woman by its peevish passionate way of barking. This paper shall serve to answer all your questions about my Journey; and I will have it printed to satisfy the Kingdom. Forsan et haec olim[10] is a damned lye, for I shall always fret at the remembrance of this imprisonment. Pray pity poor Wat, for he is called dunce, puppy, and Lyar 500 times an hour, and yet he means not ill, for he means nothing. Oh for a dozen bottles of deanry wine and a slice of bread and butter. The wine you sent us yesterday is a little upon the scum[?][11] I wish you had chosen better. I am going to bed at ten a clock, because I am weary of being up.

Wednesday. Last night I dreamt that Ld Bolingbroke and Mr Pope were at my Cathedrall in the Gallery, and that my L^d was to preach: I could not find my Surplice, the Church Servants were all out of the way; the Doors were shut. I sent to my L^d to come into my Stall for more conveniency to get into the Pulpit. The Stall was all broken; the[y] s^d the Collegians had done it. I squeezed among the Rabble, saw my L^d in the Pulpit; I thought his prayer was good, but I forget it. In his Sermon, I did not like his quoting Mr. Wycherlye by name, and his Plays.[12] This is all, and so I waked. To day we were certainly to sayl; the morning was calm. Wat and I walked up the monstrous mountain properly called Holy head or Sacrum promontorium by Ptolemy, 2 miles from this town.[13] I took breath 59 times. I looked from the top to see the wicklow hills, but the day was too hazy, which I felt to my sorrow; for returning, we were overtaken with a furious shower. I got in to a welch cabin almost as bad as an Irish one. There was onely an old welch woman sifting flower, who understood no English, and a boy who fell a roaring for fear of me. Wat (otherwise called unfortunate Jack) ran home for my coat, but stayd so long that I came home in worse rain without him, and he was so lucky to miss me, but took care to carry the key of my room where a fire was ready for me. So I cool'd my heels in the Parlor till he came, but called for a glass of Brandy. I have been cooking my self dry, and am now in my night gown; and this moment comes a Letter to me from one Whelden who tells me he hears I am a lover of the Mathematicks, that he has found out the Longitude, shewn his discourse to Dr Dobbs of y^r Colledge, and sent Letters to all the Mathematicians in London 3 months ago, but received no answer; and desires I would read his discourse. I sent back his Letter with my answer under it, too long to tell you, onely I said I had too much of the Longitude already, by 2 Projectors, whom I encouraged, one of which was a cheat, and the other cut his own throat, and for himself I thought he had a mind to deceive others, or was deceived himself.[14] And so I wait for dinner. I shall dine like a King all alone, as I have done these 6 days. As it happened, if I had gone strait from Chester to Parkgate, 8 miles, I should have been in Dublin on Sunday last. Now Michlmas approaches, the worst time in the year for the Sea, and this rain has made these parts unwalkable, so that I must either write or doze. Bite, when we were in the welch cabin, I order Wat to take a cloath and wipe my wet gown and cassock; it happened to be a meal bag, and as my Gown dryd, it was all dawbed with flower well cemented with the rain. What do I, but see the Gown and cassock well dryd in my room, and while Wat was at dinner, I was an hour rubbing the meal out of them, and did it exactly; He is just come up, and I have gravely bid him take them down to rub them, and I wait whether he will find out what I have been doing. The Rogue is come up in six minutes with my gown, and says there were but few spots (tho he saw a thousand at first), but neither wonders at it nor seems to suspect me who labored like a horse to rub them out. The 3 Pacquet boats are now all on this side; and the

weather grows worse, and so much rain, that there is an end of
my walking. I wish you would send me word how I shall dispose
of my time. If the Vicar could but play at backgammon I were
an Emperor; but I know him not. I am as insignificant here as
parson Brooke is in Dublin; by my conscience I believe Cæsar
would be the same without his army at his back. Well; the
longer I stay here, the more you will murmur for want of
packets. Whoever would wish to live long, should live here, for
a day is longer than a week, and if the weather be foul, as long
as a fortnight. Yet here I could live with two or three friends in
a warm house, and good wine—much better than being a Slave
in Ireld.[15] But my misery is, that I am in the worst part of wales
under the very worst circumstances; afraid of a relapse; in
utmost solitude; impatient for the condition of our friend; not
a soul to converse with, hindered from exercise by rain, cooped
up in a room not half so large as one of the Deanry Closets.
My room smoaks into the bargain, and the w[eather] is too
cold and moist to be without a fire. There is or should be a
Proverbe here. When M^{rs}. Welch's Chimney smoaks, Tis a sign
she'll keep her folks. But, when of smoak the room is clear, It
is a sign we sha'nt stay here. All this is to divert thinking. Tell
me, am not I in a comfortable way. The Yatcht is to be here for
Ld Carteret on the 14th of Octb^r. I fancy he and I shall come
over together.[16] I have opend my door to let in the wind that it
may drive out the smoak. I asked the wind why [he] is so cross,
he assures me 'tis not his fault, but his cursed master Æolus's.
Here is a young Jackanapes in the same Inn waiting for a wind,
who would fain be my companion, and if I stay here much
longer, I am afraid all my pride and grandeur will truckle to
comply with him, especially if I finish these leaves that remain;
but I will write close, and do as the Devil did at mass, pull the
paper with my teeth to make it hold out.

Thursday. Tis allowed that we learn patience by suffering. I
have now not spirits enough left me to fret: I was so cunning
these 3 last days, that whenever I began to rage and storm at
the weather, I took special care to turn my face towards Ireland,
in hopes by my breath to push the wind forward. But now I
give up. However, when upon asking how is the wind, the

people answer, Full in y^r teeth, I cannot help wishing a T—[17] were in theirs. Well, it is now 3 afternoon. I have dined, and invited the Master, the wind and tide serve, and I am just taking boat to go [to] the Ship: so adieu till I see you at the Deanry.

Friday, Mich^{l}mas day. You will now know something of what it is to be at sea. We had not been half an hour in the ship till a fierce wind rose directly against us. We tryed a good while, but the storm still continued; so we turned back, and it was 8 at night, dark and rainy before the ship got back and at anchor: the other passengers went back in a boat to Holyhead: but to prevent accidents and broken shins, I lay all night on board, and came back this morning at 8; am now in my Chamber, where I must stay, and get in a new stock of patience. You all know well enough where I am, for I wrote thrice after your Letter that desired my coming over; the last was from Coventry, 19th instant, but I brought it with me to Chester, and saw it put into the Post, on Thursday, 21st, and the next day followed it my self, but the Pacquet boat was gone before I could get here: because I could not ride 70 miles a day.

ON THE DEATH OF MRS. JOHNSON,
[STELLA]

THIS day, being Sunday, January 28th, 1727–8, about eight o'clock at night, a servant brought me a note, with an account of the death of the truest, most virtuous, and valuable friend, that I, or perhaps any other person ever was blessed with. She expired about six in the evening of this day; and, as soon as I am left alone, which is about eleven at night, I resolve, for my own satisfaction, to say something of her life and character.

She was born at Richmond in Surrey, on the thirteenth day of March, in the year 1681. Her father was a younger brother of a good family in Nottinghamshire, her mother of a lower degree; and indeed she had little to boast of her birth.[1] I knew her from six years old, and had some share in her education, by directing what books she should read, and perpetually instructing her in the principles of honour and virtue; from which she never swerved in any one action or moment of her life.[2] She was sickly from her childhood until about the age of fifteen: But then grew into perfect health, and was looked upon as one of the most beautiful, graceful, and agreeable young women in London, only a little too fat. Her hair was blacker than a raven, and every feature of her face in perfection. She lived generally in the country, with a family, where she contracted an intimate friendship with another lady of more advanced years.[3] I was then (to my mortification) settled in Ireland; and, about a year after, going to visit my friends in England, I found she was a little uneasy upon the death of a person on whom she had some dependance.[4] Her fortune, at that time, was in all not above fifteen hundred pounds, the interest of which was but a scanty maintenance, in so dear a country, for one of her spirit. Upon this consideration, and indeed very much for my own satisfaction, who had few friends or acquaintance in Ireland, I prevailed with her and her dear friend and companion, the other lady, to draw what money they had into Ireland, a great part of their fortune being in annuities upon funds.[5]

Money was then at ten *per cent.* in Ireland, besides the advantage of turning it, and all necessaries of life at half the price. They complied with my advice, and soon after came over; but, I happening to continue some time longer in England, they were much discouraged to live in Dublin, where they were wholly strangers. She was at that time about nineteen years old, and her person was soon distinguished. But the adventure looked so like a frolic, the censure held, for some time, as if there were a secret history in such a removal; which, however, soon blew off by her excellent conduct. She came over with her friend on the   in the year 170–;[6] and they both lived together until this day, when death removed her from us. For some years past, she had been visited with continual ill-health; and several times, within these two years, her life was despaired of.[7] But, for this twelve-month past, she never had a day's health; and, properly speaking, she hath been dying six months, but kept alive, almost against nature, by the generous kindness of two physicians, and the care of her friends. Thus far I writ the same night between eleven and twelve.

Never was any of her sex born with better gifts of the mind, or more improved them by reading and conversation. Yet her memory was not of the best, and was impaired in the latter years of her life. But I cannot call to mind that I ever once heard her make a wrong judgment of persons, books, or affairs. Her advice was always the best, and with the greatest freedom, mixt with the greatest decency. She had a gracefulness somewhat more than human in every motion, word, and action. Never was so happy a conjunction of civility, freedom, easiness and sincerity. There seemed to be a combination among all that knew her, to treat her with a dignity much beyond her rank: Yet people of all sorts were never more easy than in her company. Mr. Addison, when he was in Ireland, being introduced to her, immediately found her out; and if he had not soon after left the kingdom, assured me he would have used all endeavours to cultivate her friendship. A rude or conceited coxcomb passed his time very ill, upon the least breach of respect; for in such a case she had no mercy, but was sure to expose him to the contempt of the standers-by; yet in such a manner as he was ashamed to complain, and durst not resent. All of us, who had the happiness of her friendship, agreed unanimously, that, in an afternoon or evening's conversation, she never failed before we parted of delivering the best thing that was said in the company. Some of us have written down several of her sayings, or what the French call *Bon Mots*,[8] wherein she excelled almost beyond belief. She never mistook the understanding of others; nor ever said a severe word, but where a much severer was deserved.

Her servants loved and almost adored her at the same time. She would, upon occasions, treat them with freedom, yet her demeanour was so awful, that they durst not fail in the least point of respect. She chid them seldom, but it was with severity, which had an effect upon them for a long time after.

January 29th, My head aches, and I can write no more.

January 30th, Tuesday.

This is the night of the funeral, which my sickness will not suffer me to attend. It is now nine at night, and I am removed into another apartment, that I may not see the light in the church, which is just over against the window of my bedchamber.

With all the softness of temper that became a lady, she had the personal courage of a hero. She and her friend having removed their lodgings to a new house, which stood solitary, a parcel of rogues, armed, attempted the house, where there was only one boy: She was then about four and twenty: And, having been warned to apprehend some such attempt, she learned the management of a pistol; and the other women and servants being half-dead with fear, she stole softly to her dining-room window, put on a black hood, to prevent being seen, primed the pistol fresh, gently lifted up the sash; and, taking aim with the utmost presence of mind, discharged the pistol loaden with the bullets, into the body of one villain, who stood the fairest mark. The fellow, mortally wounded, was carried off by the rest, and died the next morning, but his companions could not be found. The Duke of Ormond hath often drank her health to me upon that account, and had always an high esteem for her. She was indeed under some apprehensions of going in a boat, after some danger she had narrowly escaped by water, but she was reasoned thoroughly out of it. She was never known to cry out, or discover any fear, in a coach or on horseback, or any uneasiness by those sudden accidents with which most of her sex, either by weakness or affectation, appear so much disordered.

She never had the least absence of mind in conversation, nor given to interruption, or appeared eager to put in her word by waiting impatiently until another had done. She spoke in a most agreeable voice, in the plainest words, never hesitating, except out of modesty before new faces, where she was somewhat reserved; nor, among her nearest friends, ever spoke much at a time. She was but little versed in the common topics of female chat; scandal, censure, and detraction, never came out of her mouth: Yet, among a few friends, in private conversation, she made little ceremony in discovering her contempt of a coxcomb, and describing all his follies to the life; but the follies of her own sex she was rather inclined to extenuate or to pity.

When she was once convinced by open facts of any breach of truth or honour, in a person of high station, especially in the church, she could not conceal her indignation, nor hear them named without shewing her displeasure in her countenance; particularly one or two of the latter sort, whom she had known and esteemed, but detested above all mankind, when it was manifest that they had sacrificed those two precious virtues to their ambition, and would much sooner have forgiven them the common immoralities of the laity.

Her frequent fits of sickness, in most parts of her life, had prevented her from making that progress in reading which she would otherwise have done. She was well versed in the Greek and Roman story, and was not unskilled in that of France and England. She spoke French perfectly, but forgot much of it by neglect and sickness. She had read carefully all the best books of travels, which serve to open and enlarge the mind. She understood the Platonic and Epicurean philosophy, and judged very well of the defects of the latter.[9] She made very judicious abstracts of the best books she had read. She understood the nature of government, and could point out all the errors of Hobbes, both in that and religion.[10] She had a good insight into physic, and knew somewhat of anatomy; in both which she was instructed in her younger days by an eminent physician, who had her long under his care, and bore the highest esteem for her person and understanding. She had a true taste of wit and good sense, both in poetry and prose, and was a perfect good critic of style: Neither was it easy to find a more proper or impartial judge, whose advice an author might better rely on, if he intended to send a thing into the world, provided it was on a subject that came within the compass of her knowledge. Yet, perhaps, she was sometimes too severe, which is a safe and pardonable error. She preserved her wit, judgment, and vivacity to the last, but often used to complain of her memory.

Her fortune, with some accession, could not, as I have heard say, amount to much more than two thousand pounds, whereof a great part fell with her life, having been placed upon annuities in England, and one in Ireland. In a person so extraordinary, perhaps it may be pardonable to mention some particulars, although of little moment, further than to set forth her character. Some presents of gold-pieces being often made to her while she was a girl, by her mother and other friends, on promise to keep them, she grew into such a spirit of thrift, that, in about three years, they amounted to above two hundred pounds. She used to shew them with boasting; but her mother, apprehending she would be cheated of them, prevailed, in some months, and with great importunities, to have them put out to interest: When the girl lost the pleasure of seeing and counting her gold, which she never failed of doing many times in a day, and despaired of heaping up such another treasure, her humour took quite the contrary turn: She grew careless and squandering of every new acquisition, and so continued until about two and twenty; when, by advice of some friends, and the fright of paying large bills of tradesmen, who enticed her into their debt, she began to reflect upon her own folly, and was never at rest until she had discharged all her shop-bills, and refunded herself a considerable sum she had run out. After which, by the addition of a few years, and a superior understanding, she became, and continued all her life, a most prudent œconomist; yet still with a strong bent to the liberal side, wherein she gratified herself by avoiding all expence in cloaths, (which she ever despised) beyond what was merely decent. And, although her frequent returns of sickness were very chargeable, except fees to physicians, of which she met with several so generous that she could force nothing on them, (and indeed she must otherwise have been undone;) yet she never was without a considerable sum of ready money. Insomuch that, upon her death, when her nearest friends thought her very bare, her executors found in her strong box about a hundred and fifty pounds in gold. She lamented the narrowness of her fortune in nothing so much, as that it did not enable her to entertain her friends so often, and in so hospitable a manner as she desired. Yet they were always welcome; and, while she was in health to direct, were treated with neatness and elegance: So that the revenues of her and her companion, passed for much more considerable than they really were. They lived always in lodgings, their domesticks consisting of two maids and one man. She kept an account of all the family-expences, from her arrival in Ireland to some months before her death; and she would often repine, when looking back upon the annals of her household bills, that every thing necessary for life was double the price, while interest of money was sunk almost to one half; so that the addition made to her fortune was indeed grown absolutely necessary.

[I since writ as I found time.]

But her charity to the poor was a duty not to be diminished, and therefore became a tax upon those tradesmen who furnish the fopperies of other ladies. She bought cloaths as seldom as possible, and those as plain and cheap as consisted with the situation she was in; and wore no lace for many years. Either her judgment or fortune was extraordinary, in the choice of those on whom she bestowed her charity; for it went further in doing good, than double the sum from any other hand. And I have heard her say, she always met with gratitude from the poor: Which must be owing to her skill in distinguishing proper objects, as well as her gracious manner in relieving them.

But she had another quality that much delighted her, although it may be thought a kind of check upon her bounty; however, it was a pleasure she could not resist: I mean that of making agreeable presents, wherein I never knew her equal,

although it be an affair of as delicate a nature as most in the
course of life. She used to define a present, That it was a gift to
a friend of something he wanted or was fond of, and which
could not be easily gotten for money. I am confident, during
my acquaintance with her, she hath, in these, and some other
kinds of liberality, disposed of to the value of several hundred
pounds. As to presents made to herself, she received them with
great unwillingness, but especially from those to whom she had
ever given any; being on all occasions the most disinterested
mortal I ever knew or heard of.

From her own disposition, at least as much as from the
frequent want of health, she seldom made any visits; but her
own lodgings, from before twenty years old, were frequented
by many persons of the graver sort, who all respected her
highly, upon her good sense, good manners, and conversation.
Among these were the late Primate Lindsay, Bishop Loyd,
Bishop Ashe, Bishop Brown, Bishop Stearn, Bishop Pulleyn,
with some others of later date; and indeed the greatest number
of her acquaintance was among the clergy. Honour, truth,
liberality, good-nature, and modesty, were the virtues she
chiefly possessed, and most valued in her acquaintance; and
where she found them, would be ready to allow for some
defects, nor valued them less, although they did not shine in
learning or in wit; but would never give the least allowance for
any failures in the former, even to those who made the greatest
figure in either of the two latter. She had no use of any person's
liberality, yet her detestation of covetous people made her
uneasy if such a one was in her company; upon which occasion
she would say many things very entertaining and humorous.

She never interrupted any person who spoke; she laught at
no mistakes they made, but helped them out with modesty; and
if a good thing were spoken, but neglected, she would not let it
fall, but set it in the best light to those who were present. She
listened to all that was said, and had never the least distraction,
or absence of thought.

It was not safe nor prudent, in her presence, to offend in the
least word against modesty; for she then gave full employment
to her wit, her contempt, and resentment, under which even

stupidity and brutality were forced to sink into confusion; and the guilty person, by her future avoiding him like a bear or a satyr, was never in a way to transgress a second time.

It happened one single coxcomb, of the pert kind, was in her company, among several other ladies; and, in his flippant way, began to deliver some double meanings: The rest flapt their fans, and used the other common expedients practised in such cases, of appearing not to mind or comprehend what was said. Her behaviour was very different, and perhaps may be censured. She said thus to the man: 'Sir, all these ladies and I understand your meaning very well, having, in spite of our care, too often met with those of your sex who wanted manners and good sense. But, believe me, neither virtuous nor even vicious women love such kind of conversation. However, I will leave you, and report your behaviour: And, whatever visit I make, I shall first enquire at the door whether you are in the house, that I may be sure to avoid you.' I know not whether a majority of ladies would approve of such a proceeding; but I believe the practice of it would soon put an end to that corrupt conversation, the worst effect of dulness, ignorance, impudence, and vulgarity, and the highest affront to the modesty and understanding of the female sex.

By returning very few visits, she had not much company of her own sex, except those whom she most loved for their easiness, or esteemed for their good sense; and those, not insisting on ceremony, came often to her. But she rather chose men for her companions, the usual topics of ladies discourse being such as she had little knowledge of, and less relish. Yet no man was upon the rack to entertain her, for she easily descended to any thing that was innocent and diverting. News, politics, censure, family-management, or town-talk, she always diverted to something else; but these indeed seldom happened, for she chose her company better: And therefore many, who mistook her and themselves, having solicited her acquaintance, and finding themselves disappointed after a few visits, dropt off; and she was never known to enquire into the reason, or ask what was become of them.

She was never positive in arguing, and she usually treated

those who were so, in a manner which well enough gratified that unhappy disposition; yet in such a sort as made it very contemptible, and at the same time did some hurt to the owners. Whether this proceeded from her easiness in general, or from her indifference to certain persons, or from her despair of mending them, or from the same practice which she much liked in Mr. Addison, I cannot determine; but when she saw any of the company very warm in a wrong opinion, she was more inclined to confirm them in it, than oppose them. The excuse she commonly gave when her friends asked the reason, was, That it prevented noise, and saved time. Yet I have known her very angry with some whom she much esteemed for sometimes falling into that infirmity.

She loved Ireland much better than the generality of those who owe both their birth and riches to it; and having brought over all the fortune she had in money, left the reversion of the best part of it, one thousand pounds, to Dr. Stephens's Hospital.[11] She detested the tyranny and injustice of England, in their treatment of this kingdom. She had indeed reason to love a country, where she had the esteem and friendship of all who knew her, and the universal good report of all who ever heard of her, without one exception, if I am told the truth by those who keep general conversation. Which character is the more extraordinary, in falling to a person of so much knowledge, wit, and vivacity, qualities that are used to create envy, and consequently censure; and must be rather imputed to her great modesty, gentle behaviour, and inoffensiveness, than to her superior virtues.

Although her knowledge, from books and company, was much more extensive than usually falls to the share of her sex; yet she was so far from making a parade of it, that her female visitants, on their first acquaintance, who expected to discover it, by what they call hard words and deep discourse, would be sometimes disappointed, and say, they found she was like other women. But wise men, through all her modesty, whatever they discoursed on, could easily observe that she understood them very well, by the judgment shewn in her observations, as well as in her questions.

A SHORT VIEW OF THE STATE
OF IRELAND

I AM assured, that it hath, for some Time, been practised as a Method of making Men's Court, when they are asked about the Rate of Lands, the Abilities of Tenants, the State of Trade and Manufacture in this Kingdom, and how their Rents are paid; to answer, that in their Neighbourhood, all Things are in a flourishing Condition, the Rent and Purchase of Land every Day encreasing. And if a Gentleman happen to be a little more sincere in his Representations, besides being looked on as not well affected, he is sure to have a Dozen Contradictors at his Elbow. I think it is no Manner of Secret, why these Questions are so *cordially* asked, or so *obligingly* answered.

BUT since, with regard to the Affairs of this Kingdom, I have been using all Endeavours to subdue my Indignation; to which, indeed, I am not provoked by any personal Interest, being not the Owner of one Spot of Ground in the whole *Island*;[1] I shall only enumerate by Rules generally known, and never contradicted, what are the true Causes of any Countries flourishing and growing rich, and then examine what Effects arise from those Causes in the Kingdom of *Ireland*.

THE first Cause of a Kingdom's thriving, is the Fruitfulness of the Soil, to produce the Necessaries and Conveniencies of Life, not only sufficient for the Inhabitants, but for Exportation into other Countries.

THE Second, is the Industry of the People in working up all their native Commodities, to the last Degree of Manufacture.

THE Third, is the Conveniency of safe Ports and Havens, to carry out their own Goods, as much manufactured, and bring in those of others, as little manufactured, as the Nature of mutual Commerce will allow.

THE Fourth is, that the Natives should, as much as possible, export and import their Goods in Vessels of their own Timber, made in their own Country.

THE Fifth, is the Priviledge of a free Trade in all foreign Countries which will permit them; except to those who are in War with their own Prince or State.

THE Sixth, is, by being governed only by Laws made with their own Consent; for otherwise they are not a free People.[2] And therefore, all Appeals for Justice, or Applications for Favour or Preferment, to another Country, are so many grievous Impoverishments.

THE Seventh is, by Improvement of Land, Encouragement of Agriculture, and thereby encreasing the Number of their People; without which, any Country, however blessed by Nature, must continue poor.

THE Eighth, is the Residence of the Prince, or chief Administrator of the Civil Power.

THE Ninth, is the Concourse of Foreigners for Education, Curiosity, or Pleasure; or as to a general Mart of Trade.

THE Tenth, is by disposing all Offices of Honour, Profit, or Trust only to the Natives, or at least with very few Exceptions; where Strangers have long inhabited the Country, and are supposed to understand, and regard the Interest of it as their own.

THE Eleventh, is when the Rents of Lands, and Profits of Employments, are spent in the Country which produced them, and not in another; the former of which will certainly happen, where the Love of our native Country prevails.

THE Twelfth, is by the publick Revenues being all spent and employed at home; except on the Occasions of a foreign War.

THE Thirteenth is, where the People are not obliged, unless they find it for their own Interest or Conveniency, to receive any Monies, except of their own Coinage by a publick Mint, after the Manner of all civilized Nations.[3]

THE Fourteenth, is a Disposition of the People of a Country to wear their own Manufactures, and import as few Incitements to Luxury, either in Cloaths, Furniture, Food, or Drink, as they possibly can live conveniently without.[4]

THERE are many other Causes of a Nation's thriving, which I cannot at present recollect; but without Advantage from at least some of these, after turning my Thoughts a long Time, I am not able to discover from whence our Wealth proceeds, and therefore would gladly be better informed. In the mean Time, I will here examine what Share falls to *Ireland* of these Causes, or of the Effects and Consequences.

IT is not my Intention to complain, but barely to relate Facts; and the Matter is not of small Importance. For it is allowed, that a Man who lives in a solitary House, far from Help, is not wise in endeavouring to acquire in the Neighbourhood, the Reputation of being rich; because those who come for Gold, will go off with Pewter and Brass, rather than return empty: And in the common Practice of the World, those who possess most Wealth, make the least Parade; which they leave to others, who have nothing else to bear them out, in shewing their Faces on the *Exchange*.

As to the first Cause of a Nation's Riches being the Fertility of the Soil, as well as Temperature of Climate, we have no Reason to complain; for, although the Quantity of unprofitable Land in this Kingdom, reckoning Bogg, and Rock, and barren Mountain, be double in Proportion to what it is in *England*; yet the native Productions which both Kingdoms deal in, are very near on Equality in Point of Goodness; and might, with the same Encouragement, be as well manufactured. I except Mines and Minerals; in some of which, however, we are only defective in Point of Skill and Industry.

IN the Second, which is the Industry of the People; our Misfortune is not altogether owing to our own Fault, but to a Million of Discouragements.

THE Conveniency of Ports and Havens, which Nature hath bestowed so liberally on this Kingdom, is of no more Use to us, than a beautiful Prospect to a Man shut up in a Dungeon.

As to Shipping of its own, *Ireland* is so utterly unprovided, that of all the excellent Timber cut down within these Fifty or Sixty Years, it can hardly be said, that the Nation hath received the Benefit of one valuable House to dwell in, or one Ship to trade with.

IRELAND is the only Kingdom I ever heard or read of, either in ancient or modern Story, which was denied the Liberty of exporting their native Commodities and Manufactures wherever they pleased; except to Countries at War with their own

Prince or State: Yet this Privilege, by the Superiority of meer Power, is refused us, in the most momentous Parts of Commerce; besides an Act of Navigation, to which we never consented, pinned down upon us, and rigorously executed;[5] and a Thousand other unexampled Circumstances, as grievous, as they are invidious to mention. To go onto the rest.

IT is too well known, that we are forced to obey some Laws we never consented to; which is a Condition I must not call by its true uncontroverted Name,[6] for fear of Lord Chief Justice *Whitshed*'s Ghost, with his *Libertas & natale Solum*, written as a Motto on his Coach, as it stood at the Door of the Court, while he was perjuring himself to betray both.[7] Thus, we are in the Condition of Patients, who have Physick sent them by Doctors at a Distance, Strangers to their Constitution, and the Nature of their Disease: And thus, we are forced to pay five Hundred *per Cent.* to decide our Properties;[8] in all which, we have likewise the Honour to be distinguished from the whole Race of Mankind.

As to Improvement of Land; those few who attempt that, or Planting, through Covetousness, or Want of Skill, generally leave Things worse than they were; neither succeeding in Trees nor Hedges; and by running into the Fancy of Grazing, after the Manner of the *Scythians*, are every Day depopulating the Country.[9]

WE are so far from having a King to reside among us, that even the Viceroy is generally absent four Fifths of his Time in the Government.

No Strangers from other Countries, make this a Part of their Travels; where they can expect to see nothing, but Scenes of Misery and Desolation.

THOSE who have the Misfortune to be born here, have the least Title to any considerable Employment; to which they are seldom preferred, but upon a political Consideration.[10]

ONE third Part of the Rents of *Ireland* is spent in *England*; which, with the Profit of Employments, Pensions, Appeals, Journies of Pleasure or Health, Education at the *Inns* of Court, and both Universities,[11] Remittances at Pleasure, the Pay of all Superior Officers in the Army, and other Incidents, will amount to a full half of the Income of the whole Kingdom, all clear Profit to *England*.

WE are denied the Liberty of Coining Gold, Silver, or even Copper. In the Isle of *Man*, they coin their own *Silver*; every petty Prince, Vassal to the *Emperor*, can coin what Money he pleaseth. And in this, as in most of the Articles already mentioned, we are an Exception to all other States or Monarchies that were ever known in the World.

As to the last, or Fourteenth, Article, we take special Care to act diametrically contrary to it in the whole Course of our Lives. Both Sexes, but especially the Women, despise and abhor to wear any of their own Manufactures, even those which are better made than in other Countries; particularly a Sort of Silk Plad through which the Workmen are forced to run a Sort of Gold Thread, that it may pass for *Indian*.[12] Even Ale and Potatoes are imported from *England*, as well as Corn: And our foreign Trade is little more than Importation of *French* Wine; for which I am told we pay ready Money.

Now, if all this be true, upon which I could easily enlarge; I would be glad to know by what secret Method it is, that we grow a rich and flourishing People, without *Liberty, Trade, Manufactures, Inhabitants, Money*, or the *Privilege of Coining*; without *Industry, Labour*, or *Improvement of Lands*; and with more than half the Rent and Profits of the whole *Kingdom*, annually exported; for which we receive not a single Farthing: And to make up all this, nothing worth mentioning, except the Linnen of the *North*, a Trade casual, corrupted, and at Mercy; and some Butter from *Cork*. If we do flourish, it must be against every Law of Nature and Reason; like the Thorn at *Glassenbury*, that blossoms in the Midst of Winter.[13]

LET the worthy *Commissioners* who come from *England*,[14] ride round the Kingdom, and observe the Face of Nature, or the Faces of the Natives; the Improvement of the Land; the thriving numerous Plantations; the noble Woods; the Abundance and Vicinity of Country-Seats; the commodious Farmers Houses and Barns; the Towns and Villages, where every Body is busy, and thriving with all Kind of Manufactures; the Shops full of Goods, wrought to Perfection, and filled with Customers;

the comfortable Diet and Dress, and Dwellings of the People; the vast Numbers of Ships in our Harbours and Docks, and Ship-wrights in our Seaport-Towns; the Roads crouded with Carriers, laden with rich Manufactures; the perpetual Concourse to and fro of pompous Equipages.

WITH what Envy and Admiration, would those Gentlemen return from so delightful a Progress? What glorious Reports would they make, when they went back to *England*?

BUT my Heart is too heavy to continue this Irony longer; for it is manifest, that whatever Stranger took such a Journey, would be apt to think himself travelling in *Lapland*, or *Ysland*,[15] rather than in a Country so favoured by Nature as ours, both in Fruitfulness of Soil, and Temperature of Climate. The miserable Dress, and Dyet, and Dwelling of the People. The general Desolation in most Parts of the Kingdom. The old Seats of the Nobility and Gentry all in Ruins, and no new ones in their Stead. The Families of Farmers, who pay great Rents, living in Filth and Nastiness upon Butter-milk and Potatoes, without a Shoe or Stocking to their Feet; or a House so convenient as an *English* Hog-sty, to receive them. These, indeed, may be comfortable Sights to an *English* Spectator; who comes for a short Time, only *to learn the Language*, and returns back to his own Country, whither he finds all our Wealth transmitted.

Nostrâ miserià magna es.[16]

THERE is not one Argument used to prove the Riches of *Ireland*, which is not a logical Demonstration of its Poverty. The Rise of our Rents is squeezed out of the very Blood, and Vitals, and Cloaths, and Dwellings of the Tenants; who live worse than *English* Beggars.[17] The Lowness of Interest, in all other Countries a Sign of Wealth, is in us a Proof of Misery; there being no Trade to employ any Borrower. Hence alone comes the Dearness of Land, since the Savers have no other Way to lay out their Money. Hence the Dearness of Necessaries for Life; because the Tenants cannot afford to pay such extravagant Rates for Land, (which they must take, or go a-begging) without raising the Price of Cattle, and of Corn, although themselves should live upon Chaff. Hence our encrease of Buildings in this City; because Workmen have nothing to do, but employ one another; and one Half of them are infallibly undone. Hence the daily Encrease of *Bankers*; who may be a necessary Evil in a trading Country, but so ruinous in ours; who, for their private Advantage, have sent away all our Silver, and one Third of our Gold; so that within three Years past, the running Cash of the Nation, which was about five Hundred Thousand Pounds, is now less than two; and must daily diminish, unless we have Liberty to coin, as well as that important Kingdom the Isle of *Man*, and the meanest Prince in the *German* Empire, as I before observed.[18]

I HAVE sometimes thought, that this Paradox of the Kingdom growing rich, is chiefly owing to those worthy Gentlemen the BANKERS; who, except some Custom-house Officers, Birds of Passage, oppressive thrifty 'Squires, and a few others who shall be nameless, are the only thriving People among us: And I have often wished, that a Law were enacted to hang up half a Dozen *Bankers* every Year; and thereby interpose at least some short Delay, to the further Ruin of *Ireland*.

YE are idle, ye are idle, answered *Pharoah* to the *Israelites*, when they complained to *his Majesty*, that they were forced to make Bricks without Straw.[19]

ENGLAND enjoys every one of those Advantages for enriching a Nation, which I have above enumerated; and, into the Bargain, a good Million returned to them every Year, without Labour or Hazard, or one Farthing Value received on our Side. But how long we shall be able to continue the Payment, I am not under the least Concern. One Thing I know, that *when the Hen is starved to Death, there will be no more Golden Eggs*.

I THINK it a little unhospitable, and others may call it a subtil Piece of Malice; that, because there may be a Dozen Families in this Town, able to entertain their *English* Friends in a generous Manner at their Tables; their Guests, upon their Return to *England*, shall report, that we wallow in Riches and Luxury.

YET, I confess, I have known an Hospital, where all the Houshold-Officers grew rich; while the Poor, for whose Sake it was built, were almost starving for want of Food and Raiment.[20]

To conclude. If *Ireland* be a rich and flourishing Kingdom; its Wealth and Prosperity must be owing to certain Causes, that are yet concealed from the whole Race of Mankind; and the Effects are equally invisible. We need not wonder at Strangers, when they deliver such Paradoxes; but a Native and Inhabitant of this Kingdom, who gives the same Verdict, must be either ignorant to Stupidity; or a Man-pleaser,[21] at the Expence of all Honour, Conscience, and Truth.

THE INTELLIGENCER

NUMBER III

—— *Ipse per omnes*
Ibit personas, & turbam reddet in unam[1]

Written in *Ireland* in the Year 1728

THE *Players* having now almost done with the Comedy called the *Beggar*'s *Opera*, for the Season; it may be no unpleasant Speculation, to reflect a little upon this *Dramatick Piece*, so singular in the Subject and Manner, so much an Original, and which hath frequently given so very agreeable an Entertainment.

ALTHOUGH an evil *Taste* be very apt to prevail, both here and in *London*; yet there is a Point which whoever can rightly touch, will never fail of pleasing a very great Majority; so great, that the Dislikers, out of Dulness or Affectation, will be silent, and forced to fall in with the Herd: The Point I mean, is what we call *Humour*; which, in its Perfection, is allowed to be much preferable to *Wit*; if it be not rather the most useful, and agreeable Species of it.[2]

I AGREE with Sir *William Temple*, that the Word is peculiar to our *English Tongue*; but I differ from him in the Opinion, that the Thing it self is peculiar to the *English Nation*, because the contrary may be found in many *Spanish, Italian,* and *French* Productions: And particularly, whoever hath a *Taste* for *true Humour*, will find an Hundred Instances of it, in those Volumes printed in *France*, under the Name of *Le Theatre Italien*: To say nothing of *Rabelais, Cervantes*, and many others.[3]

NOW I take the *Comedy*, or *Farce*, (or whatever Name the *Criticks* will allow it) called the *Beggar*'s *Opera*, to excel in this Article of *Humour*; and upon that Merit to have met with such prodigious Success, both here and in *England*.

As to *Poetry, Eloquence,* and *Musick*, which are said to have most Power over the Minds of Men; it is certain, that very few have a *Taste* or *Judgment* of the Excellencies of the two former; and if a Man succeed in either, it is upon the Authority of those *few Judges*, that lend their *Taste* to the Bulk of Readers, who have none of their own. I am told, there are as few good Judges in *Musick*; and that among those who crowd the *Opera's*, Nine in Ten go thither merely out of *Curiosity, Fashion*, or *Affectation*.

BUT a *Taste* for *Humour*, is in some Manner fixed to the very Nature of Man, and generally obvious to the Vulgar, except upon Subjects too refined, and superior to their Understanding.

AND, as this *Taste* of *Humour* is purely natural, so is *Humour* it self; neither is it a *Talent* confined to Men of *Wit*, or *Learning*; for we observe it sometimes among common Servants, and the meanest of the People, while the very Owners are often ignorant of the Gift they possess.[4]

I KNOW very well, that this happy *Talent* is contemptibly treated by *Criticks*, under the Name of *low Humour*, or *low Comedy*; but I know likewise, that the *Spaniards* and *Italians*, who are allowed to have the most Wit of any *Nation* in *Europe*, do most excel in it, and do most esteem it.

BY what Disposition of the Mind, what Influence of the Stars, or what Situation of the *Climate*, this Endowment is bestowed upon Mankind, may be a Question fit for *Philosophers* to discuss. It is certainly the best Ingredient towards that Kind of Satyr, which is most useful, and gives the least Offence; which, instead of lashing, laughs Men out of their Follies, and Vices; and is the Character that gives *Horace* the Preference to *Juvenal*.[5]

AND, although some Things are too serious, solemn, or sacred to be turned into Ridicule, yet the Abuses of them are certainly not; since it is allowed, that Corruptions in *Religion, Politicks*, and *Law*, may be proper *Topicks* for this Kind of *Satyr*.[6]

THERE are two Ends that Men propose in writing Satyr; one of them less noble than the other, as regarding nothing further than the private Satisfaction, and Pleasure of the Writer; but without any View towards *personal Malice:* The other is a *publick Spirit*, prompting Men of *Genius* and Virtue, to mend the World as far as they are able. And as both these Ends are innocent, so the latter is highly commendable.[7] With regard to the former, I demand, whether I have not as good a Title to laugh, as Men have to be ridiculous; and to expose Vice, as another hath to be vicious. If I ridicule the Follies and Corruptions of a *Court*, a *Ministry*, or a *Senate*, are they not amply paid by *Pensions*, *Titles*, and *Power*; while I expect, and desire, no other Reward, than that of laughing with a few Friends in a Corner? Yet, if those who take Offence, think me in the Wrong, I am ready to change the Scene with them, whenever they please.

BUT, if my Design be to make Mankind better; then I think it is my Duty; at least, I am sure it is the Interest of those very *Courts* and *Ministers*, whose Follies or Vices I ridicule, to reward me for my good Intentions: For if it be reckoned a high Point of Wisdom to get the Laughers on our Side; it is much more easy, as well as wise, to get those on our Side, who can make Millions laugh when they please.

MY Reason for mentioning *Courts*, and *Ministers*, (*whom I never think on, but with the most profound Veneration*) is, because an Opinion obtains, that in the *Beggar*'s *Opera*, there appears to be some Reflection upon *Courtiers* and *Statesmen*, whereof I am by no Means a Judge.

IT is true, indeed, that Mr. GAY, the Author of this Piece, hath been somewhat singular in the Course of his Fortunes; for it hath happened, that after Fourteen Years attending the *Court*, with a large Stock of real Merit, a modest and agreeable Conversation, a *Hundred Promises*, and *five Hundred Friends*, he hath failed of Preferment; and upon a very weighty Reason. He lay under the Suspicion of having written a Libel, or Lampoon against a great Minister.[8] It is true, that great Minister was demonstratively convinced, and publickly owned his Conviction, that Mr. GAY was not the Author; but having lain under the Suspicion, it seemed very just, that he should suffer the Punishment; because in this most reformed Age, the Virtues of a Prime Minister are no more to be suspected, than the Chastity of *Cæsar*'s Wife.[9]

IT must be allowed, That the *Beggar's Opera* is not the first
of Mr. GAY's Works, wherein he hath been faulty, with Regard
to *Courtiers* and *Statesmen*. For to omit his other Pieces; even
in his Fables, published within two Years past, and dedicated
to the Duke of CUMBERLAND, for which he was *promised* a
Reward, he hath been thought somewhat too bold upon the
Courtiers.[10] And although it be highly probable, he meant only
the *Courtiers* of former Times, yet he acted unwarily, by not considering that the Malignity of some People might misinterpret
what he said, to the Disadvantage of present *Persons* and Affairs.

BUT I have now done with Mr. GAY as a Politician; and shall
consider him henceforward only as Author of the *Beggar's
Opera*, wherein he hath by a Turn of *Humour*, intirely new,
placed Vices of all Kinds in the strongest and most odious
Light; and thereby, done eminent Service, both to *Religion* and
Morality. This appears from the unparallelled Success he hath
met with. All *Ranks, Parties*, and *Denominations* of Men, either
crowding to see his *Opera*, or reading it with Delight in their
Closets; even *Ministers* of State, whom he is thought to have most
offended (next to those whom the Actors represent) appearing
frequently at the *Theatre*, from a Consciousness of their own
Innocence, and to convince the World how unjust a Parallel,
Malice, Envy and *Disaffection to the Government have made*.[11]

I AM assured that several worthy *Clergy-Men* in this *City*,
went privately to see the *Beggars Opera* represented; and that
the *fleering Coxcombs* in the *Pit*, amused themselves with
making Discoveries, and spreading the Names of those Gentlemen round the Audience.

I SHALL not pretend to vindicate a *Clergy-Man*, who would
appear openly in his Habit at a *Theatre*, with such a vicious
Crew, as might probably stand round him, at such *Comedies*,
and profane *Tragedies* as are often represented. Besides, I know
very well, that Persons of their Function are bound to avoid the
Appearance of Evil, or of giving Cause of Offence. But when the
Lords Chancellors, who are Keepers of the King's Conscience;
when the *Judges* of the Land, whose Title is *Reverend*; when
Ladies, who are bound by the Rules of their Sex to the strictest
Decency, appear in the *Theatre* without Censure; I cannot

understand, why a young *Clergy-Man*, who comes concealed, out of Curiosity to see an innocent and moral Play, should be so highly condemned: Nor do I much approve the Rigour of a great Prelate, who said, *he hoped none of his Clergy were there.* I am glad to hear there are no weightier Objections against that Reverend Body planted in this City, and I wish there never may. But I should be very sorry, that any of them should be so weak, as to imitate a *Court-Chaplain* in ENGLAND, who preached against the *Beggar's Opera*; which will probably do more Good, than a thousand Sermons of so stupid, so injudicious, and so prostitute a Divine.[12]

IN this happy Performance of Mr. GAY's, all the Characters are just, and none of them carried beyond Nature, or hardly beyond Practice. It discovers the whole System of that Common-Wealth, or that *Imperium in Imperio* of Iniquity, established among us, by which neither our Lives nor our Properties are secure, either in the High-ways, or in publick Assemblies, or even in our own Houses.[13] It shews the miserable Lives and the constant Fate of those abandoned Wretches: For how little they sell their Lives and Souls; betrayed by their *Whores*, their *Comrades*, and the *Receivers* and *Purchasers* of those Thefts and Robberies. This *Comedy* contains likewise a *Satyr*, which, without enquiring whether it affects the present Age, may possibly be useful in Times to come. I mean, where the Author takes the Occasion of comparing those *common Robbers of the Publick*, and their several Stratagems of betraying, undermining and hanging each other, to the several Arts of *Politicians* in Times of Corruption.

THIS *Comedy* likewise exposeth with great Justice, that unnatural Taste for *Italian* Musick among us, which is wholly unsuitable to our *Northern Climate*, and the *Genius* of the People, whereby we are over-run with *Italian Effeminacy*, and *Italian* Nonsense.[14] An old Gentleman said to me, that many Years ago, when the Practice of an unnatural Vice grew frequent in *London*, and many were prosecuted for it, he was sure it would be the Fore-runner of *Italian* Opera's and Singers; and then we should want nothing but Stabbing or Poisoning, to make us perfect *Italians*.[15]

UPON the whole, I deliver my Judgment, That nothing but servile Attachment to a Party, Affectation of Singularity, lamentable Dullness, mistaken Zeal, or studied Hypocrisy, can have the least reasonable Objection against this excellent moral Performance of the *Celebrated Mr.* GAY.

NUMBER IX

FROM frequently reflecting upon the Course and Method of educating Youth in this and a neighbouring Kingdom, with the general Success and Consequence thereof, I am come to this Determination; That, Education is always the *worse* in Proportion to the *Wealth* and *Grandeur* of the Parents: Nor do I doubt in the least, that if the whole World were now under the Dominion of *one Monarch*, (provided I might be allowed to chuse *where* he should fix the Seat of his Empire) the only Son and Heir of that Monarch, would be the worst educated Mortal that ever was born since the Creation: And I doubt, the same Proportion will hold through all Degrees and Titles, from an Emperor downwards, to the common Gentry.

I DO not say, that this hath been always the Case; for in better Times it was directly otherwise; and a Scholar may fill half his *Greek* and *Roman* Shelves with Authors of the noblest Birth, as well as highest Virtue. Nor, do I tax all Nations at present with this Defect; for I know there are some to be excepted, and particularly *Scotland*, under all the Disadvantages of its Climate and Soil; if that Happiness be not rather owing even to those very Disadvantages. What is then to be done, if this Reflection must fix on two Countries, which will be most ready to take Offence, and which of all others it will be least prudent or safe to offend?

BUT there is one Circumstance yet more dangerous and lamentable: For if, according to the *Postulatum* already laid down, the higher Quality any Youth is of, he is in greater Likelihood to be worse educated; it behoves me to dread, and keep far from the Verge of *Scandalum Magnatum*.[1]

RETRACTING therefore that hazardous *Postulatum*; I shall

venture no further at present, than to say, that perhaps *some* Care in educating the Sons of Nobility and principal Gentry, might not be ill employed. If this be not delivered with Softness enough, I must for the future be silent.

IN the mean Time, let me ask only two Questions, which relate to *England*. I ask first, how it comes about, that for above sixty Years past, the chief Conduct of Affairs hath been generally placed in *New-men*, with few Exceptions?[2] The noblest Blood of *England* having been shed in the grand Rebellion,[3] many great Families became extinct, or supplied by Minors. When the King was restored, very few of those Lords remained, who began, or at least had improved their Education, under the happy Reign of King *James*, or King *Charles* I. of which Lords the two principal were the Marquis of *Ormond*, and the Earl of *Southampton*.[4] The Minors having, during the Rebellion and Usurpation, either received too much Tincture of bad Principles from those fanatick Times; or coming to Age at the Restoration, fell into the Vices of that dissolute Reign.[5]

I DATE from this Æra, the corrupt Method of Education among us, and the Consequence thereof, in the Necessity the Crown lay under of introducing *New-men* into the highest Employments of State, or to the Office of what we now call Prime Ministers; Men of Art, Knowledge, Application and Insinuation, merely for Want of a Supply among the Nobility. They were generally (though not always) of good Birth, sometimes younger Brothers; at other times such, who although inheriting ample Fortunes, yet happened to be well educated, and provided with Learning. Such under that King, were *Hyde*, *Bridgeman*, *Clifford*, *Osborn*, *Godolphin*, *Ashley-Cooper*:[6] Few or none under the short Reign of King *James* II. Under King *William*; *Sommers*, *Montague*, *Churchil*, *Vernon*, *Harry Boyle*, and many others. Under the Queen; *Harley*, *St. John*, *Harcourt*, *Trevor*, who indeed were Persons of the best private Families, but unadorned with Titles. So in the last Reign, Mr. *Robert Walpole*, was for many Years Prime Minister, in which Post he still HAPPILY continues: His Brother *Horace* is Ambassador Extraordinary to *France*. Mr. *Addison* and Mr.

Craggs, without the least Alliance to support them, have been Secretaries of State.[7]

IF the Facts have been thus for above sixty Years past, (whereof I could, with a little further Recollection, produce many more Instances) I would ask again, how it hath happened, that in a Nation plentifully abounding with Nobility, so great a Share in the most important Parts of publick Management, hath been for so long a Period chiefly intrusted to Commoners; unless some Omissions or Defects of the highest Import, may be charged upon those, to whom the Care of educating our noble Youth hath been committed? For, if there be any Difference between human Creatures in the Point of *natural Parts*, as we usually call them; it should seem, that the Advantage lies on the Side of Children born from noble wealthy Parents; the same traditional Sloth and Luxury, which render their Body weak and effeminate, perhaps refining and giving a freer Motion to the Spirits, beyond what can be expected from the gross, robust Issue of meaner Mortals. Add to this, the peculiar Advantages, which all young Noblemen possess, by the Privileges of their Birth; such as a free Access to Courts, and a Deference paid to their Persons.

BUT as my Lord *Bacon* chargeth it for a Fault on Princes, that they are impatient to compass *Ends*, without giving themselves the Trouble of consulting or executing the *Means:*[8] So perhaps it may be the Disposition of young Nobles, either from the Indulgence of Parents, Tutors and Governors, or their own Inactivity, that they expect the *Accomplishments* of a good Education, without the least Expence of *Time* or *Study*, to acquire them.

WHAT I said last, I am ready to retract. For the Case is infinitely worse; and the very Maxims set up to direct *modern* Education, are enough to destroy all the Seeds of Knowledge, Honour, Wisdom and Virtue among us. The current Opinion prevails, that the Study of *Greek* and *Latin* is Loss of Time; that the publick Schools by mingling the Sons of Noblemen with those of the Vulgar, engage the former in bad Company; that Whipping breaks the Spirits of Lads well born; that Universities make young Men Pedants; that to dance, fence, speak

French, and know how to behave your self among great Persons of both Sexes, comprehends *the whole Duty of a Gentleman.*[9]

I CANNOT but think this wise System of Education, hath been much cultivated among us by those Worthies of the Army, who during the last War, returning from *Flanders* at the Close of each Campaign, became the Dictators of Behaviour, Dress, and Politeness, to all those Youngsters, who frequent Chocolate-Coffee-Gaming-Houses, Drawing-Rooms, Opera's, Levees and Assemblies; where a Colonel, by his Pay, Perquisites, and Plunder, was qualified to out-shine many Peers of the Realm; and by the Influence of an *exotick* Habit and Demeanor, added to other foreign Accomplishments, gave the Law to the whole Town; and was copied as the Standard-Pattern of whatever was refined in Dress, Equipage, Conversation, or Diversions.[10]

I REMEMBER in those Times, an admired Original of that Vocation, sitting in a Coffee-House near two Gentlemen, whereof one was of the Clergy, who were engaged in some Discourse that savoured of Learning; this Officer thought fit to interpose; and professing to deliver the Sentiments of his Fraternity, as well as his own, (and probably did so of too many among them) turning to the Clergy-Man, spoke in the following Manner. *D—n me, Doctor, say what you will, the Army is the only School for Gentlemen. Do you think my Lord* Marlborough *beat the* French *with* Greek *and* Latin. *D—n me, a Scholar when he comes into good Company, what is he but an Ass? D—n me, I would be be glad, by G—d, to see any of your Scholars with his Nouns, and his Verbs, and his Philosophy, and Trigonometry, what a Figure he would make at a Siege or Blockade, or reconoitring —— D—n me,* &c.[11] After which he proceeded with a Volley of Military Terms, less significant, sounding worse, and harder to be understood than any that were ever coined by the Commentators upon *Aristotle*. I would not here be thought to charge the Soldiery with Ignorance and Contempt of Learning, without allowing Exceptions, of which I have known a few: But however, the worse Example, especially in a great Majority, will certainly prevail.

I HAVE heard, that the late Earl of *Oxford*, in the Time of his Ministry, never passed by *White's Chocolate-House* (the common Rendezvous of infamous Sharpers, and noble Cullies) without bestowing a Curse upon that famous Academy, as the Bane of half the *English Nobility*.[12] I have likewise been told another Passage concerning that great Minister; which, because it gives a humorous Idea of one principal Ingredient in modern Education, take as followeth. *Le Sac*, the famous *French* Dancing-Master, in great Admiration, asked a Friend, whether it were true, that Mr. *Harley* was made an Earl and Lord-Treasurer? And finding it confirmed, said, *Well, I wonder what the Devil the Queen could see in him; for I attended him two Years, and he was the greatest Dunce that ever I taught.*[13]

ANOTHER Hindrance to good Education, and I think the greatest of any; is that pernicious Custom in rich and noble Families, of entertaining *French* Tutors in their Houses. These wretched *Pedagogues* are enjoyed by the Father, to take special Care that the Boy shall be perfect in his *French*; by the Mother, that *Master* must not walk till he is hot, nor be suffered to play with other Boys, nor be wet in his Feet, nor daub his Cloaths: And to see that the Dancing-Master attends constantly, and does his Duty: She further insists that the Child be not kept too long poring on his Book, because he is subject to sore Eyes, and of a weakly Constitution.

By these Methods, the young Gentleman is in every Article as fully accomplished at eight Years old, as at eight and twenty; Age adding only to the Growth of his Person and his Vices; so that if you should look at him in his Boyhood through the magnifying End of a Perspective, and in his Manhood through the other, it would be impossible to spy any Difference; the same Airs, the same Strut, the same Cock of his Hat, and the Posture of his Sword, (as far as the Changes of Fashions will allow) the same Understanding, the same Compass of Knowledge, with the very same Absurdity, Impudence, and Impertinence of Tongue.

HE is taught from the Nursery, that he must inherit a great Estate, and hath no Need to mind his Book; which is a Lesson he never forgets to the End of his Life. His chief Solace is to steal down, and play at Span-Farthing with the Page, or young Black-a-moore, or little favourite Foot-boy; one of which is his principal Confident and Bosom-Friend.[14]

THERE is one young Lord in this Town, who by an unexampled Piece of good Fortune, was miraculously snatched
out of the Gulph of Ignorance; confined to a publick School for
a due Term of Years; well whipped when he deserved it; clad
no better than his Comrades, and always their Play-fellow on
the same Foot; had no Precedence in the School, but what was
given him by his Merit, and lost it whenever he was negligent.[15]
It is well known how many Mutinies were bred at this unprece-
dented Treatment; what Complaints among his *Relations*, and
other *Great Ones* of both Sexes; that his Stockings with Silver
Clocks[16] were ravished from him; that he wore his own Hair;
that his Dress was undistinguished; that he was not fit to appear
at a Ball or Assembly, nor suffered to go to either: And it was
with the utmost Difficulty, that he became qualified for his
present Removal to the University; where he may probably be
farther persecuted, and possibly with Success, if the Firmness
of a Governor, and his own good Dispositions will not preserve
him. I confess, I cannot but wish he may go on in the Way he
began; because, I have a Curiosity to know by so *singular*
an Experiment, whether Truth, Honour, Justice, Temperance,
Courage, and good Sense, acquired by a *School* and *College*
Education, may not produce a very tolerable Lad; although he
should happen to fail in one or two of those Accomplishments,
which in the general Vogue are held so important to the finishing of a Gentleman.

IT is true, I have known an Academical Education to have
been exploded in publick Assemblies; and have heard more
than one or two Persons of high Rank declare, they could learn
nothing more at *Oxford* and *Cambridge*, than to drink Ale,
and smoke Tobacco; wherein I firmly believed them, and could
have added some Hundred Examples from my own Observation in one of those Universities:[17] But they all were of young
Heirs sent thither only for Form; either from Schools, where
they were not suffered by their careful Parents to stay above
three Months in the Year; or from under the Management of
French Family-Tutors, who yet often attended them in their
College, to prevent all Possibility of their Improvement: But, I
never yet knew any one Person of Quality, who followed his

Studies at the University, and carried away his just Proportion of Learning, who was not ready upon all Occasions to celebrate and defend that Course of Education, and to prove a Patron of learned Men.

THERE is one Circumstance in a learned Education, which ought to have much Weight, even with those who have no Learning at all. The Books read at *Schools* and *Colleges*, are full of Incitements to Virtue, and Discouragements from Vice, drawn from the wisest Reasons, the strongest Motives, and the most influencing Examples. Thus, young Minds are filled early with an Inclination to Good, and an Abhorrence of Evil, both which increase in them, according to the Advances they make in Literature: And, although they may be, and too often are, drawn by the Temptations of Youth, and the Opportunities of a large Fortune, into some Irregularities, when they come forward into the great World; it is ever with Reluctance and Compunction of Mind, because their Byass to Virtue still continues. They may stray sometimes by Infirmity or Complyance, but they will soon return to the right Road, and keep it always in view. I speak only of those Excesses, which are too much the Attendants of Youth and warmer Blood: But, as to the Points of Honour, Truth, Justice, and other noble Gifts of the Mind, wherein the Temperature of the Body hath no Concern, they are seldom or never known to be misled.

I HAVE engaged my self very unwarily in too copious a Subject for so short a Paper. The present Scope I would aim at, is to prove, that some Proportion of human Knowledge appears requisite to those, who, by their Birth or Fortune, are called to the making of Laws, and in a subordinate Way to the Execution of them; and that such Knowledge is not to be obtained without a Miracle; under the frequent, corrupt, and sottish Methods of educating those, who are born to Wealth or Titles. For, I would have it remembered, that I do by no Means confine these Remarks to young Persons of noble Birth; the same Errors running through all Families, where there is Wealth enough to afford, that their Sons (at least the Eldest) may be good for nothing. Why should my Son be a Scholar, when it is not intended that he should live by his Learning? By this Rule, if what is commonly said be true, that Money answereth all Things,[18] why should my Son be honest, temperate, just, or charitable, since he hath no Intention to depend upon any of these Qualities for a Maintenance?

WHEN all is done, perhaps upon the whole, the Matter is not so bad as I would make it: And GOD, who worketh Good out of Evil, acting only by the ordinary Course and Rule of Nature, permits this continual Circulation of human Things for his own unsearchable Ends. The Father grows rich by Avarice, Injustice, Oppression; he is a Tyrant in the Neighbourhood over Slaves and Beggars, whom he calleth his Tenants. Why should he desire to have Qualities infused into his Son, which himself never possessed, or knew, or found the Want of in the Acquisition of his Wealth? The Son bred in Sloth and Idleness, becomes a Spendthrift, a Cully, a Profligate; and goes out of the World a Beggar, as his Father came in: Thus the former is punished for his own Sins, as well as for those of the latter. The Dunghil having raised a huge Mushroom of short Duration, is now spread to enrich other Mens Lands. It is, indeed, of worse Consequence, where noble Families are gone to Decay; because their Titles and Privileges outlive their Estates: And, Politicians tell us, that nothing is more dangerous to the Publick, than a numerous Nobility without Merit or Fortune. But even here, GOD hath likewise prescribed some Remedy in the Order of Nature; so many great Families coming to an End by their Sloth, Luxury, and abandoned Lusts, which enervated their Breed through every Succession, producing gradually a more effeminate Race, wholly unfit for Propagation.

A MODEST PROPOSAL

FOR *Preventing the Children of poor People in* Ireland, *from being a Burden to their Parents or Country; and for making them beneficial to the Publick*

Written in the Year 1729

IT is a melancholly Object to those who walk through this great Town, or travel in the Country; when they see the *Streets*, the *Roads*, and *Cabbin-doors* crowded with *Beggars* of the Female Sex, followed by three, four, or six Children, *all in Rags*, and importuning every Passenger for an Alms.[1] These *Mothers*, instead of being able to work for their honest Livelyhood, are forced to employ all their Time in stroling to beg Sustenance for their *helpless Infants*; who, as they grow up, either turn *Thieves* for want of Work; or leave their *dear Native Country*, *to fight for the Pretender in* Spain; or sell themselves to the *Barbadoes*.[2]

I THINK it is agreed by all Parties, that this prodigious Number of Children in the Arms, or on the Backs, or at the *Heels* of their *Mothers*, and frequently of their *Fathers*, is *in the present deplorable State of the Kingdom*, a very great additional Grievance; and therefore, whoever could find out a fair, cheap, and easy Method of making these Children sound and useful Members of the Commonwealth, would deserve so well of the Publick, as to have his Statue set up for a Preserver of the Nation.

BUT my Intention is very far from being confined to provide only for the Children of *professed Beggars:* It is of a much greater Extent, and shall take in the whole Number of Infants at a certain Age, who are born of Parents, in effect as little able to support them, as those who demand our Charity in the Streets.

As to my own Part, having turned my Thoughts for many Years, upon this important Subject, and maturely weighed the several *Schemes of other Projectors*, I have always found them grosly mistaken in their Computation. It is true, a Child *just dropt from its Dam*, may be supported by her Milk, for a Solar Year with little other Nourishment; at most not above the Value of two Shillings; which the Mother may certainly get, or the Value in *Scraps*, by her lawful Occupation of *Begging*: And, it is exactly at one Year old, that I propose to provide for them in such a Manner, as, instead of being a Charge upon their *Parents*, or the *Parish*, or *wanting Food and Raiment* for the rest of their Lives; they shall, on the contrary, contribute to the Feeding, and partly to the Cloathing, of many Thousands.

THERE is likewise another great Advantage in my *Scheme*, that it will prevent those *voluntary Abortions*, and that horrid Practice of *Women murdering their Bastard Children*; alas! too frequent among us; sacrificing the *poor innocent Babes*, I doubt, more to avoid the Expence than the Shame; which would move Tears and Pity in the most Savage and inhuman Breast.[3]

THE Number of Souls in *Ireland* being usually reckoned one Million and a half;[4] of these I calculate there may be about Two Hundred Thousand Couple whose Wives are Breeders; from which Number I subtract thirty thousand Couples, who are able to maintain their own Children; although I apprehend there cannot be so many, under *the present Distresses of the Kingdom*; but this being granted, there will remain an Hundred and Seventy Thousand Breeders. I again subtract Fifty Thousand for those Women who miscarry, or whose Children die by Accident, or Disease, within the Year. There only remain an Hundred and Twenty Thousand Children of poor Parents annually born: The Question therefore is, How this Number shall be reared, and provided for? Which, as I have already said, under the present Situation of Affairs, is utterly impossible, by all the Methods hitherto proposed: For we can *neither employ them in Handicraft* or *Agriculture*; we neither build Houses, (I mean in the Country) nor cultivate Land: They can very seldom pick up a Livelyhood *by Stealing* until they arrive at six Years old; except where they are of towardly Parts; although, I confess, they learn the Rudiments much earlier; during which Time, they can, however, be properly looked upon only as *Probationers*; as I have been informed by a principal Gentleman in the County of *Cavan*,[5] who protested to me, that he never knew above one or two Instances under the Age of six, even in a Part of the Kingdom *so renowned for the quickest Proficiency in that Art*.

I AM assured by our Merchants, that a Boy or a Girl before twelve Years old, is no saleable Commodity; and even when they come to this Age, they will not yield above Three Pounds, or Three Pounds and half a Crown at most, on the Exchange; which cannot turn to Account either to the Parents or Kingdom; the Charge of Nutriment and Rags, having been at least four Times that Value.

I SHALL now therefore humbly propose my own Thoughts; which I hope will not be liable to the least Objection.

I HAVE been assured by a very knowing *American* of my Acquaintance in *London*; that a young healthy Child, well nursed, is, at a Year old, a most delicious, nourishing, and wholesome Food; whether *Stewed*, *Roasted*, *Baked*, or *Boiled*; and, I make no doubt, that it will equally serve in a *Fricasie*, or *Ragout*.[6]

I DO therefore humbly offer it to *publick Consideration*, that of the Hundred and Twenty thousand Children, already computed, Twenty thousand may be reserved for Breed; whereof only one Fourth Part to be Males; which is more than we allow to *Sheep*, *black Cattle*, or *Swine*; and my Reason is, that these Children are seldom the Fruits of Marriage, *a Circumstance not much regarded by our Savages*; therefore, *one Male* will be sufficient to serve *four Females*. That the remaining Hundred thousand, may, at a Year old, be offered in Sale to the *Persons of Quality* and *Fortune*, through the Kingdom; always advising the Mother to let them suck plentifully in the last Month, so as to render them plump, and fat for a good Table. A Child will make two Dishes at an Entertainment for Friends; and when the Family dines alone, the fore or hind Quarter will make a reasonable Dish; and seasoned with a little Pepper or Salt, will be very good Boiled on the Fourth Day, especially in *Winter*.

I HAVE reckoned upon a Medium, that a Child just born will weigh Twelve Pounds; and in a solar Year, if tolerably nursed, encreaseth to twenty eight Pounds.

I GRANT this Food will be somewhat dear, and therefore very *proper for Landlords*; who, as they have already devoured most of the Parents, seem to have the best Title to the Children.

INFANTS Flesh will be in Season throughout the Year; but more plentiful in *March*, and a little before and after: For we are told by a grave Author, an eminent *French* Physician, that *Fish being a prolifick Dyet*, there are more Children born in *Roman Catholick Countries* about Nine Months after *Lent*, than at any other Season:[7] Therefore reckoning a Year after *Lent*, the Markets will be more glutted than usual; because the Number of *Popish Infants*, is, at least, three to one in this Kingdom; and therefore it will have one other Collateral Advantage, by lessening the Number of *Papists* among us.

I HAVE already computed the Charge of nursing a Beggar's Child (in which List I reckon all *Cottagers, Labourers,* and Four fifths of the *Farmers*) to be about two Shillings *per Annum,* Rags included; and I believe, no Gentleman would repine to give Ten Shillings for the *Carcase of a good fat Child*; which, as I have said, will make four Dishes of excellent nutritive Meat, when he hath only some particular Friend, or his own Family, to dine with him. Thus the Squire will learn to be a good Landlord, and grow popular among his Tenants; the Mother will have Eight Shillings net Profit, and be fit for Work until she produceth another Child.

THOSE who are more thrifty (*as I must confess the Times require*) may flay the Carcase; the Skin of which, artificially dressed, will make admirable *Gloves for Ladies*, and *Summer Boots for fine Gentlemen*.

AS to our City of *Dublin*; Shambles may be appointed for this Purpose, in the most convenient Parts of it; and Butchers we may be assured will not be wanting; although I rather recommend buying the Children alive, and dressing them hot from the Knife, as we do *roasting Pigs*.[8]

A VERY worthy Person, *a true Lover of his Country*, and whose Virtues I highly esteem, was lately pleased, in discoursing on this Matter, to offer a Refinement upon my Scheme. He said, that many Gentlemen of this Kingdom, having of late destroyed their Deer; he conceived that the Want of Venison might be well supplied by the Bodies of young Lads and Maidens, not exceeding fourteen Years of Age, nor under twelve; so great a Number of both Sexes in every County being now ready to starve, for Want of Work and Service: And these to be disposed of by their Parents, if alive, or otherwise by their nearest Relations. But with due Deference to so excellent a Friend, and so deserving a Patriot, I cannot be altogether in his Sentiments. For as to the Males, my *American* Acquaintance assured me from frequent Experience, that their Flesh was generally tough and lean, like that of our School-boys, by continual Exercise; and their Taste disagreeable; and to fatten them would not answer the Charge. Then, as to the Females, it would, I think, with humble Submission, *be a Loss to the Publick*, because they soon would become Breeders themselves: And besides it is not improbable, that some scrupulous People might be apt to censure such a Practice (although indeed very unjustly) as a little bordering upon Cruelty; which, I confess, hath always been with me the strongest Objection against any Project, how well soever intended.

BUT in order to justify my Friend; he confessed, that this Expedient was put into his Head by the famous *Salmanaazor*,[9] a Native of the Island *Formosa*, who came from thence to *London*, above twenty Years ago, and in Conversation told my Friend, that in his Country, when any young Person happened to be put to Death, the Executioner sold the Carcase to *Persons of Quality*, as a prime Dainty; and that, in his Time, the Body of a plump Girl of fifteen, who was crucified for an Attempt to poison the Emperor, was sold to his Imperial *Majesty's prime Minister of State*, and other great *Mandarins* of the Court, *in Joints from the Gibbet*, at Four hundred Crowns. Neither indeed can I deny, that if the same Use were made of several plump young Girls in this Town, who, without one single Groat to their Fortunes, cannot stir Abroad without a Chair, and appear at the *Play-house* and *Assemblies* in foreign Fineries, which they never will pay for; the Kingdom would not be the worse.

SOME Persons of a desponding Spirit are in great Concern about that vast Number of poor People, who are Aged,

Diseased, or Maimed; and I have been desired to employ my
Thoughts what Course may be taken, to ease the Nation of so
grievous an Incumbrance. But I am not in the least Pain upon
that Matter; because it is very well known, that they are every
Day *dying*, and *rotting*, by *Cold* and *Famine*, and *Filth*, and
Vermin, as fast as can be reasonably expected. And as to the
younger Labourers, they are now in almost as hopeful a Condition: They cannot get Work, and consequently pine away for
Want of Nourishment, to a Degree, that if at any Time they are
accidentally hired to common Labour, they have not Strength
to perform it; and thus the Country, and themselves, are in a
fair Way of being soon delivered from the Evils to come.

I HAVE too long digressed; and therefore shall return to my
Subject. I think the Advantages by the Proposal which I have
made, are obvious, and many, as well as of the highest
Importance.

FOR, *First*, as I have already observed, it would greatly lessen
the Number of Papists, with whom we are yearly over-run;
being the principal Breeders of the Nation, as well as our most
dangerous Enemies; and who stay at home on Purpose, with a
Design *to deliver the Kingdom to the Pretender*; hoping to take
their Advantage by the Absence *of so many good Protestants*,
who have chosen rather to leave their Country, than stay at
home, and pay Tithes against their Conscience, to an idolatrous
Episcopal Curate.[10]

SECONDLY, The poorer Tenants will have something valu-
able of their own, which, by Law, may be made liable to
Distress, and help to pay their Landlord's Rent; their Corn and
Cattle being already seized, and *Money a Thing unknown*.[11]

THIRDLY, Whereas the Maintenance of an Hundred Thousand Children, from two Years old, and upwards, cannot be
computed at less than ten Shillings a Piece *per Annum*, the
Nation's Stock will be thereby encreased Fifty Thousand
Pounds *per Annum*; besides the Profit of a new Dish, introduced
to the Tables of all *Gentlemen of Fortune* in the Kingdom, who
have any Refinement in Taste; and the Money will circulate
among our selves, the Goods being entirely of our own Growth
and Manufacture.

FOURTHLY, The constant Breeders, besides the Gain of Eight Shillings *Sterling per Annum*, by the Sale of their Children, will be rid of the Charge of maintaining them after the first Year.

FIFTHLY, This Food would likewise bring great *Custom to Taverns*, where the Vintners will certainly be so prudent, as to procure the best Receipts for dressing it to Perfection; and consequently, have their Houses frequented by all the *fine Gentlemen*, who justly value themselves upon their Knowledge in good Eating; and a skilful Cook, who understands how to oblige his Guests, will contrive to make it as expensive as they please.

SIXTHLY, This would be a great Inducement to Marriage, which all wise Nations have either encouraged by Rewards, or enforced by Laws and Penalties. It would encrease the Care and Tenderness of Mothers towards their Children, when they were sure of a Settlement for Life, to the poor Babes, provided in some Sort by the Publick, to their annual Profit instead of Expence. We should soon see an honest Emulation among the married Women, *which of them could bring the fattest Child to the Market*. Men would become as *fond* of their Wives, during the Time of their Pregnancy, as they are now of their *Mares* in Foal, their *Cows* in Calf, or *Sows* when they are ready to farrow; nor offer to beat or kick them, (as it is too *frequent* a Practice) for fear of a Miscarriage.

MANY other Advantages might be enumerated. For Instance, the Addition of some Thousand Carcasses in our Exportation of barrelled Beef: The Propagation of *Swines Flesh*, and Improvement in the Art of making good *Bacon*; so much wanted among us by the great Destruction of *Pigs*, too frequent at our Tables, which are no way comparable in Taste, or Magnificence, to a well-grown fat yearly Child; which, roasted whole, will make a considerable Figure at a *Lord Mayor*'s *Feast*, or any other publick Entertainment. But this, and many others, I omit; being studious of Brevity.

SUPPOSING that one Thousand Families in this City, would be constant Customers for Infants Flesh; besides others who might have it at *merry Meetings*, particularly at *Weddings* and

Christenings; I compute that *Dublin* would take off annually, about Twenty Thousand Carcasses; and the rest of the Kingdom (where probably they will be sold somewhat cheaper) the remaining Eighty Thousand.

I CAN think of no one Objection, that will possibly be raised against this Proposal; unless it should be urged, that the Number of People will be thereby much lessened in the Kingdom. This I freely own; and it was indeed one principal Design in offering it to the World. I desire the Reader will observe, that I calculate my Remedy *for this one individual Kingdom of* IRELAND, *and for no other that ever was, is, or I think ever can be upon Earth*. Therefore, let no Man talk to me of other Expedients:[12] *Of taxing our Absentees at five Shillings a Pound: Of using neither Cloaths, nor Houshold Furniture; except what is of our own Growth and Manufacture: Of utterly rejecting the Materials and Instruments that promote foreign Luxury: Of curing the Expensiveness of Pride, Vanity, Idleness, and Gaming in our Women: Of introducing a Vein of Parsimony, Prudence and Temperance: Of learning to love our Country; wherein we differ even from* LAPLANDERS, *and the Inhabitants of* TOPINAMBOO:[13] *Of quitting our Animosities, and Factions; nor act any longer like the* Jews, *who were murdering one another at the very Moment their City was taken:*[14] *Of being a little cautious not to sell our Country and Consciences for nothing: Of teaching Landlords to have, at least, one Degree of Mercy towards their Tenants*. Lastly, *Of putting a Spirit of Honesty, Industry, and Skill into our Shop-keepers; who, if a Resolution could now be taken to buy only our native Goods, would immediately unite to cheat and exact upon us in the Price, the Measure, and the Goodness; nor could ever yet be brought to make one fair Proposal of just Dealing, though often and earnestly invited to it.*[15]

THEREFORE I repeat; let no Man talk to me of these and the like Expedients; till he hath, at least, a Glimpse of Hope, that there will ever be some hearty and sincere Attempt to put *them in Practice*.

BUT, as to my self; having been wearied out for many Years with offering vain, idle, visionary Thoughts; and at length utterly despairing of Success, I fortunately fell upon this Proposal; which, as it is wholly new, so it hath something *solid* and *real*, of no Expence, and little Trouble, full in our own Power; and whereby we can incur no Danger in *disobliging* ENGLAND: For, this Kind of Commodity will not bear Exportation; the Flesh being of too tender a Consistence, to admit a long Continuance in Salt; *although, perhaps, I could name a Country, which would be glad to eat up our whole Nation without it.*[16]

AFTER all, I am not so violently bent upon my own Opinion, as to reject any Offer proposed by wise Men, which shall be found equally innocent, cheap, easy, and effectual. But before something of that Kind shall be advanced, in Contradiction to my Scheme, and offering a better; I desire the Author, or Authors, will be pleased maturely to consider two Points. *First,* As Things now stand, how they will be able to find Food and Raiment, for a Hundred Thousand useless Mouths and Backs? And *secondly,* There being a round Million of Creatures in human Figure, throughout this Kingdom; whose whole Subsistence, put into a common Stock, would leave them in Debt two Millions of Pounds *Sterling*; adding those, who are Beggars by Profession, to the Bulk of Farmers, Cottagers, and Labourers, with their Wives and Children, who are Beggars in Effect; I desire those Politicians, who dislike my Overture, and may perhaps be so bold to attempt an Answer, that they will first ask the Parents of these Mortals, Whether they would not, at this Day, think it a great Happiness to have been sold for Food at a Year old, in the Manner I prescribe; and thereby have avoided such a perpetual Scene of Misfortunes, as they have since gone through; by the *Oppression of Landlords*; the Impossibility of paying Rent, without Money or Trade; the Want of common Sustenance, with neither House nor Cloaths, to cover them from the Inclemencies of the Weather; and the most inevitable Prospect of intailing the like, or greater Miseries upon their Breed for ever.

I PROFESS, in the Sincerity of my Heart, that I have not the least personal Interest, in endeavouring to promote this necessary Work; having no other Motive than the *publick Good*

of my Country, by advancing our Trade, providing for Infants,
relieving the Poor, and giving some Pleasure to the Rich. I have
no Children, by which I can propose to get a single Penny; the
youngest being nine Years old, and my Wife past Child-bearing.

AN EXAMINATION OF CERTAIN ABUSES, CORRUPTIONS, AND ENORMITIES, IN THE CITY OF DUBLIN

Written in the Year 1732

NOTHING is held more commendable in all great Cities, especially the Metropolis of a Kingdom, than what the *French* call the *Police:* By which Word is meant the Government thereof, to prevent the many Disorders occasioned by great Numbers of People and Carriages, especially through narrow Streets. In this Government our famous City of *Dublin* is said to be very defective; and universally complained of.[1] Many wholesome Laws have been enacted to correct those Abuses, but are ill executed; and many more are wanting; which I hope the united Wisdom of the Nation (whereof so many good Effects have already appeared this Session) will soon take into their profound Consideration.

As I have been always watchful over the Good of mine own Country; and particularly for that of our renowned City; where, (*absit invidia*[2]) I had the Honour to draw my first Breath; I cannot have a Minute's Ease or Patience to forbear enumerating some of the greatest Enormities, Abuses, and Corruptions spread almost through every Part of *Dublin*; and proposing such Remedies, as, I hope, the Legislature will approve of.

THE narrow Compass to which I have confined my self in this Paper, will allow me only to touch the most important Defects; and such as I think seem to require the most speedy Redress.

AND first: Perhaps there was never known a wiser Institution than that of allowing certain Persons of both Sexes, in large and populous Cities, to cry through the Streets many Necessaries of Life.[3] It would be endless to recount the Conveniences which our City enjoys by this useful Invention, and particularly Strangers, forced hither by Business, who reside here but a short time: For, these having usually but little Money, and being wholly ignorant of the Town, might at an easy Price purchase a tolerable Dinner, if the several Criers would pronounce the Names of the Goods they have to sell, in any tolerable Language. And therefore, until our Law-makers shall think it proper to interpose so far as to make those Traders pronounce their Words in such Terms, that a plain Christian Hearer may comprehend what is cryed; I would advise all new Comers to look out at their Garret Windows, and there see whether the Thing that is cryed be *Tripes*, or *Flummery, Buttermilk*, or *Cowheels*. For, as Things are now managed, how is it possible for an honest Countryman, just arrived, to find out what is meant, for Instance, by the following Words, with which his Ears are constantly stunned twice a Day, *Muggs, Juggs, and Porringers, up in the Garret, and down in the Cellar*. I say, how is it possible for any Stranger to understand that this Jargon is meant as an Invitation to buy a Farthing's Worth of Milk for his Breakfast or Supper, unless his Curiosity draws him to the Window, or until his Landlady shall inform him? I produce this only as one Instance, among a Hundred much worse; I mean where the Words make a Sound wholly inarticulate, which give so much Disturbance, and so little Information.[4]

THE Affirmation solemnly made in the Cry of *Herrings*, is directly against all Truth and Probability; *Herrings alive, alive here:* The very Proverb will convince us of this; for what is more frequent in ordinary Speech, than to say of some Neighbour for whom the Passing-Bell rings, that *he is dead as a Herring*? And, pray, how is it possible, that a *Herring*, which, as *Philosophers* observe, cannot live longer than One Minute, Three Seconds and a half out of Water, should bear a Voyage in open Boats from *Howth* to *Dublin*, be tossed into twenty Hands, and preserve its Life in Sieves for several Hours? Nay, we have Witnesses ready to produce, that many Thousands of these *Herrings*, so impudently asserted to be alive, have been a Day and a Night upon dry Land. But this is not the worst. What can we think of those impious Wretches, who dare in the Face of the Sun, vouch the very same Affirmative of their *Salmon*; and cry, *Salmon alive, alive*; whereas, if you call the Woman who cryes it, she is not ashamed to turn back her Mantle, and shew you this individual *Salmon* cut into a dozen Pieces. I have given good Advice to these infamous Disgracers of their Sex and Calling, without the least Appearance of Remorse; and fully against the Conviction of their own Consciences. I have mentioned this Grievance to several of our Parish Ministers; but all in vain: So that it must continue until the Government shall think fit to interpose.

THERE is another *Cry*, which, from the strictest Observation I can make, appears to be very modern, and it is that of *Sweet-hearts*; and is plainly intended for a Reflection upon the Female Sex; as if there were at present so great a Dearth of Lovers, that the Women instead of receiving Presents from Men, were now forced to offer Money, to purchase *Sweet-hearts*.[5] Neither am I sure, that this *Cry* doth not glance at some Disaffection against the Government; insinuating, that while so many of our Troops are engaged in foreign Service,[6] and such a great Number of our gallant Officers constantly reside in *England*; the Ladies are forced to take up with *Parsons* and *Attornies:* But this is a most unjust Reflection; as may soon be proved by any Person who frequents the *Castle*, our publick Walks, our Balls and Assemblies; where the Crowds of *Toupees* were never known to swarm as they do at present.[7]

THERE is a *Cry* peculiar to this City, which I do not remember to have been used in *London*; or at least, not in the same Terms that it hath been practised by both Parties, during each of their Power; but, very unjustly by the *Tories*. While these were at the Helm, they grew daily more and more impatient to put all true *Whigs* and *Hanoverians* out of Employments. To effect which, they hired certain ordinary Fellows, with large Baskets on their Shoulders, to call aloud at every House, *Dirt to carry out*; giving that Denomination to our whole Party; as if they would signify, that the Kingdom could never be *cleansed*, until we were *swept* from the Earth like *Rubbish*. But since that happy Turn of Times, when we were so *miraculously* preserved by just an *Inch*, from *Popery*, *Slavery*, *Massacre*, and the *Pretender*; I must own it Prudence in us, still to go on with the same *Cry*; which hath ever since been so effectually observed, that the true *political Dirt* is wholly removed and thrown on its proper Dunghills, there to corrupt, and be no more heard of.

BUT, to proceed to other Enormities: Every Person who walks the Streets, must needs observe an immense Number of human Excrements at the Doors and Steps of waste Houses, and at the Sides of every dead Wall; for which the disaffected Party hath assigned a very false and malicious Cause. They would have it that these Heaps were laid there privately by *British Fundaments*, to make the World believe, that our *Irish* Vulgar do daily eat and drink; and consequently, that the Clamour of Poverty among us, must be false; proceeding only from *Jacobites* and *Papists*. They would confirm this, by pretending to observe, that a *British Anus* being more narrowly perforated than one of our own Country; and many of these Excrements, upon a strict View appearing Copple-crowned, with a Point like a Cone or Pyramid, are easily distinguished from the *Hibernian*, which lie much flatter, and with less Continuity. I communicated this Conjecture to an eminent Physician, who is well versed in such profound Speculations; and at my Request was pleased to make Trial with each of his Fingers, by thrusting them into the *Anus* of several Persons of both Nations; and professed he could find no such Difference between them as those ill-disposed People alledge. On the contrary, he assured me, that much the greater Number of narrow Cavities were of *Hibernian* Origin. This I only mention to shew how ready the *Jacobites* are to lay hold of any Handle to express their Malice against the Government. I had almost forgot to add, that my Friend the Physician could, by smelling each Finger, distinguish the *Hibernian* Excrement from the *British*; and was not above twice mistaken in an Hundred Experiments; upon which he intends very soon to publish a learned Dissertation.[8]

THERE is a Diversion in this City, which usually begins among the *Butchers*; but is often continued by a Succession of other People, through many Streets. It is called the COSSING *of a Dog:* And I may justly number it among our Corruptions. The Ceremony is thus: A strange Dog happens to pass through a Flesh-Market: Whereupon an expert *Butcher* immediately cries in a loud Voice, and the proper Tone, *Coss, Coss,* several Times: The same Word is repeated by the People. The Dog, who perfectly understands the Term of Art, and consequently the Danger he is in, immediately flies. The People, and even his own *Brother Animals*, pursue: The Pursuit and Cry attend him perhaps half a Mile; he is well worried in his Flight; and sometimes hardly escapes. This, our Ill-wishers of the *Jacobite* Kind, are pleased to call a *Persecution*; and affirm, that it always falls upon *Dogs* of the *Tory* Principle. But, we can well defend our selves, by justly alledging, that, when they were uppermost, they treated our *Dogs* full as inhumanly: As to my own Part, who have in former Times often attended these *Processions*; although I can very well distinguish between a *Whig* and a *Tory* Dog; yet I never carried my Resentments very far upon a *Party Principle*, except it were against certain malicious *Dogs*, who most discovered their Enmity against us in the *worst of Times*. And, I remember too well, that in the wicked Ministry of the Earl of *Oxford*; a large Mastiff of our Party being unmercifully *cossed*; ran, without Thinking, between my Legs, as I was coming up *Fishamble-street*; and, as I am of low Stature, with very short Legs, bore me riding backwards down the Hill, for above Two Hundred Yards: And, although I made use of his Tail for a Bridle, holding it fast with both my Hands, and clung my Legs as close to his Sides as I could; yet we both came down together into the Middle of the Kennel; where after rowling three or four Times over each other, I got up with much ado, amidst the Shouts and Huzza's of a Thousand malicious *Jacobites:* I cannot, indeed, but gratefully acknowledge, that for this and many other *Services* and *Sufferings*, I have been since more than over-paid.

THIS Adventure may, perhaps, have put me out of Love with the Diversion of *Cossing*; which I confess myself an Enemy to; unless we could always be sure of distinguishing *Tory Dogs*; whereof great Numbers have since been so prudent, as entirely to change their Principles; and are now justly esteemed the best *Worriers* of their former Friends.

I AM assured, and partly know, that all the Chimney-Sweeper Boys, where Members of P[arliamen]t chiefly lodge, are hired by *our Enemies* to sculk in the Tops of Chimneys, with their Heads no higher than will just permit them to look round; and at the usual Hours when Members are going to the House, if they see a Coach stand near the Lodging of any *loyal* Member; they call *Coach*, *Coach*, as loud as they can bawl, just at the Instant when the Footman begins to give the same Call. And this is chiefly done on those Days, when any Point of Importance is to be debated. This Practice may be of very dangerous Consequence. For, these Boys are all hired by Enemies to the Government: And thus, by the Absence of a few Members for a few Minutes, a Question may be carried against the *true Interest* of the Kingdom; and, very probably, not without an Eye towards the *Pretender*.

I HAVE not observed the Wit and Fancy of this Town, so much employed in any one Article as that of contriving Variety of Signs to hang over Houses, where *Punch* is to be sold. The Bowl is represented full of *Punch*; the Ladle stands erect in the middle; supported sometimes by one, and sometimes by two Animals, whose Feet rest upon the Edge of the Bowl. These Animals are sometimes one black *Lion*, and sometimes a Couple; sometimes a single *Eagle*, and sometimes a spread One; and we often meet a *Crow*, a *Swan*, a *Bear*, or a *Cock*, in the same Posture.[9]

Now, I cannot find how any of these Animals, either separate, or in Conjunction, are, properly speaking, fit Emblems or Embellishments, to advance the Sale of *Punch*. Besides, it is agreed among *Naturalists*, that no Brute can endure the Taste of strong Liquor; except where he hath been used to it from his Infancy: And, consequently, it is against all the Rules of *Hieroglyph*, to assign those Animals as Patrons, or Protectors of *Punch*.[10] For, in that Case, we ought to suppose that the Host keeps always ready the real Bird, or Beast, whereof the Picture hangs over his Door, to entertain his Guests; which, however, to my Knowledge, is not true in Fact: Not one of those Birds being a proper Companion for a *Christian*, as to aiding and assisting in making the *Punch*. For, as they are drawn upon the Sign, they are much more likely to mute, or shed their Feathers into the Liquor. Then, as to the *Bear*, he is too terrible, awkward, and slovenly a Companion to converse with; neither are any of them all *handy* enough to fill Liquor to the Company: I do, therefore, vehemently suspect a *Plot* intended against the Government, by these Devices. For, although the *Spread-Eagle* be the Arms of *Germany*, upon which Account it may possibly be a lawful *Protestant* Sign; yet I, who am very suspicious of fair Out-sides, in a Matter which so nearly concerns our Welfare; cannot but call to Mind, that the *Pretender*'s Wife is said to be of *German* Birth:[11] And that many *Popish* Princes, in so vast an Extent of Land, are reported to excel both at making and drinking *Punch*. Besides, it is plain, that the *Spread-Eagle* exhibits to us the perfect Figure of a *Cross*; which is a Badge of *Popery*. Then, as to the *Cock*, he is well known to represent the *French* Nation, our old and dangerous Enemy.[12] The *Swan*, who must of Necessity cover the entire Bowl with his Wings, can be no other than the *Spaniard*; who endeavours to engross all the Treasures of the *Indies* to himself.[13] The *Lion* is indeed the common Emblem of Royal Power, as well as the Arms of *England*: But to paint him black, is perfect *Jacobitism*; and a manifest Type of those who *blacken* the Actions of the best Princes. It is not easy to distinguish whether that other Fowl painted over the *Punch-Bowl*, be a *Crow* or *Raven*? It is true, they have both been held ominous Birds: But I rather take it to be the former; because it is the Disposition of a *Crow*, to pick out the Eyes of other Creatures, and often even of *Christians* after they are dead; and is therefore drawn here, with a Design to put the *Jacobites* in Mind of their old Practice; first to lull us a-sleep, (which is an Emblem of Death) and then to blind our Eyes, that we may not see their dangerous Practices against the State.

To speak my private Opinion; the least offensive Picture in the whole Sett, seems to be the *Bear*; because he represents *Ursa Major*, or the *Great Bear*, who presides over the *North*; where the *Reformation* first began; and which, next to *Britain*, (including *Scotland* and the *North* of *Ireland*) is the great Protector of the *true Protestant* Religion. But, however, in those Signs where I observe the *Bear* to be *chained*, I cannot help surmising a *Jacobite* Contrivance; by which, these Traytors hint an earnest Desire of using all *true Whigs*, as their Predecessors did the primitive Christians: I mean, to represent us as *Bears*, and then halloo their *Tory-Dogs* to bait us to Death.[14]

THUS I have given a fair Account of what I dislike, in all the Signs set over those Houses that invite us to *Punch*. I own it was a Matter that did not need explaining; being so very obvious to common Understanding: Yet, I know not how it happens, but methinks there seems a fatal Blindness to overspread our corporeal Eyes, as well as our intellectual; and I heartily wish, I may be found a false Prophet. For, these are not bare Suspicions, but manifest Demonstrations.

THEREFORE, away with these *Popish*, *Jacobite*, and idolatrous Gew-gaws. And I heartily wish a Law were enacted, under severe Penalties, against drinking any *Punch* at all: For, nothing is easier, than to prove it a disaffected Liquor. The chief Ingredients, which are *Brandy*, *Oranges*, and *Lemons*, are all sent us from *Popish* Countries;[15] and nothing remains of *Protestant* Growth, but *Sugar* and *Water*. For, as to Biscuit, which formerly was held a necessary Ingredient, and is truly *British*, we find it is entirely rejected.

BUT I will put the Truth of my Assertion past all Doubt: I mean, that this Liquor is by one important Innovation, grown of ill Example, and dangerous Consequence to the Publick. It is well known, that, by the true original Institution of making *Punch*, left us by Captain *Ratcliff*; the Sharpness is only occasioned by the Juice of *Lemons*; and so continued until after the happy *Revolution*. *Oranges*, alas! are a meer Innovation, and, in a manner, *but of Yesterday*. It was the Politicks of *Jacobites* to introduce them gradually: And to what Intent? The Thing speaks it self. It was cunningly to shew their Virulence against his sacred Majesty King *William*, *of ever glorious and immortal Memory*.[16] But of late (to shew how fast Disloyalty increaseth) they came from one to two, and then to three *Oranges*; nay, at present, we often find *Punch* made all with *Oranges*; and not one single *Lemon*. For, the *Jacobites*, before the Death of that immortal Prince, had, by a Superstition, formed a private Prayer; that, as they *squeezed* the *Orange*, so might that *Protestant* King be *squeezed* to Death:[17] According to the known *Sorcery* described by *Virgil*; *Limus ut hic durescit*, & *hæc ut cera liquescit*, &c.[18] And thus the *Romans*, when they sacrificed an Ox, used this Kind of Prayer: *As I knock down this Ox, so may thou,* O Jupiter, *knock down our Enemies.*[19] In like Manner, after King *William*'s Death, whenever a *Jacobite squeezed* an *Orange*, he had a mental Curse upon the *glorious Memory*; and a hearty Wish for Power to *squeeze* all his Majesty's Friends to Death, as he *squeezed* that *Orange*, which bore one of his Titles, as he was Prince of *Orange*. This I do affirm for Truth; many of that Faction having confessed it to me, under an *Oath of Secrecy*; which, however, I thought it my Duty not to keep, when I saw my dear Country in Danger. But, what better can be expected from an *impious* Set of Men, who never scruple to drink CONFUSION to all *true Protestants*, under the Name of *Whigs*? A most unchristian and inhuman Practice; *which, to our great Honour and Comfort, was never charged upon us, even by our most malicious Detractors.*[20]

THE Sign of two *Angels*, hovering in the Air, and with their Right Hands supporting a *Crown*, is met with in several Parts of this City; and hath often given me great Offence: For, whether by the Unskilfulness, or dangerous Principles of the Painters, (although I have good Reasons to suspect the latter) those *Angels* are usually drawn with such horrid, or indeed rather diabolical *Countenances*, that they give great Offence to every loyal Eye; and equal Cause of Triumph to the *Jacobites*; being a most infamous Reflection upon our able and excellent Ministry.

I NOW return to that great Enormity of City *Cries*; most of which we have borrowed from *London*. I shall consider them only in a *political* View, as they nearly affect the Peace and Safety of both Kingdoms: And having been originally contrived by wicked *Machiavels*, to bring in *Popery, Slavery,* and *arbitrary Power*, by defeating the *Protestant* Succession, and introducing the *Pretender*; ought, in Justice, to be here laid open to the World.

ABOUT two or three Months after the happy *Revolution*, all Persons who possess any Employment or Office, in Church or State, were obliged by an Act of Parliament, to take the Oaths to King *William* and Queen *Mary*: And a great Number of disaffected Persons, refusing to take the said Oaths, from a pretended Scruple of Conscience, but really from a Spirit of

Popery and Rebellion, they contrived a Plot, to make the swearing to those Princes odious in the Eyes of the People. To this End, they hired certain Women of ill Fame, but loud shrill Voices, under Pretence of selling Fish, to go through the Streets, with Sieves on their Heads, and cry, *buy my Soul, buy my Soul*; plainly insinuating, that all those who swore to King *William*, were just ready to sell their *Souls* for an Employment. This Cry was revived at the Death of Queen *Anne*, and I hear still continues in *London*, with much Offence to all *true Protestants*; but, to our great Happiness, seems to be almost dropt in *Dublin*.

BUT, because I altogether contemn the Displeasure and Resentment of *High-flyers*, *Tories*, and *Jacobites*, whom I look upon to be *worse even than profest Papists*; I do here declare, that those Evils which I am going to mention, were all brought upon us in the *worst of Times*,[21] under the late Earl of *Oxford*'s Administration, during the four last Years of Queen *Anne*'s Reign. *That wicked Minister was universally known to be a Papist in his Heart. He was of a most avaricious Nature, and is said to have died worth four Millions,* sterl[ing] *besides his vast Expences in Building, Statues, Plate, Jewels, and other costly Rarities. He was of a mean obscure Birth, from the very Dregs of the People; and so illiterate, that he could hardly read a Paper at the Council Table. I forbear to touch at his open, prophane, profligate Life; because I desire not to rake into the Ashes of the Dead; and therefore I shall observe this wise Maxim:* De mortuis nil nisi bonum.[22]

THIS flagitious Man, in order to compass his black Designs, employed certain wicked Instruments (which great Statesmen are never without) to adapt several *London* Cries, in such a Manner as would best answer his Ends. And, whereas it was upon good Grounds grievously suspected, that all *Places* at Court were sold to the highest Bidder: Certain Women were employed by his Emissaries, to carry *Fish* in Baskets on their Heads, and bawl through the Streets, *Buy my fresh Places*. I must, indeed, own that other Women used the same Cry, who were innocent of this wicked Design, and really sold their Fish of that Denomination, to get an honest Livelihood: But the rest, who were in the *Secret*, although they carried *Fish* in their

Sieves or Baskets, to save Appearances; yet they had likewise a certain Sign, somewhat resembling that of the *Free-Masons*, which the Purchasers of *Places* knew well enough, and were directed by the Women whither they were to resort, and make their Purchase. And, I remember very well, how oddly it lookt, when we observed many Gentlemen finely drest, about the Court-End of the Town, and as far as *York-Buildings*, where the Lord-Treasurer *Oxford* dwelt; calling the Women who cried *Buy my fresh Places*, and talking to them in the Corner of a Street, until they understood each other's Sign. But we never could observe that any Fish was bought.

SOME Years before the Cries last mentioned; the Duke of *Savoy* was reported to have made certain Overtures to the Court of *England*, for admitting his eldest Son, by the Dutchess of *Orleans*'s Daughter, to succeed to the Crown, as next Heir, upon the *Pretender*'s being rejected; and that Son was immediately to turn *Protestant*. It was confidently reported, that great Numbers of People disaffected to the then *Illustrious* but now *Royal* House of *Hanover*, were in those Measures. Whereupon, another Sett of Women were hired by the *Jacobite* Leaders, to cry through the whole Town, *Buy my* Savoys, *dainty* Savoys, *curious* Savoys.[23] But, I cannot directly charge the late Earl of *Oxford* with this *Conspiracy*, because he was not then chief Minister. However, this wicked Cry still continues in *London*, and was brought over hither; where it remains to this Day; and is in my humble Opinion, a very offensive Sound to every true Protestant who is old enough to remember those *dangerous* Times.

DURING the Ministry of that corrupt and *Jacobite* Earl abovementioned, the secret pernicious Design of those in Power, was to sell *Flanders* to *France:*[24] The Consequence of which, must have been the infallible Ruin of the *States-General*, and would have opened the Way for *France* to obtain that universal Monarchy, they have so long aimed at; to which the *British* Dominions must next, after *Holland*, have been compelled to submit. Whereby the *Protestant* Religion would be rooted out of the World.

A DESIGN of this vast Importance, after long Consultation

among the *Jacobite* Grandees, with the Earl of *Oxford* at their
Head; was at last determined to be carried on by the same
Method with the former: It was therefore again put in Practice;
but the Conduct of it was chiefly left to chosen Men, whose
Voices were louder and stronger than those of the other Sex.
And upon this Occasion, was first instituted in *London*, that
famous Cry of FLOUNDERS. But the Cryers were particularly
directed to pronounce the Word *Flaunders*, and not *Flounders*.
For, the Country which we now by Corruption call *Flanders*,
is in its true Orthography spelt *Flaunders*, as may be obvious
to all who read old *English* Books. I say, from hence begun that
thundering Cry, which hath ever since stunned the Ears of all
London, made so many Children fall into Fits, and Women
miscarry; *Come buy my fresh* Flaunders, *curious* Flaunders,
charming Flaunders, *alive, alive, ho*; which last Words can with
no Propriety of Speech, be applied to Fish manifestly dead, (as
I observed before in *Herrings* and *Salmon*) but very justly to
ten Provinces, containing many Millions of living *Christians*.
But the Application is still closer, when we consider that all the
People were to be taken like *Fishes* in a Net; and, by Assistance
of the *Pope*, who sets up to be the *universal Fisher of Men*,[25]
the whole innocent Nation was, according to our common
Expression, to be *laid as flat as a* Flounder.

I REMEMBER, my self, a particular Cryer of *Flounders* in
London, who arrived at so much Fame for the Loudness of his
Voice, as to have the Honour of being mentioned, upon that
Account, in a Comedy. He hath disturbed me many a Morning,
before he came within Fifty Doors of my Lodging: And although
I were not, in those Days, so fully apprized of the Designs which
our common Enemy had then in Agitation; yet, I know not
how, by a secret Impulse, young as I was, I could not forbear
conceiving a strong Dislike against the Fellow; and often said
to my self, this Cry seems to be forged in the *Jesuites* School:
Alas, poor England! *I am grievously mistaken, if there be
not some* Popish *Plot at the Bottom*.[26] I communicated my
Thoughts to an intimate Friend, who reproached me with being
too visionary in my Speculations. But it proved afterwards, that
I conjectured right. And I have since reflected, that if the wicked

Faction could have procured only a Thousand Men, of as strong Lungs as the Fellow I mentioned, none can tell how terrible the Consequences might have been, not only to these two Kingdoms, but over all *Europe*, by selling *Flanders* to *France*. And yet these Cries continue unpunished, both in *London* and *Dublin*; although, I confess, not with equal Vehemency or Loudness; because the Reason for contriving this desperate Plot, is, to our great Felicity, wholly ceased.

IT is well known, that the Majority of the *British* House of Commons, in the last Years of Queen *Anne*'s Reign, were in their Hearts directly opposite to the Earl of *Oxford*'s pernicious Measures; which put him under the Necessity of bribing them with Sallaries. Whereupon he had again Recourse to his old Politicks. And accordingly, his Emissaries were very busy in employing certain artful Women, of no good Life or Conversation, (as it was fully proved before Justice *Peyton*[27]) to cry that Vegetable commonly called *Sollary*, through the Town. These Women differed from the common Cryers of that Herb, by some private Mark which I could never learn; but the Matter was notorious enough, and sufficiently talked of; and about the same Period was the Cry of *Sollary* brought over into this Kingdom. But since there is not, at this present, the least Occasion to suspect the Loyalty of our Cryers upon that Article, I am content that it may still be tolerated.

I SHALL mention but one Cry more, which hath any Reference to Politicks; but is, indeed, of all others, the most insolent, as well as treasonable, under our present happy Establishment. I mean that of *Turnups*; not of *Turnips*, according to the best Orthography, but absolutely *Turnups*. Although this Cry be of an older Date than some of the preceding Enormities; for it began soon after the Revolution; yet was it never known to arrive at so great an Height, as during the Earl of *Oxford*'s Power. Some People, (whom I take to be private Enemies) are, indeed, as ready as my self to profess their Disapprobation of this Cry, on Pretence that it began by the Contrivance of certain old Procuresses, who kept Houses of ill Fame, where lewd Women met to draw young Men into Vice. And this they pretend to prove by some Words in the Cry; because, after the

Cryer had bawled out *Turnups, ho, buy my dainty Turnups*, he would sometimes add the two following Verses.

Turn up the Mistress, and turn up the Maid,
And turn up the Daughter, and be not afraid.

THIS, say some political Sophists, plainly shews, that there can be nothing further meant in so infamous a Cry, than an Invitation to Lewdness; which, indeed, ought to be severely punished in all well regulated Governments; yet cannot be fairly interpreted as a Crime of State. But, I hope, we are not so weak and blind to be deluded at this Time of Day, with such poor Evasions. I could, if it were proper, demonstrate the very Time when those two Verses were composed, and name the Author, who was no other than the famous Mr. *Swan*, so well known for his Talent at Quibbling; and was as virulent a *Jacobite* as any in *England*.[28] Neither could he deny the Fact, when he was taxed for it in my Presence, by Sir *Harry Dutton-Colt*, and Colonel *Davenport*, at the *Smyrna* Coffee-House, on the 10th of *June*, 1701.[29] Thus it appears to a Demonstration, that those Verses were only a Blind to conceal the most dangerous Designs of the Party; who, from the first Years after the happy Revolution, used a Cant-way of talking in their Clubs, after this Manner: *We hope to see the Cards shuffled once more, and another King* TURN UP *Trump:* And, *when shall we meet over a Dish of* TURNUPS? The same Term of Art was used in their Plots against the Government, and in their treasonable Letters writ in Cyphers, and decyphered by the famous Dr. *Wallis*, as you may read in the Tryals of those Times.[30] This I thought fit to set forth at large, and in so clear a Light; because the *Scotch* and *French* Authors have given a very different Account of the Word TURNUP; but whether out of Ignorance or Partiality, I shall not decree; because, I am sure the Reader is convinced by my Discovery. It is to be observed, that this Cry was sung in a particular Manner, by Fellows in Disguise, to give Notice where those Traytors were to meet, in order to concert their villainous Designs.

I HAVE no more to add upon this Article, than an humble

Proposal, that those who cry this Root at present in our Streets of *Dublin*, may be compelled by the Justices of the Peace, to pronounce *Turnip*, and not *Turnup*; for, I am afraid, we have still too many Snakes in our Bosom; and it would be well if their Cellars were sometimes searched, when the Owners least expect it; for I am not out of Fear, that *latet anguis in Herba*.[31]

THUS, we are zealous in Matters of small Moment, while we neglect those of the highest Importance. I have already made it manifest, that all these Cries were contrived in the *worst of Times*, under the Ministry of that desperate Statesman, *Robert* late Earl of *Oxford*; and for that very Reason, ought to be rejected with Horror, as begun in the Reign of *Jacobites*, and may well be numbered among the Rags of *Popery* and *Treason*: Or if it be thought proper, that these Cries must continue, surely they ought to be only trusted in the Hands of *true Protestants* who have given Security to the Government.[32]

SWIFT TO SIR ANDREW FOUNTAINE

S^r

This letter is sent by the hands of Mrs Mary Barber, and I was glad of the opportunity to remember our old Acquaintance and friendship, and to try the force of the latter, by my recommending that Gentlewoman to your favor and Protection. She is the best Poetess of both Kingdoms. If there be any others, they are behind her, longo intervallo.[1] She came hither onely to settle some affairs, intending to return very soon; but was caught by a long fit of the Gout, and frequent returns; but is now well enough to depart in a few days. She had so many friends of great quality who encouraged her to print her poetical works by Subscription, and went on with great Success,[2] But having been confined here much longer than she expected, hath a little stopped her progress. I believe few persons have met with more considerable friends and Patrons than she; and very well deserves their favor, by her Virtue, her humility, Gratitude and Poetical Genius: She will have it, that my Recommendations have been of some service to her, and therefore I expect and desire that they may have equal power with you, and with all those friends over whom you have any influence. The Subscription is one Guinea, and if you do not get her a hundred Subscribers at least, I shall think my self disappointed, and at least two thirds of your old friendship for me dropt by time and absence.[3] I shall write to My new Lord Pembroke on the same Subject, but in a more threating style. Is he as good an Earl as he was a Lord Herbert?[4] Is he spoylt by being a Courtier? can he still walk faster twenty miles than a Coach and six horses? Pray write to me on receit of this; and convince me by your words and actions, that you will obey my commands; and believe me to be ever, Dear Knight

Dublin. Jul. 30th 1733   Your most obedient and
most humble Servant
Jonath: Swift

Sr.

This letter is sent by the hands of Mrs Mary Barber, and I was glad of the opportunity to remember our old Acquaintance and friendship, and to try the force of the latter, by my recommending that Gentlewoman to your favor and Protection. She is the best Poetess of both Kingdoms. If there be any others, they are behind her, longo intervallo. She came hither onely to settle some affairs, intending to return very soon; but was caught by a long fit of the Gout, and frequent returns, but is now well enough to depart in a few days. She had so many friends of great quality who encouraged her to print her poetical works by Subscription, and went on with great Success. But having been confined here much longer than she expected, hath a little stopped her progress. I believe few persons have met with more considerable friends and Patrons than She: and very well deserves their favor, by her Virtue, her humility, Gratitude and Poetical Genius: She will have it, that my Recommendations have been of some Service to her, and therefore I expect and desire that they may have equal power with you, and with all those friends with over whom you have any influence. The Subscription is one Guinea, and if you do not get her a hundred Subscribers at least, I shall my self disappointed, and at least two thirds of your old friendship for me dropt by time and absence. I shall write to my new Lord Pembroke on the same Subject, but in a more threating Style. Is he as good an Earl as he was a Lord Herbert? Is he spoylt by being a Courtier? can he still walk faster twenty miles than a Coach and Six horses? Pray write to me on receit of this; and convince me by your words and actions, that you will obey my commands; and believe me to be ever Dear Knight

Dublin. Jul. 30. 1733

Your most obedient and
most humble Servant
Jonath. Swift

Plate 4. Holograph of Swift letter to
Sir Andrew Fountaine (30 July 1733)

SWIFT TO JOHN ARBUTHNOT

[November 1734]

My Dear Friend

I never once suspected your forgetfullness or want of Friendship, but very often dreaded your want of Health, to which alone I imputed every delay longer than ordinary in hearing from you. I should be very ungratefull indeed if I acted otherwise to you who were pleased to take such generous constant care of my health, my Interests, and my Reputation; who represented me so favorably to that blessed Queen your Mistress, as well as to her Ministers, and to all your Friends.[1] The Letters you mention which I did not answer, I can not find; and yet I have all that ever came from you, for I constantly endorse yours, and those of a few other friends, and date them; onely if there be any thing particular, though of no consequence, when I go to the Country, I send them to some Friends among other Papers, for fear of Accidents in my absence. I thank you kindly for your favor to the Young man who was bred in my Quire. The people of skill in Musick represent him to me as a Lad of Virtue and hopefull and endeavouring in his way. It is your own fault if I give you Trouble, because you never refused me any thing in your Life. You tear my heart with the ill account of your Health;[2] Yet if it should please God to call you away before me, I should not pity you in the least, except on the account of what pains you might feel before you passed into a better Life. I should pity none but your Friends, and among them chiefly my self, although I never can hope to have health enough to leave this country till I leave the World. I do not know among Mankind any Person more prepared to depart from us than your self, not even the Bishop of Marseilles, if he be still alive:[3] For among all your qualityes that have procured you the love and esteem of the world, I ever most valued your moral and Christian Virtues, which were not the Product of years or Sickness, but of reason and Religion; as I can witness after above five and twenty years acquaintance ... I except onely the too little care of your Fortune, upon which I have

been so free as some times to examine and to chide you; and
the consequence of which hath been to confine you to London
when you are under a disorder for which I am told, and know
the clear air of the Country is necessary. The great reason that
hinders my Journy to England is the same that drives you from
High-gate:[4] I am not in Circumstances to keep horses and
Servants in London. My Revenues by the miserable oppressions
of this Kingdom are sunk 300^{ll} a year: For Tythes are become
a Drug, and I have but little rents from the Deanry lands, which
are my onely sure paymts. I have here a large convenient
house; I live at two thirds cheaper here than I could there; I
drink a bottle of French wine my self every day, though I love
it not, but it is the onely thing that keeps me out of pain; I ride
every fair day a dozen miles, on a large Strand, or Turnpike
roads; You in London have no such Advantages. I can buy a
Chicken for a Groat, and entertain three or four friends with
as many dishes and two or three Bottles of French Wine for 10
shill[ings]. When I dine alone, my Pint and Chicken with the
Appendixes cost me about 15 pence. I am thrifty in every thing
but wine, of which though I be not a constant House-keeper, I
spend between five and six hogsheads a year. When I ride to a
friend a few miles off, if he be not richer than I, I carry My
Bottle, my Bread and Chicken, that he may be no loser; I talk
thus foolishly to let you know the reasons which joyned to my
ill health make it impossible for me to see you and my other
friends. And perhaps this domestick tattle may excuse me, and
amuse You. I could not live with My L^d Bo——[5] or Mr Pope;
they are both too temperate and too wise for me, and too
profound, and too poor. And how could I afford Horses? and
how could I ride over their Cursed roads in Winter, and be
turned into a ditch by every Carter or Hackney Coach? Every
Parish Minister of this City is Governor of all Carriages, and
so are the two Deans, and every Carter makes way for us at
their Peril . . .[6] Therefore, like Cesar I will be one of the first
here rather than the last among you . . . I forget that I am so
near the Bottom[.] I am now with one of My Prebend[aries]
five miles in the Country for 5 days. I brought with me 8 Bottles
of Wine, with Bread and Meat for 3 days, which is my Club;

he is a Bachellor with 300^{ll} a year. Pray God preserve you my dear Friend entirely.
Y^{rs} J. Swift

Pray does your Brother Robert live at Roan or Paris?[7] Some tell me that his Nephew keeps the House at Rouen, and your Brother onely comes there sometimes. He was so kind lately to send me a Hamper of near 3 dozen of Wine. I never could learn what kind of Present from hence would be acceptable in France.

DIRECTIONS TO SERVANTS

RULES THAT CONCERN ALL SERVANTS
IN GENERAL

WHEN your Master or Lady call a Servant by Name, if that Servant be not in the Way, none of you are to answer, for then there will be no End of your Drudgery: And Masters themselves allow, that if a Servant cometh when he is called, it is sufficient.

When you have done a Fault, be always pert and insolent, and behave your self as if you were the injured Person; this will immediately put your Master or Lady off their Mettle.[1]

If you see your Master wronged by any of your Fellow-servants, be sure to conceal it, for fear of being called a *Tell-tale:* However, there is one Exception, in case of a favourite Servant, who is justly hated by the whole Family; you are therefore bound in Prudence to lay all the Faults you can upon the Favourite.

The Cook, the Butler, the Groom, the Market-man, and every other Servant, who is concerned in the Expences of the Family, should act as if his Master's whole Estate ought to be applied to that Servant's particular Business. For Instance, if the Cook computeth his Master's Estate to be a thousand Pounds a Year; he reasonably concludeth, that a thousand Pounds a Year will afford Meat enough, and therefore, he need not be sparing; the Butler maketh the same Judgment; so may the Groom and the Coachman; and thus every Branch of Expence will be filled to your Master's Honour.

When you are chid before Company, (which, with Submission to our Masters and Ladies, is an unmannerly Practice) it often happeneth that some Stranger will have the Good-nature to drop a Word in your Excuse; in such a Case, you will have a good Title to justify your self, and may rightly conclude, that whenever he chideth you afterwards on other Occasions, he may be in the wrong; in which Opinion you will be the better confirmed by stating the Case to your Fellow-servants in your own Way, who will certainly decide in your Favour: Therefore, as I have said before, whenever you are chidden, complain as if you were injured.

It often happeneth that Servants sent on Messages, are apt to stay out somewhat longer than the Message requireth, perhaps, two, four, six, or eight Hours, or some such Trifle, (for the Temptation to be sure was great, and Flesh and Blood cannot always resist:) When you return, the Master storms, the Lady scolds; stripping, cudgelling, and turning off, is the Word: But here you ought to be provided with a Set of Excuses, enough to serve on all Occasions: For Instance, your Uncle came fourscore Miles to Town this Morning, on purpose to see you, and goeth back by Break of Day To-morrow: A Brother-Servant, that borrowed Money of you when he was out of Place, was running away to *Ireland:* You were taking Leave of an old Fellow-servant, who was shipping for *Barbados:*[2] Your Father sent a Cow to you to sell, and you could not get a Chapman till Nine at Night: You were taking Leave of a dear Cousin who is to be hanged next *Saturday:* You wrencht your Foot against a Stone, and were forced to stay three Hours in a Shop, before you could stir a Step: Some Nastiness was thrown on you out of a Garret Window, and you were ashamed to come Home before you were cleaned, and the Smell went off:[3] You were pressed for the Sea-service,[4] and carried before a Justice of Peace, who kept you three Hours before he examined you, and you got off with much ado: A Bailiff by Mistake Seized you for a Debtor, and kept you the whole Evening in a Spunging-house: You were told your Master had gone to a Tavern, and came to some Mischance, and your Grief was so great that you inquired for his Honour in a hundred Taverns between *Pall-mall* and *Temple-bar*.

Take all Tradesmens Parts against your Master; and when you are sent to buy any Thing, never offer to cheapen it, but generously pay the full Demand. This is highly to your Master's Honour; and may be some Shillings in your Pocket; and you are to consider, if your Master hath paid too much, he can better afford the Loss than a poor Tradesman.

Never submit to stir a Finger in any Business but that for which you were particularly hired. For Example, if the Groom be drunk or absent, and the Butler be ordered to shut the Stable Door, the Answer is ready, *An please your Honour, I don't understand Horses*; If a Corner of the Hanging wanteth a single Nail to fasten it, and the Footman be directed to tack it up, he may say, *He doth not understand that Sort of Work, but his Honour may send for the Upholsterer*.

Masters and Ladies are usually quarrelling with the Servants for not shutting the Doors after them: But neither Masters nor Ladies consider, that those Doors must be open before they can be shut, and that the Labour is double to open and shut the Doors; therefore the best, and shortest, and easiest Way is to do neither. But if you are so often teized to shut the Door, that you cannot easily forget it; then give the Door such a Clap as you go out, as will shake the whole Room, and make every Thing rattle in it, to put your Master and Lady in Mind that you observe their Directions.

If you find yourself to grow into Favour with your Master or Lady, take some Opportunity, in a very mild Way, to give them Warning; and when they ask the Reason, and seem loth to part with you; answer, That you would rather live with them, than any Body else, but a poor Servant is not to be blamed if he striveth to better himself; that Service is no Inheritance, that your Work is great, and your Wages very small: Upon which, if your Master hath any Generosity, he will add five or ten Shillings a Quarter rather than let you go: But, if you are baulked, and have no Mind to go off, get some Fellow-servant to tell your Master, that he hath prevailed upon you to stay.

Whatever good Bits you can pilfer in the Day, save them to junket with your Fellow-servants at Night, and take in the Butler, provided he will give you Drink.

Write your own Name and your Sweet-heart's with the Smoak of a Candle on the Roof of the Kitchen, or the Servants Hall, to shew your Learning.

If you are a young sightly Fellow, whenever you whisper your Mistress at the Table, run your Nose full in her Cheek; or if your Breath be good, breathe full in her Face; this I have known to have had very good Consequences in some Families.

Never come until you have been called three or four Times; for none but Dogs will come at the first Whistle; And when the Master calls [*Who's there*?] no Servant is bound to come; for [*Who's there*] is no Body's Name.

When you have broken all your earthen Drinking Vessels below Stairs (which is usually done in a Week) the Copper Pot will do as well; it can boil Milk, heat Porridge, hold Small-Beer, or in Case of Necessity serve for a Jordan; therefore apply it indifferently to all these Uses; but never wash or scour it, for Fear of taking off the Tin.

Although you are allowed Knives for the Servants Hall at Meals, yet you ought to spare them, and make Use only of your Master's.

Let it be a constant Rule, that no Chair, Stool or Table in the Servants Hall, or the Kitchen, shall have above three Legs; which hath been the antient, and constant Practice in all the Families I ever knew, and is said to be founded upon two Reasons; first, to shew that Servants are ever in a tottering Condition; secondly, it was thought a Part of Humility, that the Servants Chairs and Tables should have at least one Leg fewer than those of their Masters. I grant there hath been an Exception to this Rule, with regard to the Cook, who by old Custom was allowed an easy Chair to sleep in after Dinner; and yet I have seldom seen them with above three Legs. Now this epidemical Lameness of Servants Chairs is by Philosophers imputed to two Causes, which are observed to make the greatest Revolutions in States and Empires: I mean, Love and War. A Stool, a Chair, or a Table, is the first Weapon taken up in a general Romping or Skirmish; and after a Peace, the Chairs, if they be not very strong, are apt to suffer in the Conduct of an Amour; the Cook being usually fat and heavy, and the Butler a little in Drink.

I could never endure to see Maid-Servants so ungenteel as to walk the Streets with their Pettycoats pinned up: it is a foolish Excuse to alledge, their Pettycoats will be dirty, when they have so easy a Remedy as to walk three or four Times down a clean Pair of Stairs after they come home.

When you stop to tattle with some crony Servant in the same Street, leave your own Street-Door open, that you may get in without knocking, when you come back; otherwise your Mistress may know you are gone out, and you may be chidden.

I do most earnestly exhort you all to Unanimity and Concord. But mistake me not: You may quarrel with each other as much as you please; only bear in Mind that you have a common Enemy, which is your Master and Lady, and you have a common Cause to defend. Believe an old Practitioner; whoever out of Malice to a Fellow-servant, carries a Tale to his Master, shall be ruined by a general Confederacy against him.

The general Place of Rendezvous for all the Servants, both in Winter and Summer, is the Kitchen; there the grand Affairs of the Family ought to be consulted; whether they concern the Stable, the Dairy, the Pantry, the Laundry, the Cellar, the Nursery, the Dining-room, or my Lady's Chamber: There, as in your own proper Element, you can laugh, and squall, and romp, in full Security.

When any Servant cometh home drunk, and cannot appear, you must all join in telling your Master, that he is gone to Bed very sick; upon which your Lady will be so good-natured, as to order some comfortable Thing for the poor Man or Maid.

When your Master and Lady go abroad together, to Dinner, or on a Visit for the Evening, you need leave only one Servant in the House; unless you have a Black-guard-boy to answer at the Door, and attend the Children, if there be any. Who is to stay at home is to be determined by short and long Cuts,[5] and the Stayer at home may be comforted by a Visit from a Sweet-heart, without Danger of being caught together. These Opportunities must never be missed, because they come but sometimes; and you are always safe enough while there is a Servant in the House.

When your Master or Lady cometh home, and wanteth a Servant who happeneth to be abroad, your Answer must be, that he but just that Minute stept out, being sent for by a Cousin who was dying.

If your Master calleth you by Name, and you happen to answer at the fourth Call, you need not hurry yourself; and if you be chidden for staying, you may lawfully say, you came no sooner, because you did not know what you were called for.

When you are chidden for a Fault, as you go out of the Room, and down Stairs, mutter loud enough to be plainly heard; this will make him believe you are innocent.

Whoever comes to visit your Master or Lady when they are abroad, never burthen your Memory with the Persons Name, for indeed you have too many other Things to remember. Besides, it is a Porter's Business, and your Master's Fault he doth not keep one; and who can remember Names? and you will certainly mistake them; and you can neither write nor read.

If it be possible, never tell a Lye to your Master or Lady, unless you have some Hopes that they cannot find it out in less than half an Hour. When a Servant is turned off, all his Faults must be told, although most of them were never known by his Master or Lady; and all Mischiefs done by others, charge to him. [Instance them.] And when they ask any of you, why you never acquainted them before? The Answer is, Sir, or Madam, really I was afraid it would make you angry; and besides perhaps you might think it was Malice in me. Where there are little Masters and Misses in a House, they are usually great Impediments to the Diversions of the Servants; the only Remedy is to bribe them with Goody Goodyes, that they may not tell Tales to Papa and Mamma.

I advise you of the Servants, whose Master lives in the Country, and who expect Vails, always to stand Rank and File when a Stranger is taking his Leave; so that he must of Necessity pass between you; and he must have more Confidence, or less Money, than usual, if any of you let him escape, and, according as he behaves himself, remember to treat him the next Time he comes.

If you are sent with ready Money to buy any Thing at a Shop, and happen at that Time to be out of Pocket, sink the Money and take up the Goods on your Master's Account. This is for the Honour of your Master and yourself; for he becomes a Man of Credit at your Recommendation.

When your Lady sends for you up to her Chamber, to give you any Orders, be sure to stand at the Door, and keep it open, fidling with the Lock all the while she is talking to you, and keep the Button in your Hand for fear you should forget to shut the Door after you.

If your Master or Lady happen once in their Lives to accuse you wrongfully, you are a happy Servant, for you have nothing more to do, than for every Fault you commit, while you are in their Service, to put them in Mind of that false Accusation; and protest yourself equally innocent in the present Case.

When you have a Mind to leave your Master, and are too bashful to break the Matter for fear of offending him, the best way is to grow rude and saucy of a sudden, and beyond your usual Behaviour, until he finds it necessary to turn you off; and when you are gone, to revenge yourself, give him and his Lady such a Character to all your Brother-servants, who are out of Place, that none will venture to offer their Service.

Some nice Ladies who are afraid of catching Cold, having observed that the Maids and Fellows below Stairs often forget to shut the Door after them, as they come in or go out into the back Yards, have contrived that a Pulley and Rope with a large Piece of Lead at the End, should be so fixt as to make the Door shut of itself, and require a strong Hand to open it; which is an immense Toil to Servants, whose Business may force them to go in and out fifty Times in a Morning: But Ingenuity can do much, for prudent Servants have found out an effectual Remedy against this insupportable Grievance, by tying up the Pully in such a Manner, that the Weight of the Lead shall have no Effect; however, as to my own Part, I would rather chuse to keep the Door always open, by laying a heavy Stone at the Bottom of it.

The Servants Candlesticks are generally broken, for nothing can last for ever: But, you may find out many Expedients: You may conveniently stick your Candle in a Bottle, or with a Lump of Butter against the Wainscot, in a Powder-horn, or in an old Shoe, or in a cleft Stick, or in the Barrel of a Pistol, or upon its own Grease on a Table, in a Coffee Cup or a Drinking Glass, a Horn Can, a Tea Pot, a twisted Napkin, a Mustard Pot, an Ink-horn, a Marrowbone, a Piece of Dough, a Bundle of Shavings, or you may cut a Hole in the Loaf, and stick it there.

When you invite the neighbouring Servants to junket with

you at home in an Evening, teach them a peculiar way of tapping or scraping at the Kitchen Window, which you may hear; but not your Master or Lady, whom you must take Care not to disturb or frighten at such unseasonable Hours.

Lay all Faults on a Lap-dog, a favourite Cat, a Monkey, a Parrot, a Magpye, a Child, or on the Servant who was last turned off: By this Rule you will excuse yourself, do no Hurt to any Body else, and save your Master or Lady from the Trouble and Vexation of chiding.

When you want proper Instruments for any Work you are about, use all Expedients you can invent, rather than leave your Work undone. For Instance, if the Poker be out of the Way or broken, stir up the Fire with the Tongs; if the Tongs be not at Hand, use the Muzzle of the Bellows, the wrong End of the Fire-Shovel, the Handle of the Fire-Brush, the End of a Mop, or your Master's Cane. If you want Paper to singe a Fowl, tear the first Book you see about the House. Wipe your Shoes for want of a Clout, with the Bottom of a Curtain, or a Damask Napkin. Strip your Livery Lace for Garters. If the Butler wants a Jordan, he may use the great Silver Cup.

There are several Ways of putting out Candles, and you ought to be instructed in them all: You may run the Candle End against the Wainscot, which puts the Snuff out immediately: You may lay it on the Ground, and tread the Snuff out with your Foot: You may hold it upside down until it is choaked with its own Grease; or cram it into the Socket of the Candle-stick: You may whirl it round in your Hand till it goes out: When you go to Bed, after you have made Water, you may dip the Candle End into the Chamber-Pot: You may spit on your Finger and Thumb, and pinch the Snuff until it goes out: The Cook may run the Candle's Nose into the Meal Tub, or the Groom into a Vessel of Oats, or a Lock of Hay, or a Heap of Litter: The House-maid may put out her Candle by running it against a Looking-glass, which nothing cleans so well as Candle Snuff: But the quickest and best of all Methods, is to blow it out with your Breath, which leaves the Candle clear and readier to be lighted.

There is nothing so pernicious in a Family as a *Tell-Tale*, against whom it must be the principal Business of you, all to unite: Whatever Office he serveth in, take all Opportunities to spoil the Business he is about, and to cross him in every Thing. For Instance, if the Butler be the *Tell-Tale*, break his Glasses whenever he leaves the Pantry Door open; or lock the Cat or the Mastiff in it, who will do as well: Mislay a Fork or a Spoon, so as he may never find it. If it be the Cook, whenever she turns her Back, throw a Lump of Soot or a Handful of Salt in the Pot, or smoaking Coals into the Dripping-Pan, or daub the roast Meat with the Back of the Chimney, or hide the Key of the Jack. If a Footman be suspected, let the Cook daub the Back of his new Livery; or when he is going up with a Dish of Soup, let her follow him softly with a Ladle-full, and dribble it all the Way up Stairs to the Dining-room, and then let the House-maid make such a Noise, that her Lady may hear it. The Waiting-maid is very likely to be guilty of this Fault, in hopes to ingratiate herself. In this Case, the Laundress must be sure to tear her Smocks in the washing, and yet wash them but half; and, when she complains, tell all the House that she sweateth so much, and her Flesh is so nasty, that she fouleth a Smock more in one Hour, than the Kitchen-maid doth in a Week.

. . .

CHAP. III.
Directions to the FOOTMAN

YOUR Employment being of a mixt Nature, extendeth to a great Variety of Business, and you stand in a fair way of being the Favourite of your Master or Mistress, or of the young Masters and Misses; you are the fine Gentleman of the Family, with whom all the Maids are in Love. You are sometimes a Pattern of Dress to your Master, and sometimes he is so to you.[6] You wait at Table in all Companies, and consequently have the Opportunity to see and know the World, and to understand Men and Manners; I confess your Vails are but few, unless you are sent with a Present, or attend the Tea in the Country; but you are called Mr. in the Neighbourhood, and sometimes pick up a Fortune, perhaps your Master's Daughter; and I have known many of your Tribe to have good Commands in the Army. In Town you have a Seat reserved for you in the Play-house, where you have an Opportunity of becoming Wits and Criticks: You have no profest Enemy except the Rabble, and my Lady's Waiting-woman, who are sometimes apt to call you Skipkennel. I have a true Veneration for your Office, because I had once the Honour to be one of your Order, which I foolishly left by demeaning myself with accepting an Employment in the Custom-house.—But that you, my Brethren, may come to better Fortunes, I shall here deliver my Instructions, which have been the Fruits of much Thought and Observation, as well as of seven Years Experience.

In order to learn the Secrets of other Families, tell them those of your Master's; thus you will grow a Favourite both at home and abroad, and regarded as a Person of Importance.

Never be seen in the Streets with a Basket or Bundle in your Hands, and carry nothing but what you can hide in your Pocket, otherwise you will disgrace your Calling: To prevent which, always retain a Blackguard Boy to carry your Loads; and if you want Farthings, pay him with a good Slice of Bread or Scrap of Meat.

Let a Shoe-boy clean your own Shoes first, for fear of fouling the Chamber, then let him clean your Master's; keep him on purpose for that Use and to run of Errands, and pay him with Scraps. When you are sent on an Errand, be sure to hedge in some Business of your own, either to see your Sweet-heart, or drink a Pot of Ale with some Brother-Servants, which is so much Time clear gained.

There is a great Controversy about the most convenient and genteel Way of holding your Plate at Meals; some stick it between the Frame and the Back of the Chair, which is an excellent Expedient, where the Make of the Chair will allow it: Others, for fear the Plate should fall, grasp it so firmly, that their Thumb reacheth to the Middle of the Hollow; which however, if your Thumb be dry, is no secure Method; and therefore in that Case, I advise your wetting the Bowl of it with your Tongue: As to that absurd Practice of letting the Back of

the Plate lye leaning on the Hollow of your Hand, which some
Ladies recommend, it is universally exploded, being liable to so
many Accidents. Others again, are so refined, that they hold
their Plate directly under the left Arm-pit, which is the best
Situation for keeping it warm; but this may be dangerous in the
Article of taking away a Dish, where your Plate may happen to
fall upon some of the Company's Heads. I confess myself to
have objected against all these Ways, which I have frequently
tried; and therefore I recommend a Fourth, which is to stick
your Plate up to the Rim inclusive, in the left Side between your
Waistcoat and your Shirt: This will keep it at least as warm as
under your Arm-pit, or Ockster, (as the *Scotch* call it); this will
hide it so as Strangers may take you for a better Servant, too
good to hold a Plate; this will secure it from falling; and thus
disposed, it lieth ready for you to whip it out in a Moment,
ready warmed, to any Guest within your Reach, who may want
it. And lastly, there is another Convenience in this Method,
that if any Time during your waiting, you find yourselves going
to cough or sneeze, you can immediately snatch out your Plate,
and hold the hollow Part close to your Nose or Mouth, and,
thus prevent spirting any Moisture from either, upon the Dishes
or the Ladies Head-dress: You see Gentlemen and Ladies
observe a like Practice on such an Occasion, with a Hat or a
Handkerchief; yet a Plate is less fouled and sooner cleaned than
either of these; for, when your Cough or Sneeze is over, it is
but returning your Plate to the same Position, and your Shirt
will clean it in the Passage.

Take off the largest Dishes, and set them on, with one Hand,
to shew the Ladies your Vigour and Strength of Back; but
always do it between two Ladies, that if the Dish happens to
slip, the Soup or Sauce may fall on their Cloaths, and not daub
the Floor: By this Practice, two of our Brethren, my worthy
Friends, got considerable Fortunes.

Learn all the new-fashion Words, and Oaths, and Songs, and
Scraps of Plays that your Memory can hold. Thus, you will
become the Delight of nine Ladies in ten, and the Envy of ninety
nine Beaux in a hundred.

Take Care, that at certain Periods, during Dinner, especially, when Persons of Quality are there, you and your Brethren be all out of the Room together, by which you will give yourselves some Ease from the Fatigue of waiting, and at the same Time leave the Company to converse more freely, without being constrained by your Presence.

When you are sent on a Message, deliver it in your own Words, altho' it be to a Duke or a Dutchess, and not in the Words of your Master or Lady; for how can they understand what belongs to a Message as well as you, who have been bred to the Employment: But never deliver the Answer until it is called for, and then adorn it with your own Style.

When Dinner is done, carry down a great Heap of Plates to the Kitchen, and when you come to the Head of the Stairs, trundle them all before you: There is not a more agreeable Sight or Sound, especially if they be Silver; besides the Trouble they save you; and there they will lie ready near the Kitchen Door, for the Scullion to wash them.

If you are bringing up a Joint of Meat in a Dish, and it falleth out of your Hand, before you get into the Dining Room, with the Meat on the Ground, and the Sauce spilled, take up the Meat gently, wipe it with the Lap of your Coat, then put it again into the Dish, and serve it up; and when your Lady misses the Sauce, tell her, it is to be sent up in a Plate by itself.

When you carry up a Dish of Meat, dip your Fingers in the Sauce, or lick it with your Tongue, to try whether it be good, and fit for your Master's Table.

You are the best Judge of what Acquaintance your Lady ought to have, and therefore, if she sendeth you on a Message of Compliment or Business to a Family you do not like, deliver the Answer in such a Manner, as may breed a Quarrel between them not to be reconciled: Or, if a Footman cometh from the same Family on the like Errand, turn the Answer she ordereth you to deliver, in such a Manner, as the other Family may take it for an Affront.

When you are in Lodgings, and no Shoe-boy to be got, clean your Master's Shoes with the Bottom of the Curtains, a clean Napkin, or your Landlady's Apron.

Ever wear your Hat in the House, but when your Master

calleth; and as soon as you come into his Presence, pull it off to shew your Manners.

Never clean your Shoes on the Scraper, but in the Entry, or at the Foot of the Stairs, by which you will have the Credit of being at home, almost a Minute sooner, and the Scraper will last the longer.

Never ask Leave to go abroad, for then it will be always known that you are absent, and you will be thought an idle rambling Fellow; whereas, if you go out, and no body observeth, you have a Chance of coming home without being missed, and you need not tell your Fellow-servants where you are gone, for they will be sure to say, you were in the House but two Minutes ago, which is the Duty of all Servants.

Snuff the Candles with your Fingers, and throw the Snuff on the Floor, then tread it out to prevent stinking: This Method will very much save the Snuffers from wearing out. You ought also to snuff them close to the Tallow, which will make them run, and so encrease the Perquisite of the Cook's Kitchen-Stuff; for she is the Person you ought in Prudence to be well with.

While Grace is saying after Meat, do you and your Brethren take the Chairs from behind the Company, so that when they go to sit again, they may fall backwards, which will make them all merry; but be you so discreet as to hold your Laughter till you get to the Kitchen, and then divert your Fellow-servants.

When you know your Master is most busy in Company, come in and pretend to settle about the Room; and if he chideth, say, you thought he rung the Bell. This will divert him from plodding on Business too much, or spending himself in Talk, or racking his Thoughts, all which are hurtful to his Constitution.

If you are ordered to break the Claw of a Crab or a Lobster, clap it between the Sides of the Dining Room Door between the Hinges: Thus you can do it gradually without mashing the Meat, which is often the Fate of the Street-Door-Key, or the Pestle.

When you take a foul Plate from any of the Guests, and observe the foul Knife and Fork lying on the Plate, shew your Dexterity, take up the Plate, and throw off the Knife and Fork on the Table, without shaking off the Bones or broken Meat that are left: Then the Guest, who hath more Time than you, will wipe the Fork and Knife already used.

When you carry a Glass of Liquor to any Person who hath called for it, do not bob him on the Shoulder, or cry, Sir, or Madam, here's the Glass, that would be unmannerly, as if you had a Mind to force it down one's Throat; but stand at the Person's right Shoulder, and wait his Time; and if he striketh it down with his Elbow by Forgetfulness, that was his Fault and not yours.

When your Mistress sendeth you for a Hackney Coach in a wet Day, come back in the Coach to save your Cloaths and the Trouble of walking; it is better the Bottom of her Pettycoats should be daggled with your dirty Shoes, than your Livery be spoiled, and yourself get a Cold.

There is no Indignity so great to one of your Station, as that of lighting your Master in the Streets with a Lanthorn; and therefore, it is very honest Policy to try all Arts how to evade it: Besides, it sheweth your Master to be either covetous or poor, which are the two worst Qualities you can meet with in any Service. When I was under these Circumstances, I made use of several wise Expedients, which I here recommend to you. Sometimes I took a Candle so long, that it reached to the very Top of the Lanthorn, and burned it: But, my Master after a good Beating, ordered me to paste the Top with Paper. I then used a middling Candle, but stuck it so loose in the Socket, that it leaned towards one Side, and burned a whole Quarter of the Horn. Then I used a Bit of Candle of half an Inch, which sunk in the Socket, and melted the Solder, and forced my Master to walk half the Way in the Dark. Then he made me stick two Inches of Candle in the Place where the Socket was; after which, I pretended to stumble, put out the Candle, and broke all the Tin Part to Pieces: At last, he was forced to make use of a Lanthorn-boy out of perfect good Husbandry.

It is much to be lamented, that Gentlemen of our Employment have but two Hands to carry Plates, Dishes, Bottles, and the like out of the Room at Meals; and the Misfortune is still the greater, because one of those Hands is required to open the Door, while you are encumbred with your Load: Therefore, I advise, that the Door may be always left at jarr, so as to open it with your

Foot, and then you may carry out Plates and Dishes from your Belly up to your Chin, besides a good Quantity of Things under your Arms, which will save you many a weary Step; but take Care that none of the Burthen falls until you are out of the Room, and if possible, out of Hearing.

If you are sent to the Post-Office with a Letter in a cold rainy Night, step to the Ale-house, and take a Pot, until it is supposed you have done your Errand; but take the next fair Opportunity to put the Letter in carefully, as becometh an honest Servant.

If you are ordered to make Coffee for the Ladies after Dinner, and the Pot happeneth to boil over while you are running up for a Spoon to stir it, or are thinking of something else, or struggling with the Chamber-maid for a Kiss, wipe the Sides of the Pot clean with a Dishclout, carry up your Coffee boldly, and when your Lady finds it too weak, and examines you whether it hath not run over; deny the Fact absolutely, swear you put in more Coffee than ordinary, that you never stirred an Inch from it, that you strove to make it better than usual, because your Mistress had Ladies with her, that the Servants in the Kitchen will justify what you say: Upon this, you will find that the other Ladies will pronounce your Coffee to be very good, and your Mistress will confess that her Mouth is out of Taste, and she will for the future suspect herself, and be more cautious in finding Fault. This I would have you do from a Principle of Conscience, for Coffee is very unwholesome; and out of Affection to your Lady, you ought to give it her as weak as possible. And upon this Argument, when you have a Mind to treat any of the Maids with a Dish of fresh Coffee, you may, and ought to subtract a third Part of the Powder, on account of your Lady's Health, and getting her Maids Good-will.

If your Master sendeth you with a small trifling Present to one of his friends, be as careful of it as you would be of a Diamond Ring: Therefore, if the Present be only Half a Dozen Pippins, send up the Servant who received the Message to say, that you were ordered to deliver them with your own Hands. This will shew your Exactness and Care to prevent Accidents or Mistakes; and the Gentleman or Lady cannot do less than give you a Shilling. So when your Master receives the like

Present, teach the Messenger who bringeth it to do the same, and give your Master Hints that may stir up his Generosity; for Brother Servants should assist one another, since it is all for your Master's Honour, which is the chief Point to be consulted by every good Servant, and of which he is the best Judge.

When you step but a few Doors off to tattle with a Wench, or take a running Pot of Ale, or to see a Brother Footman going to be hanged, leave the Street Door open, that you may not be forced to knock, and your Master discover you are gone out; for a Quarter of an Hour's Time can do his Service no Injury.

When you take away the remaining Pieces of Bread after Dinner, put them on foul Plates, and press them down with other Plates over them, so as no body can touch them; and so, they will be a good Perquisite to the Blackguard Boy in ordinary.

When you are forced to clean your Master's Shoes with your own Hand, use the Edge of the sharpest Case Knife, and dry them with the Toes an Inch from the Fire, because wet Shoes are dangerous; and besides, by these Arts you will get them the sooner for yourself.

In some Families the Master often sendeth to the Tavern for a Bottle of Wine, and you are the Messenger: I advise you, therefore, to take the smallest Bottle you can find; but however, make the Drawer give you a full Quart, then you will get a good Sup for yourself, and your Bottle will be filled. As for a Cork to stop it, you need be at no Trouble, for the Thumb will do as well, or a Bit of dirty chewed Paper.

In all Disputes with Chairmen and Coachmen for demanding too much, when your Master sendeth you down to chaffer with them, take Pity of the poor Fellows, and tell your Master that they will not take a Farthing less: It is more for your Interest to get Share of a Pot of Ale, than to save a Shilling for your Master, to whom it is a Trifle.

When you attend your Lady in a dark Night, if she useth her Coach, do not walk by the Coach Side so as to tire and dirt yourself, but get up into your proper Place, behind it, and so hold the Flambeau sloping forward over the Coach Roof; and when it wants snuffing, dash it against the Corners.

When you leave your Lady at Church on *Sundays*, you have

two Hours safe to spend with your Companions at the Ale-house, or over a Beef-Stake and a Pot of Beer at Home, with the Cook, and the Maids; and, indeed, poor Servants have so few Opportunities to be happy, that they ought not to lose any.

Never wear Socks when you wait at Meals, on the Account of your own Health, as well as of them who sit at Table; because, as most Ladies like the Smell of young Mens Toes, so it is a sovereign Remedy against the Vapours.

Chuse a Service, if you can, where your Livery Colours are least tawdry and distinguishing: Green and Yellow immediately betray your Office, and so do all Kinds of Lace, except Silver, which will hardly fall to your Share, unless with a Duke, or some Prodigal just come to his Estate. The Colours you ought to wish for, are Blue, or Filemot, turned up with Red; which with a borrowed Sword, a borrowed Air, your Master's Linen, and a natural and improved Confidence, will give you what Title you please, where you are not known.

When you carry Dishes or other Things out of the Room at Meals, fill both your Hands as full as possible; for, although you may sometimes spill, and sometimes let fall, yet you will find at the Year's End, you have made great Dispatch, and saved abundance of Time.

If your Master or Mistress happens to walk the Streets, keep on one Side, and as much on the Level with them as you can, which People observing, will either think you do not belong to them, or that you are one of their Companions; but, if either of them happen to turn back and speak to you, so that you are under the Necessity to take off your Hat, use but your Thumb and one Finger, and scratch your Head with the rest.

In Winter Time light the Dining-Room Fire but two Minutes before Dinner is served up, that your Master may see, how saving you are of his Coals.

When you are ordered to stir up the Fire, clean away the Ashes from between the Bars with the Fire-Brush.

When you are ordered to call a Coach, although it be Mid-night, go no further than the Door, for Fear of being out of the Way when you are wanted; and there stand bawling, *Coach*, *Coach*, for half an Hour.

Although you Gentlemen in Livery have the Misfortune to be treated scurvily by all Mankind, yet you make a Shift to keep up your Spirits, and sometimes arrive at considerable Fortunes. I was an intimate Friend to one of our Brethren, who was Footman to a Court-Lady: She had an honourable Employment, was Sister to an Earl, and the Widow of a Man of Quality. She observed something so polite in my Friend, the Gracefulness with which he tript before her Chair, and put his Hair under his Hat, that she made him many Advances; and one Day taking the Air in her Coach with *Tom* behind it, the Coachman mistook the Way, and stopt at a priviledged Chapel, where the Couple were married, and *Tom* came home in the Chariot by his Lady's Side: But he unfortunately taught her to drink Brandy, of which she died, after having pawned all her Plate to purchase it, and *Tom* is now a Journeyman Malster.

Boucher, the famous Gamester, was another of our Fraternity, and when he was worth 50,000*l*. he dunned the Duke of B—g—m[7] for an Arrear of Wages in his Service: And I could instance many more; particularly another, whose Son had one of the chief Employments at Court; and is sufficient to give you the following Advice, which is to be pert and sawcy to all Mankind, especially to the Chaplain, the Waiting-woman, and the better Sort of Servants in a Person of Quality's Family, and value not now and then a Kicking, or a Caning; for your Insolence will at last turn to good Account; and from wearing a Livery, you may probably soon carry a Pair of Colours.

When you wait behind a Chair at Meals, keep Constantly wriggling the Back of the Chair, that the Person behind whom you stand, may know you are ready to attend him.

When you carry a Parcel of China Plates, if they chance to fall, as it is a frequent Misfortune, your Excuse must be, that a Dog ran across you in the Hall; that the Chamber-maid accidentally pushed the Door against you; that a Mop stood across the Entry, and tript you up; that your Sleeve stuck against the Key, or Button of the Lock.

When your Master and Lady are talking together in the Bed-chamber, and you have some Suspicion that you or your Fellow-servants are concerned in what they say, listen at the

Door for the publick Good of all the Servants, and join all to take proper Measures for preventing any Innovations that may hurt the Community.

Be not proud in Prosperity: You have heard that Fortune turneth on a Wheel; if you have a good Place, you are at the Top of the Wheel. Remember how often you have been stripped, and kicked out of Doors, your Wages all taken up beforehand and spent in translated red-heeled Shoes, second-hand Toupees, and repaired Lace Ruffles,[8] besides a swingeing Debt to the Ale-wife and the Brandy-shop. The neighbouring Tapster, who before would beckon you over to a savoury Bit of Ox-cheek in the Morning, give it you *gratis*, and only score you up for the Liquor, immediately after you were packt off in Disgrace, carried a Petition to your Master, to be paid out of your Wages, whereof not a Farthing was due, and then pursued you with Bailiffs into every blind Cellar. Remember how soon you grew shabby, thread-bare, and out-at-heels; was forced to borrow an old Livery Coat, to make your Appearance, while you were looking for a Place; and sneak to every House where you have an old Acquaintance to steal you a Scrap, to keep Life and Soul together; and, upon the whole, were in the lowest Station of Human Life; which, as the old Ballad says, is that of a Skip-kennel turned out of Place: I say, remember all this now in your flourishing Condition. Pay your Contributions duly to your late Brothers the Cadets, who are left to the wide World: Take one of them as your Dependant, to send on your Lady's Messages, when you have a Mind to go to the Ale-house; slip him out privately now and then a Slice of Bread, and a Bit of cold Meat, your Master can afford it; and if he be not yet put upon the Establishment for a Lodging, let him lye in the Stable, or the Coach-house, or under the Back-stairs, and recommend him to all the Gentlemen who frequent your House, as an excellent Servant.

To grow old in the Office of a Footman, is the highest of all Indignities: Therefore, when you find Years coming on, without Hopes of a Place at Court, a Command in the Army, a Succession to the Stewardship, an Employment in the Revenue (which two last you cannot obtain without Reading and Writing) or running away with your Master's Niece or Daughter; I directly advise you to go upon the Road, which is the only Post of Honour left you:[9] There you will meet many of your old Comrades, and live a short Life and a merry one, and make a Figure at your *Exit*, wherein I will give you some Instructions.

The last Advice I give you, relateth to your Behaviour when you are going to be hanged; which, either for robbing your Master, for House-breaking, or going upon the High-way, or in a drunken Quarrel, by killing the first Man you meet, may very probably be your Lot, and is owing to one of these three Qualities, either a Love of good Fellowship, a Generosity of Mind, or too much Vivacity of Spirits. Your good Behaviour on this Article, will concern your whole Community: Deny the Fact with all Solemnity of Imprecations: A hundred of your Brethren, if they can be admitted, will attend about the Bar, and be ready upon Demand to give you a good Character before the Court: Let nothing prevail on you to confess, but the Promise of a Pardon for discovering your Comrades: But, I suppose all this to be in vain, for if you escape now, your Fate will be the same another Day. Get a Speech to be written by the best Author of *Newgate:*[10] Some of your kind Wenches will provide you with a *Holland* Shirt, and white Cap crowned with a crimson or black Ribbon: Take Leave chearfully of all your Friends in *Newgate:* Mount the Cart with Courage: Fall on your Knees: Lift up your Eyes: Hold a Book in your Hands, although you cannot read a Word: Deny the Fact at the Gallows: Kiss and forgive the Hangman, and so Farewel:[11] You shall be buried in Pomp, at the Charge of the Fraternity: The Surgeon shall not touch a Limb of you;[12] and your Fame shall continue until a Successor of equal Renown succeedeth in your Place.

A COMPLEAT COLLECTION OF GENTEEL AND INGENIOUS CONVERSATION

<table>
<tr><td>THE MEN</td><td>THE LADIES</td></tr>
<tr><td>Lord Smart</td><td>Lady Smart</td></tr>
<tr><td>Lord Sparkish</td><td>Miss Notable</td></tr>
<tr><td>Sir John Linger</td><td>Lady Answerall</td></tr>
<tr><td>Colonel Atwit</td><td></td></tr>
<tr><td>Mr. Neverout</td><td></td></tr>
</table>

SECOND CONVERSATION

[Lord Smart, and the former Company at Three a Clock, coming to dine.]

[After Salutations.]

Lord Sm. I'm sorry I was not at home this Morning, when you all did us the Honour to call here. But I went to the Levee To-Day.

Lord Sp. O, my Lord; I'm sure the Loss was ours.

Lady Sm. Gentlemen, and Ladies, you are come into a sad dirty House; I am sorry for it, but we have had our Hands in Mortar.[1]

Lord Sp. O, Madam, your Ladyship is pleased to say so, but I never saw any Thing so clean and so fine. I profess it is a perfect Paradise.

Lady Sm. My Lord, your Lordship is always very obliging.

Lord Sp. Pray, Madam, whose Picture is that?

Lady Sm. Why, my Lord, it was drawn for me.

Lord Sp. I'll swear, the Painter did not flatter your Ladyship.

Col. My Lord, the Day is finely cleared up.

Lord Sm. Ay, Colonel, 'tis a Pity that fair Weather should ever do any harm. *[to* Neverout.] Why, *Tom*, you are high in the Mode.

Nev. My Lord, it is better to be out of the World, than out of the Fashion.

Lord Sm. But, *Tom*, I hear, you and Miss are always quarrelling: I fear, it is your Fault; for I can assure you, she is very good-humoured.

Nev. Ay, my Lord, so is the Devil when he's pleas'd.

Lord Sm. Miss, what do you think of my Friend *Tom?*

Miss. My Lord, I think he is not the wisest Man in the World; and truly, he's sometimes very rude.

Lord Sp. That may be true; but yet, he that hangs *Tom* for a Fool, may find a Knave in the Halter.[2]

Miss. Well, however, I wish he were hang'd, if it were only to try.[3]

Nev. Well, Miss, if I must be hanged, I won't go far to chuse my Gallows: It shall be about your fair Neck.

Miss. I'll see your Nose Cheese first, and the Dogs eating it.[4] But, my Lord, Mr. *Neverout*'s Wit begins to run low, for I vow he said this before. Pray, Colonel, give him a Pinch, and I'll do as much for you.

Lord Sp. My Lady *Smart*, your Ladyship has a very fine Scarf.

Lady Sm. Yes, my Lord, it will make a flaming Figure in a Country Church.[5]

[*Footman comes in.*]

Footman. Madam, Dinner's upon the Table.

Col. Faith, I'm glad of it; my Belly began to cry Cupboard.

Nev. I wish I may never hear worse News.

Miss. What; Mr. *Neverout*, you are in great haste; I believe your Belly thinks your Throat's cut.[6]

Nev. No, faith, Miss; three Meals a Day, and a good Supper at Night, will serve my Turn.

Miss. To say the Truth, I'm hungry.

Nev. And I'm angry, so let us both go fight.

[*They go in to Dinner, and after the usual Compliments, take their Seats.*]

Lord Sm. Ladies and Gentlemen, will you eat any Oysters before Dinner?

Col. With all my Heart. [*Takes an Oyster.*] He was a bold Man that first eat an Oyster.

Lady Sm. They say, Oysters are a cruel Meat; because we eat them alive: Then, they are an uncharitable Meat; for we leave nothing to the Poor. And, they are an ungodly Meat, because we never say Grace to them.[7]

Nev. Faith, that's as well said, as if I had said it my self.[8]

Lady Sm. Well, we are all well set, if we be but as well serv'd. Come, Colonel, handle your Arms: Shall I help you to some Beef?

Col. If your Ladyship pleases; and pray don't cut like a Mother-in-law, but send me a large Slice; for I love to lay a good Foundation: I vow, 'tis a noble Sirloyn.

Nev. Ay, here's Cut and come again.

Miss. But, pray, why is it called a Sirloyn?

Lord Sp. Why, you must know, that our King *James* I. who loved good Eating, being invited to Dinner by one of his Nobles, and seeing a large Loyn of Beef at his Table; he drew out his Sword, and in a Frolick Knighted it.[9] Few People know the Secret of this.

Lord Sp. Beef is Man's Meat, my Lord.

Lord Sm. But, my Lord, I say, Beef is the King of Meat.

Miss. Pray, what have I done, that I must not have a Plate?

Lady Sm. [*To* Lady *Answerall.*] What will your Ladyship please to eat?

Lady Answ. Pray, Madam, help your self.

Col. They say, Eating and Scratching wants but a Beginning.[10] If you will give me Leave, I'll help my self to a Slice of this Shoulder of Veal.

Lady Sm. Colonel, you can't do a kinder Thing. Well, you are all heartily welcome, as I may say.

Col. They say, there are thirty and two good Bits in a Shoulder of Veal.

Lady Sm. Ay, Colonel; thirty bad Bits, and two good ones; you see I understand you; but, I hope you have got one of the two good ones.

Nev. Colonel, I'll be of your Mess.

Col. Then, pray *Tom*, carve for your self: They say, two Hands in a Dish, and one in a Purse.[11] Hah, said I well, *Tom?*

Nev. Colonel, you spoke like an Oracle.

[*Miss to Lady* Answerall.]

Miss. Madam, will your Ladyship help me to some Fish?

Lord Sm. [*To* Neverout.] *Tom*, they say Fish should swim thrice.

Nev. How is that, my Lord?

Lord Sm. Why, *Tom*, first it should swim in the Sea; (do you mind me?) then it should swim in Butter; and at last, Sirrah, it should swim in good Claret. I think I have made it out.

[*Footman to Lord* Smart.]

Footman. My Lord, Sir *John Linger* is coming up.

Lord Sm. God so! I invited him to Dinner with me To-day, and forgot it. Well, desire him to walk in.

[*Sir* John Linger *comes in.*]

Sir John. What; are you at it? Why, then, I'll be gone.

Lady Sm. Sir *John*, I beg you will sit down; come, the more, the merrier.

Sir John. Ay; but the fewer, the better Cheer.[12]

Lady Sm. Well, I am the worst in the World at making Apologies. It was my Lord's Fault. I doubt you must kiss the Hare's Foot.[13]

Sir John. I see you are fast by the Teeth.

Col. Faith, Sir *John*, we are killing that, that would kill us.[14]

Lord Sp. You see, Sir *John*, we are upon a Business of Life and Death. Come, will you do as we do? You are come in Pudden-Time.

Sir John. Ay, this you would be doing if I were dead. What, you keep Court-Hours I see.[15] I'll be going, and get a Bit of Meat at my Inn.

Lady Sm. Why, we won't eat you, Sir *John*.

Sir John. It is my own Fault; but, I was kept by a Fellow, who bought some *Derbyshire* Oxen from me.

Nev. You see, Sir *John*, we stayed for you, as one Horse does for another.

Lady Sm. My Lord, will you help Sir *John* to some Beef. Lady *Answerall*, pray eat, you see your Dinner. I am sure, if we had known we should have such good Company, we should have been better provided; but, you must take the Will for the Deed. I'm afraid you are invited to your Loss.

Col. And, pray, Sir *John*, how do you like the Town? You have been absent a long Time.

Sir John. Why, I find little *London* stands just where it did when I left it last.[16]

Nev. What do you think of *Hanover-Square*; why, Sir *John*, *London* is gone out of Town since you saw it.[17]

Lady Sm. Sir *John*, I can only say, you are heartily welcome; and I wish I had something better for you.

Col. Here's no Salt; Cuckolds will run away with the Meat.[18]

Lord Sm. Pray, edge a little, to make more Room for Sir *John*. Sir *John*, fall to, you know half an Hour is soon lost at Dinner.

Sir John. I protest, I can't eat a Bit; for I took Share of a Beef-Stake, and two Mugs of Ale with my Chapman, besides a Tankard of *March* Beer as soon as I got out of Bed.

Lady Answ. Not fresh and fasting, I hope.

Sir John. Yes, faith, Madam, I always wash my Kettle before I put the Meat in it.[19]

Lady Sm. Poh! Sir *John*, you have seen nine Houses since you eat last: Come, you have kept a Corner of your Stomach for a Bit of Venison-Pasty.

Sir John. Well, I'll try what I can do when it comes up.

Lady Answ. Come, Sir *John*, you may go further, and fare worse.

Miss. [*To* Neverout.] Pray, Mr. *Neverout*, will you please to send me a Piece of Tongue?

Nev. By no Means, Madam; one Tongue's enough for a Woman.[20]

Col. Miss, here's a Tongue that never told a Lye.

Miss. That was because it could not speak. Why, Colonel, I never told a Lye in my Life.

Nev. I appeal to all the Company, whether that be not the greatest Lye that ever was told.

Col. [*To* Neverout.] Pr'ythee, *Tom*, send me the two Legs, and Rump and Liver, of that Pigeon; for you must know, I love what no Body else loves.

Nev. But what if any of the Ladies should long?[21] Well, here take it, and the Devil do you good with it.

Lady Answ. Well; this eating and drinking takes away a Body's Stomach.

Nev. I'm sure I have lost mine.

Miss. What! the Bottom of it, I suppose.[22]

Nev. No really, Miss, I have quite lost it.

Miss. I should be sorry a poor Body had found it.

Lady Sm. But, Sir *John*, we hear you are marryed since we saw you last. What; you have stolen a Wedding, it seems.[23]

Sir John. Well, one can't do a foolish Thing once in one's Life, but one must hear of it a hundred Times.

Col. And pray, Sir *John*, how does your Lady unknown?

Sir John. My Wife's well, Colonel; and at your Service in a civil Way. Ha, ha. [*He laughs.*]

Miss. Pray, Sir *John*, is your Lady tall, or short?

Sir John. Why, Miss, I thank God, she's a little Evil.[24]

Lord Sp. Come, give me a Glass of Claret.

[*Footman fills him a Bumper.*]

Why do you fill so much?

Nev. My Lord, he fills as he loves you.

Lady Sm. Miss, shall I send you some Cucumber?

Miss. Madam, I dare not touch it; for they say, Cucumbers are cold in the third Degree.[25]

Lady Sm. Mr. *Neverout*, do you love Pudden?

Nev. Madam, I'm like all Fools; I love every Thing that is good: But the Proof of the Pudden, is in the eating.[26]

Col. Sir *John*, I hear you are a great Walker when you are at home.

Sir John. No, Faith, Colonel, I always love to walk with a Horse in my Hand. But I have had devilish bad Luck in Horse-Flesh, of late.

Lord Sm. Why then, Sir *John*, you must kiss a Parson's Wife.[27]

Lady Sm. They say, Sir *John*, that your Lady has a great deal of Wit.

Sir John. Madam, she can make a Pudden; and has just Wit enough to know her Husband's Breeches from another Man's.

Lord Sm. My Lord *Sparkish*, I have some excellent Cyder, will you please to taste it.

Lord Sp. My Lord, I should like it well enough, if it were not so treacherous.

Lord Sm. Pray, my Lord, how is it treacherous?

Lord Sp. Because it smiles in my Face, and cuts my Throat. [*Here a loud Laugh.*]

Miss. Odd-so, Madam, your Knives are very sharp, for I have cut my Finger.

Lady Sm. I'm sorry for it; pray, which Finger? (God bless the Mark.)

Miss. Why, this Finger; no, 'tis this: I vow; I can't find which it is.

Nev. Ay, the Fox had a Wound, and he could not tell where, &c. Bring some Water to throw in her Face.

Miss. Pray, Mr. *Neverout*, did you ever draw a Sword in Anger? I warrant, you would faint at the Sight of your own Blood.

Lady Sm. Mr. *Neverout*, shall I send you some Veal?

Nev. No, Madam, I don't love it.

Miss. Then pray for them that do. I desire your Ladyship will send me a Bit.

Lord Sm. Tom, my Service to you.

Nev. My Lord, this Moment, I did my self the Honour to drink to your Lordship.

Lord Sm. Why then, that's *Hartfordshire* Kindness.[28]

Lord Sp. Why then, Colonel, my humble Service to you.

Nev. Pray, my Lord, don't make a Bridge of my Nose.[29]

Lord Sp. Well, a Glass of this Wine is as comfortable, as Matrimony to an old Maid.

Col. Sir *John*, I design one of these Days, to come and beat up your Quarters[30] in *Derbyshire*.

Sir John. Faith, Colonel, come and welcome; and stay away, and heartily welcome. But you were born within the Sound of *Bow* Bell, and don't Care to stir so far from *London*.[31]

Miss. Pray, Colonel, send me some Fritters.

[*Colonel takes them out with his Hand.*]

Col. Here, Miss; they say, Fingers were made before Forks, and Hands before Knives.

Lady Sm. Methinks, this Pudden is too much boyl'd.

Lady Answ. O, Madam, they say a Pudden is Poison, when it's too much boyl'd.

Nev. Miss, shall I help you to a Pigeon? Here's a Pigeon so finely roasted, it cries, Come eat me.

Miss. No, Sir, I thank you.

Nev. Why then, you may chuse.

Miss. I have chosen already.

Nev. Well; you may be worse offered, before you are twice married.

[*The Colonel fills a large Plate of Soupe.*]

Lord Sm. Why, Colonel, you don't mean to eat all that Soupe?

Col. O, my Lord, this is my sick Dish; when I am well, I have a Bigger.

Miss. [*To Colonel.*] Sup, *Simon*;[32] good Broth.

Nev. This seems to be a good Pullet.

Miss. I warrant, Mr. *Neverout* knows what's good for himself.

Lord Sp. *Tom*, I shan't take your Word for it; help me to a Wing.

[*Neverout tries to cut off a Wing.*]

Nev. I'gad, I can't hit the Joynt.

Lord Sp. Why, then, think of a Cuckold.

Nev. O, now I have nickt it.

[*Gives it Lord* Sparkish.]

Lord Sp. Why, a Man may eat this, though his Wife lay a Dying.

Col. Pray, Friend, give me a Glass of Small-Beer, if it be good.

Lord Sm. Why, Colonel, they say, there is no such Thing as good Small-Beer, good brown Bread, or a good old Woman.

Lady Sm. [*To Lady* Answerall.] Madam, I beg your Lady-ship's Pardon, I did not see you when I was cutting that Bit.

Lady Answ. O, Madam, after you is good Manners.

Lady Sm. Lord, here's a Hair in the Sawce.

Lord Sp. Then, Madam, set the Hounds after it.

Nev. Pray, Colonel, help me, however, to some of that same Sawce.

Col. Come, I think you are more Sawce than Pig.[33]

Lord Sm. Sir *John*, chear up; my Service to you: Well, what do you think of the World to come?

Sir John. Truly, my Lord, I think of it as little as I can.

Lady Sm. [*Putting a Skewer on a Plate.*] Here, take this Skewer, and carry it down to the Cook, to dress it for her own Dinner.

Nev. I beg your Ladyship's Pardon; but this Small-Beer is dead.

Lady Sm. Why then, let it be bury'd.

Col. This is admirable black Pudden; Miss, shall I carve you some? I am the worst Carver in the World; I should never make a good Chaplain. I can just carve Pudden, and that's all.

Miss. No, thank ye, Colonel; for they say, those that eat black Pudden, will dream of the Devil.

Lord Sm. O, here comes the Venison Pasty: Here, take the Soupe away.

[*He cuts it up, and tastes the Venison.*]

S'buds, this Venison is musty.

[Neverout *eats a Piece, and burns his Mouth.*]

Lord Sm. What's the Matter, *Tom?* You have Tears in your Eyes, I think. What dost cry for, Man?

Nev. My Lord, I was just thinking of my poor Grandmother; she dyed just this very Day seven Years.

[*Miss takes a Bit, and burns her Mouth.*]

Nev. And pray, Miss, why do you cry too?

Miss. Because you were not hanged the Day your Grandmother dyed.

Lord Sm. I'd have given forty Pounds, Miss, to have said that.

Col. I'gad, I think, the more I eat, the hungryer I am.

Lord Sp. Why, Colonel, they say, one Shoulder of Mutton drives down another.

Nev. I'gad, if I were to fast for my Life, I would take a good Breakfast in the Morning, a good Dinner at Noon, and a good Supper at Night.

Lord Sp. My Lord, this Venison is plaguily pepper'd. Your Cook has a heavy Hand.

Lord Sm. My Lord, I hope you are Pepper-Proof.[34] Come, here's a Health to the Founders.

Lady Sm. Ay, and to the Confounders too.

Lord Sm. Lady *Answerall*, does not your Ladyship love Venison?

Lady Answ. No, my Lord, I can't endure it in my Sight; therefore please to send me a good Piece of Meat and Crust.

Lord Sp. [*Drinks to* Neverout.] Come, *Tom*, not always to my Friends, but once to you.

Nev. [*Drinks to Lady* Smart.] Come, Madam, here's a Health to our Friends, and hang the rest of our Kin.

Lady Sm. [*To Lady* Answerall.] Madam, will your Ladyship have any of this Hare?

Lady Answ. No, Madam; they say 'tis melancholy Meat.[35]

Lady Sm. Then, Madam, shall I send you the Brains? I beg your Ladyship's Pardon; for they say, 'tis not good Manners to offer Brains.

Lady Answ. No, Madam, for perhaps it will make me Hare-brain'd.

Nev. Miss, I must tell you one Thing.

Miss. [*With a Glass in her Hand.*] Hold your Tongue, Mr. *Neverout*; don't speak in my Tip.

Col. Well, he was an ingenious Man that first found out eating and drinking.[36]

Lord Sp. Of all Vittels, Drink digests the quickest. Give me a Glass of Wine.

Nev. My Lord, your Wine is too strong.

Lord Sm. Ay, *Tom*, as much as you are too good.

Miss. This Almond Pudden was pure good; but it is grown quite cold.

Nev. So much the better, Miss; cold Pudden will settle your Love.

Miss. Pray, Mr. *Neverout*, are you going to take a Voyage?

Nev. Why do you ask, Miss?

Miss. Because, you have laid in so much Beef.

Sir John. You two have eat up the whole Pudden betwixt you.

Miss. Sir *John*, here's a little Bit left, will you please to have it?

Sir John. No, thankee, I don't love to make a Fool of my Mouth.

Col. [*Calling to the Butler.*] *John*, is your Small-Beer good?

Butler. An please your Honour, my Lord and Lady like it; I think it is good.

Col. Why then, *John*, d'ye see, if you are sure your Small-Beer is good, d'ye mark? Then give me a Glass of Wine. [*All laugh.*]

Lady Sm. Sir *John*, how does your Neighbour *Gatherall* of the Park? I hear he has lately made a Purchase.[37]

Sir John. Oh; *Dick Gatherall* knows how to butter his Bread,[38] as well as any Man in *Derbyshire*.

Lady Sm. Why, he used to go very fine, when he was here in Town.

Sir John. Ay, and it became him, as a Saddle becomes a Sow.[39]

Col. I know his Lady; and, I think, she's a very good Woman.

Sir John. Faith, she has more Goodness in her little Finger, than he has in his whole Body.

[*Colonel tasting the Wine.*]

Lord Sm. Well, Colonel, how do you like that Wine?

Col. This Wine should be eaten; 'tis too good to be drunk.

Lord Sm. I'm very glad you like it; and, pray, don't spare it.

Col. No, my Lord; I'll never starve in a Cook's Shop.

Lady Sm. And, pray Sir *John*, what do you say to my Wine?

Sir John. I'll take another Glass first: Second Thoughts are best.

Lord Sp. Pray, Lady *Smart*, you sit near that Ham; will you please to send me a Bit?

Lady Sm. With all my Heart. [*She sends him a Piece.*] Pray, my Lord, how do you like it?

Lord Sp. I think it is a Limb of *Lot*'s Wife.[40] [*He eats it with Mustard.*] I'gad, my Lord, your Mustard is very uncivil.

Lady Sm. Why uncivil, my Lord?

Lord Sp. Because, it takes me by the Nose, I'gad.

Lady Sm. Mr. *Neverout*, I find you are a very good Carver.

Col. Oh Madam, that's no Wonder; for you must know, *Tom Neverout* carves a-Sundays.

[*Mr.* Neverout *overturns the Saltcellar.*]

Lady Sm. Mr. *Neverout*, you have overturn'd the Salt; and that's a Sign of Anger. I'm afraid Miss and you will fall out.

Lady Answ. No, no; throw a little of it into the Fire, and all will be well.

Nev. O Madam, the falling out of Lovers, you know.[41]

Miss. Lovers! very fine! fall *out* with him! I wonder when we were *in*.

Sir John. For my Part, I believe the young Gentlewoman is his Sweet-Heart; there's such fooling and fidling betwixt them. I am sure, they say in our Country, that shiddle come sh——'s the Beginning of Love.[42]

Nev. Miss, I'll tell you one thing.

Miss. Nay, I love Mr. *Neverout*, as the Devil loves holy Water. I love him like Pye, I'd rather the Devil wou'd have him than I.

Nev. Miss, I'll tell you one thing.

Miss. Come, here's t'ye to stop your Mouth.

Nev. I'd rather you would stop it with a Kiss.

Miss. A Kiss! marry come up, my dirty Couzin:[43] Are you no sicker? Lord! I wonder what Fool it was, that first invented kissing?

Nev. Well, I'm very dry.

Miss. Then you are the better to burn, and the worse to fry.[44]

Lady Answ. God bless you, Colonel, you have a good Stroak with you.[45]

Col. O Madam, formerly I could eat all, but now I leave nothing; I eat but one Meal a-Day.

Miss. What? I suppose, Colonel, that's from Morning till Night.

Nev. Faith, Miss, and well was his Wont.

Lord Sm. Pray, Lady *Answerall*, taste this Bit of Venison.

Lady Answ. I hope, your Lordship will set me a good Example.

Lord Sm. Here's a Glass of Cyder fill'd. Miss, you must drink it.

Miss. Indeed, my Lord, I can't.

Nev. Come Miss; better Belly burst than good Liquor be lost.

Miss. Pish! well, in Life there was never any Thing so teazing; I had rather shed it in my Shoes: I wish it were in your Guts, for my Share.[46]

Lord Sm. Mr. *Neverout*, you ha'n't tasted my Cyder yet.

Nev. No, my Lord, I have been just eating Soupe; and they say, if one drinks in one's Porridge, one will cough in one's Grave.

Lord Sm. Come, take Miss's Glass, she wish't it was in your Guts; let her have her Wish for once; Ladies can't abide to have their Inclinations cross't.

Lady Sm. [*To Sir* John.] I think, Sir *John*, you have not tasted the Venison yet.

Sir John. I seldom eat it, Madam: However, please to send me a little of the Crust.

Lord Sp. Why, Sir *John*, you had as good eat the Devil, as the Broth he's boyl'd in.

Nev. I have dined as well as my Lord-Mayor.

Miss. I thought I could have eaten this Wing of a Chicken; but, I find, my Eye's bigger than my Belly.

Lord Sm. Indeed, Lady *Answerall*, you have eaten nothing.

Lady Answ. Pray, my Lord, see all the Bones on my Plate. They say, a Carpenter's known by his Chips.

Nev. Miss, will you reach me that Glass of Jelly?

Miss. [*Giving it to him.*] You see, 'tis but ask and have.

Nev. Miss, I would have a bigger Glass.

Miss. What, you don't know your own Mind; you are neither well full nor fasting. I think that is enough.

Nev. Ay, one of the enough's: I am sure it is little enough.

Miss. Yes, but you know, sweet Things are bad for the Teeth.

Nev. [*To Lady* Answerall.] Madam, I don't like this Part of the Veal you sent me.

Lady Answ. Well, Mr. *Neverout*, I find you are a true *English*-Man; you never know when you are well.[47]

Col. Well, I have made my whole Dinner of Beef.

Lady Answ. Why, Colonel, a Belly-full is a Belly-full, if it be but of Wheat-Straw.

Col. Well, after all, Kitchen Physick is the best Physick.[48]

Lord Sm. And the best Doctors in the World, are Doctor *Diet*, Doctor *Quiet*, and Doctor *Merryman*.[49]

Lord Sp. What do you think of a little House well filled?

Sir John. And a little Land well till'd?

Col. Ay, and a little Wife well will'd?

Nev. My Lady *Smart*, pray help me to some of the Breast of that Goose.

Lord Sm. Tom, I have heard, that Goose upon Goose is false Heraldry.[50]

Miss. What! will you never have done stuffing?

Lord Sm. This Goose is quite raw. Well; God sends Meat, but the Devil sends Cooks.

Nev. Miss, can you tell which is the white Goose, or the grey Goose the Gander?

Miss. They say, a Fool will ask more Questions than twenty wise Men can answer.

Col. Indeed, Miss, *Tom Neverout* has posed you.

Miss. Why, Colonel, every Dog has his Day. But, I believe, I shall never see a Goose again, without thinking on Mr. *Neverout*.

Lord Sm. Well said, Miss; I'faith, Girl, thou hast brought thy self off cleverly. *Tom*, what say you to that?

Col. Faith, *Tom* is nonplust; he looks plaguily down in the Mouth.

Miss. Why, my Lord, you see he's the provokingest Creature in Life: I believe, there is not such another in the varsal World.

Lady Answ. Oh, Miss, the World's a wide Place.

Nev. Well, Miss, I'll give you Leave to call me any Thing, so you don't call me Spade.

Lord Sm. Well, but after all, *Tom*, can you tell me what's *Latin* for a Goose?

Nev. O my Lord, I know that; Why, Brandy is *Latin* for a Goose; and *Tace* is *Latin* for a Candle.[51]

Miss. Is that Manners, to shew your Learning before Ladies? Methinks you are grown very brisk of a sudden. I think the Man's glad he's alive.

Sir John. The Devil take your Wit, if this be Wit; for it spoils Company. Pray, Mr. Butler, bring me a Dram after my Goose; 'tis very good for the Wholesoms.

Lord Sm. Come, bring me the Loaf; I sometimes love to cut my own Bread.

Miss. I suppose, my Lord, you lay longest a-Bed to-Day.

Lord Sm. Miss, if I had said so, I should have told a Fib: I warrant you lay a-Bed 'till the Cows came home. But, Miss, shall I cut you a little Crust, now my Hand is in?

Miss. If you please, my Lord; a Bit of Under-crust.

Nev. [*Whispering Miss.*] I find you love to lie under.

Miss. [*Aloud; pushing him from her.*] What does the Man mean? Sir, I don't understand you at all.

Nev. Come, all Quarrels laid aside: Here, Miss, may you live a thousand Years. [*He drinks to her.*]

Miss. Pray Sir, don't stint me.

Lord Sm. Sir *John*, will you taste my *October*? I think it is very good; but, I believe, not equal to yours in *Derbyshire*.

Sir John. My Lord, I beg your Pardon; but, they say, the Devil made Askers.[52]

Lord Sm. [*To the Butler.*] Here, bring up the great Tankard full of *October*, for *Sir John*.

Col. [*Drinking to Miss.*] Miss, your Health; may you live all the Days of your Life.

Lady Answ. Well, Miss, you'll certainly be soon married: Here's two Bachelors drinking to you at once.

Lady Sm. Indeed, Miss, I believe you were wrapt in your Mother's Smock,[53] you are so well beloved.

Miss. Where's my Knife, sure I han't eaten it? O, here it is.

Sir John. No, Miss, but your Maidenhead hangs in your Light.[54]

Miss. Pray, Sir *John*, is that a *Derbyshire* Compliment? Here,

Mr. *Neverout*, will you take this Piece of Rabbit that you bid me carve for you?

Nev. I don't know.

Miss. Why, take it, or let it alone.

Nev. I will.

Miss. What will you?

Nev. Why, take it, or let it alone.

Miss. Well, you're a provoking Creature.

Sir John. [*Talking with a Glass of Wine in his Hand.*] I remember a Farmer in our Country——

Lord Sm. [*Interrupting him.*] Pray, Sir *John*, did you ever hear of Parson *Palmer*?

Sir John. No, my Lord; what of him?

Lord Sm. Why, he used to preach over his Liquor.[55]

Sir John. I beg your Pardon. Here's your Lordship's Health; I'd drink it up, if it were a Mile to the Bottom.

Lady Sm. Mr. *Neverout*, have you been at the new Play?

Nev. Yes, Madam, I went the first Night.

Lady Sm. Well, and how did it take?

Nev. Why, Madam, the Poet is *damn'd*.[56]

Sir John. God forgive you; that's very uncharitable; you ought not to judge so rashly of any Christian.

Nev. [*Whispers Lady* Smart.] Was ever such a Dunce? How well he knows the Town! see how he stares like a stuck Pig! Well, but Sir *John*, are you acquainted with any of our fine Ladies yet? Any of our famous Toasts?

Sir John. No, damn your Fireships; I have a Wife of my own.

Lady Sm. Pray, my Lady *Answerall*, how do you like these preserved Oranges?

Lady Answ. Indeed, Madam, the only Fault I find, is, that they are too good.

Lady Sm. O, Madam, I have heard 'em say, that too good, is stark nought.[57]

[*Miss drinking Part of a Glass of Wine.*]

Nev. Pray, let me drink your Snuff.

Miss. No, indeed, you shan't drink after me; for you'll know my Thoughts.

Nev. I know them already; you are thinking of a good Husband. Besides, I can tell your Meaning by your Mumping.

Lady Sm. Pray, my Lord, did not you order the Butler to bring up a Tankard of our *October* to Sir *John*? I believe, they stay to brew it.

[*The Butler brings the Tankard to Sir* John.]

Sir John. Won't your Lordship please to drink first?

Lord Sm. No, Sir *John*, 'tis in a very good Hand: I'll pledge you.

Col. [*To Lord* Smart.] My Lord, I love *October* as well as Sir *John*; and I hope, you won't make Fish of one, and Flesh of another.

Lord Sm. Colonel, you're heartily welcome: Come, Sir *John*, take it by Word of Mouth, and then give it the Colonel.

[*Sir* John *drinks.*]

Lord Sm. Well, Sir *John*, how do you like it?

Sir John. Not as well as my own in *Derbyshire*. 'Tis plaguy small.⁵⁸

Lady Sm. I never taste Malt Liquor; but they say, 'tis well Hopp'd.

Sir John. Hopp'd! Why, if it had hopp'd a little further, it would have hopp'd into the River. O, my Lord; my Ale is Meat, Drink, and Cloth. It will make a Cat speak, and a wise Man dumb.

Lady Sm. I was told, ours was very strong.

Sir John. Ay, Madam, strong of the Water: I believe, the Brewer forgot the Malt, or the River was too near him. Faith, it is meer Whip-belly-vengeance:⁵⁹ He that drinks most, has the worst Share.

Col. I believe, Sir *John*, Ale is as plenty as Water, at your House.

Sir John. Why, Faith, at *Christmas* we have many Comers and Goers; and they must not be sent away without a Cup of good *Christmas* Ale, for fear they should p–ss behind the Door.⁶⁰

Lady Sm. I hear, Sir *John* has the nicest Garden in *England*;

they say, 'tis kept so clean, that you can't find a Place where
to spit.

Sir John. O, Madam, you are pleased to say so.

Lady Sm. But, Sir *John*, your Ale is terrible strong and heady
in *Derbyshire*; and will soon make one drunk and sick; what
do you then?

Sir John. Why, indeed, it is apt to Fox one; but our Way is,
to take a Hair of the same Dog next Morning.—I take a new-
laid Egg for Breakfast; and Faith, one should drink as much
after an Egg, as after an Ox.[61]

Lord Sm. Tom Neverout, will you taste a Glass of the
October?

Nev. No, Faith, my Lord, I like your Wine; and I won't put
a Churl upon a Gentleman:[62] Your Honour's Claret is good
enough for me.

Lady Sm. What? is this Pigeon left for Manners? Colonel,
shall I send you the Legs and Rump?

Col. Madam, I could not eat a Bit more, if the House was
full.

Lord Sm. [*Carving a Partridge.*] Well, one may ride to *Rumford* upon this Knife, it is so blunt.[63]

Lady Answ. My Lord, I beg your Pardon; but they say, an ill
Workman never had good Tools.

Lord Sm. Will your Lordship have a Wing of it?

Lord Sp. No, my Lord, I love the Wing of an Ox a great deal
better.

Lord Sm. I'm always cold after eating.

Col. My Lord, they say, that's a Sign of long Life.

Lord Sm. Ay, I believe I shall live 'till all my Friends are
weary of me.

Col. Pray, does any Body here hate Cheese? I would be glad
of a Bit.

Lord Sm. An odd kind of Fellow dined with me t'other Day;
and when the Cheese came upon the Table, he pretended to
faint. So, some Body said, Pray take away the Cheese: No, said
I, Pray take away the Fool: Said I well? [*Here a long and loud
Laugh.*]

Col. Faith, my Lord, you served the Coxcomb right enough:

And therefore, I wish we had a Bit of your Lordship's *Oxford-shire* Cheese.

Lord Sm. Come, hang saving, bring us a Halfporth of Cheese.

Lady Answ. They say, Cheese digests every Thing but itself.[64]

[*Footman brings in a great whole Cheese.*]

Lord Sp. Ay, this would look handsome if any Body should come in.

Sir John. Well, I'm weily brosten, as they sayn in *Lancashire.*[65]

Lady Sm. Oh, Sir *John*, I wou'd I had something to brost you withal.

Lord Sm. Come; they say, 'tis merry in Hall, when Beards wag all.[66]

Lady Sm. Miss, shall I help you to some Cheese? Or, will you carve for your self?

Nev. I'll hold fifty Pound, Miss won't cut the Cheese.[67]

Miss. Pray, why so, Mr. *Neverout?*

Nev. O, there is a Reason, and you know it well enough.

Miss. I can't, for my Life, understand what the Gentleman means.

Lord Sm. Pray, *Tom*, change the Discourse; in troth you are too bad.

[*Colonel whispers* Neverout.]

Col. Smoak Miss; Faith, you have made her fret like Gum Taffety.[68]

Lady Sm. Well; but Miss; (hold your Tongue, Mr. *Neverout*) shall I cut you a Bit of Cheese?

Miss. No really, Madam, I have dined this half Hour.

Lady Sm. What? quick at Meat, quick at work, they say.

[*Sir* John *nods.*]

Lord Sm. What, you are sleepy Sir *John*. Do you sleep after Dinner?

Sir John. Yes, Faith; I sometimes take a Nap after my Pipe; for when the Belly's full, the Bones will be at rest.

Lady Sm. Come, Colonel, help your self, and your Friends will love you the better.

[To Lady Answerall.]

Madam, your Ladyship eats nothing.

Lady Answ. Lord, Madam, I have fed like a Farmer; I shall grow as fat as a Porpoise: I swear, my Jaws are weary with chawing.

Col. I have a Mind to eat a Piece of that Sturgeon, but I fear it will make me sick.

Nev. A rare Soldier indeed; let it alone, and I warrant, it won't hurt you.[69]

Col. Well, but it would vex a Dog to see a Pudden creep.

[Sir John *rises.]*

Lord Sm. Sir *John,* what are you doing?

Sir John. Swolks, I must be going, by'r Lady; I have earnest Business; I must do as the Beggars do, go away when I have got enough.

Lord Sm. Well, but stay 'till this Bottle's out: You know, the Man was hanged that left his Liquor behind him; besides, a Cup in the Pate, is a Mile in the Gate; and, a Spur in the Head, is worth two in the Heel.[70]

Sir John. Come then, one Brimmer to all your Healths.

[The Footman gives him a Glass half full.]

Pray, Friend, what was the rest of this Glass made for? An Inch at the Top, Friend, is worth two at the Bottom.

[He gets a Brimmer, and drinks it off.]

Well; there's no Deceit in a Brimmer; and there's no false Latin in this; your Wine is excellent good, so I thank you for the next; for, I am sure of this. Madam, has your Ladyship any Commands in *Derbyshire?* I must go fifteen Miles To-Night.

Lady Sm. None, Sir *John,* but to take Care of yourself; and my most humble Service to your Lady unknown.

Sir John. Well, Madam, I can but love and thank you.

Lady Sm. Here, bring Water to wash; though really, you have all eaten so little, that you have no Need to wash your Mouths.

Lord Sm. But prithee, Sir *John,* stay a while longer.

Sir John. No, my Lord, I am to smoak a Pipe with a Friend, before I leave the Town.

Col. Why, Sir *John*, had not you better set out To-morrow?

Sir John. Colonel, you forget, To-morrow is *Sunday*.

Col. Now, I always love to begin a Journey on Sundays, because I shall have the Prayers of the Church, to preserve all that Travel by Land or by Water.

Sir John. Well, Colonel, thou art a mad Fellow to make a Priest of.[71]

Nev. Fye, Sir *John*, do you take Tobacco? How can you make a Chimney of your Mouth?[72]

Sir John. [*To* Neverout.] What? you don't smoak, I warrant you, but you smock. (Ladies, I beg your Pardon.) Colonel, do you never smoak?

Col. No, Sir *John*, but I take a Pipe sometimes.

Sir John. I'Faith, one of your finical *London* Blades dined with me last Year in *Derbyshire:* So, after Dinner, I took a Pipe; So, my Gentleman turn'd away his Head: So, said I, what Sir, do you never smoak? So, he answered as you do, Colonel; no, but I sometimes take a Pipe: So, he took a Pipe in his Hand, and fiddled with it, 'till he broke it: So, said I, pray, Sir, can you make a Pipe? So, he said, no: So, said I, why then, Sir, if you can't make a Pipe, you should not break a Pipe. So, we all laught.

Lord Sm. Well; but, Sir *John*, they say, that the Corruption of Pipes, is the Generation of Stoppers.[73]

Sir John. Colonel, I hear you go sometimes to *Derbyshire*; I wish you would come and foul a Plate with me.

Col. I hope you'll give me a Soldier's Bottle.

Sir John. Come, and try.—Mr. *Neverout*, you are a Town-Wit; can you tell me what Kind of Herb is Tobacco?

Nev. Why, an *Indian* Herb, Sir *John*.

Sir John. No, 'tis a Pot-Herb; and so here's t'ye in a Pot of my Lord's *October*.

Lady Sm. I hear, Sir *John*, since you are married, you have forsworn the Town.

Sir John. No, Madam, I never forswore any Thing but building of Churches.

Lady Sm. Well, but Sir *John*, when may we hope to see you again in *London?*

Sir John. Why, Madam, not 'till the Ducks have eat up the Dirt, as the Children say.[74]

Nev. Come, Sir *John*, I foresee it will rain terribly.

Lord Sm. Come, Sir *John*, do nothing rashly, let us drink first.

Lord Sp. Nay, I know Sir *John* will go, though he was sure it would rain Cats and Dogs.[75] But, pray stay, Sir *John*, you'll be Time enough to go to Bed by Candle-light.

Lord Sm. Why, Sir *John*, if you must needs go, while you stay, make good Use of your Time. Here's my Service to you. A Health to our Friends in *Derbyshire*.

Sir John. Not a Drop more.

Col. Why, Sir *John*, you used to love a Glass of good Wine in former Times.

Sir John. Why, so I do still, Colonel; but a Man may love his House very well, without riding on the Ridge;[76] besides, I must be with my Wife on *Tuesday*, or there will be the Devil and all to pay.

Col. Well, if you go To-Day, I wish you may be wet to the Skin.

Sir John. Ay, but they say, the Prayers of the Wicked won't prevail.

[*Sir* John *takes his Leave, and goes away.*]

Lord Sm. Well, Miss, how do you like Sir *John?*

Miss. Why, I think, he's a little upon the Silly, or so; I believe he has not all the Wit in the World; but I don't pretend to be a Judge.

Nev. Faith, I believe he was bred at *Hogsnorton*, where the Pigs play upon the Organs.[77]

Lord Sp. Why, *Tom*, I thought you and he had been Hand and Glove.

Nev. Faith, he shall have a clean Threshold for me; I never darkned his Door in my Life, neither in Town, nor Country; but, he's a queer old Duke,[78] by my Conscience; and yet, after all, I take him to be more Knave than Fool.

Lord Sm. Well, come, a Man's a Man, if he has but a Hose on his Head.[79]

Col. I was once with him, and some other Company, over a Bottle; and I'gad, he fell asleep, and snored so loud, that we thought he was driving his Hogs to Market.

Nev. Why, what? You can have no more of a Cat, than her Skin. You can't make a Silk Purse out of a Sow's Ear.[80]

Lord Sp. Well, since he's gone, the Devil go with him, and Sixpence; and there's Money and Company too.[81]

Nev. Pray, Miss, let me ask you a Question?

Miss. Well, but don't ask Questions with a dirty Face. I warrant, what you have to say, will keep cold.

Col. Come, my Lord, against you are disposed:[82] Here's to all that love and honour you.

Lord Sp. Ay, that was always *Dick Nimble*'s Health. I'm sure you know, he is dead.

Col. Dead! Well, my Lord, you love to be a Messenger of ill News: I'm heartily sorry; but, my Lord, we must all dye.

Nev. I knew him very well; but pray, how came he to dye?

Miss. There's a Question! You talk like a Poticary. Why, he dyed, because he could live no longer.

Nev. Well; rest his Soul; we must live by the Living, and not by the Dead.

Lord Sp. You know his House was burnt down to the Ground.

Col. Yes, it was in the News. Why; Fire and Water are good Servants, but they are very bad Masters.[83]

Lord Sm. Here, take away, and set down a Bottle of Burgundy. Ladies, you'll stay and drink a Glass of Wine before you go to your Tea.

[*All's taken away, and the Wine set down.*]

[*Miss gives* Neverout *a smart Pinch.*]

Nev. Lord, Miss, what d'ye mean? D'ye think I have no feeling?

Miss. I'm forced to pinch, for the Times are hard.

Nev. [*Giving Miss a Pinch.*] Take that, Miss: What's Sawce for a Goose, is Sawce for a Gander.[84]

Miss. [*Screaming.*] Well, Mr. *Neverout*, if I live, that shall neither go to Heaven nor Hell with you.[85]

Nev. [*takes Miss's Hand.*] Come, Miss, let us lay all Quarrels aside, and be Friends.

Miss. Don't be mauming and gauming a Body so.[86] Can't you keep your filthy Hands to your self?

Nev. Pray, Miss, where did you get that Pick-Tooth Case?

Miss. I came honestly by it.

Nev. I'm sure it was mine, for I lost just such a one. Nay, I don't tell you a Lye.

Miss. No, if you Lye, 'tis much.

Nev. Well, I'm sure 'tis mine.

Miss. What, you think every Thing is yours; but a little the King has.

Nev. Colonel, you have seen my fine Pick-Tooth Case: Don't you think this is the very same?

Col. Indeed, Miss, it is very like it.

Miss. Ay, what he says, you'll swear.

Nev. Well; but I'll prove it to be mine.

Miss. Ay, do if you can.

Nev. Why; what's yours is mine, and what's mine is my own.

Miss. Well, run on 'till you're weary, no Body holds you.

[Neverout *gapes.*]

Col. What, Mr. *Neverout*, do you gape for Preferment?

Nev. Faith, I may gape long enough before it falls into my Mouth.[87]

Lady Sm. Mr. *Neverout*, I hear you live high.

Nev. Yes, Faith, Madam; live high, and lodge in a Garret.

Col. But, Miss, I forgot to tell you, that Mr. *Neverout* got the devilishest Fall in the Park To-Day.

Miss. I hope he did not hurt the Ground. But, how was it Mr. *Neverout*? I wish I had been there to laugh.

Nev. Why, Madam, it was a Place where a Cuckold had been bury'd, and one of his Horns sticking out, I happened to stumble against it. That was all.

Lady Sm. Ladies, let us leave the Gentlemen to themselves; I think it is Time to go to our Tea.[88]

Lady Answ. and *Miss.* My Lords, and Gentlemen, your most humble Servant.

Lord Sm. Well, Ladies, we'll wait on you an Hour hence.

[*The Gentlemen alone.*]

Lord Sm. Come, *John*, bring us a fresh Bottle.

Col. Ay, my Lord; and pray let him carry off the dead Men, (as we say in the Army.) [*Meaning the empty Bottles.*]

Lord Sp. Mr. *Neverout*, pray is not that Bottle full?

Nev. Yes, my Lord, full of Emptiness.

Lord Sm. And, d'ye hear, *John*, bring clean Glasses.

Col. I'll keep mine; for I think the Wine is the best Liquor to wash Glasses in.[89]

Notes

'*BD*' after a name indicates that further information about the person may be found in the 'Biographical Dictionary'; a '*G*' after a reference indicates that further information appears in the 'Glossary'.

When I come to be old

First published 1765. A witty reversal of the conventions of 'advice' literature, in which an older man counsels an inexperienced youth about how to conduct his life, these resolutions were written just before or after the death of Sir William Temple on 27 January 1699. Copy-text: *Forster* autograph copy.

1. *or let them . . . hardly:* These words have been crossed out in the copy-text and omitted in *DS '65*.
2. *et eos . . . vitare:* 'And to hate and shun those who grasp at an inheritance' (Latin).
3. *opiniatre:* A French term then in vogue, meaning 'opinionated, or obstinate in maintaining one's view'; perhaps an ironic glance at Temple's dilettantism and preoccupation with style.

A Meditation upon a Broom-Stick

First published 1710. Written in 1702 or 1703 as a parody of Robert Boyle's *Occasional Reflections upon Several Subjects* (1665), this piece was part of a successful hoax in which it was represented to Lady Berkeley as Boyle's own reflections. The natural philosopher Boyle was an apt target for Swift because of his strongly Puritan bent, his role as co-founder of the Royal Society, and his interest in forms of hermetic thought ridiculed in *A Tale of a Tub* (1704). Swift also judged him to be 'a very silly writer' (*M.: Burnet*).

1. *a universal Reformer . . . sweep away:* Wording suggestive of the Modern critics in *A Tale of a Tub*.

2. *worn to the Stumps . . . warm themselves by:* This passage plays upon several meanings of 'stump' to suggest male impotence and inability to satisfy female desires.

The Story of the Injured Lady. Written by Herself. In a Letter to her Friend. With his Answer

First published 1746. Provoked by the Act of Union between England and Scotland, this pamphlet was probably written shortly after the Union Treaty's ratification (1707) and is Swift's earliest sustained protest against Ireland's colonial status. Influenced by Molyneux, it takes the form of an allegory, the 'Gentleman in the Neighbourhood' representing England; his 'two Mistresses', Scotland and Ireland; and the 'publick Wedding', the Act of Union. The Friend's 'Answer', chastising the Lady for attacking the Mistress rather than forming an alliance with her based on their common victimization, emphasizes the need for the Irish to help themselves through organized political action and resistance. Copy-text: *F '46*.

1. *Company of Rogues . . . Mischief:* Evokes the insubordination and unruliness associated with the Scottish Highlanders.

2. *she broke into his House . . . set it on Fire:* Glances at Scotland's invasions of England in support of Parliament during the English Civil Wars (1642–51). Swift blamed the 'cursed Hellish Scots' for many of the war's worst offences (*M.: Clarendon*).

3. *his poor Steward was knocked on the Head:* Refers to the beheading of Charles I on 30 January 1649.

4. *to act like a Conqueror:* A particularly damning accusation in light of Molyneux's insistence that King Henry II's expedition to Ireland (1172) was not a 'conquest' since the Irish received Henry in peace and were granted concessions 'of the like Laws and Liberties with the People of *England*'.

5. *an Under-Steward . . . his Directions:* That is, the Lord-Lieutenant of Ireland (*G*).

6. *my Tenants shall be obliged . . . filthy Hands:* Refers to a series of legislative acts (e.g. the Woollen Act of 1699) restricting Irish trade. See *A Proposal for the Universal Use of Irish Manufacture*.

7. *some Servants . . . on his Estate:* Refers to the absentee office-holders and landlords, a recurring target of Swift's wrath and chief among those he repeatedly blamed for Ireland's poverty.

8. *to carry it with a high Hand:* England's 'high-handed' behaviour consisted of passing the English Alien Act (1705), which mandated a ban on Scottish imports to England and the treatment of the Scots as aliens if Scotland refused to accept the Hanoverian succession or declined to enter into negotiations for a union.

9. *I would stand by him . . . upon it:* That is, Ireland's unquestioning loyalty to England—its House of Lords had declared absolute allegiance to the Hanoverian Succession—helped 'soften' Scotland into submission.

10. *a certain Great Man . . . her Will:* Refers to James Francis Edward Stuart, or 'The Old Pretender' (*BD*).

11. *an old Compact . . . I approved of:* Refers to the letters freely given to Henry II by the clerics and nobles of Ireland, 'swearing Fealty to him and his Heirs for ever' (1172); also evokes later documents supporting Ireland's parity with England, such as the Magna Charta granted to Ireland by Henry III in 1216.

12. *her Encroachments . . . direct you:* Refers to the large-scale migration of Scotsmen to Ulster.

13. *this Gentleman kept her . . . Lodging:* Refers to England's military occupation of Scotland under Oliver Cromwell after his rout of Charles II and the king's Scottish forces at Worcester in 1651.

The Bickerstaff Papers

Predictions for the Year 1708

First published 1708. These 'Predictions' follow Tom Brown's burlesque, *The Infallible Astrologer* (1700), in satirizing John Partridge (*BD*), producer of the extremely popular almanac, *Merlinus Liberatus*. Their attack is three-fold: on the pseudo-science of astrology; on the almanac as a base literary form reflective of Grub Street (*G*); and on the Nonconformist Partridge, who used his almanac to attack the Anglican church as 'only *Pop'ry* by another Name'. So successful was Swift's hoax that Partridge was in effect 'killed off', struck from the rolls of the Company of Stationers and prevented by an injunction of the Lord Chancellor from ever again printing or selling his almanac. Personages and incidents connected with the then ongoing War of the Spanish Succession (*G*) form a backdrop to many of Bickerstaff's predictions.

1. *ISAAC BICKERSTAFF, Esq.:* The headnote to *F'35* explains that the author took this name from a sign over a locksmith's house in Long-Acre; it was later used by Richard Steele in *The Tatler*.

2. *Gadbury ... Weather:* The astrologer John Gadbury (1627–1704), Partridge's mentor. Bickerstaff parodies Partridge's later attacks on Gadbury, as well as Gadbury's rejection of his own mentor, William Lilly.

3. *their Advertisements ... little to do:* A typical almanac contained not only a calendar with astronomical data, astrological charts and weather forecasts, but also items about politics, food, gardening, etc., and advertisements promoting (e.g.) quack cures for venereal diseases and sexual dysfunction.

4. *Miscarriage at Toulon ... Admiral Shovel:* After its unsuccessful campaign against the French at Toulon, an English fleet commanded by Admiral Cloudesley Shovell headed back to England on 22 October 1707 but ran aground on the Bishop Rock off the Scillies in thick fog; all aboard were lost in the shipwreck.

5. *the Battle at Almanza ... Consequences thereof:* A military engagement in August 1707 in which the Earl of Galway's troops were defeated by a Franco-Spanish army—a circumstance that eliminated the possibility that (as England had hoped) the Archduke Charles would be accepted as King of Spain.

6. *the Old Stile ... mention:* The Julian calendar was reformed by Pope Gregory XIII via a papal bull (1582) which declared that 4 October be immediately followed by 15 October. This 'New Style' was not adopted by England until 1752; until then England's calendar was eleven days behind other countries in Europe.

7. *Beginning of the natural Year:* After the Norman Conquest, 25 March was officially recognized as the first day of the new year, to mark the conception of Christ; it was replaced by 1 January in 1752. Aries, the first sign of the Zodiac, was placed at the beginning of the year from the spring equinox, 21 March.

8. *the Duke of Anjou:* Philippe of Anjou (1683–1746), grandson of Louis XIV of France, became King Philip V in 1700 after being named by the dying Charles II of Spain as his heir.

9. *Insurrection in Dauphine ... some Months:* Dauphiné, a region in south-eastern France, was the scene of unrest and rebellion stemming from Louis XIV's persecutions of the local Protestant population.

10. *Death of the Dauphin ... Kingdom:* Louis, eldest son of Louis XIV, was known as the 'Great Dauphin' (1661–1711); the title of 'Dauphin' was held by the eldest son of the King of France from 1349 to 1830.

11. *the Prophets ... Events:* Refers to the Camisards, a group of French Protestant peasants who fled to England to escape the

religious persecutions of Louis XIV. Claiming prophetic powers, they aggressively proselytized in London and published ominous predictions while attacking the Established Church.

12. *Cardinal Portocarero ... false:* Luis Manuel Portocarrero (1635–1709) reportedly influenced King Charles II of Spain on his deathbed to choose the Bourbon Philip, Duke of Anjou, as his successor over the Habsburg Archduke Charles, who proclaimed himself King Charles III after invading Spain (1704).

13. *the Duke of Burgundy's Administration:* Eldest son of the 'Great Dauphin', Louis, Duke of Burgundy (1682–1712) was serving at the time as Joint Commander-in-Chief at Oudenaarde, in Flanders.

14. *The Affairs of Poland ... the Emperor:* In 1697 Augustus II, the Elector of Saxony, was elected to the Polish throne and began a war with Charles XII of Sweden, who forced him to give up the throne in 1706.

15. *The Pope ... Sixty-One Years old:* Clement XI (1649–1721) initially supported the Bourbon claim to the Spanish throne by Philip V, but later acknowledged the Archduke Charles as King of Spain.

16. *Alter erit ... Heroas:* 'Then there will be another Tethys, and another Argo to carry chosen heroes': Virgil, *Eclogue* 4.34–5. Swift substitutes the sea goddess Tethys (for Queen Anne?) for Virgil's Tiphys, pilot of the Argo.

17. *a great Revolution ... 1688:* The Glorious Revolution (G).

18. *have it printed in Holland:* As a republic without an established religion (obviously not an ideal for the Anglican Swift), Holland had a more liberal attitude towards the free expression of ideas.

The Accomplishment of the First of Mr. Bickerstaff's Predictions

This piece was published on 30 March, one day after the predicted date of Partridge's death.

1. *Dr. Case and Mrs. Kirleus ... to him:* 'Two famous Quacks at that Time in London' (note in F '35).

2. *a mean Trade:* Partridge was originally a cobbler; Swift's 'Elegy on Mr Partrige' notes the analogy ' 'twixt *Cobling* and *Astrology*': 'How *Partrige* made his *Opticks* rise,/From a *Shoe Sole* to reach the Skies.'

A Vindication of Isaac Bickerstaff, Esq.

First published 1709.

1. *Mr. Partrige ... Learned:* Refers to Partridge's comments in his Almanac for 1709 that 'Bickerstaff' was a 'sham-name' assumed by 'an impudent lying fellow' who made false predictions about Partridge's death.

2. *the Inquisition in Portugal ... Readers of them:* 'This is Fact, as the Author was assured by Sir* Paul Methuen, *then Ambassador to that Crown*' (note in F '35).

3. *a Nation ... an Alliance:* Portugal was an ally of England in the War of the Spanish Succession and the two countries enjoyed close trading ties, which were strengthened by the Methuen Treaty of 1703.

4. *transcribing ... in my own Vindication:* 'The Quotations here inserted, are in Imitation of Dr. Bentley, in some Part of the famous Controversy between him and* Charles Boyle, *Esq; afterwards Earl of* Orrery' (note in F '35). This refers to the dispute between the 'Ancients' and the 'Moderns' over the authenticity of the *Epistles of Phalaris*, edited by Boyle but attacked as spurious by Richard Bentley (*BD*).

5. *most learned Monsieur Leibnitz:* Gottfried Wilhelm Leibnitz (1646–1716), German philosopher and mathematician, best known for his theory of monads and belief in the pre-established harmony of the universe, which gave rise to his view that this is 'the best of all possible worlds' (mocked by Voltaire in *Candide*). This view, combined with his close ties to the House of Hanover, his enthusiastic support of the New Science as practised by the Royal Society, and his mechanical experiments and inventions (e.g. the calculating machine) rendered him a ripe target for Swift's satire.

6. *Illustrissimo Bickerstaffio Astrologiæ Instauratori, &c.:* 'To the most illustrious Bickerstaff, restorer of astrology' (Latin).

7. *Monsieur le Clerc ... Ità nuperimè Bickerstaffius magnum illud Angliæ sidus:* Jean Le Clerc (1657–1736) was a Swiss theologian and biblical scholar whose scriptural commentaries laid the ground for scientific criticism of the Bible ... 'Thus most recently [has written] Bickerstaff, that great star of England' (Latin).

8. *Bickerstaffius ... Princeps:* 'Bickerstaff, great Englishman, easily first among astrologers of the present age' (Latin).

9. *Signior Magliabecchi ... Praises:* Antonio Magliabechi (1633–
    1714) was a renowned Florentine scholar and bibliophile who
    served as court librarian to the Grand Duke of Tuscany, Cosimo
    III de' Medici.

10. *Pace tanti viri dixerim:* 'I should say, in spite of the great man'
    (Latin).

11. *Vel forsan ... doctissimus, &c.:* 'Or perhaps a typographical
    error, since otherwise Bickerstaff, that most learned man...'
    (Latin).

12. *Gadbury ... the Revolution:* Almanacs were published under
    royal charter by members of the Company of Stationers, often
    under the name of a deceased astrologer who continued to be
    the legally registered author. *Poor Robin* was a satirical almanac
    founded in *c.* 1662 by William Winstanley and continued by
    other hands well into the nineteenth century; Jonathan Dove
    flourished as an almanac-maker in the 1640s and 1650s; Vincent
    Wing published a popular almanac that was continued after his
    death by family members.

13. *a new Set of Predictions:* Probably a reference to 'A Continuation
    of the Predictions for the Remaining Part of the Year 1708',
    which also purported to be by 'Isaac Bickerstaff'.

A Famous Prediction of Merlin, the British Wizard

First published 1709. Merlin, the soothsayer in the Arthurian legend,
was a name used not only by Partridge but also in earlier almanac
titles such as *Rider's British Merlin* (1636–8). To further his spoof,
Swift employs black-letter typography to give the appearance of a
sixteenth-century translation. So successful was his parody that even
Samuel Johnson was fooled into thinking it 'authentic'. Explanatory
notes were regularly used by members of the Scriblerus Club to satirize
pedantry and false learning.

1. *Johan Haukyns ... 1530:* A sixteenth-century printer, probably
    best known in England for completing the printing of a French
    grammar in London in 1530.

2. *Yonge Symnele ... Edward the Fourth:* A pretender to the throne,
    Lambert Simnel (*c.* 1475–*c.* 1535) posed as Edward, Earl of War-
    wick, not as Richard, Duke of York, son of Edward IV; he was
    crowned as Edward VI (1487) before being defeated by Henry VII.
    James Francis Edward Stuart, the 'Old Pretender' (*BD*), briefly
    held the title of Prince of Wales until his father's abdication in

1688. The prophecy that he will again 'miscarry' refers to his ill-fated attempt to regain the Scottish throne in 1708.

3. *Norways Pryd, &c.:* 'Queen Anne. *The Prophecy means, that she shou'd marry a second Time, and have Children that would live*' (note in F '35). It was Anne's failure to produce a surviving heir that ended the Stuart line. She was married to Prince George of Denmark, a country that was then united with Norway.

4. *England is now ... Britain:* As a result of the Union of England and Scotland in 1707.

5. *Geryon ... again:* Refers to the mythological three-headed winged monster; one of the Labours of Hercules was to bring Geryon's cattle from Erytheia to Eurystheus, a task he performed by killing Geryon.

6. *two Rivals for Spain ... out of Spain:* This prophecy is consistent with England's support of the Habsburg Charles over the Bourbon Philip in their competing claims for the throne of Spain.

An Argument against Abolishing Christianity

First published 1711. Written in 1708 in support of the Test Act of 1673, which mandated the taking of the Sacrament of the Lord's Supper according to Church of England practice as a prerequisite for holding public office, this ironic piece uses a persona combining aspects of a fashionable man about town and a free-thinker to expose what Swift saw as the dangers facing the Church—and society at large—from repeal of the Test, which the Whigs were then striving to bring about in Ireland. On the work's simplest level, the 'abolishing of Christianity' is synonymous with 'repeal of the Test Act', although the tract's network of ironies complicates this equation and reveals the central paradox of Swift's stance as a proponent of 'real' Christianity—one based on genuine, hence uncoerced faith—who nevertheless feels the need to defend a set of external forms and requirements not wholly unlike what the speaker is advocating.

1. *forbidden upon severe Penalties ... Majority of Opinion the Voice of God:* A reference to the 1708 law penalizing the popular pastime of wagering on the outcome of specific military engagements and the Union of England and Scotland ... This idea was associated with the Whigs—though also invoked by the Drapier, who describes 'the *Voice* of the Nation' as 'in some Manner, the *Voice of God*' (*Drapier's Letter VII*).

2. *nominal and real Trinitarians:* Theological controversies over the

relationship of the three persons of the Holy Trinity, given new life in England after the Act of Toleration (1689) and the lapse of the Licensing Act (1695) allowed the publication of heterodox views on the subject. Swift held that 'the whole Doctrine [of the Trinity] is short and plain, and in itself uncapable of any Controversy; since God himself hath pronounced the Fact, but wholly concealed the Manner' (sermon, *On the Trinity*).

3. *the Proposal of Horace . . . their Manners:* See Horace, *Epode* 16.

4. *nominal Christianity . . . Wealth and Power:* That is, 'occasional conformity', or the practice of showing only token observance of the communion requirements of the Test Act in order to become eligible for public office; an Act against Occasional Conformity, which penalized public office-holders who attended Dissenting services, was passed in 1711 . . . Some political writers at the time argued that England's ability to prosper as a nation depended on its embrace of religious toleration, hence on its repeal of the Test Act.

5. *Liberty of Conscience . . . Instance:* In his sermon *On the Testimony of Conscience*, Swift defines 'Liberty of Conscience' as 'no more than a Liberty of knowing our own Thoughts; which Liberty no one can take from us'—to be clearly distinguished from 'endeavouring to propagate [one's] Belief . . . and to overthrow the Faith which the Laws have already established'.

6. *broke only for Blasphemy:* A wry allusion to the Act for the Suppression of Blasphemy and Profaneness (1698), which imposed strict penalties on any individual who openly rejected the Doctrine of the Holy Trinity or questioned the divine authority of the Christian religion or the Bible.

7. *Deorum offensa Diis curæ:* 'An offence against the gods is the gods' concern': Tacitus, *Annals*, 1.73. Swift quotes this phrase again in *Some Thoughts on Free-Thinking* in an obviously critical way, to suggest that such offences should be the concern of men as well.

8. *Asgill, Tindall, Toland, Coward:* Examples of deistic and heterodox thinkers (see *BD*).

9. *An old dormant Statute or two . . . Execution:* Laws (such as the Test Act and the Corporation Act of 1661) that mandated religious conformity for office-holders but that ceased being enforced after the Act of Toleration in 1689. Edmund Dudley (1462–1510), lawyer and politician, served as under-sheriff of London before he teamed up with Sir Richard Empson (1434–1510) to act as financial agent for Henry VII. The two enriched the

royal coffers by millions of pounds, partly by reviving obsolete
statutes.

10. *the wise Regulations of Henry the Eighth ... Hospital:* It was
Henry's practice to give properties seized from the Roman Catholic Church to laymen rather than to the Anglican Church. In
his sermon *Upon the Martyrdom of K. Charles I* (preached at
St Patrick's on 30 January 1726), Swift accused Henry of having
'robbed' the Church; elsewhere he condemns 'that Sacrilegious
Tyrant Henry VIII' for bestowing the right to tithes 'on his
ravenous favorites'.

11. *Whether the Monument be in Danger:* Refers to the memorial
designed by Sir Christopher Wren (1632–1723) to commemorate
the Great Fire of London (1666), which blamed the disaster on
the 'Popish faction'.

12. *Margarita ... Valentini:* The Italian singer Margarita l'Epine
(d. 1746), the English soprano Catherine Tofts (*c.* 1680–1756)
and the Italian counter-tenor Valentino Urbani, aka 'Valentini'
(*fl.* 1705–15), regularly performed operas at the Queen's Theatre
in the Haymarket. It is not coincidental that Swift has the
'Trimmers', or compromisers, favour the castrato Valentini.

13. *The Prasini and Veneti ... the Blue and the Green:* Refers to
rival teams, distinguished by green and blue liveries, in the chariot
races of the Roman circus and later the hippodrome at Constanti-
nople, whose bitter antagonism culminated in civil war. Blue and
green are also the colours of the knightly Orders of the Garter
(England) and the Thistle (Scotland).

14. *prohibited Silks ... prohibited Wine:* French goods officially off
limits to the English because of the war but obtainable none-
theless through a vigorous smuggling trade between the two
countries.

15. *a Scheme for Comprehension ... all Bodies may enter:* Mocked
by Swift in his tract *The Presbyterians Plea of Merit* (1733) via
the image of disparate groups that 'all meet and jumble together
into a perfect Harmony'.

16. *a starched squeezed Countenance ... Mankind:* Evokes the
stereotyped image of the Puritan.

17. *If the Quiet of a State ... Flock:* A similar image is used to
describe the satiric strategy of *A Tale of a Tub*; its 'Preface'
explains 'That Sea-Men have a Custom when they meet a *Whale*,
to fling him out an empty *Tub*, by way of Amusement, to divert
him from laying violent Hands upon the Ship' (i.e. of state).

18. *another Securing Vote:* Refers to the Act of Settlement (1701),

which mandated a Protestant succession to the English throne 'for the happiness of the nation, and the security of our religion'.

19. *Jus Divinum of Episcopacy:* The 'divine right' of the bishopric, presumably derived from the Apostles.

20. *constant Practice of the Jesuits . . . amongst us:* Swift often suggests that Catholics and Dissenters have much in common despite their professed antagonism; in *A Tale of a Tub*, the 'Catholic' Peter and the 'Calvinist' Jack are frequently mistaken for one another due to their 'huge Personal Resemblance'.

21. *the Popish Missionaries . . . continues:* A misrepresentation of the positions of John Toland and Matthew Tindal (the 'most learned and ingenious Author'). Both men embraced Catholicism at some point in their lives but both ultimately renounced the faith.

22. *the Bank . . . One per Cent:* The Bank of England was founded in 1694 as a shareholding association that floated large loans to the government for prosecuting the war against France; the East India Company was a joint-stock company established in 1600 under Royal Charter of Elizabeth I, which granted it a monopoly over trade with Asia. The growing political power of both is attacked in *The Examiner, No. 37*.

The Tatler, Number CCXXX

First published 1710. This contribution to *The Tatler* (1709–11), the popular periodical put out by Richard Steele, comically exposes what Swift saw as the corruptions of the English language in contemporary speech and writing, a subject he also dealt with in *A Letter to a Young Gentleman, Lately entered into Holy Orders* (1720), *Polite Conversation*, and other works. An inveterate foe of cant and jargon, associated with groups he was most critical of—in this case, courtiers and people of fashion—Swift consistently counselled simplicity of expression and attacked the use of newly minted, trendy words whose meaning could be understood neither by common people nor by future generations. Swift addresses his *Tatler* letter to his own famous persona, 'Isaac Bickerstaff', recently adopted by Steele.

1. *Tom . . . Plenipo's:* Probably Thomas Harley (d. 1738), cousin of Robert Harley and a Secretary of the Treasury at the time this piece was composed. 'Plenipo's' is a shortened form for plenipotentiaries.

2. *the French King:* Louis XIV, with whom England was then at war.

3. *The Jacks . . . Phizz's:* Jacobites, or supporters of the exiled

Stuarts. 'Phizz' is short for 'physiognomy', or facial expressions that reveal qualities of mind or character.

4. *has got the Hipps:* Is 'hippish', or low-spirited, with the implication of being somewhat hypochondriacal.

5. *upon Rep:* Upon reputation (i.e. 'upon his honour').

6. *incog:* Incognito.

7. *a natural Tendency . . . Northern Languages:* Swift believed in the shaping power of climate and geography on language; *A Proposal for Correcting the English Tongue* (1712) speaks of 'harsh unharmonious Sounds, that none but a *Northern* Ear could endure'.

8. *Mob and Banter:* The term 'mob' (from the Latin 'mobile vulgus', 'the movable or excitable crowd') came into currency in the Restoration; 'banter' is described in *A Tale of a Tub* as a word 'first borrowed from the Bullies in *White-Fryars*', which 'then fell among the Footmen, and at last retired to the Pedants'.

9. *Index Expurgatorius . . . Syllables:* An official list of passages to be deleted or reworded in published works otherwise deemed permissible to read, similar to the list drawn up by the Catholic Church for its adherents. This recommendation echoes proposals put forward in *Correcting the English Tongue.*

10. *some of those Sermons . . . University:* Cf. Swift's *A Letter to a Young Gentleman*, which makes similar points.

11. *Simplex munditiis:* 'Natural elegance': Horace, *Odes*, 1.5.5.

12. *Hooker . . . Parsons the Jesuit:* Richard Hooker (*c.* 1554–1600) was best known for *Of the Laws of Ecclesiastical Polity*, a monumental defence of the Anglican Church, considered a model of both religious polemics and English prose style. Robert Parsons (1546–1610) wrote a devotional work, *A Christian Directorie*, also published in a Protestant version.

13. *Sir H. Wooton . . . Daniel the Historian:* Sir Henry Wotton (1568–1639), poet, diplomat and connoisseur, produced a diverse body of writings published after his death as *Reliquiae Wottonianae* (1651). Sir Robert Naunton (1563–1635) authored *Fragmenta Regalia: Observations on the Late Queen Elizabeth, Her Times and Favourites.* Francis Osborne (1593–1659) was a miscellaneous writer known for his *Advice to a Son* and his *Memoirs of the Reigns of Q. Elizabeth and King James I.* Samuel Daniel (1563–1619), historian, dramatist and Poet Laureate, wrote *The Collection of the Historie of England to the Death of Edward III*, a major source for Swift's 'Abstract of the History of England' (see Ehrenpreis, 2: 61).

The Examiner

First published 1710–11. *The Examiner* was a journal founded to defend the policies of the new Tory ministry headed by Robert Harley. *Number 13* marks Swift's debut as its editor and, for the next thirty-two issues, its sole author, following his estrangement from the Whig Party (see Introduction). Swift's essays defended the recent change of ministry, lamented the influence of London's newly emergent class of bankers and stockjobbers and attacked the entrenched military interests responsible for perpetuating the war against France for their own selfish ends. Copy-text: *F '46*.

The Examiner, Number 13

1. *Longa . . . rerum:* 'Long is the (tale of) injustice, long the wandering, but I will follow the high points of the story': Virgil, *Aeneid*, 1.341–2.
2. *the declining Party:* The Whigs.
3. *a General . . . his own Nomination:* The Duke of Marlborough (*BD*), a war hero from several major victories on the Continent but a recurring target of Swift's criticism and satire.
4. *to break the Settlement . . . the Pretender:* To negate the Act of Settlement (1701), designed to ensure that the English Crown would remain in Protestant hands, by recalling the Catholic James Stuart to the throne.
5. *as unknown as their Original:* That is, as obscure as their birth— a reflection on the humble origins of many who in recent years had risen to great wealth and status in the military and financial spheres, including Marlborough himself, who was the son of an impoverished squire.
6. *two Verses in Lucan:* From *Pharsalia*, 1.181–2.
7. *run up as high as the Revolution:* That is, go as far back as the Glorious Revolution (*G*).
8. *Divine-Right, Passive-Obedience, and Non-Resistance:* Doctrines associated with Tories and Jacobites; in *Examiner, No. 33*, Swift criticizes the Whigs' misuse of these terms and denies that the Tories subscribe either to the Divine Right of Kingship or to an absolute 'Passive Obedience' to a monarch's commands.
9. *A Practice as old . . . Security:* Recounted by Plutarch in his *Life of Eumenes*; an analogy was the large loans obtained by William III to carry on his wars against James II and Louis XIV.
10. *the Four-Shilling Aid . . . Kingdom:* Refers to the sum of 'four

shillings in the pound' that was first exacted from the English populace by William III in 1693 to help fund his military campaigns in Europe.

11. *if our Fathers . . . Years past:* Cf. *The Conduct of the Allies* (1711): 'It will, no doubt, be a mighty Comfort to our Grandchildren, when they see a few Rags hang up in *Westminster-Hall,* which cost an hundred Millions, whereof they are paying the Arrears, and boasting, as Beggars do, that their Grandfathers were Rich and Great.'

12. *until her Enemies . . . refuse them:* Refers to the Whigs' rejection of Louis XIV's peace offers in late 1708, at which time he agreed to all of the forty articles put forward by the Allies except one deliberately included to undermine the negotiations (in effect, to declare war on his own grandson). The clear message here is that the Tory administration will respond very differently to such peace overtures.

13. *Audiet . . . Juventus:* 'The youth, few in number because of their parents' fault (in carrying out destructive civil war), will hear of battles': Horace, *Odes,* 1.2.23–4.

The Examiner, Number 14

While on one level a satire aimed specifically at exposing the duplicity of the Whigs, in particular the Earl of Wharton (*BD*), this essay, also known as 'The Art of Political Lying', has the kind of broad application that enables each new generation of readers to find in it a striking relevance to their own time. Swift also uses the mock-genealogy in *A Tale of a Tub* (with regard to Modern Critics) and in *Examiner, No. 32,* to describe the birth of 'Faction'.

1. *E quibus . . . susurri:* 'Some of these fill their idle ears with talk, and others spread what they have heard elsewhere; while the size of the story grows, and each new teller adds something to what he has heard. Here is Credulity; here is thoughtless Error, unfounded Joy and confused Fears; here sudden Sedition and Whisperings from a dubious source': Ovid, *Metamorphoses,* 12.56–61. The passage is describing the House of Rumour.

2. *VICEROY of a great Western Province . . . Pit:* Echoes Milton's portrayal of Satan in *Paradise Lost* (1667) and evokes Wharton, 'Viceroy' (Lord-Lieutenant) of Britain's 'Western Province', Ireland.

3. *Fame:* Rumour; portrayed by Virgil, in Book 4 of *The Aeneid,*

as a monster with an eye below each feather, a tongue and mouth for each eye and twice as many ears.

4. *a prevailing Party for almost twenty Years:* The Whigs.

5. *Flower-de-Luce's ... in their Hands:* Emblems of Roman Catholicism, especially of France, are here counterposed against representations of England. The 'fleur-de-lis' was the royal arms of France; the *'Triple Crowns'* refers to the papal tiaras; *'Chains'* suggests the tyranny and absolutism of Catholic nations and evokes the Inquisition; *'wooden Shoes'* were equated with French sabots, seen to typify the miserable state of the French peasants. The contrasting 'Ensigns of *Liberty'* points to England as a Protestant nation with a limited monarchy, symbolized by the mythological Britannia holding a horn of plenty.

6. *Art of the Second Sight ... seeing Spirits:* The 'inner light' and prophetic vision claimed by the Scottish Presbyterians—the *'Hipocritical Saints'* of Swift's *Memoirs of Captain Creichton* (1731).

7. *those Legions hovering ... at Elections:* Evokes the picture of Satan's 'Legions' roused from their slumber and filling the air with their grotesque density in *Paradise Lost* (Book 1). It is not coincidental that these lies hover around *'Exchange-Alley'*—the centre for the commercial and banking interests in London.

8. *a certain Great Man ... Affairs:* Refers to Wharton. In his *Short Character of Wharton* (1711), Swift claims that dissembling and lying are 'the two Talents he most practiseth, and most valueth himself upon'.

9. *when he invokes God ... believes in neither:* According to the *Short Character*, Wharton is 'an Atheist in Religion'; he attends prayers for form's sake but 'will talk Bawdy and Blasphemy at the Chapel Door'.

10. *destroy our Constitution both in Church and State:* A possible consequence, as Swift saw it, of the Whigs' attempts to repeal the Test Act and thereby undermine the Established Church (in Ireland in particular) and increase the political power of the Dissenters, a group not known for their love of monarchical government. Wharton strongly supported such a repeal during his tenure as Lord-Lieutenant of Ireland.

11. *by powerful Motives from the City:* Implies that bribery and influence-peddling on the part of the commercial and financial interests have corrupted the election process.

The Examiner, Number 20

1. *Pugnacem ... minorem:* 'They would know a fighter (to be) less than a wise man': Ovid, *Metamorphoses*, 13.354.

2. *William Rufus ... those Days:* William Rufus (1056–1100) succeeded his father, William the Conqueror, as William II in 1087 and spent most of his reign in conflict with his elder brother, Robert, Duke of Normandy, while also fighting to suppress rebellions at home and launching military campaigns in France.

3. *as Machiavel informs us:* Niccolò Machiavelli (1469–1527), Florentine statesman best known for his authorship of *The Prince*, a discourse on the most effective methods of exercising and retaining power; his later treatise, *On the Art of War*, laid the foundations of modern military tactics. His support of a citizen's militia to replace the mercenary-army system would have struck a sympathetic chord in Swift.

4. *That no private Man ... so great:* Refers to Marlborough; in *The Conduct of the Allies*, Swift warns that 'a *General during Pleasure*, might have grown into a *General for Life*, and a *General for Life* into a *King*'.

5. *Paulus Æmilius, or Scipio himself:* Two great Roman military leaders. The former (228–160 BCE) was created consul and honoured in triumph for his victories after leading the army that destroyed Macedonia; Scipio Africanus (236–?183 BCE) helped establish Rome as a great Mediterranean power by first defeating the armies of Carthage in Spain and, later, defeating Hannibal in Africa.

6. *Cæsar ... Roman Liberty:* In *A Discourse of the Contests and Dissensions ... in Athens and Rome* (1701), Swift holds Caesar up as an example of 'the Tyranny of a single Person' and claims he contributed to 'the Ruin of the *Roman* Freedome and Greatness'. The '*certain General*' who constitutes a modern parallel with Caesar is Marlborough.

7. *petere more majorum:* 'To seek (it) according to the custom of their ancestors' (Latin).

8. *the great Rebellion ... a Trial:* The English Civil Wars that began in 1642 ... The trial before a select group of Parliamentarians that culminated in the execution of Charles I on 30 January 1649.

9. *erected a Military Government ... by Major-Generals:* Refers to the establishment in 1655 of fully fledged military rule in England under the office of a 'Protector' (Oliver Cromwell) and governed

by a new Constitution that divided England into eleven areas, each headed by a Major-General possessing extensive powers.

10. *to drink Damnation . . . Queen herself:* Swift recounts in *JS* how several officers were forced to leave the army 'for drinking Destruction to the present ministry, and dressing up a hat on a stick, and calling it Harley; then drinking a glass with one hand, and discharging a pistol with the other at the maukin . . .'

11. *short Passage to Harwich:* The most direct route between England and its ally, Holland.

12. *a Dialogue in Lucian:* Lucian, *Dialogues of the Dead*, 10. The words Swift attributes to Charon are actually uttered by Hermes to the shade Lampichus, Dictator of Gela.

Journal to Stella

Letters I and XLI–LXV first published 1766; Letters II–XL, 1768. Extracts from the earlier letters appeared in Deane Swift's *Essay upon the Life, Writings, and Character of Dr. Jonathan Swift*, in 1755. Written between September 1710 and June 1713, while Swift was in England representing the Church of Ireland, this series of sixty-five letters, which are addressed to Esther Johnson (and, secondarily, her companion Rebecca Dingley), offers a rich source of material about both the political and literary worlds of London during the reign of Queen Anne. As a member of several groups formed by the leading wits of the period, and as confidant of the most powerful men in the Tory ministry (especially the Treasurer, Robert Harley, later Earl of Oxford, and the Secretary of State, Henry St John, later Viscount Bolingbroke), Swift was an active participant in both these worlds and a wry, often perceptive—but inevitably partial and occasionally misleading—commentator on the London scene. These letters also have a significant personal dimension, especially apparent in those instances in which they adopt an intimate, playful tone towards Johnson (addressed as 'MD', or 'My Dear') and communicate through a private, invented language that Swift refers to in Letter XLIII as 'ourrichar Gangridge' ('our little Language'). Swift himself never used the title *Journal to Stella*, which was an interpolation by his subsequent editors. Copy-text for the following two Letters: *DS '68*.

Letter V

1. *Presto . . . absence:* 'Presto' is the name Deane Swift used for Swift, based on the *JS* entry which recounts: 'The [Bolognese]

duchess of Shrewsbury asked [St. John] was not that Dr. Dr. and she could not say my name in English, but said Dr. *Presto*, which is Italian for Swift.'

2.   *the Tatler that I writ . . . a pure one*: Refers to *The Tatler*, No. CCXXX, dealing with the corruptions in language.

3.   *Your Manley's brother . . . Tories of Ireland*: The Tory loyalist John Manley, just named Surveyor General, is trying to prevent his Whig brother Isaac's dismissal as Postmaster General in Ireland. Party politics likewise threaten Sir Thomas Frankland's post as joint Postmaster General in England (see *BD*).

4.   *my lampoon . . . on a certain great person*: 'The Virtues of Sid Hamet the Magician's Rod', a scurrilous satire on Sidney Godolphin (*BD*).

5.   *sir John Stanley . . . Mr. Pratt*: In other words, Swift will seek Stanley's help in soliciting support from Henry Hyde (via the assistance of Hyde's wife) on behalf of his friend, John Pratt (see *BD*).

6.   *late attorney-general*: James Montagu (*BD*); he had just resigned his post.

7.   *the cartons of Raphael . . . his house and park, and improvements*: Raphael's famous 'cartoons', based on representations of Christ and his apostles, were made for tapestries in the Sistine Chapel at Pope Leo X's behest and bought by King Charles I in 1630; during Swift's visit they were being displayed in the King's Gallery at Hampton Court . . . Halifax (*BD*) was Ranger of Bushy Park, where he pursued various building and landscaping projects.

8.   *you go dine . . . Dublin*: 'When this letter was written there were no turnpike roads in *Ireland*' (*DS* note).

9.   *your sister . . . modest sort of girl*: Anne Johnson (b. 1683), Esther's younger sister, who since her marriage in 1700 was no longer living with the Temple family at Sheen.

10. *this Mr. Dyet . . . such a man*: Richard Dyot had been acquitted of a felony charge for the actions described by Swift on the ground that his crime was a breach of trust, but he was later retried on a charge of high misdemeanour.

11. *Stella can't read*: A reference to the chronic weakness of Johnson's eyes.

12. *Joe will have his money . . . am in no fear of succeeding*: Refers to the government award bestowed on Swift's friend, Joseph Beaumont (*BD*); when the promised money failed to materialize, Swift actively lobbied on his friend's behalf . . . In the eighteenth

century, when the word 'fear' was conjugated negatively, a following negative was often illogically omitted, so that the resulting statement seems to signify the opposite of what is intended (*OED*).

13. *Don't lose your money . . . sirrahs:* By gambling; Johnson often played cards at Isaac Manley's house.

14. *another Tatler:* Probably *Tatler, No. 238*, which contained Swift's poem 'A Description of a City Shower'; in the *JS* entry for 17 October, Swift remarked, 'They say 'tis the best thing I ever writ, and I think so too.'

15. *the giver's bread, &c.:* Williams conjectures that Swift actually wrote, 'the givar's dead', with 'givars' standing for 'Devil's' in the little language; the phrase would then mean 'a long time hence' or 'never'.

16. *A Colt, a Stanhope, &c.:* Sir Henry Dutton Colt, MP for Westminster, and General James Stanhope (*BD*) were Whigs soon to be defeated by High Church candidates in the Tory landslide of October 1710.

17. *the dean, the bishop, or Mrs. Walls:* John Stearne; probably William Moreton, Bishop of Meath; the wife of the Revd Thomas Walls (all in *BD*).

18. *go out twice upon Manilio . . . your loss:* References to the card game of 'ombre' (*G*).

19. *my powers . . . the queen:* The commission Swift received from the Irish bishops, authorizing him to work on their behalf to obtain remission of the 'First Fruits' (*G*). The 'memorial' referred to was the document petitioning the government to remit the 'First Fruits' to the Irish clergy.

20. *to bring me over:* That is, to the side of the Tories.

21. *send Steele a Tatler . . . very low of late:* See n. 14, above. Steele's dejection was no doubt related to the impending loss of his position as Gazetteer due to his partisan Whig polemics and satire. A *JS* entry one week later succinctly notes, 'Well, there's an end of that: [Steele] is turned out of his place.'

22. *the you know what . . . the church:* 'These words seem to refer to the apprehension the ministry were under, that *Swift* would take part with their enemies, and therefore it was that *Harley* would do every thing to bring him over' (*DS* note). Williams, however, thinks the '*you know what*' refers to *A Tale of a Tub*.

23. *not fond . . . as I used to be:* No doubt because St James's Coffee-House was a noted Whig resort; letters addressed to Swift

were held for him there in a glass frame at the bar when he first came to London.

24. *the archbishop:* Archbishop William King of Dublin (*BD*).

25. *I've reckoned them:* 'Seventy-three lines in folio upon one page, and in a very small hand' (*DS* note).

Letter XVII

1. *the Park:* St James's Park (*G*).

2. *the memorial about Bernage ... count upon it:* Refers to the ensign's commission that Swift was helping Lt. (later Captain) Moses Bernage, a graduate of Trinity College, Dublin, procure.

3. *my head ... grow worse:* Refers to one of the recurring manifestations of Swift's Ménière's disease (*G*).

4. *We dined (says you) ... Hold your tongue, &c.:* Johnson is describing a scene at the home of John Stearne, Dean of St Patrick's (the 'dean' referred to later), which revolves around ombre-playing (*G*).

5. *colonel Fielding ... first step to it:* Probably a reference to Edmund Fielding (d. 1741), the father of the novelist Henry Fielding, who fought under Marlborough and was at this time colonel of a regiment of foot.

6. *Mrs. Vanhomrigh:* Hester Vanhomrigh (d. 1714), widow of a Dutch merchant who had successfully established himself in Dublin as commissary-general to the army in Ireland. She was now living with her daughters, Mary and Esther ('Vanessa'), in Bury Street, St James's—'but five doors off' from Swift.

7. *two lady Bettys ... a fine woman:* Lady Elizabeth Butler (d. 1750), daughter of the 2nd Duke of Ormonde and a friend of the Vanhomrighs; and Lady Elizabeth Germain (1680–1769), daughter of the 2nd Earl of Berkeley and a lifelong friend and correspondent of Swift's.

8. *the new Tatler ... epicure:* William Harrison (*BD*) became (the short-lived) editor of *The Tatler* on 13 January 1711, two weeks after Steele discontinued it. James Eckershall was Second Clerk of the Queen's Privy Kitchen and Gentleman Usher to Queen Anne.

9. *busy with poor Mrs. Walls ... I must prate, &c.:* Describes the birth of Mrs Walls' son after a difficult delivery; Swift was the reluctant godfather. 'Stoite' was the wife of Alderman John Stoyte (*BD*); 'Mrs. *Catherine*' was Catherine Lloyd, her unmarried sister. Johnson sometimes stayed at the Stoytes' residence in Donny-

brook, near Dublin, where the four of them often played cards together.

10. *Miscellanies in Prose and Verse ... they sell mightily:* Despite his profession of ignorance about this volume, Swift actively assisted in its publication by drawing up a list of works (twelve prose pieces and thirteen poems) for the printer, Benjamin Tooke (*BD*), to include; e.g. 'A Description of a City Shower', 'The Virtues of Sid Hamet', *The Bickerstaff Papers, An Argument against Abolishing Christianity* and 'A Meditation upon a Broom-Stick'.

11. *Patrick ... Leap-year:* Refers to Swift's Irish servant, Patrick, often described in *JS* as a drunk and a blunderer. The mention of his almanac points to the popularity of this type of publication among the lower classes—one of the factors motivating Swift's satiric attack on the genre in *The Bickerstaff Papers.*

12. *The duchess and [she] ... with the duke:* The 'duchess' refers to Lady Mary Somerset, second wife of the Duke of Ormonde. Swift is saying that Lady Mary and Lady Betty Butler (Ormonde's daughter) will not accompany the Duke when he returns to Ireland in the summer for his second stint as Lord-Lieutenant.

13. *Sterne's business:* The reference is to Johnson's Irish friend, Enoch Stearne (*BD*), whose 'business' with the Treasury apparently came to nothing.

14. *lord keeper:* Sir Simon Harcourt (*BD*).

15. *violent Tories on the other:* That is, the October Club, a group of Country politicians dedicated (in Swift's words) to 'drive things on to extreams against the Whigs, to call the old ministry to account, and get off five or six heads', whereas 'the ministry is for gentler measures'; cf. *Some Advice to the October Club* (1712).

16. *to play the same game ... against them:* That is, exert power by gaining the ear and trust of the Queen.

17. *I will walk like camomile:* Probably related to a proverb originating in the sixteenth century, 'The more the camomile is trodden on, the faster it grows' (*ODEP*)—the sense being that the more Swift walks, the healthier and more robust he becomes. The herb camomile has long been noted for its medicinal qualities.

18. *your new lodgings ... less than ever:* Johnson and Dingley recently moved to more upscale lodgings opposite St Mary's church in Stafford Street. Swift was critical of this move on financial grounds.

19. *all our friendship is over:* Though Swift overstates the case, a distinct coolness had developed between him and Addison (*BD*),

caused by Addison's perceived ingratitude for the assistance Swift rendered Addison's Whig friends, and exacerbated by what Swift elsewhere terms 'a Curse of Party'.

20. *one Richardson ... religion:* Refers to John Richardson (1664–1747), a graduate of Trinity College, Dublin. Swift took a dim view of both the man and his project, complaining he felt 'plagued' by Richardson.

21. *He gave me ... dpionufnad:* That is, Harley gave Swift 'A bank note for fifty pounds' (*DS* note). The coded words are deciphered by using alternate letters only (with 'bill' read for 'note'). The note, intended as recognition for his work on *The Examiner*, obviously offended Swift.

22. *Mrs. Edgworth ... last Monday se'nnight:* Refers to the departure for Ireland of the widow of Ambrose Edgeworth, a Lieutenant-Colonel in the Royal Irish Regiment of Foot. Mrs Edgeworth was entrusted by Swift with conveying chocolate and palsy water for Johnson, and Brazil tobacco for Dingley.

23. *I do read the Examiners ... as you judge:* 'Even to his beloved *Stella* [Swift] had not acknowledged himself, at this time, to be the author of the *Examiner*' (*DS* note).

24. *I do not think ... his avarice has ruined us:* Recent *Examiner* essays had charged the Duke of Marlborough with this vice. In No. 29, Swift declared that 'excessive Avarice in a General, is, I think, the greatest Defect he can be liable to, next to those of Courage and Conduct, and may be attended with the most ruinous Consequences, as it was in *Crassus*; who to that Vice alone owed the Destruction of himself and his Army.'

25. *that squinting, blinking Frenchman:* 'Presumably a relation of Mrs. De Caudres' (Williams note). De Caudres was Johnson's landlady in her new lodgings.

26. *your chancellor ... his chaplain:* Sir Constantine Phipps and Joseph Trapp (*BD*).

27. *your aukward SS*ˢ *... always SSS:* 'Print cannot do justice to whims of this kind, as they depend wholly upon the aukward shape of the letters' (*DS* note).

28. *writing in our language ... just now:* The so-called 'little language' invented by Swift. His identification of it with speaking links it to other forms of oral expression that inform many of his works.

29. *In your account ... twelvemonth:* Swift's account books began the financial year on 1 November.

30. *zoo must ... Dood mollow:* 'The meaning of this pretty language

is; "And you must cry There, and Here, and Here again. Must you imitate *Presto*, pray? Yes, and so you shall. And so there's for your letter. Good morrow"' (*DS* note). Williams suggests that there may be some inaccuracies in Deane Swift's transcript.

31. *That desperate French villain ... the archbishop:* Harley was stabbed with a penknife by Antoine, Abbé de Bourlie (b. 1658), aka the Marquis de Guiscard, a French émigré who had been granted a government pension by the Whig ministry after taking refuge in England. When the pension was later reduced by Harley, Guiscard entered into traitorous correspondence with France for monetary gain. He attacked Harley during his examination for high treason before a Committee of Council in St John's office and was himself fatally wounded by Council members. The 'archbishop' to whom Swift gave an account of the incident was William King (*BD*).

32. *the surgeon sat up with him:* Paul Buissière (d. 1739), a French Huguenot émigré who had gained a reputation in England for his surgical skills; he also wrote anatomical pieces for the Royal Society.

33. *about Mr. Clements ... place:* Swift had been asked to help Robert Clements (*BD*) retain his post as Teller of the Irish Exchequer despite the recent political changes in England.

34. *As for Bernage ... an end:* Swift is exasperated that Bernage went behind his back and secretly paid for an army commission. Henry Desaulnais ('Disney') was a French Huguenot soldier and friend of St John's.

35. *lele [i.e. there] like Presto:* The explanation in brackets is Deane Swift's.

36. *Gog and Magog:* See Revelation 20: 8. Also, in British legend, the sole survivors of a monstrous brood, imprisoned and forced into service as porters at the royal palace, on the site of the Guildhall; wickerwork models of them were carried in the annual Lord Mayor's Show (Brewer/Evans).

A Hue and Cry after Dismal

First published 1712. This piece came out as a cheaply produced 'penny paper' on a single half-sheet. Calling it a 'Grubstreet paper', Swift rushed it into print before the Stamp Act, which levied a half-penny tax on half-sheets, took effect on 1 August. The piece was written some weeks after Louis XIV agreed to let the British occupy Dunkirk and demolish the French fortifications in the port, a concession the Whigs strove to render suspect. 'Dismal', or the Earl of Nottingham (*BD*), is singled out as a satiric target because of his apostasy in throwing his weight behind the Whigs' war policy. Another, slightly enlarged version of the piece appeared under the title 'Dunkirk to be Let, Or, A Town Ready Furnish'd; with A Hue-and-Cry after Dismal'. Copy-text: London broadside of 1712.

1.　*it is better . . . stand out:* Apperson cites Camden's *Remains* (1605) as the earliest example of this proverb; cf. 'The devil himself will rather chuse to play/At paltry small game, than sit out, they say' (1759).

2.　*Collonell K–le–gr–w:* Henry Killigrew, a lieutenant-colonel of the Dragoons (Williams).

3.　*Mr. Squash . . . his Man:* Plays upon 'quashee' (or 'quashie'), a generic name for a Negro (especially a black servant); from the Ashanti or Fanti name 'Kwasi'.

4.　*Stobb . . . sight:* Despite Davis's substitution of 'hobb', the word is likelier 'stob', a pun on both a stump (as of an amputated leg) and a post or gibbet, evoking the disasters of war and proper punishment for Dismal.

5.　*nor Savoyard neither:* Swift may be playing here on the faintly comic association of Savoy natives with itinerant musicians who travel accompanied by monkeys and hurdy-gurdies (*OED*).

Swift to the Earl of Oxford

First published 1755. This letter, written from Letcombe Bassett in Berkshire, was addressed to Oxford on 3 July 1714, less than a month before the Lord Treasurer's fall from power. Its highly formal, even ceremonial tone befits a communication intended as a farewell to Oxford in his official capacity and a bowing out of the public arena by Swift. Replying to the letter on 27 July, the day of his dismissal by the Queen from office, Oxford invited Swift to visit him at his country seat in Herefordshire; but Queen Anne's death on 1 August scuttled these plans and prompted Swift to return to Ireland. Copy-text: BL autograph copy.

1.　*in your publick capacity . . . never once:* In *Some Free Thoughts upon the Present State of Affairs* (completed two days before), Swift portrays Oxford as 'a great Minister' who 'abound[s] in Secrets, and Reserves, even towards those with whom he ought to act in the greatest Confidence and Concert'.

2. *though you and somebody . . . make you:* An allusion to the failure of both Oxford and Queen Anne to help Swift obtain the post of Historiographer Royal, which went instead to the antiquary Thomas Madox.

A Modest Defence of Punning

First published 1957. Although dated 8 November 1716, this piece remained unpublished in Swift's lifetime because (Davis speculates) Swift learned that the paper it was answering, 'God's Revenge against Punning', had been written by Pope. More than just a defence of punning, the essay is itself an extended series of puns that wittily exemplify how they operate. It reveals the playful side of Swift's relationship to language: a side we see also in the 'little language' of *JS.* Pierpont Morgan autograph copy (MA 457).

1. *Punica mala leges:* A parodic echo of Virgil's 'Punica regna vides' ('You see Punic realms') in *Aeneid,* 1.338, which plays on the sound of these words to tempt the reader to (mis)translate the phrase as 'you will read bad puns'. In his *jeu d'esprit* 'The Dying Speech of TOM ASHE', Swift observes, 'I hear my friends design to publish a collection of my puns . . . therefore the world must read the bad as well as the good. Virgil has long foretold it: *Punica mala leges.*' The term *Punica mala* also means 'pomegranates', which can perhaps be seen as the classical equivalent of the 'bad apple' that brought about Man's Fall in Eden (as in the myth of Persephone).

2. *bellum Punicum . . . malum Punicum:* A joking combination of the Latin for 'Punic War' and the Latin for 'pomegranate'. The Punic Wars were fought between Rome and Carthage in the third and second centuries BCE.

3. *The Word Pun . . . Sword:* A mock-etymology. Ironically, *OED* notes that '*pun* was prob[ably] one of the clipped words . . . which came into fashionable slang at or after the Restoration'— hence precisely the type of word Swift attacks in *The Tatler, No. CCXXX* as a 'Disgrace of our Language'.

4. *Smock Simony:* Cf. *OED* example from 1705: 'Great Kindred, Smock-Simony, and Whores, have advanc'd many a Sot to the Holy-Chair'; for 'smock', see G.

5. *Πυνθάνομαι:* 'To learn by hearsay or enquiry' (Greek).

6. *our Author, J. Baker Knight . . . Chevalier de Fond Sec:* This passage refers to Charles Ford (*BD*), whose aversion to puns was

well known. Swift's nickname for Ford was 'Don Carlos', hence the references to 'a Spaniard'. Also note the words '*Quarter*', synonymous with 'fourth', homonym of 'forth', an early form of 'ford'; and '*Fond Sec*', French for 'dry bottom', a shallow place, or 'ford', for crossing a body of water.

7.   *Jews were put to their Trumps*: That is, Jews were put to their last expedient; also punning on 'Jews' trump', another term (used mainly in Scotland and Northern Ireland) for a Jews' harp.

8.   *Poor Robin . . . a Few-nest place indeed*: Robin is Robert Grattan (*BD*). The pun on 'funest' spoofs its repeated use ('these funest disasters', 'funest effects of the war') in 'God's Revenge against Punning'.

9.   *Whetstonism . . . Whistonism*: The state of being a great liar, a meaning derived from the former custom of hanging a whetstone around a liar's neck, juxtaposed alongside the ideas of the hetero-dox thinker, William Whiston (*BD*).

10.   *the Visitation . . . best Card at Comet*: Whiston's name was associated with comets; he prophesied the destruction of the world at the appearance of a comet on 13 October 1736, mocked in 'A True and Faithful Narrative' (often falsely attributed to Swift); also playing on 'comet' as the name of an old card game.

11.   *Ignorance of some Copyer . . . Occasion*: A punning reference to the claim of Richard Bentley (*BD*) that passages in *Paradise Lost* had been incorrectly transcribed by Milton's amanuensis.

12.   *Reprobat, sed non re probat*: 'He condemns him, but doesn't prove it by the matter' (Latin).

13.   *He Claps . . . Corona Veneris*: A reference to John Baron Hervey (1665–1751), made Earl of Bristol ('*Bristow stones*') in 1714; the passage contains punning play on the signs and consequences of venereal disease. According to the Bodleian copy of 'God's Revenge against Punning', the three noblemen referred to in this and the following paragraphs are Lord Hervey, Lord Stanhope and Lord Warwick (see Davis 4: 299). What all three have in common are close Whig associations: Hervey and Stanhope (*BD*) were rewarded with titles for their zealous support of the House of Hanover, and Edward Henry Rich, 7th Earl of Warwick (1697–1721), was the stepson of Addison and a member of a Whig literary group.

14.   *the Box and Dice . . . Ninepence*: A play on the several meanings of 'box' as a container for dice, a coffin, and a slang term for female genitalia. The repeated references to gaming throughout

this paragraph are meant to evoke associations with Stanhope, who was known as a heavy gambler.

15. *Var vecûm ... aere natus:* 'Born in the land of mutton-heads [*lit.*, castrated sheep] and in a dense air': Juvenal, *Satire X*, 50.

16. *The grave antient Collonell:* Identified in the Bodleian copy as 'Col. Frowd'—presumably the same person called 'Colonel Proud' and judged to be 'very ill company' in Letter VIII of *JS*. Lt.-Col. William Frowde was the uncle of Philip Frowde, an Oxford classmate and friend of Addison's, and a writer of plays and poems.

17. *Thomas Pickle:* Probably a play on Thomas Tickell (*BD*).

18. *Muley Hamet ... in his Mold:* 'Muley Hamet' is the supposed Arabic author of *Don Quixote*, Cid Hamet Benengeli ('Muley' being a variant of the Mohammedan title 'mullah'); Swift earlier used the name to satirize Godolphin in 'The Virtues of Sid Hamet'. '*[B]udge ill*' is a punning allusion to Eustace Budgell (*BD*). Daniel Button was the founder and proprietor of Button's Coffee-house in Covent Garden, which became a well-known gathering place for Whig literary figures.

19. *His Majesty's Liberality ... give us:* Refers to George I's gift of books to Cambridge University for its firm loyalty to the Protestant succession. The doctrine of 'indefeasibility', associated with Jacobites and nonjurors, held that royal titles were strictly hereditary, hence not subject to nullification.

20. *A Devonshire Man of Wit:* John Gay (*BD*). The final paragraph is a punning account of Gay's fall from a horse some months before; the only 'injury' was to his elegant snuffbox.

Sermon, On False Witness

First published 1762. This sermon is one of only twelve by Swift that have survived (eleven if we exclude one of uncertain attribution). Although he lamented to a friend that when in the pulpit 'he could never rise higher than *preaching pamphlets*', his sermons hold considerable interest, demonstrating Swift's sense of the inextricable links between the pulpit and the world beyond it, hence the close relationship between his pastoral and his civic responsibilities. This sermon, probably written early in the reign of George I, denounces the atmosphere of political repression and intimidation against Tories and suspected Jacobites which Swift found upon his return to Ireland in 1714. Copy-text: *H '62*.

1.   *False Witnesses . . . Cruelty:* Psalm 27: 12.
2.   *Jezabel . . . stoned to death:* 1 Kings 21: 10–13. Swift named his Deanery garden 'Naboth's Vineyard'.
3.   *So the two false witnesses . . . I will raise it up:* Matthew 26: 60–61 and John 2: 18–19.
4.   *The false witnesses said . . . the law:* Acts 6: 11–13.
5.   *They daily mistake . . . do me evil:* Psalm 56: 5. A few years later Swift's friend Thomas Sheridan was to see his clerical career destroyed by just such an informer; see Swift's letter to Sheridan (11 Sept. 1725).
6.   *wise as serpents . . . innocent as doves:* Matthew 10: 16.
7.   *Submit yourselves . . . supreme, &c.:* 1 Peter 2: 13.
8.   *the powers . . . ordained of God:* Romans 13: 1.

A Letter to a Young Gentleman, Lately entered into Holy Orders

First published 1720. This piece offers a unique insight into Swift's views about pulpit practices in his day, presumably shedding light on his own methods of preaching. Emphasizing simplicity of expression, it conceives of an audience of common people who would be alienated by sermons filled with excessive erudition, wit-play and abstruse theological questions. More broadly, the *Letter* is important for its reflections on language and style; for its promotion of a comprehensive model of both literary and social decorum. Moreover, its rejection of a dogmatic, narrow-minded form of Christian apologetics hostile to heathen thinkers reflects the more liberal and humanistic side of Swift's views on religion and philosophy.

1.   *barbarous Terms . . . peculiar to the Nation:* See n. 7 to *Tatler, No. CCXXX.*
2.   *Lord Falkland . . . Divines:* Lucius Cary (?1610–43), 2nd Viscount Falkland, educated at Trinity College, Dublin, was an eminent scholar who supported episcopacy but rejected the bishops' claim to divine right and all forms of religious absolutism, urging that the clergy be subject to the control of the civil magistrate.
3.   *Professors in most Arts . . . Arts:* In Book IV of *GT*, Swift ascribes to lawyers 'a peculiar Cant and Jargon of their own, that no other Mortal can understand, and wherein all their Laws are written'.
4.   *The two great Orators . . . Part:* Demosthenes (384–322 BCE)

and Marcus Tullius Cicero, or Tully (106–43 BCE), brilliant orators admired by Swift especially for their forceful denunciations of corrupt public figures. Swift's attack on Wharton in *Examiner, No. 17* is modelled on Cicero's indictment of Verres.

5. *these Northern Climates . . . next Meal:* Expresses Swift's belief (perhaps derived from Temple) in the influence of climate on character and temperament—hence the coldness of the Anglo-Saxon make-up.

6. *that divine Precept . . . Socrates:* In Book 1 of Plato's *Republic*, Socrates, in a debate on justice, gets Polemarchus to admit that 'the injuring of another [even an enemy] can be in no case just'.

7. *by shewing the Advantages . . . World:* This point is the core of Swift's sermon, *Upon the Excellency of Christianity*, which (as one might expect) presents a less favourable view of ancient philosophy. Yet even there Swift maintains that the heathen philosophers 'were as wise and as good as it was possible for them under such disadvantages, and would have probably been infinitely more with such aids as we enjoy'.

8. *those Fathers . . . Learning:* Swift may be thinking here of Tertullian (c. 150–222), a particularly zealous defender of Christianity who combined a non-classical form of Latin with an obscure style to denounce philosophers and direct personal, *ad hominem* attacks on Aristotle and Plato. Other possibilities include the Christian apologetics of Clement of Alexandria (c. 150–215) and Origen (c. 182–c. 254).

9. *as St. Austin excellently observes:* St Augustine (354–430), Bishop of Hippo, the greatest of the Church Fathers; best known for his *Confessions*, and for *The City of God*, which offers a cosmic interpretation of history rooted in the struggle between good (the City of God) and evil (the Earthly City).

10. *Pilgrim's Progress . . . Ideas:* The spiritual allegory by John Bunyan (1628–88), written in the Puritan 'plain style', is being recommended over tracts dealing with overly abstract or pedantic matters.

11. *against the Advice of St. Paul . . . Studies: Upon the Excellency of Christianity* notes that St Paul 'seems very much to despise' Epicurean philosophy, a materialist theory of the universe which posits that both the universe and individual bodies are composed of atoms; see also Acts 17: 18.

12. *Mysteries of the Christian Religion . . . Nature:* Swift's sermon *On the Trinity* likewise argues that 'our Religion abounds in Mysteries' since 'God thought fit to communicate some Things

to us in Part, and leave some Part a Mystery'. This question assumed a special urgency after the publication of John Toland's *Christianity Not Mysterious* (1696), which claimed that religious mysteries were invented by the clergy to impose upon the ignorance of their followers.

13. *impatient to be out of Play:* Anxious at being unemployed or out of office.

14. *old fundamental Custom . . . Slander:* A protest against the Septennial Act of 1716, which lengthened the normal interval between elections from three to seven years, making the offices more vulnerable to bribery and corruption. Swift advocates annual Parliaments in *A Letter from Dr. Swift to Mr. Pope*.

15. *Mr. Hobbes's Saying . . . Religion:* In the 'Epistle Dedicatory to the Earl of Newcastle' of Hobbes's *Humane Nature* (1650).

Swift to Charles Ford

First published 1935. Swift's letters to his close friend Ford (*BD*)—fifty-one of which survive—interweave public with private concerns and offer an insight into his feelings about a range of subjects. This letter of 4 April 1720, along with presenting a vivid picture of Swift's physical sufferings due to Ménière's disease, expresses his increasingly vocal anti-colonialist posture, intensified here by passage a week earlier of the Declaratory Act, which 'bound' Ireland even further to British rule. The letter is also significant for its references to a seemingly buoyant world of financial speculation (the 'South-Sea Mystery' referred to below) that would soon come crashing down in the Bubble. Copy-text: *Rothschild* autograph copy.

1. *our Missisipi Friend:* Bolingbroke (*BD*), at the time living in exile in France and about to purchase a retreat with profits from his speculation in the Mississippi Company: a financial conglomerate founded by the Scotsman John Law, which assumed France's public debt and issued money based on its monopoly of French foreign trade. Enormously successful in its initial stages, it inspired similar speculation in England.

2. *the Quarrell against Convocations . . . assemble:* The formal assembly of Anglican clergy, or Convocation, was prorogued indefinitely in May 1717, after a highly controversial sermon delivered by Bishop Benjamin Hoadly made them fear a Tory backlash; it met only once more during the century.

3. *united on their Conditions . . . ashamed of:* An allusion to the

defiant stance of the Scottish Parliament before agreeing to the Union with England in 1707.

4. *so universall a Discontent . . . to succeed:* This whole passage refers to the reactions to and consequences of the Declaratory Act (*G*).

5. *watched for his Ears . . . Inch of them:* In the seventeenth century, under Archbishop William Laud, Puritans often had their ears cut off for publishing nonconformist pamphlets—a fate Swift thinks appropriate for the notoriously unscrupulous publisher Edmund Curll (*BD*).

6. *an honest humersom Gentleman . . . mine:* Either Thomas Sheridan (*BD*) or Swift's genial Dublin companion Dr Richard Helsham (*c.* 1683–1738), with whom he exchanged riddles and puns.

7. *one about Precedence of Doctors . . . others: The Right of Precedence between Phisicians and Civilians Enquir'd into*, published in Dublin and reprinted in London in 1720; falsely attributed to Swift (Williams).

8. *Ld Harley and L^{dy} Harriette . . . Friend L— and the rest:* Edward Harley (*BD*) and his wife, the former Lady Henrietta Cavendish Holles; Erasmus Lewis (*BD*).

A Proposal for the Universal Use of Irish Manufacture

First published 1720. Carefully timed to appear in print shortly before the celebrations marking the sixtieth birthday of George I (28 May) and calculated to exploit the nationalist sentiment fuelled by the Declaratory Act passed weeks earlier, which asserted Britain's 'full power' to make laws 'bind[ing] the kingdom and people of Ireland', the 'Proposal' was Swift's first published tract devoted exclusively to Irish affairs. Calling for an economic boycott of English goods to counter a series of restrictive trade laws—particularly the Woollen Act of 1699, which prevented the exportation of Irish manufactures to other countries and limited its export of raw wool to England—the tract provoked a government prosecution against its printer by Chief Justice William Whitshed. Copy-text: first printing of 1720, collated with *F '35*.

1. *the Landlords are every where . . . Sheep:* A survey of what Swift deemed the major abuses of land management in Ireland, particularly the power of large landowners and their 'middlemen' to dictate the terms of the soil's usage by small tenant

farmers, and the conversion of tillage into pasture lands, fuelled both by the instability of land tenure and by England's strict regulation of Irish trade. In a later tract, Swift castigates 'that abominable Race of Graziers . . . ready to engross great Quantities of Land', pointing to the bitter irony that 'the more *Sheep* we have, the fewer human Creatures are left to wear the *Wool*, or eat the *Flesh*'. The maxim that 'People are the Riches of a Country' was a basic tenet of mercantilist theory that Swift declared inapplicable to Ireland due to its 'want of employment' (*Maxims Controlled in Ireland*).

2.   *our beneficial Traffick of Wool . . . to Market:* The restrictions England placed on Irish trade fuelled a clandestine trade in wool with France; an anonymous Irish pamphlet of 1721 claimed that 'our fraudulent trade in wool is the best branch of our commerce'.

3.   *Barnstable:* Barnstaple, a seaport in Devonshire; a major market for imported Irish wool.

4.   *those great Refinements . . . State of the Nation:* Refers to Parliament's preoccupation over the preceding months with proposed legislation (ultimately withdrawn) to extend the political and civil rights of Dissenters, and with the Annesley Case, a conflict between the British and the Irish House of Lords over who had appellate and final jurisdiction in Irish cases, resolved in England's favor via the Declaratory Act.

5.   *Nemine Contradicente:* No one contradicting; without a dissenting vote (Latin).

6.   *Lexicon of Female Fopperies . . . the Nation:* Like many male writers, Swift often blamed women for Ireland's ruinous dependency on expensive goods from abroad. Yet he also held responsible 'the young fops who admire them' (*A Proposal to the Ladies of Ireland*); and he blamed both sexes equally for the 'pernicious Folly' of harbouring extravagant tastes in clothing in his sermon *Causes of the Wretched Condition of Ireland*.

7.   *make burying in Woollen . . . a Law:* Nine years later, mourners at the funeral of William Conolly (*BD*) wore scarves of Irish linen to make just such a statement.

8.   *the late Archbishop of Tuam . . . Nor am I even yet for lessening the Number of those Exceptions:* John Vesey (*BD*) . . . In *F '35* this inflammatory statement is replaced by the following far less provocative statement: 'I must confess, that as to the former [the People of England], I should not be sorry if they would stay at home; and for the latter [their Coals], I hope, in a little Time we shall have no Occasion for them.'

9. *Non tanti . . . ostrum:* 'A mitre is not worth so much, nor the purple robes of a judge' (Latin).

10. *engaging not to play the Knave . . . Goodness:* A recurring complaint of Swift's, appearing also in *A Modest Proposal*; see also his sermon, *Doing Good*, and *Drapier's Letter VII*.

11. *the present Archbishop of Dublin . . . born among us:* William King, whose 'Labours for the Publick Weal' are extolled in a verse that Swift wrote during this period. The phrase 'under the rose' is usually expressed today in Latin, *sub rosa* (meaning 'secretly or in strictest confidence').

12. *The Fable in Ovid . . . to this purpose:* Ovid, *Metamorphoses*, 6.1–145.

13. *The Scripture tells us . . . wise Man mad:* Ecclesiastes 7: 7.

14. *a Person . . . from Ireland:* Arthur Annesley, 5th Earl of Anglesey (*BD*), whose 'great Estate' was Camolin Park in Co. Wexford. Anglesey fell out with Swift over this passage.

15. *Mostyn and White-haven:* British ports; Mostyn is located on the northeast coast of Wales, in Flintshire; Whitehaven, in Cumberland, is described in Defoe's *Tour Through the Whole Island of Great Britain* (1724–6) as 'the most eminent port in England for shipping off coals, except Newcastle and Sunderland, and even beyond the last'.

16. *grievous Burthen of Exchange . . . Complaint:* The effects of Ireland's lack of a fixed and stable exchange rate with England, exacerbated by Ireland's inability to mint its own currency or use British sterling, which made it dependent on foreign coins often having a different value in the two countries. Periodically, by decree from London, the English guinea was fixed at a set value in Ireland; but the resulting appreciation or depreciation of the Irish currency created opportunities for exploitation by those who could move freely between the two countries and work the exchange rate to their own advantage. See n. 18 to *A Short View of the State of Ireland*.

17. *Ballad upon Cotter . . . Government:* James Cotter, member of a well-to-do Catholic family from Cork and an alleged Jacobite, was hanged for rape in 1720; he became the subject of numerous popular ballads.

18. *a Law to bind Men . . . Matter:* Swift's first major use of the Lockean notion that men cannot be bound by laws without their consent; see *Drapier's Letter IV*. '*In foro Conscientiæ*' means, 'in the forum of conscience' (Latin). Robert Sanderson (1587–1663), Bishop of Lincoln, was a prolific writer on matters of

theology about whom Charles I is said to have declared, 'I carry my ears to hear other preachers, but I carry my conscience to hear Dr. Sanderson'. Francisco Suarez (1548–1617), a Spanish Jesuit and political philosopher, criticized the Theory of Divine Right in his *Defensio Fidei* (1613), which anticipated Locke's idea of the original equality of all men and the individual as owner of his own freedom.

19. *Corrector of a Hedge-Press . . . after him:* Thought to refer to Martin Bladen (1680–1746), soldier, politician and steadfast supporter of Walpole, who produced a popular translation of Cæsar's *Commentaries* (1712), dedicated to the Duke of Marl-borough. '*Little-Britain*' was a street in London known for its cheap clothing stalls and for second-hand bookshops patronized by Swift.

20. *Author of a Play . . . Class:* William Luckyn, 1st Viscount Grim-ston (*BD*). The praise here is ironic.

21. *my L—d W— . . . a dispensing Power in the Queen:* Lord Wharton (*BD*) . . . The power claimed by the Crown to override statutes, which was condemned when invoked by James II but later embraced when applied to statutes enacted by the Irish Parliament.

22. *Colonies of Out-casts in America:* Colonies like Virginia had become the destination points for convicted criminals, trans-ported to America as indentured servants in lieu of being hanged or imprisoned.

23. *the Vassals in Germany and Poland:* An especially charged allu-sion given that George I was German.

24. *a Thing they call a Bank . . . this Town:* Refers to the proposal in 1720 to establish a National Bank of Ireland, which was defeated by the Irish Parliament despite having received royal approval. Swift's opposition to it reflects his general hostility to the new credit economy and to any deviation from a strict gold and silver standard; see *Examiner, No. 13* and *The Drapier's Letters*.

25. *Hemp, and Caps, and Bells:* The rope used for hanging criminals, and the insignia of the fool or jester.

A Letter from Dr. Swift to Mr. Pope

First published 1741. Although dated '*Jan.* 10, 1721', it is uncertain whether this piece was actually begun on that date or on 10 January of the following year. In either case, it is likely that Swift wrote the letter over a period of months. It was never sent to its addressee, no doubt because it was intended more as a general statement of Swift's political beliefs than as a private epistle. While asserting the basic orthodoxy of Swift's views, the 'Letter' also underscores the precariousness of his position in Irish society due to ideas deemed suspect by those in power. It articulates, with a particular urgency and clarity, themes common to Swift's writings at the time: the widespread persecution of alleged Jacobites and Tories, the corruption of the judicial system, the prevalence of government informers, and the perils of being a writer in an age of surveillance and censorship. Here again a major symbol for this corruption is Chief Justice Whitshed (BD). Copy-text: F '46.

1. *gentlemen of the Long-robe . . . those in Furs:* Lawyers and judges.

2. *ten weeks before the Queen's death . . . visit:* Queen Anne died on 1 August 1714, following the collapse of the Tory ministry due to the 'incurable breach' between Harley and Bolingbroke.

3. *writ a Discourse . . . in safe hands: Some Free Thoughts upon the Present State of Affairs* (not published until 1741). The 'great Minister now abroad' is Bolingbroke, who had fled to France following his impeachment in 1715.

4. *some Memorials . . . disdained to accept it:* This is the work published posthumously as *The History of the Four Last Years of the Queen* (1758), which Swift initially hoped to complete and publish by the spring of 1713 but which fell victim to internal political dissension. The cited 'employment' was the post of Historiographer Royal, which fell vacant in 1713 upon the death of Sir Thomas Rhymer. Swift's comment that he 'disdained to accept' the post is misleading—he was never offered it. The person without 'steddiness or sincerity' was the Duke of Shrewsbury (BD), Lord Chamberlain at the time.

5. *a discourse . . . from England:* This is *A Proposal for the Universal Use of Irish Manufacture.*

6. *a person in great office here . . . law:* The three figures referred to in this passage are: Lord Chancellor Midleton, Chief Justice Whitshed and the printer Edward Waters (all in BD).

7. *the Duke of G—ft–n . . . noli prosequi:* For the Duke of Grafton, see BD. The Latin phrase, correctly *nolle prosequi* ('to be unwilling to pursue'), signifies a formal stop to further legal proceedings; it was obtained in August 1721 through the intercession of Swift's old acquaintance (and Grafton's stepfather) Sir Thomas Hanmer.

8. *how ill a taste ... introduced:* Things Swift blamed for the degenerate state of wit and morals in contemporary society. '*South-sea*' refers both to the Company (G) and to the 'Bubble' of 1720; by 'Party' is meant the extreme partisanship growing out of the conflict between Whigs and Tories. Swift's dim view of (imported) opera is expressed in *Intelligencer, No. III*; he was also critical of masquerades (G).

9. *a Dedication upon Dedications ... read:* A piece purportedly written by 'a Sparkish Pamphleteer of Button's Coffee-House' (a noted Whig gathering place) and maliciously attributed to Swift.

10. *in favour of Mr. Addison ... a remembrancer:* The writers named here (BD) were all Whigs who had benefited from Swift's patronage and friendship with Oxford when he was working for the Tory ministry.

11. *Non obtusa ... urbe:* A note in F '46 contains the following translation of this passage from Virgil's *Aeneid* (1.567–68) by Swift's friend, William Dunkin: 'Our Hearts are not so cold, nor flames the Fire/Of *Sol* so different from the Race of Tyre.'

12. *tanquam in equo Trojano:* 'As if in the Trojan horse': Cicero, *Philippics*, 2.13.

13. *Cromwell's Soldiers ... principles:* Refers to the widespread takeover of Catholic-owned lands by Protestants allied to the Puritan leader, Oliver Cromwell (1599–1658), after his Irish campaign (1649–50).

14. *a Revolution-principle ... by us:* Swift's defence here of the Glorious Revolution (G) attests to his political orthodoxy, but he clearly departs from the Whigs' uncritical adulation of it. The 'very bad effects' include the increased power of Low Church adherents and the growth of a professional military class.

15. *Standing Armies ... Interest:* The King of Brobdingnag is 'amazed to hear [Gulliver] talk of a mercenary standing Army in the Midst of Peace, and among a free People' (GT, Book IV); see also *Examiner, No. 20*. The 'artificial Necessities' recall the Whigs' pretexts for continuing the War of the Spanish Succession.

16. *if Parliaments met once a year:* By the time of this writing the interval between parliamentary elections had been extended to seven years; see n. 14 to *A Letter to a Young Gentleman*.

17. *the possessors of the soil ... kingdom:* A 'maxim' rendered somewhat ironic by Swift's growing perception of the greed and corruptness of the landed interest in Ireland; see *Use of Irish Manufacture*, n. 1.

18. *suspending any Law ... see it repeated:* Refers to the six-month

suspension of the Habeas Corpus Act (1679) in response to the Jacobite Rebellion of 1715.

19. *whole Tribe of Informers . . . plague mankind:* The chief target of Swift's sermon *On False Witness*.

Swift to Esther Vanhomrigh

First published 1766. This letter, dated 5 July 1721, is one of just over two dozen extant letters from Swift to Vanhomrigh, whom he first met, probably in late 1707, while the two were living in London, and who later followed him to Dublin, settling in nearby Celbridge. Their initial relationship was playful and flirtatious, possibly sexual, and continued after their removal to Ireland, but Vanhomrigh's increasingly passionate feelings and emotional demands alienated Swift, causing embarrassment and recriminations. Swift responded by adopting a range of tones and attitudes. This letter combines avuncular concern with a form of gallantry designed to cool rather than encourage Vanhomrigh's ardour. Copy-text: BL autograph copy.

1. *the Disposition I found you in . . . better:* Refers to Vanhomrigh's bereavement following the death of her sister, Mary (Swift's 'Molkin'), in February.

2. *Cad— . . . Imaginations:* 'Cad—' is short for 'Cadenus', the name Swift uses in his poem *Cadenus and Vanessa* (1713), which portrays 'Vanessa' as a romantic who, having become enamoured of Cadenus, 'fancies Musick in his Tongue,/Nor further looks, but thinks him young' (Swift was in his mid-forties at the time).

3. *your Law Affairs:* An allusion to the complications surrounding her father's estate, which resulted in a lengthy lawsuit against its executor in Ireland about which Vanhomrigh often solicited Swift's advice.

4. *an Irish Stage-Coach:* 'It was probably of most primitive construction. The allusion is the earliest which I know to the use in Ireland of a public conveyance by a man of Swift's rank' (note by Ball).

5. *deep employd . . . Concern:* Swift was writing this letter from Gaulstown House, Co. Meath, the country seat of Baron Robert Rochfort; his poem 'The Journal' offers a lively account of his 'employments' there.

6. *mais soyez assureè . . . par votre amie que vous:* 'But be assured that there has never been anyone in the world so loved, honoured, esteemed, [and] adored by your friend as you' (French). Swift's feminine '*amie*' should actually be '*ami*'.

7.   *I drank no Coffee . . . judge:* It has been speculated that the many
      references to 'coffee-drinking' in Swift's letters to Vanhomrigh
      have a sexual connotation. Late in their friendship he observed,
      'The best Maxim I know in this life is, to drink your Coffee when
      you can, and when you cannot, to be easy without it.'

The Last Speech and Dying Words of Ebenezor Elliston

First published 1722. Written on the occasion of the execution of
one Ebenezor Elliston on 2 May 1722, this broadside parodies the
confession and repentance speeches of criminals about to be hanged,
and sold on the day of execution. According to an introductory note
in *F '35*, 'About the time that this Speech was written, the Town
[Dublin] was much pestered with Street-Robbers; who, in a barbarous
Manner would seize on Gentlemen, and take them into remote
Corners, and after they had robbed them, would leave them bound
and gagged. It is remarkable, that this Speech had so good an Effect,
that there have been very few Robberies of that kind committed since.'
Swift was fascinated by the public and popular rituals connected with
crime and punishment, relishing the satiric possibilities they offered;
see *An Account of the Execution of William Wood* and *Intelligencer,
No. III*; also his poems 'Clever Tom Clinch going to be hanged' (1726)
and 'The Yahoo's Overthrow' (1734).

1.   *wonderfully came to Life . . . Way:* Swift may be thinking here
      of a hoax he and some friends perpetrated on the eve of All
      Fools' Day, 1713, following the execution of one Richard Noble,
      in which they circulated a story that Noble 'was but half-hanged,
      and was brought to life by His Friends . . .' (Davis, 4: 259–60).
2.   *betray one another . . . well paid:* Refers to the group of pro-
      fessional informers known as 'thief-takers', the most famous of
      whom was Jonathan Wild. In John Gay's *The Beggar's Opera*,
      the character Peachum, loosely modelled on Wild, claims that
      'like great statesmen, we encourage those who betray their
      friends'.
3.   *go snacks:* Share and share alike.

The Drapier's Letters

First published 1724. Swift wrote *The Drapier's Letters* (seven in all)
as a contribution to the widespread resistance in Ireland to the patent
obtained by the Englishman William Wood, in the summer of 1722,

for the minting of Irish half-pence, to the value of £100,800 over a period of fourteen years. Though intended as a solution to a serious problem—the shortage of specie in Ireland—Wood's patent immediately provoked opposition because of the excessive amount of coinage it authorized, the absence of safeguards to ensure the coin's value, the belief that Wood obtained the patent through government corruption and the growing anger at England's treatment of Ireland as a colony of inferiors. While the resistance to the half-pence was already well under way when Swift started writing this series of pamphlets in February 1724, *The Drapier's Letters* rapidly became a focal point and lightning rod for the controversy, with the humble tradesman 'M. B. Drapier' (possibly for 'Marcus Brutus') fomenting popular resistance while provoking the wrath of the authorities. The eventual defeat of the patent ensured Swift's status as 'Hibernian Patriot'. Copy-text: *F '35* but with title from John Harding's first printing (1724).

Letter I. To the Shop-keepers, Tradesmen, Farmers, and Common-People of Ireland

1. *ordered the Printer . . . lowest Rate:* Swift himself bore the printer's costs in order to keep the price of the pamphlet low—it was sold in quantities of three dozen for two shillings. Two thousand copies were distributed throughout Ireland in March 1724.

2. *A little Book . . . FOUND HIM GUILTY:* Refers to Swift's *A Proposal for the Universal Use of Irish Manufacture*; the 'Poor Printer' was Edward Waters (*BD*).

3. *having been many Years . . . did not succeed:* Since Tudor times, the minting of coins for Ireland was handled via patents granted to private individuals in England, often for a handsome consideration. Such a patent was granted by Charles II in 1680 and wound up in the hands of one Colonel Roger Moore, who flooded Ireland with copper half-pence, causing their devaluation. His application for renewal of the patent was denied in 1705, and no further coinage for Ireland was struck until Wood obtained the patent in 1722.

4. *did not oblige any one . . . unless they pleased:* The patent explicitly stated that Wood's half-pence was 'to pass and be received as current money by such as shall be willing to receive the same'.

5. *of such Base Metal . . . real Value:* Repudiates Sir Isaac Newton's favorable assessment of the half-pence, as Comptroller of the Mint. In *Letter III*, the Drapier says he personally witnessed the

weighing of 'a large Quantity' of the half-pence, 'which were of four different Kinds, three of them considerably under Weight'.

6. *where to give Money . . . FAIR STORY:* Refers to Wood's payment of £10,000 to George I's mistress, the Duchess of Kendal (Duchess of Munster in the Irish peerage), to acquire the patent given her by the King.

7. *The KING was deceived in his Grant . . . all Reigns:* A concept in English common law based on the presumption that the king can do no wrong, so if bad decisions are made it is his agents who are to blame.

8. *several smart Votes . . . together:* 'Humble Addresses' to the King were made by both Houses of the Irish Parliament, accusing Wood of 'Fraud and Deceit' and petitioning the Crown for relief from his patent's 'Fatal Effects'. Wood responded with arrogant and accusatory statements in several London newspapers.

9. *Bere:* 'A sort of Barley in Ireland' (note in *F '35*).

10. *in his House for Stowage:* Refers to the grand Palladian mansion, Castletown, in Celbridge, Co. Kildare, that the Italian architect, Alessandro Galilei, designed for William Conolly (*BD*).

11. *the Brass Money in King James's Time:* The base coinage that James II struck to pay his troops during his Irish campaign; known as 'gun-money' because much of it was made from melted-down cannons.

12. *run all into Sheep . . . as are necessary:* The growing practice of using agricultural land to pasture sheep instead of to cultivate crops was repeatedly condemned by Swift; see n. 1 to *Use of Irish Manufacture.*

13. *Pebble-stones . . . Coin:* Perhaps a glance at the American colonies, where items such as tobacco and shells were used as currency; a decade earlier, North Carolina had declared seventeen kinds of items legal tender.

14. *A Famous Law-Book called the Mirrour of Justice:* A compilation of common-law cases by Andrew Horne, Chamberlain of London during the reign of Edward I (1272–1307).

15. *as my Lord Coke says . . . Parliament:* Sir Edward Coke (1552–1634) was a noted jurist who defended the common law and the rights of individuals against abuses of the royal prerogative. Part II of his four-part compendium *Institutes of the Laws of England* (1628–42) is the source of Swift's quotations here.

16. *gives the King all Mines . . . other Metals:* A pointed reference to Wood's extensive holdings in copper and iron mines throughout England.

17. *Davis's Reports . . . Tyrone's Rebellion:* A collection of legal writings by Sir John Davies (1569–1626), Attorney General for Ireland, published in 1615 . . . An insurrection begun in 1594 against English rule in Ireland, led by Hugh O'Neill, 3rd Earl of Tyrone, in alliance with Philip III of Spain; the Hiberno-Spanish forces were defeated at the climactic battle at Kinsale (1601).

18. *the accursed Thing . . . forbidden to touch:* Joshua 6: 18.

19. *a Man who told the King . . . Experiment:* An example of the proverbial cruelty of the Sicilian tyrant Phalaris (*c.* 570–*c.* 554 BCE), who roasted his enemies in a brazen bull and inflicted the same punishment on the Athenian who first presented the bull to him; appears as an Ancient in *The Battel of the Books*.

Letter IV. To the Whole People of Ireland

This *Letter* was published on 22 October to coincide with the arrival in Ireland of the new Lord-Lieutenant, John Carteret. Broadening the issue of Wood's half-pence into a highly provocative challenge to British rule in Ireland, the *Letter* was deemed seditious, prompting a government prosecution against Swift's printer, John Harding, and the offer of a £300 reward for the discovery of its author—neither of which offensive against the Drapier proved successful. Reportedly the common people united behind Swift with the cry, 'Shall Jonathan die, who hath wrought this great salvation in Israel? God forbid: as the Lord liveth, there shall not one hair of his head fall to the ground . . .' (1 Samuel 14: 45).

1. *Having already written . . . at an End:* In addition to *To the Shop-Keepers*, Swift wrote *A Letter to Mr. Harding, the Printer*, published in early August, and *Some Observations upon a Paper*, addressed 'To the Nobility and Gentry of the Kingdom of Ireland', which appeared in print a month later.

2. *in the Phrase of the Report, legal and obligatory:* The official report issued by the Committee of the English Privy Council on 6 August 1724, which dismissed the complaints made about Wood's patent.

3. *When Esau came fainting . . . a Mess of Pottage:* Genesis 25: 29–34.

4. *that Word Prerogative is:* The nature and scope of royal power, or 'prerogative', was a hotly contested issue in the late seventeenth century, the Tories affirming strong support for the

prerogative while the Whigs embraced parliamentary privilege. Despite Swift's Tory leanings, the Drapier's stance is more compatible with a Whig view of limited monarchy, as espoused in Locke's *Second Treatise of Government* (1690).

5. *sending base Money hither . . . Exchange:* This action was precipitated by the need to pay the army during Tyrone's Rebellion (see n. 17 to *Drapier's Letter I*).

6. *Opinion of the great Lord Bacon . . . Prerogative:* Refers to the belief espoused by Francis Bacon (1561–1626), statesman and essayist, that nature and political policy are governed by a parallel set of rules.

7. *by a new Summons . . . after his arrival:* Parliament was not in fact reconvened until almost a year later, by which time Wood's patent had been surrendered.

8. *well known to whose Share they must fall:* That is, to Englishmen; hence the native-born Anglo-Irish cannot be bought off with promises of career advancement.

9. *All considerable Offices for Life . . . by Inheritance:* Lucrative sinecures in Ireland, perpetuated through the right of succession to a vacated office or at the discretion of the Crown. The passage seems to be conflating George Dodington, who had died four years earlier, with his nephew George Bubb (later Dodington), who inherited his uncle's rich Irish estates. For the figures mentioned here, see *BD*.

10. *Mr. Addison . . . Use:* Refers to the relatively minor post given Addison when he came to Ireland as secretary to Lord-Lieutenant Wharton (1709); Bermingham's Tower was where the records were kept in Dublin Castle.

11. *a Favourite Secretary . . . Master of the Revels:* 'Mr. Hopkins, Secretary to the Duke of Grafton' (note in *F '35*). The 'Master of the Revels' was a person appointed to organize entertainments in the Royal Household or the Inns of Court.

12. *This I speak . . . receiving:* Cf. Swift's more extended tribute in *A Vindication of Lord Carteret* (1730).

13. *seasonable Report of some Invasion . . . Danger:* Reports of a Jacobite invasion were regularly derided by Swift as 'chimerical', 'formed and spread by the Race of small Politicians, in order to do a seasonable Jobb' (*The Presbyterians Plea of Merit*). 'Acts against Popery', cited earlier, were first passed in 1695.

14. *The Gentleman . . . lately made Primate:* Hugh Boulter (*BD*).

15. *a Statute made here . . . England:* This Act, passed in 1541, changed Henry's title from 'Lord' to 'King' of Ireland. This

paragraph repudiates the Declaratory Act (G), adapting arguments made by Molyneux.

16. *my Countrymen . . . Preston:* That is, soldiers from Ireland were among the loyalist troops led by General Carpenter that defeated the Jacobite forces in the town of Preston, thus ending the 1715 Jacobite Rebellion.

17. *I would venture . . . King of Ireland:* This assertion was the primary cause of the government's censure of the *Letter* as 'a Wicked and Malicious Pamphlet' tending 'to promote Sedition among the People'.

18. *done by the same Person . . . ram them down our Throats:* Refers to Prime Minister Walpole's reported threat against the Irish.

19. *a Pamphlet . . . printed in London:* The pamphlet was entitled, 'Some Farther Account of the Original Disputes in Ireland, about Farthings and Half-pence. In a Discourse with a Quaker of Dublin'.

20. *a sort of Savage Irish . . . as they do:* A common characterization by English (and Anglo-Irish) writers since the twelfth century, invoked to justify England's 'civilizing' project in Ireland.

21. *the same Infamous Coleby . . . Under-Clerk:* Drapier's Letter III identifies Coleby as a testifier on Wood's behalf before the Privy Council in London and observes that although he was officially acquitted of the charge of robbing the Treasury in Ireland, 'yet every Person in the Court believed him to be guilty'.

22. *the True English People of Ireland . . . whenever they are asked:* An attempt to refute the prevalent rumours that an Irish 'papist' plot was behind the anti-Wood agitation. Molyneux indicated that 'the People of Ireland' for whom he was speaking were to be understood as English and Protestant.

23. *in another News-Letter . . . Fire-Balls:* The threat that the Irish would be made to swallow the half-pence was reported in *The Dublin Intelligencer* and *The Flying Post* of 12 October 1724.

24. *a Great Man:* A derisive term regularly applied to Walpole in Opposition satire.

25. *Fifty thousand Operators . . . reasonable:* An insinuation that the army would have to be called out to force Wood's half-pence on the Irish, which underscores the image of the Irish as an enslaved people.

26. *as Remote from Thunder as we are from Jupiter:* 'Procul à Jove, procul à fulmine' (note in F '35). An oft-cited Latin adage suggesting that those closest to the seats of power are subject to the greatest miseries.

A *full and true Account of . . . the Execution of William Wood, Esquire, and Hard-ware-man*

First published 1724. This broadside was written to celebrate an act of popular resistance to Wood's half-pence: the hanging in effigy of William Wood by a Dublin mob in September 1724. Like the event itself, the broadside combines various elements of street theatre and protest, including charivari—a demotic ritual marked by a serenade of 'rough music' with kettles and pans—to express opposition to Wood's half-pence in a highly comical but politically pointed format. In its inclusion of a broad range of professions, trades and social ranks, this piece concretely enacts what *The Drapier's Letters* polemically assert: that all elements in Irish society are united as 'one man' against Wood's coinage scheme.

1. *his Brother-in-law's House here in Dublin:* The residence of John Molyneux, a Dublin tradesman, to whom Wood addressed several self-incriminating letters in 1723.
2. *P—l—t Man:* Member of Parliament.
3. *cut a Caper three Story high:* Dance or leap in a frolicsome way; also playing on the phrase 'to cut a caper on nothing', meaning 'to be hanged'.
4. *sit in his Skirts:* Insult him or seek occasion for quarrel.
5. *pink his Doublet:* Pierce; hit; 'pepper'; 'dress'; plays upon the idea of ornamenting a piece of material by cutting holes or letters in it, or of puncturing the skin as an adornment.
6. *make his A— make Buttons:* 'Buttons' denoted the dung of sheep or other animals; the idea of excreting 'buttons' came to signify 'being in great terror' (see the 1702 example in *OED*); akin to the US slang, to 'shit bricks'. Perhaps also punning on the word 'button' as a type of anything of very small value (*OED*).
7. *make him set up his Pipes:* Make him desist from acting or speaking; make him 'shut up'.
8. *rub him down:* Can mean either to search a prisoner or—especially appropriate for an 'ostler'—to clean a horse; also punningly refers to the act of smoothing or grinding down (as a piece of wood).
9. *kick him to Half-Crowns:* Dun him for money; also punning on 'kick' as a term for a sixpence.
10. *have a Rubber with him:* Both play the deciding game (as in a set of bowls) and quarrel with him.
11. *water his Plants:* Urinate.

12. *pull in his Horns:* Repress his spirits; lower his pretensions.

13. *nor asking him Pardon:* It was customary for hangmen to ask the pardon of capital offenders whom they were about to execute, and for the latter to give them money as a sign that such pardon was granted.

14. *His dying SPEECH ... did not deny it:* See Swift's parody of this genre in *The Last Speech and Dying Words of Ebenezor Elliston.*

Swift to Thomas Sheridan

First published 1745. In this letter of 11 Sept. 1725, Swift is responding to the news that Sheridan (*BD*), having obtained the church living of Rincurran (Co. Cork) from Lord Carteret, unwittingly sabotaged his hopes for career preferment by preaching a sermon on 1 August, the anniversary of the accession of George I, on the text, 'Sufficient unto the day is the evil thereof', which was interpreted as a Jacobite aspersion by a zealous Whig in the audience, Richard Tighe, who reported the incident to government officials. Copy-text: *F '46.*

1. *you are too young ... the Nature of Man:* Sheridan was thirty-eight at the time (twenty years Swift's junior).

2. *quoad magis & minus:* 'More or less' (Latin).

3. *as Don Quixote said to Sancho ... hanged:* See Cervantes, *Don Quixote*, Pt. I, Bk. III, sect. xi.

4. *my Description of Yahooes more resembling:* Refers to Part IV of *GT*. Since the work had not yet been published, this comment suggests that Sheridan might have read some of it in manuscript.

5. *cum uxore neque leni neque commoda:* 'With a wife neither gentle nor suitable' (Latin). Swift's highly critical view of Mrs Sheridan appears in a number of his letters and in *A Character of Dr. Sheridan* (1738).

6. *change the Apostle's Expression ... whatever State, &c.:* Refers to St Paul's statement, 'for I have learned, in whatever state I am, in *this* to be content'; see Philippians 4: 11.

7. *si mihi credis:* 'If you trust me' (Latin).

8. *You say nothing ... but generals:* One result of Sheridan's indiscretion was that he was removed from the official list of Carteret's chaplains; but Swift doubted Carteret was responsible for such a 'mean' action.

9. *the Castle ... Balaguer:* Dublin Castle, seat of the viceregal court. To 'keep fast' is to become firmly attached to. Balaguer was

'Private Secretary to his Excellency the Lord *Carteret*, Lord Lieutenant of *Ireland*' (note in *F '46*).

Swift to Alexander Pope

First published 1741. This is one of the best-known of Swift's letters because of its references (both direct and indirect) to *Gulliver's Travels*, which include remarks about his satiric aim as well as his views on human nature. The letter, dated 29 Sept. 1725, was written during the final days of Swift's extended stay at Quilca, Thomas Sheridan's residence in Co. Cavan, as he was putting the final touches on the manuscript of *GT*. Copy-text: *F '46*, collated with later editions that restore passages (based on a Harleian transcript) originally omitted by Pope; these restored passages are indicated by brackets.

1. *He treated you ... I recommended him:* James Stopford (*BD*) had stopped in London on the first leg of his Continental travels, armed with a letter of introduction from Swift which he was supposed to (but never did) present to Pope at Twickenham. A similar situation had occurred earlier with Carteret.
2. *those dominions where I govern:* The Liberty of St Patrick's, a five-acre area surrounding the cathedral, under Swift's jurisdiction; part of a larger area known collectively as 'the Liberties', which included two other ecclesiastical 'liberties' (those of Christchurch and St Sepulchre's) as well as several 'liberties' under the aegis of the Earl of Meath. All of these were exempt from city jurisdiction. According to Letitia Pilkington's *Memoirs* (1748–54), Swift termed himself 'absolute monarch in the *Liberties*, and King of the Mob'.
3. *when a Printer ... ears:* Swift is recalling the earlier fate of his printers, Waters and Harding, imprisoned by the authorities for printing his tracts. In the event, the English publisher of *GT*, Benjamin Motte, made various emendations to Swift's manuscript in order to avoid any risk to his own ears. See n. 5 to Swift's letter to Charles Ford (4 April 1720)
4. *to vex the world, rather than divert it:* Swift is responding here to Pope's previously expressed hope that 'two or three of us may yet be gather'd together ... to divert ourselves, and the world too if it pleases'.
5. *I would be the most indefatigable writer ... without reading:* That is, it would be obvious that Swift was an indefatigable writer even if Pope didn't actually read his work.

6. *done with Translations ... time:* Pope had written to Swift: 'I
    mean no more Translations, but something domestic, fit for my
    own country, and for my own time.' The first three volumes of
    his translation of the *Odyssey* had appeared in the preceding
    April, with the remaining two slated to appear one year later.
    He had earlier published a translation of the *Iliad* (1715-20).

7. *Animale rationale ... rationis capax:* '[Man as] a rational animal
    ... [Man as] an animal capable of reason' (Latin).

8. *not in Timon's manner:* Refers to the fifth-century BCE Greek
    misanthrope Timon, the subject of a famous dialogue by Lucian
    (*c.* 120-*c.* 180 CE) and of Shakespeare's play, *Timon of Athens*
    (*c.* 1607).

9. *other hands ... drudgery:* William Broome (1689-1745) and
    Elijah Fenton (1683-1730), who assisted Pope with the Homeric
    translations.

10. *your great atchievements ... Ars Poetica:* Refers to Pope's
    ambitious landscaping projects in Twickenham, which included
    a famous grotto connecting his five-acre garden alongside the
    Thames and his residence across the road. *Ars Poetica*, 'The Art
    of Poetry', aka 'To the Pisos', is an epistle by Horace, invoked
    here for its association with *ut pictura poesis* (the parallel
    between the visual and verbal arts).

11. *The Lady whom you describe ... never hear me:* Refers to Henri-
    etta Howard, later Countess of Suffolk (*BD*), and her offer to
    help Swift via her Court connections.

12. *Dr. Arbuthnot's illness:* Pope had written that Arbuthnot 'is at
    this time ill of a very dangerous distemper, an imposthume in the
    bowels'; he survived this attack and lived for another decade.

13. *a passage in Bede ... year:* *Ecclesiastical History of the English
    People*, 3.3, by the Venerable Bede (*c.* 673-735).

14. *although not a Catholick ... as ever I knew:* Glances at the fact
    that Pope himself was Catholic.

15. *our friend Gay ... a Lord Lieutenant:* One of numerous refer-
    ences throughout Swift's writings to John Gay's difficulties in
    obtaining suitable preferment at Court. The Lord-Lieutenant is
    John Carteret (*BD*).

16. *Philips ... and others:* Refers to the verses that Ambrose Philips
    wrote to Lord Carteret's daughter, Georgiana, which began, 'Little
    charm of placid mien,/Miniature of beauty's queen,/Numbering
    years, a scanty nine,/Stealing hearts without design ...'; famously
    parodied by Henry Carey in 'Namby Pamby'.

17. *I have an ill name ... subscribe it:* Swift's reluctance to sign his

name to the letter was based on earlier confiscations of his mail
by the postal authorities, which he often complained of to corre-
spondents.

Holyhead Journal, 1727

First published 1882. Written in September 1727 in Holyhead, a port
town in Anglesey, Wales, from which boats regularly crossed the Irish
Sea, this journal records Swift's deep ambivalence about Ireland, as
well as his mounting frustrations while impatiently awaiting passage
to Dublin, where his 'dearest friend' Esther Johnson lay gravely ill (she
would be dead in four months). Swift had been in the London area
visiting Pope during the preceding months. Copy-text: *Forster* autograph copy.

1. *notice to posterity . . . now in being:* A rather ironic 'notice' given
    Swift's well-known penchant for satirizing individuals by name;
    a similar claim is made by Swift's eulogizer in *Verses on the
    Death of Dr Swift* (written 1731).
2. *heaven forgive Mr. Pope . . . Satyrs:* Elsewhere Swift complains
    of his friend's opposite tendency toward obscurity and vagueness,
    urging that he replace his asterisks in *The Dunciad* with 'some
    real names of real Dunces'. Ducklane and Grub Street were areas
    in London associated with bookselling and hack writing.
3. *Hook's Tomb . . . Inscription:* The Hooks family oversaw the
    government of the Castle of Conwy in the seventeenth century;
    an epitaph in the town's church confirms the almost-unbelievable
    prolificness of William Hooks and his son Nicholas, as recorded
    here. 'Nota bene' is Latin for 'Note well'.
4. *A.Bp Williams Life . . . [Hospes . . . celeberrimus]:* John Williams
    (1582–1650), Archbishop of York and a native of Conwy; during
    the English Civil War he initially held Conwy for the King but
    later switched sides. The Latin inscription reads: 'Visitor, read
    and reread what you would not expect in this obscure chapel.
    Here lies the most renowned of all leaders.'
5. *Wat Owen Tudor's Tomb at Penmany:* Owen Tudor (*c.* 1400–
    61) was an Anglesey landowner executed by the Yorkists during
    the War of the Roses and buried near the Welsh Tudors' ancestral
    home in Penmynydd; he was the grandfather of Henry Tudor,
    who became Henry VII in 1485.
6. *Watt's Horse . . . limp after us:* Watt (also spelled 'Wat') was the
    name of Swift's servant.

7. *Marechall Tallard . . . garden:* Camille, comte de Tallard (1652–1728) was a French general captured by Marlborough at the Battle of Blenheim (1704); he lived as a pampered prisoner in Nottingham until 1712.

8. *my giddyness . . . my hearing continues:* Suffering greatly from his Ménière's disease during the preceding weeks, Swift wrote to Sheridan on 12 August that 'I am now Deafer than ever you knew me.'

9. *would ramp on my shoulders:* Can mean either to climb over carelessly or to trample in triumph—perhaps both are implied here.

10. *Forsan et haec olim:* 'Perhaps to remember this will one day aid you' (Latin).

11. *scum [?]:* Swift's handwriting is hard to read here, though the word looks less like Davis's 'sour' than 'scum', which here would signify a film or layer of floating matter on the surface of the wine.

12. *I did not like . . . his Plays:* A glance at the reputed lewdness of the plays of Wycherley (*BD*), which would have made references to them highly unsuitable for a sermon. A further irony (unremarked here) is that the deliverer of the sermon is Bolingbroke, known for his deistic views.

13. *monstrous mountain . . . town:* Holyhead Mountain is the highest point in Anglesey. Ptolemy was a second-century CE astronomer and geographer from Alexandria; in his time Wales was under Roman control.

14. *too much of the Longitude . . . deceived himself:* The Longitude Act of 1714 offered a huge bounty to anyone who discovered a method for determining the longitude, encouraging a slew of crackpot 'solutions'. The projector who 'cut his own throat' was Swift's Irish friend Joseph Beaumont (*BD*); the 'cheat' may be referring to William Whiston (see *BD*, and *A Modest Defence of Punning*, n. 10).

15. *a Slave in Ireld:* In 'Holyhead. Sept. 25, 1727' Swift asserts that he would rather 'go in freedom to [his] grave' in Wales 'Than Rule yon Isle and be a Slave'; and he opens his poem 'Ireland' with the line, 'Remove me from this land of slaves'. Both poems were written in Holyhead at the same time as the *Journal*.

16. *The Yatcht . . . together:* Refers to the government packet, or 'yacht', used primarily to transport the Lord-Lieutenant and his entourage between Ireland and England.

17. *T—:* Turd.

On the Death of Mrs. Johnson, [Stella]

First published 1765. Esther Johnson, Swift's intimate friend for over a quarter-century, died in her lodgings near the Deanery on 28 January 1728, at the age of forty-seven. In prayers composed during her final illness several months earlier, Swift anticipated the great loss her death would mean for him: 'pity us the mournful Friends of thy distressed Servant, who sink under the Weight of her present Condition, and the Fear of losing the most valuable of our Friends'. In earlier years Swift had recorded his friendship with Johnson in works such as *JS* and a series of birthday verses to her. Copy-text: *DS '65*.

1.   *Her father . . . her birth:* Edward Johnson, a merchant and steward to William Temple, is thought to have died in Holland at a young age. As 'a younger brother of a good [English] family', he bears similarities to Swift's own father as described in Swift's fragment, 'The Family of Swift'. Esther Johnson's mother, Bridget (d. 1745), served for many years as waiting-woman to Temple's sister, Lady Giffard.
2.   *I knew her . . . her life:* Swift first met Johnson in 1689, upon his arrival at Moor Park in Surrey to work for Temple; she was actually eight, not six, at the time.
3.   *another lady of more advanced years:* Temple's cousin, Rebecca Dingley (*BD*).
4.   *the death of a person . . . some dependance:* Temple, who died on 27 January 1699.
5.   *to draw what money . . . funds:* Johnson's 'fortune' included a lease of lands in Co. Wicklow, Ireland, worth £1,000, bequeathed to her by Temple. Once she settled in Dublin, Swift added £50 a year to her support.
6.   *in the year 170– :* Probably in the summer of 1701.
7.   *For some years past . . . despaired of:* Johnson's failing health was in evidence for at least eight years prior to her death. Swift's poem 'To Stella, Visiting me in my Sickness' (1720) extols Johnson's selflessness in devoting herself to his needs 'though by Heaven's severe Decree/She suffers hourly more than me'.
8.   *Bon Mots:* 'Bons mots', literally 'good words' (French); witticisms. *Bons Mots de Stella* was first published in 1745.
9.   *Platonic and Epicurean philosophy . . . defects of the latter:* The materialist philosophy of Epicurus (*c.* 341–270 BCE) posits the pursuit of pleasure and avoidance of pain as life's principal goals

and assumes the gods' indifference (hence irrelevance) to human affairs.

10. *all the errors of Hobbes . . . religion:* The materialist philosophy and absolutist political beliefs of Thomas Hobbes (1588–1679), author of *Leviathan* (1651), which argues for submission to a centralized authority, and *De Cive* (1642), which advocates the subordination of the Church to state power.

11. *Dr. Stephens's Hospital:* Richard Steevens (1653–1710), a wealthy Dublin physician, bequeathed his fortune to building a hospital, completed in 1733, of which Swift was an early governor. Johnson's will directed that her fortune be used to provide the stipend for a chaplain for Steevens' Hospital after the death of her immediate heirs, her mother and sister.

A Short View of the State of Ireland

First published 1728. A devastating exposé of Ireland's wretched conditions, this tract (as Ferguson suggests) may have been intended as a direct response to John Browne's 'Seasonable Remarks on Trade', published several weeks earlier, which presented Ireland as a flourishing country capable of enriching England through its own wealth. The pamphlet fell victim to censorship in England when part of it was reprinted in the 20 April issue of the Opposition newspaper, *Mist's Weekly Journal*.

1. *I am not provoked . . . whole Island:* A statement to be read mainly for rhetorical effect since Swift, as Dean of St Patrick's, enjoyed an income dependent upon rents obtained from the leasing of church lands; see Landa, pp. 96–111.

2. *by being governed . . . not a free People:* An idea derived from Locke's *Second Treatise of Government*; see *A Proposal for the Universal Use of Irish Manufacture* and *Drapier's Letter IV*.

3. *where the People . . . civilized Nations:* Refers to England's refusal to allow Ireland to coin its own money and invokes the memory of the Wood's half-pence affair four years earlier; see *The Drapier's Letters*.

4. *A Disposition . . . without:* See Swift's extended argument for this position in *Use of Irish Manufacture*.

5. *denied the Liberty . . . executed:* The Woollen Act of 1699 (see *Use of Irish Manufacture*) and the Navigation Acts (1663; 1671) mandated that European goods be imported into the colonies

only via English vessels sailing from English ports, and that goods from the colonies be sent only to English ports.

6. *its true uncontroverted Name:* That is, slavery.

7. *Whitshed's Ghost . . . perjuring himself to betray both:* Whitshed (*BD*) had died about seven months earlier. His judicial tyranny and corruption are recounted at length in *A Letter from Dr. Swift to Mr. Pope*. The Latin motto '*Libertas & natale Solum*', which means 'Liberty and my native country', was also mocked by Swift in verse: 'Libertas & natale Solum;/Fine Words; I wonder where you stole 'um' ('Whitshed's Motto on his Coach').

8. *forced to pay . . . our Properties:* Because the Declaratory Act declared the British Parliament to be the court of last resort for all Irish cases, thus forcing Irishmen to 'travel five Hundred Miles by Sea and Land, to another Kingdom, for Justice', incurring great expense to decide their claims (*Drapier's Letter VII*).

9. *the Fancy of Grazing . . . depopulating the Country:* See n. 1 to *Use of Irish Manufacture*.

10. *the Misfortune . . . Consideration:* Part of Swift's ongoing attack on Irish posts being given to Englishmen.

11. *the Inns of Court . . . both Universities:* The centres of legal training in London; attendance at them was required of all those planning to practise law in Ireland. The 'Universities' are Oxford and Cambridge.

12. *a Sort of Silk Plad . . . Indian:* That is, Irish poplin, so highly regarded that when Swift sent a piece of it to Henrietta Howard it was quickly appropriated by the Princess of Wales. Swift observed that 'our Workmen here are grown so expert, that in this kind of Stuff they are said to excel that which comes from the Indies'.

13. *the Thorn at Glassenbury . . . Midst of Winter:* Legend has it that Joseph of Arimathea fixed his staff in the ground at Glastonbury in Somerset (in south-west England) on Christmas Day, and it blossomed into a plant that reappears every year on the same day. Both Joseph of Arimathea and Glastonbury are closely associated with Arthurian legend and the quest for the Holy Grail.

14. *the worthy Commissioners . . . from England:* The Commissioners of the Revenue (*G*).

15. *Lapland, or Ysland:* Apt emblems of remoteness and isolation. Lapland was a vast area of nomadic peoples that included portions of Norway, Sweden and Finland. Iceland was then under the Crown of Denmark and ruled by a private trade monopoly in Copenhagen that prohibited all foreign trade.

16. *Nostrâ miserià magna es:* 'By our misery you are great': Cicero, *Letters to Atticus*, 2.19.3.

17. *The Rise of our Rents . . . Beggars:* Similarly, Swift portrays Lord Allen as 'draw[ing] his daily Food,/From his Tenants vital Blood' ('Traulus, The Second Part'); also see *A Modest Proposal*.

18. *sent away all our Silver . . . observed:* The habitual undervaluation of silver coins in Ireland encouraged bankers (and others) to convey large amounts of silver out of the country and into England, where they could exchange them for gold coins that would turn them a profit back in Ireland. Also, the exchange rate into shillings being different in Ireland and England, it was more profitable for businessmen in Ireland to deal in cash than credit, prompting them to demand hard currency for their goods, which was then often transported to England. See *Use of Irish Manufacture*, n. 16 and Woolley's headnote to *Short View of Ireland*.

19. *YE are Idle . . . Bricks without Straw:* Exodus 5: 17.

20. *an Hospital . . . Raiment:* Swift may have in mind here the Dublin Workhouse and Foundling Hospital (founded in 1702 and reconstituted solely as the latter in 1729), an institution of which he was a governor.

21. *a Man-pleaser:* A term resonating with scriptural contempt; see Ephesians 6: 5–7 and Galatians 1: 10.

The Intelligencer

First published 1728. A short-lived weekly periodical started by Swift and Thomas Sheridan in May 1728, *The Intelligencer* (i.e. 'newsgatherer' or 'spy') aimed 'to *Inform*, or *Divert*, or *Correct*, or *Vex* the Town' as well as to publicize 'every distinguished Action, either of *Justice, Prudence, Generosity, Charity, Friendship*, or *publick Spirit*, which comes well attested' to the editors (*No. 1*). Along with the two essays printed here, Swift's contributions to the periodical included a view of the bleak prospects facing gifted and independent-minded clergymen (*Nos. V* and *VII*) and an account of the dire economic situation in the north of Ireland (*No. XIX*).

The Intelligencer, Number III

In this essay, Swift offers a witty and spirited defence of John Gay's *The Beggar's Opera*, the sensation of the 1728 theatrical season which he himself helped to inspire with his idea of a 'Newgate Pastoral'. The play draws a parallel betwen high and low society, equating politicians with highwaymen to satirize the ministry of Sir Robert Walpole (*BD*). Countering criticisms of the play's immorality in glamorizing a life of crime, Swift's essay provides a justification for satire reminiscent of the 'Apology' to *A Tale of a Tub*, and may itself be viewed as a contribution to the Opposition campaign against Walpole.

1. *Ipse . . . unam:* 'He will go through all the roles, one man representing a multitude of characters': Manilius, *Astronomica*, 5.481.

2. *Humour . . . agreeable Species of it:* In 'To Mr. Delany' (1718) Swift distinguishes between humour, as a natural gift, and wit, as a cultivated skill rooted in 'Invention'.

3. *but I differ from him . . . Rabelais, Cervantes, and many others:* Swift is disagreeing with a passage in Temple's essay 'Of Poetry' (1690) which claims that the English have excelled 'by Force of a Vein Natural perhaps to our Country, and which with us is called Humour'. '*Le Theatre Italien*' is Evaristo Gherardi's 6-volume anthology of scenes based on the *commedia dell'arte* tradition, published in Paris in 1700. François Rabelais (d. 1553) was a French Renaissance humanist best known for his comic masterpiece, *Gargantua and Pantagruel* (1532–42), which uses the bawdy adventures of the titular two giants to satirize abuses in religion and learning. He was an important influence on Swift's bodily and scatological satire. Miguel de Cervantes (1547–1616) was the author of *Don Quixote*, an immensely popular work from its initial Spanish publication in 1604, and an important influence on eighteenth-century English satire.

4. *the very Owners . . . possess:* Cf. *Thoughts on Various Subjects* (1735): 'It is in Men as in Soils, where sometimes there is a Vein of Gold, which the Owner knows not of.'

5. *By what Disposition of the Mind . . . Juvenal:* Temple argued that the English form of stage humour could be explained by factors of soil and climate as well as 'the Ease of our Government, and the Liberty of Professing Opinions' (*Of Poetry*). The distinction between the mild-mannered, amiable Horace and the more vitriolic, 'lashing' Juvenal was a common one at the time; see Dryden's *Discourse Concerning the Original and Progress of Satire* (1693).

6. *although some Things . . . Satyr:* Cf. the 'Apology': 'Religion they tell us ought not to be ridiculed, and they tell us Truth, yet surely the Corruptions in it may; for we are taught by the tritest Maxim in the World, that Religion being the best of Things, its Corruptions are likely to be the worst.'

7. *to mend the World . . . highly commendable:* Swift announced that *GT* 'will wonderfully mend the World' in a letter to Charles Ford (14 Aug. 1725), upon completing the final draft.

8. *after Fourteen Years . . . a great Minister:* Refers to Gay's thwarted efforts to gain suitable preferment at Court. Queen Caroline's humiliating offer to him of the post of Gentleman-Usher to the infant Princess Louisa was derided by Swift in his poem, 'To Mr Gay'. The 'great Minister' is Walpole.

9. *no more to be suspected . . . Cæsar's Wife:* Refers to a proverb based on Caesar's having divorced Pompeia for the mere suspicion of being involved in an accusation against P. Clodius. The saying originated in Plutarch's *Life of Julius Caesar* (Apperson, *ODEP*).

10. *even in his Fables . . . Courtiers:* In 'The Courtier and Proteus' (1727), the rejected courtier declares that 'All courtiers are of reptile race' and demonstrate a Protean ability to 'Practise the frauds of ev'ry shape'. Prince William, younger son of King George II, had been made Duke of Cumberland a year earlier, at the age of four.

11. *even Ministers of State . . . have made:* It was widely reported that Walpole himself attended the play's first performance in London. Its Dublin run, according to Swift, was seen by the Lord-Lieutenant 'often'.

12. *a Court-Chaplain in* ENGLAND *. . . so prostitute a Divine:* 'Dr. Herring, *Chaplain to the Society at Lincoln's Inn*' (note in *F '35*); Thomas Herring (1693–1757), later Archbishop of Canterbury.

13. *Imperium in Imperio . . . Houses:* The Latin term signifies a government, power or sovereignty operating within a larger government, power or sovereignty—in this case, the band of highwaymen who form their own society (while mirroring the larger one) in *The Beggar's Opera.*

14. *that unnatural Taste . . . Italian Nonsense:* A recurring object of attack, focused especially on the opera introduced on the London stage *c.* 1700. In Pope's *Dunciad*, a 'Harlot form' with 'mincing step' is glossed as representing the 'genius of the *Italian* Opera; its affected airs, [and] its effeminate sounds'.

15. *an unnatural Vice . . . perfect Italians:* Refers to the raids on 'molly houses' in 1707, which resulted in the prosecution of a large group of alleged sodomites; another such crackdown occurred in 1726. Cf. the reference to 'a large *Pederastick* School' with '*Italian* Masters' in the Preface to *A Tale of a Tub.*

The Intelligencer, Number IX

In this essay, known in its own day as both 'The Foolish Methods of Education among the Nobility' and 'An Essay on Modern Education', Swift offers a forceful rebuttal to John Locke's highly influential treatise, *Some Thoughts Concerning Education* (1693)—especially its privileging of private tutors over a public-school education and its emphasis on the creation of a 'gentleman' rather than a man of virtue and learning.

1. *Postulatum . . . Scandalum Magnatum:* Postulate or proposition (Latin) . . . 'Slander of magnates' (medieval Latin); malicious speech concerning public figures, which constituted grounds for prosecution under a series of English libel laws dating back to the thirteenth century.

2. *New-men, with few Exceptions:* Those elevated to the peerage in recent years, viewed variously by Swift depending on the occasion. He strongly supported Queen Anne's creation of twelve new peers in 1711, which gave the Tories a majority in the House of Lords and paved the way for the Peace of Utrecht.

3. *the grand Rebellion:* The English Civil Wars of the mid-seventeenth century.

4. *the Marquis of Ormond, and the Earl of Southampton:* James Butler (1610–88), 1st Duke of Ormond, Commander-in-Chief under Charles I and Lord-Lieutenant of Ireland; and Thomas Wriothesley (1608–1667), 4th Earl of Southampton, adviser to Charles I and Lord High Treasurer under Charles II.

5. *those fanatick Times . . . that dissolute Reign:* The period of Puritan rule in England, followed by the Restoration of the monarchy. In *A Proposal for Correcting the English Tongue*, Swift laments 'that Licentiousness which entered with the *Restoration*; and [which] from infecting our Religion and Morals, fell to corrupt our Language'.

6. *Ashley-Cooper:* Locke's patron, Anthony Ashley-Cooper, 1st Earl of Shaftesbury (1621–83); he was a leader of the radical Whig faction that supported the Duke of Monmouth as Charles II's successor.

7. *Under King William . . . Secretaries of State:* The individuals named here were chosen to make a point about their social and educational backgrounds, and/or to highlight their status as younger sons, who had to study for a profession because the law of primogeniture designated the eldest son as the sole heir of his

father's estate. See *BD* (under 'Clarendon' for 'Hyde'; 'Halifax' for 'Montagu'; 'Marlborough' for 'Churchil') and Woolley, 124–26.

8. *as my Lord Bacon chargeth . . . the Means:* See Bacon's essay 'Of Empire' (1597).

9. *The current Opinion prevails . . . the whole Duty of a Gentleman:* Swift's summary of Locke's main arguments. The latter phrase is a mocking swipe at Locke's emphasis on 'good breeding' and 'a gentleman's calling' as the primary aims of education; it is also a play on the title, *The Whole Duty of Man* (1658), a popular manual of moral instruction attributed to Richard Allestree.

10. *those Worthies of the Army . . . Diversions:* After the Glorious Revolution military styles became models of emulation for civilian society; e.g. a 'campaign-coat' originally worn by soldiers became fashionable city attire. A popular wig was called a 'Ramillie' after the Battle of Ramillies (1706).

11. *D—n me, Doctor . . . D—n me, &c.:* Echoes the absurd dinner conversation of the Captain in Swift's poem 'The Grand Question Debated': ' "A *Scholard*, when just from his College broke loose,/ Can hardly tell how to cry *Bo* to a Goose;/Your *Noveds*, and *Blutraks*, and *Omurs* and Stuff,/By God they don't signify this Pinch of Snuff./To give a young Gentleman right Education,/The Army's the only good School in the Nation." ' For Swift's disdain of military jargon, see *Tatler, No. CCXXX.*

12. *White's Chocolate-House . . . Nobility:* White's was a notorious venue for high-stakes gambling on St James's Street.

13. *Le Sac . . . I taught:* 'The Author's Friends have heard him tell this Passage as from the Earl himself' (note in *F '35*). 'Le Sac' is probably a misprint for the popular French dancing-master 'Isaac' (*c.* 1640–1720), though Woolley notes a Mr Le Sac (or L'Sac) recorded as a theatre dancer in 1701 and 1710.

14. *His chief Solace . . . Bosom-Friend:* A direct rebuttal of Locke's claim that it is *public* schooling that will result in a gentleman's son's idling away his time playing games with his social inferiors.

15. *one young Lord in this Town . . . negligent:* 'The Author is supposed to mean the Lord Viscount* Montcassell, *of Ireland*' (note in *F '35*). Swift no doubt chose Edward Davys, 3rd Viscount Mountcashel (1711–36), as a model because he had been an exemplary pupil of his friend Thomas Sheridan.

16. *Stockings with Silver Clocks:* An embroidered article of clothing deemed a sign of high fashion—or, to critics, of affectation and foppery. *Spectator, No.* 319 shows 'Will Sprightly' congratulating

himself as a leader of fashion because he 'made a fair push for the Silver-clocked Stocking'.

17.   *my own Observation in one of those Universities:* Largely limited to several weeks in the summer of 1692, when Swift took his MA degree at Hart Hall, Oxford University.

18.   *that Money answereth all Things:* See Ecclesiastes 10: 19.

A Modest Proposal

First published 1729. Arguably the most famous and frequently cited satire in the English language, *A Modest Proposal* was written both as a response to Ireland's worsening economic conditions, which included a serious famine caused by crop failure during the preceding two years, and as a parody of the many irrelevant and ill-informed 'proposals' then in circulation about how to solve the problem—here put in the mouth of a 'projector' whose abstract statistical calculations satirically evoke those of Sir William Petty (1623–87), author of the *Political Anatomy of Ireland* (pub. 1691). Ironically subverting the racially stereotyped depiction of the native Irish as cannibals, perpetuated in English histories from the twelfth century onwards, Swift portrays a world in which the Irish are the devoured rather than the devourers, cannibalism (a recurring trope for the practices of landlords throughout Swift's works) functioning here as a comprehensive metaphor for the systematic 'consumption' of the powerless by the powerful, the poor by the wealthy—though aided by the complicity of the Irish themselves in their own victimization.

1.   *It is a melancholly Object . . . for an Alms:* Swift's sermon *Causes of the Wretched Condition of Ireland* opens with a similarly worded picture of the impoverished state of Dublin ('this great Town').

2.   *to fight for the Pretender . . . Barbadoes:* Irish emigrants included both Catholics recruited to fight in Europe for James Stuart (*BD*) and Protestants lured to the Americas by economic hardship at home and false promises of riches abroad. Elsewhere Swift bitterly noted that 'Men in the extremest Degree of Misery and Want, will naturally fly to the first Appearance of Relief, let it be ever so vain or visionary'.

3.   *that horrid Practice . . . inhuman Breast:* Infanticide was a growing social problem during this period; one of the stated aims of the Dublin Workhouse and Foundling Hospital, founded at the beginning of the eighteenth century, was to prevent

the 'Exposure, death, and actual murder of illegitimate children'.

4. *Number of Souls in Ireland . . . one Million and a half:* Arthur Dobbs, Surveyor-General of Ireland, suggested a figure of 2 million in 1730. Later historians have tended to view both figures as being on the low side.

5. *a principal Gentleman . . . Cavan:* No doubt a tongue-in-cheek reference to Thomas Sheridan (*BD*).

6. *a Fricasie, or Ragout:* Dishes of haute cuisine, stigmatized by association with France. In 'A Panegyrick on the Dean' (1730), Swift writes that Gluttony 'sent her Priests in Wooden Shoes/ From haughty *Gaul* to make Ragous./Instead of wholesome Bread and Cheese,/To dress their Soupes and Fricassyes'.

7. *we are told by a grave Author . . . Season:* See François Rabelais, *Pantagruel*, Book V, ch. xix.

8. *Butchers we may be assured . . . Pigs:* An ironic glance at the fact that the majority of butchers in Dublin—such as those of the Ormonde Market in the Liberties—were Catholic. That the militantly Protestant 'Liberty Boys' were known on occasion to hang their Catholic nemeses, the 'Ormonde Boys', on their own meathooks adds to the immediacy of the cannibalistic trope of this work.

9. *the famous Salmanaazor:* George Psalmanazar (?1679–1763), a Frenchman claiming to be a native Formosan, who published a spurious *Historical and Geographical Description of Formosa* in 1704.

10. *lessen the Number of Papists . . . Curate:* This view that Irish Catholics were the Protestants' 'most dangerous Enemies' was unequivocally rejected by Swift, who described them as having been 'put out of all visible Possibility of hurting us' (sermon, *On Brotherly Love*). The '*good Protestants*' were the Presbyterians who emigrated to America to avoid having to pay tithes to support the Established Church.

11. *liable to Distress . . . Money a Thing unknown:* Subject to forfeiture for payment of outstanding debts . . . The scarcity of money was due to the unfavourable exchange rate between England and Ireland and the latter's inability to mint its own money; see n. 18 to *A Short View of the State of Ireland*.

12. *other Expedients:* Proposals that Swift himself had often seriously urged before, to little or no avail.

13. *the Inhabitants of TOPINAMBOO:* The Tupinamba, a tribe of Indians indigenous to coastal Brazil; made known by Jean de Léry's popular *History of a Voyage to the Land of Brazil* (1578),

which described their ritual cannibalism but presented an
ambiguous picture of their supposedly barbaric nature.

14. *like the Jews ... City was taken:* Refers to the Jews' failure to
unite in their own defence during Emperor Titus' siege of Jerusalem in 70 CE, which resulted in the destruction of the Temple.

15. *putting a Spirit of Honesty ... to it:* A frequent complaint by Swift;
see *A Proposal for the Universal Use of Irish Manufacture*, n. 10.

16. *this Kind of Commodity ... without it:* Perhaps a sly glance at
England's use of Irish salt beef to feed its navy.

An Examination of Certain Abuses, Corruptions, and Enormities, in the City of Dublin

First published 1732. This piece, which appeared in London under its
alternative title, 'City Cries, Instrumental and Vocal', is distinctively
Swiftian in its use of popular satiric modes, fascination with street
language and aspects of 'low' life, scatological humour, frequent wordplay, and employment of mock-allegorical interpretation. The satirized speaker is a rabid Whig champion of the Glorious Revolution
and a hater of Tories, whom he automatically equates with Jacobites.
The atmosphere of political paranoia and persecution that this piece
at once reproduces and exposes is depicted more seriously in *A Letter
from Dr. Swift to Mr. Pope*.

1. *what the French call the Police ... complained of:* Dublin lacked
a professional police force at this time. Policing responsibilities
were localized, falling mainly to unpaid constables and a cadre
of (usually elderly) watchmen who obtained their jobs through
the charity of parishes. By contrast, policing activities in Paris
were far more centralized, overseen by a lieutenant of police with
jurisdiction over the entire capital.

2. *absit invidia:* 'Let ill will be absent' (Latin).

3. *certain Persons ... Necessaries of Life:* The depiction of city
'cryers', or wandering hawkers of goods, was a staple of the
period's broadsides and prints. Cf. Swift's verses on 'Women
who cry Apples' and his complaint in the *JS* of 'a restless dog
crying Cabbages and Savoys [who] plagues me every
morning...'

4. *a Sound wholly inarticulate ... so little Information:* Cf. *Spectator, No. 251*, on the London Criers' 'idle Accomplishment
which they all of them aim at, of Crying so as not to be
understood'.

5. *Sweet-hearts:* 'A Sort of Sugar-Cakes in the Shape of Hearts' (note in *F '35*).

6. *our Troops . . . foreign Service:* Refers to the many Irishmen who went abroad to join other national armies, such as the French or Spanish forces allied to the Pretender.

7. *Toupees . . . at present:* 'A new Name for a modern Periwig, and for its Owner; now in Fashion. Dec. 1, 1733' (note in *F '35*). Swift satirizes their impudence and foppishness in 'The Footmen's Petition' (1732).

8. *my Friend the Physician . . . Dissertation:* The minute inspection of excrement was a common medical practice of the day, though this physician would also fit in well with the scientists of the Academy of Lagado (*GT*) and calls to mind the speaker of *A Tale of a Tub*, continually promising future publications.

9. *a Crow, a Swan . . . Posture:* Refers to the many public houses in Dublin named after animals, including the White Hart, the Swan, the Bull's Head in Fishamble Street, and the Eagle Tavern, a likely satiric target because it appealed to men of fashion and was the meeting place for the staunchly Whig Hanover Club.

10. *The Rules of Hieroglyph . . . Punch:* The fixed or recognized systems of meaning according to which signs or emblems are interpreted . . . A beverage introduced into England from India in the seventeenth century.

11. *the Pretender's Wife . . . of German birth:* Princess Maria Clementina Sobieska (1702–35), granddaughter of John III, King of Poland, who married James Francis Edward Stuart in 1719.

12. *the Cock . . . Enemy:* The cock was a symbol of France from the fifteenth century onwards, based on a conflation of the two meanings of the Latin word 'gallus', as both a rooster and a Gaul.

13. *the Spaniard . . . the Indies to himself:* British merchants attempting to carry on trade with the Spanish American colonies were continually interfered with, at times openly attacked, by the Spanish coastguard.

14. *the Bear to be chained . . . Death:* Bear-baiting was a popular eighteenth-century entertainment in which dogs were set upon chained bears and encouraged to fight to the death.

15. *The chief Ingredients . . . Popish Countries:* Brandy was obtained through Ireland's clandestine trade with France; fruit was imported from Italy with the help of an Irish merchant who had settled in Naples.

16. *King William, of ever glorious and immortal Memory:* A cant phrase used by Whigs; frequently mocked by Swift.

17. *squeezed the Orange . . . to Death:* 'To squeeze an orange' means, figuratively, 'to take all that is profitable out of something'. The phrase was also a Jacobite toast during William's reign.

18. *Limus . . . liquescit, &c.:* '[As by the kindling of the self-same fire], Harder this clay, this wax the softer grows': Virgil, *Eclogue* 8.80.

19. *As I knock down . . . our Enemies:* See Livy, 1.24.

20. *to drink* CONFUSION *. . . Detractors:* An ironic reminder of a practice followed by *Whigs*, of 'drinking confusion' to their foes—and 'charged upon [them]' by Swift himself; see n. 10 to *Examiner, No. 20.*

21. *in the worst of Times:* '*A Cant-Word used by Whigs for the four last Years of Queen* Anne'*s Reign, during the Earl of* Oxford'*s Ministry; whose Character here is an exact Reverse in every Particular*' (note in *F '35*).

22. *De mortuis nil nisi bonum:* '[Speak] nothing but good of the dead' (Latin). Cited in *ODEP* as a proverb originating in Greek with Chilon's *Diogenes Laertes.*

23. *the Duke of Savoy . . . curious Savoys:* Victor Amadeus II (1666–1732), a Protestant ally of England in the War of the Spanish Succession. Swift reduces his name to a street-cry, in which a 'Savoy' is a cabbage (see n. 3, above).

24. *sell Flanders to France:* A common Whig accusation against the Tories for their peace initiatives toward France; also punning on Flanders lace, at times called simply 'Flanders'.

25. *universal Fisher of Men:* See Matthew 4: 18–19 and Mark 1: 16–17.

26. *some Popish Plot at the Bottom:* Evokes associations with the notorious Popish Plot contrived and 'exposed' in 1678 by Titus Oates, whose false testimony was used to 'prove' a conspiracy by English Catholics to murder Charles II and restore Catholicism as the state religion.

27. *Justice Peyton:* '*A famous Whig Justice in those Times*' (note in *F '35*).

28. *the famous Mr. Swan . . . in England:* Described as 'the famous Punnster' in *Spectator, No. 61* and as the 'honest Mr Swan' who makes better puns than Horace in Dryden's *Discourse Concerning . . . Satire.* He lost his fellowship at Cambridge because he refused to take the oath of allegiance to William and Mary.

29. *Sir Harry Dutton-Colt . . . 10th of June, 1701:* Sir Henry Dutton

Colt was a minor Whig politician, mentioned also in Letter V of *JS*. The Smyrna Coffee-House was a favourite meeting-place of the Scriblerians, on the north side of Pall Mall; during the reign of George I it became a Jacobite resort. June 10 was the birthday of the Old Pretender, marked by Jacobites with a variety of street and public-house celebrations.

30. *famous Dr. Wallis ... Times:* John Wallis (1616-1703), Savilian Professor of Geometry at Oxford and Royal Society founding member, decoded Royalist cyphers for the parliamentary side during the Civil War.

31. *latet anguis in Herba:* 'A snake lurks in the grass': Virgil, *Eclogue*, 3.93; also proverbial (*ODEP*).

32. *Government:* A final paragraph added here to the London edition claims that the frequent signs of 'King George the Second' insinuate that George is 'only the second King' while 'the Pretender is the first King'.

Swift to Sir Andrew Fountaine

First printed in 1910. This letter of 30 July 1733 to Swift's old London dining companion demonstrates the seriousness with which Swift took his role as patron and promoter of the careers of those he deemed worthy, and points to the presence of women writers in his literary circle, exemplified here by the Dublin-based poet Mary Barber (*BD*). Among the many qualities he found commendable in her was that 'she is ready to take Advice, and submit to have her Verses corrected, by those who are generally allow'd to be the best Judges'—not least among these, Swift himself. Williams notes that Fountaine did subscribe to Barber's *Poems*, but for one copy only. Copy-text: Pierpont Morgan autograph copy (MA 457).

1. *longo intervallo:* 'By a long distance' (Latin).

2. *to print her poetical works ... Success:* The volume, entitled *Poems on Several Occasions*, was printed in quarto in 1734 by Samuel Richardson, who was also a subscriber.

3. *your old friendship ... time and absence:* Since the days of their intimacy in London, Swift and Fountaine had drifted apart due both to physical separation and to Fountaine's growing ties to the Hanoverian court.

4. *My new Lord Pembroke ... Lord Herbert:* The reference is to Henry Herbert (1693-1750), son of the recently deceased Thomas Herbert, 8th Earl of Pembroke, with whom Swift had

been on friendly terms in London when he was still circulating primarily in Whig circles.

Swift to John Arbuthnot

First published 1854. This letter, addressed to Swift's old London friend Arbuthnot (*BD*) was left undated by Swift but was received and postmarked in London on 22 November 1734. The letter reveals Swift's obsessive concern with the minute details of his domestic economy, along with his penchant for exaggerating the dire state of his personal finances—in part as a way of dramatizing the disastrous consequences of England's 'oppressions'. The letter is particularly significant for the insight it provides into Swift's daily activities and routines in Dublin during the final decade of his life, which made him consider Ireland rather than England as 'home'. Copy-text: *Hunter Baillie* autograph copy.

1. *that blessed Queen your Mistress . . . all your Friends:* Refers to Arbuthnot's position as physician-in-ordinary to Queen Anne and his consequent influential connections at Court.
2. *ill account of your Health:* Arbuthnot had described being 'so reduced by a dropsy and an Asthma that I could neither sleep breath eat nor move'. He died on 27 Feb. 1735, from what was called an 'inflammation of his bowels'.
3. *the Bishop of Marseilles . . . still alive:* François Xavier de Belsunce (1671–1755) gained a near-legendary reputation during the great plague of 1720 in Marseilles by disregarding the danger to his own person in order to stay behind and care for the sick and dying; he appears in Pope's *Essay on Man* (IV.106–7).
4. *High-gate:* Arbuthnot's stay was actually in Hampstead, then a fashionable spa north of London proper.
5. *My L^d Bo——:* That is, Lord Bolingbroke, who at this time was still residing in England, at his country estate, Dawley Farm; within a year he would return to France.
6. *the two Deans . . . at their Peril:* Refers to the Deans of St Patrick's cathedral and of Christ Church cathedral, the latter of whom was then Charles Cobbe (1686–1765), also Bishop of Kildare.
7. *your Brother Robert . . . Paris:* Robert Arbuthnot (1669–1741) was a noted Jacobite who established a successful banking business in Paris and became the Old Pretender's agent there.

Directions to Servants

First published 1745. Published posthumously both in Dublin and London, this piece was put together over a lengthy period of time—according to the title page, 'above twenty-eight Years'. Although several of its sections seem more or less complete, others are little more than fragments. Faulkner viewed the *Directions* as a set of ironical instructions to help gentlemen 'preserve their Estates and Families from Ruin' as a result of 'the many Vices and Faults' of the servant class, but his view fails to take into account the complexity of Swift's attitude toward servants, at least one of whom—his own servant, Alexander McGee—he thought well enough of to commemorate with a tablet in St Patrick's cathedral. A rich oral tradition recounting stories about 'Paddy and the Dane' attests to Swift's semi-affectionate, bantering relationship with members of the servant class, who provided him with personae for several of his works. Copy-text: *F '45*.

Rules that Concern all Servants in General

1. *put your Master or Lady off their Mettle:* Daunt their courage.
2. *Barbados:* A common destination for those seeking employment abroad since the island's sugar plantations required a large supply of labour, both slave and indentured; see *A Modest Proposal*, n. 2.
3. *Some Nastiness . . . the Smell went off:* The contents of chamber pots were regularly emptied onto the streets of Dublin and London from the upper windows of houses.
4. *pressed for the Sea-service:* Forced to serve in the navy, often (especially during times of war) by being physically seized and carried off by a 'press-gang' acting under the authority of an officer.
5. *short and long Cuts:* Refers to drawing lots, usually with sticks or straws of unequal length, to determine who will perform a particular act.

Directions to the Footman

6. *a Pattern of Dress . . . to you:* In 'The Footmen's Petition', men of fashion are accused of imitating footmen 'to render themselves more amiable to the Ladies'; see *An Examination of Certain Abuses, Corruptions, and Enormities, in the City of Dublin*, n. 7.
7. *Boucher . . . the Duke of B—g—m:* The noted gambler Thomas Boucher (d. 1708) was rumored to have been a footman before

he amassed a fortune and built a mansion on land he acquired in Twickenham . . . John Sheffield, Earl of Mulgrave and 1st Duke of Buckingham (1648–1721).

8. *translated red-heeled Shoes . . . Ruffles:* Fashionable but shabby attire ('translated' as in borrowed or previously owned); in *Tatler, No. 67,* the fop Didapper is reprimanded for 'wearing red-heel'd Shoes'.

9. *go upon the Road . . . left you:* The advice here is to become a highwayman.

10. *Get a Speech to be written . . . Newgate:* See Swift's parody of such a speech in *The Last Speech and Dying Words of Ebenezor Elliston.*

11. *Fall on your Knees . . . Farewel:* Cf. Tom Clinch's very different behaviour on his way to the gallows in Swift's poem 'Clever Tom Clinch going to be hanged'.

12. *The Surgeon . . . Limb of you:* That is, the footman will be spared the fate of many indigent criminals, of having their corpses seized by surgeons after their execution for use in anatomy lessons or medical experiments; depicted in grisly detail in plate IV of Hogarth's *The Four Stages of Cruelty* (1751).

A Compleat Collection of Genteel and Ingenious Conversation

First published 1738. Also known as *Polite Conversation,* this work, consisting of an Introduction followed by three conversations, was written over the course of several decades. The Introduction's persona and satiric butt, Simon Wagstaff, calls to mind Isaac Bickerstaff of the satires on Partridge, and may well have been created at around the same time. The work reflects Swift's lifelong concern with the uses and abuses of language. In its satiric exposure of the banalities and meaningless jargon of fashionable society, it evokes *The Tatler, No. CCXXX.* The work is not merely censorious, however, for it also reveals Swift's fascination with dialectal expression and forms of speech rooted in folk and oral tradition. That Swift may have made up some of these 'proverbs' himself points to the irony at the heart of this satire, which mocks verbal triteness via witty invention, making its audience laugh at the empty social exchanges while admiring the ingenuity used to convey them.

Second Conversation

The scene is a dinner party at the home of Lord and Lady Smart, near St James's Park. This Conversation parodies the conventions of Restoration comedy: its use of names that reflect specific mental or character traits, the contrast between town and country, and the frequent use of wordplay and sexual innuendo. Notes indicate proverb collection followed by date of earliest-cited entry. Copy-text: *F '38*, collated with London edition of 1738.

1. *we have had our Hands in Mortar:* Apperson, 1639; means 'We have been dabbling in building.'
2. *he that hangs Tom . . . in the Halter:* '[M]ore knave than fool; intelligent rather than stupid. A left-handed compliment of the 17th–18th centuries' (Partridge).
3. *if it were only to try:* That is, if only as an experiment to see which one he is.
4. *I'll see your Nose Cheese first, and the Dogs eating it:* Kelly's gloss: 'A disdainful rejecting of an unworthy proposal' (with 'my self the first bite' as the second clause).
5. *make a flaming Figure in a Country Church:* Ray's gloss: 'To make a fair show in a countrey Church'; Kelly's gloss: 'A jest upon a girl when we see her fond of a new suit.'
6. *my Belly began to cry Cupboard . . . your Belly thinks your Throat's cut:* Proverbial sayings expressing hunger (Ray; Apperson, 1540).
7. *Oysters . . . Grace to them: ODEP*, 1611: 'Oysters are ungodly, because they are eaten without grace; uncharitable, because they leave nought but shells; and unprofitable, because they must swim in wine.'
8. *that's as well said, as if I had said it my self:* '[E]ither a catch-phrase that has endured or, more probably, a Swiftian felicity that has become a famous quotation' (Partridge).
9. *why is it called a Sirloyn . . . Knighted it:* Sirloin's status as the upper and choicer portion of a loin of beef, combined with its French etymological meaning ('above the loin') and the Anglicized 'sir loin', gave rise to numerous stories over the years about its being knighted by various monarchs (Brewer/Evans).
10. *Eating and Scratching wants but a Beginning:* That is, once you start doing either it is difficult to stop.
11. *two Hands . . . in a Purse:* Apperson, 1605; Kelly's gloss: 'I am

pleas'd when People eat with me, but not when they invade my Property.'

12. *the more, the merrier ... the fewer, the better Cheer:* ODEP, 1530; Kelly's gloss, 'The first, because good Company exhilarate one another. The second, because there will be the more [food] to each.'

13. *kiss the Hare's Foot:* ODEP, 1598; means 'to be late'; in this case, too late to get anything to eat.

14. *fast by the Teeth ... we are killing that, that would kill us:* Deeply engaged in the act of eating ... Refers to the fact that they are eating animal flesh.

15. *You are come in Pudden-Time ... you keep Court-Hours I see:* Apperson, 1546; means 'to come at the right moment' ... Refers to the fact that people dined much later in town (3 p.m.) than in the country.

16. *little London stands ... left it last:* Playing upon the line, 'Stands Scotland where it did?' from Shakespeare's *Macbeth*, which 'has become a jocular catch-phrase' (Partridge).

17. *London is gone ... since you saw it:* That is, London has been expanding far beyond its former boundaries. Hanover Square was laid out in 1717; Defoe's *Tour Through the Whole Island of Great Britain* records 'all the new buildings by, and beyond, Hannover Square', which have greatly extended the city of London.

18. *Here's no Salt; Cuckolds ... Meat:* Tilley, 1590: 'Service without salt, by the rite of England, is a Cuckholds fee, if he claime it.'

19. *I always wash my Kettle before I put the Meat in it:* 'I always put liquor into my stomach before I eat.'

20. *one Tongue's enough for a Woman:* ODEP, 1659; Ray's gloss: 'This reason they give who would not have women learn languages'; ODEP cites Milton's application of this proverb to his daughters.

21. *what if any of the Ladies should long?:* No doubt a sly hint at a food craving associated with pregnancy.

22. *a Body's Stomach ... the Bottom of it, I suppose:* Refers to Neverout's insatiable appetite.

23. *you have stolen a Wedding, it seems:* That is, stolen it from us (since it was performed in private).

24. *she's a little Evil:* A play on the old proverb, 'Women are necessary evils'; ODEP, 1547.

25. *Cucumbers are cold in the third Degree:* Related to the pro-

verbial saying, 'cool as a cucumber', which appeared in print in 1615 in the form, 'Young Maids were as cold as Cowcumbers' (Tilley).

26. *the Proof of the Pudden, is in the eating:* Apperson traces this saying to Ovid, *Heroides*, 2, in the phrase, 'exitus acta probat' ('the outcome proves the deed'), and dates its earliest English variant at *c.* 1300.

27. *I always love to walk with a Horse in my Hand ... you must kiss a Parson's Wife:* Presumably in case one's legs give out; Kelly's gloss: 'It is good when a man of any art, trade, or profession, has an estate to support him, if these should fail' ... Cf. Ray: 'He that would have good luck in horses, must kiss the Parson's wife.' A bawdier version appears in Ben Jonson (1621): 'Youle ha' good lucke to horseflesh, o' my life, you plow'd so late with the Vicar's wife' (Tilley).

28. *Hartfordshire Kindness:* Ray's gloss: 'That is, when one drinks back again to the party who immediately before drank to him: ... commonly used only by way of derision of those who, through forgetfulness or mistake, drink to them again whom they pledged immediately.'

29. *don't make a Bridge of my Nose:* Ray's gloss: 'To intercept one's trencher, cup, or the like; or to pretend to do kindnesses to one, and then pass him by, and do it to another; to lay hold upon and serve himself of that which was intended for another.'

30. *beat up your Quarters:* Visit without prior warning or ceremony; also a military term meaning to make an unexpected attack on an enemy in camp (Brewer/Evans).

31. *born within the Sound of Bow Bell ... London:* Born within hearing distance of the steeple of Bow Church in Cheapside, hence a true Cockney.

32. *sick Dish ... Sup, Simon:* A 'sick Dish' is one eaten when one is not feeling well (*ODEP*, 1598) ... 'Sup, Simon' is 'A common ironical recommendation to any one taking medicine or anything nauseous or disagreeable' (Apperson).

33. *you are more Sawce than Pig:* 'You are more impudent (saucier) than gluttonous'; *ODEP*, 1624.

34. *Pepper-Proof:* Perhaps a pun on 'pepper' as meaning 'to inflict with venereal disease' (*OED*).

35. *this Hare ... 'tis melancholy Meat:* *ODEP*, 1558; cf. Burton's *Anatomy of Melancholy* (1621): 'Hare, a black meat, melancholy, and hard of digestion.'

36. *he was an ingenious Man that first found out eating and drinking:*

And Swift may well have been the 'ingenious man' who originated this proverb—this is the only example cited in *ODEP*.

37. *made a Purchase:* That is, of land.

38. *knows how to butter his Bread: ODEP*, 1546 ('knows on which
side his bread is buttered'); a variant of 'his bread is buttered on
both sides'; Ray's gloss: 'He hath a plentiful estate: he is fat and
full.'

39. *it became him, as a Saddle becomes a Sow:* Apperson, 1546;
cf. Brome citation (1660): 'But the title of knight, on the back of
a knave, Is like a saddle upon a sow.'

40. *it is a Limb of Lot's Wife:* That is, it is very salty (see Genesis
19: 26).

41. *the falling out of Lovers, you know:* 'Is the renewing of love';
ODEP, 1520 (earliest English example); also classical source in
Terence's comedy *Andria*. Later variants substitute 'friends' for
'lovers'.

42. *that shiddle come sh——'s the Beginning of Love:* A line from
'A Ballad of Old Proverbs' (1719): 'What tho' my Love as white
as a Dove is,/Yet you would say, if you knew all within;/Shitten
come Shite the beginning of Love is,/And for her Favour I care
not a Pin.' Samuel Pepys was so pleased with this ballad when
he first heard it sung in a tavern (1661) that he obtained a copy
of it for his own personal use.

43. *marry come up, my dirty Couzin:* Ray's gloss: 'Spoken by way
of taunt, to those who boast themselves of their birth, parentage,
or the like.' Kelly offers a somewhat different explanation: 'A
Reprimand to mean People, when they propose a Thing that
seems too saucy.'

44. *I'm very dry . . . Then you are the better to burn, and the worse
to fry:* An example of a 'crambo', a game in which one player
gives a word or line of verse to which each of the others has to
find a rhyme. There are other 'crambos' interspersed throughout
these dialogues.

45. *you have a good Stroak with you:* 'You contribute much to the
dinner', i.e. 'You're quite an eater.'

46. *I wish it were in your Guts, for my Share:* 'I'd rather my share
(of the liquor) were inside you'—a less polite version of, 'You're
welcome to my share.'

47. *you are a true English-Man . . . when you are well:* Ray; Tilley,
1616; 'A right Englishman, he cannot let a thing alone when 'tis
well' (1671).

48. *Kitchen Physick is the best Physick:* 'Home remedies are superior to any that can be bought'; *ODEP*, 1542.

49. *the best Doctors . . . Doctor Merryman:* Tilley, 1558; Ray's gloss: 'nothing but that distich of the Schola Salernitana translated'— i.e. the famous book on health written in the twelfth or thirteenth century at the school of Salerno and translated into English by Sir John Harington (1608).

50. *Goose upon Goose is false Heraldry:* A play on 'Metal upon metal is false heraldry' (Tilley, 1643); cf. Swift's 'A Serious Poem upon William Wood' (1724): 'But soft says the Herald, I cannot agree;/For *Metal on Metal is false Heraldry:/*Why that may be true, yet Wood upon Wood,/I'll maintain with my Life, is *Heraldry* Good.'

51. *Brandy is Latin for a Goose; and Tace is Latin for a Candle:* The first statement is 'An apology for drinking a dram after eating goose' (Tilley, 1588); the second, 'a hint to keep silent about something' (*ODEP*, 1676). ('Tace' is Latin for 'Be silent'.) Tilley notes that in both these sayings 'Latin' means 'slang'.

52. *the Devil made Askers:* This is the sole example cited in *ODEP* and Apperson. The sense of it is, 'It's the Devil's work to ask unnecessary questions.'

53. *wrapt in your Mother's Smock:* Born lucky; 'probably connected with the popular idea of luck attaching to a caul' (Apperson); often linked to the idea of being a favourite of the opposite sex (see Tilley, 1668).

54. *your Maidenhead hangs in your Light:* This is the first example of the saying in *ODEP*. Partridge interprets it as meaning, 'virginity is to your disadvantage'.

55. *Parson Palmer . . . used to preach over his Liquor:* According to Grose's *Classical Dictionary* (1785), 'a jocular name or term of reproach, to one who stops the circulation of the glass by preaching over his liquor, as it is said was done by a parson of that name, whose cellar was under his pulpit' (Apperson).

56. *the Poet is damn'd:* That is, the dramatist was booed; the play was received poorly.

57. *too good, is stark nought:* Swift's is the sole example in *ODEP* and Apperson; the meaning is, 'too good is no good'. Possibly meant as a play on the proverb, 'Good enough is never ought', as recorded in Ray.

58. *'Tis plaguy small:* It is too much like small-beer; it is overly weak.

59. *meer Whip-belly-vengeance:* 'Belly-vengeance' was a dialect term

for sour ale or wine (*OED*). Partridge links both this term and its variant, 'pinch-gut vengeance', to 'rot-gut', recorded as early as 1633.

60. *for fear they should p–ss behind the Door:* 'A rustic gesture of contempt for the niggardly' (Partridge).

61. *take a Hair of the same Dog . . . one should drink as much after an Egg, as after an Ox:* Apperson, 1546: 'a hair of the dog that bit you' . . . *ODEP*, 1608 (variant form); Ray's version is the same as Swift's.

62. *put a Churl upon a Gentleman:* Tilley, 1586: 'Drinke not beer after wine.' Kelly's gloss: 'Spoken when we offer ale to them that have been drinking claret.' Class snobbery is evident in this distinction.

63. *one may ride to Rumford . . . so blunt:* This passage is the earliest example in both *ODEP* and Apperson; note in *ODEP*: 'Romford, in Essex, [is] famous for breeches-making.'

64. *Cheese digests every Thing but itself:* Tilley, 1566; Ray's gloss: 'a translation of that old rhyming Latin verse, *Caseus est nequàm quia digerit omnia sequàm.*'

65. *weily brosten . . . in Lancashire:* Dialectal form for 'well-nigh burst', with the first word a variant or erroneous spelling for 'welly' (*OED*).

66. *'tis merry in Hall, when Beards wag all:* *ODEP*, c. 1300.

67. *I'll hold fifty Pound, Miss won't cut the Cheese:* That is, 'I'll wager . . .' Partridge conjectures that this might be a reference to the saying, 'cheese won't choke her', which implies physical intimacy with men.

68. *fret like Gum Taffety:* Tilley, 1604; 'Velvet and taffeta, being stiffened with gum, quickly rub and fret themselves out.'

69. *a rare Soldier . . . won't hurt you:* A sturgeon has five rows of bony plates resembling armour.

70. *a Cup in the Pate, is a Mile in the Gate . . . a Spur in the Head, is worth two in the Heel:* Tilley, 1656 . . . Cf. Kelly's gloss: 'A Man when drunk rides hard; because . . . his Heels stick in his Horse's side.'

71. *thou art a mad Fellow to make a Priest of:* 'You are hardly the kind of person one would associate with such concerns of piety.'

72. *you make a Chimney of your Mouth:* This may well be the earliest printed form of our modern-day saying, 'you smoke like a chimney'; it appears in neither *ODEP* nor Apperson.

73. *the Corruption of Pipes, is the Generation of Stoppers:* Tilley,

1576; a parody of the classical maxim, 'the corruption of one thing is the generation of another'. Cf. Swift's *Mechanical Operation of the Spirit* (1704): 'the corruption of the senses is the generation of the spirit.' Partridge's gloss: 'The corruption exercised by . . . tobacco has led to the making of pipe-stoppers (small devices for pressing the tobacco in one's pipe).'

74. *not 'till the Ducks . . . Children say:* A rural saying that means 'not until the (late) Spring' (Partridge).

75. *rain Cats and Dogs:* Tilley, 1628; see Swift's 'Description of a City Shower': 'Drown'd Puppies, stinking Sprats, all drench'd in Mud,/Dead Cats and Turnip-Tops come tumbling down the Flood.'

76. *a Man may love . . . the Ridge:* Ray's gloss: 'A man may love his children and relations well, and yet not cocker [coddle] them, or be foolishly fond and indulgent to them.'

77. *at Hogsnorton . . . the Organs:* Ray's gloss: 'This is a village properly called Hoch-Norton, whose inhabitants . . . were so rustical in their behaviour, that boorish and clownish people are said to be born there.' Apperson offers a different explanation: '. . . this saying refers to the village of Hock-Norton, Leicestershire, where the organist once upon a time was named Piggs!'

78. *a queer old Duke:* 'The unit is *queer duke*, a decayed gentleman: a late 17th–18th-century term on the borderline of underworld cant and raffish fashionable slang' (Partridge). No doubt our term 'queer duck' derives from this earlier one; see Tilley, 1523: 'Like a Duke? Like a duck.'

79. *a Man's a Man . . . a Hose on his Head:* ODEP, c. 1386 (from *The Canterbury Tales*); cf. 1708 entry: 'We may sometimes chance to meet with a Diogenes in rags.'

80. *You can't make a Silk Purse out of a Sow's Ear:* A Scottish proverb though with English variants (Ray).

81. *the Devil . . . and Company too:* Apperson, 1704: a 'laudable adage of the sage mobility' (i.e. the mob).

82. *against you are disposed:* 'Since you are inclined to merriment.'

83. *Fire and Water are . . . bad Masters:* Ray; ODEP, 1562.

84. *What's Sawce for a Goose, is Sawce for a Gander:* With a classical prototype in Varro (Apperson), this is listed in Ray as 'a woman's proverb'; but Swift himself uses it in JS.

85. *if I live . . . neither go to Heaven nor Hell with you:* 'As I live, I shall never go anywhere with you'; in a more general sense, 'I don't want to have anything to do with you.'

86. *mauming and gauming a Body so:* That is, pawing. This is the

only example noted in the *OED* definition; 'mauming' (unlike 'gauming') has no independent meaning and is probably only being used for the rhyme.

87. *gape for Preferment . . . into my Mouth:* Variants include 'You may gape long enough ere a bird fall in your mouth' (*ODEP*, 1540); Kelly's gloss: 'Spoken to those who expect a thing without reason.' It is tempting to see a relevance here to Swift's own fruitless hopes for preferment.

88. *Time to go to our Tea:* The Third Conversation records the ladies' banter at the tea table.

89. *Wine is the best Liquor to wash Glasses in:* This is the sole example cited by *ODEP*. Perhaps Swift thought it would be most fitting to end this dialogue with a newly coined 'proverb' of his own.

Glossary

absentees those owning land or holding sinecures in Ireland but living for the most part in England

adapt (*adj.*), fit; suited

ale-wife a woman who keeps an alehouse

Anabaptists radical Protestant reformers who denied the validity of infant baptism and who rejected the doctrine of justification by faith alone, stressing instead the importance of good works based on free will

animadversion consideration; judicial or critical attention; censure

applotting apportioning

at jar ajar; in a state of discord or dissension

bagnio bath house; brothel

bamboozle a cant term that first appeared in usage around 1700, meaning to deceive by trickery or impose upon; to mystify or perplex (*OED*)

bang to beat violently; to defeat

Bartholomew Fair known for its raree-shows, low farces and other popular entertainments; located in Smithfield; started by royal charter in 1133 to celebrate St Bartholomew's Day (24 August)

Bedlam the Hospital of St Mary of Bethlehem, London's asylum for the mentally deranged, where lunatics were displayed for the entertainment of spectators; figuratively, a scene of confusion or uproar

bell-man town-crier

belles-lettres *lit.* 'fine letters' (French); elegant or polite literature having a purely aesthetic function

besom (bezom) a broom made of twigs tied together around a handle; figuratively, any agent that cleanses, purifies or sweeps away things material or immaterial (*OED*)

bite hoax; trick; characterized as 'a new-fashioned way of being witty' in a 1703 letter by Swift

Black-a-moore (Black-a-more) a term commonly used in the eighteenth century for a black-skinned African, Ethiopian or other Negro, generally a member of the servant class

black-guard boy a street Arab; 'Dirty, Nasty, Tatter'd Roguish Boys' who clean shoes on street corners for a half-penny (*CD*); can also signify the lowest menial employed in a household

black-guards the lowest ranks in the army; camp-followers; also can refer to various lowly members of society, including servants, vagabonds and criminals

black money money made of brass; debased coinage

black-pudding a type of sausage made of blood and suet, sometimes with flour or meal added; a food associated with the lower classes

blade a gallant; a 'fellow' (often implying contempt); a spruce man or beau

blind obscure; hidden; a 'blind alehouse' is one without a sign, 'fit to conceal a . . . hunted Villain' (*CD*)

blow up put an end to; destroy

bob (*v.*), to rap or tap with a slight blow

bones dice

bookseller publisher

Bridewell a London house of correction founded in 1553, where lesser criminals such as prostitutes and vagrants were confined; portrayed in plate IV of Hogarth's *A Harlot's Progress* (1732)

brimmer a glass filled to the brim (with alcohol)

brogues rude shoes made of untanned hide, commonly worn by the poor in rural regions of Ireland

bubble anything fragile, empty or worthless; a deceptive show (*OED*); a fellow 'fit to be imposed on, deluded, or cheated' (*CD*); a financial swindle or deceptive scheme (e.g. 'South Sea Bubble')

bumper a cup or glass of wine (etc.) filled to the brim; usually poured for a toast

butter weight formerly eighteen or more ounces to the pound; figuratively, 'for good measure'

Candlemas the candle-lit feast of the purification of the Virgin Mary, or presentation of Christ in the Temple; the date of this feast is 2 February

cant the 'Cypher or Mysterious Language of Rogues, Gypsies, Beggars, Thieves, &c.' (*CD*); phraseology used for fashion's sake, without being a genuine expression of sentiment (*OED*); professional jargon

canting whining, or speaking in a sing-song tone; dividing up land

into small parcels and setting them out to lease, usually for short
periods of time

capite (as used in the phrase *in capite*), from the Latin for 'head'; held
immediately of the King or of the Crown, as lands held in a feudal
tenure

carter the driver of a cart, carriage or chariot

chaffering buying and selling; dealing or haggling

chair often used to signify a sedan-chair (*q.v.*)

chairman one of the two men needed to carry persons in a sedan-chair
(*q.v.*)

chapman dealer; merchant; trader

chargeable expensive; costly

chocolate-house an establishment purveying chocolate as a beverage;
e.g. White's on St James's Street, London

chop-house an eating-house where mutton chops, beefsteaks and the
like are supplied (*OED*); a house of entertainment, where provision
ready dressed is sold (Johnson)

choqued shocked; the French spelling was common in the seventeenth
century

circumvallation a rampart or entrenchment built around a place,
especially in a siege situation

City (the) the business and commercial area of central London, originally located within the old walls

civilian one who studies, writes about or is an authority on the civil
law

clap (*v.*), to infect with venereal disease; to take into custody or
imprison without formality or delay, as in 'to clap someone up'

closet a small private room or inner chamber used as a place for study,
meditation, dressing, etc.

closeting making behind-the-scenes agreements or scheming in private; exerting undue influence or intimidation through secret
meetings

clout a piece of cloth; a rag

club a contribution to defray the expense of an entertainment

Commissioners of the Revenue a board consisting of seven members—
all Commissioners of Customs, five also Commissioners of Excise—
who controlled a large patronage system of government func-
tionaries

commonplace-books compilations of noteworthy passages garnered
from reading and conversation, recorded under general headings for
future reference or use; popular from the early sixteenth century on

condescension a ready willingness to please or oblige another; gra-

cious or submissive deference shown towards another person; generally used without the pejorative connotations now attached to the
term

Confederacy (the) England's allies against France during the War of
the Spanish Succession (*q.v.*)

confident (*n.*), eighteenth-century spelling of 'confidant(e)'; one
entrusted with private information

controlled refuted; contradicted; challenged

copple-crowned crested; peaked; term originally taken from the crest
on a bird's head

coss an Anglo-Indian term derived from the Hindi word *kōs* and the
Sanskrit word *krosa*, signifying the distance at which a man's call
can be heard; also a measure between about 1¼ and 2½ miles
(*Hob-Job*)

country put seventeenth-century slang for a bumpkin or lout

Court of Requests a court for the recovery of small debts, or claims
of less than forty shillings

couzenage (cozenage) an act of deception; artifice; fraud

coxcomb a foolish, vain, ostentatiously conceited person; a fop; a
superficial pretender to knowledge or accomplishments (Johnson);
originally a cap shaped like a cock's comb worn by professional
fools

cully 'a Fop, a Rogue, [or] a Fool . . . easily drawn in and cheated by
Whores and Rogues' (*CD*)

cup (*v.*), a surgical term meaning to bleed a patient by applying an
open-mouthed glass vessel to the skin

daggled bespattered or bemired; also, as in 'daggle-tailed', having
one's skirts splashed by being trailed over wet ground; more generally, untidy or slatternly (*OED*)

dam a female parent of animals; a derogatory term for a (human)
mother

Declaratory Act an Act (1720) asserting the right of the English Parliament to enact legislation binding on Ireland and to act as a final
court of appeal in all Irish cases; based on Poynings' Law of 1494

Deist one who adheres to a form of natural religion based on reason,
which rejects the supernatural aspects of Christian belief, including
mysteries, miracles and revelation

dignities persons of high rank or estate; those who make up 'the
quality' of society

Dissenters members of various Low Church Protestant denominations who rejected episcopacy and separated themselves from the
communion of the Church of England (and Church of Ireland)

doubt (*v.*), to think or believe; to suspect; to anticipate with apprehension

drab (*n.*), a dirty and untidy woman; a slut; a strumpet

draper (**drapier**) a dealer in cloth

Dutch reckoning a verbal or lump-sum account devoid of particulars and thus open to falsification

enthusiasm a vain belief of private revelation and divine favour (Johnson); ill-regulated or misdirected religious emotion; extravagance of religious speculation (*OED*); associated with Puritans and Dissenters

epiphonemas exclamatory or striking statements used to sum up or conclude a discourse, or a passage in the discourse; Swift (via Johnson): 'a conclusive sentence not closely connected with the words foregoing'

equipages the appurtenances of rank, office or social position; that which is required to maintain an official establishment; also, carriages with horses and attendant servants (*OED*)

Exchange (the) a building in which merchants assemble for the purpose of transacting business

exploded hissed off the stage; rejected; held in contempt; out of fashion

extraordinaries extra expenses; fees or payments over and above what is usual

fain favourably disposed or inclined to; willing(ly); eager(ly)

fanatic(k) a religious zealot or enthusiast; usually equivalent to 'Puritan' in Swift's usage

farthing a coin worth a quarter of a penny, which by the eighteenth century was made of copper alloys

fatal destined; decreed by fate

fee (*v.*), to hire; to engage for a sum of money

ferret to hunt down; to worry; to drive out

fiddle faddle(s) 'meer silly Stuff, or Nonsense; idle, vain Discourse' (*CD*)

filemot a corruption of the French word *feuillemorte*, signifying the colour of a dead or faded leaf; brown or yellowish brown (*OED*)

finical affectedly fastidious; overly precise in dress or manner; fine (in the worst sense)

fireball a round projectile filled with explosive or combustible material

fireship 'a Pockey Whore' (*CD*), i.e. a diseased prostitute

First Fruits and Twentieth Parts fees, also known as 'Queen Anne's Bounty', paid to the Crown by the clergy; remitted to the Church of England in 1704 and to the Church of Ireland in 1711

flam a fanciful composition; a conceit

flambeau a (lighted) torch, especially one made of several thick wicks dipped in wax

Flanders a former countship in Europe, comprised of parts of what are now Belgium, France and Holland; a hotly contested territory during the War of the Spanish Succession

fleering sneering; smiling obsequiously; laughing coarsely or scornfully (*OED*)

flummery a kind of food made by coagulation of wheat-flour or oatmeal

flux a morbid or excessive discharge; an abnormally copious flow of blood or excrement from certain bodily organs, especially the bowel; also an early name for dysentery

foot-boy a boy attendant; a pageboy

fox (*v.*), to get drunk; to befuddle; to delude

Freemasons a secret, all-male order founded in London in 1717 and brought to Ireland in 1725, which espoused the 'mysteries' of antiquity and claimed ancestry among the ancient Egyptians and Greeks

free-thinker one who invokes his right as a rational being to question accepted religious beliefs and authority; 'a libertine; a contemner of religion' (Johnson); in the eighteenth century it often referred to a Deist (*q.v.*)

fundament buttocks or anus; originally, foundation

funest deadly; disastrous; deplorable

fustian inflated or turgid language; jargon; gibberish; bombast; claptrap (*OED*)

galley-halfpence a silver coin putatively introduced into England by Genoese sailors; made illegal in the fifteenth century

gaming gambling; card-playing (etc.) for monetary stakes

gascon(n)ade extravagant boasting; vainglorious fiction; something wholly imaginary

gauming handling, especially in some improper fashion

generals generalities; statements or propositions lacking particulars

gibbet an upright post with a projecting arm from which the bodies of criminals were hung after execution

gill-ale ale served by the gill measure, which is one-fourth of a standard pint

Glorious Revolution (the) the bloodless change of government in 1688 in which the Catholic James II was replaced by William of Orange and his wife Mary, James's daughter; restored the British Crown to Protestant hands and established the principle of a limited monarchy with a balanced Constitution

goody when placed before a surname, signifies a married woman of humble status; short for 'goodwife'

Gothic(k) pertaining to the Germanic tribes that invaded Europe in the third and fourth centuries; used either to denote a type of barbarism antithetical to the civilized Classical world, or to evoke the body of common law (the 'ancient constitution') and the mixed form of government predating the Norman Conquest, on which the concept of English liberty is based

grandee a man of great rank, power or dignity (Johnson)

groat an English coin equal to four pence, first put into circulation at the beginning of the fourteenth century but ceasing to be issued in 1662; used figuratively to signify an insignificant sum

Grub Street professional writers (named for the street in London they inhabited) who exploited the new print culture for gain; viewed by Tory satirists as hired 'hacks' appealing to the worst in popular taste

guinea an English coin first issued in 1663 and valued at 20 (later 21) shillings

hackney-coach a carriage kept for hire, used as a common mode of transportation in eighteenth-century London

halfporth, an abbreviated form of 'halfpennyworth'

Hampton Court located along the Thames about 15 miles west of London; the site of Cardinal Wolsey's palace (1514); later a favourite residence of William and Mary, who hired Christopher Wren to rebuild the Tudor structures; under Queen Anne it became as much the resort of wits as the home of statesmen

Hanoverians members or followers of the House of Hanover, which the Act of Settlement (1701) designated to supply the heir to the English throne in default of issue from Queen Anne

hawker one who sells his goods by crying them in the street; a common eighteenth-century urban figure

health (a) a toast in someone's honour

heart-burnings heated and embittered states of mind; rankling resentments or grudges

hedge(-) used as an adjunct of contempt; hence the phrase, 'by hedge or by stile', meaning 'by Hook or by Crook' (CD); a 'hedge-press' was a press operated clandestinely, implying inferiority or meanness

heydukes (heyducks) originally a term for robbers, marauders or brigands; in Hungary, a special body of foot-soldiers that attained the rank of nobility in the early seventeenth century; in Poland, attendants of the nobles

high-flyer one who has a high-flown or extravagant notion on some question of polity; used at this time to signify a High Church proponent or a Tory who supported extreme claims for the authority of the Church

hogshead a large caskful of liquor; a liquid measure containing 63 old wine-gallons, equal to 52½ imperial gallons (*OED*)

howdees salutations that enquire into the health of a person; an abbreviated form of 'how-d'ye-do'

hue and cry a legal term signifying a call raised by a constable or aggrieved party for the pursuit of a felon, or a proclamation for the capture of a criminal (*OED*)

humoursome fanciful; capricious; odd; tending to humour or indulge anyone; peevish or petulant

huzza a hurrah or cheer uttered by a large group in unison

incidents incidental charges or expenses

Independent a type of Protestant Dissenter, often associated with Congregationalism

Indian herb a now-obsolete term for 'tobacco' (*OED*)

ink-horn a small portable vessel made of animal horn for holding writing-ink

intellectuals intellectual faculties; mental powers

jack a machine for turning the spit in roasting meat

jackanapes a tame ape; an impertinent fellow who puts on airs; 'a little sorry Whipper-snapper' (*CD*)

Jacobites those, generally of Tory and High Church affiliation, who refused to accept the Revolution Settlement of 1689 and desired the restoration of the Stuart line (the offspring of James II) to the throne

jargon a medley or 'babel' of sounds (*OED*); meaningless words; the cant of a class, sect or profession

jordan chamber pot

journeyman a hireling; one who drudges for another; also a person who, having served his apprenticeship to a trade, is able to work for day-wages

junket (*v.*), to feast; to make merry with good cheer

kennel the surface drain of a street; the gutter; usually associated with an accumulation of foul matter; cf. Swift's 'Filth of all Hues and Odours', attributed to London's 'swelling Kennels' in 'A Description of a City Shower'

Kensington in Swift's day a largely rural area to the west of London proper, site of Kensington Palace, the favoured retreat of Queen Anne; its gravel pits made it a noted health resort for well-to-do Londoners

Kit-Cat Club a club founded in London at the end of the seventeenth century, made up of prominent writers, artists and public figures for the purpose of promoting Whig political and aesthetic principles

lace (*v.*), to thrash or beat; to ensnare or catch, as in a noose (*OED*)

lanthorn variant spelling of 'lantern'

levee a reception of visitors upon rising from bed; a morning assembly held by a person of high rank

literature general acquaintance with 'letters' or books; polite or humane learning

Lord-Lieutenant the chief governor of Ireland from 1700 onward, appointed by and representing the Crown, whose primary duty was to defend British interests in Ireland

lurry hubbub; confusion; 'babel'

Maintenon (a la) a way of preparing meat, named after the Marquise de Maintenon, who secretly married Louis XIV in 1685

Mall (the) a site first laid out at the time of the Restoration, running along the northern edge of St James's Park and providing a fashionable avenue for walking and socializing

malster a malt master or brewer of malt liquor

mamaluke (mameluke) a member of the military body, originally composed of Caucasian slaves, that became the ruling class in Egypt in the mid-thirteenth century; could also signify a slave in Mohammedan countries, or *fig.* a 'fighting slave' of the Pope (*OED*)

March beer a strong beer brewed in March

mareschal(l) obsolete form of 'marshal'; a military commander or general

masquerades a fashionable and popular form of masked entertainment, first organized by the Swiss promoter John James Heidegger in 1717 at the King's Theatre, Haymarket; later included the masked balls at public assembly rooms and pleasure gardens (e.g. Ranelagh)

Ménière's disease or **syndrome** a disorder of the membranous labyrinth of the ear that causes recurring attacks of deafness, vertigo and nausea; Swift suffered from a severe form of this illness

mercer a dealer in textile fabrics, especially silks; also a small-ware dealer

mess a small group of persons (usually four) who sat together at a banquet and were served from the same dishes; gave rise to the meaning of 'mess' as a place where soldiers eat their meals (Brewer/ Evans)

Michaelmas the feast of St Michael, one of the quarter days in England, Wales and Ireland; the date of this feast is 29 September

ministry a body charged with the administration of a country or state;

roughly speaking, the political Cabinet governing England, headed by a Secretary of State and a Lord High Treasurer

mobbed (*adj.*), hooded or in a 'mob-cap'; wearing flimsy or careless attire; in a state of semi-undress

mounseer an antiquated Anglicized pronunciation of 'monsieur', generally appearing in print as a vulgarism, a representation of illiterate speech, or a derisive comment on English anti-French prejudice

mountebanks charlatans; itinerant quacks selling fake cures from elevated platforms, often enhancing their audience appeal with juggling acts, storytelling, magic tricks and professional fools or clowns

mumble to bite with toothless gums

mummy a pulpy substance or mass

mumping grimacing; hinting through facial expression

Muscovy eighteenth-century name for the principality of Moscow, though it generally applied to all of Russia as well, and could on occasion refer specifically to Tsar Peter the Great

mute (*v.*), to defecate

natural parts native ability; talents that are inborn rather than acquired by learning

neat (*n.*), an ox or cow

Newgate London's principal prison from the thirteenth century onwards, notorious for its fetid and inhumane conditions; also Dublin's main prison, located in the old Cornmarket north-east of St Patrick's cathedral

Nonconformist a catch-all term for any member of a Protestant denomination or sect separated from the Church of England; often used interchangeably with 'Dissenter'

October a type of strong ale, which got its name from the month in which it was brewed

odso minced form of 'Godso'; an exclamation of surprise, emphatic assertion or solemn declaration

œconomist a manager of a household; a housekeeper; one who manages expenses effectively

ombre a Spanish card game (from 'hombre', or 'man') brought over to England in 1660; enormously popular among the fashionable set over the next six decades; played by three hands with a forty-card deck lacking eights, nines and tens, the three highest trumps being (in descending order) the ace of spades ('Spadille'), the black 2 or red 7 ('Manille') and the ace of clubs ('Basto')

ordinaries public eating-houses; 'gaming ordinaries' specialized in gambling as well as food

original(s) origins; beginnings; earliest stages

ostler (hostler) a stableman or groom; one who takes care of horses at an inn

packet (paquet) a boat plying a regular route between two ports, conveying mail, goods and passengers

Pale (the) an enclosed area safeguarded from outside intrusions; more specifically, a territory within determined bounds and subject to a specific jurisdiction, such as the 'English pale' in Ireland

palisado (palisade) a pointed wooden stake used for military fortification

palming cheating at a game, or performing a conjuring trick, by hiding something in the palm of the hand

palsy water medicinal water prescribed for the cure of palsy, made primarily from cowslip or palsy-wort

parts abilities or talents, as in 'a man of parts'

pasty a pie, usually made of a mixture of meat and vegetables

pedant a private tutor; a schoolmaster or pedagogue; 'a Man that has been brought up among Books, and is able to talk of nothing else' (Addison; cited in *OED*)

penny-post an organization that conveyed letters or packets at an ordinary charge of a penny each, established *c.* 1680 for London and its environs within a 10-mile radius (*OED*)

periwig a wig worn in the eighteenth century by both men and women as a fashionable headdress

perspective an optical instrument for viewing objects, related to the telescope and spyglass; *Spectator, No. 250* recommends it as a useful new tool for observers who want to avoid 'the Impertinence of Staring'

peruke a term that from the sixteenth century onwards became largely interchangeable with 'periwig' (*q.v.*)

philomaths lovers of learning; students of mathematics, natural philosophy and the like; a term commonly used in the eighteenth century for astrologers and prognosticators

physick medicine

picktooth a toothpick

pigeon sweetheart

pistole an old Spanish gold piece equivalent to four pieces of eight or Spanish dollars, worth between sixteen and eighteen shillings

places government offices or appointments; posts held in the service of the Crown or state

plaguy a colloquial term meaning confoundedly or exceedingly; vexatiously

play (*n.*), gambling

politeness polish; refinement; culture; generally used by Swift in an ironic or pejorative sense, to indicate the corrupt values of fashionable society

porridge a soup made with stewed vegetables and sometimes meat, often thickened with barley

porringer a small vessel made of metal, earthenware or wood, used for eating soup, broth and porridge

pose (*v.*), to puzzle, confuse or nonplus; to place in a difficult position by asking a question

pot-herb a herb grown for boiling in the pot, usually cultivated in a kitchen garden

pot-hooks curved or hooked strokes made in writing; scrawls; one of the elementary forms in learning to write; used by Swift (as in 'pot-hooks and hangers') to suggest bogus astrological symbols

poticary a variant of 'pothecary', which is itself an aphetic form of 'apothecary' (*OED*)

potshaws 'pashas', or Turkish officers of high rank (e.g. military commanders and provincial governors)

powder-horn a case used for carrying gunpowder, usually made of the horn of an ox or cow

pox venereal disease; syphilis

prebendary a canon of a cathedral or collegiate church who receives a stipend (or 'prebend') granted out of the church's estate in exchange for officiating in the church at specified times

preferment a political or ecclesiastical appointment offering social and financial rewards

premunire (**præmunire**) a penalty or liability; from the legal term *praemunire facias*, designating a writ against any person accused of prosecuting in a foreign court a suit cognizable by the law of England, or of asserting papal jurisdiction in England, thus denying the ecclesiastical supremacy of the sovereign (*OED*)

prerogative the special pre-eminence which the sovereign has over all other persons and out of the course of the common law (*OED*)

presently without delay; immediately; forthwith

pretend to profess or claim; to allege; to put forward as an assertion or statement of fact

Privy Council in England, a large body functioning as a Cabinet, with ceremonial duties such as declaring war and ratifying peace treaties; in Ireland, a body of about twenty bishops and principal office-holders, whose duties included the issuance of proclamations and the preparation and transmission of government bills to the English

Privy Council before they could proceed as bills through the Irish Parliament

probationer a novice; one who is qualifying for some position

projectors those who form 'wild impracticable schemes' (Johnson); 'Busybodies in new Inventions and Discoveries' (*CD*); attacked by Swift as economic speculators, mad scientists, etc.

prorogue to defer or postpone; to discontinue the meetings of a legislative body (e.g. the British Parliament) without actually dissolving it; to dismiss by authority until the next session

pure fine; splendid

quibbler punster

rack (*v.*), to raise rents above a fair or reasonable amount; to subject a person to the payment of 'rack-rent', or a very high rent (nearly) equal to the full value of the land

rap (*n.*), a counterfeit coin, worth about half a farthing, which passed current for a half-penny in eighteenth-century Ireland owing to the scarcity of genuine money

ravished (from) robbed; plundered; seized

receipt (receit) recipe; prescription

refinement fineness of feeling, taste or thought; elegance of manners; a piece of subtle reasoning (*OED*); usually used by Swift in a pejorative way, to suggest excessive subtlety or sophistication, manipulative use of flattery, extravagance of compliment or any form of expression intended to impose upon the hearer

remembrancer one appointed to remind others; a certain official of the Court of Exchequer (*OED*)

rent income; revenue

repetition-day a day devoted to students' recitation of pieces learned by heart

republic of letters the collective body of those engaged in literary pursuits; the field of literature itself; the earliest example cited in the *OED* is Joseph Addison's use of it in 1702

reversion the right of succession to an office after the death or retirement of the holder, often to be exercised specifically 'during pleasure [of the Crown]'

revolt (to) to change sides; to shift one's allegiance to

rug a thick woollen cloak or mantle

Sacramental Test *see* **Test Act**

St James's Park originally a deer park adjoining Henry VIII's new palace; later laid out as pleasure grounds for Charles II, who opened most of it to the public; in Swift's time a fashionable London meeting place as well as a site for less reputable activities

St Stephen's Green an ancient common in Dublin, established in the reign of Charles I as a park for the use of citizens to take the open air; during the Restoration, seventeen acres were kept as a public park while the rest were sold for upscale development; in the last years of Swift's life became completely enclosed

screwing the act of extorting money, especially from tenants; oppressing tenants with unfair exactions

scrivener one who receives money to place out at interest, and who supplies those who want to raise money on security (*OED*); also, a public copyist, scribe or clerk

scrophulous affected with or of the nature of scrofula, a disease caused by the enlargement and degeneration of the lymph glands, and marked by sores and swellings on the skin; *fig.* morally corrupt

scrupule obsolete form of 'scruple'

scullion the lowest-ranked domestic servant in a household, responsible for washing pots, dishes and utensils in the kitchen (or 'scullery'); *fig.* a low or mean person

scurvy worthless; contemptible

Scythians an ancient nomadic people originating from areas of European and Asiatic Russia, often linked to the Irish as a way of characterizing the latter's supposed primitiveness or barbarism

sectaries members of a schismatic religious sect; in the seventeenth and eighteenth centuries, Protestant Dissenters

sedan-chair a chair connected on top to a pole and carried by two men, used as a common mode of conveyance in eighteenth-century London

sennight (*se'enight*) a week (*lit.* 'seven nights'); depending on the context can also mean 'seven days old' or 'a week ago'.

sessions (the) i.e. the 'sessions of the peace', or the periodic assemblies of justices of the peace

setter an abettor of swindlers, robbers or murderers, used as a lure, decoy or spy on intended victims

shambles a place where meat is sold or where animals are butchered for food; a slaughter-house

sharper 'a Cheat, one that lives by his Wits' (*CD*); often, a fraudulent gamester

sideling moving sideways; in a sideward direction

sightly handsome; pleasing to look at

sink to make away with; to appropriate (money, etc.) for one's own use (*OED*)

sirrah a term of address asserting the speaker's authority, usually directed at men or boys

skipkennel any menial servant whose regular duties require him to jump over 'kennels', or gutters

small-beer beer of a weak or inferior quality; *fig.* a small thing or a trifle

Smithfield bargain a sharp or roguish bargain in which the purchaser is taken in; often a marriage contract based solely on financial interest; a term derived from the practices of the markets at Smithfield

smoak (smoke) to discover or suspect (a plot, hoax, etc.); to take note of; a favourite word of Swift's

smock (*v.*), to consort with women; to fornicate; (*n.*), a woman's undergarment; in allusive and hyphenated terms, suggestive of loose conduct or immorality with regard to women

snuff the portion of a drink left at the bottom of a cup; odour or scent

Society (the) also known as the Brothers Club (1711), comprised of 'men of wit' aiming 'to advance conversation and friendship, and to reward deserving persons with our interest and recommendation' (*JS*); the Tories' 'answer' to the Kit-Cat Club (*q.v.*)

Socinians a sect that denied the tenets of the Trinity, the divinity of Christ, and the proposition that man's nature is inherently sinful, and that stressed the central role of human reason in interpreting the Bible

soldier's bottle an extra-large bottle

sollary (sallary) celery, a plant indigenous to parts of England in its wild form

sophisters students in their second or third year at Cambridge University

sorites in logic, a series of propositions in which the predicate of each is the subject of the next, the conclusion being formed of the first subject and the last predicate; suggests sophistical argumentation

sottish foolish; stupid

souse (sowce) (*v.*), to steep in a pickling liquid for purposes of food preservation or preparation; to drench or soak with water; to strike or beat severely

South Sea Company a joint-stock company created in 1711 as a Tory alternative to the Bank of England; designed to take over the country's national debt through its acquisition of a monopoly of Britain's trade with Spanish America; culminated in a major stock-market crash known as the 'South Sea Bubble' (1720)

spade a eunuch

span-farthing a game in which the object of one player is to throw his farthings so close to those of his opponent that the distance between them could be spanned with the hand (*OED*)

spark one who affects to be elegant or fashionable in dress and manners; a fop or dandy

spiriting infusing life or energy into; animating or encouraging

spleen signifies a number of traits such as moroseness, hypochondria ('vapours' in women), peevishness and depression of spirits; cf. the descent into 'the gloomy Cave of *Spleen*' (Pope's *Rape of the Lock*, IV)

spunging-house a house kept by a bailiff to confine debtors before they are sent to prison

squall (*v.*), to utter or sing in a loud discordant tone (*OED*)

stay-lace a string or cord that draws together the opposite edges of an under-bodice, or corset, by being passed in and out of eyelet holes and pulled tight

stickler an active partisan or instigator; one who stirs up strife; a meddler or busybody (*OED*)

stock-jobber one who engages in the speculative dealing of stocks and shares; 'a low wretch who gets money by buying and selling shares in the funds' (Johnson, citing Swift); a recurring target of Swift's

stocks an instrument of punishment, consisting of two planks framed between posts, set edgewise one over the other, the upper plank being capable of sliding up and down, with holes at the edges of the planks used to confine the ankles (and sometimes wrists); also a jocular term for tight boots

strangury a disease of the urinary organs resulting in slow and painful urination

strol(l)ing wandering from place to place without having any fixed abode, as with beggars and vagabonds

stuff(s) woollen fabric(s); manufactured goods

superscribe to address a letter (to)

surfeit a sickness arising from excess; disgust; nausea

swingeing huge; immense

swolks a meaningless perversion of 'swounds', or 'God's wounds' (*OED*)

tack in parliamentary parlance, an extraneous clause attached as a rider to another piece of legislation, especially a money bill, in an effort to secure the former's passage

Test Act an Act passed in England in 1673 (extended to Ireland in 1704), which made the taking of Communion according to the rites of the Anglican Church a prerequisite for holding public office

threating archaic form of 'threatening', rare even in Swift's time

tincture a tinge, trace or smattering; a hue or dye; a taste or flavour; usually used by Swift in a pejorative sense, to suggest a stain, blemish or taint

tip intoxicating liquor; a draught of liquor (*OED*)

Tories members of a political party that originated in the Exclusion Crisis of 1679, when it opposed excluding the Catholic Duke of York from succession to the throne; later associated with High Church sentiments, support of strong monarchical authority, opposition to standing armies and the favouring of country and landed interests over the interests of the new moneyed class

towardly promising; well-favoured; quick to learn (especially with reference to young persons)

transported sent to the American colonies for a period of indentured servitude in lieu of imprisonment or hanging; a common punishment in the eighteenth century

trumpery deceit; fraud; trickery

uncontrollable (uncontrolled) irrefutable; not subject to dispute

underswearer one who supports another by oath (*OED*)

undertakers those dedicated to pursuing or promoting a particular scheme or business enterprise; also, local politicians who undertook to manage the Irish Parliament for the government, or the 'English interest', in exchange for a share of official patronage and political influence

Union (the) the Act of 1707 which united the governments of England and Scotland at Westminster, creating the new political entity 'Great Britain'; also, the entity thus created

uppish in high spirits; proud; arrogant; a 'low word' for Johnson; used by Swift to describe the Whigs

vails (vales) gratuities given to servants, especially by guests departing from a host's house

vapours (the) a morbid condition attributed to bodily exhalations, manifested by depression, hypochondria, hysteria and other nervous disorders; identified as a specifically female malady

varsal an illiterate abbreviation for 'universal'; 'in the varsal world' means 'in the whole wide world'

viceroy the governor of a region, acting in the name of the king; in Ireland, the Lord-Lieutenant (*q.v.*)

vicious diseased; noxious; depraved

victualler a purveyor of food and drink; an innkeeper

vogue (the) the general report or opinion

wainscot fine imported oak used to panel an interior wall

War of the Spanish Succession a European conflict (1702–13) for control of the Spanish Empire after the death of Charles II of Spain in 1700, with England and its allies (notably the Dutch) supporting the claim of the Austrian Emperor Leopold, while France backed the claim of Philip of Anjou, son of Louis XIV's heir; ended by the Treaty of Utrecht, which stipulated that the French and Spanish crowns would never be united, and gave England the monopoly ('the Asiento') of supplying slaves to Spanish America

Whigs members of a political party that originated in the Exclusion Crisis of 1679, when it supported excluding the Catholic Duke of York from succession to the throne; strong backers of the Revolution principles of 1688; associated with religious toleration for Dissenters, limits to royal prerogative and a policy of containing the French threat abroad and the perceived Catholic threat at home

whinge whine

Whitefriars a theatre and brothel district of London, bounded by Fleet Street, the Temple walls and the Thames; as a 'liberty' it enjoyed certain legal privileges and exemptions that made it a sanctuary for those fleeing the law

wholesomes wholesome things; 'good for the wholesomes' is a dialectal phrase meaning 'wholesome'

wicket a small gate (usually beside a large one) for foot-passengers, as at the entrance of a field

worrier a brutal harasser; a tormentor

Biographical Dictionary

Abercorn, James Hamilton, 6th Earl of (1656–1734). Politician and courtier; created Viscount Strabane in the Irish peerage (1701); Privy Councillor in the reigns of Anne and Georges I and II; supported by Swift in his claim to the French Dukedom of Châtelherault; ally of Swift's in the Drapier's affair.

Addison, Joseph (1672–1719). Writer and politician; Whig MP (1708); secretary to Thomas Wharton, Lord-Lieutenant of Ireland (1708–10); Secretary of State; co-editor with Richard Steele of *The Spectator* (1711–12); author of the tragedy *Cato* (1713); friendship with Swift clouded by the 'Rage of Party'.

Anglesey, Arthur Annesley, 5th Earl of (1676–1737). Hanoverian Tory politician; Treasurer at War in Ireland (1710–16); served as a Lord Justice of Ireland and a Regent appointed by the Elector; on friendly terms with Swift until their falling-out over a veiled reference to him in *Universal Use of Irish Manufacture*.

Anne, Queen (1665–1714). The last of the Stuart monarchs; Protestant daughter of the deposed James II; wife of Prince George of Denmark; assumed the throne in 1702 on the death of William III; allied with the Tories towards the end of her reign; lauded in the *Examiner* essays as a wise and popular monarch but elsewhere depicted by Swift as 'a Royal Prude' because of her disapproval of *A Tale of a Tub*, and blamed for his failure to get preferment.

Arbuthnot, John (1667–1735). Scottish-born satirist and physician who attended Queen Anne; helped form the Scriblerus Club (1713); wrote *The History of John Bull* (1712); collaborated with Pope and Gay on *Three Hours after Marriage* (1717); a valued friend and correspondent of Swift's until his death.

Argyll, John Campbell, 2nd Duke of (?1678–1743). Scottish peer and courtier; initially friendly with Swift but later joined the Whigs; angered by *The Publick Spirit of the Whigs* (1714); described by

Swift as an 'Ambitious, covetous, cunning Scot' with 'no Principle but his own Interest and Greatness' (*M.: Macky*).

Arran, Charles Butler, 1st Earl of (1671–1758). Statesman; younger brother of the 2nd Duke of Ormonde; a member of Swift's 'Society' in London; solicited to help Swift's printer Waters in the prosecution against him; deemed by Swift to have 'very good sense' but to be 'most negligent of his own affairs' (*M.: Macky*).

Asgill, John (1659–1738). Deist; pamphleteer and lawyer both in England and Ireland; author of a pamphlet interpreting the relations between God and man according to the rules of English law and concluding that death was illegal, which was deemed blasphemous and burnt by the hangman.

Ashe, St George (*c.* 1658–1718). Churchman and scholar; Swift's tutor at Trinity College, Dublin; successively Bishop of Cloyne, Clogher and Derry; professor of mathematics, interested in the new experimental philosophy; secretary of the Dublin Philosophical Society; a lifelong friend of both Swift and Esther Johnson.

Atterbury, Francis (1662–1732). Churchman; Dean of Christ Church, Oxford (1711); Bishop of Rochester and Dean of Westminster (1713); a High Church Tory known for his fiery preaching and zealous support of ecclesiastical authority; found guilty of Jacobite conspiracy and banished to France (1723).

Barber, Mary (*c.* 1690–1757). Poet; wife of a Dublin woollen-draper; won the patronage of Revd Patrick Delany, Lord Carteret, and Swift, who actively promoted her literary career and gave her the rights to the London publication of *Polite Conversation* (1738); best known for her *Poems on Several Occasions* (1734).

Barton, Catherine (1679–1739). Half-niece of Sir Isaac Newton; mistress of the Earl of Halifax; known for her brilliant conversation and wit; friendly with Voltaire; admired by Swift, who enjoyed visiting her during his stay in London and remarked, 'I love her better than any body here, and see her seldomer' (*JS*).

Beaumont, Joseph (d. 1731). Irish linen-draper; friend and sometime business agent of Swift; devised slaying tables for use in the weaving of linen, which earned him a government monetary award; driven mad in later years by his obsessive pursuit of a solution to the problem of the longitude; died by his own hand.

Bentley, Richard (1662–1742). Classical scholar and critic; Keeper of the Royal Library; Master of Trinity College, Cambridge from 1700 until his death; became a satiric target of Swift's when he exposed the *Letters of Phalaris* as a clumsy forgery; depicted as the quintessential Modern in the *Battel of the Books*.

Berkeley, Charles, 2nd Earl of (1649–1710). Lord Justice of Ireland (1699), with Swift as his chaplain; satirized as 'King Phiz' in Swift's poem 'The Discovery'; described by Swift as 'Intolerably lazy and Indolent, and somewhat Covetous' (*M.: Macky*); father of Swift's lifelong friend Lady Betty Germain.

Berkeley, William, 4th Baron Berkeley of Stratton (d. 1741). Politician; son-in-law of Sir John Temple; became Privy Counsellor in Ireland (1696) and in England (1710); First Lord of Trade and the Plantations (1714–15); held the office of Master of the Rolls in Ireland (1696–1731).

Blackmore, Sir Richard (?1655–1729). Poet and Whig political writer; physician-in-ordinary to William III and Queen Anne; author of dreary would-be epics (*Prince Arthur*) and long philosophical poems (*Creation*); attacked Swift as 'an impious buffoon'; recurring satiric butt of Pope and Swift.

Bolingbroke, Henry St John, 1st Viscount (1678–1751). Politician and political writer; Tory MP and Secretary of State in the Tory ministry (1710–14); fled to France in 1715 to join the Pretender; later returned to England, where he contributed to the anti-Walpole Opposition via essays in *The Craftsman*.

Boulter, Hugh (1672–1742). Churchman; Bishop of Bristol and chaplain to George I; Archbishop of Armagh and Primate of All Ireland from 1724; a loyal Whig and zealous champion of the 'English interest' in Ireland; a *bête noire* of Swift, who satirized him in several works.

Brown(e), Peter (d. 1735). Churchman; classmate of Swift's at Trinity College, Dublin; became Provost of Trinity College in 1699; consecrated Bishop of Cork and Ross in 1710; author of a well-regarded answer to John Toland's *Christianity Not Mysterious*; a friend of Esther Johnson's, though viewed by Swift as vain and 'capricious'.

Budgell, Eustace (1686–1737). Writer and orator; cousin of Addison; produced a translation of Theophrastus and several noted epilogues to plays; contributed some thirty essays to *The Spectator*, including a series on education; committed suicide after a string of financial and legal troubles.

Burlington, Richard Boyle, 3rd Earl of, and 4th Earl of Cork (1695–1753). Hereditary Lord Treasurer of Ireland; among the richest of the absentee landlords attacked by Swift; an architecture enthusiast who erected an Italianate villa at Chiswick; the subject of Pope's fourth *Moral Essay*.

Carteret, John, 2nd Baron and Viscount (1690–1763). Whig politician and statesman; Lord-Lieutenant of Ireland (1724–30); leader of the Opposition to Walpole; on friendly terms with Swift, who credited him with 'great natural Talents ... Comprehension, Eloquence, and Wit' (*A Vindication of Lord Carteret*).

Clements, Robert (1664–1722). Irish landowner and politician; served as High Sheriff of Cavan; MP for Newry (1715–22); Teller of the Irish Exchequer; recommended by Swift to Lord Anglesey for a lucrative post (1712); relative of Swift's friend John Pratt.

Clogher, Bishop of, *see* Ashe, St George.

Congreve, William (1670–1729). Dramatist; educated with Swift at Kilkenny School and Trinity College, Dublin; known for his Restoration comedies *The Double Dealer*, *Love for Love* and his masterpiece, *The Way of the World* (1700); member of the Kit-Cat Club; friendly with Pope and Swift in London.

Conolly, William (d. 1729). Irish Whig politician; a prosperous land speculator whose immense fortune enabled him to build Castletown House; served as Commissioner of Revenue, Lord Justice and Speaker of the Irish House of Commons; described by Swift as 'wholly illiterate, & with hardly common sence'.

Coward, William (?1657–1725). Physician; author of *Second Thoughts concerning Human Souls* (1702), which denied the existence of a soul separate from the body and maintained that immortal life will be conferred upon the whole man at the time of the Resurrection; viewed as a Deist by Swift.

Craggs, James the Younger (1686–1721). Politician; son of Postmaster General; Secretary at War (1717); MP for Tregony; Secretary of State for Southern Department (1718–21); friend of Pope and Addison.

Curll, Edmund (1675–1747). English publisher; notorious for his literary piracy, plagiarism and bowdlerization; fined and pilloried for his publication of pornographic materials; put out an unauthorized edition of works from *M 'll*; published pirated editions of Pope, who took revenge on him in *The Dunciad*.

Darteneuf (Dartiquenave), Charles (1664–1737). Civil servant; Surveyor of the King's Gardens and the Royal Roads; member of the Kit-Cat Club; valued by Swift for his witty wordplay and amiable company.

Dartmouth, William Legge, 1st Earl of (1672–1750). Statesman and politician; friend of Harley; named Secretary of State for the Southern Department (1710); signed preliminary articles of peace with France (Sept. 1711); praised in *The Examiner* as 'a Man of Letters, full of good Sense, good Nature and Honour'.

Delaval, George (1660–1723). Soldier and diplomat; served as captain under Lord Peterborough in Spain (1705–7); entrusted with the task of buying supplies for the British Army; appointed Envoy Extraordinary to the King of Portugal in October 1710; occasional dinner companion of Swift's in London.

Dennis, John (1657–1734). Dramatist and critic; known for his writings on the sublime and for his intemperate attacks on Pope, Addison and others; mocked in *A Tale of a Tub* as the Moderns' exemplar of 'the TRUE CRITICK', a descendant of Momus and Hybris 'who begat *Etcætera* the Younger'.

Dingley, Rebecca (d. 1743). Second cousin and dependant of Sir William Temple; waiting-woman to Temple's sister at Moor Park, where she developed a close friendship with the much younger Esther Johnson; accompanied Johnson to Ireland in 1701 and remained her constant companion there.

Dodington, George Bubb (1691–1762). Courtier and politician; owner of Irish lands inherited from uncle and holder of an Irish sinecure; a Lord of the Treasury under Walpole (1724); adviser to the Prince of Wales; known for his vanity, ostentatious tastes and patronage of Thomson, Fielding and others.

Ford, Charles (1682–1741). Close friend and confidant of Swift's; entertained Swift and Esther Johnson at his Meath estate; obtained the office of Gazetteer (1712) with Swift's help; figures in several Swift poems and appears frequently in *JS*; maintained an extensive correspondence with Swift.

Fountaine, Andrew (1676–1753). Virtuoso, connoisseur and courtier; an official at the viceregal court at Dublin in 1707; a frequent companion of Swift's in London; held several posts in the court of George II; a noted art collector thought to have corrected the original designs for the 1710 edition of *A Tale of a Tub*.

Frankland, Sir Thomas, 2nd Baronet (1665–1726). Politician; MP for Thirsk; Joint Postmaster General in England (1690–1715); Commissioner of the Customs (1715–18); thought well of by Swift.

Freind, John (1675–1728). Physician, author and politician; served under Lord Peterborough in Spain and wrote a defence of the latter's military conduct (1706); became Physician to the Prince of Wales and to Queen Caroline (1727); published a noted *History of Physic* (1725–6); friend of Swift's in London.

Garth, Sir Samuel (1661–1719). Poet and doctor; physician-in-ordinary to George I; author of the mock-epic poem *The Dispensary* (1699); member of the Kit-Cat Club; friend and early patron of Pope.

Gay, John (1685–1732). Poet and playwright; member of the

Scriblerus Club; author of *Trivia* (1716), *Fables* (1727), and *The Beggar's Opera* (1728), a highly successful satire on the Walpole ministry that was defended by Swift against charges of immorality; maintained an extensive correspondence with Swift.

George I, King (1660–1727). Protestant heir to the British throne through his mother Sophia, Electrix of Hanover; became monarch in 1714 on the death of Queen Anne; his poor English, his reliance on German courtiers and his indifference to high culture made him a target of derision for Swift and Pope; succeeded by his eldest son, who, closely allied to Walpole, reigned as George II from 1727 until his death in 1760.

Godolphin, Sidney, 1st Earl of (1645–1712). Politician; Lord High Treasurer in the Whig ministry (1702–10); close ally of Marlborough; attacked as 'Volpone' in a sermon by Sacheverell; despised by Swift, who complained of his 'coldness' towards him; target of Swift's lampoon 'The Virtues of Sid Hamet' (1710).

Grafton, Charles Fitzroy, 2nd Duke of (1683–1757). Whig politician; Lord-Lieutenant of Ireland (1721–4); closed down rehearsals of Gay's *Polly* (1728) as Lord Chamberlain; helped rescue Swift's printer (1724), but dismissed by Swift as 'Almost a Slobberer without one good Quality' (*M.: Macky*).

Granville, George, *see* **Landsdowne.**

Grattan, Robert (*c.* 1678–*c.* 1741). Irish clergyman; Prebendary at St Patrick's cathedral; one of seven brothers (Swift's 'fav'rite Clan') who regularly entertained Swift at their family seat north of Dublin; part of Swift's circle of punsters and writers of *jeux d'esprit*; named an executor of Swift's estate.

Grimston, William Luckyn, 1st Viscount (d. 1756). Whig politician and author; wrote poems and plays (e.g. *The Lawyer's Fortune, or Love in a Hollow Tree*) that made his name a byword for meaningless prolixity among Augustan wits; satirized by Swift as heir to Sir Richard Blackmore in 'On Poetry' (1733).

Halifax, Charles Montagu, Baron and Earl of (1661–1715). Whig statesman and politician; member of Whig Junto; First Lord of the Treasury under George I; patron of Congreve and Addison; immortalized by Swift as Pericles in *Contests and Dissensions* (1701) but later viewed by him with disfavour.

Halley, Edmund (1656–1742). Astronomer; secretary to the Royal Society (1713); Astronomer Royal (1721); known for his lunar and planetary tables, observation of solar eclipses, and method for determining the sun's distance via the parallax of Venus; predicted the comet that appeared in 1758.

Harcourt, Sir Simon, Baron and 1st Viscount (*c.* 1661–1727). Tory barrister and politician; Attorney General (1707–8); conducted the defence at the trial of Sacheverell; Lord Keeper and a member of the Privy Council (1710); later Lord Chancellor (1713–14); mentioned frequently in *JS*.

Harley, Edward and Robert, *see* **Oxford.**

Harrison, William (1685–1713). Poet and journalist; contributor to poetic miscellanies; judged by Swift to possess 'a great deal of wit, good sense, and good nature'; briefly edited *The Tatler* after Steele's departure; secretary to Lord Raby, ambassador to The Hague; returned to London penniless and died soon thereafter.

Hill, John (d. 1735). Soldier; younger brother of Queen Anne's favourite, Lady Masham; commanded a brigade at Almanza; led the unsuccessful Quebec expedition (1711); appointed governor and general of the garrison at Dunkirk (1713); a member of Swift's 'Society' in London.

Howe, John Grubham (**'Jack How'**) (1657–1722). Politician; an ardent Whig turned zealous Tory MP (1689–1705); staunch defender of the country interest; satirized by Swift as one of the 'Patriots' in *A Tale of a Tub* as well as in his poem 'A Ballad on the Game of Traffick' (1702).

Hyde, Henry, 2nd Earl of Rochester and 4th Earl of Clarendon (1672–1753). Tory politician; MP for Launceston (1692–1711); invested as Privy Counsellor (1710); Joint Vice-Treasurer and Paymaster of Ireland (1710–16); High Steward of University of Oxford (from 1711)

Jervas, Charles (?1675–1739). Portrait painter; student of Sir Godfrey Kneller; principal painter to both George I and George II; made portraits of Pope, Arbuthnot and Newton, and several of Swift.

Johnson, Esther [Hester] (1681–1728). Beloved friend of Swift, who immortalized her as 'Stella' in a series of birthday poems and through *JS*; first met Swift as a young girl in Temple's household; later settled in Ireland; praised by Swift for her exceptional qualities of mind and character.

King, William (1650–1729). Churchman; author of historical and theological works including *The State of the Protestants in Ireland* (1691); became Archbishop of Dublin in 1703; a Lord Justice of Ireland; a staunch Whig but eventually won Swift's respect as an Irish patriot and opponent of Wood's half-pence.

Kneller, Sir Godfrey (1646–1723). German-born portrait painter; numbered among his patrons a succession of English monarchs beginning with Charles II; created a baronet in 1715; a Twickenham neighbour of Pope, whose portrait he painted and who composed his epitaph.

Landsdowne, George Granville, Baron (1667–1735). Statesman and poet; Secretary at War (1710) and Treasurer of the Household (1713); among the twelve new peers created to ensure a majority for the Tory peace (1711); an early patron of Pope, who dedicated *Windsor-Forest* to him.

Lewis, Erasmus (1670–1754). Welsh-born diplomat and political operative; secretary to the English ambassador in Paris (1701); loyal political servant of Harley, to whom he introduced Swift in 1710; Under-Secretary of State (1710–14); friend to the Scriblerians; appears often in *JS*.

Lindsay, Thomas (d. 1724). Churchman; named Archbishop of Armagh and Primate of All Ireland (1714); one of the two Irish bishops to whom Swift's commission regarding the 'First Fruits' was addressed; held in low esteem by Swift, who nevertheless supported his promotion because of his Tory allegiances.

Lloyd, William (d. 1716). Welsh-born churchman; educated at Trinity College, Dublin; consecrated Bishop of Killala in 1691; one of the six signatories of Swift's commission regarding the 'First Fruits'; on friendly terms with both Swift and Esther Johnson.

Ludlow, Edmund (?1617–92). Regicide and memoirist; steadfast adherent of the republican cause and staunch defender of 'the liberty of the people'; in 1660 forced into exile to Switzerland, where he wrote his *Memoirs*, posthumously published in three volumes (1698–9).

Manley, Isaac (d. 1735). Whig functionary and civil servant; Comptroller of the English Letter Office; appointed Postmaster General in Ireland (1703); intercepted Swift's correspondence but was viewed benignly by Swift because of his (and his wife's) friendship with Esther Johnson.

Manley, John (d. 1714). Politician; MP for Bossiney and Camelford; appointed Surveyor General in 1710; cousin of the writer and satirist Delariviere Manley.

Mansell, Thomas (c. 1668–1723). Courtier and politician; Comptroller of the Household to Queen Anne (1704–12); a Teller to the Exchequer (1712–14); one of the twelve new peers named by Queen Anne to ensure a Tory majority in the Upper House (1711); mentioned often in *JS*.

Marlborough, John Churchill, 1st Duke of (1650–1722). Soldier and politician; partner of Godolphin in the Whig duumvirate; made Captain General of the Army by Queen Anne; scored major victories against the French before his dismissal (1712); repeatedly attacked by Swift for his greed and ambition.

Masham, Samuel (?1679–1758). Courtier and statesman; Groom of the Bedchamber to Prince George of Denmark; one of the twelve new peers created by Queen Anne for a Tory majority in the House of Lords (1711); a member of Swift's 'Society'; appears in *JS* as a frequent dinner companion of Swift.

Methuen, Paul (1672–1757). Diplomat and statesman; ambassador to the King of Portugal; helped negotiate the Methuen Treaty (1703), which gave England favourable-trade status with Portugal; viewed by Swift as 'a profligate Rogue, without religion or morals, but cunning enough' (*M.: Macky*).

Midleton, Alan Brodrick, 1st Viscount (?1656–1728). Whig Opposition politician and lawyer; from a rich and powerful landowning family in Ireland; Speaker of the Irish House of Commons (1703); Chief Justice (1710) and Lord Chancellor of Ireland (1714–25); against the Test Act; addressee of *Drapier's Letter VI*.

Molesworth, John (1679–1726). Diplomat and politician; Envoy Extraordinary to the Grand Duke of Tuscany (1710); Commissioner of Trade and Plantations (1715–20); envoy to Turin (1720–25); son of Robert, 1st Viscount Molesworth, addressee of Swift's *Drapier's Letter V*.

Molyneux, William (1656–98). Anglo-Irish philosopher and mathematician; educated at Trinity College, Dublin; first secretary of the Dublin Philosophical Society; best known for *The Case of Ireland Stated* (1698), which argues for the legislative independence of Ireland; a major influence on *Drapier's Letter IV*.

Montagu, James (1666–1723). Jurist and politician; one of Her Majesty's counsel (1705); solicitor general (1707); Attorney General (1708–10); Chief Baron of the Exchequer (1722).

Moore, Arthur (?1666–1730). Irish politician; MP for Grimsby; a Lord Commissioner of Trade and Plantations; a director of the South Sea Company; lost his money and credit through financial indiscretions.

Moreton, William (1641–1715). Churchman; Oxford-educated Englishman; Bishop of Kildare (1681–1705) and of Meath (1705–15); ordained Swift (1695); one of the signatories of Swift's commission from the Irish bishops to obtain remission of the 'First Fruits'.

Mountjoy, William Stewart, 2nd Viscount (d. 1728). Soldier and courtier; acquired title in the peerage of Ireland in 1692; became Lieutenant General in the army in 1709; appointed Master General of the Ordnance (1714); frequent dinner companion of Swift's in London.

Nottingham, Daniel Finch, 2nd Earl of (1647–1730). Tory politician and statesman; a leader of the High Church party during Queen Anne's reign; opposed peace with France in exchange for the Whigs' help in passing the Bill against Occasional Conformity (1711); attacked as a traitor ('Dismal') by Swift.

Ormonde, James Butler, 2nd Duke of (1665–1745). Irish soldier and statesman; Lord-Lieutenant of Ireland (from 1703); Captain General (1712); impeached for high treason (1715) and fled to France; presented Swift to the Deanery of St Patrick's (1713); lauded by Swift as a man of 'great Justice and Charity'.

Oxford, Robert Harley, 1st Earl of (1661–1724). Statesman and politician; Speaker of the House of Commons (1701–4); Lord-Treasurer of the Tory ministry (1710–14); helped Swift win remission of the 'First Fruits'; impeached and imprisoned in 1714; both admired and distrusted by Swift.

Oxford, Edward Harley, 2nd Earl of (1689–1741). Antiquary and bibliophile; son of Robert Harley; member of the Scriblerus circle; amassed a notable book and manuscript collection that later became the basis of the British Museum holdings; maintained a correspondence with Swift.

Palmerston, Henry Temple, 1st Viscount (c. 1673–1757). Politician; MP in England; nephew of Sir William Temple; son of Sir John Temple, Speaker of Irish House of Commons; appointed Chief Remembrancer of the Court of Exchequer in Ireland (1680); his title in the Irish peerage created in 1723.

Partridge, John (1644–1715). Astrologer and almanac-maker; a shoemaker before succeeding John Gadbury as the most popular astrologer of his age; his almanac *Merlinus Liberatus* (begun 1680) served as a medium for his attacks on High Church beliefs; satirized by Swift in *The Bickerstaff Papers* (1708–9).

Parvisol, Isaiah (d. 1718). Swift's steward and tithe-collector (c. 1708–18); of French extraction, possibly Huguenot; the object of recurring complaints by Swift, who dismissed him in 1714 but later rehired him.

Penn, William (1644–1718). English Quaker; strong defender of religious liberty and toleration; founder of Pennsylvania (1682); well received at the Court of Queen Anne, where he met Swift on several occasions.

Philips, Ambrose (1674–1749). Poet; member of Addison and Steele's circle; friendly with Swift in London; author of *Pastorals* competing with Pope's (1709); satirized for his poetic style by Pope and Gay; known as 'Namby Pamby' for his trochaic verses for children; secretary to Archbishop Boulter (1724).

Phipps, Sir Constantine (1656–1723). Jurist and politician; managed defence of Sacheverell (1710); Chancellor of Ireland (1710–14); known for extreme Tory and High Church sentiments; suspected of Jacobitism; defended Atterbury (1723).

Pope, Alexander (1688–1744). Poet and satirist; author of neo-classical and mock-heroic works including *The Rape of the Lock, An Essay on Man, Imitations of Horace* and *The Dunciad*; translator of Homer; member of the Scriblerus Club; editor of joint *Miscellanies* with Swift starting in 1727; opponent of the Whig ministry; a lifelong friend and correspondent of Swift's—about 100 of their letters survive.

Pratt, John (b. ?1670). Soldier and civil servant; studied with Swift at Trinity College, Dublin; became army captain (1703); Constable of Dublin Castle; Deputy Vice Treasurer of Ireland; brother of Benjamin Pratt, Provost of Trinity College; friend and financial adviser to Swift; imprisoned in 1725 for financial irregularities.

Pretender (the), *see* **Stuart, James Francis Edward.**

Prince of Orange, *see* **William III.**

Prior, Matthew (1664–1721). Poet and diplomat; switched from Whig to Tory patronage in 1702; furthered peace negotiations with France via a secret embassy to Paris (1711); known for his burlesques and his poem *Alma; or, the Progress of the Mind* (1716), ridiculing all systems of philosophy.

Pullen [Pullein], Tobias (1648–1713). Churchman; educated at Trinity College, Dublin; appointed Bishop of Cloyne (1694) and of Dromore (1695); staunchly defended the Sacramental Test and wrote against those who advocated religious toleration for Dissenters; belonged to circle of clergymen close to Esther Johnson.

Raymond, Anthony (1675–1726). Irish clergyman, scholar and antiquarian; Fellow of Trinity College, Dublin, and Rector of Trim; an avid student of Irish history and language; published a prospectus for a translation of Geoffrey Keating's history of Ireland, *Foras Feasa ar Éirinn* (1725); a frequent host of Swift's in Laracor.

Rivers, Richard Savage, 4th Earl (1660–1712). Soldier and politician; reputed to be the father of the same-named poet; fought under William of Orange in Flanders, attaining rank of Lieutenant General; branded by Swift 'an arrant Knave in common dealing and very prostitute' (*M.: Macky*).

Rowe, Nicholas (1674–1718). Poet and dramatist; editor of

Shakespeare (1709); became Poet Laureate in 1715; an ardent Whig, though friendly for a time with Swift; celebrated for his drama *Tamerlane* (1702), in praise of William III; now best known for his tragedies *The Fair Penitent* (1703) and *Jane Shore* (1714).

Sacheverell, Henry (*c.* 1674–1724). Clergyman; chaplain at St Saviour's, Southwark (1705); famous for fiery High Church sermons; attacked Godolphin as 'Volpone' in sermon at St Paul's (1709); impeached by House of Lords; his 'church martyr' status helped ensure Tory landslide of 1710; viewed with distaste by Swift.

St John, Henry, *see* **Bolingbroke**.

Sheridan, Revd Thomas (1687–1738). Schoolmaster and clergyman; educated at Trinity College, Dublin; an inveterate punster; translated the satires of Persius (1728); co-edited *The Intelligencer* with Swift (1728); enjoyed an intimate if at times querulous relationship with Swift, who often visited him at his Co. Cavan residence.

Shrewsbury, Charles Talbot, 1st Duke of (1660–1718). Courtier and statesman; Secretary of State under William III; became Lord Chamberlain in the Tory ministry; Lord-Lieutenant of Ireland (1713); a member of Swift's 'Society' in London but later viewed by Swift as lacking in probity and honour.

Somers, John, 1st Baron (1651–1716). Politician and lawyer; Lord Chancellor of England (1697–1700); impeached for secret diplomacy (1701); defended by Swift in *Contests and Dissensions in Athens and Rome*; leader of Whig Junto; dedicatee of *A Tale of a Tub*; later alienated Swift by his politics and failure to provide patronage.

Somerset, Elizabeth Percy, Duchess of (1667–1722). Courtier; married Charles Seymour, 6th Duke of Somerset, in 1682; an ardent Whig and early favourite of Queen Anne; exercised great power at Court; depicted in Swift's 'The Windsor Prophecy' (1711) as the instigator of her second husband's murder.

Southwell, Edward (1671–1730). Politician and civil servant; Secretary of State for Ireland (1702); sworn to the Privy Council of Ireland (1714); became MP for Kinsale; close friend of Archbishop King; appears in *JS* as an intermediary between Swift and the Irish bishops.

Stanhope, James, 1st Earl of (1673–1721). Soldier and statesman; commander of British army in Spain (1708); Secretary of State (1714); helped crush Jacobite Rebellion (1715); Lord of the Treasury (1717); de-facto co-head of Whig administration until implicated in the South Sea scandal (1720); intercepted letters to Swift from abroad.

Stanley, Sir John (1663–1744). Irish civil servant; created a baronet in 1699; appointed secretary to the Duke of Shrewsbury, then Lord-Lieutenant of Ireland (1713); Commissioner of Customs from 1708 until his death; on friendly terms with Swift despite his Whig associations.

Stearne, Enoch. Irish civil servant; cousin of John Stearne; served as Collector of Wicklow and Clerk to the Irish House of Lords; close friend of Esther Johnson; mentioned often in *JS*, at times for his unreliability and fall into debt and dissipation in London.

Stearne, John (1660–1745). Churchman; educated at Trinity College, Dublin; preceded Swift as Dean of St Patrick's (1702–12); Rector of Trim while Swift was in nearby Laracor; appointed Bishop of Dromore (1713) and of Clogher (1717); enjoyed the strong backing and patronage of Archbishop King.

Steele, Richard (1672–1729). Dublin-born journalist, political writer and dramatist; appointed Gazetteer (1707); member of the Kit-Cat Club; edited *The Tatler* (1709–11) and *The Spectator* with Addison (1711–12); wrote *The Conscious Lovers* (1722); early friendship with Swift destroyed by his anti-Tory 'Libels'.

Stopford, James (c. 1697–1759). Clergyman; student and Fellow of Trinity College, Dublin; a classical scholar taken under Swift's wing; made Archdeacon of Killaloe and Bishop of Cloyne (1753); praised by Swift as 'in all regards the most valuable young man of this kingdom'; an executor of Swift's will.

Stoyte, John. Irish civic leader and politician; resident of Donnybrook; Alderman of Dublin; Lord Mayor of Dublin (1715); he and his wife often dined and played cards with Esther Johnson.

Stratford, Francis (b. ?1662). Irish merchant and entrepreneur; schoolmate of Swift's at Kilkenny School and Trinity College, Dublin; a director of the South Sea Company; amassed a large fortune and lent the Government £40,000; eventually went bankrupt; a sometime companion of Swift's in London.

Stuart, James Francis Edward (1688–1766). Son of King James II; known as 'the Old Pretender'; exiled with his father to France at the time of the 'Glorious Revolution'; recognized by Louis XIV as James III in 1701; the symbolic leader of the Jacobites, who launched failed uprisings in 1708, 1715 and 1745.

Suffolk, Henrietta Howard, Countess of (d. 1767). Courtier; married Charles Howard, later 9th Earl of Suffolk (1706); mistress of George II; Woman of the Bedchamber to Queen Caroline; entertained the Scriblerus Club and anti-Walpole Opposition at Marble Hill; subject of a critical 'Character' by Swift.

Temple, Sir William (1628–99). Statesman, diplomat and writer; as ambassador at The Hague, helped arrange the marriage of William and Mary; employer of Swift at Moor Park (1689–99); wrote 'On Ancient and Modern Learning', which fuelled the controversy addressed in *The Battel of the Books*; an important influence on Swift but criticized for his 'coldness' and failure to advance Swift's career.

Tickell, Thomas (1686–1740). Poet and civil servant; served as Under-Secretary of State to Addison and later edited Addison's works (1721); became secretary to Lord-Lieutenant Carteret (1724); appointed Chief Secretary and managed affairs in Dublin Castle (1724); spent the rest of his life in Ireland.

Tillotson, John (1630–94). Churchman; chaplain to Charles II; a popular preacher known for his religious moderation vis-à-vis Non-jurors and Nonconformists; helped revise the Book of Common Prayer (1689) in response to the Toleration Act; Dean of St Paul's (1689); became Archbishop of Canterbury in 1691.

Tindal, Matthew (1657–1733). Deist and lawyer; wrote *The Rights of the Christian Church* (1706), in opposition to the High Church party; rebutted in Swift's *Remarks* (1708); published *Christianity as Old as the Creation* (1730), which argues that the Gospel is only 'a Republication of the Religion of Nature'.

Toland, John (1670–1722). Irish-born Deist and political pamphleteer; controversial author of *Christianity Not Mysterious* (1696), which argues that 'there is nothing in the Gospel contrary to Reason, nor above it'; forced to flee Ireland after the book was burnt by the common hangman; wrote anti-Jacobite pamphlets.

Tooke, Benjamin (*c.* 1642–1716). Dublin printer and publisher in London; published portions of Temple's writings posthumously; arranged the publication of the 5th edition of *A Tale of a Tub* (1710) and *M 'II*; a printer of the *London Gazette* (1711); an agent for various financial transactions of Swift's.

Trapp, Joseph (1679–1747). Scholar, writer and clergyman; first Professor of Poetry at Oxford University (1708–18); translated the *Aeneid* into English and *Paradise Lost* into Latin; wrote Tory pamphlets and indifferent verse; became chaplain to Bolingbroke on Swift's recommendation.

Travers, John (1663–1727). Clergyman; divinity degree from Trinity College, Dublin; prebendary of St Patrick's; vicar of St Andrews, Dublin; Chancellor of Christ's Church; chaplain to the Irish House of Commons.

Vanhomrigh, Esther [Hester] (1688–1723). Daughter of an Irish merchant of Dutch extraction; met Swift in London (1707) and followed him to Ireland in 1714; inspired Swift's poem *Cadenus and Vanessa* (1713), which depicts their relationship as platonic and claims that 'Things took a Turn he never meant'.

Vesey, John (1638–1716). Irish churchman; Bishop of Limerick (1673); Archbishop of Tuam (1678); appointed Vice-Chancellor of the University of Dublin (1710); served as a Lord Justice of Ireland; on friendly terms with Swift, who solicited for his son's petition in the House of Commons (1712).

Walls, Thomas (*c.* 1672–1750). Clergyman; master of St Patrick's cathedral school, Archdeacon of Achenry and Vicar of Castleknock; a good friend and correspondent of Swift's for many years; maintained close ties with Esther Johnson and Rebecca Dingley, who lived with him and his wife for periods of time.

Walpole, Horatio, 1st Baron (1678–1757). Diplomat and politician; MP (1702–56); Secretary of the Treasury (1715; 1721); top envoy to The Hague; plenipotentiary to France; brother of Robert Walpole.

Walpole, Robert, 1st Earl of Orford (1676–1745). Whig politician; de-facto leader of House of Commons after accession of George I; Chancellor of the Exchequer (1721); effectively ruled as Prime Minister until 1742, uniting Hanoverian power in the City; target of Opposition Whigs and Tory satirists.

Waters, Edward (*fl.* 1708–36). Dublin printer; associated mainly with cheap pamphlets; printed Swift's *Proposal for the Universal Use of Irish Manufacture*, for which he was imprisoned and brought to trial before Chief Justice Whitshed; responsible for the Dublin printing of *Life and Genuine Character of Dr Swift* (1733).

Wharton, Thomas, 1st Earl of (1648–1715). Politician; leading figure in the Whig Junto under Queen Anne; Lord-Lieutenant of Ireland (1708–10); led opposition to the Sacramental Test Act; attacked as a profligate, atheist and liar by Swift in his *Short Character of Wharton* and in *Examiner, No. 14*.

Whiston, William (1667–1752). Heterodox theologian; follower of Newton; Lucasian Professor of Mathematics at Cambridge; wrote *A New Theory of the Earth* (1696), attributing Noah's Flood to a comet; produced crackpot scheme for determining the longitude; satirized by Swift via the Laputans (*GT*).

Whitshed, William (*c.* 1679–1727). Lawyer and judge; Solicitor General for Ireland (1709); Lord Chief Justice of the Common Pleas (1726); prosecuted Waters for printing *A Proposal for the Universal Use of Irish Manufacture* and oversaw the case against *Drapier's*

Letter IV; vilified by Swift as a symbol of judicial bias and corruption.

Whittington, Charles (d. 1743). Clergyman; scholar of Trinity College, Dublin; prebendary of St Patrick's (1716); appointed Archdeacon of Dublin in 1719.

William III, King (1650–1702). Born and raised as the Prince of Orange in the Dutch Republic; after the expulsion of James II (1688) assumed the throne of England jointly with his wife Mary (d. 1694), James's daughter; followed policy of military containment of France abroad and religious toleration at home.

Wood, William (1671–1730). Entrepreneur and projector; owned large copper and iron works throughout England; involved in a number of questionable business speculations; in July 1722 obtained a patent from the Crown to coin copper half-pence for Ireland; attacked by Swift in *The Drapier's Letters*.

Wycherley, William (1641–1716). Dramatist; author of *The Plain Dealer* (1676) and his masterpiece, *The Country Wife* (1675), attacked by moral reformers for its alleged lewdness; later confined to Fleet Prison for debt; in 1704 befriended the much younger Pope, who dedicated his third *Pastoral* to him.

THE STORY OF PENGUIN CLASSICS

Before 1946 ... 'Classics' are mainly the domain of academics and students; readable editions for everyone else are almost unheard of. This all changes when a little-known classicist, E. V. Rieu, presents Penguin founder Allen Lane with the translation of Homer's *Odyssey* that he has been working on in his spare time.

1946 Penguin Classics debuts with *The Odyssey*, which promptly sells three million copies. Suddenly, classics are no longer for the privileged few.

1950s Rieu, now series editor, turns to professional writers for the best modern, readable translations, including Dorothy L. Sayers's *Inferno* and Robert Graves's unexpurgated *Twelve Caesars*.

1960s The Classics are given the distinctive black covers that have remained a constant throughout the life of the series. Rieu retires in 1964, hailing the Penguin Classics list as 'the greatest educative force of the twentieth century.'

1970s A new generation of translators swells the Penguin Classics ranks, introducing readers of English to classics of world literature from more than twenty languages. The list grows to encompass more history, philosophy, science, religion and politics.

1980s The Penguin American Library launches with titles such as *Uncle Tom's Cabin*, and joins forces with Penguin Classics to provide the most comprehensive library of world literature available from any paperback publisher.

1990s The launch of Penguin Audiobooks brings the classics to a listening audience for the first time, and in 1999 the worldwide launch of the Penguin Classics website extends their reach to the global online community.

The 21st Century Penguin Classics are completely redesigned for the first time in nearly twenty years. This world-famous series now consists of more than 1300 titles, making the widest range of the best books ever written available to millions – and constantly redefining what makes a 'classic'.

The Odyssey continues ...

The best books ever written

PENGUIN (🐧) CLASSICS

SINCE 1946

Find out more at www.penguinclassics.com